SKYFARER

"One of those remarkable books that consists entirely of 'the good parts.' Non-stop fun with unexpected moments of real pathos."
Neal Stephenson, New York Times bestselling author of Seveneves, Anathem *and* Reamde

"Brassey's writing is an adrenaline dump in page form."
Stant Litore, author of the Zombie Bible series

"A richly imagined story full of soaring adventure, dark intrigue, and characters you'll fall in love with."
Megan E O'Keefe, author of the Scorched Continent series

"To say that *Skyfarer* was *Firefly* meets the Battle at Helm's Deep would be to dismiss the amazing world-building that Brassey wraps us up in, or to gloss over the intricate and intense battles we are thrust into, both on high and up close. Brassey raises the bar for everyone else. More, please."
Mark Teppo, author of Earth Thirst *and* Silence of Angels

"Brassey has created an action-packed rollercoaster ride with rich characters, incredible combat scenes, and a fresh heroine audiences will love."
John G Hartness, author of the Black Knight Chronicles

W9-BPP-132

BY THE SAME AUTHOR

JOSEPH BRASSEY

SKYFARER

A Novel of the Drifting Lands

ANGRY
ROBOT

ANGRY ROBOT
An imprint of Watkins Media Ltd

20 Fletcher Gate,
Nottingham,
NG1 2FZ
UK

angryrobotbooks.com
twitter.com/angryrobotbooks
Sky's the limit

An Angry Robot paperback original 2017

Cover by Ignacio Lazcano
Set in Meridien and Mast by Epub Services

Distributed in the United States by Penguin Random House, Inc., New York.

ISBN 978 0 85766 676 5
Ebook ISBN 978 0 85766 677 2

Printed in the United States of America

9 8 7 6 5 4 3 2 1

To James and Evelyn.
May you always be
Noble and Brave,
Gentle and Kind

CHAPTER ONE
THE PORTALMAGE'S APPRENTICE

On the sun-kissed docks at the edge of the world, Aimee de Laurent awaited her freedom. In less than an hour, she would board the slender skycraft called Elysium. Then her home city of Havensreach and the Academy of Mystic Sciences would be left behind. The servitude of studentship would be gone forever, and adventure, danger, and wonder lay ahead.

Sound and sensation mingled around her. Market vendors shouted their prices in a drone overlaid by the mighty, whipping winds. Crates and workboots thudded against the ramp of the loading dock. She tasted the air, sweet and fresh.

Uncle, she thought. *If you could only see me now.*

She stood only ten feet from the lip of the bottomless sky, dressed in a long coat of faded blue with a high collar, black boots, snug pants that left her free to move, and a light shirt looser about the neck than school regulations allowed. No more uniforms. No more academy rules.

The breeze tugged stray bits of gold hair out of her braid to tickle the front of her pale, resolute face. In her left hand, she held a leather bag with her most precious personal possessions: mirror and brush, her most recent journal of mystic forms, the atlas her father had given to her, and her mother's ring. In her right hand, her burnished, silver apprentice's badge hung on its gleaming chain.

One more hour, and the full breadth of the world would open before her. Just *one more hour*.

Aimee drew in a breath of fresh wind, and drank in the trackless ocean of sky. In the distance, the nearest isle to Havensreach hovered amidst a vast bank of ochre clouds – a thin line of mountain-crowned earth, suspended in the heavens. It looked so close from here, but it was a two-day journey by behemoth or ferry to reach its ports. Her teacher boasted that a smaller, lighter ship such as *Elysium* could reach it in half a day.

She was lost in her thoughts before footfalls sounded further up the dock, and the tall, well-groomed form of Aimee's instructor stepped up beside her. "There are more productive ways to spend your time," he said, "than waiting for the loading to finish." His name was Harkon Bright, and he would hold her apprenticeship for the next several years. He folded his arms on his chest, and his gray and violet robes of mastery billowed in the breeze. His dark brown skin was marked by scars and laugh lines, and his well-trimmed hair and beard were white as moonlight.

Aimee gave the old man a sideways smile. "I thought I might snatch a few moments to take in the view," she said. "After all, when's the next time I'll get to see Drakesburg from the grand wall? It might be years." But there was so much else she *would* see.

"It'll be weeks before you see *trees* again, but I don't see you staring at those," Harkon chuckled.

"Other isles have trees, teacher," Aimee deadpanned. "I'm just eager to *go*. I've been in Havensreach for all of my nineteen years. I'm ready to be somewhere else."

"Now *there's* the storied honesty. I want more of that going forward, Miss Laurent. You will be aboard my ship for months between stops. Apprenticeship requires candor. Am I understood?"

"Absolutely," Aimee affirmed. *And thank the gods for that!*

"Come," Harkon said. "It's time to get on board."

Elysium was a long, slender skycraft, her wings swept forward and angled down from the hull. Two large exhaust ports for her top-of-the-line metadrive glowed with a faint blue light, flanking the stern gun turret. She was freshly painted a bright silver, and the two fins of her tail were short and slanted.

Aimee paused. Looking closer, the graceful curve of apertures on the nose had –if her ship lore was accurate – to be powerful ether-cannons, the sort you normally only saw on high-end military craft. Closer still, what the sorceress had initially thought to be divination sensor-pods looked more like well-concealed, *very big* guns.

Despite being designated in the official rolls as an "explorer," *Elysium* was better armed than most gunships she'd seen. That should have unnerved her, but in the brief moment of realization she felt only a surge of curiosity before they were clambering aboard.

They tromped up the loading ramp as the last of the dockworkers jogged down. Just before they entered the bay, Aimee turned to steal a last glance at home. From here, she could only see a small sliver of the port, and beyond it the expanse of Havensreach's white walls. The floating upper ring where she'd grown up was out of sight, and she couldn't *see* the mystic energy field of the portal shield enveloping the port, but her trained senses could feel it. Magic that protected. Magic that constrained.

Aimee allowed the glance to last only another moment, then turned resolutely towards the vessel's interior. No more constraints. Time to fly.

Freedom.

Aimee de Laurent was born to wealth, finery, and great privilege. Her mother was a water baron's daughter, noble born, her father a financier in Havensreach's upper ring. As a girl she'd loved puzzle games, stories of adventure, and books of ancient myth. She'd never wanted for anything but independence, and as she walked into *Elysium*'s hold she inhaled her first real breath of it. Exposed metal beams, copper piping, expensive hardwood trim and viewports ringed with brass greeted her. She walked past crates that smelled of walnut, poplar, and sandalwood oil. The ambient magic of the metadrive teased at her attuned senses.

"The bridge is straight ahead," Harkon said. "Portal work is done from there. Engine room is to the rear and down. All crew cabins and rooms are off from this central corridor on the upper deck. You'll be shown your room in a moment, after you've met the crew."

They walked through a central dining hall. The first thing that caught Aimee's attention was the beautiful observation window with its view of the clouds far below the skydocks. The floor was finished hardwood laden with fine carpets, and the galley smelled of stew cooking just past the serving ledge. As she looked, a massive gray-haired man emerged from the kitchen. His beard was braided and adorned with bronze rings. His pale face was scarred, and a stained apron was wrapped about his waist.

"This is Bjorn," Aimee's teacher said. "Cook and ship's gunner."

"So this is your apprentice?" the huge man asked Harkon.

"I am," Aimee answered. She flashed a brilliant smile and offered the cook her hand. "I am Aimee de Laurent, late of the upper ring of Havensreach."

Bjorn looked at the proffered palm and laughed. "Where'd you find this upper class lady, Hark? She sounds like an aristocrat straight from the charm schools!"

"Hah," Aimee laughed. "No, I'm not an aristocrat. *That* was my mother. But you're right about the charm school. I attended Saint Austin's for three years; it was the tradeoff that convinced my mother to let me attend the Academy of Mystic Sciences."

"Top of her class," Harkon said. "Opened her first portal at the end of her second year. Unprecedented."

Aimee saw a newfound respect in the cook's gaze. "Well, Miss Laurent, welcome to *Elysium*. I hope you like food with real flavor. These chumps in Havensreach don't know how to cook, and I learned in the Kiscadian Republic."

"Don't listen to him," a new voice said. It belonged to a woman with the slight frame of a natural-born skyfarer and an infectious smile. Her hands were delicate, her hair black, her skin tanned and jewel-toned. Her eyes were thin, dark, and intelligent.

"Bjorn *says* his cooking is spicy," she continued, "but if you've been outside the central shipping lanes of the Dragon Road at all, you know that's a lie."

She extended a hand to Aimee, grinning ear to ear. "Hi! I'm Vlana, ship's quartermaster. My brother Vant is the engineer, so you'll meet him once we get underway. He's still screaming at the portmasters. They're insisting on keeping us here for a complete inspection."

Aimee grinned and quipped back. "Can engineers and portmasters even communicate? I thought they were different species."

"Oh, you're gonna fit in great." Vlana said, and looped her arm through Aimee's. "Come on. I'll show you the bridge – Hark, do you mind?"

The old sorcerer shook his head. "Go on. It sounds like I have to keep your brother from starting a riot."

The two women walked up the corridor that spanned the spine of the skyship. "*Elysium*," Vlana explained with pride, "is a refurbished Cirrus-class air-schooner. She has a steel hull bound over ironwood, with extra enchantments for stability, lightness and speed. Her metadrive is a top of the line 7221 model with twin vents for twice the thrust. She can outrun imperial ships of the line at full burn, and out-dance two-man gunships a third her size."

"Cirrus class," Aimee mused, running through the ship classifications she'd memorized in her last year at the academy. "Don't they have a different profile?"

"Like I said," Vlana repeated. "*Refurbished*." She gave an approving smile "You know your ships."

"Required reading," Aimee answered as they climbed a short set of steps and walked through a narrow doorway. Here the sorceress paused and sucked in a breath at the vision before her: *Elysium*'s bridge was *beautiful*.

Polished hardwood and brass shone in the morning sunlight. Aimee stood atop the higher of two decks, looking down at the helm-wheel in the center of the one below. The viewport spanned the front hundred-and-eighty degrees of the room, giving the pilot an unchallenged view of the sky. Directly opposite the helm on either side were the weaponry and navigation stations. The wheel had a direct communication tube to the engine room, and the nav-station shimmered with elaborate, glowing star-charts and an astrolabe. The air here smelled of polish, hardwood, and fresh wind.

All this took Aimee a few moments to internalize, before her eyes fell upon the platform three feet in front of her, and everything else faded away: the portal dais. It was black, and rimmed in platinum, etched with the silver symbols of transportation magic. Aimee took a step forward. Her boots brushed against its lip, and she felt the potent enchantments upon the device. They pulled at her senses with a fierce insistence. This was power. This was freedom. This was the gateway to sights hitherto unimagined.

"Never seen one in person?" Vlana asked, amused.

"In the academy," Aimee answered. "But those were for student use. They were battered. Worn. This is–"

"Custom designed," Harkon said, entering the bridge behind them. "Its range is twice that of the standard circles in use nowadays. It was freshly cleaned and refurbished in preparation for our voyage."

"Twice the range," Aimee breathed. She itched to test its limits.

A brown-skinned woman in a dirty leather jacket appeared below and sidled up to the helm. She had a shock of blue hair, and the over-the-eyebrow glyph of the pilot's guild tattooed on her face. "Vant says we've got dock clearance."

"That was quick," Vlana said, surprised. "Must be eager to be rid of us." She flashed Harkon a grin.

"There are benefits to being known troublemakers," Harkon mused, and gave Aimee a sideways smile. Aimee paused. This was a different side of her teacher than she'd seen in the school. Outside the walls, in his own vessel, Harkon Bright seemed to breathe easier. There was an energy in the mage's eyes that had always seemed subdued within his academic surroundings. Now it pulsed with a static charge.

"Yeah, yeah," the blue-haired woman shot back. "Are we good to go, chief?"

Harkon looked at Vlana.

"Everything's battened down," the quartermaster said. "But they won't like this."

"That," Aimee's teacher said with a boyish laugh, "is half the fun." Turning to the blue-haired woman by the helm, he said, "Clutch, tell Vant to gun the metadrive to full power. We're going straight up."

Aimee's eyes widened. "Now?"

"If I wait," Harkon said, "we'll sit in the departure queue for three hours. I don't know about you, Miss Laurent, but I'd rather not."

Clutch grabbed the communication tube. "Vant, Hark says gun it to full. We're cutting the line."

Aimee heard an irritable voice jabber back.

"Oh," Vlana snickered, "this is gonna be *fun*."

"Hey, remember the time we gave those Kiscadian dreadnoughts the slip near Glimmermere?" the pilot asked over her shoulder. "At least nobody's shooting at us this time."

"It's the little things," Vlana confirmed.

Aimee was about to ask what in the abyss *that* meant,

when the rumble and ripple of magic passed beneath her feet as the metadrive roared to life. Clutch took the helm. The sound of loosening dock clamps rang outside the hull, and there was a lurch as *Elysium* floated free into the open air. Aimee gripped the rail for support. The deck creaked under her, and beyond the viewport, clouds swam in a sea of infinite blue.

Then her teacher said the words, and Aimee's heart leapt to a thousand paces. "Clutch," Harkon said. "Take us skyward."

The deck tilted as the ship swept clear from her berth, and Aimee had a brief view of the white walls of Havensreach sprouting from the bottom lip of the floating island. She glimpsed a line of vessels up ahead, orderly and slow in their exit. Then Clutch pulled *Elysium*'s prow up.

"I *love* this part," the blue-haired woman said. A concussive burst of arcane fury detonated at the rear of the ship, and *Elysium* shot into the sky. Outside the viewport, vessels in the queue veered from their path. The pilot's hands danced upon the wheel, and her joyful shout surged through the bridge as the silver craft tore through the clouds.

Aimee laughed and clung to the rail as the sunlight blazed ahead, and the skyship called *Elysium* carried her to heaven. Wild. Fast. *Free.*

CHAPTER TWO
HIS MAJESTY'S SWORD

Five hundred feet above the highest towers of Port Providence, Lord Azrael watched the city burn. Surrender had been offered. Surrender had been refused. The Eternal Order kept its word. Now the upper decks of the flying mountain fortress called the *Iron Hulk* were swarming with gunners and crewmen, and the massive batteries hammered the kingdom's capital from the air.

Azrael looked up. High overhead, a paltry handful of lights fought a losing battle against the onslaught of his forces. Through the visor of his angelic death's-head helm, the black-armored knight watched, impassive, as the tattered remains of the ruined royal fleet made a last gallant stand over the corpse of their city. Port Providence crouched at the edge of the isle whose name it shared, burning, and beyond its southern walls, only the darkness of the abyss waited.

The air sang with the snap of hooks and cables, or the screams of swarming crews of steel-clad boarding parties charging over wings and onto the gun decks of battered gray skyships. Here and there the errant flash of magic announced a mage's presence. Everywhere, the flares of ship-killing explosions painted the sky with fire and ruin. The air smelled of raging hull fires and the unique, olfactory-scarring stink left in the air by discharged ether-cannons.

A fresh barrage tore loose from the forward batteries fifty feet from where Azrael stood, and the side of a smaller, rectangular warship erupted, spilling cargo, wreckage, and screaming bodies into the open air. Those vessels that weren't entangled were being driven into the range of the hulk's guns. The aerial fortress wasn't maneuverable, but it was fast, and had enough firepower to savage anything smaller. The ships with smart crews were trying to make good their escape. This would be over in less than an hour.

"Lord Azrael!" Azrael heard the warning and spun on his heel to look: a smaller ship – a five-man gunboat – had swung inside the range of the hulk's batteries, and now hurtled towards the deck where he stood. Flames guttered from its damaged engines.

"She's lost control!" a crewman screamed.

"Take cover!" shouted another.

Azrael marked the path as the ship swelled in his vision: straight, unwavering, aimed low. No guns blazed. Atop the crest he glimpsed a kilted man shrieking a battle cry.

"Not out of control," Azrael murmured. "Just brave and foolish."

The ship veered right. Azrael's mystic senses hummed. He deftly jumped left, and the battered craft slammed into the gundeck. Splinters hurtled in every direction; deck-plating came apart. Debris rattled off the knight's summoned shield spell, and Azrael watched as the powerful figure in an armored kilt leaped free from the wreckage. A beautiful longsword gleamed in his fists. He had fierce eyes, a strong face, and a rough red beard. The brooch holding his tartan about his trunk marked his status, but Azrael didn't need it to recognize him. He'd seen the man's face across the vast, gilded throneroom of the king's court only weeks ago. Royalty always stood out.

"Crown Prince Collum." Azrael's voice came distorted from the depths of his skull-faced helm. He let the magic barrier dissipate and swept his own longsword from his side. No enhanced speed would be used here, nor enhanced strength. This, he would do for the challenge. "Welcome."

Collum staggered, exhausted, "You craven *cur*," the prince snarled. "The blood of my city – of my country – is on your hands, and you stand in a viewing gallery."

"I understand your highness is upset," Azrael calmly replied. "But I *did* warn your royal father: absolute oblivion. The Eternal Order keeps its word."

"Monster!" The prince lunged. His attack was pristine. Azrael was faster: he sidestepped, slapped Collum's thrust away, and drove his armored elbow into the prince's face.

Collum staggered past, eyes watering, nose broken. Azrael turned, and his blade sang through the air. Collum barely parried. Steel met. Edges caught and snagged against each other, establishing a sudden bind: a chance at leverage and sensory feedback. Quick as devils, each swordsman wound and leveraged their blade against the other to thrust from high. The prince's point darted towards Azrael's face, and his pulse quickened: Collum was better than he'd thought, but he was no Varengard master. Not even a novice.

The black knight dropped his weight; Collum's thrust sailed over his left shoulder. Too close to land his own, Azrael let go with his left hand and slammed his fist into the prince's gut. Collum doubled over, staggered back, and sliced his beautiful sword through the space between them. Azrael took one calculated step back. Both the prince's edge and point missed his armor by an inch.

Collum had barely regained his balance when the black knight set upon him with a vicious storm of blows. They flashed back and forth across the deck in a blur of dancing razors, light and dark, backlit by a burning city far below, but always the prince gave ground, and always the black knight drove in, until Collum struck from high and Azrael snapped up from below. The prince screamed. His cut had been flawless, and the sword's perfect edge –enchanted, Azrael now sensed – even cracked the front of the black knight's visor. It was close, but not enough.

Azrael's visor fell away, but his posture – legs bent, off-line, hands up, edge catching the brunt of the strike – was *perfect*. His hilt was high above his head, and his blade angled down as he drove the point of his sword through the prince's unprotected chest.

Collum stared open-mouthed. Surprise painted across his eyes as he stared at his enemy's revealed face. Blood frothed at his lips. "You're a *boy*…"

"Twenty-one winters," Azrael answered. Without his visor, his true voice sounded younger in his own ears, but still deep, and no less cold. "I admire your people's tenacious courage," he finished, and jerked his sword free. "But I did warn you: absolute oblivion. Goodbye, highness."

Collum's mouth opened wide and his eyes raked across the sky. Blood bubbled over his chin and he dropped shuddering to the deck.

Azrael knelt and pried the enchanted longsword from his enemy's fingers. It was beautiful: several inches longer than his own, the straight crossguard chased with gold, the lower half of the grip bound in silver wire and capped with a fishtail pommel. The blade was long, broad and tapering, hollow-ground, and runes traced the spine of its diamond cross-section. Azrael unbuckled the ornate belt and gilded scabbard from the dead man's body, then fastened it about his waist in place of his own.

Deckhands and gun crew ran towards him. The battle above and the burning below raged unabated. Cries of "My lord!" echoed in Azrael's ears.

"Is that their prince?" an acolyte exclaimed.

"It is!" shouted a deckhand. "I saw him before at a distance! Collum the Blessed is dead!"

"Lord Malfenshir will want his head mounted," another exclaimed. "Put on a spike till it rots in the sun."

Azrael fixed the men with a silencing look. "Quit your gawking and get back to your duties, every one of you!" he snapped. At once, they fell into line. Azrael was the master here. The conquest of Port Providence was *his* assignment.

"Go tell Malfenshir that I have killed Prince Collum. I am claiming his enchanted sword as my rightful spoils."

"My lord–"

"*Go.*"

The acolyte ran to obey. The deckhands cowered when Azrael fixed them with his green-eyed stare. Then he turned back to where Collum's corpse lay on the blood-spattered deck. Malfenshir *would* want his head mounted, yes. Lord Ogier would have wanted him blood-eagled and carried forth as a banner, if he was here. Others might have simply thrown him from the edge of the land and into the waiting abyss beneath the eternal sky.

And Azrael's own master? The black knight paused. *"Be inventive,"* Lord Roland would've said.

Collum would likely wish to be buried amongst his people, in the heart of his land, or some similarly romantic notion.

The black knight put his foot against the dead man's midsection and shoved the corpse over the edge. It fell, limp, towards the burning city far below. Then Azrael sheathed his new sword, and walked back inside.

The command solar of the *Iron Hulk* was a sparsely furnished room near the apex of the mountain, with enchanted windows that offered a one-hundred-eighty degree view of the firestorm playing out across the skies. Opposite these windows a wall was covered in maps, old parchment sheaves. Between the two was a table strewn with reports brought from officers and mercenaries below. The air here carried the smell of dry paper and metal, and Azrael's nose twitched at the oily stench of bone ink. This was where the seven knights charged with the invasion of Port Providence met in private to discuss their order's investment.

Whenever Azrael looked at Lord Malfenshir, he was struck by the man's brutal physicality. His second-in-command was huge, broad, and thick-bodied, with a cruel, square-shaped face presently twisted into a contemptuous sneer. His armor was red and scrawled with blasphemous symbols. Malfenshir towered over most men, could snap limbs with his hands, and projected a forceful menace in the air about him, even at rest.

Azrael cut a slighter figure: slightly shorter, his black armor understated and gold-accented, but elegant. He was muscular, but not freakishly large. His face was handsome, chiseled and pale, his dark hair long and thick. His nose was pointed, his chin strong, and his eyes were green.

The two men *hated* each other.

"You could have blasted him from his ship as he careened in," Malfenshir scolded as Azrael stepped into the meeting room.

"Hardly sporting," Azrael answered. "Royalty deserves the blade. And in any case, I wanted his sword."

"I hope it was worth the damage to the gunnery platform," Malfenshir growled. "We're here to butcher Port Providence, Azrael, not absorb expenses for the order."

"We're *here*," Azrael corrected him, "to seek our order's long-hunted prize. The Axiom Diamond, with which no treasure, no secret, no *person* will be hidden from our order's eyes." His mouth twisted into a frown. "And which of us was it that wasted hours in the central district with ground troops, yesterday? Which of us *insisted* on leading a raid before the bombardment began?"

"If we'd gone with *my* plan, from the beginning," Malfenshir dared. "If we'd threatened to use the Silent Scream–"

"We would've failed," Azrael said, still staring at his second.

Malfenshir stared back. Around them, the five other knights of the Eternal Order stood silently, watching the tension between the invasion's two senior officers. When the bigger warrior's jaw tightened, and his hand slipped towards his sword, Azrael took a simple step forward. Risky. In their training days, the two of them had fought to a draw more often than either had ever won, and even at his best, Azrael didn't know that he could overcome the beast before him.

But his authority had to be absolute, or it was nothing at all. Will was all. Fear was weakness. Weakness was death.

They stood facing one another for nearly a minute, then Malfenshir looked away.

"Good," Azrael said. "Now give me your reports on the state of the Investment, each in turn."

One by one they obeyed. Troop movements outside the city were laid out. The retreat of royal forces in collapse was described. The preliminary reports of settlements on the far side of the isle were given. *The Investment*, their directives called this operation. War was the Eternal Order's business.

Everything was in order except what they came for.

"But no word of the Axiom?" Azrael pressed, when they were done.

Malfenshir smirked. So he'd found something worth reporting, then.

"Don't waste my time," Azrael said.

"One of our planted spies has sent a message by spell," Malfenshir replied. His grin was hungry. "Half their forces are circling about to the far shore, but there is a smaller force making swiftly for a castle called Gray Falcon. Our spy spoke of a gray sage lurking there in the fortress's court."

A murmur passed around the circle of dark armored knights. Despite the animosity between himself and his second-in-command, Azrael felt a small flush of relief, and a smile came to the corner of his mouth. At last.

"I can be there in two days," Malfenshir pushed.

"No," Azrael said. "Use the hulk to destroy what's left of their fleet. I will take a smaller complement of ships and shock troops to bring Falcon down."

He gestured at the two to his left: "Sirs Kaelith and Cairn. You will be all I require, plus a complement of the bridge-burners, and the three frigates to get us there. I will take my healer, Esric, as well."

"A light force," Malfenshir frowned.

Azrael took a measured breath to settle his irritation. That Malfenshir considered three frigates, three Eternal Order knights, and a complement of mercenaries *a light force* spoke volumes about his belief in using maximum violence to solve minimal problems. Malfenshir would always use a sledgehammer to swat flies. And if a house possessed a single rotted beam, the red knight would gladly burn it down.

"Not everything requires the full hammer." Azrael reminded his second.

"The fleet is a distraction," Malfenshir bristled at the rebuke. "Gray Falcon is what matters."

"The fleet," Azrael countered, "is still forty-five vessels strong, and they still have allies in the Violet Imperium. Our portal shield prevents long-range communication by spell, but if even one ship gets out before we're done here, our retreat will become a rout while imperial warships face off against our *Iron Hulk*." He barely managed to keep his tone even. "Port Providence is isolated, yes, but not without friends."

"One of our knights is worth a hundred Violet soldiers," Malfenshir snarled.

"Which matters less," Azrael snarled back, "when

there are *seven* of us and millions of *them*."

"We cannot afford to lose sight of the true objective," Sir Kaelith nodded. She was a thickly built powerhouse of a woman, with dark eyes and olive skin. Male or female, the order made no distinction between genders in its titles.

Power is what matters, Roland had told Azrael, once. *Not identity.*

"The Axiom is everything," Sir Cairn affirmed.

"But not–" Malfenshir began.

"You have your orders," Azrael finished, though his eyes never left his second. "Clear the room," he said. The knights began to leave. "All but you, Lord Malfenshir. You remain."

The massive warrior stopped and fixed predatory eyes on Azrael as the others filed out. When the last one had closed the door to the command room, they faced each other, a hatred tangible in the open space between them.

Malfenshir began, "I only–"

"You will never challenge me in front of the others again," Azrael cut him off. "Am I understood?"

Malfenshir's eyes flashed. "Lord Roland assigned you the command of this invasion, but that does not mean I have no say in our stratagems."

"When I wish it," Azrael said, stepping forward, "that is *precisely* what it means. You and I do not get along. We never have, but since you seem not to understand this basic concept, I will illuminate it for you: I will tolerate no challenge to my authority. If you have views in conflict with my own, save them for private council. If you are *ever* insubordinate in front of our brothers again, I will send your master your eyes and tongue in a box, and toss what remains into the abyss. Do you understand?"

The red-armored hulk of a man clenched his fists, and Azrael tilted his head slightly, waiting to see if his second-in-command would push the limit. "Go ahead," he whispered. "I can kill more than just a prince today."

Malfenshir was silent for a long time. Then, he stepped forward. "One day," he said, "your status won't protect you from me. Then we'll see if your threats are worth a damn."

"Do you understand?" Azrael repeated. He didn't move. He didn't flinch.

"Perfectly," Malfenshir said. Then he turned on his heel and left.

Alone, Azrael relaxed, planted his hands upon the table and let his nerves unwind. Outside the viewports, he could see the ragged remnants of the fleet fleeing. Lights darted back and forth across a smoke-stained sky. Each one represented lives in the balance. Azrael reached to his hip and pulled the enchanted sword of the dead prince from its sheath. He stared at the gleaming runes, felt the thrum of magic woven into the steel. It was *old*. The blade was cold, the grip warm. Calling upon his intuitive magic, he willed the name to reveal itself.

Oath of Aurum, the runes read.

A chill ran through his blood. He closed his eyes, and the image of burning walls and smoldering flowers flashed unbidden through his mind. A shriek ripped across his thoughts. A name.

"Elias!"

For a moment, he couldn't breathe.

Nothing. It was *nothing*.

Remember your training.

It passed. He breathed again. The room was the room, and the blade was still in his hands. He sheathed it, shook his head, and walked to the far wall, where the maps of the lands around Port Providence were displayed. The kingdom was isolated, on the fringes of the Unclaimed. They had only the Violet Imperium to call upon for help, and with the portal shield up, their cries for help were gagged.

Azrael had an assault to plan.

CHAPTER THREE
THE THIRD PRIME

"... So I said to him," Harkon was saying, "if you think that the third prime is sufficient justification to ignore the mating habits of polyphages, then by all means, *stick your hand in it.*" The old mage shook his head.

He was sitting across from Aimee in the broad, windowed common area of *Elysium* while she reclined on one of the couches. Rugs were spread across the floor, and the galley was to her right. The large bay window with its unimpeded view of the cloud-speckled sky was to her left, spilling light across the warm hardwood walls with their smattering of decorative art. Vlana sat opposite Aimee. In the galley, Bjorn could be heard cutting up produce for the stew. The smell of cooking meat and spices filled the room.

"What cad is this again?" Vlana asked. "Most of the principles are going over my head, but I know the sound of an ass when I hear one."

"Professor De Charlegne," Harkon replied. "A colleague of mine at the academy. And a duke."

"And a *terrible* theorist," Aimee said with a snort.

Harkon turned to regard his student. A small smile

played about his mouth. "Do you know he asked about my choice to take you on as an apprentice? As it happens, he *didn't approve.*"

"Didn't approve?" Aimee's eyebrows raised as she chuckled. Here, far away from the walls of Havensreach and the Academy of Mystic Sciences, candor was coming more easily by the moment. "On what grounds?"

"Something about *contentiousness,*" Harkon replied, amused.

The laugh bloomed out of Aimee, caustic, half a cackle. "*Contentiousness*? Hah. That's *rich* coming from him. I don't suppose he told you about the time in fourth year dimensional principles?" Aimee shook her head, then grinned. "So," she said. "The duke walks into class – a fourth-year seminar in the advanced portalmage program, mind you – and straightfaced proceeds to give a lecture about how the twenty-third principle of structural teleportation dynamics' limited invalidation of the fourth law proposed in Sigurd's *Dichotomies of Spatial Planes* means that the third prime law doesn't apply to portal magic. Like it's all that cut and dried!"

She shook her head, standing. "He said this to a bunch of fourth year portal students. Most of whom haven't even opened their first portal yet, much less read Brivant, much less worked outside a lab." Aimee came up for air to find a room full of amused faces. "I had. So I told him that he was wrong."

Vlana was smirking now.

"He told me to sit down and show proper respect," Aimee continued, starting to pace, her hands gesticulating. "I told him that a piece of magical theory that could get his students killed didn't merit respect, it merited critique and rigor before it was just thrown out there as dogma. Yes, of course you could make the argument that the combination of Sigurd and the twenty-third principle means that because the location and the destination are both fixed points, the outcome of a controlled, carefully managed portal-casting isn't subject to the third prime, but that's just it: what casting outside of an academy lab is controlled?" Aimee threw her hands up, the laughter wry as she shook her head. "Yes, on skyships we have the amplification lenses to expand our magic and focus it, we have the dais to ground us, and the energy of a metadrive to draw upon, but none of that actually obviates the fact that the third prime still applies. Magic is not a force of reason. Telling your students that a highly circumstantial theory that hasn't been given the proper field scrutiny means they don't need to worry about the most dangerous parts of their jobs is incredibly irresponsible, all the more so when it sounds smart." She paused, then tossed out, "Plus, his cufflinks were garish."

Vlana spit her drink. Off to the side, Harkon beamed with pride. "Alright," the quartermaster said. "Before you go too far off into the library: who's Sigurd?"

Aimee felt her face flush. Gods, she'd laid it on thick, hadn't she?

"No no no," Vlana said, catching the look on her face. "I'm not a mage (don't have the gift) and I didn't go to an academy, but I love this stuff. Don't apologize, explain. Please. I'm serious. Hark makes it all sound like an encyclopedia."

"I do *not!*" Harkon protested.

"You do," Aimee and Vlana said at the same time.

Aimee took a second to gather her thoughts, then sat down opposite the quartermaster, holding a hand out to shush further protest from her teacher. "Alright, so, Sigurd and Brivant don't actually matter much. Forget them. The most important part of magic is the *three primes*. The laws that govern all sorcery, because above all others, they have the fewest exceptions. The first prime is, 'Magic wants to be used.' What it means in practice is that the energy the mage draws upon is compelled to take form. The main reason why this is important is that it means a mage has to be self-aware, self-confident, and strong-willed, or their own magic will spiral out of their control."

She cleared her throat, took a drink. She hadn't talked this much since graduation day. "The second prime is the basic explanation of how sorcery is performed: 'Gestures summon, words release.' Spells are written down as formulaic series of positions and gestures. You've probably seen the form-scrolls, with all their transitions and alternate positioning." Vlana nodded. Aimee continued. "The main thing is that the gestures summon and shape the magic. If you want to alter a spell's dimensions, range, duration, scale, you tweak the movements. But it's the *words* that actually release it. So..." she smiled. "The old adage 'Be careful what you say' is doubly true for a sorcerer."

One more drink. Vlana was attentively listening. Harkon was watching, reservedly, a small twinkle evident in the old sorcerer's eyes.

"The third prime," Aimee continued, "is 'Things do not always happen as men understand they should.' This is taken by most of us as a warning, as much as a law. Like I said before, magic is not a force of reason. Our spells use formulae, are rigorously practiced and meticulously trained, but that doesn't mean they will happen exactly as we expect. Everything, from the smallest cantrip to the mightiest grand enchantments, can have consequences the sorcerer doesn't foresee. The answer to this is that we must always be mindful. A smart mage can sense when their magic is going awry, and work to mitigate or prevent it, if they're adaptive enough."

That was when Clutch's voice came through the communication tubes. "Alright, lazy-butts. We're about twenty minutes from the shield wall."

"And that," Harkon said, "would be the cue to get ready." He rose from his chair with a stretch. Aimee and Vlana followed suit.

"So," Aimee said, clearing her throat with a nervous laugh. The reality of her job was suddenly much more immediate. "Do we flip for who gets on the dais first?"

Harkon's eyes twinkled. "Oh, no need. You're first."

"So where to?" Aimee asked as they stepped into the hall.

"Pick a place," Harkon smiled. "Not too far, but not too near. True west, perhaps."

Aimee turned and walked back down the central corridor to her cabin. Alone for a moment, she took in the surroundings. Like the rest of the ship, her private space was hardwood and brass. A single large bunk sat back against one wall, a chest of drawers integrated into another, and shelves for her texts. The wind whistled through a single, open viewport with its innumerable promises.

She walked to the circular window, pushed the brass and glass further open. The porthole was just wide enough for her head to fit through, and she pushed herself up on her toes, heart hammering in her ears at the thought of what she might see. Her uncle's words echoed across the distance of years.

"Most men will live their whole lives clinging to these fragile thrusts of land on which we make our homes, luv, but the skyfarer knows that real freedom, and real life, are amongst the clouds and the infinite blue. Home is where you make it, sweet girl, and mine was a sure deck, broad wings, and heavens beyond knowing."

"Someday," the little girl had answered him, *"it will be mine as well."*

The roar of the winds struck her face, drowning all other sound. Her hair whipped, gold and wild, about her eyes, and turning she watched as Havensreach, Drakesburg, and the other smaller isles slowly faded behind. They swam in the sea of sky, flat slabs of earth rippling with mountains, swathed in forests, dappled by lakes and sliced through with streams. The city of her birth was a distant mass of white, crouched upon the cliffs, its towers tiny pale spikes far, far away. The magic upper ring that had been her home hovered directly above the lower walls of the city. She had no idea when she'd see it again.

A wild laugh bubbled out of her as she felt the wind and lost her thoughts to its roar.

I did it, Uncle. I'm free.

The moment ended. She stepped back. Her boots thumped on the deck. A few stray breaths escaped as she caught herself. She fetched her satchel. The form-books of the types of magic she'd studied stared back at her: Portal Magic. Basic Illusions. The Fundamentals of Healing. Basic Battle and Defense Magic. She had yet to study the arts of conjuring or metamorphosis, and she knew nothing of divining, but she had time and freedom ahead.

Reaching past her spell texts, she plucked free the last gift her parents had given her before her departure: a leatherbound atlas, the title inscribed in gold leaf.

The Drifting Lands: A Comprehensive Atlas

Opening the cover, she noted the inscription in the upper left-hand corner, just inside. It was in her father's flowing script.

*May your daring ambitions carry you to every corner of
every page, and beyond.
~ All our love, Mum and Dad.*

Smiling, she turned to regard the preamble. Unlike the student versions gifted to graduates of the portalmage program, this was handwritten. The cursive lines intoned the ancient words of the First Histories. Aimee had read them a hundred times, but they still arrested her.

*"Know this: we are mankind, orphaned and exiled.
We know not whence we came, nor what apocalypse
claimed our home. Only that we may never return.
These Drifting Lands are our domain. Here we
wander, wonder, conquer, and fly, orphans among the
clouds and stars…"*

On the first page was the side-on cosmological diagram of the Eternal Sky. Above was the Celestial Veil beyond which lay the stars, moon, and sun. Below lay the incalculable depths of the Abyss, and between the two, consisting of near eternal fathoms, was the vastness of the Empyrean, the span of heaven in which man dwelt, and where the isles without number floated.

Turning the page, continents spread out before her on blotched parchment, inked lovingly in deft penmanship with directional symbols. The illustrations depicted the prevailing great winds, the political boundaries of the major powers that bordered the land where she'd grown up, and the infinite trade routes of the Dragon Road threading between. Her hands brushed over the great stretch of the landmasses ruled by the Violet Imperium, then slid down to the broad expanses of the Kiscadian Republic. The two great powers that controlled much of their corner of the sky with vast skycraft fleets and armies and treaties with lesser states.

And beyond, the vast reaches of the isles both territories called simply *the Unclaimed*. Havensreach was there, a speck of an isle, with its trade influence so much greater than its physical size.

Her finger traced the distances over which portals were needed to accelerate. Hayesha. Albatross. Sevenstons. Far-distant Althea. The tiny hinterland kingdoms: Port Providence – she'd heard they didn't even have muskets there; Ravenhaus; Ishtier; Gray Towers. So many others. Each state within the Unclaimed was a force unto itself, and even the great powers had to treat with the smaller nations, so great were the distances between them. And moving between them, intermediaries and balancing forces, were the powerful trade conglomerates and guilds simply called the Twelve.

Aimee took a breath, made her nervous heart ease its pace, and tucked an errant strand of gold hair behind her ear. Then she pulled out the navigational kit from her bag. A portal sidestepped directions – that was its nature – but the maker still needed a command of its

aim, and the limit to its distance was the mage's power.
A portal was a door without walls, a window framed by
its maker's Intent, powered by a ship's metadrive. The
vast portals that allowed the gigantic city-sized trade
ships called behemoths to make the jumps between their
destinations required more than one portalmage. For a
ship *Elysium*'s size, one would do fine. *And the duke said
the third prime didn't apply.*

She was so glad to be away from the academy.

It required the power of a metadrive and the focus
and direction of a capable sorcerer. Without a clear sense
of place and goal, the portalmage would send herself –
and her ship – hurtling into the unknown. Aimee had to
know *exactly* where she wished to go, and had to possess
the mental fortitude to direct the magic the proper way.
She picked a place and memorized the coordinates, then
jotted them quickly down.

Another breath to steady herself. She had done this
a thousand times, trained for it, practiced it. Boyfriends
had been neglected, soirees ignored, social calendar
events shunted to the backdrop of her mind, all so she
could learn the minutest of details about her chosen
trade.

"You can do this, Aimee de Laurent," she murmured
to herself, as if mere words could quell her doubt. "Now
go show them what you've got."

As she stepped out the door and walked back towards
the bridge, she wished she felt half as confident as she
looked.

"Ishtier?" Harkon regarded the small sheaf of parchment.

"North of Port Providence," Aimee confirmed. "West
of here. My uncle used to talk about it, and I've always

wanted to see it: a hundred broken fragments of land, an organic strain of emerald that grows like the trees!" She tried to keep the excitement from her voice. She only half-succeeded.

"Your apprentice wants to be eaten by dragons," Clutch deadpanned.

"There's more than dragons on Ishtier," Aimee insisted, turning. "Wyverns, cloud-whales feeding from the undersides of the broken landmasses. And I've heard tales of warbirds with lightning crackling in their beaks. My uncle told me that in the port there are sorcerers that can shape dwellings of stone with music. It doesn't work anywhere but there."

Clutch looked at Aimee for another moment, then turned back to the helm.

"Hark, she wants to be eaten by dragons."

Vlana took the paper. Considered. "It's on the survey route, chief. We haven't docked there since before Vant and I joined your crew. And it's not troubled lands, for a change. Ishtier's nice and quiet."

"Troubled lands?" Aimee turned to look at the quartermaster. "For a *change*?"

Now that was *different.*

"Those rumors are unconfirmed," Clutch countered from the helm. "If it were true, Havensreach would be in uproar."

"Unless they don't know," Bjorn said from the doorway. The big man was quiet, Aimee reflected, realizing she'd heard nothing of the cook's approach. He stood just behind Harkon, his eyes fixed on the sea of clouds outside the viewport. "International treaties are all well and good, but I've had a bad feeling about the hinterland kingdoms for months. The girl's wise, Hark, listen to her. Ishtier is a good place to go."

Harkon gave Bjorn a look. Something passed between them. Aimee realized that they'd argued about this before. A charge hung in the air between the listeners. Harkon frowned thoughtfully; Vlana looked uncomfortable. *They've been talking about this, the lot of them, before we left,* Aimee realized, *and they didn't include me.*

"Ishtier, then," Harkon agreed, scratching his white beard. "Clear the portal deck, everyone but Aimee and myself."

As Bjorn and Vlana filed out, Aimee looked at her teacher. "You haven't been telling me about what we're sailing into," she murmured. She tried to keep the slight tone of bitterness from her voice. She failed.

"There's always trouble in the world," Harkon answered, calm, defensive. "And we're not sailing into it: as Vlana said, Ishtier's nice and quiet."

"I get the sense I'm not being kept in the loop about something," Aimee said lightly.

"There's been a bit of a mess in the border kingdoms," Harkon said with a small shrug of his shoulders. "Or rumors of it, in any case. Mostly the kingdom of Port Providence. Bjorn thinks it's serious, but he's not paid to take things lightly."

Aimee frowned, crouching to familiarize herself with the raised platform she'd soon be using to cast her magic. "If it was a *real* mess, like an invasion, or a natural disaster," she said, almost to herself, "we'd have heard about it. The word would be on the lips of every newsboy and plastered across every front page."

"Yes," Harkon agreed, but his words were thick with worry. "If word got out. But things have a way of happening quickly in the hinterland kingdoms." His white brows furrowed over his dark eyes. Aimee thought she saw his fingers flex. "It's not worth worrying about."

"Uh-huh. You're going to have to explain all that later," she reminded him.

Her teacher sighed. "I promise I will. But first, the jump to Ishtier. I will assist you, but only if there is need. Now, have you memorized the coordinates?"

"I have," Aimee breathed. She stood at the edge of the dais with its platinum edging. The clamorous pull of unspoken spells danced in the forefront of her mind. Words ached to be let loose from her closed mouth. Gestures first. Magic was as dangerous as it was potent.

Another breath, and her nerves were settled. "Tell me when," she said.

The other crew had taken their places. Harkon stood behind her, his hands crossed behind his back. Calm. Observant.

"Two minutes till we leave the shield wall," Clutch said, fingers on the wheel.

"Vant," Vlana said into the tube. "Get ready for a hard burn. Amp up the drive."

Aimee heard a sharp response in reply, though she couldn't make out the exact words.

"Feet on the dais," Harkon said. Aimee stepped onto the platform. The energy pulsed under her senses, flowing up through her in a river of resplendent potential. Her hands twitched in preparation for the spell. Slowly, a series of complex lenses descended from the ceiling in front of her, focus points to amplify the magic. A portal vast enough to move a whole ship – even one so small as *Elysium* – was no easy thing. The dais let her draw upon the energy of the ship's metadrive, which she would then channel into a spell that would be amplified by the lenses, opening the portal out in front of the ship. Simple. Complicated.

She reviewed the mechanics: a portal was a doorway opened between one point and another.

"One minute," Clutch said.

"Hands in first posture," Harkon murmured. Aimee's hands rose, trailing blue fire in their wake. The air about her crackled and snapped. Pale runes danced in her palms.

"Thirty seconds," Clutch's voice had a distinct edge. "Remember, we're *not* looking for trouble, this time."

"Says you," Vlana muttered. A nervous laugh that Aimee didn't share rippled around the bridge. She had to stay focused.

"Remember," Harkon calmly said beside her, "The destination must be *firmly* in mind."

"I remember," Aimee replied.

"Shield wall behind us!" Clutch shouted. Aimee closed her eyes, envisioned the coordinates in her mind. The words of the spell pulled at her tongue, eager to be let out.

"I am the fulcrum," she intoned. The lenses gleamed. Aimee fixed her gaze through them. "I call across the void. By my command, the heavens shall part, and bear me over the span between ship and shore."

First prime. Second prime.

Her hands hammered together at the last word. She set her stance, and a flare of blazing light ripped from her palms and through the lenses. They focused it, channeled it, and magnified it until a beam ten times the size blasted forth from *Elysium*'s bridge. A vast rift, taller than the tallest tower, ripped into the heavens at her command, held open by her will, her magic. Aimee's breath left her in a gasp. An eye of darkness churned before her.

She couldn't see the other side. That wasn't right.

"Vant, *now!*" Clutch screamed.

The engines roared, and *Elysium* shot into the gap. Night yawned before them. *Ishtier,* Aimee focused. *Take us to Ishtier.*

Something was wrong. The dais beneath her trembled. Her feet stood unsteadily upon it. Abruptly, a ripple of magic energy surged upwards. She *barely* kept it from shaking her concentration apart. That wasn't supposed to happen.

The rift rippled around them. *Elysium* shook. Another surge of energy. Aimee's control wavered. She couldn't keep ahold of it. Was it her spell? Had she cast it wrong? No, she *couldn't* have. She'd done everything *right!*

"Aimee, focus!" Harkon shouted.

"Where's the other side?" Vlana shouted above the roar.

Control. Aimee's control was slipping. She tried to wrest it back, but the power was spiraling out of her command. Ishtier wavered in her mind.

"The portal is destabilizing!" Clutch screamed.

Another surge jolted her upwards. Aimee felt the power she channeled threatening to shudder out of her grasp. Her breath was uneven as she shifted her stance, desperately trying to compensate, to adjust.

The third prime: things did not always happen as men understood they should.

No, not now, she thought. *Not now!*

She fought against it, staggered to one knee as the inconsistent surges of energy pulsed through her and into the maintained spell. She was barely able to keep each individual surge from shaking the portal apart. *Elysium* shook, bucked violently, the room tilted. Instruments slid free and she glimpsed her teacher clutching the railing for support. The portal was *collapsing*. A terrible weight pushed upon her as the force of the crumbling portal threatened to crush her.

A twisted recollection of her lectures flashed through her mind: if a portal collapsed with the ship still inside, there wouldn't be enough left of the wreckage to identify.

They were all going to die, and it was her fault.

No!

Aimee pushed herself to her feet. Sweat poured from her brow. A reckless possibility flashed through her mind: recast the last half of the spell. Pick a new destination and use the next surge of energy to force the ship through. Insane. Desperate.

She had no other choice.

Her arms ached. She separated her hands, felt the power wane, felt the ship start to invert itself. The spell was in her mind. She grabbed one of the last places she'd looked at on the map, took a best guess at the coordinates. *Do it now or everyone dies.*

A fresh surge of unsteady energy rippled up through the dais. She grabbed it, made the gestures, not to *open* a portal, but to *adjust* one. A new destination.

"By my command," she shouted into the collapsing dark, "bear me over the span between ship and shore!"

Her hands smashed together. The portal flared brighter. *Elysium* flew straight. A light bloomed at the far end – *finally* – and the ship sliced through to the strange heavens on the other side. Aimee fell to her knees, breathing hard. Harkon crouched at her side, her teacher's hands rested on her shoulders. "Rest. You did well. We're alright."

A crackling blast erupted somewhere off port. *Elysium* veered starboard and a succession of staccato explosions ripped across the sky in front of the viewport.

"Sons of the Abyss!" Clutch swore. "Hang on!" She spun the wheel and set her feet. Aimee gripped the rail as the ship lurched sideways. "Vant. Hard burn!"

The engines roared, and through the viewport Aimee watched as their hard turn brought them straight into a holocaust of weaponsfire carving up the skies. Here and there, warships and civilian craft sliced through the air. Burning. Exploding. Crackling ether-cannons tore up the clouds. The world was a haze of smoke.

Hell, Aimee thought through the haze of horror and exhaustion. *I've sent us to hell.*

"Take us starboard, *starboard!*" Harkon shouted above the noise. "*Now!*"

Clutch spun the wheel again. As *Elysium* swung the way its master had commanded, Aimee caught a glimpse of a landmass far below. She saw tall mountains, deciduous trees in all the colors of early autumn, and a vast plume of smoke belching from a mass of red fire contained by walls. No. Her mouth hung open and her throat dried as the reality sank in. A city. A city was before them, engulfed in flame. Above it, a mountain hung in the sky, impossibly vast, bristling with guns spewing devastation in every direction.

Aimee felt a *massive* wall of magic energy wash over her as *Elysium* passed through a rapidly expanding, invisible barrier. "A portal shield," she breathed. "Oh Gods, we're *trapped.*"

"Burn hard and fast," Harkon said. "After the ships bearing the tartan flag."

"I don't understand," Clutch shouted back. "Where *are* we?"

"Hell, or damn near it," Harkon said.

"Port Providence." Bjorn breathed below. "The rumors are true."

CHAPTER FOUR
GRAY FALCON'S FALL

Azrael knelt in the darkness. The mystic circle surrounded him, crackling with the strain of his power. One hand was pressed to the silver and black marble, while light burst and snapped between his fingers. Yet despite the raging power of the communication spell ripping across the vast distances to its target, all the knight felt was a terrible, all-encompassing cold. The skin of his neck prickled. His breath was ragged.

The light died. The shadows descended, and Azrael took a shaking breath that scraped against raw, aching nerves. His master's presence pressed down upon him. The weight of a thousand vows.

It had worked.

"Azrael," the smooth baritone whispered, and Azrael's chest froze. "You're reporting in early."

"Forgive me, my lord," Azrael forced his voice to steady in the presence of the man that had taught him fear, and how to master it. "I am soon to venture into the field. I may be unable to send word for some time."

"Lord Ogier tells me you threatened to carve out his apprentice's eyes and tongue for defying you," the voice answered. The sentence hung, unfinished, the threat implicit. Azrael fought to steady his hands. Sweat droplets fell free from his forehead.

"Elegant," his master finished.

Azrael's eyes remained closed, his focus upon maintaining the spell. Fear clawed at his concentration, mocked his effort at maintaining the magic. The intuitive arcanism of the Eternal Order was unlike any other sorcery. They made no gestures, spoke no words. Internally, a knight called the spells he needed with thought and focus. The truly great spells that opened portals, shook islands, or split the heavens were beyond their abilities, but it didn't matter. To other mages, their power was terrifyingly fast. So long as a knight kept his focus, his strength could not waver.

"What breathes defiance must be strangled until it doesn't breathe at all." Azrael said. "I remember, Lord Roland."

"Yes," came the calm reply. "Now, I presume you have a *reason* for reaching out to me?"

"The Axiom is within my reach," Azrael said. His hand shook. "I assault the citadel of Gray Falcon today. A gray sage hides there. I will find him."

A lightening of the weight followed, but Azrael still drew each breath with difficulty. The voice sounded pleased. "And Port Providence?"

"The city is an inferno," Azrael affirmed. Shredded buildings. A sea of horror swam before his eyes. The black knight pushed the feelings down, crushed them with the weight of his own will. Fear was weakness. Weakness was death.

Burning flowers. Smoldering walls.

"We left none alive," Azrael continued. "I have slain

Prince Collum, and claimed his enchanted sword as my own."

"Good," came the response. "I am proud of your progress."

Azrael shuddered. His hands ached, still pressing against the mystic circle. "Thank you, master. Are there any further commands you have before I depart?"

Silence, then the ominous reply: "This hunt is your greatest test, student. The Axiom your personal crucible. But when you lay it in my hands, the key that our order has long sought will be in my grasp. There will be no treasure we cannot find, no enemy able to hide beyond our reach. As I rise, so shall you." The weight pressed abruptly, cruelly, down again. For a moment, Azrael remembered every blow meted upon him for failure at his master's will. Sweat pooled below him. His back felt as though it would snap.

"Do not fail," Lord Roland said.

The spell dissipated, the magic of the circle ceased. Azrael collapsed forward. He caught himself on his palms, and took a few moments to calm his ragged breathing.

Do not fail.

His heart hammered in his chest. Eyes wide. Fists clenched against the stone. Fear burned over his thoughts, setting limbs to shuddering like a child in the dark.

Elias.

Azrael squeezed shut his eyes, forced his mouth into a thin line, and clamped down on meaningless images of crisping walls, the nonsensical sounds of half-remembered music, and the burning scent of roses. The mantra flowed from his lips. "I am the hammer, the razor wind, the unfeeling storm. My breath is obedience. My only love my master's killing will. I live. I kill. I serve. My name is Azrael, and I am a knight of the Eternal Order."

Limbs slowed their shaking. His heart settled into a reasonable rhythm. At length, the black knight rose from his crouch. There was butcher's work to be done.

The frigates were light warships, built in the yards of the House of Nails under the watchful eyes of the order's master builders. Whereas Kiscadian and Violet Imperium ships of the line were designed around the philosophy of heavier armor and ever more guns, these skycraft were built along the principles for which their mother shipyards were famous: speed, power, and maneuverability.

Azrael had requested the frigate and its siblings for a reason, and now three night-dark knives roared over the landscape. Their hulls were black and slender wedges with needle points, and engine vents that glowed a hungry red. Less than three hundred feet below, trees whipped across the landscape, broken up by the occasional village. The gangway was open, and wind blasted past his armored form. Crouching in waitfullness at his back were Sir Kaelith and fifty heavily armored shock troops, braced to jump, razor-edged flame-lances in their armored fists.

"Three minutes to drop," Sir Kaelith said.

Azrael's hand tightened about Oath of Aurum's grip. Absently, he wondered at the irony of destroying the redoubt to which a third of Prince Collum's warriors had fled with the dead royal's own sword.

It seemed like something Lord Roland would appreciate.

He crouched. Up ahead, in the center of his vision, the

hilltop fortress of Gray Falcon rose from the landscape, taking its name, he supposed, from the vaguely bird-like cliff that jutted from its forward-most face. All about the citadel swarmed the ragged remnants of a small defensive fleet. Starving birds in the face of the oncoming storm. Azrael seized the end of the tube that sent his voice to the bridge, and spoke a single phrase.

"Shred them."

"As you command."

The frigate and its fellows rose higher. The trees fell away far beneath. The smooth arc of their speed took them another hundred feet up, putting them well into the sights of their enemy's spotters. Azrael saw ships starting to turn, glimpsed damaged, broad-winged civilian craft and battered gunboats with leonine figureheads struggling to bring themselves about. Too late. The forward-facing batteries of three frigates opened up, and the rhythmic pulse of red light cracked across the sky.

Gray Falcon's only line of defense erupted into a cacophonous wall of aerial fireballs. The frigates shot through the inferno, and began the turn for their second pass.

"Thirty seconds," Sir Kaelith said.

Azrael turned, looking at the men through the eye-slits of his new helm. "Crush your fear and smother your doubt. Our enemies are fleeing before us. Kaelith and I will clear the path for you. Survive the next ten minutes, and the citadel is yours to plunder."

Faces raised, lances raised in time with the chant of gruff voices. "AZRAEL! AZRAEL!"

Azrael turned towards the edge of the gangway. Gray Falcon was beneath him now, its hexagonal walls swarming with defenders. The black knight breathed and summoned three spells with a thought: one for speed, one for strength, one to slow his fall. He crouched, and leapt into the air. Silence. The wind whipped past. Azrael dropped like a shadow as the top of the wall grew in his vision. He drew his sword as he fell. The blade thrummed in his fingers.

If his mind held even the smallest kernel of doubt, his powers would falter.

Fear is weakness. Weakness is death.

His impact blasted flagstones with cracks fifteen feet to the left and right with a thundering crash, and the full weight of his landing scythed the enchanted steel through the first of the defenders. Two halves of gawking, shrieking soldier split in different directions. All around him, warriors recoiled in terror as the black knight straightened, flicking blood from his steel. Inside his helm, Azrael flashed a grim smirk.

"Next?"

Before they could find their courage, he was among them. Limbs, heads, and carved trunks of men split before him. He pushed forward, a black armored blur of gray steel trailing red and screams. Kaelith crashed down behind him, her great axe singing a dirge through shrieking warriors. The shock troops came behind. Flame-lances gleamed with mystic heat.

Pause for a moment, and he was dead.

Fear is weakness. Weakness is death.

A spear narrowly missed his face. A sword was flicked aside by Oath of Aurum before Azrael cut the man carrying it down. Focus. Willpower absolute. He paused as his troops barreled into the next cluster of defenders, taking stock of the chaos within the walls. The inner courtyard was a charnel house filled with fleeing servants and refugees. Every so often, one of them fell to Azrael's men as they rushed across the open space.

There were a lot of people dying down there.

The black knight surged forward again. No time for distractions.

In less than two minutes the wall was clear, and Azrael thundered across the red-drenched bridge towards the inner keep. Above their heads, the frigates circled, cutting vessels from the skies. At their back, a tumbling, burning gunship dropped below the outer edge of the wall before a deafening blast sent chunks of rubble raining across the inner courtyards. The air filled with the mingled scents of bile, blood, and ether-cannon afterburn.

Turning forward, stepping over a defender's corpse, a gate of oak and black iron filled Azrael's vision. A cluster of men made a mad retreat towards its closing center. Abruptly the swinging doors stopped, and the men trying to pull them shut began to panic as defenders flooded past them. Sir Kaelith was beside Azrael, now, one hand off her axe, maintaining the holding spell that kept the door from closing.

"Get on with it, my lord," the other knight snarled. "The damn thing is *heavy.*"

Azrael let go the sword with his left hand and stretched his palm towards the opening. Words of fire and hate filled his mind, and he let loose the magic with a primal scream. A hundred-foot gout of concussive force and mystic flame roared from his outstretched fingers. Men burned. Timbers crisped. Iron twisted, warped, and bent. With a stone-shaking crash, the gate of the inner keep exploded inward. Azrael staggered briefly from the effort, then straightened, raised his sword, and screamed the orders to the mass at his back. "The fortress is ours!

Woe to the conquered!" The blade dropped, pointed at the gaping hole at the bridge's end. "Take them!"

A cry rose behind Azrael. His sword swept down. A river of death flowed past.

The battle was a mad rush of dizzying adrenaline. In the heat of the blood and fury, Azrael was ablaze with feeling, a rush that made every breath real and every beat of his heart a treasure.

It came with a cost.

In the aftermath, nothing remained but exhaustion and the gnawing emptiness that settled over him in a numbing cloud. Seated upon the lord's seat of Gray Falcon's throneroom, all he felt was *nothing*. Even the slow, ponderous ministrations of Esric, his long-serving healer working over the wound in his shoulder, registered as no more than a distant sense of tugging and pulling. There should have been pain, but the black knight was too tired to feel it. The stitches binding up the sliced skin elicited no change in his expression, which must have unnerved the people cowering before him all the more.

To Azrael's right, Sir Kaelith stood, just behind the healer. To his left, a shock trooper, his flame lance dented by a soldier's axe.

The black knight took a breath and regarded the unfamiliar mass of dirty faces in varying states of tattered finery and scorched uniforms before him. Finally, he asked the healer beside him, "Who in the abyss am I looking at?"

"These are the assembled nobility and surviving officers we captured in the battle's aftermath, my lord," Esric said, calm, quiet. "Sir Cairn is bringing the last of them, forcibly extricated from the central tower."

There were twenty of them, surrounded by his soldiers. The sweaty, bloody stink of fear was everywhere. Azrael breathed, then addressed the assembled crowd. "You are defeated," he said simply. Blunt, as Roland had taught him. "Your fleet is destroyed, your warriors are dead. For your king's defiance, and your own, all lives present are forfeit."

A hush settled over the assembled faces. Some tartans still remained amidst the crowd, battered, but their brooches still shone. Azrael remembered Prince Collum's defiant eyes, his royal brooch. Some strength still lingered in these broken people. A small part of him felt a pang of admiration.

"Unless," he continued, "you give us what we want. We have learned that a member of the Order of Gray Sages called this place home. Turn him over to us, and we will spare your lives."

Silence, at first. Unsurprising. Then the first young noble tried to be a hero. He leapt from the crowd shrieking, a dirk in his fist. "Death to the conquerors!"

As the boy lunged up from the huddled masses, Azrael pivoted, sidestepped the awkward knife-thrust, and cut the youth's head from his shoulders. Red painted the marble at the foot of the throne room dais.

Blood. Blood on the floor. Azrael's head hurt. Images flashed through his mind, unbidden. Burning walls. Smoldering flowers. A song he heard in his dreams.

Enough. This is absurd.

Azrael turned back to the crowd. He should have been calm, but the words ripped out of him. "Are you finished?"

He was facing the rear of the room when the doors opened. Sir Cairn walked through. Ahead of him, he pushed three figures. The first was a young man with the same rust hair as Prince Collum, though perhaps ten years younger. Sixteen at the oldest. The second was an old man, wrapped in brown robes, blood leaking from a wound in his forehead.

Between them walked a woman whose hair had long ago gone white. She was dressed in a stately gown ripped and stained with blood – someone else's, by the look. Azrael faced them profiled, his face half in shadow.

"His Highness," Cairn said, pushing the shackled boy forward, "Prince Coulton of Port Providence. His grandmother, the Queen Mother Alahna, and their servant" – he seemed amused at this – "'Old Silas.'"

Coulton shook at his captor's leash, and straightened, staring Azrael in the face. Princely. Brave. "My brother Collum," he declared, "will punish you for this. He is in the sky, with a hundred of our late father's ships. When he reaches our allies in the Violet Imperium–"

Azrael turned to face the newcomers fully, and stepped into the light. From where they'd stood before, none of the three could have seen Oath of Aurum in the black knight's fist. The boy's eyes spotted it first, and the sight robbed him of breath.

"My brother's sword," the young prince said dumbly, fighting painful comprehension. "I... I don't understand. How do you have Collum's sword?" His tone rose, voice thick with a choking grief. "How?" he jerkily repeated. *"That's my brother's sword!"*

Azrael strode towards him. He held up the steel. It glinted in the faint light. "Was."

Coulton's hands clutched at the side of his face, and the sixteen year-old's defiant composure collapsed in a howl of pain.

The boy was caught by Silas, and the old man soothed him, manacled arms wrapped about his shoulders. His eyes darted to Azrael, and the black knight felt a chill run through him. "You fool boy," the old man said. "You don't know what you've broken. What Collum's death destroys."

Him. Azrael suddenly knew it. It was him. Silas was the sage.

The queen mother's eyes were wide with grief and pain. But it wasn't the sword she was staring at. It was Azrael's face. "Not possible," she whispered, over and over. "Not possible."

"You," Azrael leveled the point of his sword at the old man's throat. "You should've kept your mouth shut." He motioned to his warriors. "Take him."

But the queen mother moved first. She grabbed Azrael's left arm, pulled it violently. Caught off guard, he found himself staring into her amber eyes. "Your name," she demanded. "What is your *name*?"

Smoldering flowers. Burning walls. A shadow beyond the point of a sword in his hands, vast beyond reason. The music played over and over in Azrael's mind. The sides of his head ached. He tried to shake it off. Sir Kaelith moved. "My lord!" she shouted. Cairn reached for the queen mother. The black knight felt Esric's hand suddenly upon his back. It let him focus.

"I am Lord Azrael," he snapped. He jerked his hand violently from her grasp. "The steel fist of Lord Roland, reared in the House of Nails. Commander of this invasion, and *this* man," he gestured at Silas, "is now my–"

BANG!

A white light, bright and terrible, seared across his vision. Azrael was thrown back. He hit the ground, rolled, and came up with his sword in both hands. Silas stood in the center of a roaring inferno of white. A small gray shaft was in his fist that the bastard had somehow managed to hide. The black knight recognized it at once: a teleportation rod. Rare. One-use-only. The queen mother gave a violent shove and her grandson staggered into the gray sage's arms. "*Run!*" she screamed.

The light flared brighter.

"I am sorry, my queen," Silas answered. Sir Kaelith leapt down the steps. Her axe flashed through the air.

It struck carpet and shattered the flagstones beneath. Sage and prince both were gone, taken by the spell. "My lord," Esric said, helping Azrael to his feet. The old healer's voice was smooth, reassuring. "Are you alright?"

"They're gone!" Sir Cairn screamed.

"He won't be able to do that again," Azrael said. "It was a one-use rod. It'll be burnt out now."

"The spell was short range," Kaelith snarled. "They're within three miles."

"We'll *find* them," Azrael said, gaining his feet again. "Sir Cairn, secure every inch of this palace. I will hunt the boy and the sage down, myself. Then take *her*" – he gestured at the queen mother – "and send her back to the hulk."

Shaking off Esric's touch, he stormed from the room. "My lord," Kaelith said. "The other prisoners?"

"To the hulk as well," Azrael shouted over his shoulder. "Let Malfenshir have them."

His footfalls echoed on the stones. Louder. He needed the noises louder, to drown out the music, and stifle the smell of burning flowers.

It didn't work.

CHAPTER FIVE
THE GUNS OF PORT PROVIDENCE

Aimee's heartbeat pounded in her ears. She limped down from the portal deck, her hands on the railing. Failure, hot and shameful, flooded through her. Less than two hours ago she'd been lecturing Vlana on the laws of magic. Confident. Swaggering.

A muffled *BOOM* echoed outside the ship. Further away than the last had been. The thrum of the metadrive moved beneath her feet. She reached the hall ahead of her teacher, slammed a hand into the wall – out of rage, to steady her breathing. Vlana was feeding Clutch numbers. Bjorn pushed past them. She heard him shouting over his shoulder. "I can handle one gunship!"

Harkon was alongside her. She felt his hand on her shoulder. She shook him off. "Give me a job," she said. She smelled wind. Wind and the unique crisping smell mages sometimes caught from a metadrive working at maximum capacity.

"You need to rest…" Harkon started.

"No," Aimee wheeled to face him. The motion nearly made her lose her feet. It was only the pulsing pace of the metadrive racing through the ship that told her they were going very, *very* fast. "I need something to *do*."

She tried to head to the bridge. The hand caught her shoulder again. Aimee yanked her arm away from him.

"Apprentice..." Harkon's voice, though quiet, was firm enough that she couldn't look away. The formal term. She looked back into his eyes. "Tell me what happened."

Aimee stared back. The urge to explain herself, to cover for her mistakes, died in her mouth. Her heartbeat hammered painfully in her temples. Lightheaded. She might be a failure, but she wouldn't be a *dishonest* failure.

"I lost control," she said. "I opened the portal, and it never connected to Ishtier. It started to collapse. The magic surged out of my control, so I recast the second half of the spell, and picked a random location." She gestured about her. "And it brought us... here."

"That's shame talking," Harkon said. "Name it, then move along. Discard blame. Give me *specifics*."

The ship banked hard. Through the hallway up ahead, Aimee could see the other Port Providence ships flying alongside them. Clutch held the wheel. Calm. In control. Vlana was feeding her data from her navigation console. A loud *WHUMP* sounded from the rear. Bjorn was firing the rear ether-cannons at whatever pursued them.

"I had a regular flow of magic," Aimee said. "I summoned with the proper gestures. I channeled and directed. I adjusted. Then the energy started surging. Coming to me irregularly." Her jaw tightened to keep her mouth from quivering at the admission. "I couldn't control it. Third prime, sir. I didn't adapt quickly enough."

A blast sounded somewhere in the distance. Aimee heard Bjorn shout a battle cry, triumphant. "Any more on our tail?" Clutch's voice sounded over the tubes.

"None," Bjorn's voice echoed back. "At least not yet.

Keep us going, Clutch. Fast and hard. Maybe they'll give chase, maybe they won't, but for now I don't see anything."

"Check," Clutch confirmed from the bridge. Then she turned the wheel again. *Elysium* climbed. Aimee adjusted her footing.

"Sir," Aimee said again. "I need–"

"To rest." Harkon cut off further protest. "We're out of the fire for the moment. My crew know what they're doing. Maybe you made a mistake," he said. "But a portal got away from you and we're not scattered over eighty different provinces right now. You kept your head. Now put it down on something soft and recover your strength."

Somehow, Harkon was calm, collected, and supportive, even while cannons were blazing.

He gave her a gentle nudge that boded no argument, towards her cabin. "You'll need it."

It was three hours rest and two more flying before Aimee felt like she could breathe normally again. *Elysium* sailed amidst a cloud of limping vessels, some damaged, others unscathed. Even still, despite the lack of explosions rippling across the skies, there remained an air of tangible panic, draped thick and cloying over everything. Fear had a distinctive, clammy stink, and Aimee couldn't escape it.

She stood in the dining area, fingers wrapped like a vice about the rail before the viewport. Sleep had restored some of her energy, but very little of her nerves. From *Elysium*'s vantage point, the banners painted upon the nearest ships were almost legible. She saw a coat of arms she didn't recognize: two black lions rampant

on a tartan field. She'd never been much interested in
heraldry or noble lineages. She wondered if this one
would be condemned to the same obscurity and slow
death history gave to other kings who had lost their
kingdoms. The Drifting Lands were full of different
forms of government: from the Violet Imperium with its
thousand fiefs, to the Kiscadian Republic and its endless
chambers of debate, hundred-fold bureaucracies and
ritualized version of the thousand-god faith that deified
democracy. Gray Towers was a theocracy, her own
home of Havensreach was a parliamentary republic, and
neighboring Drakesburg had its lifetime-serving, elected
oligarchs. But no matter where you came from, or what
your history, one thing seemed true: the past wasn't
recoverable. No matter how people begged and wept and
clawed at old books, things never went back to the way
they were. Royals who couldn't keep their crowns didn't
get them back.

Footsteps – heavy ones – announced the presence
of the white-haired gunner and cook. Currently, Bjorn
looked more like the former than the latter. His face was
stained with soot and he was toweling grease from his
meaty hands.

"You alright, girl?" he asked. The tone was neutral.
The expression blank.

Aimee took a shaking breath. It rattled through her in
time with the pounding of her heart. She paused at the
edge of saying what was on her mind, then it tumbled
out. "This is my fault."

She let it hang there, spoken, unable to be taken back.

The old warrior sighed, then gave a nod. "Yes."

They stood opposite one another in the dimming
sunlight flooding in from outside.

"I've never screwed up like that before," she said. She didn't know the old man from a hole in the wall, nor anything about his relationship with her teacher, or the crew amongst whom she felt acutely like an outsider. "When I did, it affected you all. I'm sorry."

Bjorn stared at her, the pale eyes considering. Eventually, he simply said, "Apologies don't matter to me. I want to know what you're going to *do*."

Aimee stared back. Her throat went dry. For the first time in her life, she didn't have a quipping answer. "I don't know."

Bjorn frowned. "Well figure it out quick, girl."

"Bjorn." The new voice came from Vlana. The quartermaster walked in from the bridge, eyes lined, posture tired. "She doesn't need more admonishing."

"I'm fine," Aimee said, holding up one hand while the other brushed blonde hair out of her face. "You've got a right to be mad."

Neither of them seemed to have any answer to that, so Aimee asked a question of her own, something that had eaten at her since she first boarded the ship.

"You all looked really comfortable out there," Aimee said, referencing the ease with which the two people in front of her, and the pilot still on the bridge, had handled a firefight. "And this ship is awfully well-armed for an *explorer*."

Vlana and Bjorn exchanged a look. Aimee folded her arms across her chest. "This ship isn't a refurbished Cirrus-class air-schooner, is it? It's not even civilian grade."

Bjorn's smile was rueful.

"So what is it?" Aimee asked. "Regal-class? It has the integral guns, but the profile's too narrow. Janus-class?

It's small enough, but no ship this size can carry this sort of armament and still fly so fast."

Silence. Bjorn gave Vlana a sideways look.

"At least tell me the class," Aimee pressed.

"*Elysium*-class," Vlana said quietly.

That caught Aimee off guard. "Wait, it's the *first* of its category?"

"It's the *only* one of its category," Vlana answered. "The first of a new line of warships that was never made. One of a kind. No equal."

Aimee sagged back against the railing, her breath leaving her in a rush. "… I thought you were explorers."

"We are," Bjorn said. "But where we go, people tend to shoot at us."

"Explanations can come later," Vlana said. "But suffice to say, this isn't the first time we've been in a situation like this. We just… weren't expecting it, this time."

Aimee pinched the bridge of her nose, folded her arms across her chest, considering, then decided against pressing further, for the time being. "What's the plan?"

"For now?" Harkon said from the door to the bridge. "Talk. I've made contact with the senior officer in the remnants of this fleet, and I'm known to her. She will be on our ship in twenty minutes, then we'll have a few more answers."

Answers, Aimee reflected. Yeah. She was going to need a *lot* of those, later.

Twenty minutes later, Aimee stood in the docking bay, listening to the locks clicking into place. She wore her long blue coat, and stood beside her teacher, back straight, eyes ahead. The pressure released, and the doors slid slowly open. Two soldiers wearing battered swords and stained uniforms stepped through, eyes alight with paranoid suspicion. Behind Aimee and her teacher, Bjorn gave a low grunt. Next to him, beside his sister Vlana, was Vant. The engineer was like a slightly stockier, angrier version of his sister, with black hair and jewel-toned, tanned skin. His eyes were thin, dark, and irritated.

"Easy," came a new voice. "They're friends."

The woman who stepped through next was dressed in a worn uniform jacket beneath a green and black tartan chased with cloth of gold. She walked with a slight limp. Rusty hair covered her head, and her worn face was tired.

"I've heard the legends about the name Harkon Bright," the newcomer said. "But I didn't think to find him coming to our rescue."

"I wish I could say that was my purpose," Aimee's teacher said, his dark face regretful. "But we were just passing through. Who are you, and what happened?"

"My name," the warrior said, "is Captain Gara. I was a servant of his highness, Prince Collum, and now, by the grace of heaven, I am the commander of what little remains of this fleet. As to what happened, we're still trying to sort all that out. Weeks ago, the Eternal Order sent one of their knights to threaten our late king. When his majesty and Prince Collum threw him out, he left, promising absolute oblivion. A week later, the *Iron Hulk* appeared in our skies, and our city burned."

"What did the Order want?" Aimee asked. She tried to call to mind what she remembered of the mercenary organization called the Eternal Order. There had been references in her history books back at the academy. "The Eternal Order is just a mercenary order of magic-wielding knights." She saw Harkon twitch out of the corner of her eye. "They don't *do* this sort of thing. Invade of their own accord, I mean." She looked at her teacher. "Do they?"

Harkon was quiet for a moment. "Just once," he said, adding nothing further.

Aimee made a note to press her teacher *at length* about that, later.

"I was there," Gara said. "He demanded his brethren have access to the inner wilderness of our kingdom for a period of no less than two weeks. The king refused."

"The knight," Harkon murmured. "Tell me about him."

Gara shuddered. Her eyes closed for a moment. "Young. Different from the others. Every story I'd heard about the skull-masked freaks was of fury and rage and butchery. This one... He couldn't have been past his twentieth year: clean-shaven, cold green eyes. He stood before our king, and promised the destruction of the entire kingdom like he was telling us about the weather."

"His name," Harkon murmured. "Did he give it? Or his master's?"

"Aye," Gara said. "Lord Azrael, student of Lord Roland."

Harkon closed his eyes, let out a long breath, and gave a slow nod. "Captain Gara," he continued, before Aimee could ask a question, "whatever my crew and myself can do to help you and your people, we will."

Bjorn physically *twitched* behind the two of them. Vant actually said "Oh *come on.*"

"Thank you, Magister Bright," Gara breathed a sigh of relief, using the formal title. "I wish I could ask something simple of you, but the truth is we've wound up on the wrong side of their blockade–"

"Oh for heaven's *sake!*" Vant swore. "This *always* happens."

"–And, if you have an infirmary, we have numerous wounded–"

The engineer's voice got even more aggravated. "Of *course* you do."

"Vant," Bjorn grunted, "this is what we *do*. We help."

"I've some skill as a chirurgeon," Vlana said, cutting off her brother. "I will do what I can. Vant, stop grumbling. This isn't even the worst fight we've stuck our necks into. Skyfarers remember."

Aimee had heard her uncle say that more than once, a long time ago. Bjorn's words echoed in her head. *Where we go, people tend to shoot at us.*

She gave the quartermaster a significant look.

"Later," Vlana muttered.

Aimee turned back to the captain and his men and pulled her thoughts together. "I studied some of the basic healing spells," she added. "I can accelerate the process, so long as the wounds have been closed and the bones have been set. Basic healing magic draws some of its power from the person being mended, so they'll at least need to be able to survive it, but I'll do what I can." Then, before the conversation could proceed further, she asked, "Where do you need to go?"

"Land's Edge," Gara said. "The far side of the isle. The enemy hasn't reached it yet. From there we can hold out until Prince Collum returns."

"The prince is *missing?*" Aimee asked.

"Last seen over Port Providence's skies," Gara affirmed, "his enchanted sword in hand, rallying the fleet. But we do not fret. Prince Collum has been subject of a prophecy since his childhood. The seers are never wrong."

Aimee exchanged a glance with her teacher. Somehow she doubted that. *Don't argue with her*, the older man's eyes said. Aimee nodded, and turned her attention back to their guest. "Bring us your injured," she said. "We will help those we can."

"There's a list of things you're not telling me," Aimee said hours later. She stood before her teacher, outside an infirmary stuffed with twelve wounded men and women. Soldiers. Skyfarers.

The expression Harkon gave her was worn out and resigned, as if her words frosted a particularly unpalatable cake. "There's plenty I've not told you *yet*," he corrected. "Don't mistake a sense for what's relevant for deception, student." He regarded her, then. "But I assume you're addressing something specific."

Aimee nodded. "Specific and relevant, teacher."

Harkon watched her. Measuring. Considering. "Ask."

Aimee took a breath. Boundaries were still unclear. Harkon Bright had been one of her teachers at the academy. Had regarded her highly enough to take her on as his apprentice. But other than bonding in the dining room and their time at school, she didn't really know him. She knew he was kind, but back in Havensreach, the public understanding of Harkon was that he and his crew left on multi-year survey trips into the Unclaimed. Purely research. She was thinking now of the other rumors she'd heard – and disregarded – about him: Harkon the rebel. Harkon the troublemaker. The professional dissident. The mage who meddled. The man who used his power to start fights with countries.

It wasn't all a lie, clearly. Not by the way Gara had

reacted to him. Nor by *Elysium*'s armament. *First in a class of warships that was never made*. She was on a military vessel that she'd believed to be an explorer. Apprenticed to a man she was now coming to realize had a history of rather more violent pursuits than exploration.

But would he lie to her? Moreover, a part of her quietly considered, why didn't this bother her more?

"You know the knight who leads this invasion," she said, pushing all those complex thoughts to the side for the moment.

Harkon sighed, shaking his head. "I do not."

"His master, then," Aimee pressed. "I saw your face, and heard your voice, teacher." She knew she was entering dangerous territory, but the thought of an enemy hidden in part by her instructor's secrets worried her. "Please," she added. "If we're going to be going up against this person, I need to know."

Her teacher's expression – regretful, tired, reluctant – told her she'd hit upon the right question. But would he demur? Ever since she was a girl, the world around her had sought to protect Aimee from harm. *Please*, she thought. *Don't coddle me*.

"Eager for that, are you?" he asked at length. Blunt. Expressionless. She could feel him assessing her.

Aimee felt the test. She stared it full in the face. There was no way to meet this but head on. "Eager to lock horns with an order of murderous mercenary knights who wield magic even the academy doesn't understand?" she answered. "No. But I hate bullies and monsters, so if fighting them is what we're going to do, count me in."

"Lord Roland," Harkon said then, "is a powerful figure in the Eternal Order, unmerciful and arrogant, but wise, and cunning as well. We have a history. Have faced each other three times. Once *he* barely escaped, once *I* barely escaped. The third time was a draw, and I do not know what would happen were we to meet again. If this Azrael is his student, to call him dangerous is an understatement."

Aimee felt a lead weight settle in her chest, tied to her heart with a string and dragging it slowly down. "Thank you," she breathed. "I suppose this is where I ask, 'What now?'"

"Now," Harkon said, looking back over his shoulder at the hallway that stretched the length of the ship, "I make Vant very angry before he remembers that we've done this before. We're going to run a blockade."

"I'm not worried about whether *we* can do it," Clutch protested as Aimee's boots clicked on the deck of the bridge, an hour later. The air outside the main viewport swam with ships limping across a bleeding sky. The sunset was *achingly* beautiful: the golden haze of true west spilled forth the last rays of day to paint the clouds the colors of blood and treasure.

"*Elysium* is one of a kind," the pilot continued. "Faster and tougher than most warships. We've got the guns. We've got the speed. But we're not invincible. And if we go slow enough for these ancient Port Providence ships to keep pace, we run a much higher risk of getting hammered into the ground."

"What, my amazing pilot isn't ready to duck and weave?" Harkon asked with a smirk, following after.

"Dammit, Hark," Clutch grumbled, "there is a limit to how much I can loop-the-loop my way out of this. This is a *skyship*, not a set of tap shoes."

"That is what Miss Laurent and I are for," Harkon said

with a smile. "Making up the difference."

"What's the plan, chief?" Vlana asked. She looked exhausted from hours spent mending wounds, but her hands were steady at her navigational station.

"Go fast enough to outrun the guns," Harkon answered. "Slow enough to let the slower Port Providence ships follow. We go in with forward batteries blazing and Aimee and myself guarding us against arcane assault. The other vessels will follow behind us, and we'll be doing it all under the cover of night."

"Gods," Vant shook his head. The engineer frowned and stuffed his hands into his pockets. "I assume you want us at full burn the whole time?"

"I didn't acquire *Elysium* to fly her slowly," Harkon said with a smirk.

"No," Vant sighed, heading back down to the engine room. "Just to pick fights with devils."

"Oh come on," Vlana called back after her brother. "This is like the ninth time we've done this!"

"You're not the one who has to clean the chaos-inhibitors!" Vant yelled back.

They were turning now, the slow sweep of clouds swimming before Aimee's vision.

"Come," Harkon said to her. "It's time you learned how to cast a defensive matrix."

The two of them walked to an alcove at the front of the bridge.

"You've learned basic defensive shielding," Harkon said. "But what's taught at the academy is primarily intended for individual mage-duels or protection from gunfire."

"A cone of defense or a wall of impenetrable will," Aimee affirmed, recalling from her texts like rote.

"Shielding against ranged attack is best which covers angles reaching back across the body from a central point out front. Like the point guards of a good swordsman. Basic battle and defense magic."

"Right out of Professor Thorp's defense classes," Harkon said with an approving nod. "Far from being separate concepts, sorcery and swordplay are mirrors. The same principles that serve the one, likewise serve the other: adaptability, proper form, technique, assertiveness. The trick, then, is teaching you to widen that shield, until it is an entire vessel that is defended, and not just one person."

Aimee breathed, feeling the familiar thrill of imminent learning. Her fingers flexed in anticipation of the power she was about to master. "I'm ready."

"You're getting back that confidence. Good," her teacher remarked. He raised his hands. "Pick a point, fifty to one hundred or so feet out in front of you. The angle that proceeds past must cover the *entire* ship, at least from the point where you stand. Make that your focus point, and build the sorcery from that direction."

He showed her the hand gestures, identical to the basic defensive spells she knew, but broadened, more precise. He gave her the words next. "On these," he said, "you must be absolutely certain."

"I've learned a thing or two about certainty," Aimee answered. "How long do I have to practice?"

"An hour," Harkon said. "Then it's time to fail or fly. For all of us. You'll need both hands to maintain this thing. It's too big for one."

She took a shaky breath to steady her nerves, nodding. Turning, she picked a place out in the open air before her, and crystalized it – and its relational distance to herself and the ship – in her mind. Her fingers flexed as the energy of her magic boiled through her veins. Another large-scale spell, so shortly after she'd bungled the first. The fear pulled at her, distracted her. She forced it from her mind. There was no time for terror, or doubt, or the crippling selfishness of self-image. Violence was ahead, vast engines of destruction stalking the heavens. Hundreds of lives hung in the balance, and soon her magic would guard them.

She closed her eyes, breathed out, and spoke the words. Her rapidly moving fingers trailed streaks of light through the evening air, and with a final, potent incantation, she sent the defensive spell rippling out in front of the ship's nose. A mandala of celestial flame flashed into being, cone-shaped, warding the bow of *Elysium* as it thundered through the skies.

Success flooded through her, and relief, as hands outstretched, she held the massive defensive matrix in place. Her magic was working. War lay ahead of her, but in the moment she was ready.

"Good," Harkon said with quiet pride. "We'll make a legend of you yet."

A wild, joyous laugh burst forth from Aimee, standing at the prow of the vessel, raw and defiant against the oncoming night.

CHAPTER SIX
HIS LORDSHIP'S VENDETTA

For the first time in years, Azrael remembered his nightmares. Vast walls of mist surrounded him. He clutched an oversized sword in his hands, and stood before a vast, inexorable shadow. He tried to fight it, but it swatted his blade aside, and its icy claws closed about his throat.

He awoke choking for breath. His hand fumbled for water in the dark and knocked the glass from beside the bed. Its contents splattered across the floor. Blearily, Azrael opened his eyes. Moonlight flooded through the windows of Gray Falcon's royal bedchamber. He sat up and cursed in the dark.

The queen mother stood at the foot of the bed. Her terrible amber eyes gleamed. The shade of Prince Collum stood beside her, chest awash with blood. She pointed a hand towards Azrael's chest and spoke a word: "Elias."

Azrael's breast smoked and sizzled, and the heart within caught fire. The smell of roasting meat filled his senses. He reached for Oath of Aurum. The blade glowed bright as day, and burned his hands.

The knight's eyes opened. He awoke again – truly, this

time. He was in a tent, not Gray Falcon's state rooms. The sounds about him were those of the deep wilderness, and it was the scent of breakfast that pulled him up, not his own boiling blood.

Two days, and no sign of the prince or of the gray sage.

Azrael rose, dressed, and stepped outside the tent. The small encampment was wedged into the stone base of a natural clearing in the depths of the forests around the conquered castle. Evergreens climbed skyward in every direction, and the ground was dusted with brown needles and leaves. Everywhere was the scent of dry autumn forest, crisp and cool. Esric was tending to a cook fire, while their other raiders mended weapons and prepared for the day's hunt.

"My lord has been dreaming again," the middle-aged healer murmured.

Azrael frowned. "Lurking outside my tent is rude."

"My task is to watch over the wellbeing of the Order's members, and yours in particular, for nearly thirteen years," Esric shrugged. "Nightmares are evidence of an unquiet mind."

Azrael grunted in response, then fetched his gear from the tent. He emerged, dressed in the cloth and synthetic mesh he wore beneath his plate, the dead prince's sword hung from his hip. "They're nothing," he continued. "Just a comedown from the bloodletting."

Elias.

"Even so," Esric said. "Your mind and will must be singularly focused, and guilt in the heart or mind is a dangerous weakness. Guilt is not for such as you. Now, let me check your shoulder."

The healer stepped in unbidden, pressed his hands to

the previously wounded space. Azrael's hand snapped like a whip to his sword's hilt. His vision narrowed to a red pinprick. "Do not *touch* me."

Esric paused, hands up before him. "I merely wish," he said quietly, "to administer the proper remedies." The words carried a weight that washed over the black knight, soothing the fear. "Please, my lord, *comply*."

Azrael's vision wavered. His hand slipped from the hilt of his sword. He didn't resist the second time. He felt a brief prick of pain before the familiar relief of the healing magics flowed over him. With it came a sense of centering calm, as his attention was oriented away from the stress of the night's bad sleep, and onto the task ahead.

"You're welcome," Esric said mildly, when Azrael said nothing.

"You're a loremaster," the black knight said, as he donned his armor.

"I am," Esric nodded.

"Tell me about the Axiom."

Esric paused. "Did your master not brief you on its nature and importance?"

"He did," Azrael said, straightening. He tightened the straps of his armor before continuing. "But not in great detail. I want to know more."

Esric hesitated. He was a small man, truly. His hair was gray and his face was unremarkable. His eyes were the color of mud, and he had a pale, wispy beard on his chin. "It allows the one who masters it to perceive truth. That is what the legends say. Surely, you don't need me to explain to you *why* that's invaluable to the order. *Any* truth. Secret treasures, hidden motives, double agents, unexpected alliances. With it, nothing could stand before the order."

"Even if it was a mere trinket, it wouldn't matter," Sir Kaelith said, approaching the two, her armor donned. "Where our masters command, we go."

"Let him finish talking," Azrael said.

"The Order of Gray Sages guards its location," Esric continued. "It was not always so, however. There was a time when the Axiom belonged to the Eternal Order, or so I have read."

"And it was stolen by the sages, yes, yes," Sir Kaelith confirmed. "We all know that story."

"Do you?" Esric answered, amused.

The key that our order has long sought will be in my grasp. The words of Azrael's master echoed through his mind. The chill of freshly remembered fear crept spider-like up his neck, and the black knight suppressed a shudder.

Elias.

"Regardless of what it does," he murmured, "we still need to find it."

His master hadn't told him everything. Azrael's gloved hand balled into a fist. Irrelevant. Absolute willpower. Absolute focus.

"The damn sage and his prince will have an idea," Sir Kaelith said, assured. "We've just got to–"

The slug slammed into the back of Kaelith's armor. She flew fifteen feet forward, and her landing collapsed a tent. Esric dropped to his hands and knees. Ten feet to Azrael's right, a sword stamped with a noble crest cut the head from one of his warriors. Red gore painted the earth, and the war scream of a tartan-clad raiding party filled the air as a tide of blades came rushing from the woods.

Dammit all, they'd told him the locals didn't *have* guns.

•••

There was no time to assess numbers. A screaming man with a two-handed sword came rushing at Azrael, and the black knight hadn't had time to don his helm. The spell for speed flowed through his limbs and he flickered left. The large blade tasted earth instead of flesh. The black knight's magic sword flashed free, and he had a half-breath's glimpse of his attacker's stupefied face before the blade split the head, and the man beneath, in half.

Azrael danced right, now. A tartan-clad man held a slug-throwing pistol in an outstretched hand, his face screaming defiance. The black knight's speed was *just* enough. Fire bloomed in Azrael's vision, and he felt the wind of the bullet sail past. The shooter's face still wore the same expression as Oath of Aurum sliced through his trunk.

Red trailed in Azrael's wake. He ran for the center of the raiding party, face a mask, eyes wide and muscles suffused with his magic.

Elias. The word wouldn't leave his mind. He cut down another man, and another. Their screams echoed distorted behind him. *Elias.* Walls of impenetrable black surrounded him as nightmares bled into reality. Raiders became silhouettes; their shouts were faraway echoes underlain by the repeated, hammer-like commands of his master.

"… this hunt is your greatest test, student…"

"The Axiom your personal crucible."

Azrael's head throbbed in a vice of pain. His hands danced upon the sword's hilt. Swift hews and thrusts left white streaks across his vision. Camp and forest blurred with his movements, and the men of Port Providence shouted as he came. Blows struck him, but his armor turned them aside. Slow. Distracted. Too many thoughts in his head.

KILL.

It ended as swiftly as it began. Azrael bore down upon their leader – a broadshouldered man with a thick mustache – in a storm of attacks that drove him to his knees, pushed the noble-stamped blade from his hands, and ended with the black knight standing over him with Oath of Aurum poised at the center of his throat. Azrael's left hand was off the grip now, fingers smoking from the flames with which he'd melted another man's skull. In the aftermath of his own potent spells, his body quaked with an exhaustion he dared not let show. Weakness was death.

"Kaelith?" he asked the settled chaos behind him.

"Alive," Esric answered. "Her armor saved her, though there's bad bruising beneath. Here she comes now."

In a semicircle, Azrael's surviving warriors stood, long spears leveled at the remnants of their attackers. Twelve, he now saw, counting the corpses alongside the living. The man in front of him was breathing hard, hands at his sides, eyes staring down the length of Azrael's blade in hateful defiance.

"Cut his head off," Kaelith snarled somewhere behind Azrael.

"Go ahead," the leader defied. "Paint the ground with my blood. Consecrate the earth."

Azrael rolled his eyes. "Sir Kaelith, *shut up.*" He withdrew the point from the man's throat. *Weakness is death,* Lord Roland's teaching rang through his mind. *Show him.*

His stomach turned.

Do it.

"Comply," Esric said behind him.

Azrael let the point drop, then drove it into the joint of the man's left shoulder and twisted. Defiance turned to a high-pitched scream of pain.

"Now," Azrael said mildly, stomach revolting. "Let's start with your name."

"Useless," Azrael snarled an hour later, washing the blood from his hands. "Useless, pointless, stupid."

"I thought his rendition of his titles was hilarious," Sir Kaelith chuckled, testing her axe. "It just kept getting higher."

Behind them, their men gathered corpses into a pile. As he let the water clean the blood from his hands, the lord's blood-streaked, terrified face seemed to swim in his vision. Azrael just felt ill.

Weakness is death.

"Sir Cairn reports by spell from Gray Falcon," Esric said, approaching the two men. "The fortress's lower levels have been completely secured. There is no sign of hidden escape routes, and their hangar bays on the lower levels had no missing vessels."

"Damned teleportation rod," Kaelith growled. "The bastards could be *anywhere*."

"Anywhere on this *island*," Azrael reminded him, toweling off his hands. "And wherever he *is*, he can't go far. The man is old, and he can't use the rod again."

Kaelith frowned, her heavy brow contemplating the treeline. "So what next, my lord?"

Azrael turned. The vastness of Gray Falcon loomed above the tops of the evergreens in the distance. He could see the thin, knife-like line of one of their frigates docked with its central tower. "We return to the frigate, then make our way back to Lord Malfenshir. I must commune with my master again."

Elias.

As he turned to retrieve his things, Esric was ordering the striking of the camp, whilst a small group of the men took to the task of properly arranging their enemies' corpses into a gruesome display.

"And the fortress?" Kaelith asked.

"Loot it," Azrael replied. "Then burn it to the ground."

A frigate roared across the heavens towards the *Iron Hulk*. In its wake, a fortress that had stood for five hundred years smoldered with a heat that cracked and melted stone. Every few moments, a pocket of enchantment left within the walls by the builders caught flame, blasting plumes of liquid, multicolored fire into the sky and sending a terrible rain of debris hundreds of feet wide into the forest below.

Azrael stood and watched from the rearmost viewport of the ship. The sun was setting behind the tortured landscape. He supposed that soon the forest would catch fire. It had, after all, been a very dry summer in Port Providence. A sick, lead weight twisted in his trunk. His jaw twitched. He was not supposed to think that way. Weakness was death.

"How find you the inferno?" Esric asked, walking up beside him. The healer was toweling the blood of a recent chirurgery from his hands. "Given the fortress's age, and the power locked within it, it may burn for as many as twenty years."

The lead weight inside Azrael dropped. His breathing was briefly difficult. Esric looked at him. *Weakness is death.*

The black knight mastered himself with a shrug of his

shoulders. "Tell Malfenshir that we will be back within a day. I expect him to have made camp and begun deploying troops for proper subjugation of the ground. I must report to my master."

As he turned and walked away, Esric called after him. "You did not answer my question, my lord."

"It is a fire," Azrael replied. *It is my fault.* "It burns."

When he reached his cabin, the circle glimmered in the corner. The room was otherwise austere, consisting only of bed, trunk, and the small carpet on which he did his meditations.

You're procrastinating, he thought. *You need to make your report.*

He knelt on the circle, pressed his hands to the rune-covered surface, and used his power to call across the expanse once more. Pressure. Pain. He felt the immense strain of reaching over a vast distance, and once more the weight pressed down upon him.

"Report."

Azrael felt the fear of a thousand spiders creeping down his back. He could envision the armored warlord in his distant citadel, glimmering eyes and snide grin murky in the darkness.

"Gray Falcon burns," Azrael said. Even, careful breaths. He had delivered bad news before. Fear was weakness. Weakness was death. "The queen mother of Port Providence is my prisoner."

"And," the reply came, mild, casual, "the gray sage?"

Azrael swallowed, forced his breathing to steady. Weakness was death. "He escaped with Prince Coulton. A teleportation rod. We were caught off guard."

The weight of his master's presence pressed down. Sweat pooled on the floor beneath the black knight's brow. His hands ached as he felt as though he would be ground into paste against his own communication circle by the knight thousands of miles away.

"Forgive me," he choked, "My lord, I will not fail again."

The pressure relented abruptly. Azrael sagged downwards, his breath coming in gasps. A faint laugh echoed in his ears. "It is to be expected, student. They have centuries of experience hiding and running from us. Concerning yourself with that failure is a waste of precious time. Do *not* let him leave the isle. Take him, and remove every last scrap of information from his mind. Then dispose of what's left in whatever manner amuses you."

"As you command, master." His breathing came a little easier. Fear mingled with relief. The terrible numbness in his hands was fading. He hesitated. The question was in the back of his throat, unasked. He should not. Roland would sense it if he was perturbed. He tried to force the fear, the uncertainty, deeper into the recesses of his mind, where his master could not find it.

"Something else troubles you, my Azrael?"

Too late. Azrael's eyes closed. Hours of training ran through his mind. Dull, painful memories where the right question was rewarded, the wrong one answered with agony.

"One question, only, my lord."

"Speak."

A breath. "Who," Azrael asked, "is Elias?"

A long, terrible silence followed. The black knight forced the panic rising in him to calm, to still. Tall walls surrounded him in his mind. He held a sword too large for his hands against an immeasurably vast shadow. His knees quaked.

"A boy you killed," Lord Roland answered at last, his tone dismissive. "To prove your loyalty. Does this satisfy you, Azrael?"

The black knight released a breath. Satisfy him? It was a single sentence in the face of a growing mass of doubt and fear. It *answered* his question, but did it satisfy? Azrael felt his mouth draw into a hard line.

No.

"Yes."

"The next time you report to me, I want results. Is that understood?"

"Yes, my lord."

Silence. The light around the circle died, and the knight sagged back to the floor in the dark room. Exhaustion set in. He did not wish to sleep, for the dreams would be more terrible still. His body rebelled. Eyes closed as the steady rhythm of his shaking breathing became the only sound in his ears.

Resistance fled in the face of fatigue. *Perhaps,* he let himself think. *Perhaps this time there will be nothing.*

He was wrong.

CHAPTER SEVEN
CORINTHIAN ASHES

Night shrouded *Elysium*'s flight. The wind whipped past the viewport, all running lights snuffed. They waited on the bridge, hours out from the edge of the blockade. Aimee leaned against the wall, doing her best to settle her nerves.

Outside the viewport, the skies over Port Providence were an ocean of stars. Aimee registered that it was beautiful, but the fear ate away at her nonetheless. In a few hours, they would lead the charge with the Port Providence ships following behind, rushing past the Eternal Order's blockade and their giant flying fortress, to reach the as yet unconquered city of Land's Edge.

Aimee barely knew this crew. Her mistake had nearly cost them everything. Now their lives would be in her hands again.

"If you don't stop furrowing that brow of yours," Clutch muttered from behind the wheel, "you'll do like that other sorcerer in Albatross did a few years back, and accidentally set your hair on fire."

Aimee blinked. Looked up. "Huh?"

The pilot looked over her shoulder at her. Deadly

serious. "Hair. Burning. Pretty face. Melting."

Ever quick to quip, rare to lose a social exchange, Aimee was caught off balance. She paused.

"Oh stop making fun of her," Vlana said from the shadows. "And that lady was barely a novice at magic, according to Hark."

"*Gods* she was gorgeous, though," Clutch added. "Before her face melted, anyway."

"You've got a low bar," Vlana muttered.

"Easier to vault over," Clutch shot back. Vlana laughed.

"You're both horrible people," Bjorn grunted. He passed Vlana a flask. The quartermaster drank, then passed it to Clutch, who also took a swig and twitched. "Gods that's awful."

Bjorn snorted a quiet laugh.

"Drinking before flying hardly seems wise," Aimee said with half a nervous smile, leaning against a bulkhead.

"I once flew the Argathian gauntlet – a labyrinth of jutting rocks and jets of exploding gas – utterly shitfaced," Clutch answered. "This is just Bjorn's liquid courage."

"Don't push it on her," Bjorn grunted. "The girl's got enough on her mind and has to do complex magic soon." He took the flask back. "Or we all die."

Aimee arched an eyebrow, reading the room better now. Vlana had taken the flask back for a second swig. The short quartermaster twitched. "What's *in* this?"

"Malt," Bjorn said with a shrug. "And peat. And some weirdness that came out of the chaos dampeners awhile back."

"That's horrifying," Clutch said.

"But maybe necessary for the brave," Vlana added. She made to pass it to Clutch.

Aimee's hand intercepted the flask first. As all three watched, she unscrewed the top, and took a long, deep swig. It tasted like some sort of horrid pastiche of single malt whisky mixed with metadrive cleaner and hatred. She twitched, felt her shoulders draw in and her fists clench as the fire burned down her throat.

Then she handed it to the pilot. "Well," she said as they stared at her. "I think you've got it the other way around. You need courage to *drink* it."

Silence followed, then Bjorn let out a single, explosive laugh. "Hah!"

"Fair enough," Clutch said, taking the flask. Aimee saw the white of the pilot's smile flash in the darkness. "You'll do well here."

Hours later, she waited in the dark. The only noises were the low thrum of the metadrive, and the pounding of Aimee's own heart in her ears. She crouched near the prow of the ship, at the forward-most part of the bridge, staring into the night. Very soon, everyone's lives would be in her hands for a second time. The thoughts cascaded through her head. Doubt mingled with guilt. Since she was a girl, freedom had been equated with the power of a portalmage and the life of the skyfarer, with the innate value of performing a task crucial to the functioning of civilization: ships couldn't cross vast distances without portals.

Though she hadn't dwelt overlong on the implications, the truth was that from primary school through charm school all the way through her beginning days at the academy, power had been her pursuit.

In the privacy of darkness, she felt a shame she'd never before known eating away at her.

She had dreamed of holding lives in her hands, never imagining for a moment that she could drop them.

She took a shuddering breath as Clutch slowly counted down the time behind them. *Chin up, little girl,* she thought. *There's no time for worrying now.*

Lights glimmered ahead in the dark. The black cloak of night gave way as mountains were crested, and she saw the still-burning husk of Port Providence shining red in the distance.

From this far away, it reminded her of a campfire. The dissonant comparison made her feel ill. The fires that had consumed the city were still burning days later. Their guttering remnants still glowed in the dark.

"Where are all their ships?" Clutch murmured.

"Landed, maybe?" Vlana answered. Her voice had that high-pitched lilt it got when she was trying to reassure herself.

"They said there was a *blockade*," Clutch insisted. "*Where are the ships*?"

"We can't use sensors right now," Vlana reminded her. "They'll pick it up."

"Hiding overland?" Harkon said almost to himself. "Behind the mountains?"

Aimee stared straight ahead into the night. The starlight illuminated the edges of her fingers gripping the rail in front of her.

Then a shadow fell over them. A line of darkness swept over the entire bridge. Her eyes flashed upwards. Somewhere far above, something huge blotted out the heavens.

"They're above us," she said.

A half-second later, the iridescent beam of a mounted gun larger than their ship ripped across the night sky, fifteen feet in front of the bow. The roar made Aimee's teeth crack together and shook the bones beneath her flesh. She leaped forward without waiting for her teacher's command. Magic surged through her outstretched fingers, and a brilliant mandala of green light erupted out in the space before *Elysium*'s bow. Just in time: a second burst of light scythed towards them. Aimee pivoted, and the blast cracked wave-like against the projected arc of her power, bent around it, and diffused harmlessly behind the ship's wake.

Harkon joined her, and a second wall of flickering defense rippled into existence beside her own. In the darkness of the bridge, Harkon Bright stood, crowned with the brilliant nimbus of his tremendous power, and bellowed over his shoulder at Clutch. "They've seen us! Hard burn!"

Aimee swore she heard Vant yell "HELL YEAH!" somewhere over the tube line. Then the engines boomed, and the sorceress kept her feet only through judicious shifting of her weight. She forced her magic out ahead of them as they lanced through the center of the enemy's line. Interspersed cannon-blasts became a raging hail of hellfire. Her hands danced in response, adjusting the strength of the spell, keeping it aloft.

"Hold on, kids!" Clutch yelled. *Elysium* spun in the heavens. Up became down. Aimee forced her stomach to settle while deftly deflecting lethal slashes of light across the skies. They veered down, and her stomach rioted. The viewport filled with the dancing lights of death-spewing gunships. A single vessel exploded in a spectacular fireball that belched mystic energy and smoldering debris across the forest far below.

They veered up, and Aimee got her first glimpse

of the massive armageddon engine Gara had called the *Iron Hulk*. It wasn't a fortress, it was a *mountain*. It stood, immense and menacing, blotting out the stars as a holocaust of light ripped outwards from its shadow. Firefly muzzle-flashes of batteries illuminated tiny pieces of the whole before deafening blasts tore across the skies in their wake.

"Don't take a direct shot!" Harkon shouted beside her. "Deflect! Don't try to absorb it!"

Aimee set her feet and teeth alike. Every hour of repeated training, every brutal session spent bent over texts on combative magic, or hours spent in the gymnasium, every test, every caffeine-fueled night of endless studies – they all replayed through her mind as she stood in the eye of the storm and used her hard-earned magic to deftly turn aside the apocalyptic blasts of hundreds of gun batteries.

Then she saw it out of the corner of her eye: just off the left side of *Elysium*'s bow, she glimpsed the running lights of one of the Port Providence ships. A damaged runner, bearing wounded she'd treated with her own hands. In the blasts of weapons-fire she glimpsed the twin lions and tartan flag. A blast from the hulk nearly missed it. The next one wouldn't.

Aimee pivoted. "Not on my watch, bastards." Her hands flashed, modifying the scale of the Defensive Magic.

"What are you *doing?*" Harkon shouted beside her.

"Adapting!" Aimee shouted back. Her left hand skipped out wide, and the wall of the defensive spell flashed out with it just as the hulk's huge ether-cannons fired again. The blast veered off her extended magic with a discordant shriek. The Port Providence ship put on another burst of speed, and surged ahead, free. She pulled back her spell with a gasp and another sweep of her hand. "It *worked!*" she shouted, exultant.

"Well done!" Harkon yelled back. "Don't lose focus, we're almost through!"

Then *Elysium* spasmed, and the creaking shudder of tormented hull plates threatened to destroy her concentration.

"Bjorn!" Harkon screamed. "That wasn't an energy blast, something *hit* us!"

"Keep your focus, sir, I'm on it!" the gunner yelled. A flash of light to the left, and the bridge door to the exterior blasted open, sending the mercenary cook hurtling across the room to slump against the far wall.

Skull-helmed, clad in red and gray armor, a knight of the Eternal Order stalked onto the bridge.

"Keep your focus!" Harkon screamed. "Or we all die here!"

The knight barreled into the center of the bridge, putting its huge frame just behind Clutch and the two sorcerers. Looking over her shoulder, Aimee saw the knight's sword raise as Vlana launched herself at their attacker, leaping across the space and slamming into the knight's breastplate. A snarl echoed from behind the visor, and the armored warrior hammered his pommel into the side of Vlana's head. There was a loud *CRACK*, and the quartermaster dropped soundlessly to the deck. Bjorn was down, now Vlana was down too. Only Clutch remained, and the two sorcerers whose hands were occupied protecting the ship.

"Vlana!" Clutch screamed.

Aimee kept her focus on the defensive matrix. Behind her, the pilot gripped the wheel. The murderous figure of the armored knight rippled with mystic energy. Aimee sensed the spell a breath before it came. Her eyes widened. No words. No gestures. That wasn't *possible*.

Clutch turned. A knife whipped from her left hand as the right desperately gripped the wheel. *Elysium* bucked like a cork in the storm.

The knight's sword flashed, and he swatted the knife aside. He crossed the distance between himself and the pilot in the span of half a breath. Both of Aimee's hands were tied up keeping her defensive spell in place. What could she do?

Adapt, Aimee's mind screamed. *Adapt!* She saw the knight's sword snap up, almost too fast for the eye to follow. Now. She had to do it *now*. Her right hand left the defensive matrix and surged behind her while her left took over the double duty of holding the spell in place. The words of a desperate, simplistic holding spell ripped out of her mouth. First prime. Second prime. Gestures summoned, words released.

There was a flash of light and a cry of surprise from the knight. His arm froze in place, the blade stopped before it could cut down. Aimee's breath came in painful gasps as she held her vast defensive matrix in place with one hand. The other – freed in a single, madcap swipe – desperately maintained the holding spell that kept the knight's sword from moving. Straining against the limits of her magic, Aimee shouted. "I can only do this for a few seconds, somebody *please kill him!*"

Clutch still held the wheel. A second hail of ether-cannon fire tore at the ship from the *Iron Hulk*. The mental and physical strain of maintaining two separate, powerful spells in place at once was tearing Aimee's body and mind apart. Her teeth set and sweat poured down her brow. She couldn't sustain it. The knight's death's-head visor swiveled to stare at her. In hatred. In surprise. Aimee screamed.

In pain.

In *defiance*.

Then the furious bulk of Bjorn slammed into their enemy, smashing a long fighting knife into the mesh armpit of the armored man with every ounce of strength he had. "Port!" he screamed at Clutch. "Hard to *port!*"

Everything happened at once.

Clutch swung the wheel and *Elysium* banked hard left. The whole bridge tilted.

Knight and cook tumbled in freefall towards the open airlock.

The knight swung his sword. Bjorn caught the steel-clad elbow and punched the butt of his dagger, driving it deeper into the knight's body. Aimee heard a scream from inside the helm. "Starboard!" Bjorn screamed.

Clutch swung the wheel. The ship righted. Aimee and Harkon barely deflected another blast that would have torn the ship in half.

The knight was somehow still standing. "How the hell do you kill these things?" Aimee screamed over her shoulder.

The knight hewed at Bjorn again. Impossibly fast. Too fast to dodge without falling. So Bjorn didn't. Instead, he dropped down onto his back, slammed into the deck and kicked outwards with both legs into the center of the knight's armored chest. The red-and-gray armored killer lurched backwards, through the airlock and into the darkness.

Aimee put both hands on her defensive spell again, and let out an explosive breath of relief.

Rolling onto his side, Bjorn slowly dragged himself
to his feet, slammed shut the door, and slumped back
against it. Blood leaked down the old warrior's face from
a nasty abrasion somewhere beneath his gray hair. "You
kill them with violence," he grunted. "Lots and lots of
violence. And if that doesn't work, a ten-thousand foot
fall should do the trick."

"Hang on!" Clutch snarled. "We're almost through!"

"Vlana?" Harkon yelled.

"Alive," Bjorn answered, kneeling beside the
crumpled quartermaster. "But she'll be out for a bit. I'll
take her down to the infirmary. Just keep us alive long
enough for it to matter."

"Hang on, kids," Clutch snarled, nosing the ship
down. "This is going to be fun."

They shot straight downwards, until Aimee thought
she'd hurtle backwards and slam into the far wall of
the bridge. They jerked level. Pine trees and burning
wreckage flashed by beneath. The world was a dizzying
fugue of twists and turns as Aimee forced her spell to
remain intact.

Then, all at once, it was over. They were sailing
through open air beneath a star-speckled night sky.
The breathing of everyone in the cabin became a slow
rhythm, rising and falling in tune with the thrum of
their engines.

"I didn't know," Harkon finally said, turning to his
apprentice, eyes alight with surprise and approval, "that
you could do that. The single-handed maintenance."

Aimee leaned against the railing; sweat pooled at the
small of her back, and dampened the hair at the nape
of her neck. It was a few exhausted seconds before she
could answer through her grin. "Neither did I."

"Well," Clutch breathed, leaning on the wheel. "Thank the gods for that." She turned and looked at the old sorcerer where he stood. "Orders, chief?"

Harkon straightened, seeming to put his tiredness away as if it were nothing more than an over-warm coat. "Get communications up," he said heavily. "Let's find out how many we lost."

Exhaustion settled over Aimee as she felt the physical toll of everything she'd just done settle over her. "Yeah," she muttered, and staggered towards her cabin. "I need to lie down for a bit."

Aimee hadn't dreamed of the day her uncle died for three years, but no sooner had she collapsed into her bed that the vision returned, of standing at the docks of the grand wall as a twelve year-old girl, as a metadrive malfunction bloomed into an apocalypse flower that painted the night sky red and scattered Jester de Laurent's ship across the heavens. She didn't remember screaming, but it came fresh, regardless.

Aimee awoke in her cabin, the scent of bile and sweat filling her nose. Every muscle and bone in her body ached, and a thundering headache pulsed behind her eyes. Memories came back as she shook off a painful dream in favor of a reality just as bitter: two ships had gone down, one blasted apart by the firepower of the Eternal Order's guns, the other dashed apart on a mountainside.

Stretching seemed like a good idea for only the handful of seconds before the effort of rising sent her tumbling to the floor, choking and coughing. Her cluttered bedside table spilled its contents of notes and books across the deck with an audible crash that summoned Bjorn running into her room.

I'm sorry, she tried to say. *I fell*. What came out was a jumbled, insensible grumble that just made her head hurt.

"You overclocked yourself, Miss Laurent," Bjorn muttered, and pushed a glass of water to her lips. "You'll be alright, but you're going to have to rest for a little bit longer, understand?"

Aimee managed to nod, slumping backwards. She drank, then let the old warrior help her back into bed before sliding into a quiet oblivion. The dream did not come again.

The second time she awoke the sky was bright, and as the ship arced in a slow, graceful turn, she could see undisturbed trees and hilltops far below. Her head hurt less, and she dressed in the slashes of exterior light that pierced her cabin through the porthole. Her window was open, and an autumn wind filled the air with the smell of forest and field.

Up. She had to get up. People needed her. They were still in a nightmare, even if they'd pulled temporarily free. After a few moments of awkward staggering and the tugging on of suitable clothes, she made her way out into the main hallway. It was littered with Port Providence refugees, mostly already-tended-to wounded. She stepped gingerly over them, unsteadily making her way up to the bridge, where she found Clutch still at the helm.

"Welcome back from the dead, hero," the pilot said, amicably.

That was a nicer title to hear.

"Where are we?" Aimee croaked.

"Somewhere further inland," Clutch said. "Not much other than thick forests and some abandoned pastures out there. The farmland is mostly on the western half, I think. There's some mountains towards the isle's center. The locals say they're cursed."

Aimee leaned against the rail. "Do I want to know what happened yet?"

"A brief respite," Harkon said behind her; and turning, Aimee smiled as her tired-looking teacher approached. "Our infirmary is stuffed with wounded, and we're going to need to land soon, if only to let the engines rest."

"Vlana?" Aimee asked.

"Concussion," Harkon said. "But she'll be alright. I provided the necessary healing, but she still needs rest."

"Shit," Clutch swore.

"What?" Harkon asked.

"I'm picking up a godsdamned signal," the pilot answered. The lights on a small console next to her were blinking. "Not one I recognize, but that could as easily mean good as bad."

Harkon stepped over to look at the readings appearing as an auto-quill hastily scrawled out the ship's sensor readings on a roll of unfurling parchment. "Take us down," he said. "The nearest clearing you can find. Miss Laurent, we're going to the main cargo bay."

"Care to enlighten me?" Clutch snapped back. She nonetheless turned the ship in a graceful arc towards the trees far below. "I imagine these military types with us are gonna take issue with a sudden change of course."

"Just tell Captain Gara I have a good reason," Harkon answered. "She won't argue with me."

As Aimee followed her teacher down the long hallway, she heard Clutch grumble behind her, "I *hate* when he does this."

"What the hell do they want with this place, anyway?"
Aimee asked as they walked. "Is it really for a chunk of
wilderness?"

"I don't know," Harkon answered. His voice held
an edge of frustration, and perhaps a hint of fear. "It
doesn't quite fit their pattern," he continued. "Last time
it was…" and that had been a slip of the tongue. Her
teacher looked at her.

"Don't coddle me," Aimee said bluntly. "I nearly killed
myself for this ship and everyone on it."

"Do you know where the Eternal Order comes from?"
Harkon asked. "Their base of operations?"

Aimee looked back into her teacher's face. Rather
than hesitant, the gaze she now met was unflinching,
even haunted. "I've heard horror stories," she said.
"About a place where they build their ships and train
their warriors. The legends call it the *House of Nails*."

"They're not stories," Harkon said quietly. "And
it wasn't always called that. A long time ago it was a
kingdom known as *New Corinth*. Bright, beautiful, flawed
in its way, but prosperous, with the finest shipyards in
the Drifting Lands. It was my home, though not where
I was born."

The old mage looked tired, but his gaze didn't waver.
"There were no threats, as Gara spoke of here. Our king
wasn't given an ultimatum. We had only the barest
warning. A traitor let their assassins into the capitol; they
destroyed the portal shield, and their ships filled our
skies." Aimee's teacher's eyes had a faraway look, now.
"I heard later that when the first of the defeated nobles
were dragged before the throneroom of the palace, they
found it draped in our dead king's flesh. Then the order

set about the task of turning my adopted home into their new breeding ground for the nightmares they export across the Unclaimed."

Aimee felt the sting of guilt for asking. "Thank you," she said at length. "For telling me... How did you escape?"

"*That's* a story for another time," Harkon demurred. Silence hung between teacher and student for a long minute. Then, at last, he continued. "None of us intended to be here," he said. Aimee winced as if struck. "But now that we *are* here, we have an obligation to help these people. As you've guessed, this is not the first time my crew and I have put ourselves in the path of dangerous and powerful people. I don't know what Lord Roland's apprentice or his fellows want with this place, but whatever it is, the mere fact that they want it means we must stop them from getting it."

When they arrived in the cargo bay, more of Gara's men greeted them, many still armed, mostly with boarding swords and a handful of shock-spears. The gentle thump of the landing gear meeting earth was felt beneath their feet, and Clutch's voice could be heard through one of the communication tubes. "Whoever they are, sir, they're waiting outside. I really think this is a crap idea, but if you want to talk to them, they're here."

Harkon nodded. "Open the doors."

There was a groaning creak as the hatch to the cargo bay door slowly slid open. Wood and metal folded inward, revealing a forest clearing so empty and peaceful that the sudden quiet was jarring. Aimee's senses were assaulted by the smell of green grass and the gentle kiss of an autumn breeze.

Two figures awaited them, wrapped in stained, torn clothes splattered with mud and leaves.

"We received your signal," Harkon said. "And you're damned lucky that we did. There are few people who can read that sort of message."

"Even fewer who can send it," the more forward – and older – of the two figures said. He pushed back his hood, and Aimee saw an elderly face, recently blighted by hardship. "My name is Silas. I am a teacher, and a brother superior of the Order of Gray Sages. This–" he gestured to the other beside him, a rust-haired boy of regal bearing, no older than sixteen, "–is my ward, Prince Coulton of Port Providence."

Abruptly, every soldier in the bay fell to their knees. Whispers of joy, thanks, and praise filled Aimee's ears.

Harkon's expression was drawn, but not surprised. "I suspected as much," he murmured. "I am–"

"–Harkon Bright," Silas said. "I know. I've read the auguries, and they told me an ally was near. I beg sanctuary for myself and the boy. And more." His face drew into a grim, severe expression. "I know what the order wants, and I know how to find it. If we don't get it first, every kingdom in the Unclaimed will burn."

CHAPTER EIGHT
BACK AMIDST THE RUINS

Azrael walked down the gangplank and into the ruins of Port Providence. In the skies high overhead, the *Iron Hulk*'s gray face of steel and stone drank in the sunlight. The ring matrix at its base slowly rotated around the pulsing glow of its massive metadrive, hinting at the presence of the terrible – as yet unused – weapon within.

They had conquered the capitol of Port Providence, subdued Gray Falcon, and now Azrael had to deal once more with his officers.

Before the black knight, a vast basecamp was springing up in the wreckage of the city. Makeshift structures, tents, and repurposed buildings were labored upon by mercenaries and prisoners turned slaves. The grim eyes of taskmasters kept constant watch.

Behind them, their shoulder-mounted auto-ledgers scribbling rapid notes, came the accounters. Black-robed, dead-eyed, wherever the Eternal Order sold their swords, the accounters marched solemnly behind the carnage, noting the cost of every drop of blood and every coin of spent treasure. War was the Eternal Order's business. The chaos in Port Providence was an investment.

"Where is Lord Malfenshir?" Azrael asked the first of the taskmasters as he entered the camp. The whip-swinger looked at him, realized who he was, and blanched in fear. "Near the old palace," he said. "Engaging in some *private business*."

Private business meant only a handful of things, and all of them made the black knight's stomach turn. It was expected that knights of the order would take spoils, enjoy their plunder, and make use of the people they conquered... but even among his peers, Malfenshir was known for his broad view of those expectations. Azrael's eyes swept across the assembled host of slaves and prisoners, watching slippery hands drop bricks and fumble with ropes. "Feed them, fool," he growled at the taskmaster. "If they drop dead, they can't work."

He felt Esric's eyes on him as they walked down the devastated byways and thoroughfares of the once great city of Port Providence. "Good of you, my lord," the healer said mildly.

Azrael kept his face neutral. *Weakness is death.* "Unproductive slaves aren't useful."

In a city of flame-charred and blast-tortured ruins, the palace had survived surprisingly intact, perhaps because of the latent magic infused within its spires and stones, or perhaps some ironic jest from the gods. As Azrael approached the shattered wooden gates, he could hear the clash within the span of the main courtyard, and knew almost immediately what he'd see.

It didn't make the sight any less disgusting.

Prisoners stood in a line just inside, shivering in the cool air, wearing the tattered rags of the soldiers' uniforms in which they'd been captured. At the end of the line was an open training field, roped off, with a single mercenary standing at the entrance to the near end, a pile of weapons beside him.

The clashes came from the far end, where a half-dressed, desperate prisoner was being toyed with by Malfenshir. The knight's face spewed laughter and his red sword flicked elegantly back and forth as the desperate, starving man strove at him. Malfenshir swatted aside each attack with naked contempt.

"Your form is really quite good," the red knight said. He was not wearing his order's plate, having instead donned a light sparring vest of boiled leather that offered minimal defense. "But you're so *sluggish*."

The taunted prisoner screamed and one of his hands flopped to the ground. He dropped to one knee and clutched the stump at the wrist. Malfenshir's face screwed with contempt. "See? Slow. Aw well, then." The red sword thrust through the man's clavicle and burst sodden and dark from between the shoulder blades. He fell to the sand and blood-soaked straw and twitched for a few moments.

Malfenshir wiped his steel clean and shouted "Next!"

"What in the abyss are you doing?" Azrael's voice thundered across the courtyard. Prisoners and guards alike turned in shock.

Malfenshir flashed a wide grin and raised his sword in greeting. "Lord Azrael, welcome back. Allow me to introduce the surviving members of Collum's Hundred, the royal guard of the crown prince. I've been practicing."

"Clear the yard!" Azrael thundered. "Get these men back to their cells, then have them fed and *put to work!*"

"They *are* working," Malfenshir said.

The guards hesitated. "My lord," Esric murmured behind him.

Azrael's fist clenched and he loosed a spell. A thunderclap blasted across the courtyard. The grounds shook. People scattered. "Now!"

Malfenshir cocked his head to the side. "I take it you didn't find the sage?"

"What in the abyss have you been doing here for two days?" Azrael demanded, stalking over to him. *Careful,* he thought. *He's your equal in prowess.*

"Consolidating our foothold," the other knight said. "And keeping my skills sharp while I'm at it."

"We're not paid to butcher prisoners for *fun*," Azrael snarled. *It is the right of a knight to decide how to use his spoils,* some part of his memory reminded him. *These prisoners are spoils.* "Those men have intimate knowledge of the prince's stratagems, some of which his men are still following. Why aren't they being interrogated?"

There were different schools of thought within the order, different convictions as to how best to mete out power over others. Azrael had always known that Malfenshir believed in a brutality far exceeding the norm, but to see it in practice was another thing entirely.

"Last night," Malfenshir answered, "a group of ships ran our blockade, tearing inland and westward. Several of them were shot down, and we've had salvage crews scouring the local countryside for them all morning. As for these–" he gestured at the prisoners being led back to the dungeons "–they were all geased by the crown when they took their oaths of service. Simple magic, but potent. They'll choke on their own tongues before they tell us anything. It didn't take us long to figure that out." The big hulk of a man shrugged. "It seemed a shame to waste their bodies."

Azrael suppressed a shudder. Then he heard a rapid

series of screams from inside, high-pitched and youthful. His skin crawled, his eyes widened. "My lord," Esric murmured, stepping in front of him. "Perhaps you should hear the rest of the report–"

Azrael shoved him out of the way and stalked towards the source of the sounds. "Get out of my way or I'll tear out your throat, old man."

There was a boy in one of the state rooms. He looked as though he'd been a servant, probably common born, the child of some maid working somewhere within the stone walls. Now he lay on the floor, not moving, clutching himself. Bruised. Beaten.

Beaten in a very *specific* way. Azrael stood in the doorframe, temporarily robbed of breath. A few feet away from the child was a man. Azrael did not know him. A part of his mind registered that this was the acolyte the taskmaster had mentioned. He was one of Malfenshir's. He had a satisfied look on his face, and he was in the process of buckling his belt about his waist. It made a jingling sound that rattled in Azrael's ears.

A jingling belt.

Silence. The man seemed to belatedly realize he was being watched. His head turned, and he regarded Azrael with a curious sort of surprise. "My lord?"

A jingling belt.

The boy's eyes stared straight ahead – unwilling, unable, to look at anything else. Azrael *knew* that look. His skin crawled. Sweat ran down the base of his neck. There was a dark blotch of half-remembered haze filling up his head, like a void into which he couldn't look, but for the fact that he knew – on some level – what lurked within.

A jingling belt. Another voice. A long time ago. *"Hold still, boy."*

"I don't think he'll be of much use now," the man continued.

Memories ripped through the black knight's mind. Grasping hands. His own boyish scream.

Azrael crossed the room. Oath of Aurum slashed free from its sheath.

"My lord?" The acolyte looked surprised.

The blade leaped forward. It felt hot in his hands. The heat seared against Azrael's palm. Awareness fled as he moved. The black knight registered nothing but the look of shock on the acolyte's face as the sword punched through his chest, lifted him off his feet, and nailed him to the stone wall.

Azrael staggered back, leaving the man bolted to the stone by the gold-chased sword. Blood dribbled down his chin as he stared uncomprehendingly. The dying man's mouth opened and shut several times without sound.

Azrael stared until the life bled out of him. Then he took a step forward and pulled the sword from corpse and rock. The dead man thudded to the floor.

Malfenshir and Esric stood in the doorway behind him. The former's face twisted into a frown. "All this for a stupid child?"

Azrael reeled, his hand crackling with unexpended power. "Touch the boy, and I'll burn your still-beating heart in your chest."

He pointed at Esric. "See to his injuries. See to it that he is cared for." His breath came in rapid gasps. The heart in his chest pounded, and sensations of hot and cold alternated through his body as half-remembered afterimages of grasping hands and terrible pain licked flame-like at the corners of his senses.

"My lord–" Esric started.

"Are you *deaf*?" Azrael snapped. "I gave you an order. *Follow it*."

Esric paused for a moment, then crossed the floor to crouch beside the abused child, checking his injuries. "He will live," he murmured. "I will see to it that he is not used further." The healer's voice was soothing. A part of Azrael's mind dimly registered that it sounded as though the healer was talking to a rabid dog. "But my lord must get some rest after this. I will be along later, to help you."

The words registered. Azrael nodded. "Do it," was all he said, and the healer slowly collected the boy and carried him from the room.

Malfenshir stood opposite the black knight and watched him, incredulous. "If you're going to deny men their rightful spoils," he said after a moment, "you had best be prepared for rioting and havoc. Their part in the investment is as legitimate as anyone else's."

Azrael stared at his subordinate. In that burning moment, as his heartbeat thundered in his ears and his breath threatened to draw the life from him, he wanted nothing more than to crush the big man's throat between his armored fingers.

"We have a mission to accomplish," Azrael finally said. "If I *ever* find out that you are *wasting* our hard-earned coin and precious time butchering prisoners, or letting your men use children because they can't control themselves, I will kill the offenders, and make good on my other promise. Now get the men ready to pursue those blockade runners."

Malfenshir bristled. "Fine words, from the knight who failed to catch one old man."

"Do I have to start taking fingers?" Azrael snarled into the other man's face. "*Do it.*"

Tension. Again. The contest hovered between them. Then Malfenshir seemed to remember his position, and turned to go. At the end of the small hallway, he paused and looked over his shoulder. "You're too soft on the weak, Azrael. The boy will survive, and become stronger, or he will die, and the world will be better for one less weakling of a man."

"And where," Azrael demanded, "is the high-value prisoner I sent you?"

Malfenshir stopped, looked briefly uncertain. "The queen mother? She awaits your interrogation on the hulk. I do not overstep so far as that, my lord."

No, Azrael thought. *Only where children are concerned.*

Malfenshir was gone before another word could be exchanged. Azrael felt the breath leave him. *Weakling.* He staggered. His hand hit the wall. Fingers grasped at the stone as he caught himself. He tasted copper in his mouth, and the world spun. His eyes clenched shut, but all he saw were grasping hands, vast shadows, and all he felt was the raining of blows meant to subdue and control. His hand slipped from the stone. He sank to the floor in the state room. He couldn't breathe. He couldn't see. His pulse hammered in his ears and his body shook with what might have been sobs or screams. It built at the base of his spine, roaring upwards to an unfeeling heaven, and Azrael threw his head back, a terrible cry rending his ears in his own voice.

Every window on the second floor of the palace *shattered.*

His senses came back to him. Sluggish. Hazy. He sat opposite the filth's corpse, slumped where it had fallen when he'd pulled the blade free. All around him lay broken glass. Shaking, unsteady on his feet, his hands found the bloodstained sword of Prince Collum. The familiar enchantment stirred at his touch. A comfort, though strange.

Oath of Aurum had gone through solid stone, and there was no mark upon it. Azrael breathed. How had he done that?

He stepped over the corpse to examine the blood-smeared hole in the stone wall.

The rock was melted and charred.

Darkness lay over the ruins of Port Providence. The wispy trails of ember smoke still climbed into the starlit skies, but the night was cold and clear. It was a mercy for Azrael. The cold stars gave him just enough light to see, and the shadows were thick enough, deep enough, that his silent passage through the forests of the surrounding hills went unmarked.

The black knight was quiet, when he wished it. In his arms he carried the sleeping form of the nameless boy he'd given to Esric. The healer had retired before Azrael had slipped into the infirmary and lifted the lad from his sickbed. Now he carried him, willing him not to awaken, to a place of his choosing, far from the eyes of city, of the Eternal Order, of Malfenshir.

It was not something of which his own master would have approved. Malfenshir had said that depriving men of their spoils of conquest would induce riots amongst the rank and file. He wasn't wrong. But the man that had used this boy was dead by Azrael's own hand, and beyond following orders – as he always did – Esric cared nothing for his ultimate fate.

The black knight didn't understand why *he* cared, either. As his boots padded soft and quiet over the mossy earth, his mind warred in silence with itself, a mingling confusion of one half acknowledging that this was wrong, and the other refusing to relent in its need to know that this child would be safe.

Above all else, he understood that he would have *no rest* until this business was *finished*. Above all else, Azrael desperately needed rest. So he had done his research and interrogated prisoners from the outlying hamlets around the city, until he had the requisite name and location. Now, with night as his cover, he drew near. The trees gave way to the open fields of a small homestead, its crops already harvested and stripped bare. The family that lived here had already been visited by the raiding parties, he understood. But they'd merely had food and supplies taken. Unresisting and stoic, they'd not incurred the wrath of the order, and were left mostly alone.

Obviously Malfenshir hadn't been in charge, or everyone here would be dead. The farmhouse was nondescript, like a dozen other hovels that crouched under thatched roofs in this hinterland kingdom. A small orchard spread out on the far side, and the sight of it made Azrael stop just shy of the treeline. Familiarity tugged at his mind, painful and unwelcome. He hesitated at the sight of the homely place, trying to excise a melody from his mind that wouldn't stop playing.

Elias.

He crept silently across the yard. The boy stirred in his arms. He was near the front door now. Someone had left a primitive ward upon the battered wood. A peasant's superstition, of course. Not a hint of magic to it, but that wasn't what struck him. It was the arrangement of symbols common in charlatans' hedge magic and old wives' mysticism common throughout the Drifting Lands. He recognized the incantation: a call to heaven's angels to watch over the departed.

These people had lost a child.

Something stirred to his left. A large dog, lying in the shadows. Black. It lifted its head and stared at him. Azrael turned, a shadow holding the sleeping boy. The beast stared, but made no sound.

Slowly, the black knight laid his charge upon the stoop. Then he took the peasant's cloak he'd pilfered to mask himself, and laid it over him. He lingered a second, then took a step back. The dog barked and lunged forward only to be jerked back by the leather leash.

Beasts knew their own. Someone stirred inside the house. A candle flickered to life behind a window. It was time to go. Two steps back in softness and in silence. Then the magic. He did not stop and look back again until he was once more past the treeline.

Two figures knelt over the boy. Then one lifted him, carried him inside. The other remained on the stoop, a candle flickering in the night.

It was done. Booted feet took two more steps in retreat, then the angel of death slipped once more into the night.

CHAPTER NINE
LAND'S EDGE

A day had passed without chaos, and Aimee was starting to feel almost human again. Sleep and food had replenished the lion's share of her energy, and as she stared across the expanse of forests far below, she took a handful of breaths to steady herself.

In the past few days she'd run a blockade, healed the wounded and the dying, and botched her portal. She wasn't sure which wins made up for which losses. All she knew was that the only way was forward.

Within an hour, they would be in the smaller city of Land's Edge with their new guests of a prince on the run and his sage advisor who believed the Eternal Order was about to find a truth-telling gem that they could use to wreak untold havoc on the Drifting Lands. What awaited them, she didn't know. Their new passengers, however – mostly Gara's recovering wounded making use of the infirmary – seemed to believe that Prince Coulton's return heralded the start of a grand counterattack.

Aimee doubted that was wise. She turned from the window on the bridge and walked back down the hallway, falling into step beside Bjorn on the way to the common area where everyone was meeting.

"You look better," the old warrior nodded. His approval was reserved.

"Sleep helps," Aimee answered. "Sleep and food."

Bjorn gave a grunt of agreement, then asked, "What do you make of this Axiom Diamond business?"

Aimee thought back over the hasty, bare-bones explanation Silas had given in the hours after he and the prince had been brought aboard *Elysium*. She'd heard the old myths, but Silas's version was much more specific than the ones she knew.

"According to the version of the legend Silas told us," she said, "that it's a gemstone that serves as some sort of map to finding whatever object the bearer wants? I think he's right to want to keep it away from them."

Bjorn laughed. "You sound like Harkon."

Aimee shot the big warrior a glance. "How do you mean?"

"What was it he said earlier? *Contentious* was the word he used. Scrappy."

Aimee laughed at that. It was hard to argue with. "Given what I'm starting to understand of him," she said, "I'm not so sure. I didn't sign on thinking I was going to be flying into firefights or fighting tyrants."

"Didn't you though?" Bjorn answered.

"No," Aimee affirmed, though some part of her wondered. She'd known the rumors. "I didn't."

Bjorn looked at her with a small chuckle playing at the corner of his thin mouth. "I don't buy that. But for talking's sake, what *did* you think you were getting into?"

Aimee might have answered with any number of false

platitudes, but, when she thought about it, the past few days had stripped even the impetus of pretense from her. She couldn't muster anything but the truth.

"Reckless adventure," she said, and her voice sounded far away in her ears. "I thought I was going to be free, and become powerful, as I beheld wonder after wonder."

Bjorn snorted. "Chained, were you, back in Havensreach? Parents kept you like a bird in a gilded cage?"

Aimee shook her head, brows drawing together in thought. "Not at all. I was a rich girl who got whatever I wanted. Clothes. Books. Entertainment. When I was old enough, and lucky enough to be fit and fetching, I got the boys I wanted too." She shook her head, felt a familiar pang of guilt for boyfriends pursued and promptly ignored once acquired.

Aimee looked at her hands for a moment before looking up at the big warrior walking beside her. "I didn't sign up to be a freedom fighter."

"I think you did," Bjorn grunted in answer. "You just didn't have the living behind you to know it." He jerked his head in the direction of the main common area. "Come on, girl. You knew the rumors about Hark and you jumped at the chance to be his apprentice anyway; he told me. I remember when you came aboard. You were too smart not to realize what *Elysium* is and what we are, deep down. You knew. You stayed anyway."

Aimee opened her mouth. The law-abiding citizen within her – the person she was raised to be – wanted to protest, but no argument sprang readily to her lips.

Bjorn chuckled as they walked. "Come on. There'll be talking before we land. Best you not miss it."

•••

Gara awaited them in the common area. She stood just behind Silas, and the tired, haunted-looking, seated figure of Prince Coulton. Aimee walked down the ramp from the central hallway that spanned the ship. Her teacher was beside her, Bjorn behind them, and Vant with his folded arms and sour-milk expression, next to him.

"If we end up a gilded princeling's pleasure yacht," Aimee heard the engineer mutter, "I *quit*."

"Because your current boss is a downright pauper," Bjorn snarked back.

"There's rich," Vant whispered, "and there's rich and high-blooded. Worse, poor and high-blooded. That's entitled enough to think he's owed your work but too damn destitute to pay you."

"Children," Harkon stopped both with a word. "Please."

The crew of *Elysium* stood opposite the ragged tatters of a royal court. Silence. Then Prince Coulton said, "When I said I wanted an audience, you kept me waiting for three hours."

"Sorry, highness," Aimee answered. "Too busy patching up your injured soldiers to chat."

The look Harkon gave her approved of her spirit, but not her phrasing.

"My court shouldn't be kept waiting," Coulton said dejectedly.

"Your highness's court is very *small*," Bjorn said simply. "And presently living on charity."

"Forgive my liege," Silas answered, silencing his ward with a hand firmly gripping the prince's shoulder. "He is not as graceless as he seems, but neither is he worldly. He has lost much in the last few days, and his pride is one of the few things he has left."

"He still has a city, at least," Harkon said. "And warriors and citizens who depend upon him. At least for now. So why don't we get to the subject at hand?"

Silas gave a slow nod, then, with obvious reticence, began to explain himself. "When we land at Land's Edge, everything will be put towards two tasks: the calling for help from our allies in the Violet Imperium, and the evacuation of our people to what safe havens remain hidden in the wilderness. All military potency that we still possess must be bent towards holding the city as long as we can."

Coulton's face was pallid and tired as his advisor spoke. Behind him, Gara laid a hand on the prince's shoulder, gripping tightly as if to steady him. "We won't be able to stop them from locating the Axiom," the prince said in a pained voice. "So, with regret, in my capacity as crown prince of Port Providence, I must *beg* that you and your crew do so in our stead."

Silence. Vant's eyes bulged. Bjorn abruptly clamped a hand over the red-faced engineer's mouth.

"That's not a small request," Aimee said quietly.

"I accept," Harkon said simply.

Silas's exclamation of relief was loud. "Thank you," he breathed. "The stories do not sell your generosity short."

"I wasn't finished," Harkon said, holding up a hand. "In return for my clemency, your highness–" he gestured at Prince Coulton "–will swear not to waste the lives of any of his soldiers and people fighting to retain a crown that he has lost. In addition, my crew may lay claim to whatever treasure exists within the Axiom's vault, when we locate it. Are my terms acceptable to your highness?"

Prince Coulton stared at Aimee's teacher as though

the man before him had told him to eat manure. "Have you lost your mind?" he finally whispered.

Aimee was frozen in place as her teacher just dictated his terms to a prince. *Dictated.* Yes. That was the apt term. A part of Aimee revolted at this, shrank back as if the idea were a glowing red forge-iron. As if she had grasped it with a naked hand.

"You cannot ask that," Gara said.

Less than two weeks earlier, Aimee had delivered a speech to her graduating class, on the *realities of justice.* It had been a great speech, a thesis asserting how the convictions of freedom, respect, and tolerance were upheld by the laws of a just society with righteously appointed rulers. These were the laws she'd been raised to obey. The laws she had never questioned. The laws that secured in stone the moral convictions she'd always believed. If Port Providence was a free country, how could Harkon presume to hurl aside its sovereignty so casually?

"Port Providence is *mine,*" Coulton said, his eyes blazing. "You would have us throw aside our sovereignty?"

Aimee's hands wrung together. Out of the corner of her eye, she realized Bjorn was watching her. *You sound like him.*

Like Harkon. Her teacher. The mage who meddled. *I didn't sign on to be a freedom fighter.*

I don't buy that.

"You are asking us to risk everything we have to prevent your enemies from acquiring something you failed to protect," Harkon answered. His voice was cold. "In return, you will waste not a single life more in the pursuit of preserving your throne, and we will be paid for the risks we assume. Think of your people. That is your choice, highness. Accept my terms, or find the gem yourself."

"There is no distinction," Coulton pushed back, "between the welfare of my people and the sovereignty of my crown."

And there it was, staring Aimee in the face. Here and now, the laws with which she'd been raised, of which Coulton invoked a pale reflection, did *not* secure the convictions they claimed to uphold. Away from home, from Havensreach's protective walls, that logic didn't hold up. If the prince who sat angrily before her got his way, thousands of innocent people would die. There was no moral course but to throw the law into the trash bin.

"There is *every* distinction." The words exploded from her. She took an impulsive step forward. Guards bristled. Captain Gara reached reflexively for her sword. Bjorn growled. Aimee held up both hands to show she meant no assault. "Forgive me, highness," she said, unable to believe the words coming from her mouth. "But if you try to fight *now*, you will die. Your people will die. There is *no justice* in that, and there is no justice in asking *us* to risk our lives without compensation, either. My teacher is right."

Harkon's eyes twinkled in approval as he looked sideways at her, then shifted to lay their terrible weight upon the young prince's face. "Not a single life more," Harkon said. "Perhaps when you have collected them, fled, rallied, the time will come to speak of defiance... But now? If you want our help, you must *run*."

Silence. Aimee felt the tension hanging in the room, her own breath ragged in her lungs. She felt dizzy. In a span of a few seconds, she had done an about-face on everything the person she was a mere two weeks ago had purported to believe in.

Coulton sweated, stared back and forth between the two implacably faced sorcerers. His face burned with defiance, embarrassment, then, *finally,* with a hint of shame. "I accept your terms," he said quietly. "Will you do it?"

Harkon slowly nodded. "You have my word, highness."

The gangway slid down, and a breath of cool autumn air washed over Aimee's face, mingled with a smell of chimney fires. She took two steps down, permitted for those first few seconds to imagine a city on the verge of its harvest festival, rich with ripe fruit and cooking pies, thick with celebrations and smiling faces.

The third step killed all of that, and she saw a landing field carpeted thick with the tents, blankets, lean-tos and huddled gatherings of refugees for as far as her eyes could see. They swarmed about the gates of the city like ants in a thousand colors, and when the scent of their collected refuse struck her a second later, she had to steady herself against one of the supports at the edge of the ramp to keep from retching over the side.

This was what a city smelled like as it died.

Coulton walked past her, with Silas at one side and Gara at the other. "Gara," the prince said, "I want you to give the order for immediate evacuation. Every ship in the city, privately owned or military, is to be seized for the use of ferrying people to the outlying redoubts. There is time for neither argument, nor respect for private property."

Gara took one of her men by the shoulder. "Run, as fast as you may, and relay his majesty's orders to the inner ring of the city. Go now. The magistrate will know what to do.

"Your highness realizes," Gara continued, turning back to her prince, "that there is no way we can possibly save everyone."

"We will still try," Coulton answered. "Every ship, back and forth, until they can no longer do so without being shot down or blasted to cinders on the ground."

Aimee would have smiled at him, were it not for the fact that she was trying hard to settle her violently upset stomach. Standing there, for the first time, he looked something approaching princely. Someday, she was sure, he'd make some doe-eyed girl who wanted to be a princess very happy. He sensed her looking, and flashed nervous eyes her way. She looked back over her shoulder at the ship instead. *Sorry, highness*, she thought, *that won't be me.*

Soldiers approached, and the wounded descended the gangway as Vlana stood at the entry to the hold and noted each injured man as he passed. Aimee stepped to the side and looked at her teacher. "This is a hell of a risk we're taking," she said.

"It needs taking, Miss Laurent," Harkon said with surety. "Not only for us, but for a better future for these people. The prince's promise buys them that. I had to." His eyes darkened. "I have seen what happens when a kingdom burns. Better these people simply run."

"How do you know he'll keep it?" she asked, making sure the last of the men couldn't overhear her.

"I am not a man to cross," Harkon said with a shrug. "And for all he knows–" his eyes twinkled "–I might curse him at a distance if he does."

Aimee snorted. "You're a bad man, teacher. And the treasure?"

"Learn this well and early, my student," Harkon said. "Some things must be done simply because they are good. But that doesn't mean that they should be done for free." He smiled. "At least if payment is an option."

"I don't *ever* want to hear that payment isn't an option," Vant grumbled from the top of the gangway. "What next?"

"Next," said Silas, turning as his ward was brought towards the city gates, stopping just short of where Aimee and Harkon stood. "I tell you everything that I know, and we use what time we have to get you ready."

"You need to get better at picking your battles, Hark," the engineer said, a mixture of exasperation and affection in his voice.

"I'm very good at picking my battles," the old sorcerer said over his shoulder. "I'll take one of each."

"I will show you the way," Gara added. She wore her full uniform now, as well as her sword, as she strode up to join them. "It's where I need to go as well."

They had only a few hours, and in that time Aimee saw enough of what had become of Land's Edge to make her heart break. The city was beautiful. Silas had told her that some of its architecture was over seven hundred years old, with rooftops slatted in burnished copper and silver gothic spires stretching towards heaven. She saw beautiful storefronts, ivy-coated walls, and the stone arches of antiquated, pillared courtyards. And all around, a mad chaos was fraying the city to breaking.

The law and order she'd been raised to revere was in tatters.

Silas brought them to an old library in the wealthy districts of the city, patronized by an elderly noble whose servants were currently in the process of desperately emptying the shelves. Gara waited without, her sword hanging at her side and a ring of able-bodied warriors gathered about her.

Aimee took a few moments to look about as people hurried past her in white and gray scholars' robes and dirty regal livery, desperately stuffing priceless collections into burlap sacks and hastily appropriated trunks. It was in a part of a city just like this that she had been raised. Her parents, in their wealth, were patrons of institutions of learning just like the one in which she stood.

She was watching generations' worth of knowledge slowly funnel down the bottom of a bathtub drain.

"What will they do to this place," she asked, "when they take the city?"

"Burn most of it, I expect," Silas lamented in disgust as he led them towards another room far to the back of the main library.

"No," Harkon refuted. "They'll burn some, yes, but primarily to offend what locals survive. The truly valuable material they'll count as precious treasure, and sell for a profit."

"Have a lot of personal experience with them, do you?" Silas asked as they reached the doorway. He removed an old, arcane looking key from his robes and twisted it into the clunky, bronze lock upon the oaken door.

"Enough," Harkon said simply. "I know how they work and what they don't generally do, if not always the why."

Silas fidgeted with the lock until the deep, grinding noise of tumblers turning sounded within the mechanism. The sage gave a slow pull, and the six-inch-thick door swung slowly outward. "You don't know *why* they want it, do you? The Axiom, I mean?" the old man asked.

"I don't," Harkon murmured as the door opened.

A draft of cool air brushed Aimee's face, and she paused, her eyes sighting upon a small plaque beside the doorframe. A simple inscription was incised into the metal, faded and scarred. The first half had been time-worn nearly to illegibility, but she could make out the last part. … *Not for the fight that brings certain victory,* the words read, *but for the fight that must be fought.*

Beneath it was the simple icon of what looked like a cup.

They stepped into a chamber lit by the nearly spent light of guttering glow-globes, bathing the room in a flickering facsimile of candle flame. Across the walls, a mural spread its splendor in colors faded by time: of roses entwined beneath iconography of white and black armored figures clashing across ancient frescoes of breaking fields and burning skies. At the apex of the ceiling, Aimee saw the faded effigy of a chalice. There was a story here. An *old* one.

"You know why, though, don't you?" she said, turning to look at Silas. "You know why they want the Axiom so much."

Silas pulled scrolls from a niche cut into the wall. He shook his head. "Don't mistake membership in an order of sages for access to all its secrets," he said. Then he unfurled a large map out on the table at the room's center. "But I can tell you that the stories of white chalices and fallen heroes etched across these walls are not lies, nor merely ghost stories told by peasants." His eyes held hers a moment longer. "When my predecessors hid the

Axiom, it was to protect something the Eternal Order couldn't find. *Shouldn't* find."

They stood around a map of the expanse of the landmass, and watched as Silas planted his thumb over a spot on a large hilltop that was depicted as jutting from the surrounding landscape. "There," he breathed. "That is the place I was told of." Then he began urgently rolling the map up once more. "I can guide you there by earth or air, though the latter is preferable. When we reach the chamber, there will be two magical trials that must be passed to be deemed worthy of the diamond. I don't know what they entail, but they will be perilous."

"Two trials…" Harkon murmured thoughtfully, looking at the map. "It's not too far. A half a day's journey perhaps, with *Elysium* no longer weighed down by wounded."

"A last request," Silas said, and he began pulling scrolls and books from the wall sconces. "Help me take as much of this as we can, before the Eternal Order arrives to destroy it all."

They made their way out into the street a short time later. It was evening, and the colors of sunset splashed red and gold across the western slopes of silver steeples and copper rooftops. For a brief second, the city was a vision of daylight-kissed, traditionalist beauty: a painting frozen in a perfect moment.

Then they heard the screams. Aimee turned, her shoulders weighed down with satchels of priceless scrolls and old leatherbound tomes, and saw the first people running up the main thoroughfare. She heard Harkon swear, and raised her eyes to heaven.

"No," Silas breathed. "How did they get here so *fast?*"

The shadow of the *Iron Hulk* rode the sunset, a black

mountain against the flare of burning purples, reds, and amaranthine halcyon. Aimee looked at her teacher. The same sudden fear that gripped her chest flickered, wary and alert, in Harkon's eyes. "Back to the ship," the old mage said. "Now."

Harkon wove a swift spell of communication with *Elysium*. "Clutch," he said. "Zero in on my coordinates. Get the ship in the air and to where we are."

He was finishing his message when Aimee caught sight of a swiftly approaching lander, vulture-like in the evening haze. It deftly circled overhead, then put itself down and hammered roughly into the square, tearing up the street and collapsing a statue, forcing Aimee to throw up a shield spell to protect her companions from a spray of debris.

She lowered her arm in time to watch as two Eternal Order knights leaped casually from the lander's interior. One wore gray and black armor, his helm in the likeness of a snarling dog's skull. The other was taller, long-limbed and armored all in black, a sword with a gold hilt and silver blade held easily in his hands. His gaze settled on the group of them, and despite the angelic death's-head visor that masked his face, the deep voice that addressed them carried the weight of a triumphant smirk.

"There you are, sage. We've been looking *everywhere* for you."

Behind her, Aimee heard Silas breath a single word.

"Azrael."

CHAPTER TEN
HAIL OF HELLFIRE

Earlier

Azrael stood deep within the *Iron Hulk*, before the doors of the prison block: level fifty-seven, where the high-value prisoners were kept. The guards stood, nervous, off to the side. Neither met his eyes. He wore his full panoply of black armor and helm, the dead prince's sword hanging at his hip.

He had subdued half this wretched kingdom, despite the periodic rebellion of his second-in-command. He was *winning* by all accounts. The Axiom Diamond could yet be found. But none of that helped the gnawing in the pit of his stomach every time he remembered the piercing eyes of the queen mother, or the fact that she seemed to find him familiar. Now he wanted answers.

An armored hand turned the door handle. The door swung slowly inward, and the black knight stalked through the heavily barred cells of the detention block. He passed soldiers, minor aristocrats, peasants, and a number of other individuals without names or relevant faces. Sleep had helped to clear his mind somewhat, and the ground upon which his spirit stood was solid. In a matter of hours they would be upon Land's Edge, and the hammer would fall once more.

At last he came to her cell where, past the bars, she waited. A single glow-globe lit the dank room; a bed and chamberpot pushed up against the wall were the only furnishings. There the old woman sat, draped in the faded finery of the gown in which she'd been taken. Unwashed, tired, her white hair was stringy and laden with grease. Her hands were folded in her lap, and her eyes were closed in what looked like meditation.

For all this, Azrael could not have said that she appeared broken. Prideful defiance was etched in every stern edge of her softly aging features. Her back was straight, her shoulders relaxed.

Azrael needed answers.

The black knight's voice broke the silence. "Still the queen mother. Do you imagine that strength will save you?"

With the deliberate slowness of a royal taking audience, Alahna turned to look at him. Her amber eyes stared through the slits of his visor, straight into his own green gaze beneath. "Why are you here?" she asked.

"You are my prisoner," he said simply, meeting her stare. "The right of questioning is mine."

"And what," she asked, rising to face him with all the pride of a stoic lady, "do you imagine I have to tell you? Secrets? I was not well informed of my late son or grandson's military strategies, and considering how completely you have slaughtered our armies and burned our fleet, what little information I might know hardly seems relevant. I do not know where Silas has taken Coulton, nor where he kept his order's knowledge. I was privy to neither."

Azrael found himself smiling grimly behind the death's head visor of his helm. Blunt candor was a quality he could appreciate. "Nothing so direct, *Queen Mother*. I wish to know what possessed you to ask for my name."

This caught her off guard. Good. He noted the glint of confusion in her eyes. Perhaps off-footed, she would answer honestly. "You're not like the others," she finally said. "Your cadence. Your composure. I know a classical education when I see one."

"My master was thorough," Azrael replied, amused.

"What does it matter to you?" she said, recovering. "You gave your answer: Lord Azrael of the House of Nails, servant to the greatest butcher in the Unclaimed."

"I am all of those things, *majesty*," Azrael said with a smirk beneath the visor. "All of those and more. Yet that does not change the fact that you seemed to believe that you knew me." A part of him, in just that moment, burned to know. "Tell me why."

The queen looked at him coldly, then, after a moment, she said, "Stop hiding your face, and I will tell you what I see."

Azrael summoned a shield spell, then said, simply, "Why not?" His fingers played at the buckles, then slowly shifted the black helm from his head. His dark hair tumbled to his shoulders, and he breathed in the cold air of the cell block with a comfortable ease.

She took an involuntary step back, staring at him and shaking her head repeatedly. "Gods," she finally breathed. "Identical…"

Azrael's teeth ground. A surge of anger welled within him and he stepped toward the bars. "That's not an *answer*," he snapped.

She stepped further back. Disgust and fear flashed in her eyes.

"I see the ghost of a man far, *far* better than you, the mask of a kind man's face worn by a *monster*."

She turned. "Now unless you plan to tear into my mind for more useless information, *leave me*. You killed my son *and* my grandson."

Azrael turned towards the doors, re-donning his helm. "Suit yourself, queen. We have a long time, you and I."

He heard the first sobs racking her frame as he walked down the corridor past the despairing faces of countless others. His footfalls were resolute. He did not turn around. He *would* not turn around.

The noise disquieted him nonetheless.

Hours later, from the bridge of the *Iron Hulk*, Azrael watched as glimmering skyships fled Land's Edge, winged ants fleeing a burning colony. Behind him, a host of crew worked the vast consoles that kept the mountain fortress moving forward. On his right was Lord Malfenshir. On his left, Sir Kaelith was a wall of armor and brutal stoicism. She neither blinked nor stirred.

"I wonder," the latter said eventually, "how many of those things actually believe they can escape us?"

"Too many," Malfenshir laughed, the sound rich and harsh. "The next hour or so is going to be a lot of fun."

"If either of you lose focus," Azrael said simply, "my next report will contain a detailed explanation of your deaths. We have a specific job to do here. Now stay on task."

Malfenshir's nod of assent barely masked his hungry expression. Azrael regarded him. "You will command the aerial war," he said. "Sir Kaelith will lead the ground invasion." He looked out the sprawl of the city beyond the cavernous viewports of the vast fortress's bridge. "I will make for the great library with Sir Fenris. If the sage is anywhere in the city, he will be there. And if not him, then tomes, at least, that might be of use. I will take fifteen of our best mercenaries."

Both men nodded. Malfenshir lifted his hand as the outer walls of the city became clear. "Prepare the ether-cannons for the first volley. Their gunships will be up and making runs at us any moment."

Azrael paused, looking over his shoulders at the swarming ships over Land's Edge. A moment passed, and another, without the flare of guns or the growing sight of vessels rushing towards them. "They're not attacking," Malfenshir murmured.

"They're running," Sir Kaelith said.

"Done with their thrashings, I suppose," Malfenshir growled.

Azrael walked back to stand beside the other two. His eyes narrowed as he stared. Gunships, freighters, light escorts and pleasure yachts. All of them were flying away from the city.

"Summon the gunboats," Azrael said. "Get troops on the ground *now,* before they're able to take every scrap of valuable information with them." He gestured at Malfenshir with a menacing finger. "Don't shoot a *single* ship out of these skies unless they attack us directly. What we *need* could be on any of them. Now *move!*"

The lander struck the ground, and Azrael waded into the chaos of the internal city. Screams surrounded him, the sweaty stink of fear mingled with sewage, and the great gates of Land's Edge loomed in the distance behind. Sir

Fenris was a stalking, hungry shadow in gray and black beside him, his snarling dog's-head helm glinting in the tortured sunset. Behind them, fifteen mercenaries with flame-lances and shock-spears fanned out in a wedge-like thicket of spikes.

Their landing had pulverized a statue, torn up segments of street, and put them directly in front of the city's great library. There, descending the steps, was Silas, quivering in the company of a group of people the black knight didn't recognize: a dark-skinned old man in sorcerer's robes, and a blonde girl in a long blue coat. The girl had just thrown up a shield spell to defend herself and her companions from the debris thrown up by the lander. It was potent, the latent power teasing at the edge of Azrael's senses as he strode forward. "There you are, sage," he said. "We've been looking *everywhere* for you."

Oath of Aurum was in his hands; the blade's enchantments had gone quiet, though they yet hummed in his fingers.

"Azrael," the sage breathed, fear in his eyes. All the company were laden almost to unbalance with books, scrolls, and satchels.

"And you even emptied your order's archives, saving us the trouble," Azrael graciously continued. This was nearly over. He would soon possess *exactly* what Roland had commanded of him. Turning his eyes to the strangers he said, "Hand over the sage and his knowledge, and you'll be free to run away pissing yourselves with everyone else in this wretched city."

"He lies," the sage answered. "He'll cut us all down the moment he has what he wants."

"Now that's *rude*," Azrael quipped back. "When have I not kept my word before?"

"Sorry," the sorceress replied, her hands still maintaining the shield spell. "We don't make deals with psychopathic monsters."

Fenris released a blazing bolt of flame that shattered the girl's shield spell. Things went wrong immediately. The sorceress took two steps back as Azrael's mercenaries flooded forward, and he had a bare second's warning to throw up a barrier of his own before she unleashed a blast of coruscating light that tore outwards, frying the first three men that rushed her and sending those behind scattering across the stones of the street. Several of them did not rise again.

And abruptly, from just up the road, a group of spear-wielding city guardsmen led by a screaming red-haired woman rushed them, their points leveled and eyes fierce.

"Fine," Azrael grunted. "Blood it is."

A soldier interposed himself between Azrael and the sorceress and the sage she guarded. The girl dropped her books and satchels. A spearpoint punched at the black knight's face. He sidestepped, cut the haft in twain, and split the man behind it into two hunks of screaming meat. Casually, he stepped over the corpse and walked towards the two retreating up the steps. "This is stupid," he said. "I don't even care who you are, and you don't look like locals. Just give me the old man and make my job easier."

Fenris had joined him. The two knights stalked up the stairs as their mercenaries slaughtered the city guard behind them. "Last chance," Fenris snarled.

And suddenly, the older sorcerer was *there*, faster than Azrael could have imagined. His right hand seized Fenris's sword arm, and Azrael felt a swell of power that left him *dizzy* as the bearded mage spoke a single, mystically charged word:

"BOIL."

Fenris *screamed*. Choked on it. His hands convulsed, and melted flesh and burning oil bled from between the chinks in his armor. Azrael had just a second to reflexively bolster his armor before the sorcerer hit him with a spell that threw him twenty feet through the air. The black knight flipped, rolled. Summoned a spell for balance. A spell for speed.

Instead of having his brains dashed against the stone, Azrael landed in a crouch, and slowly stood.

"Harkon!" the girl yelled, her eyes wide with fear. "Harkon, that should've shattered every bone in his body, why is he getting back up!?"

Harkon Bright. Azrael was facing the legendary sorcerer and portalmage Harkon Bright.

There was no time to worry.

Enhanced speed roared through Azrael's body. The surviving watchmen rushed between him and the small group. He blurred through them, sword snapping too fast for their eyes to follow. A carpet of corpses splattered across the ruined street in his wake.

A blink, and he was among them. The girl sent a killing flare of red light at his head. He dropped his weight and swept his sword at her center of mass. The hastily summoned, smaller shield spell barely saved her, and the impact of Oath of Aurum shattered her enchantments in a shower of glass-like shards of light. She fell, and tried to sweep his leg as she went down. He jumped. It left him one heartbeat to pivot as Harkon hurtled a bolt of bone-melting sun-flame at his chest.

Faster than the eye could follow, Azrael's enchanted sword swept up. Reflexive. Desperate. The steel rang bell-like as he *parried* the magic. Azrael overcame his shock first. How had he *done* that? No time to wonder. The old man was slower, and his eyes widened as the black knight darted in before the mage could summon another spell and drove the point of his sword through his right shoulder.

The girl screamed. Harkon cried out in agony. "You caught Fenris off guard," Azrael snarled. "You won't have any such luck with me, *old man*."

Then a spearpoint rammed into a chink in Azrael's armor, piercing the mesh beneath the plates and putting three inches of cold metal into the flesh beneath. Azrael's eyes darted left to see the rust-haired soldier that had accompanied his enemies gripping a shock-pike by the haft. There was a cut on her forehead and she was missing a tooth, but her eyes were fierce. "This is for Prince Collum, *bastard*."

"Captain Gara!" the sage yelled.

Azrael ripped his sword free of Harkon's shoulder, too slow. "Shit."

The soldier twisted the haft, and Azrael had less than half a second to prepare himself before a bolt of lightning tore through his body.

But he didn't fall. Years and *years* of conditioning exercises, of pain, of minor enchantments woven into the flesh, paid off. Azrael shouted. His knees wanted to buckle and his heart should have stopped, but he neither fell nor flew backwards.

Instead, through the haze of pain, Azrael twisted, seized the haft of the spear with his left hand and yanked it free from his body. He heaved the soldier at the other end towards him, and hacked her head from her shoulders. Gara's eyes still looked on in fierce defiance as her head bounced across the ruined cobbles.

Azrael turned. The sage, the sorceress, and Harkon were halfway across the square, the first two dragging the third. Snarling, Azrael stalked after them. His body still tingled from the electric shock and his energy ebbed from loss of blood.

"You've lost half your scrolls and books," he said, stepping over discarded satchels, blood dripping from his gilded sword. "And your master is no longer a threat to me."

The girl stopped. The sage pleaded with her. "Don't listen to him, Aimee! He's *baiting* you! We have to run!"

Fires started by the exchange of spells now burned freely in the square.

"Aimee, is it?" Azrael said. "Pretty name. You can still walk away from this, you and your master both. Not the sage, of course. He comes with me, willing or not, but I'm *tired*, and I'd rather not waste more time killing people I don't need to."

Aimee faced him across a twenty-foot span. Her hands were by her sides. Arcane fire wisped around her fingertips and danced in her eyes. With pure, furious hate, she said, "You want them, demon, you'll have to go through me."

Azrael sighed. "Fine," he said. His sword snapped up. Her hands flashed into position, the words of a spell on her lips.

Then a hail of gunfire blasted through the square. She dove for cover. Azrael threw himself down and poured every ounce of power he had into a shield spell. The force of the blasts smashed him into the broken cobbles. His teeth set. The muffled roar of the raging explosions echoed beyond the straining border of his fraying magic.

When at last he stood, it was in time to watch as a slender, silver skyship with forward-swept wings rose from the square, its bay doors closing as his quarry vanished into its interior. It swept overhead and into the sky, keeping low over the buildings, headed not into the open air, but towards the interior of the island.

Azrael forced himself to run, dragged himself through the door to the lander and into the pilot's seat. His remaining mercenaries dashed back in as the engines roared to life and the ship shot into the sky. Fighting through the pain, he gunned the drive and roared after them. The rooftops rushed by beneath. Tall spires and steeples whipped past. He kept the skyship in his sights. He had to maintain visual contact long enough to measure their trajectory, calculate their course. The fleeing vessel was nearly past the *Iron Hulk* now – *abyss*, it was fast. Malfenshir had his orders. Do not fire. Just a few more seconds.

A storm of blasts erupted from the hulk's ether-cannons as Azrael watched, raking across the vessel's path. An explosion flared off one of its wings, and it veered off course, nearly crashing before righting itself and limping into the distance.

Azrael's fist slammed against the console, and with a sharp turn of the controls he brought the lander hurtling back towards the hulk. He had given specific, strict orders. *Don't fire on fleeing ships.*

"My lord," one of the mercenaries said. "Where are we going?"

"Back to the hulk," Azrael snapped. "To resupply and reorganize. And then to cut off Malfenshir's fingers."

CHAPTER ELEVEN
Elysium Wounded

"Son of a bitch! Son of a bitch!" The ship bucked and shuddered in the heavens. In front of Aimee, Clutch muscled the wheel and desperately strove to keep *Elysium* from dropping out of the sky. "*Son of a bitch!*"

They banked hard, wounded by an errant blast from the *Iron Hulk*. The ship dropped again. Aimee could see the treetops whipping by beneath. Harkon leaned on Silas, his expression pained, his gaze flickering in and out. "We're gonna plaster ourselves on the side of some goddamn mountain!" Clutch screamed. "Boss, I need a judgment call *now!*"

Harkon tried to say something. A fresh wave of pain overwhelmed him, and instead he groaned in agony.

"Put us down, dammit!" Vlana shouted.

"That's certain death this close to the city!" Bjorn snapped, gripping the rails.

"*Up!*" Aimee shouted, forcing herself to stay upright. The words were so loud that it caught the attention of everyone on the bridge.

"What the hell are you doing, *student*?" Clutch snapped.

"Taking command." Aimee straightened her back, staring the pilot down. There was no time for arguing about who took the lead. "Silas!" she snapped. The sage turned to her with bewildered eyes. "Give Clutch the coordinates for our approximate destination!"

She turned back to Clutch. "Tell Vant to burn as hard as he can, and take us *up*. As high as we can go, then point us at where we need to be and we'll glide the rest of the way down if we have to."

"Gods and devils," Clutch swore. "You're *not* trying to still find that dumb gem. Not when we've just taken a hit!"

"Yes, we *are!*" Aimee snapped. She forced her way across the bridge and jabbed her finger into Clutch's face. "We made a vow to the prince of Port Providence, and I've seen what our enemies are capable of. If we win, we stand to gain control of a relic we *can't let them have* and whatever treasure lies with it. If we lose, some of the biggest monsters in the Drifting Lands get their hands on an artifact that can show them whatever secret they want to see. Now are you going to follow my damn orders, or am I going to knock you flat and figure out how to fly the ship myself?"

Clutch swore, then shook her head. "Gods no, you'll kill us all. Hell. Hell. Hell. *Hell.* Silas! You heard the lady! Give me those damn numbers! Vant, give me a hard burn, we're going up, because the crazy blonde lady says so!"

Aimee stepped back and looped her arm under Harkon's. Silas nodded and stepped forward to give his information to Clutch. "Vlana!" Aimee shouted. "Help me get him down to the infirmary! I can still save him if we hurry!"

•••

The first time Aimee had been to the infirmary was mere hours after their arrival in the middle of this war zone, to prep it for Gara's wounded. She'd been so flush with terror and guilt that she'd half-staggered her way down the hallway and nearly fallen through the door.

That was *nothing* compared to the comedy of errors that was trying to haul a wounded man down the same hallway in a badly shuddering vessel currently climbing skyward. The three of them staggered about, a parody of a child's broken windup toy, whilst Harkon groaned between them, sweat on his brow and blood covering the entire front of his robes from the horrible wound in his shoulder.

Azrael had hacked off Gara's head, and nearly taken her teacher's arm off.

They kicked the door in, hauled Harkon to one of the beds, and shifted him onto it. "Hold him still," Aimee said, fighting to still the hammering of her panicked heart. Command. She had just taken command. She'd had to. After what she'd seen, it was a miracle she could still stand. As Harkon was put on his back, she forced the memory of Azrael's sword slicing Gara's head from her shoulders to stop playing over and over in her waking mind. Healing magic. She had to focus on healing magic.

"Cut his sleeve off," she instructed Vlana. The quartermaster complied. Beneath, an ugly, deep rent in the flesh pulsed fresh blood. Swallowing the rising urge to throw up, Aimee replayed everything she knew about anatomy and the laws of healing magic in her head. The healing spells she knew required bones to be set before she could mend them. Her fingers probed, finding where the blade had severed bone. Gods, this was *bad*. Harkon was breathing more normally now, but he winced in agony at the touch.

"How bad?" he asked.

"Bad," Aimee murmured. "He severed your shoulder joint. We've got to hold it together long enough for me to cast the healing spell."

"Do it," Harkon breathed.

"Vlana, the chirurgery kit," Aimee said, fighting down bile that crawled up the back of her throat. No time for fear. No time for faintness of heart. *Elysium's* climb was steeper now, and the slant of the floor was becoming a challenge.

"I thought you academy sorcerers could just point-and-fix!" Vlana breathed as she started cutting away bits of ruined flesh and cloth. Harkon's face was growing pale. Aimee couldn't help but be impressed. He was still lucid while undergoing shoulder surgery without any sort of numbing.

"The full-time healers can," Aimee said through gritted teeth. "But I only studied enough for the lesser mysteries. I need a wound cleaned and the pieces held back together, or the spell will put it back together wrong."

The ship was at a hard angle now. Aimee gripped the table with one hand. Vlana was keeping her balance with practiced ease, fingers working at cleaning the wound, and the two exchanged a look.

"Ready," Vlana murmured. "Sorry about this, boss." Her hands gripped the old man's shoulder, pushing and rotating until the severed ball-joint was pressed back into place. Harkon screamed. Aimee pressed her hands to the bloody wound and spoke the words. Healing light flared from her fingers, knitting through flesh and bone in a thousand iridescent threads. The rent in the skin closed. Bones mended with a soft *click*. Aimee's bloody hands slackened, and she sagged from the effort.

Harkon breathed in relief. His eyes opened, and he looked back and forth between the two women. "... Impressive work," he said, pained.

"If we keep this up," Aimee nervously laughed, "I'm going to have to study up on my anatomy and chirurgery."

"Or fight fewer Eternal Order knights," Vlana muttered. "That works too."

"Gods, he was fast," Harkon breathed. "Too fast."

"Your old enemy must've taught him well," Aimee said, slumping back. She just needed a few moments to regain her strength. Gods, but that healing spell had taken a lot out of her.

"Roland," Vlana murmured. At Aimee's glance, she shrugged. "I've heard the stories, too."

"Roland was never that fast, not when I knew him," Harkon grunted, carefully flexing the fingers on his healed arm. "Not when he was that young. The boy's power is less refined, but stronger."

The ship was leveling out. The deck beneath them had a gentler slope. "Can you use the arm?"

"Still hurts," Harkon answered, "I won't be as quick for a while yet. You'll have to take the lead on some bigger spells, but it will recover fully in time, I think. Good work."

And abruptly, *Elysium* shuddered hard, and the deck tilted the opposite direction. They were going down.

They stumbled onto the bridge in time to watch as the ship broke through cloud cover over the jagged, forested peaks of the inland mountains' foothills. Some were still capped with snow that had survived the oppressively dry summer. Amidst the rippling lines of wave-like crags, Aimee glimpsed the slender, blue ribbons of rivers trickling with meltwater.

For a half-second she almost forgot that she was in a wounded ship limping out of the sky over a war-ravaged land. It was beyond strange, how mere miles from the hellholes people made of their world, you'd have been hard pressed to know there was a war anywhere to begin with.

Then Clutch started swearing again. "Dammit all to hell, this is as close as we're gonna get, Silas!"

Silas – who had his map clutched in his shaking, white knuckles – was sitting in Vlana's chair, watching as the ground grew steadily larger. He babbled out his terrified response. "It will take a day to reach the place from here on foot! We've still got altitude! Why can't you go *further*?"

Aimee gripped the rail, watching as the pilot carefully managed something that would have had Skyship pilots from the Academies in Havensreach panicking and pissing themselves.

Clutch looked as though she was ready to strangle the old man. "Look out the damned windows, old-timer! Any further and there'll be nothing but pointed crags and vertical slopes, and *I can't land this bird* on *a needle!*"

"Put us down there," Harkon pointed to a strip of riverbank overshadowed by a cliff. *Elysium* was shaking again, losing altitude by the moment. Aimee felt her stomach lurching.

"You're insane," Clutch snapped.

"You can do it," Aimee affirmed. She wished she felt as confident as she sounded.

"Gods, I hate you all!" Clutch snarled. "Hold on, everyone, this is gonna be less a landing and more like a controlled crash."

Aimee felt her stomach revolt as they came in. The ship bucked from left to right. She gripped a rail. *I will not die today,* she thought. *I will not die today.* The ground rose up to meet them, at once accelerating from a slow advance to the speed of an incoming punch. Her knuckles were white, and she heard Clutch yell, "Hang on!"

Dirt and stone sprayed across the viewports. The bridge shook, and Aimee heard the sound of grinding metal and wood against stone, and fought to keep from throwing up. "Hold together," she heard Harkon swear, and she saw him pressing his hands to the hull, face awash with sweat and pain, fighting to save them even as their world felt like it was ripping apart. Aimee felt the thrum of magic. The world spun. The deck shook, tilted violently sideways, and for a terrible second it seemed that they would flip.

Uncle, Aimee found herself remembering the day Jester de Laurent's ship exploded in the Port of Havensreach. *Was it like this?*

Then they jerked back, upright, and with a hiss and the slow winding down of the metadrive, they were still. The sounds of the ship faded away to nothing, and Aimee heard her own breath coming in and out as her fingers gripped the rail for support. Alive. She was alive. They had saved the ship, and they'd saved her.

"Is everyone alive?" she managed after a moment, genuinely afraid of the answer.

"Breathing," Bjorn grunted, standing from where he'd flung himself to protect Vlana from a fallen overhead beam.

"Me too," Vlana murmured, dusting off the knees of her coveralls.

"Well *that* was smoother than expected. I'm fine," Clutch grunted.

"Alive, and so is the sage," Harkon said, rising with some difficulty. He moved to the communication tubes that led to the engine room. "Vant, tell me you're alive."

After a terrifying moment wherein Vlana looked ready to dash over to the same spot, the irritated voice came back. "I hate you all. So much."

If there was one thing Aimee now admired – fiercely – about her crewmates, it was the boundless energy and determination with which they threw themselves into the next task, only seconds after surviving what by any other count was a terrible failure.

Vlana let out a relieved laugh, then took off down the main hallway to find her brother.

"That's fine," Aimee said, straightening, relief flooding through her. "I'll take alive and hated."

Silas separated himself from Harkon, shaking his head as he collected himself. "Never had a landing like that before," he breathed, finally, then gave Clutch a respectful nod. "Your flying is magnificent."

"You're welcome," Clutch grunted, moving to the viewports and stretching until she stood on her toes to look outside. "We're by the river," she said. "Just underneath that cliff. Nailed it."

"Get down to the engine room," Harkon said. "Start taking stock of what spare parts we've got, and the damage done... We're going to need to get airborne again, somehow, or we'll all die out here."

Aimee was still settling her spirit. She'd thrown herself into a war, mended wounds, seen people die, fought, killed, all in the span of a few days. Now, as events moved rapidly past, there was almost no time to consider the shuddering, underlying changes evident in herself. If she survived, she reckoned, she would spend more than one night in her cabin hugging her knees to her chest and letting the emotions tear out of her.

But not yet. Not yet.

As the grumbling pilot followed after Vlana, the remaining four people on the bridge took a moment to breathe before Aimee broke the silence again. "So," she murmured. "Now I get to walk the walk with my idea – literally. We're going to have to hoof it the rest of the way." She'd dreaded having to follow through with it, but a promise was a promise. It was time to shoulder her worries and get things done.

"I'm afraid so," Silas murmured, leaning against the rails. "I hope we've got the supplies."

"At least a day or two's worth," Harkon nodded, moving his shoulder with a pained expression. Aimee felt a twinge of guilt that her healing couldn't obviate the need for recovery. "I can lay a spell of concealment over *Elysium*, which should deter anyone tracking us for the time being. At the least, it will keep them safe while we chase the diamond. I fear we won't be able to keep Azrael or his minions off our trail, however."

"I'm going with you," Bjorn said.

"No you're *not*," Harkon abruptly snapped. "I need you here to protect Clutch, Vlana, and Vant while they get the ship working."

"You mean the three who will be safely behind an illusion?" the old warrior shot back. "That's a waste of my talents. The three of you are powerful, but you're not fighters. You barely walked away from an on-the-ground confrontation with our enemies, and you're not at full capacity, Hark."

"He's right," Aimee added, and the iron in her own voice surprised her, though perhaps it should not have, given all she'd done in a few days. "I took the self-defense seminars at the academy, and I know my share of offensive spells, but that's not gonna cut it against them. Not with just the three of us."

Gara's head bounced across the cobbles in her mind's eye, and Aimee felt a shiver of mingled fear, horror, and hatred. She pushed it aside. They needed to listen, and she had to maintain her cool to ensure that they did. "We're going to need him," she ended. "We can't be without a proper warrior."

Harkon fixed her with a distinctly irritated stare for a moment, then sighed, looking to the other two men. She'd won, then. Good. "And this is why she's my apprentice: power, ability, and damned good sense. Very well. Bjorn, take Silas and scrounge up what equipment we can use."

He turned from the bridge and gestured for Aimee to follow him. "And I have a concealment spell to perform."

The ship didn't look that bad, from outside. The silver exterior sported the sooty scorches of glancing shots and near misses. There were dents in the tail fins and a burn mark upon the wing, but for all her groundedness, the enigmatic skyship called *Elysium* looked surprisingly unharmed.

What cut through Aimee's heart, arresting her where she stood, was that the silver ship that had cradled her for near a week *wasn't moving*. When Aimee was eleven, a boy – the child of a friend of her parents – had been taken by a rare disease just before his eighteenth birthday. It burned through him, tenaciously outpacing magical healing until nothing remained to his parents but desperate pleas and the prayers of summoned priests. Aimee had not known him well, but the last time she had seen him it had been as he lay in his sickbed, an ashen shell that hardly resembled the boy that had laughed, danced, run, and climbed.

Seeing *Elysium* immobile on the ground where even at dock it had always floated in the air, Aimee felt the same wounding cut of cosmic injustice strike her: boys that ran and jumped shouldn't fall shriveled and pale. Silver birds that flashed through heaven didn't belong broken in the dirt.

Harkon stood beside her, silhouetted against the sunlight. His eyes had the same pain, the same deeply personal wound at the sight before them, but mingled with it was a force of determination that spoke as much to the scared little girl within her as the nineteen year-old woman that girl had become.

"Don't be afraid," Harkon said. Quiet. Fierce. "She will fly again."

For a moment, Aimee had no words. Then, when she looked away from her teacher and back at the ship, they came to her. Truthful. From the heart.

"She'd better," Aimee said. "She's my *home*."

"Then let's hide her," Harkon said in assent. He looked over to their left, where Bjorn and Silas were gathering their small set of provisions into packs. The hike wasn't supposed to take long: it was less than a day's journey to their destination, but those who failed to prepare suffered for it.

Harkon stepped forward as Aimee watched. Her years

studying the rules of illusions replayed the highlights of their content through her mind as her teacher closed his eyes and breathed in. Illusion magic relied upon two things: the imagination of the caster, and the willingness of the viewer to believe. The best illusions, therefore, the most powerful, were those that masked the caster's intentions by seamlessly reflecting what the person perceiving them expected to see.

His hands flashed in a series of gestures, and Aimee watched in unvarnished admiration as the older sorcerer's precise, elegant movements summoned up a ripple of power that made the hairs at the base of her neck stand on end. She felt the formed potential of the spell hanging unreleased in the air for half a heartbeat, then Harkon spoke the word of power, and a thousand threads of light flooded from his hands, knitting themselves into a shroud that passed before their eyes. It wavered, expanded, spread across the entire space before them, from cliff edge to riverbank, then held. In place of *Elysium*'s slender, silver frame, Aimee now stood at the lip of a blasted pit riddled with tortured chunks of mangled fuselage. The sort of ruin a skyship might wreak when its metadrive erupted at the moment of a crash. It still smoked. Even knowing that it wasn't real, Aimee still had to fight the horror that revolted from her gut at the sight.

"That," she breathed, "is better than I wanted it to be."

"Convincing is what we need," Bjorn grunted, though by the look on his face he hated the sight as much as she did.

"Come on," Harkon said, rubbing his wounded shoulder as he picked up his pack. "It's time to go."

And leaving the mirage of ruin at their backs, the four made their way into the wilderness.

CHAPTER TWELVE
LOOSE THE BEASTS

"I gave you a *direct order,*" the black knight snarled. It had been a simple one. *Don't fire on any enemy ships.* They didn't know if one of them contained the sage they pursued. The black knight could bring a kingdom to its knees, slay his enemies. But he couldn't seem to keep this monstrous beast of a second-in-command in line.

Azrael sat in a chair as Esric tended to his numerous wounds. Malfenshir stood before him, eyes twin coals of fury in his cruel face.

"I specifically instructed you," Azrael continued, "*not* to fire on any fleeing vessels. Was your defiance deliberate? Or are you simply so inept that the most basic of instructions is fundamentally beyond you?"

"It was the same ship that broke our blockade," Malfenshir said. "Have you *forgotten* that there are charters in our order with very clear rules about what we do when given the chance to destroy an enemy that has escaped us before?"

"Those rules," Azrael snarled, "are ranked far below the importance of obeying your superior."

"Your lordship will simply have to *forgive* me."

Malfenshir's lip curled. "But you would do well to remember that before this invasion even began, I suggested a plan that would have forced the late king to yield."

Azrael's eyes narrowed. His teeth set. "And I had *reasons* for refusing your insane plan."

"What was it, absolute oblivion you threatened them with? My plan would have delivered." A murderous light danced in Malfenshir's dark eyes.

The black knight's fists tightened. "I told you the Silent Scream is not an option."

The big, square-faced knight laughed. Vicious. Vindictive. "Of course, when you have a weapon that can end all resistance at once, why use it?"

"You don't get it, *still*," Azrael snapped. "The king never had the diamond, nor did Prince Collum, or his grandmother. Only the sages know, and they never shared that knowledge. Your plan would have forced us to choose between destroying the whole continent – and our prize with it – or proving ourselves paper tigers, unwilling to back up our threats."

"Coward," Malfenshir accused.

Azrael stood abruptly from the chair and drilled his fist into the bigger man's face. Strong as he was, Malfenshir didn't fall, but his head snapped to the side, and he spit a tooth across the floor.

"You are a contemptible fool and a mad dog," Azrael said quietly. "And you will have no further part of the pursuit of the Axiom. Count yourself lucky to be involved further in this Investment at all."

Malfenshir slowly turned his face back towards his superior, then laughed. The sound was harsh and cruel. "Is this supposed to be a *joke*, Lord Azrael? What happened to tearing out my eyes and tongue and sending them back to our masters? Ironic, that you would accuse *my* plan of lacking teeth. This is precisely your problem: you think that unfulfilled threats are the same as action."

Malfenshir straightened to his full height – level with the black knight – and stared at him. "If you think you can force my obedience with unfulfilled threats, you're wrong. My master didn't believe you can be trusted, and the truth of why becomes more apparent by the day: you are weak, you hesitate, you are unfit for command."

Azrael's hand gripped the enchanted sword at his side and pulled, drawing the blade with a snap of his hips that drove the pommel into Malfenshir's chin. The big man's head cracked backwards, and as he staggered back, the black knight brought his knee up to his chest and smashed his heel into his second's center of mass. Malfenshir hit the deck, completely taken off guard by his superior's ferocity. Before he could roll or take his weapon, Azrael was standing over him, the enchanted sword's point hovering just above his right eye.

"If you speak again without my permission," Azrael answered, "I will kill you."

"Gentlemen," Esric's calm voice filled the room. "Let's not kill each other just yet, hmm?"

Azrael's eyes flicked left, then right. Malfenshir's hands were upraised. His fingers crackled with an arcane light, with a spell he could release in the same span of time it would take the sword to pierce his eye.

Stalemate. Slowly, Azrael straightened, drawing back his sword. Evenly matched. Still.

"That's better," Esric said. His hand rested on Azrael's shoulder. Calm settled over the black knight. He breathed out his tension and stepped back.

"Lord Malfenshir," Azrael said. "In the name of the Council of the Eternal Order, I command you to remain in the *Iron Hulk*. You will return to Port Providence, consolidate our plunder, and prepare to return to the House of Nails when I return with the Axiom. Understood?"

Malfenshir stared back at him in silence. Then he rose slowly from the floor. "Since the very beginning of this Investment you have locked me out of every task worthy of my station, blocked the execution of my duties, and treated me like little more than a mad dog on your personal chain. I will obey, *Lord Azrael*, but when this is done, you and I will have a reckoning, and you will pay, even if I must lay your jawless, well-fucked skull at the thrones of the council. That is where we stand. Understood?"

Azrael stared back into the other man's cold, dead eyes, and uttered a single word. "Perfectly."

Patched up, restored by Esric's healing and wearing his full panoply, Azrael strode across the hangar bay towards the lander. The shorter, balding man tried to keep pace with him.

"With respect, my lord," the healer pleaded, "you're not taking enough men with you."

"I have to move fast," Azrael countered. "More will slow me down." He needed to get out of here, and quickly. He needed to be free of the politicking, the backstabbing, and the oneupmanship fraying the chains of his command. He needed to be free to *do his job*. Pursue the sage. Find that silver ship. Track its crew. *Find the damn Axiom Diamond.*

"At least take me with you, then," Esric repeated. He reached to grasp Azrael by the arm. This time, the black knight reflexively swatted his hand away.

"I need you here," Azrael said. Just then, something about the healer's presence unsettled him, though he couldn't precisely say what. Esric's eyes – ninety percent of the time – were unreadable. The smooth lines of his face were unrevealing in their serene calm almost every hour of the day. But as the healer pulled his hand back from the black knight's firm rebuke, Azrael glimpsed a frightening intensity in his gaze.

In that second, Esric went from looking like a calm physician to a child robbed of the fly whose wings he was picking off. Then the serenity was back. "As you say, my lord. I still think you should take Sir Cairn or Kaelith with you."

"Twenty will suffice," Azrael said. "You'll need them to help keep an eye on Malfenshir. I want him kept in line until I get back."

A wan smile crossed the healer's face. "As though that were easy."

"I have faith in you," Azrael deadpanned, then kept walking.

Elias.

He gritted his teeth. Warriors waited for him, mercenaries with shock-pikes, flame-lances and short blades in their hands, cuirasses on their bodies, lighter armor to let them move swiftly through the thick woods of the inland. Harsh eyes. Men. Women. On some level, Azrael felt even these were too many, but it would let him cover ground more quickly. He had three trackers among them.

"Your marching orders are to capture, not kill," Azrael said to his warriors. "Now get on the ship, and let's get going."

They flared into the clouds from the landward bay of the hulk. The blazing sunset painted the sky from horizon to horizon with red-gold fire. The woods beneath them caught the molten glow, and in the lander's rear viewport, Azrael watched plumes of smoke rise from the city's interior. Another day of burning and stripping would follow. The black knight should have rejoiced inwardly at the victory, but his gut was twisted into a knot of cold numbness wrapped around feelings for which he had no name.

He simply found the aftermath of conquest unfulfilling. That had to be it. It was the fight for which he cared. The dull paperwork of the accounters and their endless blood-ledgers were simply beneath him.

It was the only possibility. The broken eyes of the defeated, of their women, and children, did not move him. They *could* not.

"My lord," the pilot asked, her tone tense, afraid. "What are we looking for?"

Azrael passed her a sheaf of paper scrawled with the trajectory he'd hastily written from memory, the calculations as to the distance and direction he'd seen the ship fleeing. "This way," he said. "And keep your eyes peeled for the signs of a crash. We'll work from there."

They found the crater after flying through the night. Beside a river, the land was torn into a furrow running hundreds of feet towards the ruins of a half-obliterated cliff-face. They paused, hovering in the air. "That doesn't look promising," the pilot muttered. "Look at the scattering of the debris, they must've hit the ground at top speed."

"By the Abyss," someone murmured. "There's almost nothing left."

All around Azrael the mutters buzzed like errant flies. The black knight moved closer to the viewport and stretched out with his own mystic senses for the signs of magic at work. There was something off about what he was looking at. A disjointedness he couldn't quite name tugged at his mind. He was about to tell the pilot to put them down so he could pick through the wreckage when the second tracker spoke up.

"I can see tracks headed into the foothills and crags," the man grunted.

"How the hell can you see *that?*" the pilot asked.

"Disturbed foliage," the first tracker – a woman – agreed, then gestured towards the far edge of the river. "They went that way."

Azrael moved to the other side and followed the arc of the tracker's finger. He ran numbers in his head, let his eyes sweep the terrain, then glanced back at the crater. If they acted now, they might be able to catch whomever had gone on, before they could reach their destination.

That also meant abandoning the investigation of the crash site. He'd need all his men in the field.

"They won't be able to stick to the woods," the first tracker said. "There's too much open ground about here, and if that's their trajectory…"

"They'll have to travel across an open space soon," Azrael nodded. He felt the thrill of the chase in his gut. "Pilot," he said. "Take us deeper into the foothills. Towards the higher peaks."

Turning, he addressed the mercenaries in the lander. "Gear up, check your weapons. Be ready to disembark at a moment's notice. The three of you–" he gestured at the trackers "–eyes on the ground. Let me know the *moment* you spot anything of worth."

All three trackers nodded and moved to the windows. If they had to go to ground and get into the mud, they would, but with a trail evident from the air there was hardly a need.

Closer. They needed to get closer, even if it meant getting into the insecure terrain of the higher mountains. This would all be over soon. Then Azrael would contend with Malfenshir, gather their forces, and return to the House of Nails in victory. The thought of being home again sent involuntary shudders of discomfort through him.

He walked back through the lander, past men and women arming themselves and tightening the straps of their armor. They were a superior force, well warded against blades and cudgels alike. They looked up as he passed, giving nods or salutes. A few shrank back in fear.

He found a small space at the back of the lander to gather his thoughts, and lost himself in the routine of checking his black armor. Oath of Aurum rested sheathed at his hip. When he touched the sword, it felt warm. That was a dissonant comfort. He released it to lift his helm, pausing a moment to look at his reflection in the polished black visor that had replaced the one Prince Collum destroyed. Azrael's distorted face stared back at him. He let out a slow breath, closed his eyes, and let his power ebb and flow within him. Fear, disjointed memory, and failure clawed their way up from deep within. They were like ghouls, their coal-ember eyes filled with memories magnified by time. *I am the master here*, he reprimanded himself. With relentless hammer blows, his will beat them back down.

Fear is weakness. Weakness is death.

Slowly, he opened his eyes.

The reflection of burning flowers stared back at him from the helmet's faceplate. In his mind, again, emerged the name: *Elias.*

He nearly dropped his helm. His heart raced and his palms sweated. It was only through will alone that he kept the sudden fear from showing. He blinked, and only his face stared back from the implacable faceplate. An illusion. A trick of the mind. Nothing more.

"My lord!" The cry came from the front of the lander. The pilot's voice. "We've spotted them!"

Azrael turned, placed the helm upon his head, and forced down doubt, fear, and pain.

It could erupt later, when he was alone, with victory to enshroud and armor him against any inconvenient questions about his sanity. It was time to do his job.

CHAPTER THIRTEEN
FROM VULTURES FLEE

Aimee wasn't used to hiking. It wasn't that she wasn't fit. She'd taken every physical conditioning course necessary at the academy. But she was learning that running around the indoor tracks, vaulting over the academy's obstacle course, or lifting weights in the gymnasium were a different animal from hauling herself double-time across the difficult landscape of Port Providence's mountainous foothills. Especially on little sleep, battered and bruised from their previous adventures, and with the fear in her gut of what would happen when their lead ran out.

The Eternal Order. Azrael. They had done this: shattered Port Providence, slain thousands, all in pursuit of the Axiom Diamond. Even Harkon and Silas didn't seem to completely agree on what the damn thing did, but that the order wanted it was reason enough to keep it out of their hands.

So they hiked, and Aimee pushed herself.

"Keep up," Harkon murmured. Aimee glared as she crested the ridge behind him. Her teacher had decided that now was the time to give her several more advanced spells. Her focus was thus further divided. Harkon seemed to read her mind.

"You will always have to divide your attention in the field. I once had to test a new spell while being chased by eagle-wasps on Zheng-Li. Best develop that skill quickly. Now repeat to me what I have told you. What is the key to an effective binding spell?"

It was the ninth new spell he'd taught her.

"The tightening of the fingers," Aimee answered through hard breathing. "If they're improperly pressed to the palm, a careless mage can ensnare *herself* rather than her target."

"Saw that happen once," Bjorn said with a grunt. He wore battered, boiled leathers and carried a two-handed sword across his back. "Kiscadian battle-mage. Tried to wrap ten men in conjured bands of his own making and wound up damn near mummifying himself."

They crested the top of a rise, and the land fell away behind them. Thick woods and rolling hills spread out across the countryside, and in the far distance the silhouetted peak of the *Iron Hulk* could be seen as the mountain that it was, looming in the heavens. Pine and sun-warmed grass teased at Aimee's nose, and air held the cold bite of higher elevation.

"Do we dare rest here?" Silas asked. The old sage breathed harder than any of them, though he endured his difficulties without complaint.

"Not yet," Bjorn shook his head, and gestured to a cluster of trees up ahead. "We get to cover first."

They set off again. Aimee's boots crunched over hard, moss-crusted rock and short grass. Her breath was a constant rise and fall in her ear, and the sun pounded down on her despite the wind, making her dizzy. She gritted her teeth, buried all urge to complain, and listened as intently as she could to what Harkon was saying.

"Repeat the gesture, without words."

Aimee's fingers ached from repetition. Her wrists raised and she twisted the index and middle fingers. Next, a gesture at the hypothetical target, then a grasp. She felt the energy rise within her, only to fade back whence it came when she gave it no verbal permission. Gestures without words released no sorcery.

"Excellent," Harkon said. "You're learning quickly. Take heart. Most of us have to do this numerous times over our careers. This is a good sign."

Good. She'd done it correctly. The second prime: gestures summoned, words released.

Except with the Eternal Order knights. She'd never witnessed so much as a single spoken word or summoning gesture.

"He never spoke words or made signs," Aimee said as they neared the treeline. "Azrael, I mean, or the one Bjorn chucked out the airlock. How is that possible? I've never heard of magic like that."

"Intuitive arcanism is the term," Silas answered. "It's not very well understood, and so far as most historians of the mystic sciences know, is only found among the Eternal Order. Nobody knows how they train it into their members, since there are no outside visitors to their citadels."

"Nobody at the academy mentioned it even once," she reflected, increasing her pace. "It wasn't in any textbooks, was never mentioned in any lectures. I only knew that their magic was of a type the professors didn't understand. Now I see why."

They'd spent months on Sigurd and Brivant, but

nothing on a trait that let sorcerous warriors *completely skip* the second prime.

"They don't have much to say about it, so they say nothing," Harkon said. There was a grim cast to his face when he spoke. "And the Academy has been threatened before. There is much to say about Havensreach that is good, Miss Laurent, don't mistake me. It is my home as much as yours." He paused. "But their government has been cowardly for a very long time, and a few generations back, their legacy is as dark as anyone else's."

They paused to take their bearings beneath the copse of trees. The wind rustled through the evergreens, and needles cascaded down around them. Aimee sagged against the trunk of a conifer. The shade was a merciful relief.

Silas pulled out his map and obsessively poured over it again.

"How many should we expect behind us?" Aimee asked. She checked the long knife strapped to her hip, and mentally reviewed the number of combative spells she had in her repertoire. Every breath felt like a fortune to be savored.

"Close to twenty," Bjorn answered. "Two search parties of ten, fanning out, following what trails they can find. We haven't had the luxury of hiding our tracks. Perhaps this *Azrael* will send one of his subordinates in charge, while he consolidates his hold on the cities."

"He won't," Silas said, quiet, still staring at his map. "This leader does things himself. He doesn't delegate anything he deems important. Not the claiming of relics, or the killing of princes." A deep bitterness poisoned his tone. "This is the last scramble. So much of what

I protected has been destroyed that it would hardly matter, but for the fact that our enemies have already taken Oath of Aurum. They can't have the Axiom as well."

The sage paused, and his pen and map fell forward onto his knees as he took a great breath in a failing attempt to gather himself. "All this would've been different," he lamented, "if Collum hadn't been so foolish. He tried to kill Azrael when he should have retreated." The old man shook his head. "But it doesn't matter now. The prophecy is broken. Its subject is dead. The sword is theirs."

Aimee fixed her gaze on Silas. "What are you talking about?"

Harkon and Bjorn watched Silas as well, now. Their faces wore the same expression of surprise. "Explain," Harkon demanded.

The old man looked at them, tired, with sad eyes on the edge of despondence. "The sword our enemy took from my prince's lifeless hand was once a holy relic. It predates the Violet Imperium itself, dating back to a time when the Drifting Lands were a different place. It was lost, and its power was thought faded, but there was a prophecy that a prince would come who would restore it to glory with acts of courage and desperate virtue. When Collum found the blade on one of his quests, we knew he was the one... But now it sits inert in the hands of the man who murdered him. I doubt it will ever blaze to life again."

Harkon's eyes widened, and his face flashed with suppressed fury. "Why didn't you *tell* me this?"

Silas gave the old mage a bitter look. "Can you raise the dead or turn back time, Harkon Bright? If not, it was hardly relevant."

Aimee stood. Her own anger blazed behind her eyes. "That our enemy is carrying around a prophesied magic sword? I'd think that's a damned relevant detail."

"Less so than either of you think," Bjorn said, calm. "He's dangerous. That's the same as it always was."

Aimee's fingers flexed in aggravation. "How many more details have you conveniently *left out*, Silas?" Her failure had brought them into this mess, but it seemed more with each passing day that the education into which she'd poured her efforts, and the city she'd fondly called home had conspired to keep life-saving truths from her at every step of her path.

"Believe it or not, Miss Laurent," Silas said, standing indignant and irritated, "there are matters that – despite the shredded state of my nation – I am still expected to remain quiet about. There are secrets that I am not free to share with anyone who helps me, and *you* are not entitled by virtue of your education and birth to know *everything*."

Aimee stared at the sage for a few seconds. Then she felt that famed control that was her hallmark at school slipping, and the girl that was the bane of Professor De Charlegne's class tore out of her. "And the conflict of your nation," she said quietly, "doesn't entitle *you* to withhold information we *need* in order to *help* you."

"Miss Laurent–" Harkon started.

"I am putting my life on the line for your kingdom!" Aimee shouted. "I mended gods-know-how-many of your soldiers! Our ship is lying beside a riverbed, protected from *your* enemies by a concealment spell my teacher could barely perform because his shoulder was nearly *sheared off* by that fabled blade you didn't warn us about. We have been shot at, threatened, pursued, hunted, blasted out of the sky, *all* in the service of your people, your prince, *your home.*" Her left hand snapped out viper-quick and fisted itself in the collar of Silas's worn shirt. "So no, you don't get the luxury of your secrets. If there's anything else that might be relevant to the risks we're assuming, you *tell me now!*"

Strong fingers grasped her shoulder, pulling her back, gentle, but insistent. "Miss Laurent," Harkon reminded her. "Control yourself."

Aimee released the sage's dirty shirt and slowly stepped back. Her breath came quick and angry.

The twenty-second silence that followed was awful, but Silas at last looked ashamed.

"I have lost everything," the sage finally said. He looked away from her. Broken. Exhausted. "I don't expect that I shall get any of it back. Forgive me if I cling to my sense of loyalty." He sighed, and his shoulders slumped with the weight of withheld grief. "It is all I have–"

Then – looking past her face – his eyes suddenly acquired a sharp focus as they fixed on something behind the group. A sudden excitement rippled across his features, and he stood, holding up the map. "Gods," he breathed. "There. *There!*"

The other three spun. Aimee's eyes raked across the landscape, hungry for a glimpse of a goal – *finally* – to reward days of pain and nights of cold-sweat terror. "I'm not seeing it, Silas," she said. "Give me something more specific."

Silas pointed, and following the arc of his arm she saw a large, moss-coated, oddly carved monolith jutting spear-like from the surrounding trees. It lay at the top of a rise beyond the far end of a rocky valley with sheer cliff faces.

"The sentinel," Silas said. "It's mentioned in about five old texts as guarding the doorway to the vault. It's our best shot."

Then a buzzing sounded from the opposite direction. Aimee turned her head and searched the empty sky with panicked eyes. She knew the noise, remembered it from Land's Edge, seconds before armored killers had descended to the city streets.

"Move," Bjorn growled. "They're here."

When Aimee was a little girl, she'd once strayed into a rougher part of the city, wandering outside the protective, upper-crust walls of her family's estate. The jaunt through the slums was uneventful, until she'd caught the attention of a group of hungry stray dogs. She'd run, filled for the first time in her life with white-knuckled terror. It was her first experience with the sort of fear that dried the throat and set the heart to panicked hammering.

She felt that fear again now. Her boots pounded over the jagged rocks of the valley floor. On either side, the cliff walls rose in flat sheets of pale, sunlit limestone. Up ahead, the canyon ended in a stone arch: a single crescent of rock linking the chunks of land through which the valley sliced. Beyond, she could see thick forest. The sound of a waterfall echoed somewhere up ahead. They just had to get *through*–

The buzzing became a roar that battered Aimee's ears. She spun in time to hear Harkon shout, "*Shield!*"

The lander filled her vision, vulture-like, its black frame silhouetted against the sun. Her teacher was beside her. Their hands wove the motions of the shield spell in flawless synchronicity. The tips of the lander's ether-cannons belched green light. The impact slammed into the summoned barrier, so hard, and so close ranged, that both Aimee and Harkon's feet were driven back through the dirt beneath them. The dull *whump* of the blast followed a half-second later.

The shot glanced off and slammed into the valley wall. Dust and rock erupted into the sky. Aimee pivoted, rotating her half of the shield to intercept a hail of flesh-pasting stone. The effort sank her to her knees. For the next few seconds, her world was all choking dirt and acrid clouds. She could neither see nor breathe.

"Up, *up!*"

Silas pulled at her arm. She followed, sluggish. Harkon ran. Bjorn ran next to him. The arch was right there. The lander had been forced to pull up, and now arced around for a second pass. No, that wasn't a pass, they were going to *land.* Aimee's feet pounded the ground, again. Faster. Chunks of still-falling stone cracked against the ground beside her. Closer. The arch was just ahead. The buzzing rose again. They would have to land at the valley's far end. The woods loomed ahead, thick with merciful shade and cover. Closer. Her heart hammered in her ears. Her chest would burst. Her legs would drop under her.

They rushed through the arch and scrambled around a sharp bend. Trees shaded them. To their left, the steep ascent of the hillside presented the first mercy Aimee had seen in days: *stairs.* Hidden beneath the ancient trees, moss-covered and root-tangled, man-cut steps climbed up the hillside towards the place where the sentinel rock poked above the treeline. Just past the arch, the ground dropped away before them into the chasm made by a waterfall on the far side.

"Come on!" she shouted, starting the ascent. Harkon

followed, and Silas. It was only when she looked behind her that Aimee realized Bjorn wasn't with them. The old warrior was down on one knee, breathing hard.

Aimee turned. Before objection could stop her or hands grab her, she was descending the stairs, running back to the crewmate who was down on his knees. He raised a sweat-stained face painted with agony as she reached him. "Come on, Bjorn," Aimee said, grabbing him by the arm. "We've gotta go, get on your feet."

He didn't rise when she pulled. Her conscious mind rebelled against what her eyes were seeing. "Bjorn," her words snapped out, irritated, "You gotta do this, I can't carry you."

"Girl," the pain in the old man's voice was a knife through her heart, "you need to get moving. There's no time for your healing magic, and it'll sap what strength I've got left." As if to settle the argument, he held up his right hand from where it gripped his side. His palm was painted red. "I'll slow them down," he said. "As long as I can."

It wasn't supposed to be like this. That was what registered with Aimee then. The *wrongness* of it. A dim understanding of a horrible weight registered within her, would fall upon her if they lived through the next few hours. Then and there, she pulled the pack from her own back. "Harkon," she said, "are the null stones in here? And the bombs?"

She looked back over her shoulder. Harkon Bright's face was an unreadable, grim-set mask, holding him together. "Yes. Be quick."

Then he looked at Bjorn and said something in a language Aimee didn't understand. Lyrical. Harsh. Bjorn grunted in acknowledgment. "Light your candle later,

Hark. Start moving."

Aimee checked the pack: concussion spheres, the null stones, unactivated, and her small share of the provisions. The last of these she removed and stuffed into her other satchel. Then she pushed the bag into his hands. "The bombs first," she said. Bjorn nodded. "Then the stones," she finished, quietly.

Bjorn managed a pained smile as he nodded. "You've got a murderous mind, for a girl who went to charm school."

Aimee looked into the aged warrior's face, then she did something rare: she hugged him. "He'll need to face you as a man," she said. "Those stones are your best chance."

"He will, girl," Bjorn said. His embrace was strong, then he let her go and pushed her away. "Now go."

Their time was up. Aimee turned, blinked the wetness from her eyes, and charged up the old moss-covered steps that jutted from the hillside like echoes of something long lost. It was a good plan. A smart plan. The best that could be made with what they had.

Every part of her *hated* it.

CHAPTER FOURTEEN
HAWK AND RAKE

The blast threw up a massive shower of stone and dust. The pilot screamed a series of curses and pulled at the controls. Azrael lurched forward. "Pull up!"

The pilot swept the vessel around in a wide arc. The horizon rotated. Azrael cursed and held on to an overhead handle to steady himself as the world tilted and spun. His warriors held on behind him, and the valley dwindled, then swelled, as the ship completed its slow turn. "Put us down!" Azrael yelled.

"It'll have to be at the opposite end!" the pilot replied. She held the wheel. "There's no room near that arch, and the cloud makes it impossible to see!"

"Fine!" Azrael shouted, and turned to address his warriors. "When we get on the ground we're making for the arch, slow and cautious. Watch your back, and the back of the fighter next to you." He drew his sword, breathed out his apprehension, and slid into his killer's skin. Minutes, and this would be over. They circled lower. The vulture swept in to pick the flesh from its kill. They hit the ground and the rear doors opened. Armed men and women flooded out past Azrael into the dissipating cloud of dust. The lingering smell of magic clung to his senses. Their shield spell had held, which meant they were alive.

"Slowly," Azrael said, stalking forward across the valley floor. "If it moves, encircle and capture." His heart pounded in his ears. The thrill of the hunt. This was about to end.

A third of the way down the valley, the rustle of armor and boots over stones echoed in his ears. Azrael had lost count of the ruined corpse-fields he'd seen, of the meat-splattered charnel grounds that ship-size guns created when they fired into groups of people, but the hairs on the back of his neck stood on end as they stalked down the rent in the earth. No blood. No shredded garments or bones pasted to the rock. His apprehension rose. Either they'd moved on – the sane choice by any measure – or they were hoping to get the jump on him.

"They survived," the first tracker snarled from up ahead. The woman had drawn a pair of long knives, and picked her way through the stones where they'd last seen their quarry. The other two trackers jogged to meet her. A pain was building in the back of Azrael's head. Esric's predatory eyes flashed through his mind.

Burning flowers. Smoke and blood. *Elias.*

He started to sweat. Not now. The sword was warm in his grasp, and his pulse raced above his comfort level. *Fear is weakness. Weakness is death.*

The arch loomed just ahead, pale stone against the sky, with forest behind. The cloud thrown up by the lander's shots was only now dissipating, and the first of the trackers had nearly reached the far end. Just beyond, Azrael saw the thick forests. If this was an ambush, it was a poorly laid one.

He turned. Something was wrong. The black knight searched for signs of where their enemy might have dodged or fled. Camouflaging themselves with hasty concealment magics might have worked, he reasoned. Azrael's eyes swept the canyon walls. Any sense he had for magic had suddenly vanished. His mind registered that only a few things could cause that. His eyes widened.

No.

The first tracker stopped abruptly, and Azrael turned as the woman called out from twenty feet before the arch. "Sir," she said, taking a step back. "I think at least one came back this way. There are some tracks that double back into the–"

A loud *snap* echoed through the valley. The tracker glanced down. Azrael had a halfsecond to recognize the pulled string stretched across the woman's ankle before it snapped and went slack. A silver sphere was at the other end, runes glowing brighter and brighter upon it.

Shit.

A bloom of fire and concussive force tore twenty-five feet upwards and outwards. The tracker and every warrior within thirty feet of her were ripped apart. Azrael reached for his shield spell. Nothing happened. No magic. A second detonation. A third. A fourth. Closer. The entire far end of the valley blew itself into an inferno, and Azrael was lifted off the ground. Whatever power had nullified his magic didn't affect the passive enchantments on his armor. It took the brunt of the blast, and he slammed into the ground, fifty feet from the doors of the lander. The pilot, standing by the open door, crumpled, her head crushed by a chunk of flying stone.

Slowly, Azrael rolled onto his side and forced himself

to stand, groaning, grasping for his sword. No magic.
Half-deafened. His helm had been knocked from his
head when he landed, but his armor was intact. The
world was spinning and his ears rang with a high-pitched
keening sound.

He'd barely found his feet when a tall, gray-haired
muscular warrior in boiled leathers hurtled towards him
from the heart of the holocaust, swinging a two-handed
sword.

Steel rang on steel, a bell-like shriek of edge meeting flat
and raking away as they came apart. The impact forced
Azrael back, and a second step prevented his enemy's
follow-up cut from touching him. He had none of his
speed or strength-enhancing magics. This man was
older, but he was also bigger, and – if the surety of his
grip and the power of his cuts told true – stronger. Azrael
had only his own skill to keep him alive. The curious
absence of magic teasing at his senses, combined with
the deadening effect on his own powers, fell into place
as he stood opposite the huge warrior.

"Null stones," Azrael addressed his enemy. "You
covered the entire valley in a magic-dampening field.
Clever."

The old warrior waited now, his hands near his waist,
the point of his sword leveled at Azrael's face. It tracked
the black knight as he slowly circled. Azrael let the back
edge of his sword rest against his armored right shoulder,
the blade angled slightly behind him, his arms close and
tight to his body.

"I didn't think your men would walk right into the
blast," the warrior admitted. His voice was deep, graveled.
His clear eyes watched without focusing, taking in the

whole of what he was seeing. Azrael's heart raced. This one wouldn't make mistakes.

"You were smart," the old warrior finished. "Quick, as well. Few knights in your order can fight as well without their magics covering for their weaknesses."

"My master believes in a holistic approach," Azrael replied. "Let's see if you can guess the style in which I was trained, before I split your skull." Lord Roland's teachings screamed in his mind. *Disdain that which purely defends. Attack in a way that includes defense. Cover the line. Move laterally. Strike first, and you decide the terms of the fight.*

Azrael kicked off with his back leg, surged forward, and the magic sword sheared down at his opponent's left shoulder. The old man's sword snapped up from a low guard and across the center. The action was purely defensive. Azrael wrenched his hilt right as the blades rang against each other, feeling in the bind, sensing where his opponent's pressure went and going around it, then drove his point at the big man's chest. Azrael's skill was calculated relentlessness. Attack, and attack again. Mutate when he tried to fight back. Allow no counter to manifest.

But instead, the old man's hilt shot high, taking Azrael's point with it. The gray-haired warrior's left hand came off the grip and drilled into the side of the black knight's face. Azrael staggered. His world spun. He felt his blade slide off his enemy's as the old man let his point trail off to the side. Azrael's world reeled. He could barely understand what his senses were telling him. All he knew was that the sudden release of pressure meant his enemy was free to rotate his sword into an overhand chop at his exposed head. *Get your sword in the way!* his mind screamed.

Azrael's hands flashed high and the parry rang like a bell. The whip-crack cut was so hard it jarred his arms down to his shoulders. He pivoted backward, trying to recover his ground as the old man's sword slid off Oath of Aurum. A cut from just beneath followed, along the exact same line. It was only the black knight's knowledge and athleticism that saved him. He dashed back and away and stood beyond the range of the two-handed sword, breathing hard as he and the old man circled once more.

"You studied under Lord Roland of the House of Nails," the old man said casually, unperturbed. His clear eyes were peaceful, intent, and fearless. "And *he* is a student of the Varengard style, which the order has honed and perfected. The old secrets of the blade passed down from antiquity. Your system teaches relentlessness in the attack, defense by way of superior offense that accounts for your enemy's actions, and an assertive aggression that allows him no quarter. If parried, you will always drive in."

Azrael's breath came hard. It was the first time in a long while that he'd ever been so cleanly assessed. "Astute," was all he could say.

"I have been fighting upstarts for forty years," the old man said. "You are not the first."

"Who the hell *are* you?" Azrael demanded.

"Just an old soldier," the man smiled. "But Bjorn works fine."

"Never heard of you," Azrael spat back.

"You wouldn't have."

The old man's attack was so fast, so clean, that Azrael barely got out of the way. He voided by stepping swiftly sideways, head still spinning. Not enough time to recover. The smooth arc of the blade from left to right opened up

Bjorn's left shoulder to attack, and Azrael rammed his point in, keeping the blade high.

Bjorn pivoted backwards, outdistancing the thrust by centimeters. The two-handed sword's back edge *crashed* into Azrael's right side, hammering into the weaker armor under his armpit. The enchanted steel saved him, but his feet were lifted from the ground by the force of the blow, and he rolled away, coughing and clawing for breath. He forced himself up, jabbed the sword into the air before him to keep the inevitable follow-through at bay.

None came. Bjorn turned towards him, but slowly. His face was pale with pain, and sweat marked his brow. At this angle, Azrael could now see blood on the old man's right side, just above his hip. He'd begun this duel already wounded.

"You're bleeding, old man," Azrael breathed, straightening. "What is it, deep lacerations in your sides?" He spit blood into the dirt between them. "Turning must *really* hurt."

He launched forward again. Bjorn was still just as quick. The swords clashed. Edges bound and skipped. With every attempt to bind and thrust, Azrael was forced to maneuver as Bjorn's blade flicked away to cut at another opening. The bigger, longer sword outdistanced him, and the larger man's strength let him dance with it through the air, fast as a willow cane. Dirt churned up under their feet, and the sun pounded down on their heads as they strove. Azrael chased the openings, Bjorn blunted him at every turn. His defensive motions gave opportunities that over and over the black knight couldn't reach, whilst hammering two attacks for every one meted out by Oath of Aurum. They separated. Bjorn retreated, his footsteps giving ground, and his broad, quick cuts keeping Azrael from getting too close. Still the black knight gave chase.

They neared the arch. The sun cut contrasting lines of light and darkness between them, and they slowed so as not to slip on the blood-slick killing ground where the corpses of Azrael's warriors painted the rocky earth. Azrael advanced. He was bruised beneath his armor, could feel a numbness in the side of his face where Bjorn had landed his one solid punch. But as he walked, he let himself smirk for the first time in the fight.

"You're a student of the sword laws of the ancient blade princes of old Skellig," Azrael breathed. "You'll never come to a bind. You'll never stay in one place. You'll dance, and dance again, with downward hawks and upward rakes, coming at me from every angle at once."

Bjorn's smile was almost admiring. "Your gifts are *wasted* on the Eternal Order, boy."

Elias. Burning flowers, crisping walls. A soft melody that wouldn't leave his thoughts. Azrael's head hurt. He forced himself forward. The old man looked near exhaustion.

When Azrael paused in his advance, no assault came. His eyes closed in a painful blink as the world got fuzzy. *Wrong. This is wrong,* a part of his mind – long buried – snapped at him. The ghouls of fear and terror pushed themselves up after it. Azrael nearly staggered, remembered Esric's hand on his shoulder. The world seemed to right itself. He snarled as he advanced on Bjorn. "Shut up, and get out of my way, so I can find your wretched friends."

"Perhaps not, then," the old man said. He slid into a

high guard, arms over his head, sword poised to drop, cleaver-like, with tremendous power and incredible reach. The threat of the Hawk was that even seen and expected, it was still hard to evade, and blocking a sword like that, straight on, was nearly impossible.

Bjorn smirked, and took one more step back, through the arch. There was only one way forward, now, and it was guarded by a massive man who warded the path with an attack that couldn't be avoided, that outdistanced him, with a sword that would shatter his bones.

Azrael breathed hard. It didn't matter if the way forward was impossible. He had a duty to perform.

"Go on, boy," Bjorn said with quiet intensity. "We both know you'll never back down. Get this damn thing over with. My arms are tired."

Azrael's heart hammered in his chest. Conflicting thoughts flashed through his mind. For the first time in living memory, his killer's instinct hesitated.

The old man stared into his eyes. He *saw*. He *knew*.

It was *unforgiveable*.

Esric's hand was on his shoulder in his mind. *Do it*. Roland's warning screamed in his skull. Ghouls crawled from the depths of his nightmares. *Fear is weakness. Weakness is death*.

"Poor fool boy," Bjorn said sadly. "What have they *done* to you?"

Unforgiveable.

Azrael launched himself forward. *"Be silent!"* he screamed. "You know *nothing* of me!"

The sword dropped like a hammer. Azrael pivoted as hard as he could, not away from the cut, but *into* it. His sword dropped low, then snapped up over his head. The enchanted blade took the entire force of the blow on the base of its hilt, just above the crossguard. It drove Azrael down to his knees, but he kept his arms overhead, his hilt skyward, his point angled at the center of Bjorn's body.

Then he *lunged*. Oath of Aurum punched through leathers, clothes, skin, and flesh, halfway through the left side of the man's abdomen. The force of the thrust carried both men through the arch and straight to the edge of the precipice on the other side.

Bjorn dropped his sword over the edge. His eyes bulged with pain. His face paled. His blood leaked onto the ground. The roar of the falls thundered in Azrael's ears. Then the big warrior's hands closed like a vice around the black knight's throat. "No," the old man whispered. "Fight a man, and know him. You're still trying to live, and I never needed to, to win this. Everyone dies, young man. And I've lived a very long time."

Azrael couldn't breathe. His vision began to cloud. His hands still clutched his blade. He tried to turn it. Twist it. Anything. The world was taking on bizarre colors, and his mouth opened as he desperately clawed for breath.

"I've seen your type before," Bjorn hastily rasped. "Broken. Twisted. Remade. Perhaps one day you might have saved yourself… But I can't let you stop my friends. I'm truly sorry, boy, but if you won't see reason, then we die together."

They teetered towards the edge. Azrael's back was to the falls. The sound of water hammered in his ears. Panic flashed through his head. A last chance. He jerked the sword as hard as he could, and let his weight fall back. Surprise and pain painted Bjorn's face as the big man fell forward atop him. The grip of his hands loosened. Azrael pulled his knees in and kicked as hard as he could. The old warrior gave a terrible scream of pain as the blade jerked free of his body and his momentum carried him over the edge. Azrael rolled onto his side in time to see the big man's silhouette vanish into the frothing spray far below.

Alone, Azrael lay gasping on the ground, desperately dragging in fresh breaths. The sounds of water and woods filled his senses, and his heart pounded a rhythm of fear and pain through his still rising and falling chest.

After what seemed too long, he forced himself to his feet, alone, with the red-stained sword in his hand. Confusing thoughts burned through his mind. The blood of the kill on his hands that brought him no pleasure.

He swayed. Nearly fell again. Then forced himself to steady. Beyond him, stairs wound up into the forested hills. This, then, was where they had run. He had no backup. He was now outnumbered, and they had a head start.

Roland loomed large and terrifying in his mind. The hand of Esric was like a force against his back pushing him forward. Absently, he wiped clean the sword with a cloth in a belt-pouch, and feverishly began the long ascent up the winding stairs into darkness. His worth was predicated on one thing only: whether he succeeded or failed.

He could not fail.

CHAPTER FIFTEEN
LORD OF THE IRON MOUNTAIN

Malfenshir's armor made hardly a sound, enchanted as it was for silence. The technician in front of him was one of the bizarre caste of workers that maintained the immense, aeonian power source at the beating heart of the mountain of death. The tech was hairless, with gaunt limbs and hands like spiders. The elders said they were descended from the men that built the hulk and its nine brothers, that their needs had long ago grown alien to anyone that did not reside so close to the heart of their lovingly tended, utterly dependent god. This particular tech had long ago replaced his eyes with steel orbs.

"How *soon*," Malfenshir repeated, "can the Scream be sounded?"

The tech cocked his head to the side, listening to an imperceptible sound. "A day at least, dread lord. Whether it is a man with needles in his hands or the god-sphere with its sacred call, a scream cannot be done without breathing in first."

The technician's neck abruptly twitched. "It will be winter soon. The rose will bloom in twenty-three hours, twelve minutes, and forty-two seconds."

"Notify me the moment the Scream is ready," Malfenshir replied. He didn't comment on the rest of it. Nobody understood what the technicians said most of the time anyway.

The *Iron Hulk* – they said – had been in operation for a thousand years. Staring at its exterior walls, covered as they were in rust, dirt, and the forest of guns later added, perhaps a person might have guessed it, but nowhere was it more *truly* clear than in the one-hundred story, cavernous core of the fortress's vast metadrive chamber. Standing upon a mystically suspended catwalk hundreds of feet above the churning orb of a mystic furnace hundreds of feet across, Malfenshir took a deep, reverent breath and bathed in the heat of its power.

A day.

He had one day to array everything before the Scream would tear this wretched continent apart, and he could watch as every man, woman, and child upon the ground whose bones were left unliquified, whose eyes were left unmelted, fell into the infinite black below. Chaos was Malfenshir's only god, destruction his dearest lady love, and this would be his greatest offering yet. That they were simpering weak things that died was all the better. Life had taught Malfenshir early that those who could not hold their ground against strength and force didn't deserve its protection. No amount of mewling philosophy could disprove that experience.

And the "civilized" world, just now, was *infested* with an overabundance of weakening compassion. A purging was long overdue.

He took his time circumnavigating the circular catwalks, observing the small swarm of technicians and workers about the beating heart of the monster he commanded in Azrael's absence.

In Azrael's absence.

When Malfenshir had been commanded by Lord Ogier to second the black knight in this illustrious mission, his master had left him with a specific instruction:

"Lord Roland's protege must be watched, rigorously. Many are blinded by his seeming perfection and graceful efficacy, but the elders are worried. Serve. Obey. But Roland's angel of death is not to be trusted."

Amidst the senior circles just beneath the elders, Roland was foremost in glory, strength, and cunning. They called him the dread lord of ashes, and of his three apprentices, Azrael was most respected, feared, and protected, and of the three he was likewise the one about which everyone else knew the least. Balance within the order was a delicate thing, carefully placed pieces upon a chessboard resting not upon solid bases, but upon the needlepoint pedestals of power: if the board moved even a little, then the pieces upon it began to shift.

Malfenshir placed his hands upon the rail, watching as the immense coils were maneuvered beneath the glowing power source below. Destroying Port Providence would do more than shift the board; it would *smash* it. He straightened. The process had been started. Now he simply needed to give the orders.

"Where have you been?" Sir Kaelith growled as Malfenshir arrived on the command deck. "We've got a big problem."

Malfenshir paused. All about them, the sweeping, multi-tiered decks with their flickering control stations were manned by techs and crews. "You mean other than the perpetual failure of our leader to secure our objective?" he sneered. "Please, do tell."

"The portal shield still holds," Sir Kaelith explained. The big woman's expression was intent. Worried. "No ship within its sphere can open a swift escape, but there's nothing preventing vessels outside that range from coming here, and it seems someone managed to send a signal from a short distance away from near Land's Edge as we were arriving to take the city."

Malfenshir frowned. "So?"

"My lord," Sir Kaelith continued, "the reason we know this is because we intercepted the *reply*. It came from the Third Battle Fleet of the Violet Imperium. They are coming here. By my estimate, we have days, perhaps less."

When the order had invaded Port Providence, they had done so knowing that the kingdom's only ally worth considering was the Violet Imperium – the aging, conservative empire to the skyward north. They had also known that the Imperium was far away, and that communication via spell would be made impossible by the same portal shield that kept ships from making the jump to safe harbors. They had planned on being able to secure their objective and vanish before the Imperium even became a factor.

But the plan hadn't been foolproof. Someone, it seemed, had flown far enough from the isle to send a message. And that meant the Imperium was coming to honor their defense obligations.

Malfenshir felt his eyebrows raise in an involuntary display of emotion. An imperial battle group, here. He could see their vast dreadnoughts and squadrons of gunboats in his mind's eye. Their boarding craft with grapple guns, their dreaded spinal-mounted beam weapons called *cloud-crackers*. The *Iron Hulk* was able to withstand tremendous punishment. It was older than some nation states, more powerful than the Leviathan-class ships of the line that would doubtless be the heart of their new foe's array. But there would be many, many warships coming, with legions, and escorts in vast numbers.

Sir Kaelith didn't seem to expect Malfenshir's smile when it came. "Good," the red knight said. He turned and walked to the edge of the observation deck, sweeping his eyes across the people feverishly manning the workstations. Bee-like. A hive of furious workers unknowingly facing annihilation.

"My lord," Sir Kaelith continued. "They will overwhelm us."

Malfenshir turned and seized the other knight by the shoulder, a grin splitting his face so hard it hurt. "Not," he said, "if we destroy this entire landmass first."

Sir Kaelith stared at him. The hum of activity whorled around them. "You're preparing the Scream," she finally said.

"If we face the Third Battle Group," Malfenshir explained, "we'll lose. They outnumber us; their collected firepower can break us, even if it's at great cost." His hand on the other knight's armored shoulder tightened. "If we fight them, our order *loses*, the one thing it categorically *must* not do. But if we destroy this entire island, the message is sent: threaten us, and we will burn you down, savage what you cherish, and salt what remains. Total oblivion, just as we originally promised."

"And the Axiom?" Sir Kaelith asked. Her tone was casual, assessing the risks and the rewards. "It would be a high price to lose it in the process."

"If Lord Azrael fails to return with it," Malfenshir said, "it won't matter. He erred in not taking either of us with him. Sir Fenris is dead, and Sir Cairn lies in the care of Esric after that damned Land's Edge sorcerer melted his face off. Sir Vhaith was thrown from that ship's airlock, and Sir Nemaris is overseeing the plunder ships the accounters are preparing to return to the House of Nails. This has become a mop-up operation. Our Investment is running its course. We have overextended ourselves here and paid for it. But nobody will remember that if we leave a ruined field of shattered rocks in our wake. They will call us *Earth-slayers*. The Violet Imperium itself will quiver before us."

Kaelith regarded him with an even stare. "Bold," she said. "But we can't do that from the coast."

"Which is why we're going inland," Malfenshir said. "The last of the plunder and slaves should be loaded in an hour, yes?"

"So I have been told," Kaelith nodded with a smirk. Good, Malfenshir acknowledged. She was compliant, then.

"Give the order to accelerate the process, with a special emphasis on art and manuscripts from the library," Malfenshir said. "Then I want everyone and everything back aboard, with the frigates providing escort." He passed a small sheaf of paper to the other knight. "Then set a course for these coordinates. The center of the landmass. I've done the math. It should take no longer than a day to reach."

He turned on his heel. There was one more thing he needed to do before matters were firmly in hand.

•••

A short time later, Malfenshir knelt on the large, raised dais, breathing out as the powerful spell tore across vast distances to where the council of elders awaited in the heart of the House of Nails. He breathed, maintaining the spell, inviting the mind-searing, skin-crawling presences that reached out from the darkness at the far end to touch and caress his soul. This was highly irregular. Normally, a knight-lord in the field was supposed to report to their master directly, passing knowledge up the chain of command without bypassing those whose blood and treasure entitled them to know it first.

But this was a matter of special circumstance. Lord Ogier didn't have the authority to override the commands of Lord Roland, and without that censure, Malfenshir might face agony and torment upon his return to their sanctuary. But the elders could command anything. Their words were iron law, and all those beneath obeyed or died screaming.

The spell flared and rose, filling the room with incandescent light. Then the darkness descended and noise fled. There wasn't time to wonder what might happen next: Malfenshir *felt* the slow rise of nine, *terrible* minds in a circle about him. Projected across the incalculable distance by magic and joined by sorcery to his thoughts, they manifested as pillars of pure night, rising forever into the high vaulted ceiling of the communication chamber.

"Masters in shadow," Malfenshir addressed them. "Forgive my intrusion, but I have news most dire to report."

Nine voices responded at once. Their words carried a crushing weight that momentarily robbed Malfenshir of all breath.

"Proceed."

Malfenshir raised his head, gasped for breath in the darkness. When he found it, explanations poured out of him, swift and fearful.

"Lord Azrael has left us listless," he said. "Every command he has given has been in error from the first day of our invasion, and now his quest to claim the Axiom Diamond sits upon the cusp of failure. The Violet Imperium's third battle fleet is coming, and will be upon us in a matter of a few short days. I need your permission to sound the Silent Scream."

The nine voices deliberated among themselves. Malfenshir had to fight to prevent himself from pressing his face to the floor until he crushed the noises out of his skull. He had heard another knight say once that the elders had taken their pursuit of perfection, mastery of the order's intuitive magic by which their powers were manifest, to such an extent that they were more energy than man, their bodies little more than vessels for the tremendous power that burned within them. But that power had come at a cost: as their needs grew further and further from mortals, so too had their desires, their thoughts grown more alien. No one could know what they might do when presented with news to their displeasure.

Nor could one any longer know what might displease them.

"He seeks permission to destroy the continent of Port Providence," said one voice.

"What is land?" asked another dreamily. "A slab of stone and wood, floating in air above the abyss. What do we care?"

Malfenshir twitched as the words whirled around him

in the dark. Their callous whimsy whispered knife-like across his skin, the sensation like cuts to the meat of his mind.

"The line must be walked carefully," said yet another voice. "The grand design is not yet a third complete."

"What of the Axiom?" the voices asked all at once. "Roland was charged with acquiring it, and he gave that task to Lord Azrael."

Malfenshir winced. His head swam and he felt a pain at the base of his neck. Sustained contact with the elders was doing more damage by the moment.

"I do not know," Malfenshir admitted. "But Lord Azrael pursued it without thought or foresight. He is the one in charge of this invasion, yes, but he has behaved senselessly ever since he slew Prince Collum and laid claim to his sword. Some gold-chased blade called *Oath of Aurum*."

"The sword!" a voice cried, and it echoed from voice to voice, far and near. "The sword!"

"The sword!"

"If Lord Azrael returns with the blade," they said as one, "you must return both it and him to us, with the Axiom. When the sword is melted to slag, and Azrael's mind is open to our searching, you shall be rewarded. Destroy Port Providence. Leave it as nothing but a field of dust. Complete the Investment. Kindle its remaining lives as a pyre flame to our glory. Return with the plunder."

The connection was severed. Malfenshir sat breathing hard upon the dais. The base of his nose was wet, and when he brushed his fingers against his upper lip, they came away red. Slowly, the laughter slipped from him, echoing high-pitched in the chamber. "Survived," he breathed around his giggles. "I have stood toe to toe with the elders, and I have *survived*."

The laughter boiled out, upwards towards the ceiling, shaking his large frame with convulsive cackles. Then he set forth to put his plans into motion.

Absolute oblivion. Just as promised.

CHAPTER SIXTEEN
A Glimmer in the Dark

Clutch was ready to kill someone. Strike that, she'd been ready to kill someone for *days*. Now her anger was well past the boiling point. She pushed herself slowly on her back across the access tunnel beneath the vast exhaust vents of *Elysium*'s rear engines, a light source in one hand and a balled-up fist full of hate in the other.

"I swear to all the gods of the thousandfold choirs," she cussed. "Vant, you *better* be right about this or I'm going to shave your head while you sleep and burn the hair to curse your family for six generations."

"Good luck with that," Vant's reply echoed up through the hatch. "I hate kids. Just find the smear. If I'm right, it's only going to be about half a foot across."

Clutch shuffled forward, the glow-stone in her hand illuminating the inner cylinder of the vent. There, just ahead, a burn mark across the ensorcelled metal. "Yeah," she called back. "It's right here!"

"What *color* is it?" Vant's voice came back.

"Hell," Clutch grunted, squinting in the dim light. "Vant, I can only see so much in this light."

"Is it brown?" Vant pressed. "That's all I need to know.

If it's not brown, then I'm right and we'll be back in the air in a few hours."

Clutch squinted in the dark. For a few terrified seconds she thought she was staring at exactly the shade Vant described, but as she pulled the light source closer and blinked several times... No. "Green," she said with a sigh of relief. "It's green."

"Alright get back down here," Vant replied. "All I need to do is jumpstart the metadrive and flood the chamber. And, y'know, it's best you're not *in* there when I do."

"You're a regular charmer, Vant," Clutch grunted as she pushed herself back down the vent wall and slipped through the access hatch. Vant and Vlana were waiting for her, the former dressed from head to foot in stained coveralls, the latter holding an immense toolbag over her shoulders.

"So, you want to explain that one to me?" Clutch added. "I'm not a *complete* novice, but since when does the color on a blast-point matter?"

"Basically," Vant said, "it means that we didn't actually take a direct hit from the hulk's big guns, like I was afraid of. It was a close graze, and the detonation was powerful enough to scramble the drive for a bit, which, combined with that bit of wing damage, made everything go to hell until we could get down and reset things."

Vlana's white-knuckled fingers eased their grip on the strap for the first time since the three of them had been left in the ship to make repairs. They had sat by the viewports, watching as the vulture-like lander had seemed to contemplate them, only to hurtle over the treeline in pursuit of its quarry.

Their crewmates. Their friends.

If Clutch thought about it for more than a few seconds,

she got nauseous. No. She looked away from it. Like the
teachers in the navigator's loft said to her as a little girl:
Find your star, kid. Find your star and focus.

"What's next, mop-top?" she asked Vant.

"You two get up to the bridge," he said, running a
hand through the dark tangles of his hair. "I restart the
metadrive, do a system flush, and see if that wing we
patched will get us in the air."

"Come on, bristle-cut," Clutch said, grabbing Vlana by
the arm. "Time to save the day."

The dirt had been cleared from the viewport on the
bridge, and as they strode into the empty room Clutch felt
the reverberations of their footfalls as painful reminders
of her sweet girl's present state. *Elysium* was silent. She
wasn't *supposed* to be silent. She was a beautiful bird, as
alive and thrumming as any human heart. When Clutch
held the wheel and guided her across the heavens, she
saw herself as a caretaker, not a master. Now the pulse
was dead, the vessel still. It was like walking through a
corpse, and it drove her crazy. She loved *Elysium* more
than any kin. More than any man or woman she'd been
with. More – perhaps – than life.

"Alright," Vlana murmured, stepping around the
place where Bjorn had kicked that armored knight out
the airlock days ago, "full check. Top to bottom. Hit the
nav-systems and the main console. I need to go one up
and check the portal dais."

"Why?" Clutch asked over her shoulder. "It's probably
the safest thing on this ship. Nothing's touched it but
Aimee, not since the workers finished doing the once
over before we left Havensreach."

"You focus on your part and let me do mine, alright?"

Vlana shooed her away, vanishing out the lower door
and emerging a few moments later on the upper portal
deck. Clutch knelt, throwing herself into the meticulous
work of console-checking and obsessive nitpicking. She
was fastidious in her pre-flight checks, and took every
opportunity she had to clean her station in the few
breathers this trip had given her. By her third go-over,
the checks were losing any real value.

Then Vlana started cursing like a proper skyfarer from
the upper deck. The sound was dissonant, coming from
the slip of a cheerful quartermaster. "Oh Sons of the
fucking Abyss!" she snarled.

"You gonna share what just happened up there?"
Clutch asked, "or are you planning to make it through
the whole profanity alphabet?"

Vlana hauled herself to the edge. "Aimee didn't make
a mistake."

Clutch shook her head, still muddied by time spent
checking a hundred knobs and dials. "Dammit, bristle-
cut, gimme that again," she said, holding up a hand, "but
with *context.*"

Vlana shook her head in irritation. "Aimee's error!
The thing that ended with us here in Port Providence
instead of Ishtier, it wasn't a mistake!"

Clutch just stared at the younger woman incredulously.
"…You're saying the new girl *meant* to bring us here?"

Vlana stared back, blank-eyed for a moment, then
understanding dawned. "No, no! Not what I meant:
I mean she had nothing to do with it, except that she
probably saved all our asses. Someone messed with the
portal dais before we left. It's just slightly off, and the
enchantments underneath were *altered.*"

Clutch's eyes slowly widened. Sabotage. Someone

had intentionally sent them here, into this hellhole of a warzone.

If she ever found them, she'd nail their hand to the outer hull with a boot knife and fly through a sand gale until only bones were left.

Vlana seemed to read her mind and shook her head. "No, Clutch, you don't understand. I'm not a mage, but I understand how these things work. It's because of Aimee's quick spellwork that we're alive at all." She exited the door, and seconds later she was dragging Clutch up to the upper deck where the beautiful dais sat, looking much the same to Clutch as it always had, save for the fact that Vlana had moved it to examine the delicate, crystalline mystic amplifiers in the deck beneath.

"Look," Vlana knelt, and pointed out a series of spots. Now that Clutch looked, she could see that something was wrong. One of the crystals had been split in half, and another had been deftly moved to another part of the array. A chill went through her. She didn't know *exactly* how these things worked, but she knew enough about the principles of amplification to recognize what one of those nodes in the wrong spot would do.

"Holy hells," the pilot breathed.

"I don't know *how* Aimee did it," Vlana said, "but her quick bit of adjustment actually stopped this sabotage from doing what it was supposed to do: blast the whole ship into cloud-dust."

"So the question is," Clutch said to the twins a few minutes later, "can we *fix* it?"

Vant knelt beside the portal dais, staring at the crystal amplifiers beneath with a practiced eye. After a few moments, he looked up at his sister and affirmed what she'd said. "She's right. These were moved very deliberately. The good news is whoever did it clearly didn't factor our survival into their plans. If they had, maybe they'd have done more damage to ensure we couldn't make it right."

Vlana took a deep breath. "I'm not an expert at these things. I've only toyed with them under supervision, and I've never rearranged the amplifiers before... But if it's a choice between that and our escape attempt scattering pieces of us across several different dimensions? Yeah, I kinda have to take the risk."

Vant nodded, though Clutch watched the engineer's face pale slightly. The siblings had been on *Elysium's* crew for several years longer than she had. More than anyone else, this vessel was their full-time home, and for all the bickering, their bond was deeper than any other on board.

"Well," Vant said, "I'll get the tools, then. The drive's off, so there's no need to worry about feedback, just–"

"Just the possibility that the whole ship blows up if I do it wrong, when you turn it back on," Vlana said.

"Right," Clutch muttered. "So just, you know, do it right."

A few moments later, Vant was handing Vlana a small batch of tools that Clutch had only seen a handful of times before, used for the delicate work of amplifier modification. Half of them were crystalline instruments, more delicate than aristocratic tableware. "Vant, gimme a hand," Vlana said as she crouched on the deck. Her brother obediently obeyed. For the next few seconds, Clutch leaned against the upper deck rail, watching as the slender young woman slowly went about a process that more closely resembled ritual incantation than delicate handiwork. The two siblings fell into a hushed rhythm in their collaboration, and for a little while the pilot was more mesmerized than she was fearful, reminded of the fact that while she'd spent well over two-thirds of her twenty-five years on and off a ship, *true* skyfarers – those born, reared, and entirely educated on ships – were a different sort altogether.

Skyfarers remember, the phrase went. It could be the most heartfelt promise or the most ominous threat.

The two were younger than she by several years, maybe a little older than Harkon's new apprentice, Aimee de Laurent. In moments like this, she realized that Vant and Vlana had an understanding of life in the infinite sky that would always be just beyond the grasp of someone like her.

Vlana abruptly took a deep breath, and Clutch found herself holding hers. She wasn't a religious woman, but every superstition from her time in the navigator's loft came rushing back to her mind as she watched the younger woman slowly extract the single crystal that had been moved. She held it between tweezers before her thin, intent eyes, then looked up at Clutch and grinned. "Right, no going back now."

Clutch's pulse raced, and her lips moved, soundlessly forming the pilot's mantra from when she was a kid.

But if the winds should cease and the starlight flee
Let me die in the heavens, soaring and free.

The amplifier clicked back into place in its original, pre-sabotage position. Clutch still held her breath as Vlana slowly got to her feet, her brother sliding the dais back into place. "Well," the quartermaster said with her best attempt at cheerfulness, "now I guess we find out if we're all going to die or not."

Vant stood. The three of them exchanged nervous, fearful glances. For all that, there was no hesitation in what happened next. "Do it," Clutch said. "So we know if we're on the move again, or blasted to hell and back."

The engineer's footsteps receded down the length of the silent ship, and Clutch walked to the pilot's wheel, standing there for a few moments as the golden rays of the midday sun illuminated the dust motes between viewport and pilot station. Off to the side, Vlana stood before her navigational panel. They exchanged a look, a nod, then it was time, and Clutch picked up the mouthpiece to the comm tube. "Do it, Vant," she said, her voice steadier than she felt.

Silence. Then a series of clicks. Then a *wave* of energy rippled beneath their feet. The pilot waited for oblivion.

Instead, the thrum of the roaring, active metadrive filled the bridge. Panels came alive. Instruments buzzed to full capacity. The wheel beneath her fingers shifted. Every single one of her dials glowed as the glimmer of the active bridge whirled around her in a cascade of golden jewels. The deck moved beneath them as the ship lifted to float several feet above the ground that had been its jailer. Mobile. Free. Restored.

Vlana's cheer rang bell-like through the air as the quartermaster leaped up, fist pumping the air with wild and loud laughter.

Clutch sank back, relaxing against the wheel. For just a few seconds, she let the tears held in reserve wet her eyes, her shoulders drooping and her weight falling against the wheel. She didn't cheer. Instead, her hand just patted the paneling of her pilot station, whispering, "Welcome back, old girl. Never scare me like that again."

She was about to grab the tube, call back down with congratulations before taking them up into the air, when a loud *bang* sounded from the aftward hold. So loud she jumped.

"Stay here," she grunted to the shorter woman, grabbed the boarding hatchet from beside her station, and started down the long hallway to the rear of the ship.

"Like hell," she heard Vlana say behind her. There wasn't time to argue. She careened into the rear hold in time to hear a second *bang*. It came from the side airlock, not the main door, the one that only the crew knew about. Creeping forward, Clutch reached for the handle and turned it.

Outside, swaying on his feet, ashen-pale, and clutching a horrible wound in his lower abdomen, was Bjorn.

"Infirmary," he groaned, and fell forwards through the door.

CHAPTER SEVENTEEN
Who Dares the Vault

One step before the other. The trees blurred by him. Still, Azrael ran up the long, winding stairs that cut through the forested peaks. He was well beyond the range of the null stones, but held his power close, not wanting to exhaust himself before there was need to use it. Speed would be invaluable when he reached the summit. Armor didn't slow him, bruises didn't slow him. The jogging ascent was a low burn of energy maintained by steady, even breaths and a singular, tunnel-like focus.

He had endured worse than this.

One step after another, Roland's voice chased him up the long winding stairs cut into the rock. In his mind's eye, his master, teacher, and surrogate father was as immense as when he first remembered him, even though they now stood at even height. Still, Roland was a titan swathed in steel, his cold gray longsword a darting wisp of silvery light when he trained. His pale eyes were frigid stars in the depths of his helm, and the dark smirk urged on Azrael's desperate need for approval, even as Lord Roland's rebukes and punishments were the stuff of nightmares.

Fear was weakness. Weakness was death.

A step up the path. Another. Another. The trees he passed now wore coats of mist, fed by the fog that clung to the peaks even in the driest summers.

The sword was warm, again, in Azrael's hands. He didn't dare sheath it, not knowing if at any second the legendary Harkon Bright would leap from the shadows and grasp his arm, turning his blood to boiling oil. Bjorn's horrible death-scream filled his mind, drove his rage, gave him more energy for his ascent.

Fear was weakness. Weakness was death.

"Kneel, nameless." Roland's voice echoed in his mind. Age fifteen, wrapped in robes of black samite, surrounded by a host of armored men, Azrael had bowed before his master. *"Death to the weak. Mercy to none. You are harder than iron, more flexible than steel. Quicker than the fury of the storm,"* Roland had pronounced. He had raised his enchanted, gray sword to dub his apprentice, the youngest made knight in a generation. Roland had paused: the naming – it meant everything. *"You shall be my angel of death,"* Roland had said to the boy with no name. *"You shall be my Azrael."*

The blade had struck his shoulder.

"Elias!"

Azrael almost stopped. This time it had sounded like a physical cry, echoing from somewhere far away, in the anguished voice of a woman. He staggered forward and cast panicked eyes about in the woods. Nothing. No voices whispered from the shadowy evergreens to torment him, no mocking cries without source, nor screams without faces to make them. At a ledge, he stopped, turned in a circle, heart pounding, mind reeling.

He held his sword out before him, as if doing so would keep the terror at bay.

Collum. At once, the prince's face seemed to swim before his own, as it had in his nightmares at Gray Falcon. The eyes of the dead prince simply stared back at him, knowing something at which Azrael's mind couldn't seem to grasp. A fog clouded his thoughts. Then Esric's hand was on his back, in memory. Purpose flooded back, even as the healer's predatory gaze filled the black knight's mind. Both hands gripped the sword, which had lost its heat.

"You're *dead,*" he spat at the vision before him. "Have the courtesy to *stay* that way." Oath of Aurum slashed out in front of him. The illusion of the prince was torn in half, and faded away.

Breathing hard, alone, Azrael stood on the ledge, surrounded by a panoramic view of the landscape in all its beauty. It was this wretched place. Ever since he had come here, dreams had dogged him; voices he couldn't place had scratched at his every waking thought, making him doubtful, afraid, unsure.

"Poor fool boy," Bjorn said sadly in his memory. *"What have they done to you?"*

Elias.

Azrael turned in a circle, and his own voice tore out in a furious cry at the emptiness. "Be silent!"

Silence. Stillness. Nothing surrounded the black knight but the ambient whispers of the forest and his own, wrathful breathing. Good. He turned, and resumed his ascent. A large, spire-like rock loomed just ahead. The trail was fresh. He was almost there.

It was almost *over*.

•••

It wasn't a spire, it was a statue, placed atop a natural outcropping centuries ago. The wind had weathered its outward face, once carved into a cloak draped over armored shoulders, but the effigy was clearly of a man swathed in plate. His helmed head somber and downcast, and his hands clutched a sword that rested point down in the earth.

As Azrael drew near, something about the detailing on the ancient carvings pulled his attention and tugged at his sense of familiarity in a way that chilled his heart: the armor was of the same make and style as the old effigies of long dead knights of the Eternal Order displayed in Roland's citadel, but the styling was different. About the warrior's feet curled the faded carvings of stone roses rising from a simple cup. Something about the ancient visage disquieted him, as though the unseeing stone eyes watched him with shame. After a moment, Azrael had to look away.

The trail. They had come this way. He walked in a circle about the ledge upon which the effigy was planted. There, obvious boot prints. Three, still. All were living. None, it seemed, were wounded. He would have to come upon them quickly and without hesitation, or the two mages might outfox him. He took a moment to breathe, marshaling his strength and taking stock of which way they'd gone. It took only a few seconds. Beyond the spire, the mouth of a cave split the face of the rock. From anywhere but this ledge, or perhaps in the air just above, it would have been impossible to see. Certainly, there was no putting a ship down here.

He faced the cave: lightless, dank. To be afraid was absurd. There was no way but forward, and failure wasn't an option. He flexed his fingers about the hilt of his sword, and pushed himself towards the maw in the earth. The gaze of the statue chased him. He did not look back.

Darkness swallowed him. He made his way as far as he could, until the ground sloped down, and the natural light from without faded. Here, at last, he could no longer justify going without a light source. He summoned a globe of silver light into his left hand, and crept forward through the dark, keeping pace with the prints upon the ground as best as he was able.

After an indeterminate time, the walls of the cave widened, and he found himself faced by a small, open cavern. Light danced from jewels set into sconces held in the outstretched hands of stone statues. One of these was a knight of the same make as the sentinel without; the other wore stone robes similar to the traditional vestments of the gray sages as they dressed in the old days, before the Eternal Order killed or drove them into hiding.

Dark burns marked the stone floor, such as might have been made by a beam of scorching light. Azrael traced the trajectory back to the remnants of a great, cyclopean eye ensconced in the walls high above. Its center was cracked. So whatever trap lay here, they had either sprung or defeated it. It was also possible that they'd been vaporized. And wouldn't that make his job easier?

The path continued between the two statues, and a few seconds' examination showed that there were disturbances in the dust passing through them. So at least some had survived. Harnessing his power, the black knight followed.

•••

He passed two more bizarre formations. A stream took over the path, and he had to do his best to keep his feet from the water while tracing it further down into the ground. He lost track of time, passed a monolith of amethyst split down its center and a smoke without source. The deeper he went, the more his mind began to play tricks on him.

The face of the queen mother loomed before his eyes as his boots crunched over graveled stream-bank. *"... The mask of a good man's face worn by a monster."*

He had no answer but the will to keep walking.

Words echoed inside his mind, amplified by the strangeness of this place. After a time, he canceled his light spell, his way lit by the shimmer of phosphorescent lichen that clung to the dank walls. It reflected off the surface of his black armor, fired the edge of his sword in white. Strange shadows played off the ground at his feet, cast by the warm waters and obscuring the trail. Silence became impossible when the tunnel narrowed, eliminating the bank. His armored feet sloshed through the shallows.

Abruptly, a side tunnel diverged, carved steps rising from the stream and into a broader chamber from which a soft, natural white light flooded. He paused, inspected the lowest steps for any sign of tracks. Here, boots had disturbed gravel and sand. There, dust had been knocked aside by the passage of a long coat or a robe. He called his spells to mind, flexed his fingers in preparation for conflict. He would have to be faster, stronger, and more ruthless by far than any of the three. He could not let them touch him. Stepping carefully so as not to project sound, he ascended the stairs and entered a vast, illuminated cavern.

Even tensed, worn, and pained as he was, Azrael froze, stricken at once by the beauty spread out before him. Nowhere else in his travels had he seen anything half as lovely: beyond a shoreline of pearlescent sand, a placid, underground lake shone like a mirror. A single stone pathway connected the white beach to a circular stone dais at the lagoon's center, and from its middle rose a pedestal of black marble. And upon its apex, at last before him, was a pale white jewel that shone with an inner light.

He took a full step into the cavern, both hands upon the sword. A shadow darted to his left, and he turned reflexively. His left hand released the hilt to loose a bolt of flame across the span.

The binding spell hit him so hard it made him dizzy. Perfectly delivered, he only registered that the words had been spoken half a heartbeat after bands of mystic force slammed into him, coiled about his body, and held his arms to his sides, hard and fast. His balance gave out, and he slammed sideways into the hard ground. Stars blasted across his vision as his head struck stone. For the next few seconds he could neither think, nor properly process, limited only to staring hatefully as his captors stepped forth from the shadows.

Footsteps crunched over the ground, and the gray sage named Silas reached down to pluck the beautiful sword from where Azrael had dropped it. The old man looked haggard. He'd lost weight in the few days since the black knight had first seen him at Gray Falcon. His hair and beard were matted, his torn clothes and ragged hands blotched with dirt and grime. Nobody, not the queen mother, not Prince Coulton, nor Prince Collum as he died, had ever stared at Azrael with half as much hate.

"This sword," Silas said, holding Oath of Aurum before him, "doesn't belong to you."

The legendary sorcerer Harkon Bright came next. His eyes were lined and tired, his face dark-skinned, his hair and beard like moonlight. His gaze still held the slightest tinge of apprehension, of knowing what the knight on the floor before him was capable of. His wound had to have been healed… But the positioning of his hands was wrong. He hadn't cast the spell currently holding Azrael in place. The black knight looked to the sage's right, and he saw her.

She stalked towards him, her movements graceful and deliberate. The sorceress from Land's Edge. Slender. Pale and gold-haired. Quick. Determined. Beautiful. She faced him, spear-straight and poised. An apprentice's badge hung on a silver chain about her neck, and her hands were frozen in the perfect position of the spell that had ensnared him. An apprentice. He'd been beaten by *an apprentice*.

For the first time, the black knight had nothing to say.

Aimee smiled, and addressed him in a quiet, angry alto.

"Got you, bastard."

CHAPTER EIGHTEEN
WHAT IS TO GIVE LIGHT

White-knuckled, breathing hard, Aimee stood in the shimmering light of the cavern, her hands in the terminating position of the binding spell. Years of academy training, hours spent studying texts in the libraries, missing soirees and social events, repeating patterns, paid off here and now. Her friend Aryanna had once asked her what individual spell available to novice portalmages could possibly be worth the sacrifice of so much?

"None," Aimee had answered. *"I am training myself to learn quickly."*

They had run, fought, chased, planned, reacted, battled in the heavens and on solid ground, and now – here in the Axiom's vault – they had *won*. The conqueror of Port Providence was their prisoner.

She twisted her fingers, and the threads of binding spell wrenched Azrael from the ground to sit with his back against the stone wall of the cavern.

Aimee breathed out, lowered her hands, and completed the incantation to make the bindings permanent. He wasn't going anywhere. Harkon stepped back and regarded their prisoner with a look that belied just how much pain the warrior had caused them, how much untold horror and bloodshed lay at the feet of this one battered young man.

Young. That was the first thing that struck her as she stepped forward, relaxing her nerves enough to take stock of her imprisoned enemy. It seemed almost impossible that everything they had faced could be traced to the commands and actions of a man who could not have been more than a year or two older than she was. His helmet was gone, so she took the measure of his bruised face: angular, framed by thick dark hair. His skin was pale, his jaw strong, and his mouth was a hard, tight line. The eyes, however, arrested her: green, bright, and burning with a barely caged *something* behind a wall of iron discipline.

If she didn't hate him so much, she'd have thought he was very handsome.

Silence followed, as the knight neither answered her initial words, nor offered threat of his own. Just when Aimee was about to speak, Silas beat her to it. Still clutching his dead prince's sword, the old sage took a shaking step forward.

"I should kill you, for all you've done," Silas hissed.

Azrael's face turned to fix his burning green gaze on the old man. Bored. Slow. "Free me," he said, "and you're welcome to try."

The sage took an involuntary step back.

"Where is the old warrior?" Harkon demanded, and Aimee caught the distinct undertone of pain in her teacher's voice. "Where is Bjorn?"

Azrael's head slowly turned to regard him. Again, his tone was bored. Contemptuous. "Somewhere downriver,

I imagine. I didn't stop to see where he *landed*."

Aimee's blood thundered through her ears, and she stepped towards the bound black knight. His eyes fixed on her. "Go ahead, apprentice. See what I can do even bound as I am. You saw what I did to your teacher in Land's Edge." He smirked. "Nice healing work, by the way. I assume it was yours?"

"Shut *up!*" Silas had found his courage. His hands gripped the beautiful longsword that had once belonged to his prince and hewed at Azrael's head as hard as he could. The blade stopped an inch from the bound knight's face. Harkon's outstretched hand held the warding spell that had blocked the blow. "Silas," Aimee's teacher said quietly. "Put the sword away."

Azrael was still staring at the old man that had tried to kill him. His expression was harsh, defiant. A caged animal ready to die ripping its captors to shreds. The blade had stopped less than an inch from his face, and he hadn't so much as flinched.

"Harkon," Silas said. He stepped back, reluctant. "This man is *single-handedly* responsible for the butchering of my kingdom, the destruction of untold homes and lives without number, among them my king, my brethren, and our prophesied prince."

"And he is a valuable prisoner," Harkon answered in a voice full of quiet steel. "He is Lord Roland's apprentice, Silas. Think of the things he knows."

"You're awfully *quiet*," Azrael murmured, addressing Aimee directly. "What, no threats? No promises of punishment?"

Aimee folded her arms across her chest and met his gaze. She wouldn't look away. "I don't talk to genocidal monsters."

"This is a waste of time," Harkon said, then turned to face his student and the old sage that had taken them this far. "I imagine it's not as simple as crossing the water to claim the jewel, is it?"

"No," Silas muttered. "But the stories are vague, past this point. My predecessors didn't feel like sharing that information. Clearly they felt that anyone who could get this far would have to prove their worth. I only know that there are two tests, and only one person may try each."

Aimee stepped to the shoreline, and stretched out with her senses. Just beyond the water's edge, she sensed a quiet, subdued power. Intense. Patient. A wire waiting to be tripped. As her teacher and the sage spoke behind her, she considered what she remembered of puzzle boxes and logic games from her childhood. Her mother had adored them, always the expert with unconventional problems, where her father's mind was bound to iron numbers. Aimee had spent endless hours playing with simple traps and mental exercises on the sun-drenched balconies and gardens of her family's villa. What lay before them was much the same – only bigger. More perilous by far.

If there was one thing she remembered about such challenges, it was that the second test was always harder than the first.

She looked at the water again, then reached into her pocket and plucked out a simple copper coin. She turned it over in deft fingers, then flicked it out into the pool. The second it struck the surface, a whirl of frost erupted outwards from the immediately frozen splash. The entire lake, from top to bottom, hardened into a lattice of frosted spikes. Silence followed. The frost receded as quick as it came. Aimee gulped, and calculated whether a person could have survived that. Unlikely.

She straightened. So triggering the *first* test was a matter of taking the right path. She really only had one choice: trip the wire. Start the process. If she passed the first her master could save his strength to complete the exponentially more difficult second.

Her teacher's shout of objection was too late to stop her. Her feet set upon the stone pathway that led to the pedestal, and she felt the wave of magic wash over her as dormant enchantments roared to life.

"Aimee, what are you *doing?*"

She looked over one shoulder, and forced a smile. "Taking the initiative, teacher."

Walls of magic closed behind her.

She stood alone in an endless field of stars. The ground beneath rippled at the touch of her feet, and there was neither pedestal, nor discernible cavern wall within sight. A night sky more detailed, deep, and brilliant than any she had ever seen stretched over her head, reflected perfectly across the ground. She smelled water and wind, and the undefinable scent that always came with night.

"… Alright," Aimee said "Not what I was expecting."

She tested the floor, tapped her foot in a complete circle around her. Just ripples. No path. No freezing water, either. The faint smell of water and night rose about her. Whether this was an illusion or a creation wholly of the test she faced, it didn't seem that she needed to worry about where she stepped. She tried to recall everything she could remember from classes on old myths, mystic trials, and extradimensional phenomena. She seemed – for the moment – to have time.

One of Harkon's old lectures sprang to mind, about alternate planes and constructed mass illusions so precise they functioned as truly divergent realities, and might have been considered as such, but for the fact that they ceased when the enchantments that birthed them ended.

"To exist within such a construct is to contend with a reality that is malleable. In such a place, the power of thought alone to shape, conjure, or craft, is exponentially greater. The trick is knowing it."

Aimee closed her eyes. *You want me to see something.* She reached out into the vast dark. *Show me.*

Silence. She breathed in and out, quieted her mind as best she could, and tried not to be overwhelmed by the immensity of an infinite universe spread out before her. Wonder could save, but it could also kill.

When she opened her eyes, the pedestal loomed before her.

Unlike its counterpart in the center of the cavern, this was an organic spire of black, oily basalt jutting from the mirror floor beneath her. A primal thrust of ebon stone that reached into the vast starscape above. Near the top, she glimpsed a flash of pale white light.

Somehow, she knew, she was seeing not just the conjuring of an illusionary test, but something far older, even if it no longer persisted in the present. This was, perhaps, the place from which the Axiom had first come.

"... I've never seen anything so beautiful," she breathed.

And a voice, mouthless, breathless, echoed inside her mind. *"You wanted to see the truth and wonder, Aimee de Laurent. Best hurry. Such visions rarely last for long."*

She turned in a circle, seeking the source of the

speaking. She found none, and with a simple sigh, addressed the emptiness. "I can't tell if that's a warning or a threat."

Silence followed, and after a few seconds of it, Aimee started towards the black upthrust of rock.

When she reached its base, she searched for an easy path of ascent, finding none after a cursory walk once around the exterior. She breathed out her frustration and fear, the terror that their mission would fail because she couldn't hash out the puzzle before her.

"So suspicious," the voice said again. *"Do you still not understand? You need not deceive, Aimee de Laurent. You need only see."*

She turned. It had come from her right, this time. But looking, she found not a person, but a narrow staircase incised into the rock, winding its way upwards into the starry heavens above. Aimee hesitated for only a moment, then began her climb.

It took hours, or so it felt. Her limbs were tiring and the air seemed thinner. One step before the other. The beauty blurred by her, settling into a focus of steps taken up and around the black exterior of the tower. When she crested the peak, she couldn't have said how long she'd been climbing.

An armored facsimile of a man awaited her. Behind him, a silver pedestal crowned the tower's apex. He was indistinct. His armor shifted when he moved, designs altering, and style, and age. He said nothing, so Aimee took a step towards the pedestal. The figure shifted to bar her path.

"So," she said after a moment. "You're my opponent, then? I have to defeat you. Is that how this works?"

Silence was his only answer. Now his armor was

black, now white, now covered in blood, now pristine and unstained. Aimee was not a warrior. She had never trained at the sword, nor learned the art of bow or spear, though she knew a little hand-to-hand. A list of spells, offensive and deadly, sprang to mind. She measured the personage before her. She had overcome more dangerous before, certainly, even bound Azrael against his will. She was powerful. She had it in her.

"You assume so much," the figure said. Its voice was familiar, though distorted, as if echoing from a place far away. "Assume, and *presume*. What makes you believe that you are worthy?"

Aimee frowned. "I don't have time to debate ethics with a gatekeeper," she said. "Whether I'm worthy or not isn't important. Dangerous, powerful men are seeking what you protect. I *have* to stop them." She started forward.

The armored face of the knight stared back, and an armored palm raised to bar her way. "Urgency doesn't make worth. Not where truth is concerned."

People were dying. Aimee's mind was assaulted by the memory of burning cities, of the dozens of wounded men she'd helped to mend, and the gnawing, obsessive wondering she'd barely kept in check of how many of them had gone on to be hacked to pieces, burned alive, or tortured and enslaved. Finally, Gara's decapitated head, rolling across the cobbles as the black knight lowered his bloody sword, flashed through her mind. The way her whole body had *jerked* when she fell.

Aimee grabbed the hand that held her. Worth did not matter. Urgency did. She was *done* with this. Her hand lashed out and struck the armored knight's helm. To her surprise, the visor split, falling away to reveal a face staring back. Green-eyed. Handsome. But for the serene, mournful expression, it was Azrael's.

Aimee screamed, and hurled a killing spell right between his eyes. Flesh burned, skin blackened and curled. The illusion flashed to nothing in a second and the clattering remnants of armor fell to the ground. She dashed towards the gem upon its pedestal, but pain seared white-hot through her hand until she pulled it away with a scream.

"*Poor child,*" the voice from before said in her mind. "*Too much hatred and pain. You don't understand... But you will. You must.*"

A rumble passed overhead, and a ripple passed beneath her feet. A cold chill cut through Aimee's heart as the jewel receded from her sight. She'd failed. Gods and demons, she'd *failed.*

"Wait!" Aimee screamed, and as she raised her eyes above, the stars fell.

With a gasp, she found herself sitting upon the stone walkway onto which she'd stepped. A glimmer of enchantment was collapsing around her, as the remnants of the test burnt and dissolved into nothing. From the far shore she heard Silas calling. "Did it work?" he asked. "Did you pass?"

Harkon's hands were upon her shoulders, helping her up. She was dizzy, felt nauseous, the energy sucked from her. *A side-effect of the illusion,* she reminded herself. *I'll be fine in a few minutes.*

"Are you alright?" Her teacher's voice was quiet, but when he looked in her eyes, Aimee could tell immediately that he knew.

"I'm sorry," she whispered.

"This doesn't make any sense," Silas breathed, still keeping his prince's sword pointed at Azrael's throat. "If the test failed, why has the enchantment fallen away? How is it that only one test remains?"

"I heard a voice," Aimee murmured. "It said that I didn't understand," she shot a venomous look at the imprisoned black knight, "but that I would."

The sage's eyes widened with a brilliant, desperate hope. His laugh cracked, the voice high pitched. "Then only one test is left!" he cried. "We're *saved!*"

"It's not so simple," Harkon said, patting Aimee on the shoulder and rising slowly to his full height. He looked at the central pedestal, and Aimee followed his gaze, slowly pushing herself up. A weight of frustration and fury burned within her – to have studied so hard for so long, to have come *so* far in the years since her schooling began, only to fail what seemed like every test of note. She forced down tears of frustration, of the burning sense of inadequacy that reared its head at the back of her mind.

"There is one test remaining," Harkon said, staring at the pedestal. "But if I fail it, the Axiom will not be yielded to anyone. *That* is how it works."

Silas stared at the two of them. Aimee watched as his hands shook. The old sage stuttered several times, his head dropped, and a full ten seconds passed before he managed to wrest up the emotional fortitude to reply. "With respect to all you have done for myself, and my country," he said, and his eyes raised to look at Aimee and her teacher. They were wide as twin moons, and something wild and broken hovered in their depths. "Do. Not. Fail."

Aimee took an involuntary step back. She was

about to say something to her teacher when Harkon took a breath, and stepped further down the path. The whole room rumbled with the release of caged magic, and Harkon Bright was lost to the thrall of the test, surrounded in flickering pale light.

CHAPTER NINETEEN
Must Endure Burning

Twice now, Azrael had watched as the sage nearly talked himself into killing him. Twice, he had done nothing but keep his gaze fixed on the old man. Had watched as Silas held Oath of Aurum in his trembling, spotted hands. The black knight sat in his bindings, his back against the wall of the cavern. As Harkon Bright stepped forth and triggered the second test, he found himself now outnumbered by only one.

This was going to be a delicate, difficult process.

"We cannot fail," Silas murmured, over and over as his mind seemed to crack. "We cannot fail."

"We won't," Aimee said. She appeared to be doing her best to comfort her companion, but the effort barely masked her own sense of failure and uncertainty. It was written all over her face.

If Azrael could just get *free*, he could still pull a victory from this horrible mess of a situation. He was a prisoner of two emotionally unbalanced people who were forced to divide their attentions. And Harkon Bright, the most dangerous person there, was now completely occupied with a test that would consume the lion's share of his energy.

"I'd ignore the girl, if I were you," Azrael said mildly to the sage. "Her estimation of your chances is optimistic *at best*."

"Shut up," Silas hissed. He turned to face Azrael. His hands gripped the enchanted sword. The black knight felt the point hovering a breath away from his throat. He kept his green eyes locked on the sage's. Fail now, and all was lost. *Failure is weakness. Weakness is death.*

"You're not accustomed to the idea of killing, are you?" he asked the old man.

"No," Silas snapped. "I'm not like *you*."

Easier than he thought. Azrael lifted his chin. "No, that I can see. You have the eyes of someone who's spent his life clinging to bright ideals. How does it feel, sage, to watch them crumble?"

Lord Roland's teachings ran through his head as he spoke, lessons on how to read men and understand them. How to read the cues of their bodies, the way they held themselves, responded when challenged. *Find his weakness, and he will do as you wish.*

"You know *nothing* of my ideals, of virtue," Silas spat. The sword pricked closer. Azrael didn't flinch. He needed the blade to move.

"My education included ethics," Azrael said, shrugging. "And I've known plenty of men who imagined themselves thus." He let the smile slide up one corner of his mouth. "Like your prince. What was his name again? Canton?"

Silas *recoiled*. The blade dropped as he shook with incandescent fury. "Don't you *dare* speak to me of Collum."

"Collum, that's right, I think I remember him shouting

it at me before he died." Azrael shrugged. "Sorry. I've killed so many of your people since we came here that I can't be arsed to remember names and faces. I *do* remember his, though."

"Silas, take a step back," Aimee's voice cut across the conversation, and her cold blue eyes filled Azrael's vision.

"I can handle one arrogant boy–" Silas protested.

"Not if you don't step back and *take a moment*," she answered, addressing the sage.

"Jealous?" Azrael asked, slipping smoothly from one tactic to another. He turned his head to fix his grin on her, one eyebrow raised with practiced grace. "Don't worry, I have plenty of time for both of you." He let his laugh slip free, mocking and deep. "As you've so skillfully ensured: I'm not going anywhere."

Aimee turned to meet his stare. Unflinching. Determined. It struck him, absently, just how rare that was. Most of his enemies couldn't hold his gaze for long. "You talk a strong bluff," she finally said, "for someone as afraid as you are. I can't *imagine* your masters will be too happy to see how spectacularly you've failed. Just how long is the life expectancy for a member of your order who doesn't deliver? Is it measured in years? Months?" Her probing tone dropped to a whisper. "Hours?"

Her eyes looked into his. They saw. There was no time for reservations, falling short, or letting himself become disarmed. Azrael kept his focus, and gave a simple tilt of his head, meeting the blue gaze with tenacity. "One of us has brought an entire nation to its knees in a matter of days," he said. "The other has failed to pass a single magical test requisite to find a shiny *rock*."

Aimee's eyes closed. Her fists clenched. "I think,"

Azrael said quietly, "that it may be your turn to *step back*."

"This man," Silas breathed, "is a *serpent*."

"Calm down," the girl urged the sage.

"Yes," Azrael added, "mustn't lose our temper."

"Shut up!" Silas took a step forward.

"Don't," Aimee grabbed him by the arm. "Think about what makes him *different* from us."

"For starters," Azrael snarked, "I am restrained, and you are not."

Silas strained against Aimee's grip on his arm. "Silas!" she snapped. The old man turned to look at her. "Keep it *together*," she said.

Before any of them could speak again, the conversation was interrupted by a sharp, agonized cry from Harkon Bright.

Azrael craned his neck to watch as Aimee and Silas turned. Walls of enchantment stood translucent, and the powerful mage about whom so many legends had been told stood riveted to his place on the stone walkway, eyes wide, face drained and pained. Azrael watched as Aimee took a compulsive step towards her teacher.

Harkon breathed with difficulty. Sweat poured from his brow, and he stared into the iridescence of the Axiom Diamond. Silas straightened. Aimee's attention was now *fully* upon her teacher.

"Don't," Harkon whispered. The sound carried throughout the whole cavern. "Please, I beg you, do not show me."

The light flared a second time, and the mage winced as if struck. A beam of pure silver pulsed from the center of the gem to Harkon's forehead, and the mage went rigid. Azrael felt his heart pounding in his chest. Succeed or fail, the old man's test would be over momentarily. He had minutes, likely less, to get himself free. Every mental effort at shattering the bonds Aimee had set upon him had failed. Like it or not, her spell was more powerful than he could break in the time he had. They would have to be cut, and there was only one tool in the room that could do it. His eyes leveled on Oath of Aurum, resting in Silas's hands as the old man watched Harkon's struggle unfold. The black knight steadied his heart, forced his focus down to a pinprick, and set his course. The old sage was a pacifist, like all the other members of his order. He was a believer in peace, in wisdom, in justice.

He would not be driven to strike easily, but Azrael had to get free.

The old man had to be made to break.

The girl gave him his golden opportunity. "Stay here, Silas," she admonished him. "I've got to try to help, if I can. *Stay here* and don't let him do *anything*."

Silas nodded, took a breath to steady himself, and slowly walked back towards the black knight. Azrael fixed him with his green gaze. His stomach churned in knots. *Elias.*

Esric's hand was on his back. Roland was in his mind. Weakness was death.

"Tell me, sage," Azrael said after a moment. "How long have you served the royal family of Port Providence?" Esric's face filled his mind's eye. The black knight felt sick. Something in the back of his mind was tearing. Ripping.

Silas slowly turned his hateful gaze towards Azrael. Gods, but that expression looked so familiar.

"Since early in the reign of the late king," Silas answered. "Long before you were born, I imagine. Since before New Corinth fell to your wretched order."

"Knew them well, did you?" Azrael asked mildly. "The royals, I mean. Their names, faces, habits, loves, hatreds."

Silas's eyes were wet. He stared at Azrael transfixed, unable to look away. Elsewhere in the cavern, Harkon cried out again. A line of white erupted from the aura around him, forming a figure at the edge of the lake. A woman in mage's robes. She looked beautiful, grief-stricken. "Don't make me see them," Harkon whimpered. "Please, don't make me watch."

"I knew them all," Silas whispered.

More figures formed at the edge of the water. Harkon's knees trembled. Azrael heard Aimee addressing her master. "These aren't your old enemies," she said with realization. "They're the people you've failed to save."

"So many," Harkon whimpered. "So *many.*"

"How did your king die?" Azrael asked. He kept his voice even. *Eyes on me*, he thought as Silas seemed as though he would look away. *Eyes on me.* "I never actually learned the truth." When Silas stared back at him in pain, he pressed, calmly. "I'd assumed he burned to death in our initial bombardment, you see, but then we found the palace intact, and when we were looting all its artwork, we found no remains, *so–*"

Azrael winced. The mental image of the boy upon the floor hovered in his vision. He almost choked on his words. He had to do this. He had to *win.*

"He died upon the walls," Silas said quietly. He watched Azrael differently now. Much of the conflict in his eyes had vanished. It was as if he stared at a particularly loathsome insect. One he *longed* to squash. Vows of pacifism and peace were mere formalities. All

Azrael had to do was *keep pushing*.

"He died," Silas continued, "trying to get as many people out of the city as he could... Certain that the survival of his line was secured in the lives of his sons."

Azrael shook his head and sighed. "Pity, that."

Both of Silas's hands gripped the longsword, trembling. Its unblemished blade flickered in the silver light of the cavern. The old sage's wise eyes were rimmed with tears as the things he had believed in cracked and splintered and tumbled away from him whilst Azrael watched. *Me*, the black knight mentally urged. *Blame me*.

Silas's lips moved. The whisper was almost too quiet to hear. "What *are* you?"

Azrael tilted his head slightly, let the crooked smile slip out. "The man who killed your prince," he finally answered after a few minutes faking consideration. "Which, when you think about it, means I am also the man who knows his essence, his spirit, better than anyone else in the world. Better even than you."

Now for the finisher. He had one chance at this. One. Azrael leaned forward as much as he could, looked the sage in the eye, and whispered: "Do you want to hear how he begged for mercy?"

Silas stared at him. There was noise elsewhere in the cavern. Aimee had made it halfway down the walkway towards her teacher. The risk she was taking was unimaginably great. A small part of the black knight registered being impressed.

The sage's head dropped. A wave of sobs overtook him, then became the great, racking cries of a man whose soul was coming apart at the seams. He shook. The sword drooped and its point rang against the cave floor.

Then Silas's head snapped up. His red-rimmed eyes were bloodshot and furious. Sobs became great, shuddering screams. He seized the sword in both hands and wheeled it high up over his head. His tear-streaked face twisted into a hideous mask of grief-stricken rage.

"To hell with vows!" He screamed. "To hell with the order! And *to hell with you!*"

The sword dropped like a cleaver.

Azrael rolled. Silas was not a warrior. His strike was *terrible*, insufficient to cut anything, but for the fact that Oath of Aurum was not a normal sword.

It was exactly what the black knight needed. His roll shifted him just enough, exposing the magical bonds holding him. The magic sword sliced through them. Azrael felt his limbs come free, and he sprang to his feet. The sage still wore a look of stupefied surprise on his face as the black knight's armored fist cracked into the side of his head. Silas crumpled, groaning. Azrael retrieved the sword, and rose.

Starting at the noise, Aimee turned. Horror flashed across her face. "Silas!" she screamed.

Azrael hefted the blade in both hands, and grinned. "Never trust an unstable old man with guard duty, little girl."

The timing was perfect. A mass of illusionary figures surrounded the edge of the lake, now, legacies of whatever tormented history the Axiom's trials had dragged from Harkon Bright. At once, they all seemed to nod, and the final walls of enchantment broke. The older mage collapsed to his knees, breathing hard. Exhausted. Good. Azrael had but one opponent.

Aimee glanced between him and the diamond, perfect

upon its pedestal. Her hands flashed to summon a spell. Azrael was already moving, his spell for speed a breath between heartbeats. He tore up the path. She dashed at the same time. Slower, but closer. She reached the edge of the dais. Turned. One hand groped for the gemstone as the other hurled a bolt of flame at his exposed head. Azrael sidestepped. The dodge cost him his balance.

He crashed into the pedestal. Pain rushed through his shoulder beneath the armor even as it spared him the worst. In his periphery, the jewel for which untold crimes had been committed and countless lives lost, tumbled free. It struck the stone. The noise echoed like a hammer blow through the cavern.

Aimee lunged for it. Azrael rolled forward and grasped at the same time. He felt his fingers touch a perfectly faceted, warm edge, and he put forth every ounce of willpower he had.

Resplendent light filled his vision. Agony raged behind his eyes, seared up his arms. It was everywhere, all around him.

Azrael's world burned away.

CHAPTER TWENTY
LORD ROLAND'S DEMON

When Aimee's eyes opened, the cavern was empty. Of people. Of bolts of whirling spells. Of the line of endless manifestations of her teacher's ghosts. And of the woman that had strode towards Harkon, a horrible wound in her chest.

Aimee scrambled to her feet, dusted off her hands, and cast about for any sign of her companions. "No," she breathed. "No no no no this is wrong, where are they?"

"They are where you left them."

She felt the words, and turning saw their source. The voice from her first test, at last, revealed. The Axiom Diamond hung above the lake of water. Its light – seconds ago a baleful, agonizing glow – was now a soft, even pulse.

"Please," Aimee begged, the absurdity of addressing a gemstone forgotten. "If you brought me here, I have to go back!" Tears of exhaustion rolled down her cheeks. If they died while she languished here...

"They are no longer in danger."

The Axiom's voice was calm, smooth.

"The contest is over."

Several unsteady steps carried Aimee forward. She was once more upon the shore, and the signs of the horrors unleashed only seconds ago were now wholly absent. It was as if nobody had ever disturbed this place at all, but for the fact that the diamond now hovered mid-air.

And seemed to be speaking.

"There were three tests, Aimee de Laurent," it answered in a calm, kind voice, *"not two. First was a test of intention. Next, a test of fortitude. Third–"*

"Was a test of will," Aimee breathed, relief flooding through her. When she had grasped the diamond at the same time as the escaped Azrael, she had put forth every ounce of her willpower. It had worked. She sank to her knees at the edge of the lake. "This is in my head," she realized.

"Yes," came the answer. *"But you need not fear. Your companions are alive and well, your enemy subdued."*

Aimee's eyes closed. "I won," she breathed. "My will was stronger than Azrael's."

Silence, then the gem spoke again.

"No," it said.

Fear, white-hot, cut through her. Aimee's face snapped up. "What?"

"In that moment, his will was stronger," it said. *"He will now receive all that I can confer upon him."*

Aimee's mouth hung open, the truth a lance through her heart. How many had died to stop this? How many had striven, struggled, bled, and suffered? Gara. Bjorn. Soldiers without number.

She had let them all down.

But the voice was not done with her. *"Do not despair, Aimee de Laurent,"* it said. *"Like so many before, you sought without knowing, and grasped without understanding. As did he. But it is not the ruin of your cause that failure brings, young sorceress. Not all worth is measured by passing tests. Why do you think I permitted your company to grow closer still? Some truths need to be seen. The world is changing."*

Behind the hovering gemstone, a tear of light opened in the air. Within it, images played, unfamiliar, repeating. Indistinct, but sharpening by the second as the rift grew. "What are you? What are you doing?" Aimee asked.

"I am neither a map to secret treasure, nor a perfect viewing gallery for those who wish to see across distance," it said. *"What I am is a compilation of knowledge more vast than any library, deeper than any extant tome. I am a storehouse of the truth of souls, a refracting mirror for the realities of self."* The Axiom's voice filled with terrible sadness. *"And I am conferring my blessing."* The tear had nearly encompassed the entire cavern. Aimee's sense of anything else but the sights and sounds within were fading. *"Now pay attention, Aimee de Laurent, for I must show a young man called Azrael the truth about himself, and I think it is important that you watch as well."*

The light of the diamond flared once more, devouring the cavern, burning away the world. Sweet-scented rose petals blew across Aimee's face.

Throughout her education in the Academy of Mystic Sciences, and since coming to the nightmare that the Eternal Order had made of Port Providence, Aimee had seen many horrible things. None of that compared – even in the abstract – to the experience of witnessing Azrael's life in reverse. She watched as the black knight goaded Silas to madness, traced his flight through the woods to reach them. She watched as he crossed swords with Bjorn, then further back. Her heart lurched as the old warrior disappeared over the falls.

Memories swirled around Aimee, and as she strove to focus, to drive out the noise, the bloodshed, the horrifying chaos, she heard another voice screaming amidst the cacophony. "Let me go!" Azrael shouted. "I know my own life!"

"Poor boy," the voice said back. *"You sought truth, and now you shall have it."*

They stood in a bay, vast, filled with mercenaries in service to Azrael and his masters. Arrayed in armor, the black knight stood before a man robed in the trappings of a middle-aged healer – she heard someone call him Esric – who reached out to touch him. The black knight swatted his hand away, and in that second, a line of enchantment connecting healer to knight snapped. Esric's appearance flickered, *changed*. Aimee watched as Azrael beheld the man's predatory gaze. The healer's eyes hardened, deepened. His pupils swelled until Esric stared at his momentarily-denied plaything with a gaze of solid black. A knife-like stab of fear cut through the apprentice portalmage. The thing that called itself Esric wasn't human.

She heard Azrael scream. Turning, she saw the black knight as he was, watching as all this unfolded before him. A layer of filmy light formed about his head, then cracked as if it were glass, and peeled away, falling to shatter upon the bay floor. Shock and surprise struck her: her arrogant, dangerous enemy was terrified.

"Elias."

"Please," Azrael begged. His voice cracked in pain. Aimee watched as gauntleted hands reached up to desperately clutch at the sides of his head. The steel dissolved even as she watched. A part of her felt a grim satisfaction, but the rest couldn't dismiss the sharp pang of pity somewhere deep in her chest.

"No," the Axiom answered. *"There is more that you must see."*

Backwards. Aimee watched as Azrael hid a wounded child at a farmhouse. As he drove his sword through the body of a brute that had abused the same small boy, her anger, her hate, hesitated. These weren't the actions of a monster. The wall in her heart trembled. Aimee marked – though Azrael in the past did not – the flickering gleam that faded from the blade as it punched through man and into stone. She watched the brilliant colored windows of an entire palace floor shatter. The breath nearly left her body as shards of glass fell around her like drops of remembered rain. She winced at the release of power in the young man's tormented scream. She watched in shuddering, wide-eyed horror as Malfenshir butchered prisoners to hone his swordplay. The Azrael beside her stood transfixed. When Esric, still further back, healed him at Gray Falcon, another piece of glass-like light formed, cracked, and fell away from his body. The chink in the wall of Aimee's heart widened. This time Esric's whole form contorted as his healing spell wove dark threads of sinister magic into the black knight's mind. His coal eyes sprouted veins of inky darkness across his face. Nobody about them in the memories noticed. Aimee felt her stomach lurch in horror. She knew mind-control magic when she saw it. In her own heart, in the wall of implacable hatred she'd built around her enemy, a chink appeared. *How long,* she thought, *have they been doing that to you?*

"Angel of death," the diamond addressed the black knight. *"How you have been used."*

"Please," Azrael pleaded. "Please…"

Further back. The invasion. Skyships warred across the skies over Port Providence. Aimee had to force herself to hold her ground, to not leap away from phantom wreckage and blasts of searing heat. She smelled the afterscent of ether-cannon fire, felt the kiss of the unforgiving sun, heard every scream as its own private horror. And in the midst of it, Prince Collum – fabled and grieved for – rode his vessel down to crash upon the *Iron Hulk*. Black knight and prince dueled across the battered ruins. Collum's corpse fell into the flaming abyss. Aimee watched the body turn into a silhouette against the flames, watched as the implacable face of the black knight's remembered self picked up his sword. The moment the hand touched the steel, the black bands of Esric's enchantments upon him trembled.

"The arc of inevitability does not bend only towards evil," Aimee heard the Axiom say. *"Virtue is just as relentless."*

Further back. The green-eyed knight stood before the throne of a king, throwing a brutal promise at his feet.

"Absolute oblivion, your majesty."

Earlier. Malfenshir and Azrael argued, standing together before the red-lit pulsing heart of the *Iron Hulk*: a metadrive more vast than any Aimee had ever seen.

"If you promise the king oblivion," Malfenshir argued, "you had best be prepared to make good. I warn you, Azrael. Do not underplay our hand. The Silent Scream is our ultimate tool. Do not fail to use it."

Aimee crept closer. Plans lay written on parchment before her. A weapon. A cold cyst of fear clenched in her chest.

"You must see, Aimee de Laurent," the Axiom said in her mind.

Her eyes widened. If it could do what those plans *said* it could…

"No," Azrael answered in the past. "If we lead with this, we risk the chance that they don't know where the Axiom is, either. If they then refuse, we are forced to either destroy our prize along with the rest of the isle, or prove ourselves unwilling to back up our threats."

The past Azrael turned back towards them, looking away from the metadrive core in all its vastness. A conflict played out behind his eyes. He shook his head. "Where is Esric?" he asked.

"You have fought your whole life," the Axiom said. *"Even from beneath the weight of a thousand oppressive blows."*

"Above," Malfenshir murmured. "He doesn't come down here, remember? The techs are frightened of him."

Crack. Light split. Another glass shard shattered. The black knight shuddered in pain.

"Elias."

"Stop saying that name!" Azrael screamed, in the present.

"You still don't understand," the Axiom pressed. *"But you will."*

Azrael turned away from the memories before him. Aimee turned with him. A pain, a mad terror, rolled off the young man who had done so much, and to whom so much had been done. In her heart of hearts, Aimee felt the chink in the wall become a deep crack.

They stared now into a void. Shapes moved within it. Murmurs. Occasional sounds of things yet more terrifying. From within its depths, memories sprang to life, swirling around her. "Please," Azrael whispered. "Don't make me look."

The voice of the Axiom was pitiless. *"You wanted truth."*

A realm more nightmare than reality rose up before them, full of black towers and shadowed parapets, built upon the bones of something once great and beautiful. Aimee felt the dark sadness of the place as a stinging affront that wetted her eyes with an unspeakable grief. There weren't words for the crimes meted out within this tortured place.

The House of Nails, she realized. *This is what New Corinth became after the order conquered it.*

Whips cracked. Screams resounded from vast, labyrinthine hellscapes. In a cathedral that had once played host to the upraised, worshipping hymns of the thousand gods, banners black, red, and gold hung with the heraldry of innumerable, infamous butchers. There, before a mass of robed and armored knights, a younger Azrael – no more than sixteen – knelt before a dread lord. In the memory, the figure was more nightmare than real, the stuff of horrible dreams given form and flesh by the vague, incoherent recollection of the one who had lived through his presence. Aimee's heart pounded fearfully in her chest as she looked upon the smirking, helm-shadowed face of her teacher's enemy. His cold eyes glittered in the dim light of burning braziers like distant stars.

Lord Roland.

"Arise, my angel of death," she heard the deep voice echo, as if from far away. "Arise, my Azrael."

The sword touched his shoulders, and she saw the magic again, surrounding him, sickly and black, seeping into every pore of his flesh, knitting itself into the fabric of his mind. Behind the curtain Esric lurked. She saw *it* – she could no longer believe it possessed any human traits – exchange a nod with Lord Roland, and the threads of magic suffusing the newly made knight *tightened*. Aimee felt abruptly ill.

"No," Azrael breathed, beside her. "No, I swore my vows *willingly*."

"To swear under coercion and pain of death is not 'willingly,'" the Axiom answered.

Whips sounded again. Brutal laughter. Aimee watched with a twisting heart as further back, the boy who would become Azrael was trained. Beaten. Made to obey. Green eyes filled with fear and hate stared up at trainers, defiant. Once, he began to speak a name. A blow from Roland's fist landed before it could leave his mouth. "She is *dead*, Nameless. That boy is a memory," the dread lord said. "You will be punished in sufficient manner to drive it from your mind."

The cyst of fear in Aimee's chest tightened. *No.*

A dark room came, then. Candlelight. The once-defiant boy huddled alone, broken in a corner. Bruised. Beaten. Violated. The adult Azrael suddenly, *violently* recoiled from what he was seeing. His eyes were wide, his expression *terrified*. The crack in the wall in Aimee's heart widened.

At the far end of the room, Lord Roland spoke to a silhouette of a man, his name and face forgotten, pressing a gold coin into his hands.

"He'll never say that name again," the faceless man said.

Aimee could only stand and stare, her mouth momentarily unable to form words in response to the atrocity.

Later, the boy lay upon a table. His green eyes stared unseeing at the ceiling. Lord Roland stood by as a healer shook his head. "He will not wake," he said. "He will not rise. The power to live is there, but the will is gone."

"Get out of my sight," Roland said. In the darkness and the silence, he stood, staring contemptuously down at the dark-haired, broken boy. "Dammit child," he snarled. "I need you *alive*."

Slowly, resignedly, the dread lord turned and addressed a shadow that lurked in the back of the tent, deeper than the others. "You win," he finally said. "I call you forth from the endless night."

The shadow slithered from the black, a darkness that assumed a faintly man-like form on the opposite side of the child's bed. "Suppress his memories. Heal him. *Fix* him," Roland snarled. "Keep him functional, able to serve. Keep him compliant, and obedient, and you can do whatever you want to whomever, or whatever, crosses his path as you journey together. Is this acceptable?"

The shadow nodded. Then it twisted, warped. Skin grew, hair, clothes took shape from its protean chaos, until the *thing* had become the man called Esric.

"Completely," it whispered.

Aimee's hand covered her mouth. She felt the sick urge to void her stomach all over the floor. Azrael fell to his knees, his fists clenched, tears running down his face, his breath coming in gasps.

"You cannot be free," the diamond said. *"Until the Truth that they have taken from you is laid bare."*

Silence descended. The void of memory yawned before them. Azrael slowly looked up and stared horrified into the black abyss that had slowly grown as each memory emerged. Now it loomed before them, the titanic pupil of a burning, cyclopean eye. Aimee turned, standing side by side with her enemy before the whirling void. Her heart pounded in her ears, sweat stained her neck. The rush of emotions, each as painful as the one before, flooded her senses.

"One truth remains," the diamond whispered.

From the depths of the void a woman's voice whispered. *"Elias."*

A tempest of white rose petals whirled across the black.

The petals settled. The darkness lifted.

Aimee opened her eyes in a sun-drenched orchard. The rays of the warm summer sunset painted the edges of fruit, leaves, and branches a brilliant, molten gold. Standing among buzzing insects, her feet upon sweet-smelling, soft grass, was so dissonant that Aimee had to rub her eyes to swear that what she saw was real, *had* been real, once upon a time. She turned in a circle, heart still pounding after everything to which she'd borne witness. White rose petals spread outward from where her feet and Azrael's had touched the memory's ground. She crouched, felt them soft between her fingers, more real than the vision. The pounding of her heart slowed, fear and terror replaced with confusion and a disoriented warmth.

"Elias!"

The name cut across Aimee's thoughts like a white knife. She turned, disoriented and surprised as the same green-eyed boy from the previous memory dropped to the ground from a nearby tree branch. He landed in a laughing crouch, then ran down the aisle beneath the arches of gold-tinted apple trees under the warm summer sun. He couldn't have been older than six. Aimee stared, momentarily dumbstruck. It seemed inconceivable that the boy she looked at now could have become the black knight that stood, tormented, beside her.

As if in a dream, the adult Azrael's lips moved in time with the little boy's answer.

"I'm coming, Mama!"

Aimee stared at the exhausted, broken, bewildered man beside her, watched as the child laughed and ran his way towards a cottage. The crack in the wall split open. Pity turned to sadness, and deep beneath, she felt the first surge of rage on the black knight's behalf.

"Elias," she whispered. "That's your name... Your *real* name."

She didn't know if he could hear her. Whether or not the magic that allowed her to bear witness to this distant moment permitted them communication, or if she was simply permitted to see, but when the black knight's lips moved again, the voice that spoke was broken, pained, and small.

"... I had a mother." He grasped for the next words. "I had a name."

"You cannot know who you are," the Axiom said, *"until you know what was taken from you."*

Unsure if he could see or hear her, Aimee nonetheless followed the adult Azrael through the dreamlike blur of a recollection long past. Her mind struggled to wrap itself around the monstrous nature of everything this man had done, even as she grappled with the immensity of what had been done *to* him. Moreover, how much of it could he be said to have done of his own free will?

He was as much of a victim as everyone in Port Providence.

The rage within her burned brighter.

The boy rushed into the arms of a pretty young woman with dark hair as thick and wavy as that of her adult son. She was dressed in simple peasant's clothing, and scooped up the boy in pale arms not born to the beating sun or naturally callused from hard work. *She wasn't born to this life,* Aimee realized.

"Were you climbing the trees again?" the woman asked. Her green eyes, deep and bright as her son's, twinkled with amusement. Aimee felt her heart twist in empathy as the man beside her stared at the pair with a look of bewildered agony on his face.

The crooked grin the child flashed was so identical to the look the adult sometimes wore that Aimee nearly staggered.

"No, Mama," the boy giggled. "I would never."

"You're a poor liar, Elias Leblanc," his mother laughed. "You mustn't lie. Remember what I told you?"

The little boy grinned, and repeated six words with the lilt of memorization: "Noble and brave," he said. "Gentle and kind."

The woman smiled, approving, and ruffled his dark hair. "That's right. Now come on, little monkey. Your supper is ready."

Something stirred within the adult Azrael as the pair walked towards the house. The woman hummed an old lullaby as she walked.

"Don't," Aimee heard him whisper, and the wall around him in her heart split down the middle. Glass cracked and splintered in the air about him. His remaining armor fell away. Each step forward that he took seemed to cause him physical pain, and yet, still, he pushed himself after them. "Please," the black knight begged. "*Please!* Don't go into that house!"

The door creaked open, and a churning void yawned on the other side. Azrael paused, and when Aimee found that her feet could carry her no further than where his lead boot had landed, she realized, abruptly, that there were limits to the Axiom's power to reveal. At the threshold of truth, Aimee felt her own fear as a painful knot bunched in the center of her chest, threatening to freeze her heart.

"Beyond this lies the last thing that has been hidden willfully from you," the voice said. *"It is there, waiting. The choice is now yours, you who are called Azrael, who was once Elias. Truth or ignorance?"*

Azrael stared into the abyss of the doorway. Strange sounds came from the other side. Cries. Shouts. Aimee stood beside him, beside this monster she had tried to kill, the man that she had hated, for whom her heart now ached despite all sense.

"The ancients had a saying," she whispered. His green eyes flicked briefly towards her, hearing her for the first time. She made herself look back, drawing upon a well of compassion that would have seemed impossible minutes earlier. "Elias," she said, iron in her voice. "The truth will set you free."

His eyes held hers for a moment. She didn't know if he looked past her, or into her. Then, with steps that clearly pained him, he forced himself through the door, and Aimee walked with him.

"I choose the truth."

Darkness washed over them again, and she heard him screaming. Straining against bonds that had bound his mind for *years*.

"This," said the voice, *"is what Lord Roland has mutilated your mind and violated your body to force you to forget."*

A room came into focus. Aimee staggered, caught herself, and felt her eyes widen at the chaos and horror she saw. Inside the cottage, the furniture was smashed. The woman lay upon the floor, blood seeping from her mouth as she stared up at the armored titan of Lord Roland. He was younger here. His armor was the battered finery of some sort of regal guardsman, and a bloody sword was in his fist. But his eyes were the same cold stars Aimee had seen in the later memories. Still murderous. Still arrogant. And here they were unrestrained, their ravening hunger for violence satiated for the first time.

Aimee's fists tightened as she straightened, and revulsion built like bile at the back of her throat. The presence of the man was a disgusting taste sticking to the air.

The woman's eyes, for all their pain, were defiant in a way that mirrored her adult son's.

"I always wondered," Roland snarled, "what madness drove you from the city that adored you. The lights. The fine china, the *parties*. Theliana, the belle of New Corinth. Princess. Vanished like smoke. Now I know. To think, with all you might have had, *this* was all it took." A spiteful hatred danced in his eyes as he circled her. "Were you happy, in this wretched hovel? Were songs and gardens all it ever *really* took?"

The iron in the woman's voice arrested Aimee where she stood, and the defiance evident on Theliana's face filled her heart with a fire. Even beaten upon the ground, she was the strongest presence in the room.

"You might have sung a thousand songs," Theliana said, and her voice made Roland recoil as if struck, "or owned a thousand castles. I refused you then. I refuse you now. Nothing could make you other than what you are, Ma–"

The back of Roland's gauntlet crashed into the side of her face. The big man seemed to momentarily lose his mind. "Do not say that name, *whore*. Don't you say it. Don't you *speak* it." On his knees, he clutched her face between armored fingers as he half-sobbed, half-screamed at her. "You have no grasp of what you gave up. What you might have had. You have denied me, but *you will not mock me!*"

Theliana spit into the dread lord's face. Roland lurched away, then screamed and raised his fist to strike her again.

The concussive blast of breaking magic tore through the room. Roland was knocked back and crashed into a broken chair. Theliana's eyes – defiant until now – snapped to the explosion's source, suddenly afraid. There, standing in the ashes of the dissipating illusion his mother had used to hide him, stood the little boy named Elias Leblanc.

"Elias," Theliana choked. "*Run.*"

Beside her, Aimee heard Azrael give a mangled cry.

Roland regained his feet. His eyes watched the boy with a predatory intensity. Elias looked frightened, but then Aimee saw what was in his hand. An old, notched sword taken from some peg on the wall beside a battered lute. It was too big for his hands, and he struggled to hold it up. The boy's eyes were tear-streaked and *angry.*

"Get away from my mother." The defiance was every ounce his mother's. Aimee's fingernails dug so hard into her fists that her palms hurt.

The vision began to warp as Roland moved forward, became more vast shadow than man. "So this," he whispered, "is what you were hiding. You had a son with him. A boy with the gift of Intuitive Arcanism."

The woman forced herself up on one arm, fighting the agony of her wounds. Aimee somehow knew what was coming, but that didn't stop her from silently begging the memory to play out a different way.

"And your spell of secrecy couldn't even hide him," Roland said. "I think I've found a form of revenge even better than killing you."

The boy rushed forward at the same time that his mother forced herself up. Her eyes *flared* with light, and she clutched at a charm about her neck. A blast of power, a perfectly crafted killing spell, bloomed from her hand.

Roland twisted. The speed Aimee had seen Azrael use several times now saved his life. The blast tore a hole through the roof. Masonry fell downwards. Aimee reflexively dodged. Elias lunged forward. His sword slammed uselessly against the armor on Roland's legs. Growling, the future dread lord backhanded the boy and drove his own sword down through Theliana's neck. Her cry cut short, her bright eyes stared into her son's as her mouth moved soundlessly, forming a word Aimee couldn't understand. Blood frothed at her lips.

Roland's free arm seized the six year-old boy around the middle as he struggled, kicked, fought. "Come, boy," Roland snarled, a mixture of grief, disgust, and hate upon his face as he straightened over the woman's corpse. "You're *mine*, now, and you will be my monument in blood to *everything* that I was denied."

Flames spewed from Roland's fingertips, consuming the cottage, the tapestries, the white roses in the gardens. The furniture, and the body that lay within. Elias screamed as his captor carried him out and into the shadows. The cry deepened, matured, rose in volume and in pain, until it roared up from the depths of the soul of the adult man who stood beside Aimee. He fell to his knees, cast his eyes to heaven, and screamed in defiance, grief, and rage, at the truth burning all the lies away.

The last vestiges of glass enchantment surrounding the black knight fell away, and *shattered*.

Aimee's eyes snapped open. They were in the cavern again, and Harkon was shouting her name. Less than a second had passed. The racking pain of the memories ripped through her, and she found that her fingers were still clenched.

Azrael was opposite her. Both their hands still held the Axiom Diamond. Then the black knight lurched backwards. One hand retracted as if burned. He clutched the side of his head, and he *screamed*. Harkon forced himself up, his hands weaving gestures that flowed with magic. "Get away from her!" he thundered. His hands flared with light, the opening gestures of the binding spell he'd taught her only hours earlier.

Aimee's mind was mush, her thoughts sludge. She tried to stand.

Suddenly Azrael moved, staggering, but still fast. The binding spell missed, and bands of light closed on nothing at all. The knight stumbled swiftly past her, clutching one side of his head with his left hand, his sword in his right. Harkon turned. Azrael was on the other side of her now. An animalistic cry of pain and anger tore loose from him as he teetered on the edge of the stone walkway and nearly tumbled into the water.

Harkon paused. Hesitated. Azrael stood mere feet from her. In a horrible flash, Aimee realized that she had no defensive spells readied. No weapon with which to defend herself. From where he stood, he could cut her head from her shoulders, and she couldn't stop him. There was no way out.

Checkmate.

Then their eyes met. The proud, arrogant knight's face wore a sick look that hovered on the edge of madness.

He stared at her. Then he *ran*. A spell of speed sparked halfway across the cavern as he fled, and he was gone.

"What…" Harkon breathed, leaning on the pedestal. "…What just happened?"

Slowly, Aimee realized that there was a weight still in her hand. She looked down, and stared through tear-clouded eyes into the soft, pulsing glow of the perfect jewel for which so much killing and dying had been done.

"… He fled," she managed, her voice thick and pained. "And he left the Axiom behind."

CHAPTER TWENTY-ONE
THE GOOD MAN'S FACE

Azrael *ran*. Armored feet pounded tunnel floor. The darkness blurred about him, and he found his way by sense, by a light source summoned into one hand. Jutting bits of rock barely missed his unprotected face. It hardly seemed to matter. No matter how hard he ran, how hard he pushed, how loud he screamed, the demons still gave chase. They still caught up.

His mother died before his eyes, over and over. Esric swam before his gaze, now a man, now a horror stitched together from discordant memories. And how many of *those* were real? He ran harder. Faster. Bits of identity fell away like paper on the wind. The laughable mockery that he was crumbled second by second.

Elias.

Azrael.

His armored left hand clutched at the side of his head. Freed of the powerful spells of mental conditioning, sensation and sensory feedback flooded into him, a cacophony of discordant sounds. His fingers dug into his skin until it hurt, and screaming, he burst forth from the cave, tripping, staggering to his knees before the spire of the ancient statue he'd passed before.

The dull blur through which he'd viewed the world was gone, and a lifetime stretched out fresh before him, crystalline in the perfection of its vision. His hands dropped to the dirt as he heaved forward. His mother's eyes burned back at him, even as Esric's repeated commands echoed in his skull. Robbed of their mystic compulsions, the healer's voice registered now only as violating whispers that had left patches of oily contamination on his mind: patches the Axiom had burned away, leaving something raw, red, and cauterized behind.

"Who was Elias?" he had asked his master.

"A boy you killed." Lord Roland had answered.

For the second time, he heaved back his head and screamed in rage and despair.

In his mind's eye, Roland drove the sword into his mother's neck, summoned a monster to violate him for the crime of remembering her, and a fiend to violate him again and again and again.

"Keep him functional, able to serve, keep him compliant, and obedient."

Functional.

Able to serve.

Compliant.

Obedient.

"My angel of death. My Azrael."

How many people had he murdered? How many lives had he ended? Port Providence burned in his mind. Collum's eyes died, and the prince's corpse fell away into the inferno. Innocents burned. Gray Falcon burned. Soldiers without number fell beneath his sword. The queen mother's eyes stared into his own. *"I see a monster, wearing a good man's face."*

Compliant.

Obedient.

Flames consumed the flowers in the cottage he and his mother had lived in. The walls crisped and burnt. The shadow loomed before the little boy with the sword in his hands.

Azrael rolled onto his back in the dirt, and stared into the pale blue sky.

All that he was was coming apart. As the pieces began to split, rip away from one another, he felt the abyss open beneath him. A void of oblivion beckoned, into which everything was being pulled. Personality, memory, everything teetered on the edge. *Mad*, he thought. *I am going mad.*

It would be so easy to simply let go, to slip into the yawning shadows. Forget. Even the name by which he had gone seemed laughable now. Azrael was a macabre facsimile of a person, stitched together by a demon's hand on a foundation of lies from the remains of a boy broken beyond repair. Cracks widened. The darkness beckoned.

Slip away.

Compliant.

Obedient.

Azrael's eyes closed. There was no undoing what he had done. There was no making it right. Collum. Port Providence. The queen mother.

The queen mother.

She was still alive – a prisoner on the *Iron Hulk*. Her and thousands of others, about to be hauled to the House of Nails to be sorted as slaves, women given to the inhuman techs aboard the *Hulk* for their appetites. The fragments of his soul trembled. The glass vibrated. An armored fist clenched against the dirt. Malfenshir would know that the mission had failed. He would use the Silent Scream. But in the face of that, what did he have?

"Elias, remember what I told you?"

"Noble and brave. Gentle and kind."

An armored right hand clenched about the hilt of Oath of Aurum. The blade felt warm at his touch. Its power thrummed in his grip. He couldn't make this right. He couldn't change what he had done. But he could prevent worse – by far – from happening. The lander... he could still make it to the lander. His power was not yet spent, and wells of strength lay within him that he could tap without fear of death.

It wasn't as if he expected to survive anyway.

The lips of his dying mother moved in his mind's eye. They formed a word.

Fight.

Elias's eyes opened, and the black knight rose.

The lander flashed through the sky. In the pilot's seat, Elias forced himself to swallow the last emergency healing draught. His hands trembled at the controls.

It had taken a day and a half to get here.

The explosion Bjorn had set off in the valley had damaged the craft, but it was still airworthy. He'd never been the finest skyfarer, and he was at best a middling pilot, but his target was large, easy to find at range, and getting inside would be a simple thing.

What happened next would be complicated. He forced nerves raked raw to steady themselves. The *Iron Hulk* loomed in the distance, visible through clouds as the mountain of death that it was. It took him a moment's assessment to realize what was different: it had moved further inland, nearly at full speed by the look of it, and had taken itself nearly double its distance upwards. Slowly, the fortress of stone and iron was rotating, and beneath the vast underbelly of its base, something immense and terrible glowed with a rhythmic light.

A shock of fear cut through Elias's chest. He had expected Malfenshir to use the Scream if he did not return in a matter of days, possibly weeks.

The monster had already begun the process. The black knight's breath quickened. His fingers fidgeted at the lander's controls, numbers running through his mind. How long did he have? He couldn't say. They had spoken of *how* to use it. He had an understanding of the theoretical concepts, but Elias had never actually used the weapon, nor witnessed it fired.

Given what he was seeing, he had a *day* at most. He hit the throttle and took the lander closer. The goal – he had to keep his mind fixed upon the goal. To succeed, he would have to slip in unnoticed, and that meant using one of the landing platforms not currently in use. He turned the lander in a slow arc. Escort ships took no notice. Outwardly, the hulk was a forest of ether-cannons, deterring anything that came close with apocalyptic overkill.

The truth was that behind the screen of weapons fire, it was ridiculously easy to put individuals on the surface of the fortress, provided they knew what they were doing. The black knight had commanded it, directed it in war and on its long journey from the House of Nails.

He knew *exactly* where to go. He guided the lander in past the reach of the guns. There was a platform just outside the prison block he sought. Landing gear hissed as the ship set down.

He waited, sitting in the empty quiet of the pilot's seat for a few terrified moments. A deafening silence pressed down upon him and drowned out everything but the pounding of his heart. There was no going back.

The next few minutes passed as if within a dream. He slipped through the platform doors like a shadow. Recollections of patrol patterns and security details ran through his head like clockwork. These were protocols he had put in place, that he had organized. They weren't *easy* to evade, but a discerning pause at the edge of one corner, soft footfalls down another cavernous hallway, and a few moments counting in his mind, waiting for the shift change, and he was outside the door he sought.

He faced the prison block where the queen mother and the other high value Port Providence prisoners were being kept. The doors normally required proper keys, but were enchanted to open without complaint for one of the seven knights of the order on the hulk, that they might be free to conduct their business with prisoners of their choosing at will. When the door opened, he was confronted with a dour-faced guard, holding a truncheon in his hands.

It was known that Azrael was gone. The guard's face registered a look of surprise. "My lord–" he started. Elias's foot kicked the door shut behind him. His hands snapped out. A spell for strength. He seized the guard by the face and broke his neck with a *crack*.

The body fell, and the black knight walked further into the prison block. Oath of Aurum slid free from its sheath. In their cells, warriors, nobles, and the handful of sorcerers imprisoned shrank back from his passage. The name and face of the invasion's leader was known to

all. He was the slayer of Prince Collum. The conqueror of
Gray Falcon. The destroyer of Port Providence.

Elias barely registered the looks of shock on their faces
as he walked down the line, cell by cell by cell, and used
the enchanted blade to cut every single lock in half. The
sword was warm in his hands now. It moved like a living
thing, slowly awakening. Elias didn't understand why,
and did not pretend to, but the way it sang in his fingers
was a small, welcome comfort.

They staggered out of their cells. Men. Women.
Capable, but unarmed. Some of them looked as though
they were contemplating attack. Others just stood back
and stared.

"There is an armory for the guards down one hallway
and through a door of oak and iron," he said. "The dead
man at the far end has the keys. Go two floors down, and
you will find where your other people are being held.
Get them to the landing bays, steal landers, and *flee.*"

He didn't wait to see if they would listen. Turning,
he kept walking, until he reached the room where the
queen mother was imprisoned. She didn't mark his
presence until he announced it. Oath of Aurum sheared
through the locking mechanism and dropped the handle
and a cluster of iron bars to the floor. The door swung
slowly open, and the old woman turned to look at him
in shock.

"What are you doing?" she demanded, unafraid.

"Freeing you," Elias answered. "Your people are
leaving. I would have you go with them."

Regal, composed, the old woman nonetheless wore
an expression of utter disbelief upon her face. For a
moment that stretched a painful eternity, her mouth
hung open.

"Majesty," Elias said at last. His voice was thick. Seeing her face, he could think only of the dying eyes of her grandson: the man that he had killed, with whose sword he now made her free. "You called me a monster. You were right."

His voice broke as he stepped aside, leaving ample room for her to pass. "Let me wear the good man's face. Get your people out while you still can."

Slowly, she walked through the door, past him, and paused in the hallway. Further down, people called her name in hushed voices, urging her to go, to hurry. Instead, she turned and looked up into the black knight's face. There was fear in her eyes, but also something else: empathy? Kindness? Elias couldn't begin to imagine how to process either. He reached for the proper response, but found nothing but a little boy whose mother was dead. He couldn't use that. It was as distant as the name he awkwardly wore.

"I don't understand," she said. "Why are you doing this?"

Elias closed his eyes in momentary frustration. "Highness, please," he begged. "I've been made to see things differently. There's no time for anything else."

"Come with me," the old woman said. Her eyes suggested her words surprised her as much as they surprised him.

The offer was like a knife to the heart. To be free. To live elsewhere, to know this person who supposedly knew more about him. It was more than he deserved. But there was no time. "No," he said. "I can't fix what I have done. There's no mending what I've broken. But there is *much* worse still coming. If there's a chance that I can prevent it, I have to try."

The queen mother's face flickered with the ghost of a sad smile. "Should you live, find me again, and I will tell you everything I think I know." Reaching up, she touched his face, and the man and boy within him closed their eyes. He bent his head, and felt her lips brush his brow. Then she stepped away, and the black knight straightened. "Were it not for the glow about the blade in your hands," she said, "I would doubt... But prophecies have been wrong before, or misunderstood."

Looking down, it only then registered with Elias that the blade in his hands was lit from within by a soft, white light tinged with pale gold. He didn't know what it meant, and there was no time to ask.

"Majesty," he said as she moved to rejoin the others. "My name is Elias Leblanc." His voice caught in his throat. "My mother was Theliana of New Corinth." The words petered out after he said them. "I just want *someone* to remember that."

She held his eyes, a flicker of recognition in her gaze, then spoke across the widening span between them, before she slipped out of the cell block with her people, her last words ringing in his mind.

"I will not forget, Elias."

CHAPTER TWENTY-TWO
GAMBLE MOST DESPERATE

Aimee had never been so glad to see the sun. Golden light washed over her face from a pale blue sky, suffusing her tired limbs with an energy she hadn't thought to feel again – not after everything she had seen.

As Harkon and Silas emerged into the daylight behind her, she felt a pang of guilt. Her teacher looked tired but resolute, the grime of cave dirt on his face doing nothing to dim the determination in his eyes. But Silas, by contrast, seemed barely stable. The old sage had been muttering to himself the entire walk back. Now his wide eyes stared around, hungrily searching the shadows. "Can't have gone far," he muttered under his breath. "Can't have gone far."

"Silas, he's *gone* by now," Harkon said. "Especially at the pace he was moving."

Aimee's fingers still held the coveted diamond, its glow fainter, but still pulsing like a fist-sized heartbeat in her hands. She still hadn't told either of them what she'd seen, only that it had been confusing and twisted, and that she *knew*, beyond a shadow of a doubt, that the man they called Azrael wouldn't be returning.

Inwardly, her own emotions were a potent mix of fear, empathy, and bitter anger that she should feel sympathy for a person who had committed so many heinous crimes. She had seen his life – all of it. Every torturous, painful moment he had been made to endure since the order took him by force and made him theirs.

No, she shook her head. *Azrael committed those crimes, and he was hardly a person at all. Elias… There aren't words for what was done to him.*

"We will find him," Silas rasped, turning in a circle in the clearing at the base of the weathered spire-statue. "When this is all come to an end, Prince Coulton will hunt him to the ends of all the Unclaimed. Port Providence will make a *flag* out of his skin."

"Lovely," Aimee muttered, searching the sky with her eyes. As hungry as she was to see daylight again, the wonder was wearing off. "We need to get back," she said. She didn't add the next part of what she was thinking – that if *Elysium* was still as they'd left it, there was next to no hope. "If we don't," she added, "we may never get out of here at all."

"What are you talking about?" Harkon said.

"He will *pay*," Silas was muttering to himself. "And pay and pay and pay and pay…"

Ignoring the sage and his fraying sanity, Aimee turned to her teacher. "Short version: when Azrael and I both touched the diamond, a battle of wills between us ensued."

"And you passed," Harkon said dismissively. "That's why he fled. I understand–"

"No," Aimee cut him off. "That's just it, you *don't*. He passed the test, and I failed. But the Axiom doesn't just yield up whatever truth you want to see when you pass its final test, it turns that truth on *you*, and shows you the truth about yourself. I saw… everything, his whole life, what they did to him, how he was manipulated, used, abused…" She shook her head, aware at once of the sage's eyes upon her, and the incredulous look on her teacher's face.

"Look," she pushed, straightening her back and fixing her gaze authoritatively on both men. She wasn't about to be dismissed. "I'm not telling you this to advocate for our former enemy, alright? But when I was in his head I *saw* things. He has a second-in-command named Malfenshir, who's in charge of that gigantic flying mountain they brought with them. Before they even came here, the two of them argued about whether or not to use a weapon that mountain has at its base, called the Silent Scream. It has the power to destroy this entire landmass. Azrael didn't want to use it, Malfenshir salivated at the thought. We have to find Prince Coulton and warn him, because with Azrael gone, Malfenshir is going to use that thing, and *everyone still living in this kingdom will die.*"

Silence hung thick between them. Aimee watched realization click into place behind her teacher's eyes, but it was Silas that spoke first, in the most inane way possible. "*Former* enemy?"

"Shut up," Harkon snapped at the sage. "Do you know how it works?" he asked her. "How to *stop* it?"

Aimee recalled the plans she'd seen in Elias's memories – why, *why* was she calling him that now? – and considered how complicated they were. After a moment's consideration she took a deep breath and blew it out, blowing strands of golden hair away from her face with a sigh. "I don't know. I mean yes, I remember the plans, but as to whether or not the thing can be

stopped... can Vant work on a metadrive that big? How
many pounds of explosives can you give me?"

Harkon stared at her for a moment, threw his head
back, and laughed uproariously. He didn't get to deliver a
full answer, because seconds later a rushing sound filled
their ears, growing in volume until it was deafening.
Casting their eyes to heaven, they watched as the sleek,
winged form of *Elysium* descended from the sky – flying
unhindered, flying free. Its wounds bandaged and its
body whole, the ship grew in their vision until it hovered
only a short distance above the apex of the spire.

Aimee had never seen anything half as beautiful in
her life. With a rumble, the bay door slid open, and a
rope ladder dropped down. Vlana's face appeared over
the lip of the ramp, grinning. "Staring is rude, you guys.
Get your asses up here."

There was, in that moment, no greater joy imaginable
than to be flying. No sooner was she up the ladder
than Aimee was embracing the shorter quartermaster,
laughing even as she wept, not having words at first for
the thanks, the sheer relief she felt to be alive, on a ship
that until moments before she had believed permanently
chained to the ground. With *Elysium* in the sky once
more, they had a chance, however slim.

When you were drowning, even the slightest breath
of air was to inhale the whole sky. "Get communications
up and running," Harkon said. Less than a minute after
they were aboard, and his orders were hurtling left and
right.

Aimee followed her teacher to the bridge, but Vlana
held her back. "Not yet," she said. "There's someone in
the infirmary who needs your help."

Heartbeats and footsteps later, she stood in the doorway of *Elysium*'s sickbay, staring at the massive, shallowly breathing frame of gray-haired Bjorn, a red-soaked bandage about his middle. He was pale, with bruises joining old scars all over his body, but there was a faint rise and fall to his chest. Alive.

Aimee rushed to the big man's side, looked him over and checked the hastily applied dressings.

"Between the three of us, we did the best we could," Vlana murmured. "It was a stab wound, and deep... Simple enough to sew, but who knows how long he was out there, floating in the river, or dragging himself through the wilds to reach us? If we didn't find you, what Azrael did to him..." Her voice burned incandescent with hate for just a moment, then the quartermaster let it go. "Can you save him?"

Aimee slowly undid the bindings, sucked in a breath at the ugliness of the wound beneath. She checked it. It wasn't perfect, but between the three of them, Clutch, Vant, and Vlana had done a decent enough job of making it survivable. She summoned her power and pressed her palms to the wound. "Come on, old dog," she breathed as the white light flared. "Your battles aren't done yet."

The wound closed. Bjorn breathed easier. Aimee sagged back. Relief mingled with pain somewhere far away in the back of her mind, but the revelations were piling up, and the need to keep her focus crushed other feelings back into some dark place where they wouldn't get in the way.

Her mother would have arched her stupid eyebrow and asked in that drawling aristocratic tone of hers if Aimee was *really* sure that this was the life that she wanted.

"Well," Vlana said. "Whatever else happens, it doesn't matter how little you've been with us. You're one of us now, Aimee de Laurent. And there's no going back."

Aimee looked at her friend, and felt the grin, and attendant tears, on her own face.

Without a doubt, the answer was *yes*.

They found Prince Coulton after a day and a half, on a battered ship of the line at the far edge of the Isle. Communication spells led them over mountains, valleys, and a handful of settlements before they rejoined the battered, pathetic remnants of Port Providence's fleet. Older-model gunships with their straight wings and battered ether-coils limped through the air alongside two badly damaged, spear-shaped frigates providing escort to the only thing approaching a capital ship that the kingdom had left.

After Land's Edge had fallen, Coulton and his advisors had fled here, rallied the remnants of their fleet, and now waited, preparing for something – she didn't know what.

Aimee didn't realize until they were disembarking from *Elysium* aboard the vast gundeck of Coulton's flagship just how badly damaged the vessel was. Half its ether-cannons were gone. Rudimentary patching hadn't even mended half the gaping blast holes and burn marks on the sleek, bird-shaped hull, and an entire section of the superstructure was a mangled mass of twisted metal and charred wood. There was a sort of painful irony in the fact that its roaring, leonine figurehead remained unscarred at the vessel's prow. It was an old ship, too. A design at least one generation out of current battlefield models.

It was honestly a miracle that the damn thing was flying at all. Aimee's feet stepped off *Elysium*'s ramp and onto the battered deck. The wind whirled about her, and she reflexively pulled her coat tighter. Two soldiers in familiar tartan livery approached. Aimee checked to see if either were ones she'd healed. Neither was.

"Harkon Bright," the first woman said to her teacher. "Come. The king and his advisors would speak with you immediately."

Silas pushed past them, his face a mask of implacable determination. "His grace needs to know," he said, "that that monster – Lord Azrael – is still free in our homeland, with Collum's sword clutched in his unworthy fist."

Aimee and Harkon exchanged a look as they followed. Vant and Vlana came in tow, with Clutch minding the ship. "That guy's lost his damn mind," Vant muttered.

The prince awaited them in a war-room draped with dissonant splendor. Gold fringe upon heavy velvet curtains glinted in the light from the glow-globes and candles. Medal-bedecked nobles resplendent in their tartans and capes clustered about a too-small table. Men and women wore equal arms and finery. Aimee swallowed. The expressions on their faces were like that of Silas: hungry, battered, humiliated, and above all, *angry*.

Sitting at the far end of the table, Coulton wore a golden crown, his slight shoulders draped in the robes of his office. His hands clutched the arms of his chair. His knuckles were white, and his fingers bore jeweled rings. His eyes sank into dark circles, and his face was both petulant and imperious.

"The third battle group of the Violet Imperium is coming," he said to them. "The Eternal Order and its

mountain fortress will be burned to ash, and my people
– my family – will be avenged. In return for your service,
you may wait here, with us, until they and their portal
shield are destroyed. When this happens, you will be
free to go."

"Highness–" Harkon started.

"The proper term of address," a noblewoman corrected
him, "is *majesty*. Coulton the Third has received his father's
crown, his coronation held in this ship's very chapel. Have
a care, Harkon Bright. You speak now to a king."

"A king," Harkon deadpanned. "Wonderful."

"Majesty," Aimee took a step forward. "We have
retrieved the Axiom, and with it I was granted a brief
glance into our enemy's mind. They have a weapon,
called the Silent Scream, in the base of their mountain.
They're going to use it to destroy the whole landmass
and everything on it."

The looks that spread across the assembled faces
were at first incredulous, but Aimee caught the sudden
apprehension as well, the fear that could only come from
her words confirming already extant suspicion.

"I believe," Silas said quietly beside the king, "that she
speaks the truth."

"Yesterday morning," a nobleman said, "our scouts
and sensors confirmed that their mountain fortress was
moving further inland. We braced for an attack, but
when it reached the center of the isle, it just... *stopped*.
Escorts surround it, but no further move has been made.
We assumed they were looking for a place of advantage
from which to fight the approaching battle group."

"The weapon can't simply be fired at a moment's
notice," Aimee confirmed. "They have to have the right
angle, and it has to have time to charge."

"Majesty, if the girl is right–" another noblewoman said.

"–She is," Harkon interjected.

"Then we cannot wait for our allies," Coulton murmured, and his head sank. Then he looked back and forth between Aimee and her teacher. "What, then, do you advise?"

"Attack," Harkon said bluntly. "With everything you have. It is desperate and perhaps foolhardy, but there is no other option available, and with their portal shield still up, nobody can flee."

"Days ago," Coulton's eyes flashed dangerously, "you made me swear *not* to fight."

"At risk then was your crown and lordship over this land," Harkon said. "Now the survival of everything on this isle is at stake."

Coulton's eyes stirred with something fierce, but he didn't argue further. "Go on, then," he said.

"While you provide a diversion," Harkon continued, "my crew will get inside, and stop the weapon before it can fire."

"Just two of us," Aimee said, bluntly. Even Harkon looked at her in surprise, this time. "I know its layout. I know where its metadrive is located, and–" she gestured at the engineer standing behind her "–I have a metadrive expert who can help me overload it."

"Aimee–" Harkon began.

"No," Aimee said with a shake of her head. "More than two of us and we will be seen. We will be caught. I can get him there, and protect him while he gets the job done. Any more and it gets too complicated and *Elysium* is too undercrewed. If we're going to do this, best it be two of us."

The boy king fixed them with a look somewhere between incredulousness, anger, and desperate hope. After a few costly seconds, he looked at Harkon. "Is this possible?"

Through his teeth, Aimee watched her teacher answer, "It is dangerous, but if my engineer agrees, I will not argue with him, or with my brave, *foolish* apprentice."

Aimee's smile pricked involuntarily at the corner of her mouth. As one, all eyes in the room turned to Vant.

The short, scowling engineer looked back and forth between Harkon and Aimee. "I'll have you know," he growled, "that I hate you both... but if she can get me in there, and watch my back?" He nodded, resigned. "Then yeah. I can do it."

She had botched her first portal, flown through a blockade, battled in the streets of Land's Edge, rescued a prince, secured a mythical relic, and borne witness to the soul of a broken enemy who perhaps – in the end – was no enemy at all. Still, it was hard for Aimee to keep her hands from shaking.

This would be Aimee's fourth battle in fewer weeks, she reflected. A simple goal: infiltrate the *Iron Hulk*. Overload and destroy its metadrive. Flee. She stood in her cabin, staring at her own tired, grime-smeared face in the mirror. She'd changed her usual long coat and traveling clothes out for borrowed field gear: a bodysuit under a set of form-fitting leathers enchanted for silence and durability. She tightened the buckles on her boots and tested her movement. Then she took a breath and let go of fear, of regret, of the nameless dread that she might never again see home. Then she walked out of her room.

They were cruising through the late afternoon sky, running at top speed, long departed from the fleet. The plan was brazenly simple: Coulton's ships would attack from the north while *Elysium* slipped up from below. They would land on one of the many abandoned platforms on the *Iron Hulk*'s exterior – this would have been impossible without all the information she'd retained from the Axiom encounter – and she and Vant would make for the inside while Harkon concealed the ship with his magic, until it was time to cut and run.

Now they were getting close. She made her way down the hallway to the loading bay. It was only a little while ago that she'd climbed up its ramp, bright-eyed and so eager for adventure that she hadn't much thought about what it might mean, what it might entail. Now she knew.

She blew out a breath, closed her eyes, and looked up at the ceiling. "Gods forgive me," she murmured out loud. "But I *love* it."

"Good," Vant muttered, walking into the room. The engineer wore light leathers, fingerless gloves, a bag of tools around his back, and a pair of metal bars hanging from his hips. Shock sticks. "Because this plan is unhinged and ridiculous, and at least *one* of us should be having fun."

A rumble echoed from without. It was hard to tell from within the cold, windowless confines of the main bay, but Aimee knew they were hurtling through the sky at incredible speeds.

"Two minutes," Clutch's voice echoed from the projection horns high over their heads. "You'll have to move *quick* when we touch down."

"How the hell can you remember the whole layout, anyway?" Vant asked.

Aimee thought of the shining diamond now being kept on the bridge. "Something about the Axiom," she finally said, voicing her suspicions out loud. "It's sentient. I... It's hard to explain, but it *wanted* me to remember these things, so it writes deep within you. I don't think I'll be able to forget what I saw in there–" She swallowed, the bloody hellscape of the black knight's mind still clear in her memory "–or that I *should*."

The ship veered. They heard blasts outside. The thrum of magic energy teased at Aimee's senses. She'd slept. She'd eaten. She'd done everything she could to restore herself. It was time to get moving. "Coming in!" Clutch's voice echoed over the tubes. There was the abrupt, shaking *thud* of landing gear hitting the deck.

The bay door slammed open. Aimee vaulted down the gangway, Vant at her back. They burst into the daylight, feet pounding on a deck long and flat and mercifully free of guards. Up ahead, the endless face of the mountain of death stretched eternally in every direction. Straight ahead was a door of wood and iron. She took off at a run, fingers dancing and voice hissing, summoning a shield spell to ward them both. As they charged, she stole a glance to the northern side: all around them was the vision of a gorgeous, cloud-thick sky in late afternoon, painted across with the flashing, explosive firestorm of two fleets of skyships battling in knife-fighting range. The air smelled of smoke and burnt oxygen, and in the heartbeat span of her glance, she watched one of Port Providence's green and black gunships drop out of the sky, torn to pieces by the mountain's vast guns.

They neared the door now. Vant at her heels. There wasn't time to unlock the thing. *Gestures summon, words release.* She summoned a spell of concussive force, added motions to focus and narrow it, aimed it at the lock, and released the magic with a single, powerful word. There was a small burst and the sound of rending metal, and the door swung open. They careened into an empty hallway. In one direction, Aimee heard distant shouts and footfalls, the sounds of fighting below. Someone was screaming: "The prisoners are loose! The prisoners are loose!"

"Hey," Vant said. "It's a stroke of luck. I'll take it. Where now?"

Memories of plans, of directions left by the Axiom flashed through her mind. It just took a few seconds to orient herself, then Aimee gestured left. "This way. There's an access shaft. It's used to vent excess heat, but if they're charging up to fire the Scream–"

"It won't be used right now," Vant said. "Dangerous, but the best bet. Lead on."

The shaft seemed to go on forever. It bypassed floors, boring straight through the rock. Despite the downward slope, a combination of gravity enchantments gave the sense of only a gradual decline. Once they slipped in through a hatch in the floor, they found themselves on the relatively even surface of a tunnel so immense that the ceiling was hard to see. They moved at a jog, trying not to burn themselves out, horribly cognizant of the rhythmic echo of their footsteps through the vast space.

Twice, they evaded what appeared to be men making their way at a clipped pace through the same tunnel. Twice, their attempts to hide themselves turned out to be unnecessary: not only were the individuals content to ignore them, they barely seemed human at all. Solid metallic eyes stared from gaunt, hairless heads, and words were exchanged between them in low, buzzing tones and clicks.

Gradually a dull red glow grew ahead of them, a second sunset that filled the far end of the chamber. Closer, they started to feel a tangible heat. "That," Vant breathed, "is one *hell* of a metadrive." Her companion kept pace with her, sweat on his face and a serious, determined look in his eyes. "You were right," he continued. "I know these things, scaled up or scaled down. I was working on drives when I was *seven*. They're pulling every ounce of its power inward."

His eyes got a haunted look in them. "And that... that is a *lot* of power."

Aimee nodded. She felt it herself. The raw magic energy teased at her senses with the promise of everything – virtuous and vile – that could be done with it.

Another hatch loomed up ahead. If they followed the venting tunnel all the way to its source, they'd drop directly onto the surface of the core and die instantly. But this would put them into the chamber, and from there it was just a matter of finding the right control station.

Through the door, a small ladder led down. Then they dropped onto a catwalk stretching out through an incalculably *vast* space bathed in crimson light. Hot air blew around them, and Aimee had to take a moment to catch her breath so as not to collapse from dizziness. This place was so immense that every part of her was terrified. In the distance, more of those inhuman "techs" could be seen, taking readings, doing last-minute, incomprehensible work to vast machines.

Down below them, it loomed: a red sun surrounded by thousands of needle-like walkways. Here Vant crouched and pulled a spyglass from his pack. His moment's scanning allowed Aimee to get a good look around. She ran through her index of utility spells, things she could use to navigate this space, all the while fighting a nausea that churned in her stomach – from the vastness of the room, from the risk of what they were doing, from the incredible power that almost eliminated her ability to sense anything else.

"There," Vant murmured, pointing at a catwalk some two hundred feet down, the source of a hive's nest of wires and crystalline structures. "Can you get me down there?"

Aimee sucked in a breath and fought off a bout of dizziness. "Yeah. Hold on." She took Vant by the shoulder, stepped to the edge of the catwalk, and cast a spell to slow their descent before leaping into space. Holding on to her shoulder, Vant spat a steady stream of whispered curses the whole way down.

They were greeted by one of the techs. Its metallic eyes fixed upon them. Its hands raised, and Aimee started to say the words of her shield spell, but something else caught its attention. Its impenetrable gaze moved past them, and it did the last thing Aimee expected: it *fled*. The bizarre creature turned and dashed down an adjacent catwalk.

Aimee spun on her heel, raising her hands, a list of spells running through her mind, only to freeze in place as overwhelming panic surged through her at the sight of what approached.

A footstep. He was a man. Another. He was a man-shaped outline containing something pitch dark. Another. He was a creature of viscous, bubbling flesh. Eventually, the war between the illusion it projected and

Aimee's recollection from Elias's memories forced her to perceive it as something halfway between the two: a man of middling height and middle age, draped in healer's robes, with the calm demeanor of a physician, and solid, coal-black eyes spawning veins of night that split his face like a sickness.

On a catwalk over their heads, a figure in red armor appeared, a drawn, black sword in his hands. Aimee felt the cold in her gut tighten into a fist of ice. *Malfenshir.*

"So you're the one," Esric said, advancing, "who found the Axiom. I can *smell* it on you. You are *very* interesting."

"Do what you want to them, *healer,*" the red-armored knight sneered. "I'll watch."

Esric took a step forward. Aimee shoved Vant behind her and summoned a shield spell.

Then a blast of arcane light seared into the catwalk, and Esric leaped back, staggering. His image flickered, distorted for a moment as the monster was forced to choose between maintaining its illusion and protecting itself.

Aimee's eyes flashed right. On the catwalk above them, a figure approached. Black-armored, green-eyed, dark-haired, and melting from the shadows, his frame was illuminated by the faintly glowing sword in his hand. Silas's words echoed in her head.

"...a prince would come, who would restore it to glory with acts of courage and desperate virtue."

"Overload the drive," he called down to them. "It's minutes from firing. Overload it, and it will bring the whole mountain down."

Malfenshir turned on his heel, and Aimee detected in his voice the briefest hint of apprehension. "Lord

Azrael," he snarled. "So *there* you are."

The black knight stopped short, and fixed his eyes on his counterpart in red. "My name," he said, "is *Elias.*"

And the faint glow of Prince Collum's sword, clutched in the black knight's fist, blazed to an incandescent white.

CHAPTER TWENTY-THREE
THE FALLEN ANGEL

Elias stood on a narrow strip of metal, high above the apocalyptic radiance of a pulsing red sun. He tore his eyes away from Aimee, her ally, and Esric. He had done what he could, and now the inevitability that he had dreaded since long before he even touched the Axiom waited ahead: the lynchpin of a fate long avoided, but as inescapable as the oncoming storm.

Malfenshir.

They faced each other in silence. The winds generated by the pulsing metadrive roared around them, driving steam upwards in whirling pillars of white. Malfenshir stared for another second, then Elias saw a smirk form on the red knight's cruel face. Lights flashed below, as battle between Aimee and Esric was joined.

"When Esric told me about your *connection*, that he'd lost track of you, I didn't believe him," Malfenshir said. "Lord Roland's angel, insipid, sentimental coward that he was, knew loyalty, at least."

"Yet still you prepared," the black knight said.

"I disbelieved," Malfenshir said. "But I still *hoped*. Don't play, *Elias*–" he *spat* the name "–you've wanted this as long as I have."

Elias took his sword in both hands. The blade glowed with a blazing white light from within, so bright that it left after-flickers across his sight. Oath of Aurum flicked into a point guard, a perfect line of white in the center of his vision. Since he'd come to Port Providence, he'd been a man at war with himself, torn in conflict, rent with memories trying to claw their way up from a mind long beaten into submission.

But here and now, faced with the monstrous knight in red, his mind was clear. Elias smiled sadly. "I was just lost, Malfenshir," he said. "But here at the end, I will be what I should've been from the start."

Malfenshir's eyes blazed with hate, and he slipped into guard. The sound of his neck popping echoed across the space between them. "Don't you *dare* disappoint me, traitor."

A breath of silence hung between them for half a second, then both men summoned spells of speed, and *exploded* forward. In every battle thus far on Port Providence, Elias had fought opponents he vastly outpaced, and had fought without the aid of magic only twice. Against Collum it had been for arrogance, honor, and the joy of the challenge. Against Bjorn it had been circumstance.

Now he faced a foe who was his equal in skill *and* in power, armored in enchanted steel that didn't slow him, and moving with a strength and a speed that could rend metal and pulverize stone. There was no time for fear, for hesitation, for doubt. Stripped of the identity foisted upon him, Elias hardly knew who he was. But he knew precisely *what*: a weapon, among the finest in the world, skilled above all else at ending lives. And here and now, a weapon was precisely what was needed. He let go of everything but the moment, and sank into the raging surge of violence.

They crashed together. The blades shrieked and skipped apart. Elias went for the high thrust; Malfenshir offset and countered. Faster than normal eyes could follow, they separated. Sparks crackled across the floor in the wake of their collision. A breath, and this time Elias hammered forwards. The swords flashed, white and black, in the red glow of the chamber. Bind and thrust, counter and wind, their speed increased. The ringing of their blades was the rapid scream of discordant bells.

Then Elias feinted left. Malfenshir took the bait, and the black knight hammered in at his opening. The white sword cut across from right to left, a blow that would have split stone. Malfenshir's sword was there, blocking, but at a price. The force of the blow blasted him through the flimsy rails and sent him hurtling into the open air.

Laughing, the monster in red turned the fall into a leap, and sent a lightning spell tearing upwards. Oath of Aurum danced in Elias's hands and caught the brunt of the force on the flat of the blade. Gritting his teeth, he willed the energy to lance off and away from him. It crackled into a power conduit. Clouds of billowing smoke spewed into the air between them.

Elias crouched, summoned his magic, and dropped through the fog. Halfway down, a shearing black blade rose to meet him.

They met mid-air. The blades sounded a scream of crackling enchantments smashing against one another. Edges caught, the bind existed for a fraction of a second. Elias leveraged it as they fell and wrenched Malfenshir's sword aside as he tried to cut his head from his shoulders.

The red knight's head jerked back and he pushed out. Instead Oath of Aurum's point traced a line of red across his forehead.

Malfenshir's eyes bulged with hate. His left hand snapped up and flickered with arcane fire. Point-blank range – Elias saw it coming, brought his own left hand up in mirror image. They loosed their spells at the same second, and a blast of concussive force sent them hurtling away from each other.

The black knight barely slowed his descent enough to turn a flesh-pasting slam into an impact on a nearby platform that drove the breath from his lungs. He kept his hand on his sword, rolled up gasping for breath, and cast about to get his bearings. He was hundreds of feet from where they'd started.

An incomprehensible duel unfolded far away near the control platform. He thought he caught a glimpse of the engineer Aimee had brought with her, crouched at the controls.

Then Malfenshir was upon him. A second lightning bolt blasted across the platform on which he stood, electrifying the metal. Elias leaped up, letting the jolt pass beneath him, and loosed a bolt of his own. Malfenshir barely sidestepped.

"It was *you* that freed the prisoners," the red knight snarled. He was breathing hard now, though more with excitement than exertion. "Just like you killed a perfectly useful acolyte for the sake of one stupid, worthless palace boy."

"I did," Elias answered. "I would again."

Malfenshir's shoulders shook with rage as Elias watched, an uncomprehending, terrible, spiteful fury. "Gods… You've proven my every suspicion true. And yet *you* were the one deemed so *worthy* to lead this mission, you who choke in the face of hard choices. You who shirk true violence, and put the lives of your enemies above your own brothers." Malfenshir's face twisted into a hateful mask as he screamed. "And now you fight me, for *what?* To defend the wretches seeking to destroy us all? For the sake of degenerates little better than worms in the ground? You won't walk away from this, *Elias.* There is no peace awaiting you."

Elias met his old ally's eyes with a level stare. "I don't need to walk away," he answered. "You don't understand, Malfenshir. I need neither respite, nor forgiveness. I need only live long enough to kill you."

The white sword blazed incandescent, and for the first time since Elias had known the monster in red, Malfenshir looked *afraid.*

Elias surged forward. The first principle of his art: the one who struck first dictated the terms of the fight. Malfenshir barely made his parry, and staggered backwards. Elias breathed out his fear, and gave himself to the whirling chaos of the duel.

At speed, they blazed across the platform, driving at one another through the thick fog of smoke loosed by the fires their conflict had started. Malfenshir leaped to another platform; Elias followed. Catwalks were cut in half by missed strikes. Spellfire tore railings into mangled masses of melted metal. They tore apart, clashed together, and drove one another back. Blows landed. Elias bled from five different places where Malfenshir's sword slipped past his defenses. Light wounds, but adding up. A strap on his armor had been severed; his breastplate was loose. He fought on.

The teachings of Lord Roland rang through his mind.

His duel with Prince Collum, with Bjorn, both at much slower speeds, let their lessons flow through his limbs. Elias cut and cut again, wounded, thrust, mutated and chased. Ever he drew nearer the red monster's center. Malfenshir, more blur than man, viciously attacked in response, and strove with all his might to regain initiative. Oath of Aurum danced in Elias's hands, blunted him at every turn, cut off his paths of egress, and forced him to fall back or die. The space between them narrowed, and Elias pushed into it – occupied it – fought to forbid any advance into any space his blade threatened. Moving thus, sword and man in perfect harmony, it seemed that his glowing white steel was everywhere at once.

Malfenshir sweated, now only one of every three of his furious strokes threatening. He retreated and lashed across open space. Then he vaulted clear and slid into a defensive stance as Elias pursued, and loosed a furious bolt of spellfire – not at Elias, but at the platform where Vant worked at the metadrive controls.

No.

Elias was quick enough, barely, to change direction. He lunged into the air, kicked off another catwalk mid-leap, and surged into the path of the spell. Oath of Aurum desperately lashed out to block as it had so many times before.

Sword and spell connected. The force nearly drove the weapon from the black knight's hands. Elias crashed into the catwalk. His shoulder hammered into the metal. Pain exploded through his upper body. The spell flickered into the distance as he forced himself upward, trying to regain his orientation.

White hot agony burned through his center of mass as Malfenshir's black sword found the opening made by his loosened armor and punched straight through the left side of Elias's gut. Control evaporated. Spells collapsed. He tasted blood on his tongue, then the black knight opened his mouth and screamed.

"This is the finish," Malfenshir laughed. The red knight's blunt, cruel face swam in Elias's vision as he twisted the blade. Muscle fiber shredded and blood bubbled down over the armor on his legs. Numbness started to spread through his body. Elias's right leg collapsed under him. Blood loss. Malfenshir stood over him now.

"Don't fight it, traitor," the monster whispered. "We both know this was how it was always going to end. Join the weak and degenerate. Die with them."

Elias clenched red-stained teeth. *Just one more push. Just one more.* His sword was low, still held in both hands. He looked up into Malfenshir's face, then his left hand shot up and grabbed his enemy by his pauldron. The red knight's armor was tight, but with Oath of Aurum, it didn't matter. With a defiant scream, Elias's hips snapped forward, and with his right hand, he drove the white sword upwards, ramming it through Malfenshir's chest plate, ribs, and lungs. The point of the glowing blade burst out the backplate, just below the base of the monster's neck.

"I told you," Elias whispered. "I just need to live long enough to *kill you*."

Malfenshir's eyes bulged. The cruel face contorted. He opened his mouth to speak and choked on a red froth. He let go of his own sword with one hand, and clawed ineffectually at his throat. The red knight stumbled backwards, slid off the white sword, and fell to his knees at the edge of the catwalk. He leveled a hateful finger as if to cast a final spell.

Then, as Elias watched, Malfenshir collapsed, and didn't rise again.

The black knight sank to his knees, pulled Malfenshir's sword from his body. It would make everything worse, hasten the end, but that wasn't so bad. Not truly.

The metadrive core pulsed and twisted. Its red light flashed in shades of blue and purple. He didn't know what that meant, but he knew that he had tried. The darkness closed in. Malfenshir was dead. There was no walking away.

The memory of his mother flashed through his mind: smiling, laughing, beckoning a boy with green eyes to run across the grass in a peaceful orchard kissed by sunlight.

Noble and brave. Gentle and kind.

He saw her lips move as she died on Roland's sword. Her mouth formed a word.

Fight.

It had taken him sixteen years of darkness and ignorance, but in the end, he had remembered. Elias would slip into oblivion with the memory of the one person that had loved him on his lips, and the precious knowledge of his own name. As far as deaths went, this one wasn't bad.

"Mother," he whispered. "I'm free."

A smile spread across his numbing face, and he fell onto the catwalk. The white sword clattered on the steel. The warm sound of his own laughter echoed in his ears as his eyes closed, then the darkness took him.

CHAPTER TWENTY-FOUR
PORTALMAGE

In the heart of the *Iron Hulk*, mere feet away from the control station of the blazing metadrive, Aimee de Laurent faced a demon and fought for her life. She was no stranger to duels of sorcery. Back in the academy, she had faced her fellow students across the hall, waited for the thunderclap to signal the start. She'd confronted her juniors, her seniors, and even a guest lecturer she'd managed to offend.

The monster called Esric was something else entirely. The crackling light of her first offensive spell faded away, and the *thing* stood unfazed, an arm still in the position of the counterspell. Its form, its positioning, everything was *perfect*.

"Fascinating command of Combative Principles, for one so *young*," it said, and Aimee realized that it wasn't actually addressing her. Its voice sounded warped and twisted, now deep and cavernous, now man-like, as it continued. "Specimen is capable, aggressive, assertive, and well-practiced in traditional forms of sorcery." A twisted smile passed across its face. "It is also very, *very* afraid. We will study."

It raised a hand, and a mass of silver spines formed from its body before they blasted towards her. Aimee stepped back, swept her hands into a defensive form, and slapped them away with a gust of mystic wind. One slipped through and stuck in her leathers.

Once when she was a little girl, she'd put her finger into the standing flame of a candle on her mother's desk. The pain had made her scream. This was worse, and it was *everywhere*. Esric stepped forward. A hand reached out to grab her. Aimee's hands sliced through a second defensive form, deflected the gesture and loosed blazing flames into its center of mass. This time it warped itself, changing shape to avoid the point-blank spell. It didn't entirely succeed, and Aimee heard a high-pitched, keening shriek rip out of the creature as it was hurt.

Then its palm struck her in the center of the chest. Aimee hurtled back across the platform. In the half-second it touched her, she saw a flash of her own memories ripped forth from her mind against her will. Havensreach. Her parents. The academy. Her first boyfriend. The gull pup she'd played with on her seventh birthday. The day her friend Rachelle had fallen off the edge of the Isle. The voice of Esric was in her head, toxic, grave-like.

"Fascinating recollection. Such unique individuals, experiences. A location, fascinating. A name: Havensreach. Added to lists."

It approached. Vant turned from his work at the controls and let out a scream of horror as he caught sight of what was coming.

Aimee shook off the fugue. The damage done by her initial spell was already sealed. She forced herself up. Her fingers sliced through adapted offensive forms, compounding incantations. Words flowed from her lips, and a barrage of killing spells ripped out at the advancing monster. *Gods*, it was fast. Limbs flowed like water, deflected, counterspelled, dismissed. Only one in every three struck home, and Aimee watched as right in front of her eyes, each wound closed in less than seconds.

The *thing* was healing itself faster than she could hurt it.

She threw up a shield spell between them, walling off the entire far end of the platform. She put her hands forward, poured every ounce of power and strength she had into maintaining it. Her gestures widened and intensified. Twice the thickness. Twice the size. "Vant!" she screamed to the engineer behind her. "How's it coming?"

"Working on it!" Vant snapped back. A pulse of energy vibrated at the edge of Aimee's senses, just as when she'd stood upon the portal dais. The engineer gave a cry of elation. "The containment field is down! Just a few more seconds!"

The thing called Esric reached the boundary of Aimee's defensive barrier. It stopped, and considered. "Skillful," it said. "But we are tired of play. Now you will *come* to us, and *comply*."

The sheer force of its command *slammed* into Aimee's mind, so hard that her hands almost dropped. At the same moment her senses were nearly overwhelmed by the raw power of the metadrive as the containment field that kept its power in check was deactivated.

Esric extended a hand. A powerful, dizzying spell pulled Aimee through the air towards grasping claws of shadow. Panic seized her. Her boots dragged across the floor as she fought to stand her ground. For all her knowledge and skill, this thing was out of her league.

A sudden realization. A mad idea… no it *wasn't*. She *did* have a spell for this. She had no dais, no lenses. No navigation formula to help her, nor her mentor's assistance to save her at the last second. She couldn't make it stable. But that was the beauty of it: it didn't *need* to be stable.

Time to *adapt*.

Aimee's boots shrieked across the floor as the monster pulled her towards it. She summoned the words and gestures into her mind, mentally adjusted the spell to scale.

"… What is it doing?" The thing called Esric looked confused.

The portalmage answered through gritted teeth. "Learning *quickly*."

The first prime: Magic wanted to be used.

Aimee dropped her shield.

The second prime: Gestures summoned, words released.

Hands in first position.

Aimee's hands rose, trailing blue fire. Pale runes danced in the air. The coordinates burned in her mind. Random numbers. The end result didn't matter. Her left hand snapped out, summoned as much raw magic from the churning red sun of the coruscating metadrive as she could, wrenched it into her spell with a scream of effort.

The third prime: Things did not always happen as men understood they should.

She stared the monster in the eyes. "Go back to the abyss that spawned you, you monstrous *fiend.*"

Aimee's palms crashed together, and the words of the spell thundered from her lips. A line of brilliant blue light blasted Esric full in the chest, and the monster *howled* as a portal blasted open in the middle of his center of mass. It slashed outwards and upwards as Aimee held forth both hands. An iridescent line of blue flame connected her to the dimensional aperture shredding the monster apart. Esric became a man, became a silhouette, then something else altogether, a slimy, black mass of ichorous flesh riddled with pale lights. Aimee flexed her fingers, wrenched the portal wider, ripped the monster called Esric into a thousand pieces, and blasted them into the void.

With a tremendous act of will, she pulled her hands apart, slammed them together again, and killed the spell with a concussive *bang*. Her knees collapsed to the platform. Aimee's blood pounded in her ears, and her heart hammered in her chest as the raw power of the metadrive she'd drawn upon sizzled out in her veins. She'd done it.

Vant pulled her up by the arm. Behind them, the metadrive pulsed and flickered, unconfined, overloading. "That was amazing, Miss Laurent, but it's *time to go!*"

Aimee got to her feet unsteadily, her head clearing as the excess energy faded from her system. Dimly, she was aware of the fact that what she'd just done – drawing upon the magic energy of a functioning metadrive of that size to weaponize an unstable portal – had never been recorded before. "It's done?" she asked.

"Yeah," Vant said, grabbing his bag. "And with that *thing* gone, and that killer in red elsewhere, we might just be able to cut and run. Come on!"

Aimee looked about, against inclination, against the tug of fear. Perhaps she just wanted to be sure that Malfenshir was *dead*. That was what she told herself as she turned, putting a hand on the edge of the platform railing to steady herself. Then she saw them, further down the same catwalk on which they now stood. Two bodies. One armored in black, one red.

Aimee's impulse took over and she charged towards where the two men lay.

Elias.

"Aimee!" Vant shouted after her. "*Wait!*"

She skidded to a stop on her knees in between the two bodies. Malfenshir lay on his side, sightless eyes staring into nothing, blood frothed down the lower half of his face.

Elias lay on his back. His face was pale. His eyes were closed.

Shaking, she checked him. Illogical relief flooded through her. He was breathing. It was shallow, faint, but it was there. It didn't take long to find the wound: through the right side of the abdomen. Vant jogged up behind her now. She did the preliminary check. It was… Gods, it was *bad.* He'd lost a lot of blood. She couldn't fix this here. But she could do a temporary staunch to keep him alive.

Aimee pressed her hands to the wound, calling up her healing spell. "A few days ago I hated you and wanted you dead," she whispered in an urgent tone that unnerved even her. "Now I know there's so much more to your mind than just the monster they made you. Now get your shit together, Elias. Don't you *dare* give your old masters – or the person I was just a few days ago – what they want. Don't you *dare* die on me."

Soft white light flared from her touch. The wound closed. The man's breathing eased.

"Aimee," Vant said behind her, "what the *hell* are you doing?"

She reeled on him. "Returning a favor." She pried the magic sword from the unconscious man's grasp and shoved it through her own belt. "Now grab an arm. We're taking him with us."

Vant jammed one of his shock sticks into the control panel of the station. He growled, "Fix that, jackasses."

They hauled Elias through the tunnel by which they'd entered. Conduits exploded. Flames belched from trapdoors. Techs fled and mercenaries ran. Cries that the mountain was dropping out of the sky echoed around them. Fear that *Elysium* would be a blasted, twisted ruin upon the deck when they returned, seized her, gave her the energy to keep going. They passed the signs of what looked like a prison riot when they came out of the tunnel.

Then they burst out through the door and onto the landing platform, and emerged into a blazing sunset presiding over an apocalyptic sight of battling skycraft. The deck tilted violently, and Aimee felt her stomach leap into her throat as she realized that the *Iron Hulk* was, indeed, starting to drop out of the sky.

Elysium's bay door was down. Vlana stood there, screaming something incomprehensible. They ran, drag-pulling the unconscious man behind them. Her footfalls pounded up the ramp, and then they were inside. Aimee registered the hiss of closing locks, and the cracking blasts of dying ships dulled to muffled thumps.

"Are you alright?" Vlana asked.

"I'm good," Aimee answered. "We need to get him to the infirmary–" she started hauling the still-unconscious form of their dragged former enemy "–and get his wound bandaged up. Now!"

Vlana belatedly recognized who it was they were carrying. She'd never actually met him before, but a glance across the detailing on the bloodstained black-and-gold armor summoned a look of pure hate that Aimee knew all too well.

"What," Vlana hissed, "is *he* doing here?"

"Beats me," Vant grunted, "but he saved our lives, so we're returning the favor."

Vlana bit her lip so hard it looked like she might draw her own blood, then finally nodded. "Fine. Get him in there, then get up to the bridge. I'll... do my best to explain."

They hauled him to the infirmary. Aimee felt *Elysium* lifting off into the sky as she and Vant put the pale knight down on the bunk opposite Bjorn. Dull explosions echoed in the distance, muffled thumps that made the floor tremble and the lights flicker. She checked his wounds again. He was stable. She'd have to do more work later, but for now... She glanced briefly at the other bed where Bjorn lay, likewise sleeping. Then she dashed down the long hallway towards the bridge.

She just hoped neither of them woke up before she got back.

When she vaulted through the bridge door, she was confronted by the sight of Clutch gripping the wheel, steering the ship through a hailstorm of weaponsfire. They were back amidst the Port Providence ships now, themselves being shredded and in retreat. *Elysium* turned in a long arc, and as Aimee watched, the *Iron Hulk* dropped ever lower towards the continent below. The ground beneath was a churning mass of wrecked earth.

The Scream had already *started* before they'd managed to overload the drive. Now the underside of the massive mountain sputtered and flashed with destabilizing explosions. Gouts of flame and bursts of light tore outward from its faces, and a swarm of escape craft flooded outwards in all directions.

But what held her attention was a spell-projection of Prince – no, she reminded herself, *King* Coulton standing in the center of the bridge. "They are breaking," he was saying. "Their frigates are falling back as the fortress falls. Return to my command ship."

The command was *jarring*. Vlana's eyes widened. Clutch gritted her teeth. Only Harkon's face was impassive in the face of the king's orders. "I remind you, majesty," he said, "that my crew and I are *not* your subjects."

"But you carry *our* property," Coulton snapped back. "The Axiom comes from Port Providence, which makes it *ours*, and–" He seemed to see Aimee for the first time. Dammit. She must have stepped into range of the spell, visible like her teacher was. Then the realization hit her: Coulton wasn't looking at her face, but at her belt.

She'd forgotten to remove Oath of Aurum from her person. Coulton's eyes bulged with anger. "And that sword is *mine*. How did you get it? Is Azrael dead? Have you killed him? Did you take him prisoner? *Turn him over at once!*"

Aimee looked at her teacher. Harkon seemed to read her face in a second. His eyes widened. "You didn't…"

"Run," Aimee pleaded. "We can't turn him over to them. We have to *run*."

"Hey *guys!*" Clutch snapped from the helm. "Got Port Providence guns turning towards *us* now. A decision would be *great!"*

"If you do this," Coulton's projected image threatened, "you will make an enemy of my entire kingdom. My people will *hunt* you, and no matter how far you go, we will *find* you, and reclaim what you have taken from us!"

"Hark," Vlana breathed, afraid.

The old mage's eyes flashed, and for a moment everything hung in the balance. Aimee held her breath.

"I trust my apprentice's judgment more than that of any king, your majesty," Harkon answered. "Our business is concluded. As for catching us–" a small smile pricked at the corner of his mouth "–you're certainly welcome to *try."*

He waved his hand, and the furious visage of King Coulton vanished.

"Clutch," Harkon said. "I assume the portal shield is down?"

"It vanished when their metadrive started malfunctioning," the pilot confirmed.

"Then get us to portal distance as fast as you can," the old mage answered. "We're *running."*

The ship surged forward, lanced away from land, from battle, from forsaken allies and hated enemies, like a bolt of lightning, and Aimee braced herself, clutched a railing as clouds and ruined ships flooded by the viewport. For all the peril and danger, the havoc blazing through the golden-purple sunset about them, a feeling of mingled relief and exultation flooded through her, heightening her senses and stamping the moment into memory. They were going to make it. They were going to escape.

Then she heard her teacher, and her heart froze in her chest. "Aimee, Vant told me about what happened. Get up to the top deck; you're opening the portal," Harkon said. "My arm's still not up to the task."

Aimee reeled, her eyes wide, her throat dry. "Sir," she started. "I... What I did in the hulk was a last minute solution. It wasn't *stable*, I had a wealth of loosed energy to draw on." An explosion burst near *Elysium*. The ship trembled. "The last time I did this, I nearly killed us all."

"No," Clutch said, not turning from behind the wheel. "You didn't. While we were down, Vlana and I discovered that the dais had been tampered with. *Someone* back in Havensreach tried to kill us, and they nearly succeeded. But it wasn't you. In fact, if you hadn't done as well as you *did*, we'd have all been blown straight to the abyss before we even got here."

The pilot looked over her shoulder at Aimee, her eyes fierce in her dark face. "We fixed it. Now get back up on that dais, portalmage, and *do your job*."

Aimee ran to her duty, heart in her throat. Her mind told her that she shouldn't fear. There hadn't even been time for the revelation to sink in. She raced up the stairs as the ship bucked and swayed and maneuvered out of the path of long range batteries. She caught a glimpse out of the side viewport of Port Providence, floating suspended in an endless sky as the large, mountain-sized fortress – now a small lump against the vastness of her interior – plummeted through the air. Ships were flickering bursts of light.

She surged onto the portal deck. The lenses lowered from above. Harkon caught her by the arm, helped her onto the dais. They exchanged a brief look. He nodded.

Aimee called to mind the coordinates for their original destination, still burnt into her memory by weeks spent mulling over what she'd thought had been her greatest failure, and what had, in truth, been her greatest success. She was tired, battered by battle and mental strain, but as she stared into the sunlit skies with their infinite possibilities, her heart soared and her hands tingled with the magic. More than ever before, she knew without doubt or fear that *this* was the life for which she was meant.

She pictured the destination, pictured Ishtier, as blue fire trailed about her flashing hands and runes danced in the air. Then Aimee aimed the spell through the amplification lenses, put forth her power, and spoke the words that split the sky in half.

A brilliant portal ripped open, a gossamer eye of coruscating magic, gleaming perfect and immense in the space before the rushing skycraft called *Elysium*. Ringed with gold, filled with purples, blues, greens, and every color she could have imagined, it stood before them, stable and true, with the shimmering light of another place on the other side.

She was aware of commands being shouted around her, of the deck thrumming as *Elysium* gunned its engines. She heard Clutch give a defiant, victorious cry as her creation swelled in the viewport, then felt the gut-churning alteration of space and time as their ship lanced through the portal she'd opened, and maintained: a celestial arrow trailing golden fire.

They shot out the other side, into a strange, quiet sky filled with soft clouds. She brought her hands together, ended the magic. The portal closed behind them.

Vlana and Clutch embraced below. Over the tube, Aimee heard Vant laughing. She sagged against the railing on the upper deck as lenses retracted and the dais ceased its soft glow. Then turning, the apprentice raised tear-streaked eyes and a smiling face to look at her teacher. Harkon Bright's tired, worn face cracked in a relieved, warm smile, and she felt his hand come to rest on her shoulder.

"Congratulations, Aimee," the old mage said, the corners of his eyes wet. "Well done."

CHAPTER TWENTY-FIVE
INTO THE INFINITE SKY

Elias awoke in a warm bed. His eyes opened and saw a ceiling illuminated by the dim radiance of glow-globes suspended in the air. The only noise was that of his own rhythmic breathing. He blinked several times. He was no longer armored, but was dressed in basic shipboard fatigues. The wound in his abdomen ached, but he also recognized the faint tinge of healing magic. It set his heart pounding. Esric. No. He'd been taken again. He tried to surge upwards, but it proved a mistake. A sharp pain spasmed through his upper body, and he closed his eyes, wincing.

"I wouldn't advise that," a male voice said. "You still aren't well."

Elias turned, aware now of the distant thrum of a metadrive. His senses recognized its mystic aroma as a man born to storms knew the scent of coming rain. The next thing he sensed was the powerful, *shimmering* magic presence beside him, its source evident as he found himself meeting the reserved, level gaze of Harkon Bright. The old sorcerer looked tired, his hair was silver, and his dark face was lined. But there was a resolute, incredible power within him, radiating from his calm, relaxed posture in waves.

Azrael had gotten *lucky* when he'd managed to wound the old man.

Elias leaned back against the wall. One hand probed the bandage that wrapped his middle. The wound beneath was still tender, but it was healed. "Where am I?" he croaked, throat dry.

"Aboard my ship, *Elysium,*" Harkon allowed. "Far away, now, from Port Providence and your friends."

Elias closed his eyes, ran his hands across his face. There was a dark irony, if ever he'd heard one. It likely didn't help his case, but he couldn't contain the rueful, bitter laugh that slipped out in answer to Harkon Bright's pronouncement. "They're not my friends."

"So I hear," Harkon answered. He handed the young man a cup of water. At the incredulous look that followed, the old mage shook his head. "You've been in my infirmary for three days, dear boy. If I was going to kill you, I would have."

Elias took it, and drank. Cool water soothed his throat. He breathed a little easier. *Hadn't* killed him. They *hadn't.* Why? Did they not know what would follow? "You should have," he finally answered. At the slight arch of the old man's eyebrow, Elias looked Harkon in the eyes and said, simply, "They'll come for me. All of them."

Silence hung in the air, the thrum of the metadrive the only noise. Then Harkon's face flickered with the ghost of a smile. "Be less concerned with your former order," Harkon said, "and more concerned with *me.*"

Elias brushed dark hair away from his face, and met the old man's eyes. A terrible weariness settled over him, exhaustion past reasoning. "Why am I alive?" he asked.

"My apprentice saved you," Harkon said, simply, and the old man watched how Elias reacted to that *very* carefully. "She brought you back here, and insisted that you be nursed back to health. Make no mistake, Elias Leblanc," he said, and the last name startled the young man. "Without Aimee as your savior and advocate, you would, indeed, be dead."

"… Leblanc," Elias breathed. His fingers clenched against the mattress beneath him, and he felt as though his head would drop from his shoulders from the weight of the word.

"Yes," Harkon said quietly, and here the old mage's face showed its first sign of genuine compassion. "My apprentice told me what she saw within the Axiom when your minds were joined. That, also, is part of why you are still alive. Your mother–" here the old man paused, and Elias realized that the woman's name was difficult for Harkon to speak "–was… a dear friend of mine, once."

Elias closed his eyes. The weight of it settled in. Not only of what had happened to him in the past two days… But the sheer immensity of the theft of sixteen years of his life, of atrocities without number committed under the name of Azrael, crushed down on him. When he had rushed Malfenshir, thrown himself into freeing prisoners and betraying his former masters, it had been with no expectation of survival. Now the gnawing emptiness of despair ate away at his insides. There was no making up for what he'd done – no mending the crimes committed under the name of Azrael. He didn't even understand how to *try*.

Noble and brave. Gentle and kind.

Perhaps he had more than he thought.

After what seemed an inappropriately long time, he raised his eyes to once more look at Harkon Bright. "So," he said. "What happens now?"

"That depends on you," Harkon said quietly. "As you pointed out, there are many powerful people who believe you deserve death for either treachery or mass atrocity."

"What do you believe?" Elias asked.

"I believe," Harkon answered, "that you were denied a choice for a long time, and that when finally presented with one, you opted to fight back. You showed yourself willing to die rather than permit further crimes to be committed against those who were your enemies mere days before." He leaned forward, assessing the young man on his infirmary bed. "Azrael may have been a monster, but my apprentice believes, and I believe, that Elias Leblanc is worth saving."

The old mage stood from his seat, and offered Elias a hand, extended from the same shoulder that Azrael had cloven with his blade mere days before. "You saved the lives of two of my people, and enabled the success of our mission at great personal cost. I cannot mend the damage behind you, but if you want it, there is a place for you on my crew, and a home for you on my ship."

The young man paused for just a second, met the gaze of the benefactor he had nearly killed, then clasped the proffered palm of his former enemy.

"I accept," Elias said.

It was another day before he saw anyone else. Exhaustion kept him bedridden for most of that time, and in the end, he rose only when he couldn't justify staying in one place any longer. Barefoot, unarmored, unarmed, he stepped out of the infirmary and made his way through a place he had never seen before. Halls of polished hardwood and brass greeted him. Whereas the *Iron Hulk* had been cold, mechanical austerity mingled with the pilfered finery of stolen wealth, the interior of *Elysium* was warm. His feet padded softly across the floor as he walked down a long, central hallway, lined with cabin doors and a few hanging works of priceless art.

He'd never been in a place more alien in his life. The young man walked until he pushed a door aside into what looked like a central living area. There were couches and a few windows presenting a beautiful view of the skies without. Rising banks of clouds billowed, vast beyond imagining in a sky tinged with the golden sheen of sunrise. As if in a dream, Elias walked towards the window and simply *stared* at it. Resplendent and wondrous, he let his gaze drift away from anything around him but the seemingly limitless expanse of sky, in all its color and radiance. How had he never noticed it before? Never stopped to consider the aching beauty of the heavens?

How much time had he lost? He felt wetness at the corners of his eyes as he took it in. Then he closed them, and drew in a long, free breath. Perhaps there was no fixing what had been broken. But for the first time in a very long while, he felt a small sense of hope.

"You'd think," the young woman's voice said behind him, "that you'd never seen a sunrise before."

Elias turned. Aimee de Laurent slowly approached. She wore a long robe and slippers. Her face still displayed the sleepy expression that the mug of coffee between her slender hands was doubtless meant to chase away. Her long golden hair was pulled away from her face in a messy bun, and her slight, athletic frame was relaxed. He was unarmored, barefoot, and dressed in ill-fitting fatigues. It was the complete opposite of every context in which they had faced one another before.

For all that, her blue eyes were inquisitive, and the look with which she fixed him held not a trace of hate.

It took him a moment to remember that she'd spoken to him. "I haven't seen one... not truly," he admitted after a few moments. His voice was sleep-graveled and tired. Strange to his own ears. "Not for a very long time."

"Well," she said, coming to stand beside him. "You get up early enough, and you'll see plenty from this deck. It's the best place to see them, other than the bridge, and Clutch and Bjorn are up there right now. They had night shift."

Bjorn. Elias's memory flashed with the recollection of the big man screaming, hurtling over the falls. Relief at the survival of a man he thought he'd killed mingled with the sudden apprehension of what such a man might do when he saw him again.

She saw him tense. "Harkon's talked to everyone," she said, reflexively reaching out to touch his arm. Memories of grasping hands cut like a knife through his mind, and he flinched away.

"I'm sorry," Aimee said after a moment. Her outstretched hand closed along with her eyes. Her face screwed up in an apologetic look. "I... I really should've known better."

"It's alright," Elias said. He shook his head, holding up a hand to forestall further objection. "It is a lot for one person to remember."

"No," Aimee said, and this time her eyes met his intently. "It's not. Look, I can't promise that the people on this ship are going to like you. Or that they will even be kind, but I can tell you that Harkon, and I, convinced them all that you deserve a chance to figure out who you really are. And if you can go through everything you have, and come out a person at least willing to try to do right by others, then the least I can do is keep in mind what you've endured," she swallowed what must have been a lump in her throat, "and be kind."

Elias took a moment to process all that she'd said. He felt that there was so much more he *should* say, after all that had happened, but in the end, all he could do was say "thank you."

"I have something for you. Stay here," Aimee said, and she vanished around a corner. Her footsteps receded as Elias stood alone in the room with the window, feeling for all the world like a naked man left exposed to the elements. Sense and perception were raw. The identity through which they'd once been filtered was gone, and a gaping hole remained in its absence.

When she returned, she carried a familiar object of shining steel in her hands. It took a second for Elias's overwhelmed mind to absorb what he was seeing, but before he could raise objection, she lifted Oath of Aurum in its scabbard and pressed the sword with its gold-chased hilt into his hands.

"I don't really care what the sage and Coulton say," she murmured quietly as his fingers closed around the hilt. The familiar feel of the grip in his right hand came with a thrumming warmth, and when he pulled the first few inches from the sheath, the blade gave off a pale glow.

"That it's still glowing in your hands is proof enough to me," Aimee continued. "That sword is an ancient relic, long dormant, and prophesied to be restored to power by a prince wielding it with acts of desperate virtue. I don't know what that means about who you are, Elias," she said, "but I do know that it means that sword belongs to you." Silence hung for a moment between them, then she simply said, "And I trust you, so I'm giving it back. We saved your armor, too, but Vant should probably fix it before you put it on again."

A small laugh escaped Elias. "You don't want me walking about in it again. They'll be coming for me, when they learn that I survived. All of them."

Aimee shrugged. "And we'll fight them when they do," she said. "You were theirs for a long time, Elias, but then the Axiom took you back, and you became your own. Then, when you accepted Harkon's offer, you became one of ours."

"One of yours," Elias repeated, the words bizarre in his mouth.

Aimee cleared her throat, briefly awkward. The slightest hint of a blush colored her cheeks. "The crew, I mean." Then she looked at him, earnestly, seriously. "We won't let them have you. The others may complain, but they'll come around. After all, we're crew."

"I don't have sufficient words to thank you," Elias said after a moment. "But if it takes the rest of my life, I will repay you." The next words had to be said around a lump in his throat. "You have my word."

Again, a slight blush tinted her face. She turned once more, to regard the dazzling radiance of the heavens before them. "Welcome to freedom, Elias Leblanc. And welcome to *Elysium*."

Elias didn't answer, but in that moment, by the way she glanced sideways at him, he didn't need to.

Instead they stood together in silence and peace, as the ship traveled on and on, through the brilliance of the morning, and into the infinite sky.

In the darkness, Truth is your candle. Burn bright.

THE ADVENTURE CONTINUES IN...

DRAGON ROAD

READ THE FIRST THREE
CHAPTERS NOW

PROLOGUE
The Autumn Compromise

The fate of the kingdom of Port Providence was decided on the morning of the first day of the second month of autumn. It was done in a small room with a closed door, by twelve eccentric captains of industry. None of them had titles of birth or elected office, and none of them were from the land of the tartan flag.

Twelve inked signatures on a single piece of parchment signed away the fates of over one million people. The conversation began in argument. They sat – the twelve of them – about a table of finest ironwood, the grains of steel shining out burnished from the natural rings of what had once been a vast tree. Fingers bedecked with rings drummed upon a table, as the master of the Shipping Guild made his case. His name was Claus, and he was presently bored with debate.

"Port Providence might seem, at first glance, to be an opportunity," the man said, dabbing the smears of cloudfish sauce from the corner of his pudgy, wormlike mouth. "But the isle is, itself, a hinterland. Yes, perhaps, incentivizing some sort of building projects to restore its economy might be profitable in the *long* run, but is it truly? Coulton's kingdom never exported anything other than a pittance of timber and a particularly rowdy brand of kilted skyfarer. Let their sovereignty die, and the timber can simply be harvested by those of us who need it, without having to deal with the appeasing of a proud monarch who may not always be *pliable*. Better money is had in the long run if the tartan flag is just left burnt."

"And what of the Violet Imperium?" The follow-up question came from a broad-chested, wattle-necked man named Vincentus. His ring marked him as head of the Guild of Laborers, and he was one of the least liked men at the table. Officially, the vast organization which he represented acted as the go-between and representative structure for skilled laborers in their dealings with prospective employers from royalty to freemen business conglomerates.

Unofficially, everyone knew that the Guild of Laborers was the single greatest slave-market in the known isles. Workers throughout the Unclaimed knew them as the Chain-Makers. Vincentus adjusted the ring upon his hand and leaned forward. "What if they take up young Coulton's claim, and prop him back up on his little oak throne?"

A rapid murmur rippled through the heads of the Twelve. Faces exchanged thoughtful glances. Mumbles echoed from mouths that commanded fortunes beyond imagining. Shoulders burdened with the heavy cloaks of industry and trade shifted in discomfort.

"They won't," said yet another voice, and this one came from the thin lips and gaunt face of the sunken-eyed head of the Financiers Conglomerate. "Port Providence enjoyed a patronage primarily out of charity, and a smidgen of shared history. They've already proven themselves to be more trouble than they're worth by getting themselves invaded. The Imperium might grant Coulton and his court an honorary asylum, but they will bury what to do about his kingdom in bureaucracy until his grandchildren are dead. Port Providence will be left to whatever fate we choose for it."

Then the financier turned in his chair, and stared into the face of the thirteenth individual present at this meeting. An impressive feat, as the robed man at the far end of the table with his pale face and bald pate represented interests that even the mighty guildsmen feared. The representative of the Eternal Order had lived for a very long time, and none could say exactly how long he had visited these councils. Only that none possessed the authority – or perhaps the spine – to turn him away. His eyes were red-rimmed. His forehead bore the stamped symbol of his masters: a ring of nine black stars. His hands were folded within his sleeves, and they all shrank from him when they met his gaze. Even his name was not properly known. The other guildmasters present simply called him *the Envoy*. He looked back into the face of the head financier, and he smiled.

"Yes, *banker*?"

The head financier held his ground, meeting the red-rimmed, heavy-lidded gaze. "Envoy, leave us not be coy. There is no pretending that this present mess is not *your order's fault*."

The Envoy leaned forward. The smile disappeared. "Have you forgotten the nature of my order's bargain with the Twelve? Let me remind you: the Eternal Order kills only whom they are paid to kill. Fights only whom they are paid to fight. We take no part in your internal politics. In return, when it comes to the order's private business, and the securing of our own property, The Guilds *stay out of our way*. Port Providence was a matter of order business. *Private* business. My recommendation is it be allowed to remain that way."

He paused. His head cocked to the side. "Unless," he added quietly, "you are implying that we don't have the right to secure what *belongs to us*?"

Claus held up a pudgy hand in dismissal. "Nonsense, Envoy. The terms of your illustrious order's contract are known to all. Our principal objection is to the fact that none of us were *warned*."

"Indeed," Vincentus added. "And with all that said, this begins to look disturbingly similar to the New Corinth business from years ago."

The Envoy laughed. The sound echoed through the room, and the twelve representatives alternately shrank back or looked chilled in their seats. "I recommend you reexamine your history books and your own records," he said. "The House of Nails was always our property. That it was occupied by a nation of squatters and chaff does not change the fact that it was ours. Port Providence merely had possession of an item we had long sought to reclaim. Surely your wise minds can grasp how these situations are distinct."

"Surely," said the head of the Financiers Conglomerate, "but consider that it is not your invasion that troubles this group so much as your utter failure to contain the fallout."

And here, the head of the Skyspeakers' Guild leaned forward. Her name was Lysara, and her long, bare arms rested upon the table, fingertips etched with the pale blue skin enchantments of her order. "When the *Iron*

Hulk obliterated itself upon Port Providence's central hinterlands, it left two hundred square miles of land uninhabitable, and the surviving *things* your people kept living within it have since begun running roughshod over the landscape. Killing. Defiling." Her augmented, prismatic eyes regarded the envoy with a piercing, indignant stare. "My Guild has censored more desperate cries for help in the past month from that region than in the past seven years combined. More than seventy-five percent were cut short. Before this debacle, we did not even know that these *techs* – as you call them – existed, and now they are running amok over half an island."

"These creatures constitute a new threat for which none of us have contingency plans," Vincentus said. "Preliminary reports suggest that they reproduce by violating the bodies of ordinary humans they encounter. We were never warned about their existence, so how can we possibly know what their net effect will be on continued operations, should any of them escape?"

The Envoy listened to each objection in turn, his impassive expression taking in the Twelve's concerns with perfected stoicism. When Vincentus had finished speaking, however, he leaned forward, letting the sleeves slip from his laced, heavily tattooed fingers. "See this, then, as a chance to learn. Place Port Providence under Guild-enforced quarantine. The Violet Imperium will be glad to have the mess taken from their overburdened hands. I am even authorized to offer you a small team of the order's experts to assist in your observations and studies. The techs have been groomed for generations for a specific purpose, and we, too, are curious as to the implications of an incident such as this one. Why fret, guildsmen, when you can *learn?*"

Reaching within his robes, he produced a piece of parchment upon which was outlined a contract for his proposal. Twelve pairs of eyes watched as the Envoy let his hands drift across it, the wordless nature of his magic projecting a reflection of its words before the faces of each of the assembled guildmasters.

"A simple signature," the envoy said, "and you can all move on to more pressing business."

They read. Minor quibbles were made, and answered. For the next hour, twelve guildmasters and one robed envoy debated the minutia of a contract that would dictate the fate of a kingdom. In the end, all twelve signatures were etched in expensive ink across the space at the base of the original parchment. Deaths were acknowledged as unfortunate collateral. The price of Eternal Order assistance was established at a sum fit to feed three thousand starving for two years. Jokes were made. Congenial remarks passed back and forth between the casual brokers of power about an ironwood table made from the cross-section of an ancient tree.

Then they broke for lunch.

It was in the hallway outside the room that the Envoy cornered the head of the Shipping Guild. Imposing man though he was, the heavy-set magnate was nonetheless off-put as the robed man with the nine-star mark upon his brow waylaid him in the absence of the others. Even Claus's expensive, Imperium-trained mercenary bodyguards couldn't truly protect him from the figure he now faced.

"Guildmaster," the Envoy said. "I have another matter to speak to you about. Rather, I should say, a notification. Something of which my masters wish you to be informed in your dealings over the next several months."

Standing thus, the guildmaster did his best to remain straight and tall, meeting the red-rimmed Envoy's gaze with difficulty. "I am not accustomed," he said, "to be dictated to."

"That is of no concern to me," the Envoy said. "But my masters require that you listen. As master of shipping, your voice holds more sway in the affairs of port operations throughout the Drifting Lands than any other. There is a skyship traveling the Dragon Road, if rumors tell true, called *Elysium*. It carries several individuals the order has declared marked."

"The order can deal with its own enemies, surely," Claus replied. "Your honor has made that more than clear."

A wan smile passed over the Envoy's face. "Certainly. But I am not making a request. I am passing on notification: My masters wish you to understand that they require any interactions your guildsmen have with this vessel to be passed on to us. If you fail to do so, the order will view it as a deliberate act of disrespect and breach of contract."

The guildmaster's face paled. "You cannot *possibly* expect me to have such encyclopedic knowledge of the doings of *one ship*."

"I expect *nothing*," the Envoy said. "My orders were simply to ensure that you were informed." A wicked light gleamed in the red-rimmed eyes. "The winds are blowing, Guildmaster. Change is coming. Understand that when it arrives, the Eternal Order will remember their friends." He cocked his head to the side. "And their enemies."

CHAPTER ONE
THE PALE APOSTATE

Ishtier was beautiful. Purple rays of a setting sun vaulted off the crystalline structures of the port far below the skydock, and the riot of colored specks that made up the countless people basking in the sunlight of a free port were like the drunken splotches of a painter throwing his brush at a blank canvas. They were as chaotic as they were jarring.

For all this, Elias couldn't process much of it beyond the fact that it was beautiful. He was very, *very* drunk. He hadn't meant to be. But in the face of a swarm of overwhelming recollections reaching up from the black void of his memory, the bottle he'd acquired on one of his few portside strolls since *Elysium* docked had become too easy a solution to ignore. Now he stood at the railing of the skydock, white knuckles gripping a metal bar and staring into an endless sea of sky, wishing for numbness.

Elias Leblanc had never expected to survive. That he was alive at all was a quandary that he couldn't understand. Not understanding was even worse than living.

His breath came in a slow drag as the viscous fire

of the alcohol burned its way through his system. His
eyes were red, and his posture slack. He had never been
one to indulge in drunkenness before, so it had taken
relatively little of the poison to put him in his current
state. When he had been Azrael, when he had served
the Eternal Order as its willing, brainwashed killer, he
had treated his body as a temple. That now freed, he
was heaping abuse after abuse upon it in an effort to
kill his thoughts was an irony that didn't go unnoticed.
But it was hard to argue himself out of it, either. When
waking moments were spent walking the razor's edge of
avoiding his crewmates' implacable, stoic stares, it took
most of his mental energy to keep his own temper in
line. That energy expenditure left him exhausted at the
end of each day, and would have required a solid night's
sleep to recover, no matter the circumstances.

It had been weeks since Elias had gotten any
meaningful sleep. He would lie awake in his cabin – one
of the smaller ones normally meant for guests – staring
up at the ceiling for hours and hours, praying for sleep
to take him. When he closed his eyes, the nightmares
would rise again, a different, horrific flavor depending
on the evening. He would awake exhausted, his head
pounding and limbs aching, and begin the whole affair
again.

The bottle rested on the planks next to him, the winds
whistling mournfully over its open lip. Elias's left hand
gripped the rail, trembling as it did. The right was holding
his long knife. The sunlight danced off it in a hundred
dirty shades of gold. As he watched, each of them slowly
darkened to a familiar, dull red. He hadn't come here to
contemplate what he was about to do... The truth was
he hadn't come here with any specific purpose at all,

other than to be somewhere other than *Elysium*. The ship, floating suspended in the heavens, was several hundred feet away, longer by the winding catwalks of the skydocks he'd wandered to get where he was.

But now he considered it. Beyond the railing there was only open sky, and a long, long fall to the lands far below, or simply eternity, if the stone and dirt was missed. Absently, he thought about what it would be like to fall forever into the darkness beneath the sky. There were only ghost stories to answer that. Ghost stories, old myths, and the fearful mumblings of madmen.

And wasn't Elias Leblanc just the picture perfect specimen of the madman?

It wasn't the first time he'd thought about doing it. But every time before, it had just been conjecture. An idle thought that happened to have the weight of inevitability. *I'll get to it later*, he'd told himself. *If I have to.*

Now he was alone, drunk, and had only his knife for company. He held it up before his face, staring at it with a dull gaze. It was the thinking about it that was pulling him up short. That was the problem. He needed to just get on with it.

Everyone would be better off.

"What're you doing, boy?"

The words, jarring, gruff, cut across his thoughts, and the young man turned to see the big, burly figure of Bjorn standing not ten feet from him. He'd dressed for the wind, a thick coat of sheepskins and big clomping black boots that made Elias wonder how he'd been able to approach unheard. The alcohol, he told himself. That was why his senses weren't what they should be.

"Isn't it obvious?" Elias heard himself answer. His voice was slurred. "I'm *voting*."

The big man's bearded face sized him up and down, the pale eyes holding something halfway between disgust and worry in their depths. He crept closer, then he held out his hand. Elias looked at it, then at his knife with its infinite shades of red.

"Give me the knife, boy," Bjorn said. Insistent. Quiet.

"You're not letting me walk away with it, are you?" Elias asked. His fingers caressed the hilt.

Bjorn's level gaze remained on him. "No. I'm not."

Vision blurry, Elias turned to fully face the man, meeting the older, more experienced stare. His head was pounding and he felt unsteady on his feet. "I could just put it in your throat, then finish myself, you know," he finally said. "I'm fast enough."

"I know," the big man said quietly. "But you won't. Because you're not Azrael. Spite isn't what drives you."

"You don't know me," Elias answered. "You don't even *like* me."

"I don't *trust* you, boy," Bjorn snorted. "There's a difference. I don't trust you because you're half-cocked and a walking mess. I don't trust you because you don't trust yourself. But give me time – give them all time – and that'll come. Now give me the knife."

The last time Elias stood opposite the big man, they'd both held swords in their hands, facing one another across a rocky, blood-splattered valley floor. Bjorn still bore the bandage from the near-mortal wound Elias had given him when he'd gone by the name of Azrael. He'd left that life, and that name, behind. The recollections burned in his mind, an aching, raw wound on his thoughts and emotions, but he still had the ability to say of himself that it was *the past*, and not the present. The blade longed to cut into something. His hands shook.

Then he flipped it, caught it on the flat, and presented the handle to the bigger man. When Bjorn slowly clasped the grip, however, Elias didn't let go. He met the big man's gaze, and said, "There's something I need you to help me with."

Elias staggered up the gangway and into *Elysium*, his head pounding, leaning on the bigger man's arm so as not to topple off and into the heavens. Bjorn now held the knife, but with a specific set of instructions. The moment they stepped into the bay again, Elias staggered away from the bigger man, catching himself on one of the recently loaded crates. His hands caught on the smooth surface, then he pushed himself up, taking his bearings. The interior of the ship was nicer, by far, than any he'd ever traveled in before his time here. Even the cargo bay had an aesthetic charm to it that the interiors of Eternal Order warships and the *Iron Hulk* had simply lacked. Warm hardwood, exposed steel beams and burnished brass were everywhere, and the viewports were positioned to give the interior the maximum amount of natural light.

He turned to regard Bjorn. In the month since Elias had joined *Elysium*'s crew – since he had turned against his former masters and turned away from the name of Azrael and all the horrors he'd committed while he wore it – the big man had hardly spoken to him. Even on their last mutual days spent in the infirmary, they'd avoided acknowledging one another's presence, as if even a spare glance might summon the unfinished duel from the valley floor in Port Providence.

A duel that Elias had won, albeit when he was still calling himself Azrael. A name that he still struggled *not* to call himself, even in his dreams.

"Get your clippers," Elias grunted. "We're going to the viewing deck after I hit my cabin."

"If you try to jump," Bjorn grunted. "I swear to the gods of my ancestors I'll drag you back up by the collar of your shirt and beat you senseless."

"Too drunk to jump," Elias muttered as he started up the corridor that spanned the spine of the slender skyship. He managed a wry smile. "I'd just fall."

The primary cabins of *Elysium* had already been occupied when Elias became a permanent member of its crew, so one of the passenger cabins in the belly of the vessel had become his. Whereas the others opened their doors onto the central corridor of the upper deck, the simple, metal door to Elias's room opened directly into the cargo hold, and when he stepped through, he stood for a few moments in silence as the sunlight spilled in through the viewport, illuminating his living space. As far as places to lay your head went, it wasn't bad. The floor was polished hardwood, the bed a double pushed against the wall. A bookcase sat opposite the viewport, bare, and a washing station and latrine were retracted into the wall. The sound of his breath and heartbeat filled the silence. Opposite him, in the room's farthest, darkest corner, a hastily made rack held the polished, black steel of Azrael's armor, minus the helm, lost back on Port Providence.

He hadn't worn it since he came onboard. His reflection stared back at him from the burnished black and gold, perfectly maintained out of compulsive habit. Elias stared. The armor stayed where it was.

Someday, he thought, *you will have to put it on again*.

And on that day, he would be recognized, and *they*

would find him. All of them.

The thought sent a shudder through him, and he reached, instead, for the longsword that hung in its scabbard from a peg on the wall beside the bed. Its straight crosspiece was gold-chased, the lower half of its two-handed grip wrapped in wire. The broad fishtail pommel glinted immaculate in the sunlight as Elias gingerly lifted the sword called Oath of Aurum from where it hung, and began slowly buckling the blade about his waist. When his hand touched the hilt, the familiar warmth flooded up his arm as its enchantment responded to his touch. He let the first few inches of hollow-ground, diamond-spined silver blade slide from the sheath, and the steel gleamed, as if lit from within by a pale golden light. This, at least, he could still carry. Though it was legend in some circles, few people knew what Oath of Aurum *looked* like.

That Elias had taken it from the dead hands of a virtuous man he'd killed would haunt him for the rest of his life. No, *not* Elias. Azrael.

He shook his head, his breathing fearful and measured in the empty room. Was there a difference?

Yes. There had to be, he reminded himself. There *had* to be. And now, with Bjorn's help, he would make that difference a little more dramatic.

He headed back up towards the viewing deck, still unsteady on his feet, but helped along the way by a simple conviction to get where he was going without painful embarrassment. When he got there, he found Bjorn waiting, the winds of Ishtier's vast port bay blowing his coat all about him in a chaotic swirl. A sea of smaller craft hung suspended in the sky from the thousand branches of the vast, wooden dock apparatus.

From this far away, the immense structure looked like a beehive bristling with thorns. It would be dark soon. The evening sky had faded from golds and reds to the deep purples and blues of twilight, and amidst the darkness of the port, the running lamps of countless ships twinkled.

Bjorn had caught the gist of what Elias intended, and the big man regarded him now, his tools stuffed into his long coat pockets. Nonetheless, the expression on his face was somber. "You sure about this, boy?"

Elias swayed. He gripped the railing with his left hand to steady himself. After everything that he'd been through, it hardly seemed appropriate to be as disconcerted as he was by what he was about to do... but there it was. He had to do the first part himself. It was important. Symbolic.

He let go the rail, reached up with both hands, and gathered his long, thick dark hair up, pulling it into a tail at the back of his head. Then, clutching that in his left fist, he drew Oath of Aurum with his right. The blade gleamed in the growing darkness. A brief vision of Lord Roland swam before his eyes. Implacable. Relentless.

"I renounce you," Elias whispered. "And *everything* you represent."

With a graceful slice, he sheared the ponytail from the back of his head, and flung it into the darkness. Then he sat back on a stool that Bjorn had fetched, and submitting himself to the trust of the man that had been his enemy only a month past, closed his eyes. Bjorn drew his clippers, grunting, "Yeah, can't have you looking like *that*, boy."

The snipping of shears and scissors filled Elias's ears, as bits of hair fell to the deck like rain.

CHAPTER TWO
Revels Ended

Being free and in the open, with nobody trying to kill her, was still a bit of a luxury so far as Aimee was concerned. So as the sun dipped out of sight, and the night fell over Ishtier's port, she walked beneath the soft glow of innumerable lanterns suspended from cables high overhead. As if in a dream, her booted feet carried her over the long dirt road past a bazaar of shopfronts, fruit vendors, and buildings half formed of earth sculpted by the local sorcerers, who the locals called the *rocksingers*.

When Aimee had asked Harkon why such a useful discipline had never been exported, the older mage had shrugged. "It doesn't seem to work on other lands. Only people born on Ishtier can do it, and only on Ishtier. The best minds in magic have never sussed out why."

The third prime of magic: things did not always happen as men understood they should.

She wore her long blue coat, recently cleaned, and her knee-high boots had mud from the previous day's expedition with her teacher to the crystal cliffs, there to measure the growth of emerald obelisks that pushed further from the earth every year. Ishtier was less a

whole landmass, and more a collection of hundreds of
close-floating islands, each with its own unique biome,
and the name *Ishtier* itself referred primarily to the main
isle with its Crystal Port on which Aimee now stood. The
locals had their own names for the hundreds of other,
smaller islands, but she'd never learned them.

"Hey Aimee," Clutch said behind her. "Hold up.
Vlana's gonna hurl again."

The pilot's dark face wore an amused expression as
she brushed back blue hair from her eyes and adjusted
her leather jerkin. A short distance away, Vlana leaned
over the edge of a fountain, her thin eyes shooting glares
at the pilot. The normally pale face of the natural-born
skyfarer looked slightly green. "Shut up, halfer," she
muttered. "You know being on the ground makes me
nauseous."

"You spent most of a day on the ground when we
crashed in Port Providence," Clutch fired back. "And
watch your mouth, ship rat."

Ship rat – Aimee had learned – was skyfarer slang
for natural-born skyfarers, such as Vlana and her twin
brother Vant, that had spent their whole lives on skycraft.
Halfer referred to people like Clutch: skyfarers that lived
and worked on ships, but came from land. Normally
both terms were considered deeply offensive, but Clutch
and Vlana tossed them back and forth with affection.

Vlana stuck out her tongue. "I never actually *left the
ship*."

"Details." Clutch laughed.

"Do I want to know what someone like *me* is called?"
Aimee asked.

"No," both answered.

They walked on, laughing. The trip portside hadn't

started as an intentional girls' night for the three women, but with Harkon and Vant currently talking to the portmasters and Elias and Bjorn determinedly staying shipside, it had ended up that way. They'd already had dinner at a restaurant uptown that served a sort of shelled crustacean the locals called crystal crab in a spicy sauce. Now they were perusing the shopfronts as the last light in the vast east faded behind the banks of immense clouds. They wandered further inland, past the immigration offices with their universal symbols of doors and hands, past the various guild chapterhouses and the long, opal-tiled walkway that led to the Governor's manor. Then they stopped at a repair shop where Clutch and the owner haggled for close to ten minutes over a rare tool that Aimee didn't recognize: a steel rod inlaid with gold filigree and capped with a multifaceted emerald that faintly glimmered in the shop's light.

It cost enough money that when Vlana handed over the slats, Clutch raised her eyebrows. "Where'd you get that kinda money?" the pilot asked as the three of them strode once more out onto the street.

"Unlike *some* people," Vlana said, "I *save* my earnings, rather than blowing months' worth on two days with an expensive prostitute."

"It's high class courtesan," Clutch corrected her with a grin. "And for your information, his name is Juno, and I'm very fond of him."

"Hey I'm not judging how you spend your time or your payment," Vlana said, holding her hands up, the bag of her new acquisition dangling from one thumb. "I'm just saying – we each have our priorities. And this is going to make cleaning out the nav-panels *so* much easier. The head of this thing is pure Ishtier organic emerald. I checked. Anywhere but here, an ounce of that stuff is a year's takings of a paygrade much higher than mine. Here, though? They just grow more."

"Why haven't the Guilds monopolized the production so that the price doesn't hit the locals?" Clutch asked, a curious eyebrow arched.

"That," Aimee interjected, "would be because of the Barrakha Accords. The locals get to control how much of their resources they sell, and how much they keep in free circulation here. Guilds ignore that constantly in other places, but it helps that Ishtier has all sorts of weird magic protecting the place."

Aimee followed her words by looking up into the sky. The stars were coming out in the heavens, despite the lantern glow of the city and its port.

"Still wishing you'd seen a dragon?" Vlana asked, stepping up alongside her.

"Honestly?" Aimee answered, "after everything that happened in Port Providence, I've been glad things are low-key for a change." She paused, let out a genuinely relieved sigh. "The dragons will keep."

They were a few feet further down the street when Aimee realized Clutch wasn't with them. Both women turned. Their pilot was standing amidst several other people, staring up at the sky, her eyes wide. As Aimee watched, Clutch's mouth fell open. The young sorceress turned herself, and immediately beheld the reason: against the darkness of the night sky, a deeper shadow – impossibly vast – blotted out the stars.

Aimee rarely lacked words. Her upbringing was steeped in literature, in the fine speaking forms of charm school, in the academic halls of the Academy of Mystic Sciences.

The thing that now approached Crystal Port brought her up short. Only in Port Providence, months ago, faced with the immensity of a flying mountain known as the *Iron Hulk*, had she seen something more impressive… but the hulk – for all its terror – had been a *mountain*. A flying fortress built into the interior of an immense chunk of rock moving like another island through the sky.

This wasn't a mountain, it was a *ship*. A ship that – while still smaller than the *Iron Hulk* – was nonetheless bigger than the entire port it now approached. Her mind reeled, grasped about for the term she'd memorized in her hours upon hours spent studying ship types back in the Academy days. She still came up short. Only Vlana's laughter shook her free of it.

"What?" the shorter quartermaster said. "Never seen a behemoth before?"

"Sure," Clutch said before Aimee could get words out. "But isn't it a bit early in the year for a proper flotilla to be showing up around here?"

Behemoth. Flotilla. That was right. Aimee shook her head to rid it of the fog summoned by the vision of something so vast. Behemoths were the huge trade ships that plied the skylanes of the Dragon Road, as big as cities, filled with crews who were born, lived, and died upon them. They carried everything from bulk foodstuffs to the rare and exotic, all across the Drifting Lands. But normally, they never came this close. They – and the flotillas of other such ships they traveled with – would station themselves well away from the edges of the smaller ports such as Ishtier and send smaller skycraft with their goods to hock. Even in Havensreach, she'd only glimpsed vessels like this at a distance. Only at the vast, mythical ports of the

great powers could a behemoth hope to dock directly
with the earth.

"It–" Aimee's words briefly failed her as she took
several steps forward, then recovered "–it's *beautiful*."

Abruptly, she took off jogging towards the proper
docks, away from the shopfronts and the vendors and
the restaurants and the roadside stands. Away from
paper lanterns and familiarity towards – as she *always*
did – the unknown. The pilot and the quartermaster
ran behind, chasing her until she reached an unused
skyjack, all battered wood and rusted metal, thrusting
out into the empty heavens, a would-be bridge unto
the clouds.

From here the view was much clearer. Standing at
the rail, Aimee could see the behemoth's colossal frame
illuminated by piecemeal splashes of light amidships, and
from beneath by the soft glow of Ishtier. High up above,
the top of its hull vanished into the night, identifiable
only by the way its outline cut off the stars, and the
running lights and windows intermittently viewable as
specs along the length. It was shaped roughly like a brick:
long, rectangular, the bow a flat face of huge bay doors at
the bottom and multi-storied, cathedral-esque viewports
towards the top. A city's length away, her tail end could
be noted by the muffled glow of multiple exhaust ports,
each larger than the biggest buildings in Havensreach's
upper ring.

From where she stood, Aimee could see only a few
windows with any clarity, but behind those, she caught
glimpses of movement, and along awning-covered outer
walkways and tiered, external decks, she glimpsed the
shadows of countless swarming crewmembers.

Just above the bow, running lamps illuminated a

name painted onto a pitted, scarred hull. Each letter was as tall as *Elysium*.

ISEULT

Aimee let out a breath she'd held unnoticed. Turning, she flashed her crewmates a grin. "It's named after one of the mythical lovers," she said. "From the pre-scriptures!"

"And she's *damn* close," Clutch was saying as she eyed the slowing, enormous vessel.

"Battle damage?" Vlana asked the pilot. "Here out of emergency?"

"If so," the pilot mused, frowning, "she's in the wrong damn place. There's not a drydock in all of Ishtier that could take a behemoth."

A sudden rushing noise assaulted their ears, the now-familiar blast of forward engines firing to bring the immense vessel to a halt. "Well," Clutch muttered dryly. "At least they're not planning to crush the whole port. That's good of them."

"I don't see any damage," Vlana added as her eyes traced the length of the ship. "Nothing more than the usual wear and tear of long-term service. She's been patched a lot, but most of these things get completely rebuilt over the course of their lives."

Despite the wonder of the colossal skyship blotting the night out before her, Aimee stepped back from the rail. She stretched her memory to recall what she'd learned about ships like this: their crews and passenger populations numbered in the tens, sometimes hundreds of thousands. Among them could be any number of ears, informants, or – conversely – sources of information. And before they did anything else, she wagered, they should get back to *Elysium*.

"Yeah," Clutch was saying slowly as she squinted at the Iseult. "She *definitely* shouldn't be here right now. Not this time of year, and *definitely* not this close."

"We need to get back to the ship," Aimee said. "I need my books, and there'll be no view like the one from the common area."

Her hands itched to get the texts in hand, to review her lists of ship types, to see if one of *Elysium*'s vast ledgers had the known behemoths written down by name and history. If it didn't, she could always ask her teacher.

And if he didn't know, she thought abruptly… she could always ask Elias. The image of green eyes and a handsome face at once the crux of a host of disputing emotions floated momentarily through her mind before Aimee dismissed it. Not right now.

And that was when it happened: a discharge of arcane energy from the prow of the ship erupted into the air hundreds of feet above and before it. Lines of magic shot from several different tiered decks, and Aimee thought she glimpsed the silhouettes of sorcerers at the base of each flash. Twelve of them, she counted, mingling their sorcery to create a visible display high above the tallest buildings of Ishtier's port. First came a rapid series of glyphs burning in the night sky – guild symbols, identifying the ship, her affiliations with the flotilla, the shipping guilds, the Skyspeakers' Guild, the Pilots' Guild. All the necessary credentials were flashed.

Then a face; robed, tired, immense, chalk-pale, strong-browed, and marked with a single black bar across the left eye, was projected into the heavens. It spoke, every phrase repeated in both the common and local tongues. Words flashed beneath the moving mouth to ensure the deaf could understand – and heed – what was being said.

"Ishtier, who is bountiful and beautiful," the voice rippled, grief-thick and formal, across the port. "We are *Iseult* of Flotilla Visramin. We come to you in grief for the death of your son, Amut, who was our captain. Amut of the kind hand. Amut of the strong arm. Amut of the wise eyes. Lion of Heaven. He has passed from this world, and we have come as the wind, to lay him in his native soil."

The message began to repeat itself. Aimee stepped back. "Yeah," she murmured, "back to the ship."

"I agree," Clutch muttered. "Don't like being far from my own helm and sitting in the shadow of something that imposing."

"There is *all* sorts of subtext in that statement, Clutch," Vlana said with a wry laugh.

"Shut up, ship rat," Clutch said.

The three women jogged up the ramp and into the cargo hold. Aimee didn't stop to take stock of things, she simply hoofed it up the ladder and into the central corridor that spanned the spine of the prototype warship-turned-exploratory-vessel that was her home.

"Alright!" she yelled. "Who's onboard?"

Clutch jogged past her when she reached the common area, headed for the bridge. "Vant!" the pilot called. "Did you fall asleep on your bridge hammock again?"

"Calm your damn boots," a muffled voice came from the exterior viewing deck. Aimee squinted, recognizing Bjorn's voice. "We're just finishing up."

Against the dim light of the port, two silhouettes could be seen out on the viewing deck. Aimee did a double-take. Bjorn – discernible by his size – was standing over the angular frame of another man, seated, his back to the common area. Bjorn was holding scissors. The other silhouette – Elias, his voice confirmed – touched the side of his head. "That was *really loud*."

"Hold still, you big baby," Bjorn forced the other man to straighten before going back to grooming his hair, apparently. "Just give us a moment, Miss Laurent."

"You know what, never mind," Aimee answered, continuing up to the bridge, washing her hands of that… weirdness. "I don't want to know."

The bridge flickered to life as she stepped onto it, just in time to watch as Clutch jerked the cord at one end of a hammock hung between bulkheads, and sent a squawking Vant tumbling to the floor. "Are you shitting me?" the pilot barked. "You have a cabin!"

The engineer vaulted upwards and unleashed a cloud of curse words, half of which Aimee didn't yet know. She caught a few, though. *Sky Jockey* was in there, also *Cloud-Fucker*.

Aimee had been on *Elysium* for months and she still wasn't sure if the engineer and pilot were mortal enemies or the best of friends. It was possible they didn't know either.

"You're on night shift!" Clutch snapped back. "Sleeping is the opposite of what you do on night shift!"

"I was resting my eyes, crazy halfer!"

"In a hammock, Vant," Vlana said mildly, crossing the room to her navigation station.

"Look, just because I know how to *optimize*," the engineer grunted.

"Where's Harkon?" Aimee cut in. As funny as this was, she couldn't justify what she wanted to do without his permission.

"He's either portside giving one of those lectures he gives any school that will take him for money," Vant said, "or he's sleeping. So go find him or risk waking him up."

"The latter, if you must know," the sleep-heavy, deep voice of Harkon Bright said from behind them all, a look on his face halfway between irritated and amused. "But thank you for your discretion. It's comforting to know that my crew still can't do anything quietly."

"This one is Aimee's fault," Vlana said from her console. "A behemoth showed up and she insisted we come back. Shouting."

"Traitor," Aimee muttered.

"I keep telling people you can't trust my sister," Vant beseeched the ceiling. "Nobody *ever* believes me."

"To be fair," Clutch said, "it's close enough to port that I'm surprised there isn't panic in the streets."

"It's right up against the docks," Aimee affirmed.

"Practically fucking them," Clutch added. "The catwalks look all sorts of uncomfortable."

Harkon's brows drew together. He looked at Vant expectantly.

"What?" the engineer asked. "It's a ship coming into port. They do that."

The master portalmage turned his gaze to Aimee next, with an expression that said "please justify waking me up. Now."

Aimee drew herself up to her full height, flashed that same smile that had owned the valediction at graduation, and said, "I want to do a flyby."

Harkon frowned, considering. "Reasons?"

"One," Aimee said, "she's away from her flotilla. That's highly unusual. Two – as Clutch mentioned – she's clogging up the whole port, which has got to be making people angry. Three, according to the magical projection they just sent into the sky, their captain just died and they're looking to bring him home. I think it merits a closer look."

Harkon weighed that. He arched a single eyebrow. "And it doesn't hurt, I imagine, that you've never seen a behemoth this closely before?"

"Oh not at all," Aimee said with a grin. "But since we've got reason anyway..."

Silence. The crew looked on. Then Harkon straightened the collar of his evening robe and said, "Do it."

Vant unhooked his hammock from the bulkheads and threw it over his shoulder in the most indignant way possible. "Someone better tell the hair stylist and his client that it's about to get windy out there," he said before he vanished down the hall.

The metadrive thrummed to life moments later. There was a brief, clamorous exchange between Clutch and the dockmasters before the mooring clamps released, then the ship was sweeping free, turning in a soft arc through the starlit sky. *Elysium* had been docked quite a distance from the central port, so they now approached *Iseult* from the rear, and well above. Vast rear exhaust vents glowed blue in the darkness, their dull roar audible even at range. Clutch angled the wheel forward, then aimed the ship starboard. *Elysium* dropped, turned, then began to arc along the side of the city-sized skycraft. Aimee saw a vast upper deck carved deep with verandas, rich balconies, and the swells of domed structures that could be anything from houses of worship to star-gazing labs to internal gardens.

"Typical behemoth," Clutch muttered. "Huge. Lower level covered in scaffolding and ad-hoc ramshackle crazy. Upper levels looking like a bunch of pretentious architects vomited all over a flying brick."

The sounds of heavy footfalls announced the arrival
of Bjorn and Elias on the bridge. The former wore a long
leather apron that he used for cooking and barber work.
Aimee did a brief double-take. Elias's hair, previously
long, thick, and falling to his shoulders was now cut
short, highlighting the angular lines of his long, thin
face. There were dark circles beneath his green eyes, and
the hand that gripped one of the bridge rails was white-
knuckled. He caught her glance, gave her a small nod.
Her small smile in response was reflexive.

"Now that thing's a sight," Bjorn muttered from the
back. "Less hodgepodge than typical."

"*Iseult* is co-flagship of Flotilla Visramin," Harkon
explained from just behind Aimee. "Her sister ship is the
Tristan, but it seems she came here alone."

"Not worth diverting an entire flotilla for one man's
funeral?" Vlana posited.

"I imagine not," Harkon considered. "But it's still a
big detour. The Dragon Road demands strict schedules."

"There are no lights running on the upper deck," Elias
murmured. "Odd."

"Why?" Aimee asked over her shoulder.

"The lamps of a behemoth's upper deck are a signal
to smaller craft," Elias explained quietly. "They alert
other ships in the flotilla, or port, that there's something
immense and covered with dwellings out there." He
frowned, peering across the darkened expanse before
them. "They only kill the lamps if their grid is down, or
if they're paranoid about raiders."

"Raided behemoths often, did you?" Vlana muttered
bitterly.

Elias fell immediately silent. A quick glance at his
face showed Aimee a rapid spasm of shame, regret, and

pain, before the iron curtains of discipline and control dropped, and his face was a mask, again.

The panel to Clutch's right abruptly flashed, and the auto-quills started furiously scribbling across their parchment. Aimee crossed the bridge as the pilot focused on keeping them straight, checked the reading, then looked back at her teacher in surprise.

"Uh, teacher? We've got a communication incoming. Addressed to you by name."

Harkon frowned. "Let it through."

A half second later, the spell-projected image of a copper-skinned man with a wispy, pale beard hovered in the center of the bridge. A ragged scar traced from forehead to cheek on the left side of his face, the eye a jarring milk-white. When he saw Harkon, his smile – if Aimee could call it that – looked genuine. "I'll be damned. I thought I recognized *Elysium's* signature. Hark, what in the name of the thousand gods are you doing here?"

"What I always do, Rachim: explore, fly, get into trouble. What are you doing on a behemoth?"

The man named Rachim seemed to shift, glanced behind him, and lowered the tone of his voice. "Long story, but suffice to say I'm in charge of a few things on *Iseult* these days. Intership relations falls under the purview. We should talk."

Harkon seemed to catch something in the tone. As Aimee watched, her teacher's frown deepened, and he said, "Name the place."

"Here," Rachim answered. "I'm issuing you and your crew a formal invitation to the funeral of Captain Amut. I'll be in touch with more details soon, but for the moment you might want to veer off. My superiors are twitchy tonight."

"We'll be there," Harkon said, and without a further nod or comment, the projected image vanished.

"... Well *that's* not nothing," Aimee said thoughtfully in the silence that followed.

"Clutch," Harkon said. "Take us back to berth. We've got some errands to run."

His eyes swept *Elysium's* assembled crew. "... And you all need to find something suitable to wear."

CHAPTER THREE
The Grief of Iseult

There had to be a phrase, Elias reflected, in at least *one* of the languages he knew, for the supreme, self-conscious awkwardness of being a mass murderer attending the funeral of a good man. More likely, he acknowledged, it didn't yet exist because it hadn't yet been invented. His situation was unique.

Two days since the flyby of the behemoth called *Iseult*, and now he stood with *Elysium*'s crew upon a vast marble-tiled platform that floated between the port docks and the behemoth behind them. They stood in a line, along the edge of an open column between two clusters of mourners, waiting beneath the sun-shading vastness of *Iseult*'s immense, cathedral-like bow. All to his left, Elias's new crewmates waited in somber silence, whilst around and in front of them were spread a panoply of figures draped in importance both genuine and presumed. Many were the oddly shaved heads, the elaborate jewels and spell-fashioned hodgepodge of fine, expensive clothes worn by shipboard courtiers in the company of stoic, uniformed officer-aristocrats. The black knight saw lips painted gold, guild brands outlined in body gems, silver and platinum adorning the delicate fingertips of men and women alike. Upon their city-ship, these people were wealthier than some landborn kings.

And Elias Leblanc couldn't stop noticing how murderously on edge every damned one of them was. Oh, none of them desperately clutched at the – largely ceremonial, occasionally real – blades hanging at their hips, nor did they finger the elaborately designed, custom firearms upon their belts with the familiar terror of people about to start shooting, but to the senses of a trained killer there were cues in abundance, when a group of people thrummed with the energy of unease and paranoia.

The smell of fear, Lord Roland had called it. Elias felt his jaw tighten at the recognition, and the dark, sardonic acknowledgement of where the skill to sense it had come from. He was surrounded by a riot of mournful color, and couldn't shake the sense that it was ready to erupt into a whirlwind of red.

Then a horn sounded, and the focus changed. Elias turned and watched as two lines of crimson-robed, mask-wearing figures approached, the billowing cloth of their vestments stirring in the unique way garments did when heavy armor was worn beneath. These, then, were the Captain's Guard: the highly trained, elite warriors responsible for the defense of the behemoth's late commander. Their gauntleted hands bore tall banners, the first of which bore only the simple black glyphs of the guilds known as the Twelve. After them, however, came a riot of heraldry as the principal households of *Iseult's* officer class were carried forward.

Behind them came six figures bearing a bier on which rested the silk-draped form of Captain Amut's corpse.

The petals of aurora orchids were artistically draped over the dead man, and little objects – the keepsakes of crew and family, Elias supposed – were laid on either side of him in reverence. A glass apple. A simple long knife. A crudely carved wooden comb.

Elias shifted from foot to foot, putting his hands in the pockets of the black and green long coat he'd acquired for the occasion. Oath of Aurum's pommel brushed against his arm from where the sword hung on his hip. The steel was warm today, though Elias didn't feel particularly virtuous. In the face of vast ceremonial grief, his own emotions were muted by exhaustion and overexposure. For all that it seemed wrong to feel that way, sometimes a body was just a body. He'd seen plenty.

They carried it past him. The first two pallbearers were men in black robes, silver-lipped, heavy-eyed, bearing short, silver boarding swords. Behind them, a pair of officers in pale blue uniforms walked stoically, and last came what seemed to be a priest, and the man that had addressed Harkon on the bridge of *Elysium*. Rachim, Elias seemed to recall. He was shorter in person, with rounded shoulders, and a limp that slowed his fellow pallbearers. He must have been dear to the late captain, to be afforded such an honor at the attendant expense of the aesthetic these people clearly prized.

Elias wondered how the man had lost his left eye. He didn't seem accident prone, nor did he look like the sort of man who went hunting. But the stance, the way his face surveyed his surroundings, the lilt of his hard-edged stoicism, those told a story. Elias felt a wan smile tug at the corner of his mouth. So, Rachim was prone to getting into fights, and often enough to pay a price for it.

No wonder he and Harkon were friends.

Elias turned and watched as they passed him, headed for the place where the delegation from Ishtier would receive the body. Glancing down the line, he had a perfect sequential view of his crewmates: the twins, Vant and Vlana, wore simple black fatigues, their boots freshly shined, brooches he'd never seen them wear before on their chests.

Clutch stood immediately to their left. The brown-skinned pilot was a study in practiced aloofness. Her blue hair was braided in an elaborate knot down the center of her head, and her leather flight jacket had been freshly patched and cleaned. Her arms were folded. Her gray eyes watched the proceedings with a lazy sort of interest.

Next was Bjorn. Him Elias understood, mostly. The old white-haired mercenary was of even height with Elias, with a barrel chest and immense hands that had once closed around his throat before the man he had been had run him through and thrown him over a waterfall. His beard was thick and – at least today – set with rings, and his big coat was furs and leathers sewn together. They'd hardly spoken since he'd cut Elias's hair.

Beside Bjorn, Harkon Bright cut an understated, imposing figure. Perhaps it was the legends that clung to him, or the mixture of gravitas and mischief inherent in the mage's dark eyes. Perhaps it was that Elias owed him an unpayable debt. Either way, the young man couldn't look at him for long, so instead he shifted his gaze to Harkon's apprentice.

Aimee de Laurent had laid aside her long blue coat for dark apprentice's robes that draped flatteringly over a slender, athletic figure that somehow managed to stand relaxed, poised, and yet brimming with a fierce curiosity all at once. Her gold hair was bound up in an elaborate knot at the back of her head, and her silver apprentice's chain was clasped behind her pale neck. She was looking away from him just then, her bright blue eyes fixed on the procession currently passing her with a somberness that didn't *quite* hide her academic fascination. Alone among the crew, she knew the full extent of the crimes he had committed, the things he had endured, and the nebulous, still foggy time before the Eternal Order had taken him.

He had taken care not to dwell overmuch on what that fact meant. The emotions it evoked were tempestuous at best, sharp in their pain at worst. After a handful of seconds, Elias looked elsewhere. It was no more complex than it was with her teacher: a debt was owed. He could never repay it.

Perhaps that was a lie, but lies had their uses.

A voice sounded from the priest as the coffin was laid down, and Elias turned to watch. The ceremony was beginning.

An hour later, and the young man in green and black was doing his best not to get lost in an ocean of painted faces. The ceremony had been brief. The ruling class of the *Iseult* cleaved to a strain of the thousand-god faith that held the soul of the departed as a righteous burden that had to be carried to where it would rest. Having given Amut to his own people in Ishtier, they now celebrated his life with the candid relief of those who were no longer burdened.

Or, at least, that was what he'd managed to divine from the handful of conversations he'd had. Elias stood now on the black marble steps at the far end of a vast ballroom with a ceiling enchanted to display the open

sky. All around him, the officer and courtier classes
rubbed elbows and spoke with the unique affectations
of an upper class that fancied themselves meritocratic,
but guarded the gates to their status with invisible vipers.

Elias was on edge. During his time as Azrael he had
watched places like this burn to cinders in the heavens.
There was no accounting for that and, deeper down, a
part of him acknowledged that every second he lived was
stolen time. Nonetheless, the fear pulled at him, making
him tense. If any of these people should recognize his
face...

It was best not to obsess. Instead, he did his best
to pick out who the power players in the room were.
He watched courtiers move, their gestures and their
posture. The secret language of head lilts, eye twitches,
and gesticulating fingers that all people spoke with their
bodies. *Learn*, Roland's recalled voice repeated in his
head, *to find the most powerful people in the room. Learn what
they want.*

His wry grimace was involuntary. *I will never be rid of
you, my lord, will I?*

It took him a few moments, a careful circuit of the
room, affecting the stance of a simple courtier. Men
and women stared at him as he passed, eyes raking him
from boots to face. That wasn't unusual. Birth had given
him physical beauty, and a lifetime of hard training had
honed it into an effortless grace and charm, but these
traits came with as many potential difficulties as benefits.
It wasn't that it made going unnoticed impossible; the
world was full of empty heads with pretty faces, but that
managing that attention was something that required
nuance. One form of carriage could make him the focus
point of everyone in the room; a small adjustment, and

only *certain* people would pay any mind to the handsome man in black and green. The key was being aware of what was needed, and managing it accordingly.

He adjusted his posture: slack, relaxed – Gods that wasn't easy right now – and molded his smile into something casual, self-absorbed, and not-as-smart-as-it-presumed. The looks he received changed almost immediately. Only certain sorts of people eyed him now, and none of them in a dangerous way. Now he could move.

It took him the better part of twenty minutes to discern who in this room had real power, but once he'd memorized a few faces, he stopped short, briefly off-footed standing beside a refreshment table. He was still falling into the old patterns: learn who the powerful people were, assess them, examine them, and then what?

His own words as Azrael echoed back in his ears, as if they were still ringing in the throneroom of Port Providence. *"Absolute oblivion, majesty."*

He shifted from foot to foot, nearly felt his veneer crack, wrested it back into place. Azrael had been trained to assess everyone in the room, find the powerful, discern what they wanted, and use it to destroy them. Elias still had the skill, but he didn't know what to *do* with it. He scanned the crowd again. Vlana and Vant were talking with the brooch of the Engineers' Guild on his shoulder. No good. One of them was ambivalent to him, the other wished him only death. Clutch he barely knew, and she was being happily chatted up by a high-collared helmsman. Bjorn was by the window getting solidly drunk.

Harkon. Harkon could make use of this. He spotted

the old mage standing on the opposite side of the hall, sipping a glass of some dark, amber alcohol. Elias started towards him, only to stop halfway across the elaborately tiled floor when Rachim and two other men stepped between them, and the three began a quiet, urgent conversation that was quickly carried out onto a balcony. It was well that Elias was trying to seem a bit like an empty-headed courtier. Standing stumped in the center of a funerary soiree, empty-headed was how he felt.

Damn.

Move, fool, his mind reminded him. Standing here in the open like this was conspicuous. He turned, casting his eyes about for the only other person he could give this information to, when suddenly there she was, right in front of him. Aimee arched an eyebrow at the look on his face. "You look lost."

Elias stumbled for a moment. Her eyebrow climbed higher. He awkwardly offered her his arm. "Just go with it," he muttered. She took it.

Once they'd walked to the side of the room previously occupied by Harkon, Aimee looked up at him, fixing him with the curious stare of her blue eyes. "Alright," she said. "I don't know if it's just because I know you—" they both looked briefly askance at that, it was an awkward subject "—or if you're just *that* high strung, but you look like you're ready to jump through the nearest window. Explain, please, because it's making me *nervous*."

Elias looked away, scanning the room again. "Well," he answered, measuredly, "not the *window*..."

"Oh for the Gods' sake," Aimee placed a slender hand on her forehead. "That wasn't an invitation."

"And that wasn't an offer," Elias replied. Before they could digress again, he launched into as clean an explanation as could be mustered. "I was trained in the arts of the court," he said, "rigorously, from just as early as… everything else. I have a trained reflex to size up the room, figure out who the resident power players are, and what they might want."

Aimee nodded, following his gaze, as if by so doing she could suck that information out of the air with her eyes. Information was a siren call to the young sorceress. "Alright," she said, folding her arms under her chest and leaning against a black pillar, "I'm not understanding the problem though. That sounds useful."

"I learned how to do it so I would know who in the room I needed to manipulate or kill."

Understanding registered in her gaze. "… Ah."

"You see my problem."

She eyed him mildly. "Assuming you're not going to…"

He frowned. "Of *course* not." Then he sagged back against the pillar opposite her, resting the back of his head against the cool stone. "But that's part of the problem. Absent that mission I… I don't know what to *do* with that information."

She processed that. Aimee de Laurent had a way of looking unnervingly calm when she was assessing a thing. "Well *that's* obvious, then. Tell me."

"That was plan B," he admitted.

"I'm assuming plan A wasn't 'kill everyone in the room,'" she said.

"Hilarious," he deadpanned. "No. Plan A was telling Harkon."

Aimee's smile was catlike. Both in that it was curious, *and* irritated. "And now he's not here. So *spill*."

Elias nodded. "Fine." He shifted so he faced the crowd,

DRAGON ROAD

and gestured across the room. "Do you see the white-haired man covered in medals?"

Aimee shifted closer, the better to follow his finger. She was wearing some sort of perfume. It was distracting. "Yes," she said, nodding.

"Notice the way he's responding to everyone?" Elias said. "Reserved–"

"–but cold. There's no warmth behind the smile," Aimee finished. "I track. But the way those people are surrounding him–"

"–He's someone who matters," Elias confirmed, "who holds position, but elicits conflict."

Her smile was cunning. "So," she said, giving him a sideways look. "Who's he fighting?"

"When you see a grudge," Elias said, "check the shadow first."

She didn't need him to point. Her eyes flicked to the second figure. "So he's got issue with that pale-haired Violet-Imperium fellow in the red uniform," she murmured. "And... The woman in the ochre dress, with lapis lazuli hairpins. The former of those two is more ambitious than the latter, but pretends he isn't."

Elias smiled. "That's a step further than I'd taken it."

"I'm astute."

"Perhaps," Elias suggested, "you don't actually *need* me to point out the others."

She frowned sideways at him, her blue eyes narrowing just slightly. "Not fair."

"You're already taking my observations several steps forward," he said, folding his arms and leaning against the pillar, leveling his gaze on her. "You're smart enough."

"That's the *fun* of it," she sighed in mock exasperation. "How am I supposed to enjoy myself if I'm not one-upping your assessments?"

Elias shrugged. "Birdwatching?"

She swatted his arm. The first real laugh he'd had in weeks rumbled up from his chest in retort. "The others," he said then, "are a group of identically robed individuals being sought out by half the important people in this room. They're all wearing samite and rings with opals in them."

"A soldier," Aimee said, "a nobleman, a wise woman, and a council of some sort." The sorceress brought a hand to her chin and pursed her lips in thought. "With the captain dead," she said, "everything in the webs of power will be bending towards who influences the choice of the new one." She held up a hand to forestall his objection. "You said the next step was figuring out what they *wanted,* and that's the obvious lead-in."

"Please don't follow my process to its logical conclusion," Elias said. "I don't do that anymore."

She waved away the remark, focused intensely now upon the speculation. "Everything I've heard today is that Amut's death was sudden and unexpected."

"And then there was Rachim's tone in his communique with Harkon," Elias added. "There are wheels turning here. Immense ones. The trick is seeing them."

"Why ask us here," she continued, "if not because of that?"

They suddenly looked at each other, and Elias realized in the snap of the moment that they'd both come to the same conclusion.

Then Harkon Bright reemerged from the same direction he'd initially gone, and sighting them, made a direct line to the pair. "Get everyone together," he said in low tones. "I've just accepted a request to mediate the ruling council's deliberations to appoint *Iseult*'s new captain. When this behemoth leaves port tomorrow morning, we're going with them."

Elias's eyes flashed to Aimee's. And at the same time, they both muttered: "Shit."

DRAGON ROAD

COMING SOON

ACKNOWLEDGMENTS

No work worth its weight is done alone, and this book had plenty of helpers. First, to Dad who figured out my passion before I did, and Mom who always supported it. To Matt for sharing the creative fever-haze and being a sounding board. To Mike Underwood for having faith in this story, to Marc and the Angry Robot crew for shepherding it to publication. To Mark Teppo, Neal, and Greg, and many others. The thanks I owe you all could fill a hundred volumes. To Meg: your brilliance and kindness continue to inspire me.

To the music of Rage Against the Machine, Two Steps from Hell, Yasuharu Takanashi, Celldweller, and Tchaikovsky for breathing life into the Drifting Lands.

And to you, for reading this thing and sharing the journey with me, if only for a while. Now get up, pick a cause, and go make a difference. The world doesn't wait, and it needs you. Stand up. Find your courage. Fight.

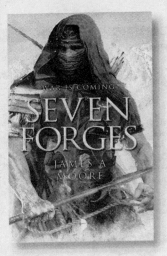
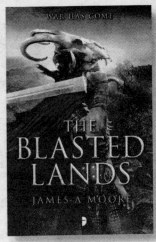
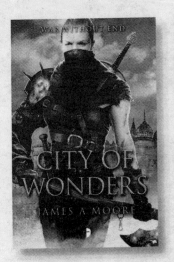
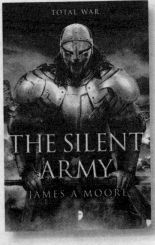

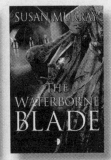

ANGRY
ROBOT

TRAVEL THE DRAGON ROAD

angryrobotbooks.com

twitter.com/angryrobotbooks

RAVES FOR
JAMES PATTERSON

"Patterson knows where our deepest fears are buried . . . There's
no stopping his imagination."
—New York Times Book Review

"James Patterson writes his thrillers as if he were building
roller coasters."   —Associated Press

"No one gets this big without natural storytelling talent—
which is what James Patterson has, in spades."
—Lee Child, #1 *New York Times* bestselling author of the
Jack Reacher series

"James Patterson knows how to sell thrills and suspense in
clear, unwavering prose."   *—People*

"Patterson boils a scene down to a single, telling detail, the
element that defines a character or moves a plot along. It's
what fires off the movie projector in the reader's mind."
—Michael Connelly

"James Patterson is the boss. End of."
—Ian Rankin, *New York Times* bestselling author of the
Inspector Rebus series

THE PARIS DETECTIVE

THREE DETECTIVE LUC MONCRIEF THRILLERS

JAMES PATTERSON
and RICHARD DiLALLO

GRAND CENTRAL
PUBLISHING

NEW YORK   BOSTON

Copyright © 2021 by James Patterson

Hachette Book Group supports the right to free expression and the value of copyright. The purpose of copyright is to encourage writers and artists to produce the creative works that enrich our culture.

The scanning, uploading, and distribution of this book without permission is a theft of the author's intellectual property. If you would like permission to use material from the book (other than for review purposes), please contact permissions@hbgusa.com. Thank you for your support of the author's rights.

Grand Central Publishing
Hachette Book Group
1290 Avenue of the Americas, New York, NY 10104
grandcentralpublishing.com
twitter.com/grandcentralpub

Originally published in trade paperback and ebook in December 2021
First oversize mass market edition: October 2022

French Kiss was first published by Little, Brown & Company in October 2016
The Christmas Mystery was first published by Little, Brown & Company in December 2016
French Twist was first published by Little, Brown & Company in February 2017

Grand Central Publishing is a division of Hachette Book Group, Inc. The Grand Central Publishing name and logo is a trademark of Hachette Book Group, Inc.

The publisher is not responsible for websites (or their content) that are not owned by the publisher.

The Hachette Speakers Bureau provides a wide range of authors for speaking events. To find out more, go to hachettespeakersbureau.com or call (866) 376-6591.

ISBNs: 9781538718841 (oversize mass market), 9781538718865 (ebook)

Printed in the United States of America

OPM

10 9 8 7 6 5 4 3 2 1

CONTENTS

FRENCH KISS

JAMES PATTERSON
AND RICHARD DiLALLO

CHAPTER 1

THE WEATHERMAN NAILED IT. "Sticky, hot, and miserable. Highs in the nineties. Stay inside if you can."

I can't. I have to get someplace. Fast.

Jesus Christ, it's hot. Especially if you're running as fast as you can through Central Park *and* you're wearing a dark-gray Armani silk suit, a light-gray Canali silk shirt, and black Ferragamo shoes.

As you might have guessed, I am late—very, very late. *Très en retard,* as we say in France.

I pick up speed until my legs hurt. I can feel little blisters forming on my toes and heels.

Why did I ever come to New York?

Why, oh why, did I leave Paris?

If I were running like this in Paris, I would be stopping all traffic. I would be the center of attention. Men and women would be shouting for the police.

"A young businessman has gone berserk! He is shoving baby carriages out of his path. He is frightening the old ladies walking their dogs."

But this is not Paris. This is New York.

So forget it. Even the craziest event in New York goes unnoticed. The dog walkers keep on walking their dogs. The teenage lovers kiss. A toddler points to me. His mother glances up. Then she shrugs.

Will even one New Yorker dial 911? Or 311?

Forget about that also. You see, I am part of the police. A French detective now working with the Seventeenth Precinct on my specialty—drug smuggling, drug sales, and drug-related homicides.

My talent for being late has, in a mere two months, become almost legendary with my colleagues in the precinct house. But…oh, *merde*…showing up late for today's meticulously planned stakeout on Madison Avenue and 71st Street will do nothing to help my reputation, a reputation as an uncooperative rich French kid, a rebel with too many causes.

Merde…today of all days I should have known better than to wake my gorgeous girlfriend to say good-bye.

"I cannot be late for this one, Dalia."

"Just one more good-bye squeeze. What if you're shot and I never see you again?"

The good-bye "squeeze" turned out to be significantly longer than I had planned.

Eh. It doesn't matter. I'm where I'm supposed to be now. A mere forty-five minutes late.

CHAPTER 2

MY PARTNER, DETECTIVE Maria Martinez, is seated on the driver's side of an unmarked police car at 71st Street and Madison Avenue.

While keeping her eyes on the surrounding area, Maria unlocks the passenger door. I slide in, drowning in perspiration. She glances at me for a second, then speaks.

"Man. What's the deal? Did you put your suit on first and *then* take your shower?"

"Funny," I say. "Sorry I'm late."

"You should have little business cards with that phrase on it—'Sorry I'm late.'"

I'm certain that Maria Martinez doesn't care whether I'm late. Unlike a lot of my detective colleagues, she doesn't mind that I'm not big on "protocol." I'm late a lot. I do a lot of careless things. I bring ammo for a Glock 22 when I'm packing a Glock 27. I like a glass or two of white wine with lunch…it's a long list. But Maria overlooks most of it.

My other idiosyncrasies she has come to accept, more

or less. I must have a proper *déjeuner*. That's lunch. No mere sandwich will do. What's more, a glass or two of good wine never did anything but enhance the flavor of a lunch.

You see, Maria "gets" me. Even better, she knows what I know: together we're a cool combination of her procedure-driven methods and my purely instinct-driven methods.

"So where are we with this bust?" I say.

"We're still sitting on our butts. That's where we are," she says. Then she gives details.

"They got two pairs of cops on the other side of the street, and two other detectives—Imani Williams and Henry Whatever-the-Hell-His-Long-Polish-Name-Is—at the end of the block. That team'll go into the garage.

"Then there's another team behind the garage. They'll hold back and *then* go into the garage.

"Then they got three guys on the roof of the target building."

The target building is a large former town house that's now home to a store called Taylor Antiquities. It's a place filled with the fancy antique pieces lusted after by trust-fund babies and hedge-fund hotshots. Maria and I have already cased Taylor Antiquities a few times. It's a store where you can lay down your Amex Centurion card and walk away with a white jade vase from the Yuan dynasty or purchase the four-poster bed where John and Abigail Adams reportedly conceived little John Quincy.

"And what about us?"

"Our assignment spot is inside the store," she says.

"No. I want to be where the action is," I say.

"Be careful what you wish for," Maria says. "Do what they tell you. We're inside the store. Over and out. Meanwhile, how about watching the street with me?"

Maria Martinez is total cop. At the moment she is heart-and-soul into the surveillance. Her eyes dart from the east side of the street to the west. Every few seconds, she glances into the rearview mirror. Follows it with a quick look into the side-view mirror. Searches straight ahead. Then she does it all over again.

Me? Well, I'm looking around, but I'm also wondering if I can take a minute off to grab a cardboard cup of lousy American coffee.

Don't get me wrong. And don't be put off by what I said about my impatience with "procedure." No. I am very cool with being a detective. In fact, I've wanted to be a detective since I was four years old. I'm also very good at my job. And I've got the résumé to prove it.

Last year in Pigalle, one of the roughest parts of Paris, I solved a drug-related gang homicide and made three on-the-scene arrests. Just me and a twenty-five-year-old traffic cop.

I was happy. I was successful. For a few days I was even famous.

The next morning the name Luc Moncrief was all over the newspapers and the internet. A rough translation of the headline on the front page of *Le Monde*:

OLDEST PIGALLE DRUG GANG SMASHED BY YOUNGEST PARIS DETECTIVE – LUC MONCRIEF

Underneath was this subhead:

Parisian Heartthrob Hauls in Pigalle Drug Lords

The paparazzi had always been somewhat interested in whom I was dating; after that, they were obsessed.

Club owners comped my table with bottles of Perrier-Jouët champagne. Even my father, the chairman of a giant pharmaceuticals company, gave me one of his rare compliments.

"Very nice job…for a playboy. Now I hope you've got this 'detective thing' out of your system."

I told him thank you, but I did not tell him that "this detective thing" was not out of my system. Or that I enjoyed the very generous monthly allowance that he gave me too much.

So when my *capitaine supérieur* announced that the NYPD wanted to trade one of their art-forgery detectives for one of our Paris drug enforcement detectives for a few months, I jumped at the offer. From my point of view, it was a chance to reconnect with my former lover, Dalia Boaz. From my Parisian *lieutenant* point of view, it was an opportunity to add some needed discipline and learning to my instinctive approach to detective work.

So here I am. On Madison Avenue, my eyes are burning with sweat. I can actually feel the perspiration squishing around in my shoes.

Detective Martinez remains focused completely on the street scene. But God, I need some coffee, some air. I begin speaking.

"Listen. If I could just jump out for a minute and—"

As I'm about to finish the sentence, two vans—one black, one red—turn into the garage next door to Taylor Antiquities.

Our cell phones automatically buzz with a loud sirenlike sound. The doors of the unmarked police cars begin to open.

As Maria and I hit the street, she speaks.

"It looks like our evidence has finally arrived."

CHAPTER 3

MARTINEZ AND I RUSH into Taylor Antiquities. There are no customers. A skinny middle-aged guy sits at a desk in the rear of the store, and a typical debutante—a young blond woman in a white linen skirt and a black shirt—is dusting some small, silver-topped jars.

It is immediately clear to both of them that we're not here to buy an ancient Thai penholder. We are easily identified as two very unpleasant-looking cops, the male foolishly dressed in an expensive waterlogged suit, the woman in too-tight khaki pants. Maria and I are each holding our NYPD IDs in our left hands and our pistols in our right hands.

"You. Freeze!" Maria shouts at the blond woman.

I yell the same thing at the guy at the desk.

"You freeze, too, sir," I say.

From our two pre-bust surveillance visits I recognize the man as Blaise Ansel, the owner of Taylor Antiquities.

Ansel begins walking toward us.

I yell again. "I said freeze, Mr. Ansel. This…is…a…drug…raid."

"This is police-department madness," Ansel says, and now he is almost next to us. The debutante hasn't moved a muscle.

"Cuff him, Luc. He's resisting." Maria is pissed.

Ansel throws his hands into the air. "No. No. I am not resisting anything but the intrusion. I *am* freezing. Look."

Although I have seen him before, I have never heard him speak. His accent is foreign, thick. It's an accent that's easy for anyone to identify. Ansel is a Frenchman. Son of a bitch. One of ours.

As Ansel freezes, three patrol cars, lights flashing, pull up in front of the store. Then I tell the young woman to join us. She doesn't move. She doesn't speak.

"Please join us," Maria says. Now the woman moves to us. Slowly. Cautiously.

"Your name, ma'am?" I ask.

"Monica Ansel," she replies.

Blaise Ansel looks at Martinez and me.

"She's my wife."

There's got to be a twenty-year age difference between the two of them, but Maria and I remain stone-faced. Maria taps on her cell phone and begins reading aloud from the screen.

"To make this clear: we are conducting a drug search based on probable cause. Premises and connected premises are 861 Madison Avenue, New York, New York, in the borough of Manhattan, June 21, 2016. Premises title: Taylor Antiquities, Inc. Chairman and owner: Blaise Martin Ansel. Company president: Blaise Martin Ansel."

Maria taps the screen and pushes another button.

"This is being recorded," she says.

I would never have read the order to search, but Maria is strictly by the book.

"This is preposterous," says Blaise Ansel.

Maria does not address Ansel's comment. She simply says, "I want you to know that detectives and officers are currently positioned in your delivery dock, your garage, and your rooftop. They will be interviewing all parties of interest. It is our assignment to interview both you and the woman you've identified as your wife."

"Drugs? Are you mad?" yells Ansel. "This shop is a museum-quality repository of rare antiques. Look. Look."

Ansel quickly moves to one of the display tables. He holds up a carved mahogany box. "A fifteenth-century tea chest," he says. He lifts the lid of the box. "What do you see inside? Cocaine? Heroin? Marijuana?"

It is obvious that Maria has decided to allow Ansel to continue his slightly crazed demonstration.

"This—this, too," Ansel says as he moves to a pine trunk set on four spindly legs. "An American colonial sugar safe. Nothing inside. No crystal meth, no sugar."

Ansel is about to present two painted Chinese-looking bowls when the rear entrance to the shop opens and Imani Williams enters. Detective Williams is agitated. She is also *très belle*.

"Not a damn thing in those two vans," she says. "Police mechanics are searching the undersides, but there's nothing but a bunch of empty gold cigarette boxes and twelve Iranian silk rugs in the cargo. We tested for drug traces. They all came up negative."

I think I catch an exchange of glances between Monsieur and Madame Ansel. I *think*. I'm not sure. But the more I think, well, the more sure I become.

"Detective Williams," I say. "Do you think you could fill in for me for a few minutes to assist Detective Martinez with the Ansel interview?"

"Yeah, sure," says Williams. "Where you going?"

"I just need to…I'm not sure…look around."

"Tell the truth, Moncrief. You've been craving a cup of joe since you got here," says Maria Martinez.

"Can't fool you, partner," I say.

I open the shop door. I'm out.

CHAPTER 4

THE SUFFOCATING AIR ON Madison Avenue almost shimmers with heat.

Where have all the beautiful people gone? East Hampton? Bar Harbor? The South of France?

I walk the block. I watch a man polish the handrail alongside the steps of Saint James' Church. I see the tourists line up outside Ladurée, the French *macaron* store.

A young African American man, maybe eighteen years old, walks near me. He is bare-chested. He seems even sweatier than I am. The young man's T-shirt is tied around his neck, and he is guzzling from a quart-size bottle of water.

"Where'd you get that?" I ask.

"A dude like you can go to that fancy-ass cookie store. You got five bills, that'll get you a soda there," he says.

"But where'd you get *that* bottle, the water you're drinking?" I ask again.

"Us poor bros go to Kenny's. You're practically in it right now."

He gestures toward 71st Street between Madison and Park Avenues. As the kid moves away, I figure that the "fancy-ass cookie store" is Ladurée. I am equidistant between a five-dollar soda and a cheaper but larger bottle of water. Why waste Papa's generous allowance on fancy-ass soda?

Kenny's is a tiny storefront, a place you should find closer to Ninth Avenue than Madison Avenue. Behind the counter is a Middle Eastern–type guy. Kenny? He peddles only newspapers, cigarettes, lottery tickets, and, for some reason, Dial soap.

I examine the contents of Kenny's small refrigerated case. It holds many bottles, all of them the same— the no-name water that the shirtless young man was drinking. At the moment that water looks to me like heaven in a bottle.

"I'm going to take two of these bottles," I say.

"One second, please, sir," says the man behind the counter, then he addresses another man who is wheeling four brown cartons of candy into the store. The cartons are printed with the name and logo for Snickers. The man steering the dolly looks very much like the counterman. Is he Kenny? Is anybody Kenny? I consider buying a Snickers bar. No. The wet Armani suit is already growing tighter.

"How many more boxes are there, Hector?" the counterman asks.

"At least fifteen more," comes the response. Then "Kenny" turns to me.

"And you, sir?" the counterman asks.

"No. Nothing," I say. "Sorry."

I leave the tiny store and break into a run. I am around the corner on Madison Avenue. I punch the button on my phone marked 4. Direct connection to Martinez. All I can think is: *What the hell? Twenty*

*cartons of candy stored in a shop the size of a closet?
Twenty cartons of Snickers in a store that doesn't even
sell candy?*

She answers and starts talking immediately.
"Williams and I are getting nowhere with these two
assholes. This whole thing sucks. Our intelligence is all
screwed up. There's nothing here."

I am only slightly breathless, only slightly nervous.

"Listen to me. It's all here, where I am. I know it."

"What the hell are you talking about?" she says.

"A newsstand between Madison and Park. Kenny's.
I'm less than two hundred feet away from you guys.
Leave one person at Taylor Antiquities and get every-
one over here. Now."

"How—?"

"The two vans, the garage…that's all a decoy," I
say. "The real shit is being unloaded here…in cartons
of candy bars."

"How do you know?"

"Like the case in Pigalle. *I know because I know.*"

CHAPTER 5

ONE MONTH LATER. IT'S another sweltering summer day in Manhattan.

A year ago I was working in the detective room at the precinct on rue Achille-Martinet in Paris. Today I'm working in the detective room at the precinct on East 51st Street in Manhattan.

But the crime is absolutely the same. In both cities, men, women, and children sell drugs, kill for drugs, and all too often die for drugs.

My desk faces Maria Martinez's scruffy desk. She's not in yet. Uh-oh. She may be picking up my bad habits. *Pas possible*. Not Maria.

I drink my coffee and begin reading the blotter reports of last night's arrests. No murders, no drug busts. So much for interesting blotter reports.

I call my coolest, hippest, chicest New York contact—Patrick, one of the doormen at 15 Central Park West, where I live with Dalia. Patrick is trying to score me a dinner reservation at Rao's, the impossible-to-get-into restaurant in East Harlem.

Merde. I am on my cell phone when my boss, Inspector Nick Elliott, the chief inspector for my division, stops by. I hold up my "just a minute" index finger. Since the Taylor Antiquities drug bust I have a little money in the bank with my boss, but it won't last forever, and this hand gesture certainly won't help.

At last I sigh. No tables. Maybe next month. When I hang up the phone I say, "I'm sorry, Inspector. I was just negotiating a favor with a friend who might be able to score me a table at Rao's next week."

Elliott scowls and says, "Far be it from me to interrupt your off-duty life, Moncrief, but you may have noticed that your partner isn't at her desk."

"I noticed. Don't forget, I'm a detective."

He ignores my little joke.

"In case you're wondering, Detective Martinez is on loan to Vice for two days."

"Why didn't you or Detective Martinez tell me this earlier? You must have known before today."

"Yeah, I knew about it yesterday, but I told Martinez to hold off telling you. That it would just piss you off to be left out, and I was in no rush to listen to you get pissed off," Elliott says.

"So why *wasn't* I included?" I ask.

"You weren't necessary. They just needed a woman. Though I don't owe you any explanations about assignments."

The detective room has grown quieter. I'm sure that a few of my colleagues—especially the men—are enjoying seeing Elliott put me in my place.

Fact is, I like Elliott; he's a pretty straight-arrow guy, but I have been developing a small case of paranoia about being excluded from hot assignments.

"What can Maria do that I can't do?" I ask.

"If you can't answer that, then that pretty-boy face

of yours isn't doing you much good," Elliott says with a laugh. Then his tone of voice turns serious.

"Anyway, we got something going on up the road a piece. They got a situation at Brioni. That's a fancy men's store just off Fifth Avenue. Get a squad car driver to take you there. Right now."

"Which Brioni?" I ask.

"I just told you—Brioni on Fifth Avenue."

"There are *two* Brionis: 57 East 57th Street and 55 East 52nd Street," I say.

Elliott begins to walk away. He stops. He turns to me. He speaks.

"You *would* know something like that."

CHAPTER 6

WHAT'S THE ONE QUESTION that's guaranteed to piss off any New York City detective or cop?

"Don't you guys have anything better to do with your time?"

If you're a cop who's ever ticketed someone for running a red light, if you're a detective who's ever asked a mother why her child wasn't in school that day, then you've heard it.

I enter the Brioni store at 57 East 57th Street. My ego is bruised, and my mood is lousy. Frankly, I am usually in Brioni as a customer, not a policeman. Plus, is there nothing more humiliating than an eager detective sent to investigate a shoplifting crime?

I'm in an even lousier mood when the first thing I'm asked is, "Don't you guys have anything better to do with your time?" The suspect doesn't ask this question. No. It comes from one of the arresting officers, a skinny young African American guy who is at the moment cuffing a young African American kid. The minor has been nabbed by store security. He was trying to lift three cashmere sweaters, and now the kid is scared as shit.

"You should know better than to ask that question," I say to the cop. "Meanwhile, take the cuffs off the kid."

The cop does as he's told, but he clearly does not know when to shut up. So he speaks.

"Sorry, Detective. I just meant that it's pretty unusual to send a detective out on an arrest that's so…so…"

He is searching for a word, and I supply it. "Unimportant."

"Yeah, that's it," the young officer says. "Unimportant."

The officer now realizes that the subject is closed. He gives me some details. The kid, age twelve, was brought in for petty robbery this past February. But I'm only half listening. I'm pissed off, and I'm pissed off because the cop is right—it's unimportant. This case is incredibly unimportant, laughably unimportant. It's ridiculous to be sent on such a stupid little errand. Other NYPD detectives are unraveling terrorist plots, going undercover to frame mob bosses. Me, I'm overseeing the arrest of a little kid who stole three cashmere sweaters.

As Maria Martinez has often said to me, "Someone with your handsome face and your expensive suit shouldn't be sent on anything but the most important assignments." Then she'd laugh, and I would stare at her in stony silence…until I also laughed.

"We have the merch all bagged," says the other officer. The name Callahan is on his nameplate. Callahan is a guy with very pink cheeks and an even pinker nose. He looks maybe thirty-five or forty…or whatever age a cop is when he's smart enough not to ask "Don't you have anything better to do with your time?"

"Thanks," I say.

But what I'm really thinking about is: *Who the hell gave me this nauseatingly* petite *assignment?*

I'm sure it's not Elliott. Ah, *oui,* the inspector and I aren't exactly what they call best buds, but he's grown used to me. He thinks he's being funny when he calls me Pretty Boy, but he also trusts me, and, like almost everyone else, he's very pleased with the bust I (almost single-handedly) helped pull off at Taylor Antiquities.

I know that my partner, Maria Martinez, puts out good press on me. As I've said, she and I are simpatico, to say the least. I like her. She likes me. Case closed.

Beyond that, anyone higher than Elliott doesn't know I exist. So I can't assume that one of the assistant commissioners or one of the ADAs is out to get me.

"There's a squad car outside to bring him in," Callahan says.

"Hold on a minute. I want to talk to the kid," I say.

I walk over to the boy. He wears jeans cut off at mid-calf, very clean white high-top sneakers, and an equally clean white T-shirt. It's a look I could live without.

"Why'd you try to steal three sweaters? It's the god-damn middle of summer, and you're stealing sweaters. Are you stupid?"

I can tell that if he starts talking he's going to cry.

No answer. He looks away. At the ceiling. At the floor. At the young cop and Callahan.

"How old are you?" I ask.

"Sixteen," he says. My instinct was right. He does start to cry. He squints hard, trying to stem the flow of tears.

"You're a lousy liar *and* a lousy thief. You're twelve. You're in the system. Don't you think the officers checked? You were picked up five months ago. You and a friend tried to hold up a liquor store on East Tremont. They got you then, too. You *are* stupid."

The kid shouts at me. No tears now.

"I ain't stupid. I kinda thought they'd have a buzzer or some shit in the liquor store. And I kinda felt that fat-ass guy here with the ugly-mother brown shoes was a security guy. But I don't know. Both times I decided to try it. I decided…I'm not sure why."

"Listen. Good advice number one. Kids who are assholes turn into grown-ups who are assholes.

"Good advice number two. If you've got smart instincts, *follow them*. You know what? Forget good advice. You've got a feeling? Go with it."

He sort of nods in agreement. So I keep talking.

"Look, asshole. This advice is life advice. I'm not trying to teach you how to be a better thief. I'm just trying to…oh, shit…I don't know what I'm trying to teach you."

A pause. The kid looks down at the floor so intensely that I have to look down there myself. Nothing's there but gray carpet squares.

Then the kid looks at me. He speaks.

"I get you, man," he says.

"Good." A pause. "Now go home. You've got a home?"

"I got a home. I got a grandma."

"Then go."

"What the fu—?"

"Just go."

He runs to the door.

The young officer looks at me. Then he says, "That's just great. They send a detective to the scene. And he lets the suspect go."

I don't smile. I don't answer. I walk to a nearby table where beautiful silk ties and pocket squares are laid out in groups according to color. I focus on the yellow section—yellow with blue stripes, yellow with tiny red dots, yellow paisley, yellow...

My cell phone pings. The message on the screen is big and bold and simple. CD. Cop Down.

No details. Just an address: 655 Park Avenue. Right now.

CHAPTER 7

COPS AND LIGHTS AND miles of yellow tape:
POLICE LINE DO NOT CROSS.

Sirens and detectives crowd the blocks between
65th and 67th Streets. Even the mayor's car (license
NYC 1) is here.

People from the neighborhood, doormen on break,
and students from Hunter College try to catch a
glimpse of the scene. Hundreds of people stand on the
blocked-off avenue. It's a tragedy and a block party at
the same time.

Detective Gabriel Ruggie approaches me. There will
be no French-guy jokes, no late-guy jokes, no Pretty
Boy jokes. This is serious shit. Ruggie talks.

"Elliott is up there now. The scene is at the seventh
floor front. He said to send you up right away."

I walk through the fancy lobby. It's loaded with cops
and reporters and detectives. I hear a brief litany of
somber "hellos" and "hiyas," most of them followed by
various mispronunciations of my name.

Luke. Look. Luck.

Who the hell cares now? This is Cop Down.

Detective Christine Liang is running the elevator along with a plainclothes officer.

"Hey, Moncrief. Let me take you up," Liang says. "The inspector's been asking where you are."

What the hell is the deal? Ten minutes ago I'm supervising New York's dumbest little crime of the day. Now, all of a sudden, the most serious type of crime—officer homicide—requires my attention.

"Good—you're here," Elliott says as I step from the elevator. I feel as if he's been waiting for me. It's the typical chaos of a homicide, with fingerprinting people, computer people, the coroner's people—all the people who are really smart, really thorough; but honestly, none of them ever seem to come up with information that helps solve the case.

I'm scared. I don't mind saying it. Elliott hits his phone and says, "Moncrief is here now."

"Who's that?" I ask.

"Just headquarters. I let them know you were here. They were trying to track you down."

"But you knew where I was. You sent me there," I say, confused.

"Yeah, I know. I know." Elliott seems confused, too.

"What's the deal?" I ask.

"Come with me," Elliott says. The crowd of NYPD people parts for us as if we're celebrities. We walk down a wide hall with black and white marble squares on the floor, two real Warhols on the walls. Suddenly I have a flash of an apartment in Paris—the high ceilings, the carved cornices. But in a moment I've traveled back from boulevard Haussmann to Park Avenue.

At the end of the hallway, an officer stands in front

of an open door. Bright lights—floodlights, examination lights—pour from the room into the hallway. The officer moves aside immediately as Elliott and I approach.

Three people are huddled in a group near a window. I catch sight of a body, a woman. Elliott and I walk toward the group. We are still a few feet away when I see her. When my heart leaps up.

Maria Martinez.

A black plastic sheet covers her torso. Her head, blood speckling and staining her hair, is exposed.

Elliott puts a hand on my shoulder. I don't yell or cry or shake. A numbness shoots through me, and then the words tumble out.

"How? How?"

"I told you this morning, she was on loan to Vice. They had her playing the part of a high-class call girl. It seems that...well, whoever she was supposed to meet decided to...well, take a knife to her stomach."

I say nothing. I keep staring at my dead partner. Elliott decides to fill the air with words. I know he means well.

"The owners of this place are at their house in Nantucket. No servants were home...no..."

I've stopped listening. Elliott stops talking. The police photographers keep clicking away. Phil Namanworth, the coroner, is typing furiously on his laptop. Cops and detectives come and go.

Maria is dead. She looks so peaceful. Isn't that what people always say? But it's true. At least in this case it's true. In death there is peace, but there's no peace for those of us left behind.

Elliott looks me straight in the eye.

"Ya know, Moncrief, I'd like to say that in time you'll get over this." He pauses. "But I'd be a liar."

"And a good cop never lies," I say softly.

"Come back to the precinct in my car," Elliott says.

"No, thank you," I answer. "There's someplace I've got to be."

CHAPTER 8

IT'S THE SOUTHWEST CORNER of 177th Street and Fort Washington Avenue. Maria and Joey Martinez's building. I had never been there before, although Maria kept insisting that Dalia and I had to come by some night for "crazy chicken and rice," her mother's recipe.

"You'll taste it, you'll love it, and you won't be able to guess the secret ingredient," she would say.

But we never set a date, and now I am about to visit her apartment while two cops are standing guard outside the building and two detectives are inside questioning neighbors. I was her partner. I've got to see Maria's family.

A short pudgy man opens the apartment door. The living room is noisy, packed. People are crying, yelling, speaking Spanish and English. The big window air conditioner is noisy.

"I'm Maria's brother-in-law," says the man at the door.

"I'm Maria's partner from work," I say.

His face shows no expression. He nods, then says, "Joey and me are about to go downtown. They wouldn't let him—the husband, the actual husband—go to the crime scene. Now they'll let us go see her. In the morgue."

A handsome young Latino man walks quickly toward me. It has to be Joey Martinez. He is nervous, animated, red-eyed. He grabs me firmly by the shoulders. The room turns silent, like somebody turned an Off switch.

"You're Moncrief. I know you from your pictures. Maria has a million pictures of you on her phone," he says.

"Yeah," I say. "She loves clicking away on that cell phone."

I can't help but notice that he calls me by my last name. I don't know why. Maybe that's how Maria referred to me at home.

I try to move closer to give Joey a hug. But he moves back, blocking any sort of embrace. So I speak.

"I don't know what to say, Joey. This is an incredible tragedy. Your heart must be breaking. I'm so sorry."

"Your heart must be breaking also," Joey says.

"It is," I say. "Maria was the best partner a detective could hope for. Smart. Patient. Tough…" Joey may not be weeping, but I feel myself choking up.

Joey gestures to his brother. It's a "Let's go" toss of his head.

"Look, my brother and I are going down to see Maria. But Moncrief…"

There's that last-name-only thing again. "I need to ask you something."

Now I'm nervous, but I'm not at all sure why. Something is off. The room remains silent. Brother is now standing next to brother.

"Sure," I say. "Ask me. Ask me anything."

Joey Martinez's sad and empty eyes widen. He looks directly at me and speaks slowly. "How do you have the nerve to come to my house?"

I feel confusion, and I'm sure that my face is communicating it. "Because I feel so terrible, so awful, so sad. Maria was my partner. We spent hours and hours together."

Joey continues speaking at the same slow pace. "Yes. I know. Maria loved you."

"And I loved her," I say.

"You don't understand. Or you're a liar. Maria *loved* you. She really loved you."

His words are so crazy and so untrue that I have no idea how to respond. "Joey. Please. You're experiencing a tragedy. You're totally...well...you're totally wrong about Maria, about me."

"She told me," he says. "It's not a misunderstanding. She didn't mean you were just good friends. We talked about it a thousand times. She *loved* you."

Now he pushes his face close to mine. "You think because you're rich and good-looking you can get whatever you want. You think——"

"Joey. Wait. This is insane!" I shout.

He shouts even louder. "Stop it! Just shut up. Just leave!" He shakes his head. The tears are coming fast. "My brother and I gotta go."

CHAPTER 9

WHEN I GET HOME, Dalia is waiting for me in the apartment foyer. Her hug is strong. Her kiss is soft—not sexual per se—just the perfect gentle touch of warmth. The tenderness of Dalia's kiss immediately signals to me that she's already heard about Maria Martinez's death. I'm not surprised. The DA's office has access to all NYPD information, and Dalia knows her way around her job.

Dalia is an ADA for Manhattan district attorney Fletcher Sinclair. She heads up the investigation division. The two qualities that the job requires—brains and persistence—are the two qualities Dalia seems to have in endless supply. Nothing and no one stands in her way when she's hot on an investigation.

Every day at work she tones down her tall and skinny fashion-model look with a ponytail, sensible skirts, and almost no makeup. When Dalia's at her job, she's all about the job. Laser-focused. Don't mess with the ADA.

Some evenings, when Dalia's dressed for some

ultrachic charity dinner, even I have a hard time believing that this breathtakingly *belle* woman in her Georgina Chapman gown is one of the toughest lawyers in New York City.

"We got word about Maria at the DA's office late this morning," she says. "I was going to call or text or something, but I didn't want to butt in. I didn't want to nudge you if you didn't need me...."

"You can always nudge me, because I always need you," I say.

"I opened a nice Chilean Chardonnay. You want a glass and we can talk?" she asks.

"Yes," I say. "Mix a glass of wine with a quart of tequila and we'll have a drink that *might* make me forget what a miserable day this has been."

"Maria, Maria, Maria," Dalia says. She shakes her head as she pours the wine into two wineglasses. Then she says, "I hate to ask, but...any ideas yet?"

"I sure don't have any guesses. I don't even have all the details yet. Plus Maria's husband is a crazy mess right now." I decide to skip the details.

"Understandably," Dalia says.

I cannot shake the mental picture of Joey Martinez's hurt and anger as he spat out the words "She *loved* you."

Then Dalia says, "But what about you? How are you feeling?"

"How *can* I feel? Maria was my partner, and she was as good a partner as anyone ever had. She was damn near perfect. As my rugby coach used to say, 'The best combination for any job is the brains of an owl and the skin of an elephant.'"

"What was the name of the genius who came up with that little saying?" Dalia asks.

"Monsieur Pierre LeBec. You must remember

him—the fat little man who was always smoking a pipe. He coached boys' rugby and taught geometry," I say. A reminiscence is about to open up.

Dalia and I speak often about the school in Paris we both attended. We became girlfriend and boyfriend during our second year at Lycée Henri-IV. And we fell in love exactly the way teenagers do— with unstoppable passion. There wasn't enough time in the day for all the laughter and talking and sex that we needed to have. Even when we broke up, just before we both left for university, we did it with excessive passion. Lots of door slamming and yelling and crying and kissing.

Ten years later, when Act II of *The Story of Dalia and Luc* began, it was as if we were teenagers all over again. First of all, we "met cute." Dalia and I reconnected completely accidentally three months ago at one of the rare NYPD social functions—a spring boat ride on the Hudson River. I was standing alone at the starboard railing and must have been turning green. About to heave, I was one seasick sailor.

"You look like a man who needs some Dramamine," came Dalia's voice from behind me. I'd know it anywhere. I turned around.

"Holy shit! It's you," I said. We hugged and immediately agreed that only God himself could have planned this meeting. It may not have been an actual miracle, but it was certainly *une coïncidence grande.* Two former Parisian lovers who end up on a boat and then…

Dalia reminded me that she was not Parisian. She was Israeli, a sabra.

"Okay, then it's a fairy tale," I said. "And in fairy tales you don't pay attention to details."

By the time the boat docked at Chelsea Piers, we were in love again. And—holy shit indeed—had she ever turned from a spectacular-looking teenager into an incredibly spectacular-looking young woman.

She invited me back to her ridiculously large penthouse at 15 Central Park West, the apartment that her father, the film director and producer Menashe Boaz, had paid for. That night was beyond unforgettable. I couldn't imagine my life if that night had never happened.

After the first week, I had most of my clothes sent over.

After the second week, I had my exercise bike and weights sent over.

After a month I hired a company to deliver the three most valuable pieces from my contemporary Chinese art collection: the Zao Wou-Ki, the Zhang Xiaogang, and the Zeng Fanzhi. Dalia refers to them as the Z-name contemporary art collection. She said that when those paintings were hung in her living room, she knew I planned to stay.

But now we have *this* night. The night of Maria's death. A night that's the emotional opposite of that joyful night months ago.

"Will you be hungry later on?" Dalia asks.

"I doubt it," I say. I pour us each another glass of wine. "Anyway, if we get hungry later on, I'll make us some scrambled eggs."

She smiles and says, "An eight-burner Garland range and we're making scrambled eggs."

That statement should be cute and funny. But we both know that nothing can be cute and funny this evening.

"I want to ask you something," I say.

"Yeah, of course," she says. She wrinkles her forehead a tiny bit. As if she's expecting some scary question. I proceed.

"Are you angry that I'm so sad about Maria's murder?"

Dalia pauses. Then she tilts her head to the side. Her face is now soft, tender, caring.

"Oh, Luc," she says. "I would only be angry if you were *not* sad."

I feel that we should kiss. I think Dalia feels the same way. But I also think something inside each of us is telling us that if we did kiss, no matter how chaste the kiss might be, it would be almost disrespectful to Maria.

We sit silently for a long time. We finish the bottle of Chardonnay.

It turns out that we never were hungry enough to scramble some eggs. All we did was wait for the day to end.

CHAPTER 10

THE PERSON RESPONSIBLE FOR whatever skill I have in speaking decent English—very little French accent, pretty good English vocabulary—is Inspector Nick Elliott. No one has mastered the art of plain speaking better than he has.

"Morning, Pretty Boy. Looks like it's going to be a shitty day" is a typical example.

This morning Elliott and a woman I've never seen before appear at my desk. Looks like I'm about to receive an extra lesson in basic communication skills.

"Moncrief, meet Katherine Burke. You two are going to be partners in the Martinez investigation. I don't care to discuss it."

I barely have time to register the woman's face when he adds, "Good luck. Now get the hell to work."

"But sir…" I begin.

"Is there a problem?" Elliott asks, clearly anxious to hit the road.

"Well, no, but…"

"Good. Here's the deal. Katherine Burke is a

detective, a *New York* detective, and has been for almost two years. She knows police procedure better than most people know their own names. She can teach you a lot."

I go for the end-run charm play.

"And I've got a lot to learn," I say, a big smile on my face.

He doesn't smile back.

"Don't get me wrong," Elliott says as he turns and speaks to Burke. "Moncrief has the instincts of a good detective. He just needs a little spit and polish."

As he walks away, I look at Katherine Burke. She is not Maria Martinez. So, of course, I immediately hate her.

"Good to meet you," she says.

"Same here." We shake, more like a quick touch of the hands.

My new partner and I study each other quietly, closely. We are like a bride and groom in an arranged marriage meeting for the first time. This "marriage" means a great deal to me—joy, sorrow, and whether or not I can smoke in the squad car.

So what do I see before me? Burke is thirty-two, I'd guess. Face: pretty. No, actually *très jolie*. Irish; pale; big red lips. A good-looking woman in too-tight khakis. She seems pleasant enough. But I'm not sensing "warm and friendly."

And what does she see? A guy with an expensive haircut, an expensive suit, and—I think she's figured out already—a pretty bad attitude.

This does not bode well.

"Listen," she says. "I know this is tough for you. The inspector told me how much you admired Maria. We can talk about that."

"No," I say. "We can forget about that."

Silence again. Then I speak.

"Look. I apologize. You were trying to be nice, and I was just being...well..."

She fills it in for me: "A rude asshole. It happens to the best of us."

I smile, and I move a step closer. I read the official ID card that hangs from the cord around her neck. It shows her NYPD number and, in the same size type, her title. These are followed by her name in big bold uppercase lettering:

K. BURKE

"So you want to be called K. Burke?" I ask her as we walk back to the detective room.

"No. Katherine, Katie, or Kathy. Any of those are fine," she says.

"Then why do you have 'K. Burke' printed on your ID?"

"That's what they put there when they gave me the ID," she says. "The ID badge wasn't high on my priority list."

"K. Burke. I like it. From now on, that's what I'm going to call you. K. Burke."

She nods. For a few moments we don't speak. Then I say, "But I must be honest with you, K. Burke. I don't think this is going to work out."

She speaks, still seriously.

"You want to know something, Detective Moncrief?"

"What?"

"I think you're right."

And then, for the first time, she smiles.

CHAPTER 11

THE LOBBY OF THE Auberge du Parc Hotel is somebody's idea of elegance. But it sure as hell is not mine.

"Pink marble on the walls *and* the floor *and* the ceiling. If Barbie owned a brothel it would look like this." I share this observation with my new partner as I look out the floor-to-ceiling windows that face Park Avenue.

K. Burke either doesn't get the joke or doesn't like the joke. No laughter.

"We're not here to evaluate the decor," she says. "You know better than I do that Auberge du Parc is right up there with the Plaza and the Carlyle when it comes to expensive hotels for rich people."

"And it affords a magnificent view of the building where Maria Martinez was killed," I say as I gesture to the tall windows.

Burke looks out to the corner of 68th Street and Park Avenue. She nods solemnly. "That's why we're starting the job here."

"The job, you will agree, is fairly stupid?" I ask.

"The job is what Inspector Elliott has assigned us, and I'm not about to second-guess the command," she says.

Elliott wants us to interview prostitutes, street-walkers, anyone he defines as "high-class lowlife." Enormously upscale hotels like the Auberge often have a lot of illegal sex stuff going on behind their pink marble walls. But asking the devils to tell us their sins? I don't think so.

This approach is ridiculous, to my way of thinking. Solutions come mostly by listening for small surprises—and yes, sometimes by looking for a few intelligent pieces of hard evidence. Looking in the *unlikely* places. Talking to the *least* likely observers.

Burke's theory, which is total NYPD style, is way more traditional: "You accumulate the information," she had said. "You assemble the puzzle piece by piece."

"Absolutely not," I replied. "You sink into the case as if it were a warm bath. You *sense* the situation. You look for the fingerprint of the crime itself." Then I added, "Here's what we'll do: you'll do it your way. I'll do it mine."

"No, not *your* way or *my* way," she had said. "We'll do it the NYPD way."

That discussion was a half hour ago. Now I'm really too disgusted and frustrated to say anything else.

So I stand with my new partner in a pink marble lobby a few hundred yards from where my old partner was murdered.

Okay. I'll be the adult here. I will try to appear cooperative.

We review our plan. I am to go to the lobby bar and talk to the one or two high-priced hookers who are almost always on the prowl there. You've seen them—

the girls with the perfect hair falling gently over their shoulders. The delicate pointy noses all supplied by the same plastic surgeon. The women who are drinking in the afternoon while they're dressed for the evening.

Burke will go up to the more elegant, more secluded rooftop bar, Auberge in the Clouds. But of course she'll first stop by the hotel manager's office and tell him what he already knows: the NYPD is here. Procedure, procedure, procedure.

If Maria Martinez is watching all this from some heavenly locale, she is falling on the floor laughing.

After agreeing to meet Burke back in the lobby in forty-five minutes, I walk into the bar. (I once visited Versailles on a high school class trip, and this place would have pleased Marie Antoinette.) The bar itself is a square-shaped ebony box with gold curlicues all over it. It looks like a huge birthday present for a god with no taste.

At the bar sit two pretty ladies, one in a red silk dress, the other in a kind of clingy Diane von Furstenberg green-and-white thing, which is very loose around the top. I don't think von Furstenberg designed it to be so erotic. It takes me about two seconds to realize what these women do for a living.

These girls are precisely the type that Nick Elliott wants us to speak to. Yes, a ridiculous waste of time. And I know just what to do about it.

I walk toward the exit and push through the revolving door.

I'm out. I'm on my own. This is more like it.

CHAPTER 12

K. BURKE THINKS A good New York cop solves a case by putting the pieces together. K. Burke is wrong.

You can't put the pieces together in New York because there are just too goddamn many of them.

One step out the revolving door onto East 68th Street proves my point. It's only midday, but everywhere I look there's chaos and color and confusion.

Bike messengers and homeless people and dowagers and grammar-school students. Two women wheeling a full-size gold harp and two guys pushing a wheelbarrow full of bricks. The Greenpeace recruiter with her clipboard and smile, the crazy half-naked lady waving a broken umbrella, and the teenager selling iPad cases. All this on one block.

The store next to the Auberge bar entrance is called Spa-Roe. According to the sign, it's a place you can visit for facials and massages (the "spa" part) while you sample various caviars (the "roe" part). Just what the world has been waiting for.

Right next to it is a bistro...*pardon*...a bar. It's called Fitzgerald's, as in "F. Scott." I stand in front of it for a few moments and look through the window. It's a re-creation of a 1920s speakeasy. I can see a huge poster that says GOD BLESS JIMMY WALKER. Only one person is seated at the bar, a pretty young blond girl. She's chatting with the much older bartender.

I walk about twenty feet and pass a pet-grooming store. A very unhappy cat is being shampooed. Next door is a "French" dry cleaner, a term I'd never heard before moving to New York. There's an optician who sells *discounted* Tom Ford eyeglass frames for four hundred dollars. There's a place to have your computer fixed and a place that sells nothing but brass buttons. I pause. I smoke a cigarette. The block is busy as hell, but nothing is happening for me.

Until I toss my cigarette on the sidewalk.

CHAPTER 13

A MAN'S VOICE ISN'T ANGRY, just loud. "What's with the littering, mister?"

Littering? That's a new word in my English vocabulary.

The speaker is a white-bearded old man wearing brown work pants and a brown T-shirt. It's the kind of outfit assembled to look like a uniform, but it isn't actually a uniform. The man is barely five feet tall. He holds an industrial-size water hose with a dripping nozzle.

"Littering?" I ask.

The old guy points to the dead cigarette at my feet.

"Your cigarette! They pay me to keep these sidewalks clean."

"I apologize."

"I was making a joke. It's only a joke. Get it? A joke, just a joke."

This man was not completely, uh...mentally competent, but I had to follow one of my major rules: talk to anyone, anywhere, anytime.

"Yes, a joke. Good. Do you live here?" I ask.

"The Bronx," he answers. "Mott Haven. They always call it the south Bronx, but it's not. I don't know why they can't get it right."

"So you just work down here?"

"Yeah. I watch the three buildings. The button place, the animal place, and the eyeglasses place. They call me Danny with the Hose."

"Understandably," I say.

"Good, you understand. Now stand back."

I do as I'm told until my back is up against the optician's doorway. Danny sprays the sidewalk with a fast hard surge of water. Scraps of paper, chunks of dog shit, empty beer cans—they all go flying into the gutter.

"Danny," I say. "A lot of pretty girls around here, huh? What with the fancy hotel right here and the fancy neighborhood."

He shuts off his hose. "Some are pretty. I mind my business."

A young man, no more than twenty-five, comes out of the pet-grooming shop. He has a big dog—a boxer, I think—on a leash. Danny with the Hose and the man with the dog greet each other with a high five. The young man is tall, blond, good-looking. He wears long blue shorts and a pathetic red sleeveless shirt.

"Hey," I say to him. "Danny and I have just been talking about the neighborhood. I'm moving to East 68th Street in a few weeks. With a roommate. A German shepherd."

"Cool," he says, suddenly a lot more interested in talking to me. "If you need a groomer, this place is the best. Take a look at Titan." He pets his dog's shiny coat. "He's handsome enough to be in a *GQ* spread.

I've been bringing him here ever since we moved into 655 Park five years ago."

My ears prick up. I go into full acting-class mode now.

"Isn't 655 the place where that lady cop got killed?"

"They say she was a cop pretending to be a hooker. I don't know."

"Luc...Luc Moncrief," I say. We shake.

"Eric," he says. No last name offered. "Well, welcome. I said 'pretending,' but I don't know. Women are not my area of expertise, if you know what I mean. All my info on the local girls comes from one of the doormen in my building. He says all the hookers hang out at the Auberge."

"That's where I'm staying now," I say.

"Well, anyway, Carl—the doorman—says most of the girls who work out of the Auberge bar are clean. Bang, bang, pay your money, over and out. He says the ones to watch out for are the girls who work for the Russians. Younger and prettier, but they'll skin you alive. I dunno. I play on a whole other team."

"Yet you seem to know a great deal about *mine*," I say. "Nice meeting you."

The guy and the dog take off. Danny with the Hose has disappeared, too.

I look at my watch. I should be meeting up with K. Burke.

But first I'll just go on a quick errand.

CHAPTER 14

IF YOU EVER NEED to get some information from a New York doorman, learn from my experience with Carl.

A ten-dollar bill will get you this: "Yeah, I think there's some foreign kind of operation going on at the Auberge. But I'm busy getting taxis for people and helping with packages. So I can't be sure."

I give Carl another ten dollars.

"They got Russians in and outta there. At least I think they're Russian. I'm not that good with accents."

I give him ten more. That's thirty so far, if you're keeping track.

"I heard all this from a friend who works catering at the Auberge. The Russians keep a permanent three-room suite there…where they pimp out the hookers."

Carl gives me a sly smile. It would seem my reaction has given away my motives.

"Oh, I see where you're headed. You wanna know if the Russians had anything to do with the murder on seven. The cops talked to me, like, twenty times. But I wasn't on the door that day. And how the girl got in? No clue."

Perhaps that's true. But I have a feeling Carl might be leading me to some other clues. I give him ten bucks more.

"Strange, though. Those Russians specialize in young, pretty, all-American blondes. You know. Fresh, clean, sort of look like innocent little virgins. Nothing like the woman who got iced. But…there is something else."

I wait for Carl to keep talking, but he doesn't. Instead, he hustles outside the building just as a yellow cab pulls up. He opens the door, and a weary-looking gray-haired man in a gray pin-striped suit emerges. Carl takes the man's briefcase and follows him down a long hallway that leads to an elevator. The old man might as well be *crawling,* he's going so slowly. Finally Carl returns.

"Sorry. Now, what was I saying?"

Damn this sneaky doorman. I know he's playing me, but I'm hoping it's worth it. Because all I've got left is a fifty. I give it to Carl with a soft warning: "This better be worth fifty bucks."

"Well, it's a little thing, and it's from my buddy at the Auberge, and you never know when he's telling the truth, and…"

"Come on. What is it?"

"He says that the girls never wait in the lobby or the suite or the back hallways. The Russian guys keep 'em in the neighborhood somewhere. I don't know where. Like a coffee shop or a private house. Then the girl gets a phone call and a few minutes later one of the blondies is taking the elevator up to the special private suite."

Bingo. I'm ready to roll. And—if you're keeping track—it cost me ninety bucks.

But it was *definitely* worth it.

CHAPTER 15

I WALK INTO THE lobby of the Auberge. Standing there is K. Burke. She's easily identifiable by the smoke coming out of her ears.

"Where have you been?" she demands. "I checked the bar, then the restaurants, then…anyway. What did you find out?"

"Nothing," I say. "And you?"

"Wait a minute. Nothing? How many people did you talk to?"

"Beaucoup."

"And nothing?"

"Oui. Rien."

She shakes her head, but I'm not sure she believes me.

"Well," she says as she gestures me out the front door, "while I was standing around, waiting for a certain someone I won't name, I texted a contact in Vice, who gave me access to some of their files. And I have a theory." Detective Burke begins to speak more quickly now, but she still sounds like a first-grade teacher explaining simple arithmetic to the class.

"There have been three call-girl murders in the past three months, including Maria Martinez. All Vice cops posing as call girls. The first was…"

I cannot keep quiet. We've already looked into this.

"I know," I say. "Valerie Delvecchio. Murdered at a construction site. A *rénovation* of a hotel. The Hotel Chelsea, on 23rd Street and Seventh Avenue. The second cop was Dana Morgan-Schwarz. She was offed in a hotel on 155th and Riverside. A drug-den SRO so bad I wouldn't go there to take a piss."

This does nothing to dampen Burke's enthusiasm for her theory.

"Don't you see, Moncrief? You're not putting the pieces together. This is a pattern. Three Vice cops posing as call girls. All of them murdered. This is—"

"This is ridiculous," I say. "This is *not* a *pattern*. It is at best a *coincidence*. The Chelsea murder is unsolved, yes. But the detective's body was dumped there *after* she was murdered. And Morgan-Schwarz was probably involved in an inside drug deal. No high-class hooker would go to that hotel."

But Burke is simply not listening.

"I set up a meeting for us with Vice this afternoon at four. We're going to get the names, numbers, and websites of *every* expensive call-girl service in New York."

"Good luck with that," I say. "That should only take a few weeks."

"Then we're going to meet all the people who run them. I don't care if it's the Mafia, Brazilian drug lords, Colombian cartels, or other cops. We're going to see every last one."

"Great. That should only take a few *months*."

"You've got a bad goddamn attitude, Moncrief."

I'm not going to explode. I'm not going to explode. I'm not going to explode.

"I will see you at four o'clock for our meeting with Vice," I say calmly.

"Where are you going till then? We've got work to do."

"I'm going to work right now. Want to come along?"

Burke folds her arms and frowns. "You lied to me, didn't you? You did find out something."

"Come with me and see for yourself."

CHAPTER 16

"WELCOME TO THE ROARING Twenties," I say to K. Burke as we enter Fitzgerald's Bar and Grill, on East 68th Street.

"Not much roaring going on," Burke says. The room is empty except for the bartender and one female customer.

The same girl I watched through the window earlier.

The lone woman at the bar is young. She's blond. She's pretty. And after we flash IDs and introduce ourselves as detectives with the NYPD, she's also very frightened.

"Try to relax, miss," says Burke. "There's a problem, but it's nothing for you to worry about. We're just hoping you can help us out."

I'm astonished at the genuine sweetness in Detective Burke's voice. The same voice that was just loud and stern with me is now soothing and gentle with the pretty blonde.

"Could you tell us your name, please?" I ask, trying to imitate Burke's soft style.

"Laura," she says. Her voice has a quiver of fear.

"What about a last name?" Burke asks.

"Jenkins," says the girl. "Laura Jenkins."

"Let's see some ID," I say.

The girl rustles around in her pocketbook and produces a laminated card. Burke doesn't even look at it.

"You're aware, Ms. Jenkins, that in the state of New York, showing a police officer false identification is a class D felony punishable by up to seven years in prison."

Holy shit. I'm in awe of Burke. Sort of.

The girl slips the first card she removed from her purse back into it and hands over a second. It reads: LAURA DELARICO, 21 ARDSLEY ROAD, SCARSDALE, NEW YORK.

"What do you do for a living, Miss Delarico?" I ask.

"I'm a law student. That's the truth. I go to Fordham. Here's my student ID." She holds up a third plastic identity card.

"Do you work?" I ask. "Perhaps part-time?"

"Sometimes I babysit. I do computer filing for one of the professors."

"Look, Miss Delarico," I say, raising my voice now. "This is serious business. Very serious. Detective Burke was being genuine when she said you have nothing to worry about. But that only happens if you help us out. So far, not good. Not good at all."

Laura looks away, then back at me.

"We know that you work for a prostitution ring," I continue. "A group that trades in high-priced call girls. We know it's controlled by a Russian gang."

Laura begins to cry. "But I'm a law student. Really."

"A few days ago a female detective posing as a call girl was murdered. Somebody who meant a lot to me. We need your help."

I pause. Not for dramatic effect but because I feel myself choking up, too.

Laura stops crying long enough to say, "It's just something I'm doing for a little while. For the money. I live with my grandfather, and law school costs so much. If he ever found out…"

A few seconds pass.

Then K. Burke says, "Off the record."

K. Burke is staring deep into Laura's eyes. But Laura is frozen. No response.

"Let me show you something," I say.

Laura looks suspicious. K. Burke looks confused. I reach into my side pocket. Next to my ID, next to the place where I kept the cash for Carl the doorman, are two small photographs. I take them out. One shows Maria Martinez on the police department's Hudson River boat ride. I took that picture. The other shows Maria Martinez dead. It was taken by the coroner.

I show Laura the photos. Then she looks away.

Finally, she says, "Okay."

CHAPTER 17

PROSTITUTES DON'T KEEP traditional hours.

Laura Delarico tells us that she's "on call" at Fitzgerald's for another thirty minutes. She's certain she'll be free by late afternoon. "Even if I do get a client," she says, "I'll be in and out quickly." (No, I don't think she was trying to be funny.)

I suggest that Laura, K. Burke, and I meet at Balthazar, where a person can get a decent *steak frites* and a pleasant glass of house Burgundy. "This will put everyone at ease," I say.

K. Burke suggests that we schedule an interview at the precinct this evening. "This is an investigation, Moncrief, not happy hour. Plus, *I'm* going to that meeting with Vice."

Because proper police procedure always trumps a good idea, at six o'clock the three of us are sitting in an interrogation room at the precinct.

Laura is surprisingly interested in the surroundings. The bile-colored green walls, the battered folding chairs, the crushed empty cans of Diet Coke on the table. I don't think I'm wrong in thinking that Laura is also interested in me.

"So this is, like, where you bring murderers, drug dealers, and…okay, prostitutes?"

"Sometimes," I say. "But today is strictly informal, off the record. No recordings, no cameras, but as much of the cold tan sludge my colleagues call coffee as you can drink."

Laura is wearing a black T-shirt, jeans, and a gold necklace with the name *Laura* on it. She could be a barista at Starbucks or a salesgirl at the Gap or, yes, a law student.

"We're very glad that you agreed to try to help us," K. Burke begins.

Laura interrupts: "Listen. I don't think I want to do this anymore. I think I've changed my mind."

"That would not be a good idea," I say. My goal is not to sound threatening, merely disappointed.

"We're counting on you," K. Burke says. Where does she hide that beautiful soothing voice?

"I don't think there's much I *can* tell you," Laura says. "I get a call. I turn a trick. That's how it goes."

"Tell us anything," I say.

"Anything?" Laura says. Her voice is suddenly loud, suddenly scared. "Like what? What does 'anything' mean? What I ate for lunch? What classes I went to? Anything?"

The conversation needs K. Burke's smooth-as-silk voice. Here it comes.

"Maria Martinez was found murdered on Tuesday," K. Burke says. "Were you working Tuesday morning or Monday night?"

Laura closes her eyes. Her lips curl with disgust. She spits out three little words: "Paulo the Pig."

Burke and I are, of course, confused. I picture a cartoon character in a Spanish children's television program.

But Laura repeats it, this time with even more venom. "Paulo the Pig."

"That's a person, I assume," Burke says.

"A person who deserves his nickname. If you're a girl on call and you get assigned to Paulo the Pig, you never forget it."

Her hands shake a bit. Her eyes begin to water.

"That's where I was the night your friend was murdered. I was with Paulo. Paulo Montes."

"Tell us, Laura," I say. "We need to know what happened that night with you and Paulo. Everything you remember. You're safe with us."

Her story is disgusting.

CHAPTER 18

PAULO MONTES, A BRAZILIAN drug dealer, is usually followed everywhere by two bodyguards. Tonight, however, he sends them away and waits alone for the arrival of his hired girl.

The fat middle-aged man has dressed appropriately for the occasion—a sweat-soaked sleeveless undershirt. Thick curly black hair grows like an unmown lawn over both Paulo's chest and back. The hairs crawl up and down his shoulders and neck. He wears long white silk shorts—longer than boxers, almost long enough to touch his fleshy pink knees. Montes has greased himself up with a nauseating combination of almond oil and lavender cologne. He has used this same overwhelming oil-and-cologne concoction to slick back the greasy hair above his fat round face.

Paulo answers the door himself. "You're much prettier than that dark-haired bitch they sent up an hour ago," he says.

He is speaking to Laura Delarico—tall, slim, blond. With her fine youthful features, Laura is easily Paulo's fantasy come to life—a combination of Texas cheer-leader and Italian fashion model. Fresh and clean, lithe and athletic. Just what Paulo is longing for.

He begins quickly, clumsily unbuttoning Laura's white oxford-cloth shirt. "The first one they sent was the kind I could find for ten dollars in an alley in São Paulo. Dark hair, dark skin. Screwing her would be like screwing myself."

Paulo Montes laughs uproariously at his little joke. Laura smiles. She's been taught to smile at a client's jokes.

Paulo pulls her onto the bed. His fingers are fat, and he has become bored with trying to unbutton Laura's shirt. So he pulls it up and over her head. He tugs at Laura's panties, ripping them.

Soon she is naked. Soon Paulo the Pig is naked. Every inch of Laura's flesh is disgusted by him. She feels he might crush her with his weight, but she's skilled at positioning her shoulders and hips in such a way as to minimize all discomfort. She tries to ignore the garlicky alcohol smell as he roughly kisses her face and lips, as he squirms slowly downward to kiss her breasts. He suddenly slaps her face. For some sick reason this makes him laugh. Paulo Montes then pulls hard at her hair.

"Stop it," Laura says. "You're hurting me."

"Like I give a shit," Paulo says. Now he grabs her genitals. His filthy fingernails travel harshly around her vagina. She feels scratching, bleeding. With his other hand he pulls hard at another handful of hair. "I'm paying good money for this!" he yells. "I'm in charge."

He pushes himself back up, again closer to her face. His saliva is dripping onto Laura's cheeks and lips. The kisses begin to feel more like bites. She is certain the skin on her right cheek has been punctured by his teeth. Then more hair pulling. Her vagina is full of pain.

This time Laura screams. "Stop. Slow down!" She pushes at his fat neck.

Then suddenly Paulo makes a huge noise—a kind of explosive grunt. His breathing immediately slows down.

Laura realizes that she doesn't need to protest any longer. It's over. He's finished. He never even entered her. Paulo the Pig begins panting like a tired old horse. He is resting, she thinks. He remains on top of her for a few minutes.

Finally Paulo rolls off and rests at her side.

For a moment, Laura becomes a kind of waitress in a sexual diner. "Can I get you anything else, sir?"

But Paulo Montes merely keeps his heavy breathing pumping. "That was good, very good. Go into the next room. Take what you want. Within reason, of course." He laughs again. What a comedian!

Like all the girls who work for the Russian gang, Laura knows Paulo Montes is one of the most significant importers of what are called travel packages: drugs that are smuggled along strange geographic routes—say, from Ankara to Kiev to Seoul to New York to São Paulo—in order to confuse and evade the narcs.

"No, thank you," Laura says, slipping into her torn underwear, her jeans, and her shirt. She plucks a few of his many sweaty curly hairs from her stomach.

"Don't be ungrateful, bitch," Paulo says. This time he's not sounding funny. He doesn't laugh. "Scag, maybe. I got it in the plastic containers. Or some good China white."

"I just need to use the bathroom," Laura says.

Paulo snaps at her quickly. "Use the maid's bathroom

at the end of the hall. You can't use this one. I have personal items in there."

Laura simply says, "Okay." She's tired and frightened and disgusted.

"Now go in the next room and treat yourself. Even something simple. Take a little C. Have a party later with your friends."

To appease him she says, "Do you have some weed? I'll take some weed."

He laughs again, the loudest of all his laughing jags.

"Weed? You're joking. Like Paulo would ever deal low-class shit like that."

She watches Paulo on the bed, naked, laughing.

As Laura leaves the room all she can think of is that line from the Christmas poem: "...a little round belly / That shook when he laughed, like a bowl full of jelly."

CHAPTER 19

LAURA DELARICO HAS FINISHED her story.

"So that's it. The clients don't pay us girls directly. It's all online, I guess. I don't really know. When it was over, I just left."

Burke speaks. "Detective Moncrief and I want to thank you. We know this has been tough."

"I wish I could have helped more," Laura says. "I'm not afraid. I just...well, that's what happened."

"You've helped us more than you can imagine," I say. Sincerely, softly. "What you gave us was big. I'm fairly certain Maria Martinez visited Paulo's room as well."

Burke agrees. "There's a very real possibility she was the dark-haired girl he rejected before you."

"You don't know that for sure," Laura says.

"You're right," I say. "Not yet. But it is a logical deduction. He may have killed her and disposed of her. *Or* he may have put her body in the bathroom."

"The one he wouldn't let me use," she says quietly. "I guess that makes sense."

K. Burke holds up her hand. "Or we may be completely off base. Maybe it was not Maria Martinez. Maybe we've got it all wrong."

I cannot resist. I say, "Ah, K. Burke, ever the jolly optimist."

I reach over and gently touch Laura Delarico's hand. She does not pull away. She is so much less frightened than she was a few hours ago.

"And that is why…" Suddenly, I must stop speaking. Oh, shit. Oh, no.

I feel my throat begin to burn. I'm having trouble breathing. Maria is on my mind, in my heart. Because of Laura's information, we may actually have a shot at solving Maria's murder.

K. Burke senses the emotional hole I've fallen into. She finishes my remarks.

"And that's why…we need you to help us just a little bit more."

CHAPTER 20

LAURA SAYS NOTHING FOR a few long moments.

"Well?" I say.

Laura is suddenly businesslike. Sharp. Composed.

"I know what you'll do if I don't keep helping you," she says.

"You *know* what we'll do?" I ask. "I don't even know what we'll do except ask you to help us."

"No," Laura says. "You'll play the Grandpa card."

"The what?" I ask.

K. Burke is far quicker than I am in this matter.

"Laura thinks we'll tell her grandfather how she's been making money," says Burke.

For the first time I see a toughness in Laura. I am beginning to think that Laura Delarico is not so naive and innocent as I first thought. She'll make a good lawyer someday.

"Believe whatever you want, Laura," I say, "but I promise you with my heart that we will never do such a thing."

"I guess I'll believe you because…well, because I *want* to believe you," Laura says. "I want to help…at least, I think I want to help. Oh, this sucks. This whole thing sucks."

Time for a bottom line. Laura agrees to continue to help. "But just one more time."

Later, after Laura leaves, K. Burke and I walk the dirty gray hallway back to the detective room.

"Nice job," Burke says. "Your performance won her over."

"Did you think that was a performance, K. Burke?" I ask.

"To be honest, I don't know."

Back at our desks, we learn that Paulo Montes will not be in New York for three days. He is on a quick drug trip through San Juan, Havana, and Kingston.

I tell Burke that I'm going to take one of those three days off.

"Impossible!" she exclaims. "Your presence is critical. We have Vice files to examine. We have a reinspection of the murder scene as well as forensics at Montes's suite. I need you to—"

I cut her off immediately. "Hold it," I say sharply. "Here's what I need from *you*. I need you to stop thinking that you're my boss. You're my partner. And I don't mean to throw this in your face, K. Burke, but we would not be progressing if I had not pursued my very *un*professional way of doing things."

K. Burke gives me her version of a sincere smile. Then she says, "Whatever you say, partner."

CHAPTER 21

A MAN KNOWS HE'S in love when he's totally happy just watching his girlfriend do even the simplest things—peeling an apple, combing her hair, fluffing up a bed pillow, laughing.

That is precisely how I'm feeling when I walk into the ridiculously tricked-out media room of Dalia's apartment: the Apologue speakers, the Supernova One screen, the leather Eames chairs. A room that is insanely lavish and almost never used.

As I walk in I see Dalia standing on a stepladder. Her back is to me. She is frantically sorting through the small closet high above the wet bar. She neither sees nor hears me enter. I stand and watch her for a moment. I smile. Dalia is wearing jeans and a turquoise T-shirt. As she stretches, one or two inches of her lower back are exposed.

I walk toward her and kiss her gently on that enticing lower back.

She gives a quick little yell.

"Don't be scared," I say. "It's only me."

She steps off the ladder and we embrace fully. I know a great kiss cannot wash away a bad day, but it surely can make the night seem a little bit brighter.

"When did *this* closet become the junk closet?" she asks as she climbs back up the ladder and begins tossing things down to me.

A plastic bag of poker chips. These are followed by three Scrabble tiles (*W, E,* and the always important *X*). A plastic box containing ivory chess pieces, but no chessboard in sight. And a true relic from the Victorian era: a Game Boy.

"This is for you," she says as she pretends to hit me on the head with a wooden croquet mallet. I add the mallet to the ever-expanding pile of items next to me.

"And you'll like *this*," she says with a smile. Dalia leans down and hands me a small gold box. I open it. It contains two little bronze balls the size of small marbles. Never saw them before. I shrug.

"Give up?" she asks. "They're those Chinese things they use for sex, for the vagina."

"The vagina?" I say. "Yes. I think I've heard of it." She laughs and punches me lightly on the arm. I decide not to ask where she got them—or how often she used them or with whom.

"Well," she says. "At least we've solved *one* mystery. This closet is not a junk closet. It is obviously a game closet."

"What exactly are you looking for, anyway?" I ask.

"This," she says as she steps down off the ladder. She is holding a slim burgundy leather book. I recognize it immediately. It's the yearbook for our class at Lycée Henri-IV.

She opens it and turns to the page that has her graduation picture. "I was thinking of getting bangs. The last time I had them was when I was a kid. I

wanted to see if I was as goofy-looking as I remember."
She frowns. "Guess I was."

I say exactly what is expected of a man in this
situation. The only difference is that this man means it
with all his heart.

"You were beautiful," I say.

"You're mad. Braids on the side and bangs in the
front. I look like a goatherd."

I reach toward her and touch her face.

"If so, then you are *la plus belle* goatherd since the
beginning of time." I lean in and kiss her. Then I speak.
"How about we have something nice to drink?"

"How about a nice warm bath, with lavender perfume?" she says.

"A bath?" I say. "I don't know. I don't think I'm
that thirsty."

Dalia taps me playfully on my nose. Then she heads
toward the bathroom.

CHAPTER 22

LAURA KNOCKS ON THE hotel-room door.
Everything feels just as it did the last time she visited
Paulo.

She wears a white oxford-cloth shirt. Just as she did
the last time. The tiny entrance hall where she waits
stinks of liquor and bad cologne. Just as it did the last
time. One other thing that's the same, one other thing
she cannot deny: she's horribly frightened. Her arm
shakes as she knocks on the door again.

Yes, Moncrief and Burke have assured her that
everything is set up to keep her perfectly safe. This
time, hidden in Paulo's bedroom are two minuscule
video surveillance cameras: one is attached to a large
bronze lamp on the writing desk, the other to the fake-
gold-leaf-and-crystal chandelier hanging directly over
the king-size bed. The videos play on monitors that
are being watched two doors away by five people: Luc
Moncrief, K. Burke, Inspector Nick Elliott, and two
officers from Vice.

Paulo opens the door and steps back. He smiles at her.

This time Paulo manages to look even more disgusting than before. Laura Delarico quietly gasps as she takes in the repellent sight: Paulo the Pig is completely naked except for a pair of short brown socks.

"So," he says. "They sent you back like I asked. I'm glad. You're the best."

Laura and the five people watching in the other room realize immediately that Paulo Montes is drunk or drugged or both. He stumbles. He slurs his words. His feeble erection collapses as he lunges toward her, and he begins half spitting and half kissing, half hugging and half groping her.

"Hold on. Come on. Just hold on," Laura says. Then she uses one of the first conversation starters that a woman learns in "prostitute school."

"Let's get to know each other."

Laura wonders how she will ever get Paulo to talk about the dark-haired woman, the woman who may have been Maria Martinez. Laura wafts in and out of that nightmare. She must keep reminding herself she is there to help uncover the truth of the death of a woman she never even knew.

Paulo is even more impatient this time at bat. He tugs hard at Laura's shirt. Two buttons snap off and onto the floor. He pushes his greasy face into her breasts as if he is trying to suck in oxygen from the space between them.

Within a few seconds, he has her on the bed. They are, for the moment, side by side, facing each other. The slobbering. The saliva. The boozy breath.

"So," Laura ventures, trying to cajole him into a calmer, gentler mood. "Just tell me how much more you like me than that dark-haired girl who was here."

Paulo is in no mood for conversation. He is somewhere between crazy drunk and crazy turned on.

"Dark?" he shouts. "Was her hair dark? I don't remember. Does any bitch have the color she's born with?
In Brazil they all lie. Lie and dye. That's the joke in Rio
and São Paulo. Let's check you. Let's see if you're telling
the truth."

Laura fears a harsh inspection of her pubic hair.
Instead Montes rolls over and on top of her. He grabs
a great chunk of her hair and pulls it hard with his fat
heavy hands. She yells for him to stop.

"I have to find the roots!" he screams and laughs
simultaneously.

In the surveillance room, Inspector Elliott speaks
loudly: "We've got to stop this immediately, Moncrief.
We can haul him in right now for aggravated assault."

"I don't want him arrested. I want him to talk," says
Moncrief. "I want to get the story on Maria."

"I swear, Moncrief. This whole thing is a half-assed
setup. I should never have let it get this far."

"Inspector! Look!" K. Burke says. All five in the
surveillance group peer intently at the screen. Paulo
Montes is grunting and making animal-like noises as
he pinches one of Laura's nipples hard and fiercely
bites the other.

"That's it!" yells Elliott.

"Give it five seconds," says Moncrief as he grabs
Elliott by the arm to urge him to remain. "The guy
might calm down."

Almost as if Montes actually heard Moncrief speak,
Paulo begins gently massaging Laura's breasts.

"There, there," Paulo says softly. "You are beautiful.
I could love a woman like you."

Paulo gently brushes his lips against Laura's beautiful soft cheeks. He touches her chin and runs his hand
down her neck.

"Kiss me," Paulo says. "Kiss me like you love me."

Laura knows her job. She kisses him softly on his lips.

Then suddenly, horribly, Montes slaps Laura against her right cheek, so violently that her head snaps to the side. She lets out a scream.

"You are just another dumb bitch!" Montes shouts, saliva dripping from his mouth onto Laura's face.

"Get away!" Laura screams. "Get the hell off of me!"

Paulo slaps her again, then holds her down by her wrists. She is fighting as hard as she can. But it's useless.

Again she screams, "Get off! Stop it!"

As Paulo is about to sink his teeth into her, the door to the room swings open.

"NYPD! Freeze!" The voice belongs to Moncrief.

Moncrief, Burke, and both Vice officers are holding guns. They all rush toward the bed.

With the help of one of the Vice cops, Moncrief pulls Montes away from Laura.

Laura quickly rolls away from her attacker. Then she grabs a pillow and holds it up to cover her nakedness. Montes thrashes about in a futile attempt to free himself from Moncrief and the cop. He keeps struggling and manages to push his one free hand under another pillow. He pulls out a pistol. He shoots it once. The bullet hits the TV screen. It shatters into a small mountain of glass pieces. Moncrief pushes his own index and middle fingers into Montes's face. The drunken Montes manages to get off one more shot. The bullet hits a Vice officer's forearm. As Moncrief and the two officers struggle to pull the naked fat man to his feet, Montes struggles to bring his arm around. Montes aims the gun at Laura.

A final shot. It comes from Moncrief's gun.

The bullet goes right into Montes's neck via his Adam's apple.

Laura Delarico is sobbing. K. Burke is on her cell,

calling for reinforcements, forensics, the coroner, police attorneys, the DA's office. Nick Elliott closes his eyes and shakes his head back and forth.

When she finishes her phone calls, K. Burke takes a gray jumpsuit from one of the police kits. She walks to Laura and helps her slip into it. For just a moment Burke's eyes meet Moncrief's.

The two of them are thinking the same thing. They are no closer to solving the case of Maria Martinez. And the one person who might have helped them is now dead.

CHAPTER 23

PHOTOGRAPHERS AND MORE photographers. Detectives and more detectives. Statements are made and then repeated. Hotel guests wander into the hallway.

We go to the precinct. More detectives. Two police attorneys. Everyone agrees: my bullet was justified. The surveillance video verifies what happened. My colleagues can easily rationalize that the world is a better place without Paulo Montes. I want to rationalize it also, but I cannot ignore the fact that I'm the cop who made it happen.

I go home.

"I'm awake," I hear Dalia shout. "Be right out."

I move toward the bedroom.

We meet in the hallway, and we stand directly in front of a black-and-white Léger poster, a drawing of four people artfully intertwined. Dalia and I do not kiss, but we hug each other with all our strength, as if we are afraid that the other person might slip away.

A few minutes later we are seated on a sofa. We

watch the city sky slowly brighten. We both sip a snifter of Rémy. I devour a bowl of cashews. I tell her about my evening. Her face fills with horror, her eyes widen when I her about the horrific ending.

"Oh, my God, Luc. You must feel … I don't know … I don't know how you must feel."

"I don't think I know, either," I say. "I've never killed anyone."

I find myself remembering the shooting range near Porte de la Chapelle, where I spent so many hours learning how to load and shoot, load and shoot. The paper dummies, the foolishly big ear protectors. One-handed aim, two-handed aim, shoot from a prone position, shoot from a standing position. But shoot, always shoot. You got him. You got him. You missed him. You got him.

My plan for Montes would have worked. I am sure it would have worked.

I take the last gulp of my Cognac. I swipe the inside of the cashew bowl with my index finger. I touch my salty finger to the tip of Dalia's tongue. She smiles. I hold her tightly.

I tell Dalia that all I want to do now is sleep. She understands. We begin walking toward the bedroom. I stop for a moment. So Dalia stops also.

I have an idea. A very good idea. So good I want to share it with someone. But I'd be a fool to share it with Burke and Elliott. What about Dalia? I usually tell her everything, but not this time, not this idea. She'd kill me if she knew.

Dalia looks up at me.

"You're smiling," she says. "What are you thinking about?"

"Just you," I say. And as we fall on the bed, I consider crossing my fingers behind my back.

CHAPTER 24

I CALL GARY KUEHN at Vice. He's one of the few guys in that department who's smart enough to appreciate what he calls my shenanigans.

Shenanigans. English is a wonderful language.

Gary emails me a list of names of "superior sex workers" (translation: high-class hookers) and their managers (translation: drug-dealing abusive johns). I specifically request names of girls who regularly service the toniest areas of the Upper East Side.

I tell my new plan to no one—not K. Burke, not Nick Elliott, not even Gary. At midafternoon, I take an Uber car across town and check into a room at the Pierre, on Fifth Avenue at 61st Street. A mere seventeen hundred dollars a night. I silently thank my father for the large allowance that makes this expensive escapade possible.

I arrange for a series of these high-priced call girls to visit my room—one girl every thirty minutes. I do all the scheduling—the phoning and texting and emailing—myself.

At three o'clock a girl with incandescent mahogany skin appears. Her skin is so shiny it looks polished. Her hair is short and dark. She smiles. I am sitting in a comfortable blue club chair. She approaches me and touches my face.

"Please have a seat over there," I say, pointing to the identical blue club chair opposite my own. No doubt she thinks we're about to begin a freaky fantasy.

"Here is the first piece of news: I'm not going to touch you, but I will, of course, pay you for this visit." I hand her three hundred-dollar bills. (The agreed-upon price was two fifty.)

"Here is the second piece of news, and perhaps it is not quite so welcome. I am going to ask you some questions."

She smiles. I quickly add, "Nothing uncomfortable—just some simple talking and chatting. I am a detective with the NYPD."

Her face becomes a mask of fear.

"But I promise. You have nothing to worry about."

The questions begin:

Have you ever serviced a client at 655 Park Avenue?

Have you ever serviced a client at the Auberge du Parc Hotel?

Have you ever serviced a client who acted with extreme violence?

A client who hurt you, threatened you, brandished a weapon, a gun, a cane, a stick, a whip? A client who tried to slip a tablet or a powder or a suspicious liquid into a beverage?

Have you ever met with a client who was famous in his field—an actor, a diplomat, a senator, a governor, a foreign leader, a clergyman?

The answers are all no. And the pattern remains the same for every woman who follows.

A few of them tell me about men with some odd habits, but as the woman in the tight yellow jeans says, "A lot of guys have odd habits. That's why they go to prostitutes. Maybe their fancy wives don't want to suck toes or fuck in a tennis skirt or take it up the ass."

Other statements are made.

A tall woman, the only woman I've ever seen who looked beautiful in a Mohawk haircut, says, "Okay, there is this congressman from New Jersey that I see once or twice a month."

A very tan woman in a saronglike outfit says, "Yeah, one guy was *sort of* into whips, but all he wanted was for me to unpin my hair and swing it against his dick."

A woman who shows up in blue shorts cut off at mid-thigh, her shirt tied just above the navel, gives me some hope, but she, too, is a waste of time. "I think I was at 655 Park once. But it was for a woman. I hate working chicks. The few I've done were all, like, just into kissing and touching and petting. They're more work than the guys."

No information of any value. Yes, two of the girls have been slapped—both of them by men who were drunk. Yes, the girl-on-girl prostitute at 655 Park works for the Russian gang, but she knows nothing about the death of Maria Martinez, and she has never even heard of Paulo Montes.

What I am learning from these few hours of wasted interviews is the knowledge that the world is filled with men who are happy to pay to get laid. That's it. That's the deal. Over and out. It is a gross and humiliating way for a girl to make money, but, in most cases, each has made her separate peace with it.

The interviews end. Thousands of dollars later I have nothing to show for my work.

It is definitely time for me to leave the Pierre.

It is definitely time for me to return home to Dalia.

CHAPTER 25

EVERY MORNING AT THE precinct, K. Burke and I have the following dialogue.

Instead of saying the words "Good morning," she looks at me and says sternly, "You're late."

I always respond with a cheery "And good morning to you, *ma belle.*"

It has become a funny little routine between the two of us, the sort of thing two friends might do. Who knows? Maybe K. Burke and I are becoming friends. Sometimes a mutually miserable situation can bring people together.

But this morning it's different. She greets me by saying, "Don't bother sitting down, Moncrief. We have an assignment from Inspector Elliott."

All I know is that unless Elliott has had an unexpected stroke of genius (highly unlikely) I am not interested in the assignment. I must also face the fact that my mood is terrible: interviewing the call girls has led to absolutely nothing, and I can share my frustration with no one. If I were to tell Burke or

Elliott about my unapproved tactic they would both be furious.

"Whatever it is the inspector wants, we'll do it later."

"It's already later," Burke says. "It's one o'clock in the afternoon. Let's go."

"Go where? It's lunchtime. I'm thinking that fish restaurant on 49th Street. A bit of sole meunière and a crisp bottle of Chablis…"

"Stop being a Frenchman for just one minute, Moncrief," she says.

I can tell that K. Burke is uncomfortable with what she's about to say, but out it comes: "He wants us to visit some high-class strip clubs. He's even done some of the grunt work for us. He's compiled a list of clubs. Take a look at your phone."

I swipe the screen and click on my assignments folder. I see a page entitled "NYC Club Visits. From: N. Elliott."

Sapphire, 333 East 60th Street
Rick's Cabaret, 50 West 33rd Street
Hustler Club, 641 West 51st Street

Three more places are listed after these.

As a young man in Paris, full of booze and often with a touch of cocaine in my nose, I would occasionally visit the Théâtre Chochotte, in Saint-Germain-des-Prés, with some pals. It was not without its pleasures, but on one such visit I had a very bad experience: I ran into my father and my uncle in the VIP lounge. That was the night I crossed Chochotte and all Parisian strip clubs off my list. Even a son who has a much better relationship than I have with my father does not ever want to end up in a strip joint with the old man.

As for clubs in New York…I am no longer a

schoolboy. I am no longer touching my nose with cocaine. And I now have Dalia waiting at home for me.

The fact is that my assignment would be the envy of
most of my colleagues. But I am weary and frustrated
and pissed off and…it seems impossible for me to
believe, but I am growing tired of so much female flesh
in my face.

"I won't do it," I say to Burke. "You do it alone. I'll
stay here and do some detail analysis."

"No way am I going alone, Moncrief. C'mon."

"I cannot. I will not," I say.

"Then I suggest you tell that to Inspector Elliott."

I feel my whole heart spiraling downward. The
entrapment with Laura. The death of Paulo. The futile
interviews with the call girls. Now I am expected to go
to these sad places, where a glass of cheap vodka costs
thirty dollars, and try to talk to women with breast
implants who are sliding up and down poles.

"I am sick. I am tired," I tell Burke.

"I know you are," Burke says. And I can tell she
means it. "But you need to do it for Maria. This is—"

I snap at her. "I do not need a pep talk. I know
you're trying to be helpful, but that kind of thing
doesn't work with me."

Burke just stares at me.

"Tell Inspector Elliott we will make these 'visits'
tomorrow. Maria will still be dead tomorrow. Right
now, I'm going home."

CHAPTER 26

BURKE WILL TELL ELLIOTT that I went home because of illness. And, of course, Elliott won't believe it.

But I think that K. Burke and I are now simpatico enough for her to cover for me.

"Suddenly he's sick?" Elliott will say. "That's pure bullshit."

The answer Burke might produce could go something like, "Well, he was out sick all day yesterday."

It makes no difference. For the moment I am engaged in a very important project: I am in a store on Ninth Avenue selecting two perfect fillets of Dover sole. The cost at Seabreeze Fish Market for a pound of this beautiful fish is one hundred and twenty dollars. I have no trouble spending that much (or more) on a bottle of wine. But—Jesus!—this is fish. In the taxi uptown to Dalia's apartment I hold the package of fish as if it were a newborn infant being brought home from the hospital.

The moment I walk through the door of the

apartment I feel lighter, better, stronger. It's as if the air in Dalia's place is purer than the air in the dangerous, depressing crime scenes I frequent.

I place the precious fish in the refrigerator.

I unpack the few other items I've bought and remove my shirt. I'm feeling better already.

In a moment I'll start chopping the shallots, chopping the parsley, and heating the wine for the mustard sauce. This preparation is what trained chefs call the *mise en place.*

I decide to take off my suit pants. I toss them on the chair where my shirt is resting. I am—in my mind—no longer in a professionally equipped kitchen overlooking Central Park. I am in a wonderfully sunny beach house on the Côte d'Azur. I am no longer a gloomy angry detective; I am a young tennis pro away for a week of rest, awaiting the arrival of his luscious girlfriend.

I press a button on the entertainment console. Suddenly the music blares. It is Dalia's newest favorite: Selena Gomez. "Me and the Rhythm." I sing along, creating my own lyrics to badly match whatever Selena is singing.

Ooh, all the rhythm takes you over.

I chop the shallot to the beat of the music. I scrape the chopped pieces into my hand and toss them into a sauté pan.

I am moving my feet and hips. I drop a half pound of Irish butter into the pan, and now I feel almost compelled to dance.

I sing. I dance. When I don't sing I am talking to an imaginary Dalia.

"Yes," I am saying. *"Your favorite. Dover sole."*

"Yes, there is a bottle of Dom Pérignon already in the fridge."

"Yes, I left early to make this dinner."

"The hell with them. They can fire me, then."

The music beats on. I rhythmically slap away at the parsley leaves with my chef's knife.

In the distance I hear the buzzing of a cell phone. The sound of the phone at first seems to be a part of Selena's song. Then I recognize the tone. It is my police phone. For a moment I consider ignoring it. Then I think that perhaps there is news on Maria Martinez's case. Or it might merely be Nick or K. Burke calling to torment me. But nothing can torment me tonight.

I let the music continue. Whoever my caller is can sing along with me.

I yank my suit jacket from the pile of clothing. I find my phone.

Ooh, all the rhythm takes you over.

"What's up?" I yell loudly above the music.

My prediction is correct. It is Inspector Elliott on the line.

He speaks. I listen. I stop dancing. I drop the phone. I fall to my knees and I scream.

"*Noooooooo!*"

CHAPTER 27

BUT THE TRUTH IS "yes." There has been another woman stabbed, another woman connected to the New York City police. Only this time the woman is neither an officer nor a detective. This time the woman is also connected to me.

"Who is it, goddamn it?"

Elliott's exact words: "It's Dalia, Moncrief."

A pause and then he adds quietly, *"Dalia is dead."*

I kneel on the gray granite floor and pound it. Tears do not come, but I cannot stop saying "no." If I say the word loudly enough, often enough, it will eradicate the fact of "yes."

For a few moments I actually believe that the call from Nick Elliott never happened. I am on the floor, and I pick up the phone. I observe it as if it were a foreign object—a paperweight, a tiny piece of meteorite, a dead rat. But the caller ID says N/ELLIOTT/NYPD/17PREC.

An overwhelming energy goes through me. Within seconds I am back in my pants and shirt. I slip on my shoes, without socks. I go bounding out the door, and the madness within me makes me certain that running down the back stairs of the apartment building will be faster than calling for the elevator.

Once outside, I see two officers waiting in a patrol car.

"Detective Moncrief. We're here to take you to the crime scene. Take the passenger seat."

I don't even know where the crime scene is. I grab the shoulders of the other cop and shake him violently.

"Where the hell are you taking me? Where is she?" I shout. "Where are we going?"

"To 235 East 20th Street, sir. Please get into the car."

Within moments we are suffocated in midtown rush-hour traffic. How can there be so much traffic when Dalia is dead?

At Seventh Avenue and 45th, the streets are thick with sightseeing buses and cabs. Some people are dressed up as Big Bird and Minnie Mouse. The sidewalks teem with tourists and druggies and strollers and women in saris and schoolchildren on trips and...I tell the driver to unlock the doors. I will walk, run, fly.

"This traffic will break below 34th Street, Detective."

"Unlock the fucking door!" I scream. And so he does, and I am on the sidewalk again. I don't give a shit that I am pushing people aside.

Within minutes I am at Seventh Avenue and 34th Street. The streets remain packed with people and cabs and cars and buses.

I cross against the light at 34th Street, Herald Square, Macy's. Where the hell is Santa Claus when you need him?

Sirens. Cars jostle to clear a route for the vehicle screeching out the sirens.

I am rushing east on 32nd Street. I am midway between Broadway and Fifth Avenue, a block packed almost entirely, crazily, with Korean restaurants. Suddenly the sirens are fiercely loud.

"Get in the car, Moncrief. Get back in the car." It is the same driver of the same patrol car that picked me up earlier. They were right about the traffic, but I am vaguely glad that I propelled myself this far.

In a few minutes we are at 235 East 20th Street. The police academy of the New York City Police Department. The goddamn police academy. Dalia is dead at the police academy. How the hell did she end up here?

"We're here, Detective," says one of the officers.

I turn my head toward the building. K. Burke is walking quickly toward the car. Behind her is Nick Elliott. My chest hurts. My throat burns.

Dalia is dead.

CHAPTER 28

"THIS WAY, LUC," K. Burke says. Both Burke and Nick Elliott guide me by the elbows down a corridor—painted cement blocks, an occasional bulletin board, a fire-alarm box, a fire-extinguisher case.

The usual cast of characters is standing nearby: police officers, forensics, the coroner's people, two firemen, some young people—probably students—carrying laptops and water bottles. A very large sign is taped to a wall at the end of the corridor. It is a photograph of four people: a white male officer, an Asian female officer, a black male officer, a white female officer. Above the big grainy photo are big grainy blue letters:

SERVE WITH DIGNITY. SERVE WITH
  COURAGE.
THE NEW YORK CITY POLICE
  DEPARTMENT

Burke and Elliott steer me into a large old-fashioned lecture hall. The stadium seating ends at the bottom with a large table at which a lecturer usually stands. Behind it are a video screen and a green chalkboard. In this teaching pit also stand two officers and two doctors from the chief medical examiner's office. On the side aisles are other officers, other detectives, and, as we descend closer to the bottom of that aisle, a gurney on which a body rests.

K. Burke speaks to me as we reach the gurney. She is saying something to me, but I can't hear her. I am not hearing anything. I am just staring straight ahead as a doctor pulls back the gauzy sheet from Dalia's head and shoulders.

"The wound was in the stomach, sir," she says.

She knows I need no further details at the moment.

Need I say that Dalia looks exquisite? Perfect hair. Perfect eyelashes. A touch of perfect makeup. Perfect. Just perfect. Just fucking unbelievably perfect.

How can she be so beautiful and yet dead?

In my mind I am still screaming "No!" but I say nothing.

I look away from her, and I see the others in the room backing away, looking away, trying to give me privacy in a very public situation.

I must touch Dalia. I should do it gently, of course. I take Dalia's face in both my hands. Her cheeks feel cold, hard. I lean in and brush my lips against her forehead. I pull back a tiny bit to look at her. Then I lean in again to kiss her on the lips.

The room is silent. Deadly silent. I have heard silence before. But the world has never been this quiet.

I will stand here for the rest of my life just looking at her. Yes, that's what I'll do. I'll never move from this spot. I stroke her hair. I touch her shoulders. I stand erect, then turn around.

Nick Elliott is looking at the ground. K. Burke's

chin is quivering. Her eyes are wet. I speak, perhaps to Nick or K. Burke or everyone in the room or perhaps I am simply talking to myself.

"Dalia is dead."

CHAPTER 29

"DO YOU WANT TO ride in the ambulance with her?" Elliott asks. And before I can answer he adds, "I'll go with you if you want. We've got to get Dalia to the research area."

The research area. That is the NYPD euphemism for "the morgue." It is what they say to parents whose child has been run over by a drunk driver.

"No," I say. "There's nothing to be done."

K. Burke looks at me and says what everybody says in a situation like this: "I don't know what to say."

And me? I don't know what to say, either — or what to think or feel or do. So I say what comes to mind: "Keep me posted."

I walk quickly through the lineup of colleagues and strangers lining the cement-block hallway. I jump over the giant stone barricades that encircle the police academy in case of attack. I am now running up Third Avenue.

"May I help you, monsieur?" That is the voice I hear. Where have I run? I don't recall a destination.

I barely remember running. Did I leave Dalia's dead body behind? I look at the woman who just spoke to me. She used the word *monsieur*. Am I in Paris?

She is joined by a well-dressed man, an older man, a gentleman.

"Can I be of some help, Monsieur Moncrief?"

"*Où suis-je?*" I ask. Where am I?

"*Hermès, Monsieur Moncrief. Bonsoir. Je peux vous aider?*"

The Hermès store on Madison Avenue. It is… was…Dalia's favorite place in the entire world to shop.

"*Non. Merci, monsieur. Je regarde.*" Just looking.

On the glass shelves is a collection of handbags, purses, and pocketbooks in red and yellow and green. Like Easter and Christmas. I feel calm amid the beauty. It is a museum, a palace, a château. The silk scarves hanging from golden hooks. The glass cases of watches and cuff links. The shelves of briefcases and leather shopping bags. And then the calm inside me dissipates. I say, "*Bonsoir et merci*" to the sales associate.

I have neither my police phone nor my personal cell. I do not have my watch. I do not know the time. I know I am not crazy. I'm simply crazed.

It's early evening. I walk to Fifth Avenue. The sidewalks are crowded, and the shops are open. I walk down to the Pierre. I was recently inside the Pierre. Was I? I think I was. I continue walking south, toward the Plaza. No water in the fountain? A water shortage, perhaps? I turn east, back toward Madison Avenue, then start north again.

Bottega Veneta. I walk inside. No warm greeting here. A bigger store than Hermès. Instead of a symphony of leather in color, this is a muted place in grays and blacks and many degrees of brown. Calming, calming, calming, until it is calming no longer.

I leave. My next stop is Sherry-Lehmann, the museum of wine. I walk to the rear of the store, where they keep their finest bottles—the Romanée-Conti, Pétrus, Le Pin, Ramonet Montrachet, the thousand-dollar Moët. The bottles should all be displayed under glass, like the diamonds at Tiffany.

I am out on the sidewalk again. I am afraid that if I don't keep moving, I will explode or collapse. It is that extraordinary feeling that nothing good will ever happen again.

A no-brainer: I cannot return to Dalia's apartment at 15 Central Park West. Instead I will go to the loft where I once lived. The place is in the stupidly chic Meatpacking District. I bought the loft before I renewed my life with Dalia. I sometimes lend the place to friends from Europe who are visiting New York. I'm pretty sure it is empty right now.

Will I pick up the pieces? There is no way that will ever happen.

Move on, they will say. Mourn, then move on. I will not do that, because I can't.

Get over it? Never. Someone else? Never.

Nothing will ever be the same.

As I give the address to the cabdriver, I find my chest heaving and hurting. I insist—I don't know why—on holding in the tears. In those few minutes, with my chest shaking and my head aching, I realize what Elliott and Burke and probably others have come to realize: first, my partner, Maria Martinez; then my lover, Dalia Boaz.

Oh, my God. This isn't about prostitutes. This isn't about drugs. This is about me.

Somebody wants to hurt me. And that somebody has succeeded.

CHAPTER 30

A LOFT. A BIG space; bare, barren. Not a handsome space. It is way too basic to be anything but big.

I lived here before Dalia came back into my life. Even when I lived here, I was too compulsive to have allowed it to become a cheesy bachelor pad—no piles of dirty clothing; no accumulation of Chinese-food containers. In fact, no personal touches of any kind. But of course I was spending too many of my waking hours with the NYPD to think about furniture and paint and bathroom fixtures.

I turn the key and walk inside. I am almost startled by the sparseness of it—a gray sofa, a black leather club chair, a glass dining table where no one has ever eaten a meal. Some old files are stacked against a wall. Empty shelves near the sofa. Empty shelves in the kitchen. I have lived most of my New York life with Dalia, at Dalia's home. That was my real home. Where am I now?

I stretch out on the sofa. Fifteen seconds later, I am

back on my feet. The room is stuffy, dry, hot. I walk to the thermostat that will turn on the air-conditioning, but I stare at the controls as if I don't quite know how to adjust the temperature. I remember that there is a smooth single-malt Scotch in a cabinet near the entryway, but why bother? I need to use the bathroom, but I just don't have energy enough to walk to the far side of the loft.

Then the buzzer downstairs rings.

At least I think it's the buzzer downstairs. It's been so long since I heard it. I walk to the intercom. The buzz comes again, then once more. Then I remember what I'm expected to say. A phrase that is ridiculously simple.

"Who is it?"

For a split second I stupidly imagine that it will be Dalia. "It was a terrible joke," she will say with a laugh. "Inspector Elliott helped me fool you."

Now a hollow voice comes from the intercom.

"It's K. Burke."

I buzz her inside. Moments later I open the door and let her into the loft.

"How did you know where to find me?" I ask.

"I called your cell twenty times. You never picked up. Then I called Dalia's place twenty times. You weren't there, *or* you weren't picking up. So I found this place listed as the home address in your HR file. If I didn't find you here, I was going to forget it. But I got lucky."

"No, K. Burke. *I got lucky.*"

I have no idea why I said something so sweet. But I think I mean it. Again, an idea that comes and goes in a split second: whoever is trying to destroy me — will he go after K. Burke next?

She gives me a smile. Then she says, "I'm about

to say the thing that always annoys me when other people say it."

"And that is…"

"Is there anything I can do for you?"

I take a deep breath.

"You mean like brewing a pot of coffee or bringing me a bag of doughnuts or cleaning my bathroom or finding the son of a bitch who—"

"Okay, I got it," she says. "I understand. But actually, Nick Elliott and I did do something for you."

My forehead wrinkles, and I say, "What?"

"We tracked down Dalia's father. He's in Norway shooting a film."

"I was going to call him soon," I say. "But I was building up courage. Thank you." And just thinking about father and daughter begins to break my already severed heart.

"How did he accept the news?" As if I needed to ask.

"It was awful. He wailed. He screamed. He put his assistant on, and he eventually…well, he sort of composed himself and got back on the line."

My eyes begin filling with tears. My chin quivers. I rub my eyes. I am not trying to hide my emotions. I am merely trying to get through them.

"He sends you his love," K. Burke says. I nod.

"He is as fine a man as Dalia was a woman," I say.

"He asked me to tell you two things."

I can't imagine what Monsieur Boaz wanted to tell me.

"He said, 'Tell Luc that I will come to America when I finish my film, but he should bury Dalia as soon as possible. That is the Jewish way.'"

"I understand," I say. Then I ask, "And the other?"

"He said, 'Tell Luc thank you…for taking such good care of my girl.'"

This comment should make me weep, but instead I explode with anger. Not at Menashe Boaz, but at myself.

"That's not true!" I yell. "I did *not* take good care of her."

"Of course it's true," K. Burke says firmly. "You loved her totally. Everybody knows that."

"I…let…her…die."

"That's just stupid, Moncrief. And it smells a little of…" K. Burke abruptly stops talking.

"What? Finish your thought. It smells of what?" I say.

"It smells of…well…self-pity. Dalia was murdered. You could not have prevented it."

I walk to the floor-to-ceiling windows of the loft. I look down at Gansevoort Street. It's this year's chic hot-cool place to be—the expensive restaurants and expensive boutiques, the High Line, the cobblestone streets. It is packed with people. I am disgusted with them because I am disgusted with me. Because Dalia and I will never again be among those people.

I turn and face Detective Burke, and suddenly I am more peaceful. I am truly grateful that she is here. She has stopped by to offer the "personal touch" and I was hesitant at first. Afraid I would feel nervous or embarrassed. But K. Burke has done a good thing.

I walk back toward her and speak slowly, carefully.

"There is one thing we need to discuss very soon. You must realize that these two murders had nothing to do with prostitutes or Brazilian drug dealers or…well, all the things we have been guessing at."

"I realize that," she says. I continue speaking.

"The first murder, at a rich man's home, was to confuse us. The next murder, at a school where people learn to be police professionals — that was to torment us."

K. Burke nods in simple agreement.

"These murders have to do with *me*," I say.

"In that case," K. Burke says, "these murders have to do with *us*."

CHAPTER 31

"WHAT THE HELL IS the story with these two murders?"

This question keeps exploding off the walls of NYPD precincts. It is the commissioner's question. It is Nick Elliott's question. And—obsessively, interminably, awake or asleep—it is my question.

The question is asked a thousand times, and a thousand times the answer comes back the same.

"No idea. Just no goddamn idea."

Forensics brought in nothing. Surveillance cameras showed us nothing. Interviews at the scene turned up nothing.

So it is now time for me to do the only thing left to do: turn inward and rely entirely on my instincts. They have helped me in the past, and they have failed me, too. But instinct is all I have left.

I confront Nick Elliott. I tell him that the answer to the murders is obviously not in New York. The answer must be in Paris.

"Paris?" he shouts.

Then I say, "I need to go to Paris—look around, nose around, see if I can find something there."

Nick Elliott gives it a long pause and then says, "Maybe that's not a bad idea."

Then I tell him that I want to take K. Burke with me.

He pauses again, another long pause. Then he speaks. "Now, *that's* a bad idea."

"Inspector, this is no holiday I'm planning. This is work. K. Burke and I will be examining cases that—"

"Okay, okay, let me think about it," Elliott says. "Maybe it'll help. On the other hand, it might end up being a waste of time and money."

I think quickly and say, "Then it will be a waste of *my* time and *my* money. I'll supply the money for the trip. I only care about getting to the bottom of these murders."

"I guess so," says Elliott.

I say, "I'll take that as a yes."

A minute later I am telling K. Burke to go home and pack.

Her reaction? "I've never been to Paris."

My reaction? "Why am I not surprised?"

CHAPTER 32

K. BURKE AND I are sitting at a steel desk in a small room with bad internet service at Les Archives de la Préfecture de Police, the dreary building on the periphery of Paris where all the old police records are kept. Here you can examine every recorded police case since the end of the Great War. Here you can discover the names of the French collaborators during the Vichy regime. You can examine the records of the Parisian bakers who have been accused of using tainted yeast in their bread. Here are the records of the thousands of murders, assaults, knife attacks, shootings, and traffic violations that have occurred in the past hundred years in the City of Light.

It is also here that K. Burke and I hope to find some small (or, better yet, large) clue that could connect us to whoever is responsible for the brutal deaths of Maria Martinez and my beloved Dalia.

To find the person who wishes to hurt me so deeply.

"Here," says Detective Burke, pointing to my name

on the screen of the archive's computer. *"L. Moncrief était responsable…"*

I translate: "L. Moncrief was responsible for the evidence linking the Algerian diplomat to the cartel posing as Dominican priests in the 15th arrondissement."

I press a computer key and say to Burke, "Listen: after years of being dragged to church by my mother, I know a real priest when I see one, and no *prêtre* I'd ever seen had such a well-groomed beard and mustache. Then I noticed that his shoes…eh, never mind. See what's next."

We study my other cases. Some of those I worked on are ridiculously small—a Citroën stolen because the owner left the keys in the ignition; a lost child who stopped for a free *jus d'orange* on his way home from school; a homeless man arrested for singing loudly in a public library.

Other cases are much more significant. Along with the phony Dominicans, there was the drug bust in Pigalle, the case I built my reputation on. But there was also a gruesome murder in Montmartre, on rue Caulaincourt, during which a pimp's hands and feet were amputated.

In this last case my instincts led me to a pet cemetery in Asnières-sur-Seine. Both the severed hands and feet were found at the grave of the pimp's childhood pet, a spaniel. Instinct.

But nothing in the police archive is resonating with me. I do not feel, either through logic or instinct, any link from these past cases and the awful deaths of my two beloved women.

"I think I need another café au lait, Moncrief," K. Burke says. Her eyelids are covering half her eyes. Jet lag has definitely attacked her.

"What you need is a taxi back to Le Meurice," I say. "It is now *quatorze heures....*"

K. Burke looks confused.

I translate. "Two o'clock in the afternoon."

"Gotcha," she says.

"Go back to the hotel. Take a nap, and I will come knocking on your door at *dix-sept heures*. Forgive me. I will come knocking at five o'clock."

I add, "Good-bye, K. Burke."

"Au revoir," she says. Her accent makes me cringe, then smile.

"You see?" I add. "You're here just seven hours, and already you're on your way to becoming a true *Parisienne*."

CHAPTER 33

WE MEET AT FIVE.

"I am not a happy man," I say to K. Burke after I give our destination to the cabdriver. Then I say, "Perhaps I will never be a completely happy man again, but I am *un peu content* when I am in Paris." Burke says nothing for a few seconds.

"Perhaps someday you will be happi*er*." She speaks with an emphasis on the last syllable. Perhaps someday I will be.

Then I explain to her that because we will have to get back to our investigation tomorrow—"And, like many things, it might come to a frustrating end," I caution—this early evening will be the only chance for me to show her the glory of Paris.

Then I quickly add, "But not the Eiffel Tower or the Louvre or Notre Dame. You can see those on your own. I will show you the special places in Paris. Places that are visited by only the very wise and the very curious."

Detective Burke says, *"Merci, Monsieur Moncrief."*

I smile at her, and then I say to the cabdriver, *"Nous sommes arrivés."* We are here.

Burke reads the sign on the building aloud. Her accent is amusingly American-sounding: "Museé… des…Arts…Forains?"

"It is the circus museum," I say. And soon we are standing in a huge warehouse that holds the forty carousels and games and bright neon signs that a rich man thought were worth preserving.

"I can't decide whether this is a dream or a nightmare," Burke says.

"I think that it is *both*."

We ride a carousel that whirls amazingly fast. "I feel like I'm five again!" shouts K. Burke. We play a game that involves plaster puppets and cloth-covered bulls. K. Burke wins the game. Then we are out and on our way again.

This time out I tell our cabdriver to take us to Paris Descartes University.

"Vous êtes médecin?" the cabdriver asks.

I tell him that my companion and I are doctors of crime, which seems both to surprise and upset him. A few minutes later we are ascending in the lift to view the Musée d'Anatomie Delmas-Orfila-Rouvière. The place is almost crazier than the circus museum. It's a medical museum with hundreds of shelves displaying skulls and skeletons and wax models of diseased human parts. It is at once astonishing and disgusting.

At one point Burke says, "We're the only people here."

"You need special permission to enter."

"Aren't we the lucky ones?" Burke says, with only slight sarcasm.

From there we take another cab ride—to the Pont des Arts, a pedestrian bridge across the Seine. I show her the "love locks," the thousands of small padlocks attached to the rails of the bridge by lovers.

"They are going to relocate some of the locks," I tell Burke. "There are so many that they fear the bridge may collapse."

So much love, I think. And for a moment my heart hurts. But then I hail another cab. I point out the Pitié-Salpêtrière hospital, and we both laugh when I explain that it was once an asylum for "hysterical women."

"Don't get any ideas, Moncrief," Burke says.

Since our bodies are still on New York time, it is almost lunchtime for us, and I ask K. Burke if she is hungry.

"*Tu as faim?*" I ask.

"*Très, très* hungry. Famished, in fact."

Ten minutes later, we are in the rough-and-tumble Pigalle area. I tell Detective Burke that she can always dine at the famous Parisian restaurants—Taillevent, Guy Savoy, even the dining room in our hotel. But tonight, I am taking her to my favorite restaurant, Le Petit Canard.

"Isn't this the area where you made your famous drug bust?" Burke asks.

"*C'est vrai,*" I tell her. "You have a good memory."

She is looking out the taxi window. The tourists have disappeared from the streets. The artists must be inside smoking weed. Only vagrants and prostitutes are hanging around.

"Ignore the neighborhood. Le Petit Canard is amazing. I used to come here a great deal when I lived in Paris. With friends, with my father, with…"

She says, "With Dalia, I'm sure." She pauses and says, "I am so sorry for you, Moncrief. So sorry."

Softly, I mutter, "Thank you."

Then I add, "And thank you for allowing me to

take you to the crazy tourist sights. It lifted my spirits. It made me feel a little better, Katherine."

Burke appears slightly startled. We both realize that for the first time I have called Detective Burke by her proper first name.

I look closely at Burke's face, a lovely face, a face that goes well with such a lovely evening in such a beautiful city.

"Okay," I say loudly and with great heartiness. "Let me call for the wine list, and we shall begin. We will enjoy a glorious dinner tonight."

I fake an overly serious sad face, a frown. "Because you know that tomorrow...*retour au travail.* Do you know what those three French words mean?"

"I'm afraid so," she says. " 'Back to work.' "

CHAPTER 34

MONCRIEF AND K. BURKE return to the hotel. If you were unaware of the details of their relationship, you would assume that they were just another rich and beautiful couple strolling through the ornate lobby of the Meurice.

Much to Moncrief's surprise and pleasure, K. Burke had brought along an outfit that was quite chic— a long white shirt over which hung a gray cashmere sweater. That sweater fell over a slim black skirt. It was finished with short black boots. Burke could *possibly* pass as a fashionable Parisian, and she could *certainly* pass as a fashionable American. Moncrief had told her how "snappy" she looked.

"You look snappy yourself, Moncrief," she had said to him. This was, of course, true: a black Christian Dior suit with a slight sheen to it; a white shirt with a deep burgundy-colored tie.

Moncrief walked K. Burke back to her room and said good night. He listened while Burke locked her door behind her. Then he walked to the end of the hallway, to his own room.

It was a dinner between friends, between colleagues. K. Burke had expected nothing more. In fact, K. Burke *wanted* nothing more. It had been a spectacular day—the odd museums, then the extraordinary dinner: foie-gras ravioli, Muscovy duckling with mango sherbet, those wonderful little chocolates that fancy French restaurants always bring you with your coffee (or so Moncrief told her).

The night had turned out to be soothing and fun and friendly. He referred to Dalia a few times, and it was with nostalgia, sadness. But there was no darkness when he reminisced about his late girlfriend.

Now, as Burke unscrews and removes her tiny diamond studs, she wonders: *Can you have such a wonderful time with a charming, handsome man and not think about romance?*

Of course you can, she tells herself. But then again, it's impossible to put a man and a woman together—the electrician who comes to fix the wiring, the traffic cop who stops you for speeding, the attorney who is updating your will—and not consider the possibilities of *What if…at another time…under different conditions…*

Burke removes her shirt and sweater. She sits on the bench at the white wood dressing table and removes her boots. As she massages her toes she shakes her head slowly; she is ashamed that she is even having such thoughts. Despite the pleasant dinner, she knows that Moncrief has not remotely begun to recover from Dalia's awful, sudden, horrible death. *And yet here I am, selfishly thinking of how great we look together, like one of those beautiful couples in a perfume ad.*

"Enough nonsense." She actually says these two words out loud.

Then she goes into the bathroom, removes her

makeup, brushes her teeth, and takes the two antique combs out of her hair. She slips her T-shirt (GO RANGERS) over her head, then she removes her contact lenses and drops them into solution. There is only one more thing to do.

She goes to her pocketbook to do what she does instinctively every night before bed: check the safety on her service weapon. Then she remembers—she doesn't have a gun. The French police said that she and Moncrief were on official business for New York, *not* for Paris. No firearms permits would be issued.

She remembers what Moncrief said to her when she complained.

"Do you feel naked without your gun, K. Burke?"

"No," she had answered. "Just a little underdressed."

CHAPTER 35

THE SAME CRAMPED AND ugly little room. The same primitive air-conditioning. The same stale air. The same inadequate internet service. But most of all, the same rotten luck in finding "the fingerprint," the instinctive connection between one of my past investigations and the tragedies in New York.

Detective Burke and I keep working. We are once again seated in the police archives building, outside Paris. We have been studying the screen so intently that we decided to invest in a shared bottle of eyedrops.

The screen scrolls through old cases, some of which I had actually forgotten—a molestation case that involved a disgusting pediatrician who was also the father of five children; a case of a government official who, not surprisingly, was collecting significant bribes for issuing false health-inspection reports; a case of race fixing at the Longchamp racecourse.

"This looks bigger than fixing a horse race," she says. "The pages go on forever."

"Print them," I say. "I'll look at them more thoroughly later."

Forty pages come spitting out of the printer. Burke says, "It looks like this was a very complicated case."

"Not really," I say. "No case is ever *that* complicated. Either there's a crime or there isn't. The Longchamp case began with a horse trainer. Marcel Ballard was his name. Not a bad guy, I think, but Ballard was weary of fixing the races. So he fought physically—punching, kicking—with the owner and trainer who were running the fix. *And* Ballard had a knife. *And* Ballard killed the owner and cut the other trainer badly."

K. Burke continues scrolling through the cases on the screen. She says, "Keep going, Moncrief. I'm listening."

"I met with Ballard's wife. She had a newborn, three months old, their fourth child. So I did her a favor, but not without asking for something in return. I persuaded Ballard to confess to the crime and to help us identify the other trainers who were drugging the horses. He cooperated. So thanks to my intervention—and that of my superiors—he was allowed to plead to a lesser charge. Instead of *homicide volontaire,* he was only charged with—"

"Let me guess," says K. Burke. "*Homicide* in*volontaire.*"

"You are both a legal and linguistic genius, K. Burke."

I grab some of the Longchamp papers and go through them quickly. "I'm glad I did what I did," I say. "Madame Ballard is a good woman."

"And the husband? Is he grateful?" K. Burke asks as she continues to study the screen intensely.

"He has written to me many times in gratitude. But one must keep in mind that he did kill a man."

Burke presses a computer key and begins reading about a drug gang working out of Saint-Denis.

"What does this mean, Moncrief? *Logement social.*"

"In New York they call it public housing. A group of heroin dealers had set up a virtual drug supermarket in the basement there. Once I realized that some of our Parisian detectives were involved in the scheme, it was fairly easy—but frightening—to bust."

"How'd you figure out that your own cops were involved?" she asks.

"I simply *felt* it," I say.

"Of course," she says with a bit of sarcasm. "I should have known."

We continue flipping through the cases on the computer. But like the race fixing and murder at Longchamp, like the drug bust in Saint-Denis, all my former cases seem to be a million miles away from New York. No instinct propelled me. No fingerprint arose.

We studied the cold cases also. The kidnapping of the Ugandan ambassador's daughter (unsolved). The rape of an elderly nun at midnight in the Bois de Boulogne (unsolved, but what in hell was an elderly nun doing in that huge park at midnight?). An American woman with whom I had a brief romantic fling, Callie Hansen, who had been abducted for three days by a notorious husband-and-wife team that we were never able to apprehend. Again, nothing clicked.

We come across a street murder near Moulin Rouge. According to the report on the computer screen, one of the witnesses was a woman named Monica Ansel. Aha! Blaise Ansel had been the owner of Taylor Antiquities, the store on East 71st Street. Could Monica Ansel be his wife? But Monica Ansel, the woman who witnessed the crime at Moulin Rouge, was seventy-one years old.

"Damn!" I say, and I toss the papers from the

Longchamp report to the floor. "I have wasted my time and yours, K. Burke. Plus I have wasted a good deal of money. And what do I have to show for it? *De la merde.*"

Even with her limited knowledge of French, K. Burke is able to translate.

"I agree," she says. "Shit."

CHAPTER 36

K. BURKE SITS OUTDOORS at a small bistro table on rue Vieille du Temple. She is alone. Moncrief had asked if he could be by himself for a while. "I must walk. I must think. Perhaps I must mourn. Do you mind?" Moncrief had said.

"I understand," she had said, and she did understand. "I don't need a chaperone."

She sips a glass of strong cider and eats a buckwheat crepe stuffed with ham and Gruyère. It is eight o'clock, a fairly early dinner by French standards. At one table sits a family of German tourists—very blond parents with two very beautiful teenage daughters. At another, an older couple (French, Burke suspects) eating and chewing and drinking slowly and carefully. Finally, there are two young Frenchwomen who appear to be...yes, K. Burke is right...very much in love with each other.

Burke's own heart is still breaking for Moncrief, but she must admit that she is enjoying being alone for a few hours.

Back in her hotel room, she takes a warm bath. A healthy dose of lavender bath oils; a natural sea sponge. Afterward, she dries herself off with the thick white bath sheets and douses herself with a nice dose of the accompanying lavender powder.

She slips on her sleep shirt, and she's about to slide under the sheets when her phone buzzes. A text message.

R U back in yr room? All is well?

She imagines Moncrief in some mysterious part of Paris, at a zinc bar with a big snifter of brandy. She is thankful for his thoughtfulness.

Yes.

But then, for just a moment she considers her own uneasiness. She simply cannot get used to not having a gun to check. So she does the next best thing: she checks that the door is double-locked. She adjusts the air-conditioning, making the temperature low enough for her to happily snuggle under the thick satin comforter. Within a few minutes she is asleep.

Two hours later, she is wide awake. It is barely past midnight, and Burke is afraid that jet lag is playing games with her sleep schedule. Now she may be up for hours. She takes a few deep breaths. The air makes her feel at least a little better. Maybe she will get back to sleep. Maybe she should use the bathroom. Yes, maybe. Or maybe that will prevent her from falling asleep again. On the other hand...

There is a sound in the room. At first she thinks it's the air conditioner kicking back into gear. Perhaps it is the noise from the busy rue de Rivoli below. She sits up in bed. The noise. Again. Burke realizes now that the sound is coming from the door to her hotel room. Some sort of key? What the hell?

"Who's there?" she shouts.

No answer.

"Who's there?"

Goddamnit. Why doesn't she have a gun?

She should have insisted that Moncrief get them guns. He was right. She feels naked without it.

She rolls quickly—catching herself in the thick covers, afraid in the dark—toward the other side of the bed. She drops to the floor and slides beneath the bed just as a shaft of bright light from the hallway pierces the darkness. Someone else is in the room with her. She moves farther underneath the bed. *Jesus Christ,* she thinks. *This is an awful comedy, a French farce—the woman hiding beneath the bed.*

As soon as she hears the door close, the light from the hallway disappears.

"Don't move, Detective!" a muffled, foreign-sounding voice hisses.

Then a gunshot.

The bullet hits the floor about a foot away from her hand. There's a quick loud snapping sound. A spark on the blue carpet. She tries to move farther under the bed. There is no room. It is so unlike her to not know what to do, to not fight back, to not plot an escape. This feeling of fright is foreign to her.

Another bullet. This one spits its way fiercely through the mattress above her. It hits the floor also.

Another bullet. No spark. No connection.

A groan. A quick thud.

Then a voice.

"K. Burke! It is safe. All is well."

CHAPTER 37

HOTEL MANAGEMENT AND GUESTS in their pajamas almost immediately begin gathering in the hall.

K. Burke emerges from under the bed. We embrace each other the way friends do, friends who have successfully come through a horrible experience together.

"You saved…" she begins. She is shaking. She folds her arms in front of herself. She is working to compose herself.

"I know," I say. I pat her on the back. I am like an old soccer coach with an injured player.

Burke pulls away from me. She blinks—on purpose—a few times, and those simple eye gestures seem to clear her head and calm her nerves. She is immediately back to a completely professional state. She has become the efficient K. Burke I am used to. We both look down at the body. She moves to a nearby closet and wraps herself quickly in a Le Meurice terry-cloth bathrobe.

The dead man fell backward near the foot of the bed. He wears jeans, a white dress shirt, and Adidas sneakers. His bald head lies in a large and ever-growing pool of blood. It forms a kind of scarlet halo around his face.

The crowd in the hallway seems afraid to enter the room. A man wearing a blue blazer with LE MEURICE embroidered on the breast pocket appears. He pushes through the crowd. He is immediately followed by two men wearing identical blazers.

I briefly explain what happened, planning to give the police a more detailed story when they arrive.

K. Burke then kneels at the man's head. I watch her touch the man's neck. I can tell by the blood loss, by simply looking at him, that she is merely performing an official act. The guy is gone. Burke stands back up.

"Do you know him, Moncrief?" Burke asks.

"I have never seen him before in my life," I say. "Have you?"

"Of course not," she says. She pauses. Then she says, "He was going to kill me."

"You would have been…the third victim."

She nods. "How did you know that this was happening here, that someone was actually going to break in…threaten my life…try to kill me?"

"Instinct. When I texted you I asked if all was well. So I drank my whiskey.

"But fifteen minutes later, when I am walking back to the hotel, I found myself walking faster and faster, until I was actually running…I just had a feeling. I can't explain it."

"You never can," she says.

CHAPTER 38

THE NEXT MORNING.

Eleven o'clock. I meet K. Burke in the lobby of the hotel.

"So here we are," she says. "Everything is back to *ab*normal."

Even I realize that this is a bad play on words. But it does perfectly describe our situation.

"Look," I say. "A mere apology is unsuitable. I am totally responsible for the near tragedy of last night."

"There's nothing to apologize for. It goes with the territory," she says, but I can see from her red eyes that she did not sleep well. I try to say something helpful.

"I suspect what happened a few hours ago is that the enemy saw us together at some point here in Paris and assumed that we were a couple, which of course we are not."

I realize immediately that my words are insulting, as if it would be impossible to consider us a romantic item. So I speak again, this time more quickly.

"Of course, they might have been correct in the assumption. After all, a lovely-looking woman like you could—"

"Turn it off, Moncrief. I was *not* offended."

I smile. Then I hold K. Burke by the shoulders, look into her weary eyes, and speak.

"Listen. Out of something awful that almost happened last evening…something good has come. I believe I have an insight. I think I may now know the fingerprint of this case."

She asks me to share the theory with her.

"I cannot tell you yet. Not for secrecy reasons, but because I must first be sure, in order to keep my own mind clear. *On y va.*"

"Okay," she says. Then she translates: "Let's go."

We walk outside. I speak to one of the doormen.

"Ma voiture, s'il vous plaît," I say.

"Elle est là, Monsieur Moncrief."

"Your car is here?" Burke asks, and as she speaks my incredibly beautiful 1960 Porsche 356B pulls up and the valet gets out.

"C'est magnifique," Burke says.

The Porsche is painted a brilliantly shiny black. Inside is a custom mahogany instrument panel and a pair of plush black leather seats. I explain to Detective Burke that I had been keeping the car at my father's country house, near Avignon.

"But two days ago I had the car brought up to Paris. And so today we shall use it."

I turn right on the rue de Rivoli, and the Porsche heads out of the city.

After the usual mess of too many people and

triple-parked cars and thousands of careless bicycle riders, we are outside Paris, on our way south.

K. Burke twists in her seat and faces me.

"Okay, Moncrief. I have a question that's been bugging me all night."

"I hope to have the answer," I say, trying not to sound anxious.

"The gun that you used last night. Where did you get it?"

I laugh, and with the wind in our hair and the sun in our eyes I fight the urge to throw my head back like an actor in a movie.

"Oh, the gun. Well, when Papa's driver dropped off the car two days ago, I looked in that little compartment, the one in front of your seat, and voilà! Driving gloves, chewing gum, driver's license, and my beautiful antique Nagant revolver. I thought it might come in handy someday."

In the countryside I pick up speed, a great deal of speed. K. Burke does not seem at all alarmed by fast driving. After a few minutes of silence I tell her that I am taking the country roads instead of the A5 *autoroute* so that she might enjoy the summer scenery.

She does not say a word. She is asleep, and she remains so until I make a somewhat sharp right turn at our destination.

K. Burke blinks, rubs her eyes, and speaks.

"Where are we, Moncrief?"

Ahead of us is a long, low, flat gray building. It is big and gloomy. Not like a haunted house or a lost castle. Just a huge grim pile of concrete. She reads the name of the building, carved into the stone.

PRISON CLAIRVAUX

She does a double take.

"What are we doing here, Moncrief?"

"We are here to meet the killer of Maria Martinez and Dalia Boaz."

CHAPTER 39

A FEW YEARS AGO, a detective with the Paris police described the prison at Clairvaux as "hell, but without any of the fun." I think the detective was being kind.

As K. Burke and I present identification to the entrance guards, I tell her, "Centuries ago this was a Cistercian abbey, a place of monks and prayer and chanting."

"Well," she says as she looks around the stained gray walls. "There isn't a trace of God left here."

Burke and I are scanned with an electronic wand, then we step through an X-ray machine and are finally escorted to a large vacant room—no chairs, no tables, no window. We stand waiting a few minutes. The door opens, and an official-looking man as tall as the six-foot doorway enters. He is thin and old. His left eye is made of glass. His name is Tomas Wren. We shake hands.

"Detective Moncrief, I was delighted to hear your message this morning that you would be paying us a visit."

"Merci," I say. "Thank you for accommodating us on such short notice."

Wren looks at Detective Burke and speaks.

"And you, of course, must be Madame Moncrief."

"Non, monsieur, je suis Katherine Burke. Je suis la collègue de Monsieur Moncrief."

"Ah, mille pardons," Wren says. Then Wren turns to me. He is suddenly all business.

"I have told Ballard that you are coming to see him."

"His reaction?" I ask.

"His face lit up."

"I'm glad to hear that," I say.

"You never know with Ballard. He can be a dangerous customer," says Wren. "But he owes you a great deal."

With a touch of levity, I say, "And I owe him a great deal. Without his help I would never have made the arrests that made my career take off."

Wren shrugs, then says, "I have set aside one of the private meeting rooms for you and Mademoiselle Burke."

We follow him down another stained and gray hallway. The private room is small—perhaps merely a dormitory cell from the days of the Cistercian brothers—but it has four comfortable desk chairs around a small maple table. A bit more uninviting, however, are the *bouton d'urgence*—the emergency button—and two heavy metal clubs.

Wren says that he will be back in a moment. "With Ballard," he says.

As soon as Wren exits, Burke speaks.

"I remember this case from the other day, Moncrief. On the computer. Ballard is the horse trainer who killed some guy and wounded another at the Longchamp racecourse."

"Yes, indeed, Detective."

"But I don't totally get what's going on here now."

"You will," I say.

"If you say so," she answers.

I nod, and as I do I feel myself becoming…quiet… no, the proper word is…frightened. A kind of soft anxiety begins falling over me. No man can ever feel happy being in a prison, even for a visit. It is a citadel of punishment and futility. But this is something way beyond simple unhappiness. Burke senses that something is wrong.

"Are you okay, Moncrief?" she says.

"No, I am not. I am twice a widower of sorts. And now I feel I am in the house where those plans were made. No, Detective. I am not okay. But you know what? I don't ever expect to be okay. Excuse me if that sounds like self-pity."

"No need to apologize. I understand."

CHAPTER 40

A CREAKING SOUND, LIKE one you would
hear in an old horror movie, comes from the door. It
opens, and a burst of light surges into the bleak room.

Wren has returned, and with him is a young prison
guard. The guard escorts the prisoner—Marcel Ballard.

Ballard is ugly. His fat face is scarred on both cheeks.
Another scar is embedded on the right side of his
neck. The three scars show the marks of crude surgical
stitching. Prison fights, perhaps?

His head is completely bald. He is unreasonably
heavy for a man who dines only on prison rations; he
must be trading something of value for extra food.

The guard removes the handcuffs from Ballard.

Ballard comes rushing toward me. He is shouting.

The guard moves to pull Ballard away from me, but
Ballard is too fast for him.

"Moncrief, mon ami, mon pote!" he yells. Then he
embraces me in a tight bear hug. In accented English,
the guard translates, "My friend! My best friend!"

Then Ballard kisses me on both cheeks.

CHAPTER 41

IT IS BALLARD WHO enlightens K. Burke.

"You wonder why we embrace, mademoiselle?"

"Not really," says K. Burke. "I know about you and the detective. I know that you received a lesser sentence because of *him,* and I know that he received some valuable information because of *you.*"

Ballard smiles. I look away from the two of them.

"Detective Moncrief, you have not told your colleague the entire story of our relationship?" Ballard asks, his eyes almost comically wide.

For a reason I can't explain, I am becoming angry. With a snappish tone I respond, "No. I didn't think it was necessary. I thought it was between the two of us."

"But many others know," Ballard responds. "May I tell her?"

"Do whatever you like," I say. The bleakness of the prison, the memory of the Longchamp arrests, and the indelible pain of Maria and Dalia's deaths all close in on me. I am sinking into a depression. There is no reason why I should be angry that Burke will be hearing the story of Ballard and me. Still, he hesitates.

I try to restore a lighter tone to the conversation. "No, really. If you want to tell her, go right ahead."

After a pause, Ballard tells her, "When I was arrested I was the father of an infant, and I was also the father of three other children, all of them under the age of five years."

He pauses, and with a smile says, "Yes, we are a very Catholic family. Four children in five years." Burke does not smile back.

Then he continues. "Life would have been desperate for my wife, Marlene, without me. The children would have starved. When I was sentenced to the two decades in the prison, I worried and prayed, and my prayers were answered.

"In my second month inside this hell, Marlene writes to me with news. She is receiving a monthly stipend, a generous stipend, from Monsieur Moncrief."

He pauses, then adds, "I was overwhelmed with gratitude for his extreme generosity."

Burke nods at Ballard. Then she turns to me and says, "Good man, Detective."

I do not care to slosh around in sentimentality. I gruffly announce, "Look, Ballard. I am here for a reason. An important reason. You may be able to pay me back for that 'extreme generosity.'"

CHAPTER 42

THE GOSSIP NETWORK IN a prison is long and strong.

Ballard confirms this. "I was overcome with sadness and anger when I heard about your police friend and your girlfriend, Detective. I could not write to you. I could not telephone. I did not know what to say. And, I am ashamed to admit, I was afraid. If the other prisoners found out that I was speaking to a member of the Paris police, I might be in danger."

"I understand," I say. "Besides, Marlene wrote me and expressed her outrage and sympathy."

"*Très bien,*" he says. "Marlene is a good woman."

I am silent. I want to speak, but I cannot. Suddenly everything is rushing back—the sight of Maria in the lavish Park Avenue apartment, the sight of Dalia on the gurney, the crazed run that I made through Hermès and the wine shop.

I think Burke senses that I have wandered off to a deeper, darker place. She keeps a steady gaze on me.

Ballard looks confused. He is waiting for me to say something. My tongue freezes as if it's too big for my mouth. My brain is too big for my head, and my heart is too broken to function.

Ballard reaches across the little table and places his rough hand on mine.

"The heart breaks, Detective."

I remain silent. Ballard speaks.

"What can I do, my friend?"

My head is filling with pain. Then I speak.

"Listen to me, Marcel. I believe that someone being held in this prison arranged for the executions of my partner, Maria, and my lover, Dalia. I think whoever it was also planned to kill my current partner, the person sitting here."

I cannot help but notice that Ballard does not react in any way to what I'm saying. He finally removes his hand from mine. He continues to listen silently. If he is anything, he is afraid, stunned.

"It is pure revenge, Ballard. There are men here in Clairvaux who detest me. They don't blame their crimes for their imprisonment. They blame *me*. They think that by killing the people I am close to…they are killing me…and you know something, Ballard? They are right."

Again silence. A long silence. The minute that feels like an hour.

Ballard interrupts the quiet. He is calm. *"C'est vrai, monsieur le lieutenant.* Someone who hates you is killing the women you love."

"Tell me, Marcel. Tell me if you truly have gratitude for what I've done to help your wife and children: do you have any idea who ordered these murders?"

Ballard looks at Burke. Then he looks at me. Then he looks down at the table. When he looks back up again a few moments later his eyes are wet with tears. He speaks.

"Everyone inside this asylum is cruel. You have to learn to be cruel to survive here."

I am awestruck at Ballard's intensity. He continues.

"But there is only one man who has the power to buy such a horror in the outside world. And I think you know who that is. I think you know without my even saying his name."

And I know the person we should bring in.

CHAPTER 43

BURKE AND I WAIT for Adrien Ramus.

We wait in a smaller, bleaker room than the one in which we met with Ballard. This room is located within the high-security area, where the most treacherous prisoners are kept. It is not solitary confinement, but it is the next worst thing. Isolation, only relieved for food and fifteen minutes of recreation a day in the yard.

The room has no table, no chairs. It is bare except for the emergency button, three clubs, and three mace cartridges that hang on the wall.

The door opens with the same horror-film creak as the door in the previous interview room. Tomas Wren once again accompanies the prisoner, but Ramus apparently warrants *three* guards to keep him under control. What's more, I suspect that the handcuffs behind Ramus's back will not be removed.

Ramus is gaunt, thin as a man with a disease. His nose is too big for his face. His eyes are too small for his face. Yet all his characteristics come together to form a frightening but handsome man. He could be an aging fashion model.

Years ago, during his booking, his trials, and his sentencing, Ramus spat on the floor whenever he saw me. When this vulgarity earned him a club to the head from a policeman or a prison guard, Ramus didn't care. It was worth a little pain to demonstrate his hatred for the detective who had brought him down.

Ramus does not disappoint this time. Upon seeing me he immediately lobs a small puddle of spittle in my direction.

I sense madness—not only in Ramus but also in myself. I reach across and grab him by the chin. I push his head back as far as it will go without snapping it off. I know the guards probably hate Ramus as much as I do. I know they won't stop me. I could beat Ramus if I wished to.

"My partner! My lover!" I shout. "It was you!"

He just stares at me. He twists his neck forcefully, trying to relieve the pain of my assault. I let go of his chin, then shout again.

"You have sources on the outside who can do such things!"

Now Ramus smiles. Then he speaks. The voice is rough, the words staccato.

"You are a fool, Moncrief. I have sources, yes. But anyone inside this pit of hell can buy influence outside. Put the pieces together, Moncrief. Are you so stupid?"

He spits again. Then he just stares at me. I speak more softly now.

"You will burn in hell…and I cannot wait for that time! I cannot wait for God to burn you. And you will do more than die and burn. You will first *suffer*. And then die and burn. I will see to it."

He says, "When I heard that your two women friends were killed I was happy. I was joyful."

My heart is beating hard. My chest is heaving up and down. Ramus continues.

"Some men are very powerful...sometimes even *more* powerful in the shadows of a prison than they are on the streets of the city."

I feel my hand and both my arms tense up completely. In seconds I will be at him once again. This time I will force my hand around his neck. Then I will force my fingers around his Adam's apple. Then...

He speaks again.

"Believe whatever you want, Moncrief. It is of no meaning to me. As I say, you are a stupid, pathetic fool. When will you learn? Where I am concerned, you are powerless. The boss? He is Ramus."

The tension and strength suddenly drain from my body. My arms fall to my side. I am the victim of a perfect crime.

I bow my head. *I have solved the case, but the women closest to me are gone.*

I try to control my shaking limbs. I try to hold my feelings inside me.

"Get him out of here," I say to the guards.

Ramus says nothing more. They lead him out. It's over.

CHAPTER 44

THE NEXT AFTERNOON K. Burke and I fly back to New York City.

Closure. K. Burke is smart enough and now knows me well enough not to talk about "closure," a glib and wishful concept. Nothing closes. At least not completely.

Friends and colleagues and family will say (and some have said already), "You're lucky. At least you're young and rich and handsome. You'll get over this. You'll find a way to learn to move on."

I will nod affirmatively, but only to stop their chatter. Then my response will be simple: "No. Those qualities—youth, wealth, physical attributes— are randomly distributed. They protect you from very little of life's real agonies."

Menashe Boaz and I speak on the telephone. He is still in Norway with his film—"wrapping in three days." His voice, predictably, is somber. I am one of the few people who knows precisely how he feels. With my complete agreement, he decides that he will send two assistants to New York to oversee clearing out Dalia's apartment. Sad? It is beyond sad. Menashe and I cannot have this conversation without the occasional tear. It is a miracle that we can have the conversation at all.

"I don't want a thing from Dalia's apartment," I tell him. I never want to enter the place again.

Any book I've left there I will never finish reading. Any suit in her closet I will never wear again. The real keepsakes are all inside me. A handful of wonderful photographs are on my phone.

Full of jet lag, fatigue, tension, and sorrow, K. Burke and I speak with Inspector Elliott at the precinct. I describe in broad strokes our time in Paris. Burke describes the same thing, but in much greater detail. I say the words I've been aching to say: "The case is solved."

When our two hours with Elliott are over, I tell K. Burke, that her memory is "astonishing. I mean it."

She says, "Almost as good as yours. I mean it."

We return to the detective pool—piles of files, the endless recorded phone messages, the crime blotter. I see that Burke is not her usual ambitious self. She is shuffling papers, typing slowly on her computer.

"Something is troubling you, Detective?" I say.

She looks up at me and speaks. "I'm angry that Ramus has brought us down. I know that's stupid. I know the case is solved. But he *has* committed the perfect crime. He can kill and get away with it. It really pisses me off. I can only imagine how you must feel."

"Life goes on, K. Burke. Who knows? Maybe tomorrow will be a little bit better," I say.

Detective Burke smiles. Then she speaks.

"Exactly. Who knows?"

CHAPTER 45

La maison centrale de Clairvaux

ALL PRISONERS ARE EQUAL in the mess hall. At least that's the way it's supposed to be. Same horrid food, same rancid beverages. But in prison, those who have money also have influence. And those with money and influence live a little better.

Marcel Ballard supplies two kitchen workers with a weekly supply of filtered Gauloises cigarettes. So the workers show their gratitude by heaping larger mounds of instant mashed potatoes on Ballard's plate and by giving him a double serving of the awful industrial cheese that is supplied after the meal. On some lucky occasions, Ballard goes to take a slug of water from his tin cup and finds that a kitchen ally has replaced the water with beer or, better still, a good amount of Pernod.

Adrien Ramus has even more influence than Ballard. Ramus, you see, has even more bribery material at his disposal. Even Tomas Wren has snapped at the bait Ramus dangles. Because he gives Wren the occasional gift of a few grams of cocaine, Ramus has a relatively easy time of it in isolation—a private cell, a radio. Ramus sells many things to many prisoners. He always has a supply of marijuana for those who want to get high and access to local attorneys for those who want to get out.

It is Tuesday's supper. The menu never changes. Sunday is a greasy chicken thigh with canned asparagus spears that smell like socks. Monday is spaghetti in a tasteless oil. And then Tuesday. Tuesday at Clairvaux is always—unalterably, predictably—white beans, gray meat in brown gravy, canned spinach, and a thin slice of cheap unidentifiable white cheese.

Guards patrol the aisles.

No conversation is allowed. But that rule is constantly broken, usually with a shout-out declaring, "This food is shit." Sometimes there's a warning from someone just on the edge of sanity, a "Stop staring at me or I'll slice off your balls" or "You are vomiting on me, *gros trou du cul*." That charming phrase translates as "you big asshole."

This evening is relatively quiet until one man slashes another man's thigh, and as both victim and abuser are hauled away, most of the other prisoners cheer like small stupid boys watching a game. Two other men fight, then they are separated. Two more men fight, and the guards, for their own amusement, allow the fight to proceed for a few minutes until, finally, one man lies semiconscious on the floor.

Suppertime, an allotment of twenty minutes, has almost ended. Some men, like Marcel Ballard, have, for a few euros, bought their neighbor's beans or cheese. Ballard stuffs the food into his round mouth.

Other prisoners have not even touched their plates. Most likely they have chocolate bars and bread hidden in their cells; most likely such luxuries have been supplied—for a price, of course—by Adrien Ramus.

Hundreds of years ago this mess hall was the refectory of Clairvaux Abbey. Here the hood-clad monks chanted their *"Benedic, Domine,"* the grace said before meals. The faded image of Saint Robert of Molesme, the founder of the Cistercian order, is barely visible above the doors to the kitchen. Often, when some angry prisoner decides to throw a pile of potatoes, the mess ends up on Saint Robert's faded face.

The men are ordered to pass their individual bowls to the end of each table. Most do so quietly. Others find that this chore gives them the opportunity to call a fellow diner a prick or, sometimes more gently, a bitch.

Lukewarm coffee is passed around in tin pitchers. Nothing is ever served hot. Too dangerous. Boiling soup or steaming coffee could be poured over an enemy inmate's head. Almost everyone pours large amounts of sugar into their cups. Almost everyone drinks the coffee, including one of the most prominent and influential prisoners, who sits silently at the end of a table.

That prisoner takes a gulp of coffee. He then places the cup on the wooden table. Suddenly the man's right hand flies to his neck, his left hand to his belly. He lets out a hoarse and stifled gasp. His head begins shaking, and a putrid green liquid surges from his mouth. The prisoners near him move away. Two guards move in on the victim. As trained, two other guards rush to protect the exit doors. This might easily be a scheme to start an uprising.

This, however, turns out not to be a trick. The stricken prisoner falls forward onto the wooden table. His head bounces twice on the wood. His poisoned coffee spills onto the floor. He is dead.

Prisoners are shouting. Guards are swinging their clubs.

Adrien Ramus remains seated. No smile. No anger. No expression. He is satisfied.

At this exact same time, the rest of the world continues turning.

In Paris, a group of French hotel workers are busy replacing the bullet-scarred carpeting where K. Burke was attacked.

In Norway, Menashe Boaz is calling "Cut" and then saying, "Fifteen-minute break." He must be alone.

In New York, Luc Moncrief, who has just come in from running four miles on the West Side bike path, sits in a big leather chair in his apartment. He is sweaty and tired and sad. But for some unknowable reason he finds that he is suddenly at peace.

CHAPTER 46

"I THOUGHT YOU WERE out today," K. Burke says to me, as crisp and confident as ever. Whatever jet-lag body-clock adjustment she had to make has been made.

"I was," I say. "But I had to see you. I must show you something on the computer."

"What's with you, Moncrief? You sound a little—I don't know…creepy. It's like your energy level is down a few notches."

"Yes, Detective. I am stunned. I am walking in a dream. Maybe half a dream and half a nightmare."

As always, about a dozen other New York City detectives are very interested in our conversation. Everyone is aware of the murders. Now many are aware of the attack on Burke in Paris.

"Interview room 4 is free. I checked. Let's go there," I say.

Perhaps for the benefit of our police colleagues, Burke shrugs her shoulders in that I-dunno-maybe-he's-a-little-crazy way. Then she follows me down the hall to the interview room.

I close the curtain to prevent anyone from spying on us through the two-way mirror. I place my laptop on the table, open it, and tap a few buttons.

"I've read it maybe fifty times," I say. "Now it's your turn. Please read. Then I am going to delete it."

K. Burke looks vaguely frightened, but she is also curious. I can tell. Her eyes widen, then they relax. Then her forehead wrinkles. She begins to read.

Monsieur Moncrief:

I believe that the following information will be of interest to you.

Three hours ago, at 1800 hours Paris, an inmate in my charge died, the direct result of poison administered to his coffee.

He was a man of your acquaintance: Marcel Ballard.

Burke looks away from the screen. She looks directly at me.

"Ballard?" she says. "But I thought…no. Not Ballard!"

"Keep reading," I say.

Ballard's death was obviously planned and perpetrated by someone inside La maison centrale de Clairvaux.

I know that it was your belief that the murders of Maria Martinez and Dalia Boaz were ordered by another prisoner, Adrien Ramus.

I must inform you, however, that evidence taken here at this scene after today's murder proves otherwise.

An investigation of Ballard's cell revealed a laptop computer hidden within a broken tile beneath the toilet.

An examination of the laptop's contents showed frequent correspondence between Ballard and two Frenchmen who were in the United States on visitor visas. One of them, Thierry Mondeville, returned to France a few days ago. Mondeville has now been identified as the attacker in the incident involving Katherine Burke and yourself.

Further correspondence indicates Ballard's extreme anger at his imprisonment and the role you played in causing it. Ballard explicitly held you responsible for "destroying my life and destroying my family."

Upon its release by the police I will forward a file containing the complete contents of Ballard's computer as well as the findings and conclusions of the official investigation.

Je vous prie d'agréer, Monsieur, mes
respectueuses salutations,
Tomas Wren

Burke and I say nothing for a few moments.

Then she looks at me and speaks. "Do you believe this is true?"

I nod, and, for assurance, I say, "I am certain."

I walk to the other side of the room. I look out the perpetually dirty window. The tops of the brownstones look like figures drawn in charcoal when seen through the dirt on the glass.

"But, Moncrief, you mean…all these years you were helping Ballard, and all these years he was planning to destroy your life?" she says. "You must be amazed at this."

"To be honest, I am not amazed. *I knew.*"

Now Burke is the one who is amazed. She is speechless.

"Ramus is indeed a wretched excuse for a human being. But if he had ordered the executions he would have happily bragged to me about them. He would have told me directly that he was the talent behind the killings. But…he stopped just short of bragging.

"That is why I assaulted him. But I could not drive him to say what he would have been glad to say. He would not admit to being the force behind the killings.

"Then we add the fact that Ballard was so effusive in his thanks to me. Bah! I put him in prison for most of his life. Do you think he cares what happens to his family? Do you think he cares about their welfare? I instinctively knew he was throwing the *connerie,* the bullshit, at me."

I can tell she wants to smile, but this moment is too serious.

"But most important, *I could not have put Ramus in prison if Ballard had not given me information on him.* I knew that someday Ramus would punish Ballard. This was timing *parfait.* Ballard falsely pinned the crimes on Ramus *and* Ballard had previously betrayed him. So, *le poison dans le café.*"

"So the case is solved," she says. But she speaks softly, cautiously.

"I guess so," I say. I know, however, that there is sorrow in my voice.

I walk back to the table where the opened laptop rests. Then I push the button marked DELETE.

CHAPTER 47

I LEAVE THE PRECINCT and head toward Fifth Avenue and 52nd Street. I am standing outside a fabulous shop, Versace. I pause and then walk through the great arched center door.

This was one of Dalia's favorite stores. I can remember almost every single item Dalia ever bought here.

The black skirt. If I looked hard I could see through the tightly woven material and catch a glimpse of Dalia's exquisite legs.

The shoes with thick cork platforms that made Dalia a half inch or so taller than I am. We always laughed at that.

The belts with golden buckles. The black leather shopping totes. The crazy shirts with variously colored geometric shapes that shout at you.

"Signor Moncrief. It has been a thousand years since we have seen you," says the store manager, Giuliana. "Welcome. You have been away, perhaps?" she adds.

"Yes. I've been away. Far away."

Giuliana tilts her head to one side. "I heard of the tragedy of Miss Boaz, of course. We were all so sad."

"Thank you," I say. "I read your condolence note. I read it more than once."

"We liked her so very much," says Giuliana. Then she says, "I will leave you alone. Call on me if I can help you."

"I will," I say. *"Grazie."*

She walks away, and I remain still, moving only my head. I take in the lights from the golden fixtures. The multitude of wallets laid out in their cases in neat overlapping rows.

It is late summer. So they are showing fall coats, fall dresses, fall scarves. Reds and browns and dark yellows. Black jeans and white jeans. And lots and lots of sunglasses. Even the mannequins are wearing sunglasses.

"Sunglasses are always in season," Dalia used to say.

I am about to move deeper into the store. I am calm. Not completely calm, but I am calm.

Then my phone rings. The caller is identified as "K. Burke."

I answer.

"Good afternoon, K. Burke. Don't tell me. There's been a murder."

"How did you know?" she says.

"I just knew. Somehow I just knew."

THE CHRISTMAS MYSTERY

JAMES PATTERSON
AND RICHARD DiLALLO

PROLOGUE

ONE

CHAOS AND CONFUSION reign in New York City's most glamorous department store, Bloomingdale's.

A dozen beautiful women—perfect makeup, perfect clothing—are strutting around the first floor, armed. No one escapes these women. They are shooting customers... with spritzes of expensive perfume.

Enough fragrance fills the air to create a lethal cloud of nausea. The effect is somewhere between expensive flower shop and cheap brothel.

"Unbelievable! This place is packed," says K. Burke.

"Yes," I say. "You'd think it was almost Christmas."

"It *is* almost Chris—" Burke begins to say. She stops, then adds, "Don't be a wiseass, Moncrief. We've got a long day ahead of us."

K. Burke and I are police detective partners from Manhattan's Midtown East. Our chief inspector, Nick Elliott, has assigned us to undercover security at this famous and glamorous department store. I told the inspector that I preferred more challenging assignments, "like trapping terrorists and capturing murderers."

Elliott's response?

"Feel free to trap any terrorists or capture any murderers you come across. Meanwhile, keep your eyes open for purse-snatchers and shoplifters."

K. Burke, ever the cooperative pro, said, "I understand, sir."

I said nothing.

In any event, K. Burke and I at this moment are standing in a fog of Caron Poivre and Chanel No. 5 in Bloomingdale's perfume department.

"So, how are we going to split up, Moncrief?" asks Burke.

"You decide," I say. My enthusiasm is not overwhelming.

"Okay," Burke says. "I'll take the second floor… women's designer clothes. Why don't you take high-end gifts? China, crystal, silver."

"May I suggest," I say, "that you take women's designer clothing on the *fourth* floor, not the *second*. Second floor is Donna Karan and Calvin. Fourth floor is Dolce & Gabbana, Prada, Valentino. Much classier."

Burke shakes her head. "It's amazing, the stuff you know."

We test-check the red buttons on our cell phones, the communication keys that give us immediate contact with each other.

Burke says that she'll also notify regular store security and tell them that their special request NYPD patrol is there, as planned.

"I've got to get out of this perfume storm," she says. She's just about to move toward the central escalator when a well-dressed middle-aged woman approaches. The woman speaks directly to Burke.

"Where can I buy one of these?" the woman says.

"I got the last one," Burke says. The woman laughs and walks away.

I'm completely confused. "What was that lady asking about?" I say.

"She was asking about you," Burke says. "As if you didn't know."

Burke walks quickly toward the up escalator.

TWO

WITHIN THREE MINUTES I'm standing in the fine china and silver section of Bloomingdale's sixth floor. If there is a problem with the economy in New York City, someone failed to tell the frantic shoppers snapping up Wedgwood soup tureens and sterling silver dinner forks. It's only ten thirty in the morning, yet the line at gift-wrap is already eight customers deep.

My cell phone is connected to hundreds of store security cameras. These cameras are trained on entrance areas, exit doors, credit card registers—all areas where intruders can enter, exit, and operate quickly.

I keep my head still, but my eyes dart around the area. Like Christmas itself, all is calm, all is bright. I make my way through the crowd of wealthy-looking women in fur, prosperous-looking men with five-hundred-dollar cashmere scarves.

Then a loud buzz. Insistent. Urgent. I glance quickly at my phone. The red light. I listen to K. Burke's voice.

"Second floor. Right now," she says. She immediately clicks off.

Damn it. I told her to go to the fourth floor. Burke makes her own decisions.

Within a few seconds I'm at the Bloomingdale's internal staircase. I skip the stairs three at a time. I burst through the second floor door.

Chaos. Screaming. Customers crowding the aisles near the down escalators. Salespeople crouched behind counters.

"Location Monitor" on my cell notifies me that Burke is no longer on the original second floor location. Her new location is men's furnishings—ties, wallets, aftershave. Ground floor.

I reverse my course and rush toward the rear escalator near Third Avenue. I push a few men and women out of my path. Now I'm struggling to execute a classic crazy move—I'm running *down* an escalator that's running *up*.

I land on the floor. I see K. Burke moving quickly past display cases of sweaters and shirts. Burke sees me.

She shouts one word.

"Punks!"

It's a perfect description. In a split second I see two young women—teens probably, both in dark-gray hoodies. The pair open a door marked EMPLOYEES ONLY. They go through. The door closes behind them.

Burke and I almost collide at that door. We know from our surveillance planning that this is one of Bloomingdale's "snare" closets—purposely mismarked to snare shoplifters and muggers on the run. This time it works like a Christmas charm. We enter the small space and see two tough-looking teenage girls—nose piercings, eyebrow piercings, tats, the whole getup. One of them is holding an opened switchblade. I squeeze her wrist between my thumb and index finger. The knife falls to the ground. As K. Burke scoops up the knife, she speaks.

"These two assholes knocked over a woman old enough to be their grandmother and took off with her shopping bag," Burke says. "They also managed to slash her leg—the long way. EMU is taking care of her."

"It ain't us. You're messed up. Look. No shopping bags," one of the girls says. Her voice is arrogant, angry.

"Store security has the shopping bag. And they've got enough video on the two of you to make a feature film," Burke adds.

It's clear to the young thieves that they'll get no place good with Burke. One of them decides to play me.

"Give us a break, man. It probably isn't even us on the video. I know all about this shit. Come on."

I smile at the young lady.

"You know all about this shit? Let me tell you something." I pause for a moment, then continue quietly. "In some cases, with the holidays approaching, I might say: give the kids a warning and release them."

"That'd be way cool," says her friend.

K. Burke looks at me. I know that she's afraid my liberal soft spot is going to erupt.

"But this is not one of those cases," I say.

"Man, no. Why?" asks the girl.

"I believe my colleague summed it up a few minutes ago," I say.

"What the hell?" the girl says.

I answer. "Punks!"

THE CHRISTMAS MYSTERY

CHAPTER 1

Almost Thanksgiving

WHEN DALIA BOAZ died a few months ago, I believed that my own life had ended along with hers.

Friends suggested that, with time, the agony of the loss would diminish.

They were wrong. Day after day I ache for Dalia, the love of my life. Yet life rattles on. Unstoppable. Yes, there are moments when I am joyful. Other times are inevitably heartbreaking: Dalia's birthday, my birthday, the anniversary of a special romantic event. Holidays are a special problem, of course, because I am surrounded by celebration—Easter baskets overflowing, fireworks erupting, bright lights hanging from evergreen trees.

Thanksgiving Day is a unique problem. There is nothing remotely like it in France. When Dalia was alive, if I was not on duty, we stayed in bed and streamed a few movies, whipped up some omelets, topped them with beluga caviar, and were thankful that we did not have to eat sweet potatoes with melted marshmallows.

This Thanksgiving proved a challenge. A few detective colleagues generously and sincerely invited me to join them. No, that wasn't for me. So I volunteered for holiday assignment. But Inspector Elliott informed me that Thanksgiving was well staffed with both detectives and officers (mostly divorced parents who traded seeing their children on Thanksgiving Day for seeing them on Christmas Day).

For a moment I wondered how my partner would be spending her holiday. Although my knowledge of K. Burke's private life was sparse, I knew that both her parents were deceased.

Casually I asked her, "Where are you going for Thanksgiving?"

"The gym," was her answer.

In an unlikely explosion of sentiment that surprised even myself I said, "Come to my place. I'll fix Thanksgiving dinner for both of us."

"Yeah, sure," was her sarcastic reaction. "And I'll bake a pumpkin pie."

"No. I'm serious."

"You are?" she said, trying to hide her surprise.

With only a hint of confusion she spoke slowly and quietly. "Oh, my God. This feels like a date."

"I assure you, it is not," I said.

Both Burke and I knew that I meant it.

Then I added, "But please do *not* bake a pumpkin pie."

CHAPTER 2

Thanksgiving

"THIS PLACE IS . . . well, it's sort of unbelievable,"
K. Burke says. She stands in the entrance gallery to my
new apartment and spreads her arms in amazement.

"Merci," I say. "I had to find a new home after Dalia
died. I could not stay in her place. I could not stay in
mine. Too many..." I pause.

Detective Burke nods. Of course, she knows. Too
many memories. I take her on a brief tour of the place.
A loft on Madison Square, a single three-thousand-
foot room with a view of the Flatiron Building to
the south and the Empire State Building to the north.
The huge room is sparse—purposely so. Steel furniture, glass side tables, black-and-white Cartier-Bresson
photographs of Paris.

We eventually move to the table for Thanksgiving
dinner. The small black lacquered table is set with my
great-grandmother's vintage Limoges.

As we begin the main course of the dinner, K. Burke
says, "The only thing more impressive than this apartment is this meal."

Another *Merci*.

"Moncrief, I've known you almost a year. I've spent hundreds of hours with you. I've been on a police case in Europe with you. I...I never knew you could cook like this. I just can't believe you can make a meal like this."

"Well, K. Burke. I *cannot* make a meal like this. But fortunately Steve Miller, the senior sous-chef at Gramercy Tavern, was happy to make such a meal."

And what a feast it is.

Burke and I begin with a truffled chestnut soup. Then, instead of a big bird plopped in the middle of the table, Miller has layered thin slices of turkey breast in a creamy sauce of Gruyère cheese and porcini mushrooms. Instead of the dreaded sweet potatoes, we are dining on crisp pommes frites and a delicious cool salad, a combination of shredded brussels sprouts and pomegranate seeds.

"This is what the food in heaven tastes like," K. Burke says.

"No, this is what the food in Gramercy Tavern tastes like."

I pour us each some wine.

"What shall we toast to?" she says.

I say, "Let us toast to a good friendship during a difficult year."

She hesitates just for a moment. Then K. Burke says, "Yes. To a good friendship."

We clink glasses. We drink.

She holds up her glass again.

"One more thing I want to toast to," Burke says.

"Yes?" I say, hoping it will not be sentimental, hoping it will not be about Dalia, hoping...

"Let's toast to you and me really trying to see eye to eye from now on."

"Excellent idea," I say. We clink glasses again. We continue to devour the wonderful food.

And then her cell phone rings. Burke quickly puts down her fork and slips the phone out of her pocket. She reads the name.

"It's Inspector Elliott."

"Don't answer it," I say.

"We've got to answer it, Moncrief."

"Don't answer it," I repeat. "*We* are having dinner."

"*You* are a lunatic," she says.

I roll my eyes and speak.

"So much for trying to see eye to eye."

CHAPTER 3

OF COURSE, K. BURKE triumphs. She takes Inspector Elliott's call.

Fifteen minutes later we're in the detective squad room of Midtown East watching Elliott eat a slice of pie. K. Burke later tells me that it is filled with something called mincemeat, made out of beef fat and brandy. *Incroyable!*

"This could have waited until tomorrow, but you both told me that you wanted to work today. So I assumed you'd be free," Elliott says.

Then he looks us both up and down closely, Burke in a simple, elegant gray skirt with a black shirt; me in a navy-blue Brioni bespoke suit.

"But you both are dressed like you've just come from the White House."

Neither Burke nor I speak. We are certainly not going to tell our boss where we were dining fifteen minutes earlier.

"In any event, I decided to come in and do some desk work. My wife packed me some pie. And I figured I could watch Green Bay kick the Bears' ass on my iPad instead of watching it on TV with my brother-in-law."

Then he gets down to business.

"I thought this problem might go away, but it's real. Very real. Potentially dangerous. And it involves some New York City big shots."

Elliott swallows the last chunk of his pie. Then he continues speaking. He's energetic, anxious. Whatever it is, it's going to be a big deal.

"You two ever heard of the Namanworth Gallery up on 57th Street?"

"I think so," says Burke. "Just off Park Avenue."

"That's the one," says Elliott. "You know the place, Moncrief? It sounds like something you'd be down with."

"As a matter of fact, I *do* know that gallery. They handled the sale of a Kandinsky to a friend of mine a few months ago, and a few years back my father was talking to them about a Rothko. Nothing came of it."

"Well, your dad might have lucked out," says Elliott. "We've got some pretty heavy evidence that they've been dealing in the most impeccable forgeries in New York. A lot of collectors have been screwed over by them."

I speak.

"Namanworth hasn't owned that place for thirty years. A husband and wife are the owners. Sophia and Andre Krane. I think she claims to have been a countess or duchess or something."

"We don't know about her royal blood. But we do know that Barney Wexler, the guy who owns that cosmetics company, paid them thirty-five million dollars for a Klimt painting. And he thinks it was…"

I finish his sentence for him. "…not painted by Klimt."

Elliott says, "And Wexler's lined up two experts who can back him up."

"Although the case sounds really exciting…" Burke says, "there's a special division for art-and-antique counterfeit work."

"Yeah," says Elliott. "But with these big players, there may be more to it than simple forgery. Where there's smoke, there's usually fire. And where there's valuable artwork, there's possible fraud, possible money-laundering—ultimately, possible homicides. So they want us to stick our dirty noses in it. We can call on counterfeit if we want."

I speak. "I don't think we'll want to do that."

"That's what I thought you'd say, Moncrief." Then he taps a button on his computer. "There, I've just sent you all the info on the case. You'll see. It's not just Wexler. These are the money-men *and* the money-women who rock this town.

"By the way, there's a special pain in the ass about this case…"

"Isn't there always?" Burke says.

"This is particularly painful," says Elliott. "The Kranes aren't talking. They're comfy in their eight-hundred-acre Catskills estate."

"The hell with that," says Burke. "We'll get an order from justice."

"No, you won't, not when the attorney general of the state of New York says they don't have to cooperate."

"What the hell is that all about?" I say.

"Exactly," says Elliott. "What the hell is that all about?"

He lets out a long breath of air and swivels to face his PC.

As we walk away from Elliott's desk, K. Burke lays out her plan to download all information on the Namanworth Gallery, all information on Barney Wexler, all information on Sophia and Andre Krane, and all classified insurance information on important international collectors.

"What's your plan, Moncrief?" she asks.

"First, I think we should return to my home and finish our dinner."

"And then?" she asks.

"And then I'll call my friends who collect art."

CHAPTER 4

K. BURKE LIKES to do things by the book. I like to do things by the gut. This is our professional relationship. This is also our ongoing problem.

"It looks like we'll be spending the day at this desk, Moncrief," she says. Do I detect a note of smug satisfaction in her voice?

But of course I do.

Black Friday, the day after Thanksgiving. Almost everyone will be open for what America calls door-busting sales, but the truly fashionable establishments—certainly the 57th Street galleries—will be locked up tight. No wealthy collector is going to be shopping for a Jasper Johns today.

"I have been at this desk for thirty minutes, and I've accomplished nothing," I say to Detective Burke.

"Try turning the computer *on*," Burke says.

I stand and inform her that I'll be doing a little "on-the-street wandering." Burke simply shakes her head and smiles. She knows by now that both of us will be better off if I'm out doing "my kind of police work."

Twenty minutes later I am entering a shop at the corner of Lexington Avenue and 63rd Street, J. Pocker, the finest art framer in New York City.

"I think you may have used us before," says the very gracious (and very pretty) Asian woman who greets me.

"Yes," I say. "A few years ago. You framed two photographs for me."

"Yes, you're the Frenchman. You brought in those Dorothea Lange portraits. Depressing, but very beautiful," she says.

"Isn't that sometimes the way?" I ask. I feel myself shifting into Automatic Flirt.

I look through the glass partition behind the huge measuring table at the rear of the shop. Two bearded young men are working with wood and glass and metal wire.

"So, how may I help you today, sir?" the woman says.

I pull out my personal cell phone. A photograph of a painting by Gary Kuehn comes up. It is essentially a pencil, ink, and oil drawing of a slice of the moon. The moon is a deep dark blue. It hangs against an equally dark gray-brown sky. It is beautiful, and it hung in the bedroom that Dalia and I once shared.

"I need to have this piece reframed. The frame is a cheap black thing. I had it done in Germany some time ago, when I bought the piece."

"It's a Kuehn," she says. "I like his work."

She walks to the measuring table and pulls out a sample of maple and one of thin shiny steel.

"I think either of these would be worth considering. I prefer simple subject matter to have a corresponding simple frame. I know that the French prefer contrast— a Klee inside an ornate Renaissance-type frame, but consider…"

I cut her off. "The Frenchman agrees with your suggestion."

"Please take the samples with you. You can return them after you've made your choice."

I thank her, and as I am about to leave she says, "I've seen a lot of Kuehn's work lately. He's older. But he's become very popular recently."

"As a fan of his, I must ask, how much of his work have you seen recently?"

"Certainly three or four canvases," she says. "Many of them — I think — are similar to the one you own. Curves. Circles. A sort of defiance of space."

Ah, the babble and bullshit of the art world.

"Yes," I repeat. "A defiance of space."

She smiles.

I tell her that I will be back. Yes. I will definitely be back.

CHAPTER 5

I WATCH THE SHOPPERS. Today's shopping could be classified as a sort of athletic event. People barely able to carry their exploding shopping bags. Huge flat-screen television sets lugged by happy men. Packs of happy people, angry people, exhausted people.

I have seen the videos of women punching one another to snatch the last green Shetland sweater at H&M. Entire families—mothers, fathers, wailing children—waiting outside Macy's since four in the morning so they can be the first to race down the aisles.

I take in all the madness as I walk the six blocks down and one avenue over from 63rd Street to 57th Street. I turn right. Yes, Namanworth Gallery will be shut tight, but I am so close that I must visit.

An ornate carved steel door covers the entrance. The one front window holds a single easel that holds a single large impressionist canvas. It is famous. A painting by Monet. The painting is framed with baroque gold-leaf wood. It is one painting in Monet's series of haystacks.

The subtle beauty of color and craft eludes me. I cannot help myself. I examine it purely as a possible forgery.

I pull up the series of paintings on my phone and quickly find the one I'm looking at. I know I am on a fool's errand. The tiny phone photo and the gorgeous real painting cannot be compared. Is a straw out of place? Is *that* smudge of cloud identical to *that* smudge of cloud?

Wait. What about the artist's signature?

I recently read that a woman had a Jackson Pollock painting hanging in her entrance hall for twenty years. No one—not the woman, not her guests—ever noticed that the artist's signature was spelled incorrectly: "Pollack" instead of "Pollock."

No such luck. A big bold signature: Claude Monet. Not Manet. Not Maret.

"Monet" is "Monet." How could I expect to be so lucky?

I decide to take a few photographs of the painting. I am not sure why I need photographs, but they might somehow someday come in handy. I move to the left, then right. I try to avoid the glare on the window.

Now I hear a voice from behind me. "You taking a picture for the folks back home?"

Mon Dieu! I have been mistaken for a tourist.

I turn and see a portly middle-aged man. He is wearing an inexpensive gray suit with an inexpensive gray tie. He wears a heavy raincoat and a brown fedora. He is smoking a cigarette.

"Beautiful painting," the man says.

"It certainly is," I say, as I slip my phone into my suit jacket.

"I'm one of the security people for Namanworth's," the man says. "You've been looking at that picture for quite a while."

There is no threat in his voice, no anger.

"I have a great interest in Monet," I say. "The Haystacks series in particular."

"Apparently a lot of people have an interest in this stuff," the man says. "I work out of that second floor front office. Just me and my binoculars."

He gestures in the direction of the elegant stationery store across the street. It is the same store where I have my business cards engraved.

"I just thought I'd come ask what's so intriguing about that painting. It seems to have caught a lot of attention today. Not just the usual shoppers and tourists," he says.

"Well, who else, then?" I ask as casually as I can.

"Well, there was a man and a woman, a young couple. They were driving a Bentley. Double-parked it. Then they began shooting their iPhones at the painting. Little later two guys in one of those Mercedes SUVs jumped out; these guys had big fancy cameras, real professional-looking. Then I saw you...and anyway, I needed a smoke."

"And do you have any idea what the others wanted?" I ask.

"Just art lovers, I guess. Anyway, they looked kinda rich. Sorta like you—now that I see you close up. I guess you're too fancy to be a tourist."

A twinge of relief. Then the security man flicks his cigarette onto 57th Street.

"Did you record the license numbers of the cars?" I ask.

"No. They weren't doing anything *that* unusual. Could be they were thinking of buying it. I'm just here to make sure nobody breaks the window…though it's as unbreakable as you can get."

"I'm sure it is," I say.

"Well, you have a good day," the man says. He walks to the curb, looks both ways. He turns back toward me and speaks.

"You're French, right?"

"I am, yes."

"I thought so."

I am so obviously French that I might as well have a statue of the Eiffel Tower on my head. But the man is pleased with his detective work. Then he crosses the street.

I take a final look at the Monet.

I am about to make my way to Madison Avenue when, without warning, I think about Dalia. I freeze in place. People walk around me, past me.

Suddenly I am overwhelmed by sadness. It is not depression. It is not physical. It is…well, it is a sort of disease of the heart. It always comes without warning. It is always dreadful, painful.

Fortunately, I know just what to do.

CHAPTER 6

SHOPPING IS THE ANSWER. For me it is almost always the answer. So I join the holiday madness. An uncontrolled shopping spree, for some unfathomable reason, always brings me peace.

My mind clicks madly away as to how I can best visit the many extraordinary stores on 57th Street.

Like a recovering alcoholic who studiously avoids bars, I almost always avoid this area. The merchandise is so tempting, so upscale, so expensive.

Where to start? That's so easy. The Namanworth Gallery is a block away from Robinson Antiques. Surprisingly, it's open. This shop is only for the wealthy cognoscenti of New York — eighteenth-century silver sugar shakers, Sheffield candelabras that hold twelve candles, a rare oil painting of a cocker spaniel or a hunting dog, another of a Thoroughbred at Ascot. A mahogany wig stand, one whose provenance says that it was one of twenty that once stood in the Houses of Parliament. The distinguished-looking old salesman says, "May I help you?" Five minutes later I have become the proud owner of four sterling silver Georgian marrow scoops. Seventy-three-hundred dollars.

The salesman wants to explain the insignia of King George III on the reverse side of the scoops. I tell him to please hurry. "I have to be someplace."

The place "I have to be" is also nearby—Niketown. One of the first things K. Burke said when we began working together was, "You are the only person I've ever met who can find sneakers that look as if they were made by a Renaissance artist."

Burke was right. The sneakers she had seen were black high-tops with a small brass clasp, Nike by Giuseppe Zanotti. Today the store manager escorts me to "The Vault," a small room in the back of the very busy store. When I leave the Vault I am wearing a pair of black Ferragamo Nikes—black with thin white soles, the distinctive Gancini buckle. As I exit Niketown I think, *I must be insane. Except to play an occasional game of squash, I never wear sneakers.* This thought, however, lasts only for a minute. By then I am back across 57th Street at Louis Vuitton where I'm examining an oversized overnight bag. It is made with simple soft brown leather. It does not have the ostentatious LV pattern on it. It is beautiful. It is perfect. Not at all like my life.

Now I am only a few yards from the Van Cleef & Arpels entrance at Bergdorf Goodman. I can do some real damage here.

The Van Cleef doorman is still holding the door open when my phone buzzes. The red light. Burke.

"Your day's just beginning, Moncrief," she says.

"What's going on?"

"I see you're at 57th and Fifth."

"Right," I say.

"Get over to 61st and Park, number 535. Somebody

decided to murder the elderly Mrs. Ramona Driver Dunlop. Or as they still call her on the gossip blogs, Baby D."

"Ramona Dunlop?" I say. "I didn't know she was still alive."

"She's not," Burke says.

"Good one, Detective. Very good."

CHAPTER 7

I EXPECT THE usual homicide pandemonium. But this is over-the-top madness. Twice the sirens, twice the flashing lights, twice the news reporters. I should not be surprised.

After all, this was Baby D. In 1944 she was Debutante of the Year. In 1946 she married Ray Dunlop, a Philadelphia millionaire who had inherited extremely valuable patents on ballpoint pens and mechanical pencils. In 1948 she divorced Dunlop and took up with a waiter from the Stork Club.

The lobby of 535 Park is cluttered with the usual detectives and forensic folks. An NYPD detective holds up four fingers. Then he nods toward the elevator. An elevator man takes me up to the fourth floor. The elevator doors open directly into the foyer of the Dunlop apartment. K. Burke is standing with four senior officers. She waves at me, and then approaches.

"You waved?" I say. "Did you think I wouldn't be able to find you in that ocean of blue?"

Burke ignores my comment, glances at my shopping bags, and says, "Little man, you've had a busy day."

"In a manner of speaking, yes," I say.

"Follow me," she says. Burke and I turn right and walk down a long narrow hallway.

These hall walls are cluttered with photos and paintings and framed documents: an invitation to President Kennedy's inauguration; a cover of LIFE magazine that verifies Baby D as "New York's Debutante of the Year." Then I see a large Lichtenstein cartoon panel. It hangs next to a much smaller Hockney diving board and swimming pool. I linger for a moment and take in the paintings.

Then we are in Mrs. Dunlop's bedroom. Also in the bedroom are Nick Elliott and assistant ME, Dr. Rosita Guittierez.

"Where's Nicole Reeves?" I ask. Elliott understands, of course, that I am referring to the fact that Guittierez is an *assistant,* while Reeves is the big boss.

"She must be out shopping," Elliott says.

"Like everyone else," Burke adds.

The late Mrs. Ramona Driver Dunlop is resting, very dead, in her king-sized bed with the powder-blue satin-covered headboard. Mrs. Dunlop is covered with protective plastic police cloth, from her shoulders down to and including her feet. What's left exposed is the dry bloody slash that begins at the jawbone below one ear and extends the entire width of the neck to the other ear. The face is thin and, as with many women of a certain age, has the high-puffed chipmunk-like cheeks that only a significant facelift can guarantee.

Burke asks Elliott for the details. Elliott hands the floor over to Rosita Guittierez.

"Looks like we're talking about six o'clock this morning when this happened. Sharp-bladed instrument, probably a knife. You can see the wound is U-shaped. So it got all the jugulars—internal, external, posterior. It got the carotids. She partially bled out. No sign of force. They got the old girl while she was still asleep."

Burke listens carefully. I pretend to listen, but I am more interested in looking around the room—light-blue walls matching the satin on the headboard, an ornate crystal chandelier more appropriate for a ball-room, mock Provincial side tables, and bureaus with random dabs of white and gray paint to give a dis-tressed antique look. And one odd detail: Except for a full-length mirror behind the bathroom door, nothing is hanging on the walls. Absolutely nothing.

CHAPTER 8

WE LEARN WHAT little else is left to learn.

Mrs. Dunlop spent most of Thanksgiving Day at her son and daughter-in-law's house in Bedford. The only other person who was in the apartment after her return was a maid. The maid discovered the victim at the time she always woke Mrs. Dunlop.

Three medical staff police now pack up Mrs. Dunlop and wheel her out.

Elliott speaks.

"What do you guys think?"

"My guess is that it's a burglary gone bad," says Burke. "Holiday weekend. Lots of places empty. The intruder could have had inside information. What do you think, Moncrief?"

"Perhaps," I say. "Always perhaps. I see nothing to prove otherwise, but I also see nothing to support the theory. So for the time being, let's embrace Detective Burke's theory."

Elliott nods and says—as only an American detective

can say easily and without irony—"I'll see you guys back at the morgue."

He leaves, and K. Burke speaks. "Thanks for supporting my theory. I wasn't really expecting that."

I smile. "Don't get used to it, K. Burke. I am not so concerned with this murder as I am concerned with the circumstances *surrounding* this murder."

"And that means?" says Burke.

"The victim was almost ninety years old. May God bless her and welcome her into His paradise. Baby D has lived a life of enormous pleasure and wealth. *But*...fresh off our investigation of the Namanworth Gallery...I notice something interesting. Hanging outside her bedroom are paintings by Lichtenstein and Hockney. Only they are forgeries. The small dots in the 'talk bubbles' on the Lichtenstein are too neatly spaced to be authentic. And the swimming pool in the Hockney should be more rectangular."

Burke says exactly what I am expecting her to say.

"You can't be the first person to have noticed that."

"Perhaps. Perhaps not. But I don't think that too many art connoisseurs traverse that hallway. The possibility may also exist that Baby D knew that her pieces were forgeries and it made little difference to her. Like a print of the *Mona Lisa* in a small apartment in Clichy. It brings the owners joy. Perhaps the same was true with Madame Dunlop and her modern masterpieces."

"We need to tell Elliott about this," Burke says.

"I don't want him breathing down our necks. At least not yet. We will return tomorrow morning, let the others finish the interviews. We'll have more information and more space to examine the apartment closely, see what we can see, find what we can find."

"This is not going to end well, Moncrief. I don't like doing things this way."

"I know you don't," I say. "That's what makes it such an adventure."

CHAPTER 9

THERE ARE ONLY three things in this world that I truly hate: overcooked vegetables, flannel sheets, and whenever K. Burke is right about something.

This next day is one of those times.

We arrive at 535 Park Avenue at 8:00 a.m. There is still a "modified police presence"—one NYPD officer at the corner of Park and 61st Street, a second officer in the small mailroom, a plainclothesman in the lobby. It's the usual setup for a post-homicide scene.

Burke and I bring with us two big evidence cases marked "NYPD." These will be used to carry the forged Lichtenstein and Hockney. When the elevator opens at the Dunlop apartment we exchange hellos with Ralph Ortiz, a smart up-and-coming rookie who's stuck guarding the crime scene.

"Allons-y," I say. "Let's go."

"I know what *allons* means, Moncrief," she says. "I've only told you a few thousand times. You do *not* have to translate for me. I know French. That's one of the reasons they teamed us up."

"Ah, oui," I say. Then I say, "That means 'yes.'"

Burke ignores me as we walk toward the hallway.

And then...son of a bitch! The paintings are missing.

Softly Burke says, "Goddamnit."

I turn quickly and rush down the hallway to Officer Ortiz.

"How long have you been on duty?"

"Since midnight," he says. Ortiz senses that something's not right. He immediately answers the question I would have asked.

"Nobody's been in or out. Nobody. Not a soul," he says. And then, because he's as sharp as any kid I know in the NYPD, he says, "And I never heard anyone. I never saw anyone. I checked on the master bedroom and the other rooms every hour. I know..."

"Okay, okay," I say. "I'm sure nothing got by you."

"Only something *did* get by him," Burke says. "A bunch of officers and detectives on surveillance and two paintings disappear."

"Listen, these things happen. These things..." But she cuts me off.

"Goddamnit," says Burke. "I should never have listened to you. We should have gotten the info to Elliott and *then* together the three of us could proceed. But you. You have your own ways. The goddamn *instinct.*"

My anger about the paintings, along with Burke's rant, now makes me explode.

"Yes. And my ways are good ways, smart ways. History proves it. My ways usually work!"

Burke shakes her head and talks in a calm, normal voice.

"The operative word here is 'usually.' I'm going back to the precinct house."

"I'll join you shortly," I say. We are quiet.

I know this brief two-sentence conversation is as close as Burke and I will come to signing a peace treaty.

As soon as K. Burke leaves, Ortiz and I check the apartment, walking the rooms for any detail that might stand out. Nothing. Pantry. Maid's rooms. Butler's pantry. Service hall. *Nothing*. Silver closet. China closet. Powder rooms. *Nothing*. Dressing rooms. Kitchen (and impressive wine collection). Office. Dining room. *Nothing. Nothing. Nothing.*

I rush back to the hallway wall where the Lichtenstein and Hockney once hung. I study the two empty spaces of the wall—as if the paintings might magically have reappeared, as if I could magically "wish" them back to the wall.

Finally, I say to Ortiz, "I cannot stay in this apartment any longer. If I do, I will explode like a human bomb."

CHAPTER 10

IT IS BARELY ELEVEN in the morning when I leave Baby D's apartment. The day is cold and crisp, and to the happy person...Christmas is in the air. The sadness that I've come to know so well begins to descend. As the doctors say, "Rate your pain on a scale of one to ten, ten being the most painful." I would call it a six or seven.

I walk down Park Avenue and turn left on 59th Street. I am at a store I enjoy enormously, Argosy, the home of rare maps and prints, antiquarian books. Perhaps a $30,000 volume of hand-colored Audubon birds will lift my spirits. Perhaps a letter addressed to John Adams and signed by Benjamin Franklin will cheer me up. I touch the soft leather on the binding of a first-edition *Madame Bovary*. I study a fifteenth-century map of my native land—a survey of France so misshapen and inaccurate, it might as well be a picture of a dead fish. But I buy nothing.

The same happens to me in Pesca, a swimsuit shop, where Dalia once bought a pale-yellow bikini for five hundred dollars, where I could buy an old-fashioned pair of trunks with a bronze buckle in front for $550 and look just like *mon grand-père* on the beach in Deauville. I move on to other shops.

But nothing is for me. Not the art deco silver ashtrays, not the leather iPad cases that cost more than the iPads that they hold.

No. Not for me. But also not for me are the street corner Santa Clauses, the exquisite twinkling white lights in the windows of the town houses, the impromptu Christmas tree lots on Third Avenue.

In the season of buying I have, for once, bought nothing.

CHAPTER 11

I REALLY DO intend to return to Midtown East and meet with K. Burke. Really. But then other instincts take over. I decide to return to 535 Park Avenue. I must make a dent in this case. I must redeem myself.

I walk back toward Baby D's building. This morning I interviewed the super, a handsome middle-aged guy named Ed Petrillo. Like most Park Avenue supers Petrillo wears a suit, has an office, and thinks he's running a business like General Motors or Microsoft. He says he was at his weekend house (the super has a weekend house!) for Thanksgiving.

I also spoke with the first-shift doorman, Jing-Ho. He was not aware of anything unusual. He suggested that I talk to George, the doorman who came on after him. I let other detectives speak to George, but now I need to stick my own fingers into this pie.

I arrive at the building and exchange a few words with the police guard at the corner of Park and 61st. "Nothing suspicious, nothing extraordinary." He's seen a bunch of limos outside the Regency Hotel across the street. He's seen a celebrity—either Taylor Swift *or* Carrie Underwood. He's not sure. (Hell, even I would know the difference.)

George the Doorman has the full name of George Brooks. The dark-blue uniform with gold braid fits him well. He wears black leather gloves.

"In winter we wear leather gloves. Other times of the year it's strictly white gloves. White gloves are what separates the 'good' buildings from the 'cheesy' buildings."

He is a polite guy, maybe thirty-five.

"Listen, Detective, not to be uncooperative or anything, but two other detectives have already asked me a bunch of questions—all I can do is tell you what I told them. I really don't know much. I mean, Mrs. Dunlop didn't have many guests. Just the usual deliveries through the service entrance—groceries, flowers, Amazon, liquor."

"Just tell me anything unusual about the day she died," I say. "Even if you think it's not important, just tell me."

"Nothing. Really nothing. She had come back Thursday night from the country. Her regular driver dropped her off." He pauses for a moment. "I didn't like the driver, but who the hell cares about what I think."

"I care quite a bit about what you think. Why didn't you like him?"

"He wasn't here long, but he thought he was better than the building staff. Because he drove a rich lady around in a car. A big black Caddy, an Escalade. Who gives a shit? Here's a good example: drivers are not supposed to wait in the lobby. That's the rule. They either stay in the car or go downstairs to the locker room. The driver was always standing outside smoking or sitting on the bench right here by the intercom phone. So I tell Mr. Petrillo about it…"

"The super," I say.

"The super, yeah. So Mr. P. tells him he can't do it anymore, and Simon says that that's bullshit. He says he's going to tell Mrs. Dunlop. Mr. Petrillo says go right ahead. Well, I guess Mrs. Dunlop agrees with the rules of the building. So the next thing you know—*bam!*—Mrs. Dunlop is getting a new driver."

I've read all this previously, in the interviews taken down by the other detectives, but I do notice a small trace of triumph in George Brooks's face when he arrives at the climax of his story.

I also know that the driver, whose full name is the very impressive moniker "Preston Parker Simon," did *not* say he was fired. According to his manager, he'd quit. K. Burke had checked Simon out with Domestic Bliss, an employment agency that places maids, laundresses, chauffeurs, and the occasional butler. Simon hadn't answered her calls, but a manager at Domestic Bliss, Miss Devida Pickering, told Burke that Simon was honest and dependable. But, she said, Mrs. Dunlop only used him part-time, and Simon wanted to be a full-time chauffeur. So that was that. But as that is never *really* that, we would need to track him down. He was the last person to see Baby D alive. I thank George. He offers me his hand to shake. I, of course, shake it.

I tell him thank you.

He says, "It's been great talking with you, absolutely great."

CHAPTER 12

A MINUTE LATER, I am in the basement of the building. My interviewee is fifty-four years old and is wearing khaki pants with a matching shirt. The shirt has the words "535 Park" emblazoned in red thread on the pocket.

The man's name is Angel Corrido, and Angel stands in the doorway of the service elevator. As we talk he removes clear plastic bags of very classy recycling. Along with the newspapers and Q-tips boxes are empty bottles of excellent Bordeaux and Johnnie Walker Black Label, empty take-out containers from Café Boulud.

I've already been briefed on his initial interviews on the scene, so my first question is the old standby: "Could you tell me anything I might not know about Mrs. Dunlop?"

He shrugs, then speaks. "No, nothing. Mrs. Dunlop never sees Angel Corrido."

"Never?"

"Eh, maybe sometimes." He removes a bundled stack of magazines.

"When I see her...Mrs. Dunlop...she is nice. She says, 'Hello, Angel. How are the wife and the children?'"

Angel laughs and says, "I have stopped telling her that I don't have a wife and I don't have children. She don't remember. She is nice, but a man who runs the back elevator blends in with the other men who run back elevators and shovel snow and take out garbage."

Angel does not sound angry at this. He actually seems to think it's amusing.

"Were you working here on Thanksgiving?" I ask.

"No, I come to work early the next morning. No back elevator on Thanksgiving."

He takes the last bag of recycling from the elevator. Then he throws a glance at the stairs leading down from the lobby above.

"But Angel *can* tell you something you do not know. But it is not about Mrs. Dunlop. It is about someone else."

"Yeah?"

He says nothing.

"So what is it?"

Still silence.

Then I do what no NYPD detective is ever supposed to do. I take a fifty-dollar bill from my pocket and hand it to him.

"So?"

"So maybe you should know something about that big-shot *el cabrón* who holds the door open for people, George Brooks," says Angel.

"Go on," I say.

"You know the way you just tipped me?"

"Yeah."

"That is the way the *chofer* for Mrs. Dunlop used

to tip George every week. One hundred dollars when he delivers Mrs. Dunlop the big packages from the art gallery."

"The Namanworth Gallery?" I ask.

Angel speaks.

"Yes, maybe that is the name. I am not always good when I try to remember names. You know, when you are not born in this country—it is sometimes hard."

"Yes," I say. "It is sometimes *very* hard."

I thank him. I run up the stairs.

I text K. Burke: Need more info on driver P Simon. Let's find him.

CHAPTER 13

BURKE TELEPHONES DOMESTIC Bliss again. They have no current address for Preston Parker Simon, but she finds out that he is now driving for the CEO of a large and very successful comedy video website.

Making up for their failure to maintain addresses for their employees, Domestic Bliss does have the capability to track their drivers while they're driving clients. In a few minutes Burke finds out that the Escalade, presumably with Preston Parker Simon in the driver's seat, is parked outside the Four Seasons Hotel.

All roads in this case seem to lead to 57th Street. The Four Seasons is neatly bookended with Brioni, the men's fashion hot spot, on one side and Zilli, the French luxury brand, on the other side.

Burke and I meet up outside the hotel. A parade of limos, SUVs, and two Bentleys are waiting there. Their engines are running, poised to whisk away some business tycoon or rap star or foreign princess.

Burke punches some buttons on her phone, and soon we're asking Simon to step out of the Escalade.

He turns out to be a good-looking blond guy, certainly no older than thirty. He's charming, cooperative, and he has a fancy British accent that fits perfectly with his fancy British name.

Burke tells him that we're investigating the murder of Mrs. Ramona Dunlop. As soon as we do, a look of horror crosses his face.

"I heard. I saw it on the telly yesterday. Quite horrid. You know, I worked briefly for Mrs. Dunlop."

"Up until yesterday, you were her chauffeur," Burke says.

"Lovely woman. Remarkably spry for her age," Simon says.

He pulls out a tortoiseshell cigarette case from his jacket and offers us a cigarette.

"Have a fag?" he asks. Then he adds, "I love saying that to Americans. Always good for a laugh."

Burke and I decline the cigarette. We also decline to laugh.

"How long did you work for Mrs. Dunlop?" Burke asks.

"Not more than a month. She had a home in East Hampton. So a few times I took her out there. But she only really needed me for an occasional trip to the Colony Club for lunch, sometimes the opera, once or twice to her son's house in Bedford. It was not working out financially for me. I sought other clients."

"You drove her up to her son's house Thanksgiving Day, correct?" I ask.

"Quite correct."

"Though you had already given your notice?"

"Yes. She had hired a new driver, but we agreed I'd work through the holiday."

"How long were you and Mrs. Dunlop up there?" I ask.

"About four hours. We left for the city around six o'clock. I think I had her back on her doorstep by seven fifteen, maybe seven thirty."

Burke says, "Did you help her into the building with her things?"

"Things?" Simon asks, confused.

"Yeah," says Burke. "Things. Luggage. Packages. Leftover stuffing."

"Oh, no, no, no. There was a doorman. Very posh place. Lovely mansion," says Simon.

"535 Park Avenue is an apartment building, a co-op," says Burke.

I speak. "In England an apartment building sometimes is called 'a mansion.'"

"Live and learn, I guess," says Burke.

When did he officially resign from his job with Mrs. Dunlop? Yesterday.

Has he had reason to return to 535 Park since her death? No.

Who's he working for now?

"Danny Abosch, a dot-com prince," he says. "Lovely young chap."

As if on cue, a guy who looks like a college student who's late for class exits the hotel.

"Mr. Abosch is approaching," says Simon. "I really have to dash."

K. Burke responds to a crackle from her radio. I tell Simon that we may want to talk to him again. He says, "Surely," but his attention is on his boss, the young man in a blue Shetland sweater and a red ski parka walking toward us.

As Preston Parker Simon moves to open the car door he hands me a "calling card"—name, number, email. Engraved. Beige paper. Garamond type.

A chauffeur with his own calling card.

And they say I'm fancy.

CHAPTER 14

K. BURKE AND I begin walking from the Four Seasons Hotel down Fifth Avenue. We're headed back to police headquarters on East 51st Street.

A few minutes pass in silence. Then I speak.

"Preston Parker Simon is not an Englishman," I say.

"He sure does a good imitation of one," K. Burke says.

"Precisely," I answer. "His accent is purely *theatrical*. It is not authentic. In England someone from Yorkshire sounds distinctly different from someone from Cornwall. *Monsieur le chauffeur* has an all-purpose stage accent, the kind Gwyneth Paltrow uses in the cinema."

"You're good, Moncrief," Burke says. "Very good."

"*Merci,*" I say.

"But you aren't telling me anything I don't already know."

"You could detect it also?" I ask.

"No. Simon might as well have been Prince Charles as far as I could tell."

We stop to look at the Christmas display in the

windows of Bergdorf Goodman. It is sparkly and sexy and crazy. Neptune and half-dressed female statues and the Baby Jesus. Toward the back of all this opulence is a crystal Eiffel Tower—homage to the horror of the hideous Paris terrorist attacks. I turn away.

"So, go on," I say to Burke. She speaks.

"While we were finishing up with Simon I received a 'birth and background' file from downtown. They found out that Preston Parker Simon's real name is Rudy Brunetti. He's from Morristown, New Jersey. He was born and raised there, and then…"

"And then he became an actor," I venture.

"Don't try to speed ahead of me, Moncrief."

"Forgive my enthusiasm," I say.

"*Then* Simon went to Lincoln Technical Institute. That's in Edison, New Jersey. *Then* he became a karate instructor. *Then* he became an actor."

"And after that he became a chauffeur," I say.

"What did I tell you about speeding ahead of me? No."

She takes out her iPad and consults it for the rest of Simon's bio.

"Then he signed up with Domestic Bliss. He got a job as a personal assistant to one of Ralph Lauren's designers. Then for a year he was a butler at the French consulate…."

"And he fooled the French?" I exclaim as if I were shocked. *"Mon Dieu!"*

"*Then* he became a driver. First to Mrs. Dunlop. Now to this Abosch kid at the comedy website. By the way, neither the police nor Domestic Bliss has an address for him, just a post office box in Grand Central."

Burke and I are about to turn onto 51st Street. We pause to admire the huge wreath on the front of

St. Patrick's Cathedral. It is lighted with thousands of lights.

Then I lose interest in the wreath. My mind still lingers on the window of Bergdorf Goodman—the crystal *Tour Eiffel* a few blocks away, the wrought-iron *Tour Eiffel* a few thousand miles away.

I should be used to Burke's amazing sensitivity, but this time I am truly astonished.

"You're thinking of the Paris attacks, aren't you, Moncrief?" she says.

"You are a very wise woman, K. Burke."

"My heart breaks for you and your countrymen."

I nod. Then I say, "I know. I know it does. But enough gloom for now. Tell me. What do you think the next steps should be with Rudy Brunetti?"

"Let's go pick him up and find out what the story is, yes?"

I speak slowly, thoughtfully.

"No. I have another idea. Let us wait a few hours. My plan may turn out to be more helpful."

CHAPTER 15

NINE O'CLOCK THAT EVENING.

Burke and I sit in a car on Tenth Avenue and 20th Street in the shadow of Manhattan's newest beloved tourist attraction, the High Line.

I had wanted to drive my 1962 light-blue Corvette for this job. K. Burke's reaction to that idea?

"Forget it, Moncrief. You might as well have a brass band marching in front of that Corvette. They designed that car to attract attention," she said. Grudgingly, I told her she was correct.

So we sit in an unmarked NYPD patrol car. A Honda? A Chevy? Who cares? We are watching Preston Parker Simon, who is sitting in his black Escalade outside a brand-new thirty-five-story building. The three of us are waiting for the same thing—the young internet video tycoon. Once Simon picks up the "rich kid" we will tail them. Domestic Bliss can only track him when he's on the clock; our objective is to discover the location of the place that Simon calls home.

Fifteen minutes later we see Simon get out of his

SUV. He holds the door open for Danny Abosch. They exchange what appear to be some pleasant words. The kid steps inside the car. They take off.

Simon's car turns right onto 20th Street. Another right onto Ninth Avenue. Whether the tycoon is going to dinner or just going home he is, of course, going to Alphabet City. Apparently every person in New York below the age of thirty goes to the Alphabet City.

The car eventually stops on Saint Marks and Avenue A. Abosch is home. Or possibly at a friend's home. Or possibly at a girlfriend's home. Or…it doesn't matter. Whatever might come next is what matters.

Shortly I'm tailing Simon's car on the East River Drive, heading north. A fairly heavy snow begins. I stay "glued by two." I learned that this is the expression for tailing a car while allowing one other car in front of you for camouflage.

Simon exits the Drive and starts moving west all the way across Manhattan, then north on the Henry Hudson Parkway, across the Henry Hudson Bridge into the Bronx.

My tour guide, Detective Katherine Burke, explains the Bronx to me in two easy sentences.

"Riverdale is the fancy-ass part of the Bronx. Everything else is meh."

Traffic lightens, then slows. The snow dusts the road. "Glued by two" has to end. Now I keep some space behind Simon. He pulls off the main road, crosses even farther east. The street sign says "Independence Avenue." Then Simon pulls into a long circular driveway of a very elegant apartment building.

Two men come out of the building. One is clearly a doorman—the hat, the coat, the gloves. The other is smaller, in a black wool pea coat, a dark woolen ski cap pulled down over his head.

Simon hands the doorman a very large, flat, wrapped package.

"You don't have to be a detective to figure out that Simon just gave the doorman a painting," says Burke. "I wonder if…"

But I interrupt her. I speak loudly.

"Son of a bitch!" I say.

"What's the matter?"

"The other man," I say.

We watch as Simon hands the other man a similar-looking wrapped package.

"Do you know him?" she asks.

"I sure as hell do."

"Who is he?" asks Burke.

"It's the little guy on the back elevator. It's Angel Corrido."

CHAPTER 16

ANGEL AND THE DOORMAN CARRY the paintings into the building. The doorman returns immediately. Angel remains inside.

We watch Simon and the doorman closely. They seem to be having a very intense conversation. The pantomime goes like this: The doorman moves close to Simon. The doorman looks like he is screaming. Then it appears that Simon is having none of it. Simon, using both hands, pushes the doorman. Although the doorman is larger than Simon, and the shove doesn't seem particularly violent, the doorman staggers backward and falls to the sidewalk.

As the doorman staggers to his feet, Simon puts his hand in his coat pocket. I am expecting a knife or a gun to be pulled out. Instead he hands the doorman something I don't recognize.

"Looks like Simon may have just slipped the doorman some cash," I say.

"I'm not sure, Moncrief. He handed him something. It looked like a tiny package."

"Some rolled-up bills," I say.

"No," says Burke. "My guess is he gave him a good noseful of coke." Then she adds, "And by the way, don't you think we should call him by his real name? He is *not* 'Preston Parker Simon.' He is Rudy Brunetti. Let's stop calling him Simon."

I think that this is a...what?...the kind of correction that Burke enjoys. Ah, well, it is easier for me to agree. So I nod. Then I say, "Brunetti it is."

Now we watch Simon...er, Brunetti...go back inside the building. The building doorman gets into the car and drives it into an attached building marked GARAGE.

He's back on the door in less than five. I immediately drive up to the building entrance.

"Who are you here to see, sir?" says the doorman, a very thin man, two days' growth, a dark stain on the lapel of his heavy brown coat.

He's only spoken a few words, but I can tell that he has an accent. My guess is Danish.

I lean across Burke and say, "We're here to see you."

"Me?" he says. And he looks genuinely confused. He blinks his eyes quickly. He wipes his lips with his gloved right hand.

"Yes, we'd like to talk to you about the gentlemen who you just assisted with the paintings...." I begin.

"What paintings?" he says.

I realize that this guy has a bad attitude *and* a drug problem. I am sure that Burke is onto this also. The symptoms are simple and obvious—quivering hands, milky pink eyes, perspiration on his upper lip. Dirty, matted wisps of blond hair stick out from beneath his hat.

K. Burke gets out of the car and stands next to the doorman. She flashes her ID.

I get out of the car and stand next to Burke. I touch the inner suit pocket where I carry the Glock I'm not supposed to carry.

"NYPD, sir," she says. "We'd like to see some ID immediately."

"What for? For helping a tenant with packages?"

"No. Possible possession of drugs. ID, please," I say.

I don't know a bit of Danish, but I think this guy just taught me the Danish word for "Shit."

CHAPTER 17

THE DOORMAN-DRUGGIE'S NAME IS Peter Lund. He was in the Royal Danish Navy. He jumped ship seven years ago. I guess I can buy that story.

Early on in the interview he says, "Yes, I like the heroin too much." A minute later, with very little prodding from us, he adds, "And yes, it is possible that Mr. Brunetti and Mr. C. bring the works of art in and out of the apartment."

He rubs his lips.

Major rule of an interview: If a suspect starts talking, let him keep talking. Don't interrupt.

"Mr. Brunetti tips me generous, and he sometimes gives me my H, and it is none of my business to ask the tenant what are his parcels in and out. Not my job."

I believe him. Burke nods. A signal to me that she also believes him. Okay, now we know that Brunetti is storing artwork here. But we need more.

Then I have an idea, an idea that might get us information.

"It would be a great help if you would take us to see Mr. Brunetti's car," I say.

"But he would be angry," says Lund.

"Then you will be arrested for drug possession," says Burke. "How's that for a trade-off?"

"Come on," I say. "Show us where Brunetti's car is parked."

Lund answers quickly. "Which one?"

Three minutes later we are standing in the underground garage of 2737 Independence Avenue, Riverdale, Bronx, New York.

Peter Lund points to three identical black Escalades parked side-by-side-by-side. We look in the windows. Just the usual: black leather seats, high-tech dashboards. Burke takes a quick picture of the cars, the interiors, the plates. With one client, what does Brunetti need a fleet of SUVs for? This, and the involvement of Angel Corrido, suggests that the operation is bigger than we thought.

Burke tells Lund that we'll probably be back to talk some more. She suggests he try to stay as clean as he can *and* try to keep his mouth shut.

On the ride back to Manhattan, Burke says to me, "I'll do the write-up when we get back. We can't keep screwing around, avoiding Nick Elliott. We've got to build a file for him."

"Do you have reason to believe he's become impatient?" I ask.

"Yeah, I do. Let me read you a message." Then she reads from her cell phone: "What the hell are you two doing? Barney Wexler is up my ass. And the commissioner is standing right next to Wexler." Then Burke looks up at me and adds, "Maybe if you read your messages…"

"We will have something for him tomorrow. Next day at the latest," I say.

"No, Moncrief. We've got to get something to Elliott now."

"You are much too worried about the upper echelon, K. Burke."

"No. I'm worried that we are getting in way over our heads. Put a choke hold on your arrogance, Moncrief. We don't know for sure what we've got. Art forgeries? Drugs? It's time we got the rest of the team caught up."

"Give me one more day without any interference."

"No. Listen. It's not me. It's the case. We've got the facts—the stolen art, Rudy, Angel, a dead society dame, drugs. But we don't know where it's leading or how the hell to put it all together."

"I know how to put it together. Please, K. Burke. One more day to follow my arrogance. Please. Don't make me beg."

"You're not *begging* me, Moncrief. You're *bullshitting* me. But fine, I'll give you one more shot, one more day to piss in the ocean. Then we call in the cavalry."

CHAPTER 18

ETIENNE DUCHAMPS IS a billionaire and a very important art collector. He is also my friend. I have known Etienne since we were both four years old and attended *la petite école*.

Etienne has arranged a private viewing of the Monet at the Namanworth Gallery. Only the best of customers receive this kind of treatment.

I tell K. Burke that she and I will be introduced to the gallery owners as Mr. and Mrs. Luc Moncrief, *les amis intimes de Monsieur Duchamps*. Burke is angry with such a charade. She is even angrier by what I say next.

"So, it would be good for you to dress in the style of a wife of a man who can afford to purchase a Monet," I say.

"In that case I'll wear clean chinos," she says, then curls her lips with annoyance.

Amazingly, when she shows up at my apartment the next morning she looks…well…*chic*. In fact, *très chic*. Slim black slacks, black silk blouse, beige cashmere cardigan sweater. Her black hair is shiny, piled up fashionably carelessly. A brown silk scarf and a short sheared beaver jacket pull the look together.

"What have you done with Katherine Burke?" I say as I open the door.

"Don't expect me to ever look like this again, Moncrief. Everything but my underwear is borrowed from my friend Christine, who happens to be a buyer at Neiman Marcus."

"You look like a woman who has a château that is chock-full of Monets. But I would add one or two little touches, if Madame Moncrief does not mind."

"What exactly are those 'touches'?"

"You'll see in a moment." Then I walk into my bed-room and quickly return.

"Here, put these on," I say.

I hand her a bracelet with two rows of twenty small square-cut diamonds on each row. The clasp that keeps it together fastens onto a large citrine stone. I also hand her a thin gold chain from which hangs an antique ruby and diamond pendant.

"This type of jewelry is what my mother used to call 'daytime jewelry,'" I say, forcing a smile.

"I don't feel comfortable wearing these things," she says, as I help her with the necklace clasp.

"You look exactly like the wife of a wealthy art collector," I say. Then I look away from her.

"Moncrief," she says. "I can't. Didn't this jewelry belong to…?"

"Yes, of course. But they have been sitting like sad orphans in Dalia's jewelry safe," I say.

Is my voice cracking? Can Burke hear my heart beating? What the hell am I doing?

"Think about this. It's not right," Burke says.

I glance at her. She does look lovely. Then I speak loudly.

"Enough with the jibber-jabber. Let's go," I say. "We have a Monet to examine."

CHAPTER 19

THE OWNERS, SOPHIA and Andre Krane, are waiting for us at the shop door.

"I drove in from the country this morning. I so wanted to greet you myself," Sophia Krane says. She is a phony, but the kind that Dalia used to call "a *real* phony."

Sophia looks to be about seventy-five years old. Elegant, well preserved, slow-moving, fake-golden hair pulled back tight. She says she's a countess. Even if she is lying, she carries herself like royalty.

Her husband, Andre, must be at least ten years older. Andre is not nearly so well preserved. Overweight, balding, he wears a herringbone sports jacket with leather elbow patches. Later K. Burke will say, "The coveted New England college professor look."

The Monet has been moved from the window to a large easel. It is a wonder of the impressionist's art. When we stand close to the canvas we see a blur of overlapping colors, a clown's scarf, a paint-by-numbers set. A few steps back the viewer is transported to a breathtakingly beautiful field in Giverny.

Just as Sophia Krane appears to be a real countess, so, too, does this painting appear to be a real Monet. But what do I know? Burke and I are not there as art experts; we are there as sniffing-around detectives.

Andre Krane speaks: "And how does Madame Moncrief like the piece?"

To my astonishment Burke speaks with a graceful and very believable French inflection. I am amazed at her acting. I've seen her "play" tough. I've seen her "play" sentimental, but I've never seen her transform herself into a woman of high society.

"As expected, it is magnificent," Burke says, a charming and slight smile enhancing her performance.

"I will tell you," says Sophia, "that we have had an offer of forty. The offer is from an American, seventy-five percent is in cash, the remainder in stock holdings…dot-com stock, of course."

"Of course," Burke says.

I nod and stifle the urge to stroke my chin in contemplation.

"Not to change the subject too much," I say, "but are you by chance representing any of the Moderns?"

"Not many," says Andre.

"A minor Utrillo," says Sophia. "A few other things."

Andre speaks conspiratorially, lowering his voice. "Follow us. We'll take you someplace very special—the Back Room. It's where we keep the work that we don't show just anybody."

CHAPTER 20

THE "BACK ROOM" turns out to be nothing more than a kind of storage space. On the near wall are two unframed canvases. Both have the graffiti touch of a Basquiat. Sophia Krane flicks her hand dismissively toward the unframed pieces.

"You won't want these," she says. "They're second-rate examples. I knew Basquiat well."

As if to prove her friendship, she now refers to him by his first name. "Jean-Michel has much better work. We just don't have any of it at the moment."

Then she walks to three framed canvases on the floor. They lean against the opposite wall, behind one another.

"Now these..." she says. Andre flips on an overhead fluorescent bulb. Sophia continues in her casual tone.

"This is a good Hopper. It comes from a private collection in Philadelphia. I think there was something going on between Hopper and the woman who originally owned it."

She slides the painting to the side. She reveals a three-dimensional painting of a toy fire truck.

"Feldman. He's hot again," says Sophia.

"Whoever thought he'd be back on top?" says her husband. Sophia shoots Andre a mean glance, then says, "I did, darling."

The third painting is a series of bowls on a shelf—simple, geometric, flat.

Sophia speaks.

"Ed Baynard is back, too. At least he's back for the wealthy couples in Sanibel and Palm Beach. The rich people in Florida can't decorate a media room without one of these pretty little Baynards hanging near their recliner chairs."

Sophia's art lesson has ended, and, although I find the Baynard paintings quite appealing, I am smart enough to remain silent.

Suddenly my fake–French wife speaks.

"I really would like to look at them further…but at a later time," Burke says. "Luc and I are meeting our mutual friend, Etienne, for drinks.…"

"Etienne is in town? I didn't know that," says Andre.

Burke is, I think, becoming a bit too impressed by her own charade. We need to get out. Burke speaks.

"Just for the day. An unexpected business meeting. So we will be in touch about the Monet and perhaps the Feldman. But, you know, I do have a question."

"Of course," says Sophia.

Burke continues.

"Isn't it unusual to have such valuable pieces stacked one on top of another, leaning against the wall, on a dirty floor?"

"That's how the artists often keep them in their studios," says Andre.

"But this is not a studio," Burke says, her charming smile in place.

Detective Burke and Mrs. Krane exchange tense smiles. But I know Burke well enough to realize that she is heading somewhere in this conversation.

"I was so hoping," she says, "that you would sift through those three paintings and reveal a fourth canvas. I was foolishly hoping for a piece by Frida Kahlo. One of the self-portraits."

"Yes, everyone loves the self-portraits," says Andre. "The perfect scarves, the interesting headdress…"

"You know…" says Sophia.

"I know what you're thinking," says Andre. (I prepare myself for an avalanche of bullshit.)

Sophia speaks directly to K. Burke. Here it comes.

"You know, there is a collector, a very discreet individual, who has acquired three Kahlos over the years. The collector is away for the Christmas holidays. Saint Martin, I think. The French side, of course. I can get in touch, though. Would you be interested?"

"It would be a dream come true for Madame Moncrief," I say.

Burke touches my shoulder. She smiles at me. She speaks.

"What a sweet Christmas gift that could be…." Her voice trails off. And we say our good-byes.

As soon as we step onto 57th Street I say, "A magnificent performance, K. Burke."

"I'd like to thank the Academy…." she says. "And we might get a fake Frida Kahlo piece out of this."

But I am already plotting our next steps.

"I hope you are not too exhausted for tonight's job, when we follow Simon again," I say.

"No, we're not flying solo anymore. It's time to brief Elliott on our suspicions."

"Tonight will be our last time, K. Burke," I say.

"No way," says Burke. "No freakin' way." She is angry.

I smile my most charming smile and say, "Tonight if we get Simon we will be able to arrest him."

Burke speaks slowly, firmly.

"If you go on surveillance again, Moncrief, you're doing it without me."

I speak, barely able to spit out the words. I am angry also.

"If that's the way you want it, then stay back tonight. Stay and punch the numbers, search the file. I will do real police work. Go on back to Elliott now. Tell him whatever you like. As for me, I'm going into the Sherry-Netherland for a martini."

CHAPTER 21

I SIT WITH a frosty gin martini—straight up—at the bar of the Sherry-Netherland. The happy quiver of the first sip calms me, at least for a moment. Then my phone buzzes. A message from K. Burke. She texts: Read this. Then call me or come to precinct.

I read the following, from the *New York Post*'s website:

Bye-Bye, Baby D

Mrs. Ramona Driver Dunlop, the society matron known popularly as "Baby D," was bid farewell today at a lavish memorial service at St. Thomas Episcopal Church on Fifth Avenue and 53rd Street. White lilies and Bach cantatas filled the air as friends and family remembered the glamorous life of the social queen. Understandably, none of the speakers mentioned Baby D's earthly farewell—a particularly gruesome murder.

"There are more detectives and cops here than there are friends," said nightlife gossip blogger Teddy Galperin. "Let's hope one of them can finally make some headway in the case."

His comment was a reference to the NYPD's inability to make any progress in solving the murder of Mrs. Dunlop Friday. NYPD has thus far offered no clues as to the story behind the grisly death of the elderly woman.

In her youth Mrs. Dunlop was named New York Debutante of the Year. In recent years, the wealthy widow had turned her considerable energy and fortune to helping charities involved with the scourge of drug abuse. A lover and collector of fine art, Mrs. Dunlop also served on the boards of many museums, including the Frick and the Metropolitan Museum of Art. She is survived by her son and daughter-in-law.

I do not call K. Burke. I know what she will tell me: *No more screwing around, Moncrief! We must get help!*

I text K. Burke: Hold Elliott off until tomorrow. Don't be angry.

Burke texts me back: Not angry. Just worried.

CHAPTER 22

I'M WAITING EXACTLY where I waited the previous night. But this time, I'm waiting in the car that Dalia had christened "The Baby Blue from '62." And K. Burke isn't here to tell me that driving a flashy Corvette is a foolish idea.

Simon/Brunetti sits in his Escalade. The "rich kid" comes out of the building and slides into the backseat. When they take off, I take off after them.

Okay. A slight variation this time around: Simon deposits Abosch at Dirt Candy, a hip vegetarian restaurant on Allen Street.

This time Simon heads back to the Henry Hudson, only we take the George Washington Bridge into New Jersey. Simon speeds…85…90.…I speed, too. It seems like Simon knows all the speed traps. He slows down three times, always unexpectedly. Then back up to 85…90.…The Baby Blue from '62 and I are loving it. *Detective Burke, you don't know what you're missing.*

An hour and a half later, we're in Monticello, New

York. A few minutes later we're maneuvering around dark roads in the Catskills.

I turn off my headlights and drop back to a safe distance. The guardrails and ditches on the country roads become my guide. If I lose track of Simon's car, I'll be adrift.

Occasionally I see a house decorated with Christmas lights. A few Nativity scenes on front lawns. Neon wreaths. But mostly murky darkness.

Ten…fifteen…twenty minutes. Amazingly at a certain point I see Simon's car flash a right-turn signal. Is it a driver's reflex? Or, as Americans say: Is this guy just messing with me?

CHAPTER 23

A TOUCH OF winter moonlight provides just enough illumination to watch the Escalade pull into a very long dirt driveway. At the end of the driveway is a large Tudor-style mansion. I park on the road.

Two in the morning, but most of the windows are bright with lights. Simon leaves his car. He carries two packages. I'm assuming that they're the same paintings from last evening in Riverdale. But why drop them in storage instead of coming straight here? Maybe for discretion.

He rings the doorbell and looks around him. Yup, he's nervous. In a few moments Andre Krane opens the door. Simon disappears inside.

Now I exit my car. I stretch. I step into the woods a few feet. I survey the area. Woods and woods and then more woods. Giant trees—bare oaks, bare elms, hundreds of pines and evergreens. Tiny-sized to majestic-tremendous. The ground is covered with snow, tree limbs peeking out. Not far from the house is an ice-gray lake. More evergreens surround the lake, a lake so big that I can't even tell where it ends.

I return to the car and open the glove compartment. I unwrap a perfectly ripe piece of Camembert. I push a piece of sliced baguette into the soft cheese and enjoy my meal. A crisp Belgian ale, a perfect heirloom apple. A good snack along with this simple fact: I love solo detective work so much that even these bizarre and boring stakeouts are enjoyable to me. I'm a hunter after the game. There is a prize at the end for my perfect patience.

I crack the car window open an inch. The cold air rushes in.

Then I turn on the engine and warm the car. This on-and-off engine procedure occurs four times in the next hour. My eyes remain fixed on the house. I watch the lights go out. The mansion is draped in darkness. But I will not sleep.

At three o'clock I exit the car again. I bend and touch my toes a few times. I tie my silk scarf snug around my neck and chin. The snow begins again. The night is relentlessly cold.

I decide to move closer to the Krane house. *Histoire de voir.* I'll see what I can see.

CHAPTER 24

THROUGH THE LEAD-FRAMED windows of the dining room, when my eyes adjust to the dark, I see a giant oak table with chairs that look like Tudor thrones. If I expected to see a Matisse or an O'Keeffe hanging on the wall, I am disappointed. Four British fox-hunting prints. Nothing else.

I walk to the rear of the house and look into the huge kitchen. Two old stoves. Two deep sinks. A refrigerator from the 1950s. A marble-topped pastry table. A butler's pantry.

The ground is frozen hard, yet beneath the snow are deep hidden holes. I look toward the lake. The dock is covered with layers of tarp.

I move cautiously through the ice and snow. I now stand at the windows to the living room. Nothing on the wall except some African carvings and bronze antique sabers.

I decide to head back to my car. Too cold. Too icy. Also I must be there if Simon suddenly leaves.

I hear the door to the house open, and voices. There

he is. I begin to run—then I trip. A hole? A branch? A discarded fake Picasso? I am not hurt. I get up quickly. But my fall has apparently tipped someone off to my presence.

Suddenly the unmistakable sound of a bullet cracks the air. It shatters a piece of the stucco wall near where I stand and lands significantly away from where I'm standing. But a bullet can never land far enough away.

Then another bullet.

Another shot. Because the woods appear thicker near the lake I try to run there as fast as possible. To hide. To escape. I take out my gun, but I'm not acting in a Western. Real life offers no chance for me to spin on my heels and actually shoot my pursuer.

My knees are bent. I run close to the ground. If I fall I have less chance of getting hurt.

Then a scream in the darkness.

"I *will* get you, Moncrief."

The dumbest detective in America could identify the British-sounding voice. It is, of course, Preston Parker Simon/Rudy Brunetti.

I keep running as fast as possible toward the lake. What once looked like a short distance seems like a marathon challenge.

Another bullet. Then immediately another.

My shoes and ankles and calves are soaked with melted snow and ice.

Another bullet.

As I get closer to the lake, a voice comes at me: "You'd better be able to swim that lake, asshole." He's stalling. Probably reloading.

Simon is closer. But now he sounds simpler, cruder, American. I get it. He's slipped into being his real self. He's not Preston Parker Simon. He's Rudy Brunetti.

Now I am at the water's edge. In the dim moonlight I can see Simon. He is getting closer.

He fires three more bullets in succession. The bullets land close enough to where I stand that I can see sections of the icy surface shatter.

He fires two more shots.

He suddenly shouts, "Who the hell…? Angel, is that you?"

No response.

"Angel? Angel?"

Still no response.

Another yell from Simon: "Krane. Is it you? Are you there?"

I can see Simon clearly now. I watch him raise his gun. He fires in my direction. He fires again. He misses. He aims carefully. I fall to the snowy icy ground. He lowers his aim just a bit. He sees me.

He raises his arm slightly. He reevaluates the situation.

I am like a scared child. I close my eyes tightly.

Then…one more bullet shot. It comes nowhere near me.

I wait for the next bullet. And I wait. I only hear the sounds of nature. Winter birds cackling in the sky. Strong winds whipping through the pine trees.

Then a voice calls out.

"You okay, Moncrief?"

I know that voice. It is K. Burke.

CHAPTER 25

THE CHEESY TUDOR-STYLE living room— like something out of Disneyland—fills up quickly with lots of local law enforcement.

The New York State police arrive: seven burly men and two substantial-looking women. The local Monticello police arrive: two detectives, two coroners, four police officers. This may be the entire town police department. The local press arrives, as eager and noisy as anything in Manhattan or Paris. The coroners do a quick on-site examination of Rudy Brunetti. Then they begin to transfer the body to an ambulance.

I stand at an open window and watch them speedily move the body to the ambulance. The coroner sees me and explains what I already know: "We need to minimize dermal contamination."

Why do American officials enjoy using big words? Couldn't he just have said "skin decay"?

Detective Burke and I are at different corners of the room. We see each other, and I immediately join my colleague, the person who just saved my life.

"So, K. Burke," I say. "You *did* accompany me after all." I squeeze her shoulders, as close to a loving gesture as we have ever shared.

"You probably predicted that I'd be following you," she says.

I tell her the truth.

"Not this time, I must say. This time I thought our disagreement was too great for it to mend quickly."

There is a pause. Then she looks at me with intense eyes. Softly she says, "I could never let you down, Moncrief."

My head turns to the ground. My throat aches with anxiety. I know that I should be lying dead on the icy ground. I shake. My neck hurts. I speak.

"*Merci, merci beaucoup.* You have saved my life. I am beyond grateful."

Burke smiles. Her eyes sparkle.

"As you should be."

I smile. This will not grow any further into a sentimental moment. That is simply not the way Burke and I behave.

And anyway, we must not allow the local police to take over. No. Now we must take control, as all the little puzzle pieces of the investigation begin to fall into place.

The results turn out to be fairly much as we expected. The elegant Sophia and Andre Krane are the masterminds in this grand fraud scheme. They maintain a large basement studio at this home. It looks like a classroom at a university's fine arts painting course. Easels with half-finished canvases dot the room—a large Picasso here, a tiny Rubens there, a Schnabel that looks like every other Schnabel, a Warhol "Liz Taylor" that looks like a thousand others.

Handcuffs are locked onto the Kranes. Sophia Krane

is calm, stoic, almost bored, as she stands with three police officers guarding her.

"Rudy was a fool. I told him all he had to do was steal some goddamn paintings, from her bedroom. He didn't have to kill the old lady," she says.

"But he did," K. Burke says.

Now the Kranes are led out of their gloomy house to join Angel, who is already in a police car.

Burke and I question and Andre quickly admits that they sold the Hockney and Lichtenstein forgeries to Baby D. Only too eager to sell out their pal Rudy, he described how they had planted him—already an accomplice in art forgery sales—as her driver, when other clients of the gallery had started to raise alarm about the legitimacy of their pieces.

Rudy was supposed to gain access and steal the paintings back, but she'd sniffed him out and fired him before he had the opportunity. Desperate, after their last drive Rudy had killed her—but was too cowardly to take the paintings then, sniffed Sophia.

So they'd enlisted Angel Corrido to "retrieve" them from the apartment after her death. Their fear at that point, of course, had become that Mrs. Dunlop's estate would identify the pieces as forgeries. "You might as well look in Baby D's second maid's room," Sophia tells us. "She has a box spring with a secret compartment. Right now you'll probably find a Giotto wood panel and a group of architectural drawings from Horace Walpole's country home that Angel couldn't manage to get out. And…oh, yes…ten animation cels from Disney's *Snow White and the Seven Dwarfs*."

"No one can say we don't offer a variety," says Andre.

The local chief of police, the Monticello district attorney, and the sergeant of the county police approach us like a pumped-up sports team. I know what they want: a quarrel. Will these three criminals be tried in Sullivan County where they were arrested? Or will they be tried in Manhattan where their crimes were committed? I'm way too weary to deal with this.

"K. Burke, you have given me the greatest gift that one person can possibly give another. Thanks to you, I am still alive."

"All in a day's work," she says, with only a trace of irony in her voice.

"Now I must ask for one more favor, a small favor," I say.

She simply rolls her eyes.

"What is it, Moncrief? Do you want me to give you a kidney?"

"Actually, worse than that. Would you please deal with these three local police people? I have an errand to run."

"An errand? It's five thirty in the morning. We're at a crime scene in the middle of the woods a hundred miles from home base…and you've got an errand to run?"

"*Merci,* K. Burke. *Merci, merci,* and for good luck, one more *merci.*"

CHAPTER 26

IT IS DARK as midnight when I walk outside. The late-November morning is misty and cold. It is snowing lightly, just enough to make the air wet and icy. It is a perfect environment for sadness. The frozen lake, the dark night, the icy air…it should be ideal for depression. Yet I am strangely buoyant. I am calmer than I have been in months. I know it is the result of a successful end to the art forgery case. The usual sense of smugness that runs through me is stronger than ever. I look forward to discussing the details with Elliott. I know that some of my New York colleagues will have a touch of envy that this French interloper cracked the case. But most of all I am deeply warmed by Katherine Burke's extraordinary role in saving my life. Beyond friendship, and even, in a certain way, beyond romantic love.

I look down toward the lake. I stand still. I imagine the scene of a few hours ago, a scene of terror as a man with a gun pursued me through the dark. Now the entire area is one of peace and beauty.

A wooden shed sits not far from the main house. I have seen sheds like this outside some of the very old châteaux of France; they are remnants from hundreds of years earlier—outdoor bathrooms, basically toilets for the servants.

I look through the one small glass window in the shed's wooden door. The tiny household's gardening equipment—old-fashioned hand mowers, clippers, axes, shovels. I open the door and see a rusty bow saw hanging on a hook. I take it down and walk toward the lake.

In this forest of dead winter branches and hundreds of evergreens, I find a pine tree that is precisely the same height as myself—six feet, no taller, no shorter. It is not a tree from a storybook—not a scrawny lonely tree, yet not a great thick beauty. A tree. Simple. Lovely. A good representation of the work of God…if you are happy enough with life to still believe in God.

The trunk is soft. I cut through easily. As I do, I notice how completely ruined my shoes and trousers are—stained with water and ice and snow and the feces of deer and dogs.

I give the severed trunk an easy shove, and the tree falls forward. Just as I slip the bow saw over my shoulder and lift the bottom end of the trunk to drag the tree back toward the house, I hear a man's voice calling.

He shouts my name. He calls, "Detective Moncrief. Over here."

I wave at him, and he continues toward me. I recognize him as one of the Monticello police officers on the crime scene. He is no boy. He may be as old as thirty. As he comes closer I see that he is tall and blond and handsome, no doubt a local girl's dream.

But as is always the way with me, I am hesitant, suspicious. Perhaps the Kranes and Rudy Brunetti had a cabal of helpers up here. It would not be incredible—a few facilitators in the police force, in city hall, in the highway department.

I drop the tree and slip the bow saw from my shoulder to my hand. I grip the saw handle tightly.

The police officer stands next to me.

"I can give you a hand with that," he says. "I saw you from way up there."

"Ah, you caught me in the act of thievery," I say.

"I think you can help yourself to anything you want around here. You and Detective Burke are heroes. This is pretty amazing, the way you solved this case."

He nods his head nervously. He looks a bit goofy.

"Persistence," I say. "All it takes is persistence…and a great deal of patience."

"Yeah, I'm sure," he says. Then he speaks quickly.

"I was talking to your partner," he says. "Um…I asked her…well, I hope you won't be mad, but I asked her if you and her were anything more than partners."

I know exactly what the young man means, but I pretend otherwise.

"More than partners?" I ask.

"You know…God, I can't believe I'm doing this…like…" He cannot get it out.

"What did Detective Burke say?" I ask.

"She said 'absolutely not,' but then she told me to ask you."

"She is teasing you, *monsieur*. Detective Burke and I are partners professionally, but we are just friends."

"Just friends," he repeats. "So I could see her, go on a date with her?"

"You could go to the moon with her," I say.

"I'll help you with the tree," he says. Then he adds, "You take the lighter end."

"I'm fine with this end," I say. So we carry the tree. I see K. Burke is standing, waiting for us near the toolshed.

"*That's* where you were, Moncrief. Cutting down a tree?" she says with a smile. "I can't believe it."

The police officer, K. Burke, and I are standing, admiring the tree.

"Christmas is a few weeks away, K. Burke. Here is my gift to you. For Christmas and for saving my crazy little life. We can tie the tree to the roof of the car and bring it back to the city. This strapping young man can help us."

She looks at me. I speak.

"Merry Christmas, Detective," I say.

"Merry Christmas, Detective," she says.

Then K. Burke begins to cry. I also feel my eyes fill with tears.

The young police officer speaks.

"Just friends," he says. "Sure. Just friends."

CHAPTER 27

CHRISTMAS IS COMING. And as my favorite American expression goes:

I couldn't care less.

In the past I would have been in deep consultation with Miranda, my traditional Cartier shopping assistant. Miranda had a 1.000 batting average in helping me select the perfect Christmas gift for Dalia. Not too flashy, but not too boring. Something with sparkle, but something that did not call attention to itself…like Dalia herself.

It is December 20, and whatever gift-giving I am doing these few days is taken care of with a checkbook. I write gift checks for the daily maid, the twice-a-week laundress, the wine merchant at Astor who advises me when a particular Bordeaux is at its peak, Xavier who cuts my hair at Roman K, and…and that is it.

I consider giving something special to Detective Burke. But what do you give a person who has saved your life? An expensive car, an expensive trip, an expensive bracelet? They each sound ridiculous, and I think perhaps that any of them would insult Katherine Burke.

The days since the arrests of the art forgery gang have been dull. Elliott suggested that we take some time off. I tried to do so, but a man can only play so much squash and attend so many exhibitions at MoMA and the Morgan.

K. Burke takes a few days to do some Christmas shopping with her nieces and nephews in New Jersey. I decline to accompany them to the Short Hills mall.

When we return to work we catch up on the paperwork for the forgery case. We make an easy arrest of a drug dealer outside Julia Richman High School on East 67th Street. Elliott asks us to spend two days renewing our former Bloomingdale's assignment. We are reluctant and grumpy and unpleasant about the assignment, but the department store is a block away from Le Veau d'Or, where we have lunch this afternoon. The impeccably old-fashioned French restaurant on 60th Street still knows how to make perfect veal kidneys in a mustard sauce. And this afternoon Le Veau d'Or becomes the first (and most likely, last) restaurant where K. Burke has *tripes à la mode de Caen*. When I tell her that tripe is the stomach lining of a cow, she simply shrugs and says, "All I know is that it tastes good. Thanks for the reco." I think she is lying. But such a lie means that she must finish eating the dish.

Bloomingdale's closes at 10:00 p.m. Fifteen minutes later I am sitting in my apartment, sifting through Christmas cards wishing me *Joyeux Noël et Bonne Année*.

I stand and pour myself a small glass of Pepto-Bismol. Have I grown too old for veal kidneys?

The phone rings. The Caller ID shows the familiar

161 area code for Paris, but the remainder of the phone number means nothing to me.

As I reach for the phone I remember that it is about five in the morning in Paris.

"Luc," she says. "It is Babette."

Babette Moreau is my father's personal secretary. She has been his secretary for forty years, maybe longer.

My instincts tell me why she is calling.

"Votre père est mort."

Your father has died.

My first instinct is to feign sadness. I do not want Mademoiselle Babette to have proof of what she already knows: my father and I had a distant, sometimes angry relationship. He was a man of great financial achievement and great emotional distance. Early on—when it became clear that he and I had nothing in common except that we were related—he, a young widower, dispatched me to the care of nannies and tutors and tennis instructors and private schools. He thought that my interest in police work was ridiculous, and, while he was extremely generous with his money, he was extremely sparing with his love and companionship. This system worked. He did not care much about me. And I surely did not care very much about him.

A different son might burst into tears. A different son might express over-the-top shock at the news. But I am not that son. And I am a detective, not an actor.

"A heart attack," Babette says. "No pain. He was at his desk, of course."

"Of course," I say.

"The arrangements?" I ask.

"Notre Dame," she says. "That is what he would have wanted."

"Yes," I reply. "That is certainly what he would have wanted."

A pause, and then she asks what she is afraid to ask.

"Will you attend?" she says.

I do not pause.

"Of course," I say. It is an honest response. No, I am not moved by his death. But for a son not to attend his father's funeral is an extraordinary offense.

I tell her that I will leave tomorrow for Paris. She tells me that she will schedule the funeral after my arrival. I tell her to call me if there is anything else I need to know. The conversation ends.

What do I do next? I telephone K. Burke.

"That's awful, Moncrief," she says. Then a pause. Then…"Listen. I know you and your father didn't have the best relationship. But *he was your father*. Nothing changes that. Do you want me to come by and be with you?"

"No," I say. "No. But there is something you can do to help me through this."

"Of course. What is it?"

"Tomorrow afternoon…come to Paris with me."

CHAPTER 28

"I AM EMBARRASSED to be enjoying this flight so much," says K. Burke.

The premier cabin is spacious and elegant. Aside from an exotic-looking sheik who is traveling with a valet, Burke and I are the only other passengers in the first-class compartment of this Air France flight to Paris. The luxury is, even for a spoiled brat like me who has flown first class his entire life, extraordinary. It is slightly intoxicating to be above the Atlantic Ocean with so much *stuff* at one's disposal: flatbed seats for perfect sleeping, each bed with a small dressing room attached; perfectly chilled bottles of Dom Pérignon; access to first-run movies.

"And you are embarrassed...why?" I ask.

"Because we are going to Paris for a funeral. Not a wedding, not a birthday party, not even a business meeting. A funeral."

"Just pretend that it is one of the pleasanter events you just mentioned," I say. "Or call it business. I'm certain business will be discussed. I have already received two emails from my late father's personal assistant Babette and *three* emails from his protégé, Julien Carpentier."

"Julien Carpentier," Burke repeats. "That's a new name for me."

"Julien is his 'business assistant.' Julien is the new and improved version of the son I was supposed to be. If I had turned out to be the person my father wished me to be—ambitious, serious, businesslike—I would have been Julien. Instead I became what my father called *un policier fou,* a foolish policeman."

"And Julien is an asshole, I suppose?" K. Burke asks as she piles a generous spoonful of beluga caviar onto a warm blini.

"Surprisingly not. I do not know him well, but the few times I've seen or spoken with Julien, he has been quite…I don't know the word precisely…pleasant… authentic…yes, that is it, authentic. I think he is happy with his luck to have such an important position. Plus he diverts my father's attention from me. Julien and Babette are both probably truly saddened by my father's death. While you and I are sitting in luxury, sipping the bubble-water, soon to go to sleep on Pratesi bed linens, Julien is tending to the comings and goings of the company."

The flight attendant stops at our seats. She is carrying the 500mg tin of beluga with her. Pointing at the tin with her mother-of-pearl caviar spoon, she asks if we would like some more.

Burke hesitates.

"Go ahead," I say. "Have some more. Caviar builds strength. You will need all you can get for our important meetings."

I smile, but the flight attendant takes my remarks seriously.

"Ah, you are in France on business?" she says.

"In a manner of speaking," I say.

"I hope you will meet with great success," she says.

When the pretty young woman leaves us, Detective Burke speaks.

"By the way, Moncrief. I did do something that *you* forgot to do," she says.

"Whatever we failed to pack will be available at my father's house," I say.

"Don't be so smug. It's nothing as simple as dental floss or underwear. You forgot to tell Inspector Elliott that we are disappearing for three days."

"We are not *disappearing,* K. Burke. We are on holiday," I say.

"Well, maybe you can be cavalier about this. But not me. I need this job. Anyway, I called Elliott earlier and told him that he was right, we both needed a real break, that the work from the forgery case finally caught up with us. So we were taking a few days off."

"And he said what?"

"He said 'You two guys deserve it. Have fun.'"

I begin to laugh. Burke looks confused. My laughter grows louder.

"What's so funny, Moncrief?"

"Don't you see? Our boss thinks that we're off on a romantic journey."

I keep on laughing. Detective Burke does not.

CHAPTER 29

EIGHT O'CLOCK IN the morning at Charles de Gaulle airport.

Burke and I are fast-tracked through customs. We are suffering from "Dom Pérignon Syndrome," an alcohol-fueled sleep followed by a walloping morning headache.

In the reception lounge K. Burke says to me, "There he is. There's Julien Carpentier." She points to a handsome man in his late twenties, perhaps his early thirties. Six feet tall or so. Light-brown hair. A well-cut, dark-blue overcoat, a dark-blue silk scarf.

"How did you know that man is Julien?" I ask. "You've never seen him before."

"Correct. But I know it's Julien Carpentier because he looks exactly like you."

It has been at least a year since I have seen Julien, but for some reason this time, in the bright unflattering light of the airport, I see the truth of K. Burke's observation. He is not a mirror image of me, not a twin, but we both have a sharp nose, straight long hair, green eyes.

Julien is accompanied by a beautiful woman who is formally dressed in a chauffeur's uniform—black suit, brass buttons, large cap. I cannot help but think that this is the beginning of a pornographic film.

Julien moves toward me quickly and embraces me like a brother, which perhaps he thinks he is. I return the hug with a lot less vigor.

"*Mon ami, Luc.* Welcome. Welcome." He turns to Katherine Burke and makes a small quick bow from the waist. "And this, of course, is Mademoiselle Burke, a fine companion to have at this sorrowful time."

Julien takes Burke's hand, bows once again, and— well, he doesn't quite *kiss* her hand—he gently *brushes* Burke's hand beneath his lips.

"I only wish that we might have met under happier circumstances," Julien says. K. Burke says that she agrees.

"Huguette and I will go gather your luggage," Julien says. "We will meet you at the doorway marked D-E." As they leave for the luggage carousel Burke mumbles, "No. Don't…it's all right. I…" In the noise of the terminal they do not hear her.

"Let them go," I say. "We will have to listen to Julien chatter all the ride into Paris. Let's take a short break from him right now."

"But, Moncrief. There's only one little suitcase, mine. You said you didn't need to bring anything, that you had a lot of clothing at your father's. Julien and that hot-looking driver are going to be looking for your stuff. And then they'll…"

"Listen. I have only been with Julien about sixty seconds, and he is already annoying me with yak-yak-yak."

"You're wrong. I think he's genuinely glad to see

you. *And* I think he's far more broken up about your father's death than you are."

"The woman who served us dinner on the plane was more broken up about my father's death than I am," I say.

I take a deep breath. I squeeze a few eyedrops into my eyes and say to K. Burke, "Very well. Let's go to the luggage area and find them. We'll tell them that we were so jet-lagged that we forgot we only had one small piece of luggage."

"You're impossible, Moncrief."

"Let's go find them, but…"

"But what?" Burke says.

"But let us walk very, very slowly."

CHAPTER 30

AS PREDICTED, JULIEN talks incessantly on the ride into Paris.

"Your father was a tough boss, but a fair boss."

"The factory workers in Lille and Beijing are all anxious about their future."

"*Monsieur le docteur* said the heart attack came fast. He did not suffer."

"I wanted the funeral at Sacré-Cœur. Babette wanted Notre Dame. She, of course, got her way. It is only right. She knew him best."

"The American ambassador, the ambassadors from Brazil and Poland, even the Russian ambassador, the one your father detested, will be there."

"We are prepared with security for the paparazzi. They will come for the television and cinema personalities."

"The presidents of *all* your father's offices are attending, of course."

"I am so grateful that the heart attack came quickly.

Not that it was not expected after the two bypass surgeries and the ongoing atrial fibrillation."

"There will be a children's choir at the mass as well as the regular Notre Dame chorus."

K. Burke listens intently. I think she may actually be intrigued by the details of this grand affair. Julien and Babette have planned my father's funeral as if it were a royal wedding—red floral arrangements, Paris Archbishop André Vingt-Trois to officiate, Fauchon to cater the luncheon after the burial.

I tune out of Julien's lecture early on. His words come as a sort of sweet background music in my odd world of jet-lagged half sleep.

Then I hear a woman's voice.

"Luc," she says. "Luc," she repeats. It sounds very much like Burke's voice, but...well, she never uses my Christian name—"Luc." I am always "Moncrief" to her. She is always "K. Burke" to me.

"Luc," again. Yes, it *is* Burke speaking. I open my eyes. I turn my head toward her. I understand. With Julien and the driver here she will be using my first name. I smile and say, "Yes. What is it...Katherine?"

"Monsieur Carpentier asked you a question."

"I'm sorry. I must have dozed off," I say.

"Understandable. The jet lag. The long flight. The sadness," says Julien. "I merely wanted to know if you cared to stop and refresh yourselves at your father's house before we go to the *pompes funèbres* to view your father's body."

I have already told Burke that we would be staying at my father's huge house on rue de Montaigne, rather than my own apartment in the Marais. Burke knows the reason: I cannot go back to my own place, the apartment where I spent so many joyful days and nights with Dalia.

"Yes, I *do* want to go to the house," I say. "A bath, a change of clothes, an icy bottle of Perrier. Is that all right with you, *Katherine?*"

K. Burke realizes that I am having entirely too much fun saying her name.

"That's just perfect for me, *Luc.*"

"So, Julien," I say. "That's the plan. Perhaps we can allot a few hours for that, but then…well, I think we can hold off on the viewing of the body…"

I pause and suppress the urge to add, *"My father will not be going anywhere."*

"I see," says Julien. "I just thought that you would…"

I speak now matter-of-factly, not arrogantly, not unpleasantly.

"Would this perhaps be a better expenditure of time instead to meet with Valex attorneys, get a bit of a head start on the legal work?" I ask.

"You're in charge, Luc," says Julien, but his voice does not ring with sincerity.

"Thank you," I say. "What I'd like you to do is assemble my father's legal staff. Invite Babette, of course. We can meet in my father's private library on the third floor. I am sure there are many matters they have to discuss with me. Ask anyone else who should be there to please be there. Only necessary people— division presidents, department heads. This may also be a convenient time to reveal the main points of the will."

Julien is furiously tapping these instructions into his iPad. I have one final thought.

"The important personages who are not here for the funeral—North America, A-Pac, Africa—Skype them in."

I am finished talking, but then K. Burke speaks up.

"What about other family members, Luc?" she asks.

There is a pause. Then Julien speaks.

"Luc is the only living family member."

"As I may have mentioned, *Katherine,* my father had two daughters and a son out of wedlock. I never met them. The girls are younger than I. The boy is a bit older. But arrangements have been made. Correct, Julien?"

"Correct. The lawyers settled trust funds upon them years ago," he says. He nods, but there is no complicit smile attached to the statement. "They have been dealt with quite a while ago."

Meanwhile Julien continues to tap away at his iPad. The car is now closing in on Central Paris. Julien looks up and speaks again.

"I have texted the IT staff. They are on their way to the house now. They will set up Skype and two video cameras, a backup generator…the whole thing."

"What about sleeping arrangements?" I ask. I look to see if there is a change of expression on Julien's face. Nothing.

"All the bedrooms are made up. You may, of course, do what you wish," says Julien.

"What I wish is for Mademoiselle Burke to have my old bedroom. It is quite large. It has a pleasant sitting room, and it looks out over the Avenue."

I look at Burke and add, "You will like it."

"I'm sure," she says.

"As for me, I will sleep in the *salon d'été.*" The summer room. It is spacious and well ventilated and close to my father's library. It was where I always slept during the summer months when I was a child. It is no longer summer. And I am no longer a child. But I can forget both those facts.

"Very well, Luc. As you wish. I will have a Call

button installed, so you can summon a maid if you need one," Julien says as he flicks his iPad back on.

"Thank you," I say. "But that won't be necessary. I doubt if I'll have any need to summon a maid."

Julien smiles and speaks.

"As you wish, my friend."

CHAPTER 31

BABETTE ENTERS THE LIBRARY. She is dressed entirely in black, the whole mourning costume—stockings, gloves, even *une petit chapeau avec un voile*. Drama and fashion are her two passions, so my father's funeral is a glorious opportunity to indulge those interests.

"*Luc. Mon petit Luc,*" she says loudly. She embraces me. She flips the short black veil from her forehead. Then she kisses me on both my cheeks. She is not an exaggerated comic character. She is, however, one of those French women trained to behave a certain way—formal, slightly over-the-top, unashamed.

She keeps talking.

"*Mon triste petit bébé.*"

"I will agree to be your *bébé,* Babette, but not your '*sad* little baby.'"

She ignores what I say and moves on to a subject that will interest her.

"And this, of course, must be the very important

police partner, Mademoiselle Katherine Burke of New York City."

"I'm delighted to meet you, Mademoiselle Babette," says K. Burke.

Detective Burke extends her hand to shake, but Babette has a different idea. She goes in for the double-cheek kiss.

The attorneys are arranging stacks of papers on the long marble table in the center of the room. Two of the housemaids, along with my father's butler, Carl, are arranging chairs facing that table. Three rows of authentic Louis XV chairs. We will be like an audience at a chamber music recital.

The attorneys introduce themselves to me. They extend their sympathies on "the loss of this magnificent man, your father." "He was one of the greats, the last of his kind."

One of the attorneys, Patrice LaFleur, the oldest person in the room, the only attorney I actually know, asks me if I would like to join him and his colleagues at the library table. I decline.

The doors to the book-lined room remain open. Well-dressed men and women enter and take seats.

"They are employees of Valex, important employees," Julien says.

Some of them smile at me. Some give a tiny bow.

"I'm a New York City cop, Julien. I'm not accustomed to such respect."

Julien Carpentier takes me by the shoulders. He looks directly into my eyes. He moves his head uncomfortably closer to mine. He speaks.

"This is a gigantic company. Sixteen offices. Twelve factories. Valex manufactures everything from antacids to cancer drugs. Thousands of people are dependent on Valex for their employment, hundreds of thousands are dependent on Valex for their health. You are their boss's son. *Allow* them to respect you."

I am a little nervous. I am a little confused.

"But this is not my company," I say. "It's my father's enterprise."

"But it is your responsibility," Julien says. I want very much to trust his sincerity, to trust Babette. But I have spent so much time in my life listening to the lies of heroin dealers and murderers that I cannot wholly embrace the sincerity of my father's two most trusted employees.

I nod at Julien. He smiles. Then I sit. Front row center. The best seat in the house.

Julien is to my left. K. Burke is to my right.

"What are you thinking, Moncrief?" whispers Burke.

"You know me too well, K. Burke. You can perceive that my instincts are telling me something."

The room is settling down. All is quiet. Burke leans in toward me. She whispers.

"Can you ask the lawyers to hold off for a few minutes, so you and I can talk?"

"No. What you and I have to say can wait."

CHAPTER 32

THE LEAD TRUSTS, wills, and estates attorney is Claude Dupain, a short-nosed, large-eared methodical little man who has devoted his entire life to my father's personal legal matters.

"Good afternoon to the family, friends, and business colleagues of my late, great friend, Luc Paul Moncrief. Monsieur Moncrief's funeral memorial, as you know, will take place tomorrow. Today, however, at the request of his family, we are deposing of Luc's...forgive me...Monsieur Moncrief's will...forgive me once again...I am, of course, referring to Luc Moncrief père, Moncrief the elder. He is the Moncrief I shall be speaking of here.

"In the upcoming months, Monsieur Moncrief's bureau of attorneys will begin the complex filing of all business documents, debt documents, mortgages, and other Valex-related items. As you all know, Monsieur Moncrief paid strict attention to detail. While his death was terribly unexpected, he recently had become...shall we say...somewhat preoccupied with preparations for death. He brought his will and estate planning up to date in the last few weeks. And that recent planning is reflected in what I announce at this gathering.

"I must add that while it will take many months, even years, to honor all legal procedures in company matters, Monsieur Moncrief's wishes in other matters, personal matters and bequests, are quite simple and very clear."

I realize easily what Dupain's legal babble means: Valex is a monstrosity of a company, so it will take a great deal of time to sort out its future. However, my father's personal directions about his estate will be, like my father himself, easy to understand.

Dupain opens a leather portfolio and removes a few pieces of paper. I bow my head. I look down at the floor. The attorney speaks. And, as promised, the information is simple.

Babette will receive a yearly income of 150,000 euros with annual appropriate cost-of-living increases. She will also receive rent-free housing in her current house at Avenue George V. After her death, her heirs will receive the same annual amount for one hundred years.

Julien Carpentier is to continue at his annual salary of 850,000 euros annually. And, subject to the approval of the board of directors, Julien will be named Chairman and CEO of Valex and its subsidiaries.

The American phrase comes to mind again: I could not care less.

There now follows a long list—at least forty names—of disbursements to office personnel and household staff members in Paris, as well as at my father's London house, his château in Normandy, his house in Portofino, and—a stunning surprise to me— his apartment at 850 Fifth Avenue in New York.

The amounts of the disbursements are generous,

excessive by traditional standards. Housemaids will be able to stop scrubbing and dusting. Butlers will retire to Cannes. Gardeners will become country squires. Frankly, I am delighted for all of them.

After the listing of the bequeathals to the staff members, Dupain dabs at his forehead with a handkerchief. An assistant presents him with a large glass of ice water. He drinks the water in one long gulp. Then he says, "There is but one item left. I shall read it directly from Monsieur Moncrief's testament."

Dupain removes a single paper from yet another leather envelope. He reads:

"To my son, Luc Paul Moncrief, I leave all my homes and household goods, all attachments to those homes and household goods, all real estate, all attachments to that real estate. I further leave to him all monies and investments that I may own or control.

"*With the following stipulation:* After assigning this distribution to my son Luc Paul Moncrief, any monies remaining *in excess of three billion euros* will be divided equally among the Luc and Georgette Moncrief Foundation, the Louvre Museum, the Red Cross of France, and the Museum of Jewish Heritage in the United States."

There is a long pause, a very long pause. It is the kind of pause that comes when you hear that someone has just inherited three billion euros.

My head remains bowed. I continue to stare at the floor. The silence is punctuated by an occasional sob, a smattering of whispering. Finally, Dupain the attorney speaks again.

"I believe that it is now appropriate for the remainder of this meeting to be conducted, not by me, but by Luc Moncrief the younger."

I hold up my head. But I do not rise from my seat.

"Monsieur Dupain. I think that there is nothing more for me to add to the proceedings. However, I would like to ask a question of you," I say. "And I ask it here in the presence of all assembled, because it has troubled me since I was first informed of my father's death."

"But of course, monsieur."

"Are there police reports *or* medical reports *or* coroner reports *or* any kind of reports available concerning the death of my father?"

Dupain appears startled by the question, but he does not hesitate to answer.

"As you must know, Luc…er…Monsieur Moncrief, your father was a man in his late seventies. He had suffered from heart disease. He was discovered dead at his desk. Of course, there is an official death certificate signed by Doctor Martin Abel of the French Police Department."

"And that is all?" I ask.

"That is all that seemed necessary."

It is then…finally…that I feel my eyes fill with tears.

CHAPTER 33

WHEN I WAS YOUNGER, much younger—ten years old, fifteen years old—I visited magnificent homes of my school friends: huge châteaux in western France, thirty-room hunting lodges in Scotland, outlandishly large London town homes smack in the middle of Belgravia.

Many of these houses had rooms dedicated solely to pastimes like billiards and swimming and cigar-smoking and wine-tasting. Many had entire floors that housed ten to twenty servants. Some of the houses had stables with rooms put aside for tanning saddles and polishing stirrups.

But I had never seen in any other home the sort of room that we had in our house on rue du Montaigne.

Our house had a "silver room."

This room was about the size of a normal family dining room. It had perhaps fifty open shelves. These shelves were loaded with sterling silver serving pieces—everything from finger bowls to soup tureens, asparagus servers to butter pats, charger plates the size of platters, water goblets as ornate as altar chalices. Open bins were neatly filled with stacks of dinnerware assorted into categories like "Cristofle" and "Buccellati" and "Tiffany." Subcategories were sets of silver dinnerware wrapped with red velvet ribbon, each bin marked with a note signifying when the pieces had been used:

1788, one year before the Revolution
1872, one year after the ending of the Franco-Prussian War
1943, a dinner for General Eisenhower and his secretary, Kay Summersby
Babette, Birthday
Luc, Partie de Baptême

In the middle of the room is a simple pine table. It can easily seat eight butlers to polish and buff silver. It can also seat eight people for a party.

This early evening it seats only K. Burke and myself.

We sit facing each other. We sip a St. Emilion. The wine's château and vineyard names mean little to me and nothing to K. Burke.

Our moods are...well, I can only speak for me. I am slightly touched now with sadness, and yet I am happy that the process of the will has ended. Tomorrow is the funeral to get through, but then—after perhaps a day or two of shopping and museum-hopping—we will return to our favorite pastime—NYPD detective work.

We ignore the fruit and cheeses and charcuterie that the kitchen has assembled for us. We drink our wine.

Finally, Burke speaks.

"I see the newspaper headline now," Burke says. "Luc Moncrief, the Gloomiest Billionaire on Earth. Sob. Sob. Sob."

"K. Burke, surely you, of all people, are smart enough to know that a great big pot full of money does not make a person happy. Too many people in my position have jumped from skyscrapers, overdosed on drugs, murdered their lovers, died alone…money is a fine thing, especially if you do not have it, but it guarantees nothing other than money."

"Skip the lecture, Moncrief. Of course I know all that. And I also know that your heart was broken into pieces when Dalia died. There's no amount in the world—no money, no work of art, no beautiful woman—who can repair that."

A pause, and then I say, "It is because of that wisdom that you and I are such fine friends."

"So, what's the problem, Moncrief? Is it just that your father has been good to you in death and that you wish that he had…"

"No. No. It is not the usual, not the obvious."

I decide to be blunt. I speak.

"I believe that my father was murdered."

Burke does not flinch. She barely reacts. Her eyes do not pop open. Her jaw does not drop. If anything she is a woman acting as if she's heard a very interesting piece of casual gossip.

"Hence, your one and only question to the attorney. The question about the doctor's report," she says.

"Of course. I knew you would deduce that."

"What makes you believe that…other than your impeccable instinct?" she asks.

"Sarcasm does not flatter you, K. Burke." I pause. Then I say, "Yes, it is my instinct, of course. But there are two small issues. *One,* my father was a man of great importance and great wealth. You know that the newspapers and political blogs referred to him as *le vrai président,* the real president. Surely the police and detectives would require an autopsy or some sort of medical investigation to assure that there was no foul play. That would be done for a cabinet minister or an ambassador's wife. But it was not done for one of the most important men in France? *Ridicule!*"

K. Burke takes a long gulp of her wine. She nods, but she says nothing. I have something else to add.

"Now, another thing, something perhaps a bit subtler, but not to be overlooked: Julien Carpentier mentioned innumerable times that my father died of a heart attack, that my father had heart disease, that my father passed painlessly because of the speed of his heart attack. How many times was it necessary to tell us that? Likewise, from Babette's very first phone call to me in the States, she too kept insisting that it was a heart attack, a heart attack, a heart attack. Dupain the attorney mentioned it.... Why so much attention to this? Yes, surely he may very well have died from a heart attack, but is it necessary to mention it so many times?"

I pour us more wine. Then Detective Burke lifts her purse from the floor. It is her big black leather satchel of a purse. She unzips the bag and puts her hand inside. She retrieves a business-sized envelope. It is cream-colored. It looks like fine heavyweight paper.

Burke hands the envelope to me. On the reverse side, just below my father's engraved initials, the envelope is held closed by a bit of red sealing wax.

"I found this envelope where I am staying, in your bedroom. It was leaning against the bronze inkstand on your desk. The envelope was meant to be discovered," she says.

I flip the envelope over. There, in my father's precise handwriting, are these words: *à mon fils.* To my son.

I grab a dinner knife from one of the bins. Then I slit the envelope open. I read the letter aloud.

My Dear Luc,

This letter assumes that you are now in Paris for my funeral, that you are in our house, in your former bedroom.

Here is what I wish you to know.

In April I received word from Julien Carpentier that our most important new product—Prezinol, a breakthrough treatment for childhood diabetes— was facing serious problems. Prezinol was to be my last great achievement. Valex had worked on it for decades.

Then this awful news arrived. Thirty percent of three hundred juvenile test volunteers in Warsaw suffered a dreadful reaction to the drug—kidney failure or stage one cancer of the liver.

Julien immediately (and without consulting me) dispatched a team of doctors to Poland. By the time Julien involved me in the matter, the doctors reported back that the kidney and liver damage were irreversible. They advised that we stop all testing immediately, and that we cancel our plans for a similar test in São Paulo.

I disagreed with this strategy. I could not allow Prezinol to fail. I posited that we might receive different results in São Paulo. I also knew from experience that it would take the Polish bureau of health a few months to take action against Valex.

I instructed Julien to proceed with everything as planned. He refused. In fact, he accused me of being—and I quote—"a senile old devil." He said that my entire life was driven by greed and ego.

The fact is this: Julien was correct. I realized the truth of his observation. It is one that you yourself had sometimes made.

That evening I instructed Julien to stop all testing in Warsaw, to cancel plans for the testing in São Paulo, and to arrange significant compensation for the Polish children who suffered such unspeakable damage.

I then considered what else I might do to compensate for my history of abhorrent behavior. Sadly I realized that there was no suitable punishment.

I realized I was just another old man with arthritis and heart disease. My financial success was everything and nothing.

I decided to address my situation as follows.

First, to name Julien as my successor at Valex. Julien has the skills and moral fiber to act in a way that will allow Valex to create pharmaceuticals that will advance worldwide health.

Second, to leave to you the vast portion of my wealth. Out of guilt certainly for my years of paternal neglect, but also because you will use my fortune not merely to live well, but to live wisely.

Finally, to have delivered to me a shipment of fifty capsules of Prezinol.

My dear Luc, more than anything, I wish you the love I kept locked in my heart.

Votre père

CHAPTER 34

THE SONGWRITER WAS wrong when he wrote the lyrics that said he even loved "Paris in the winter, when it drizzles." I tell this to K. Burke as she and I walk the Boulevard Haussmann toward the enormous shopping cathedral known as Galeries Lafayette, after my father's funeral.

"The drizzle, it even gets through the finest wool coat," I complain.

"You should wear a good puffy ski jacket like mine," says Burke.

"I would rather wear a circus clown costume than a ski jacket."

"Say what you want, but I'm warm and dry, and you're cold and wet."

The morning had been a blur, but it was a mercifully short, respectful service with no gathering after. Except that I called Julien and Babette to meet with us. We ate homemade breakfast brioche and discussed my father's suicide.

Julien and Babette readily admitted that they knew

the *full* story, and, yes, they had been complicit in hiding the method from me. They swore that they were going to tell me the truth and to put that truth "in context." That my father was suffering from advanced heart disease, that the children's diabetes drug had caused grave damage to many in the test group, that my father had, in fact, ended his own life by taking more than four dozen Prezinol capsules.

"We merely wanted to get through the funeral, Luc. With so many business matters and the will, it seemed like the right thing," Julien said. "I am sorry if we miscalculated."

I was inclined to believe him. I still am. You see, the simple truth is: What difference does it make? We move on. My father is gone. Babette is a sad old lady. Julien is set for a lifetime of overwhelming work. We move on. At least we try.

As for me, I am and will always be without my beloved Dalia. To have a death that meaningful in your life is to always have the tiniest cloud over even the greatest joy. My police work may fascinate me. Good friends like Burke will support me. France may win the World Cup. I may sip a magnificent Romanée-Conti. I may even fall in love again. Even that I cannot rule out. But: no matter. Dalia will not be here with me.

K. Burke and I continue our walk. Now we are within a block of the Galeries Lafayette. Christmas lights hang from the chestnut trees. Candles sit shining in the shop windows.

"You know, Moncrief. You're a real Frenchman," she says.

"Did you ever doubt it?" I ask.

"No. Here's why: you do what many Frenchmen do. I noticed. You don't walk. You *stroll*. Long strides, a little hip swing, head back. You're like a little cartoon of a French guy."

"There's a compliment hidden somewhere in those words, K. Burke. I just haven't found it yet."

So we stroll. We approach the Haussmann entrance to the store. Burke asks that we pause for a moment. We do, and she says, "So, you were right. Your instincts were true. Your father was murdered."

"But, of course not, K. Burke. Not murder. My father committed suicide."

"I guess, but…" she says. "He was a murderer who… murdered himself."

I tell Burke how I feel. That sometimes I believe his suicide was an old-fashioned noble gesture; that he had committed sins that could never be forgiven. So, *poof*. He punished himself.

"But then," I tell her, "I think he was an old-fashioned coward. The mere thought of *earthly* punishment— jail, humiliation—told him to escape. He up and left us. He left Babette, a woman who loved him. He left Julien, a young man who idolized him. And he left me, his son, the boy he barely knew, the man he *never* knew."

We walk inside the gilded department store. It looks like a Christmas tree turned upside down. Sparkle and glitter and thirty-feet-high gift boxes suspended from the vaulted ceiling. Burke looks upward, her neck stretching backward, as if she were standing in the Sistine Chapel. Her mouth literally opens in awe. The Christmas shoppers crowd the floor.

Then she says, "Let's start shopping before you start wanting to move on. I want to buy a few things to take back."

"I can assure you, K. Burke, there is almost nothing worth purchasing here."

"Well, thanks for the advice, Moncrief. But I think I'm about to prove that statement wrong."

I limit her, however, to one hour. In that short time she purchases a green Mark Cross Villa Tote bag, a pair of real silk stockings (the sort that also requires her to buy simple but quite intriguing garters), two tiny bronze replicas of the Arc de Triomphe (*"Vous touriste!"* I tell her), and four silk scarves (blue for her cousin Sandi, red for her cousin Elyce, yellow for her cousin Maddy, white for her cousin Marilyn). The scarves are my treat. I insist.

I also came out of the store with a purchase of my own. A five-pound tenderloin of venison.

"I shall give this venison to my father's cook, Reynaud, and you shall feast in a way you never have before."

"I'll say that it was interesting being in a butcher store inside a department store. But really…venison? Deer meat?"

"What is so odd about that?" I ask.

"I can tell you in one word: Bambi."

CHAPTER 35

I MUST ADMIT the truth: I am enjoying my day with K. Burke.

She is constantly refreshing, authentic. She has a complete honesty to her behavior. On the job she is not always charming, but here she always is. Burke is like a provincial schoolgirl on her first trip to Paris—wide-eyed and enthusiastic, but never irritating or vulgar. Burke has the purity that I have experienced in one other woman.

"We are going someplace really special now," I say.

"Galeries Lafayette was special enough for me," she says.

"Cease the humility, K. Burke. Where we are going next is…is almost…"

"*Incroyable?*"

"*Oui.* Almost unbelievable."

"It is only a short walk. It is on the Place Vendôme. But the drizzle is still drizzling. I'll try to get us a taxi."

"No, we'll walk," she says.

"But the rain. It is cold. It is icy."

"We'll walk."

So we walk, and I try to remember not to "stroll." K. Burke can't get enough of the Parisian excitement. Her head seems as if it's attached to a well-oiled fulcrum that allows her to snap her eyes from side to side in only a second.

We pass the furriers and jewelers and even the occasional hat store on our walk. Then, in front of a chocolate shop, of all places, I make a grave error.

"If there's anything you want, just say so, and we can get it," I say.

She stops walking. The smile leaves her face, and her head remains motionless.

"I don't want you to buy me anything…anything. I shouldn't have let you buy those expensive scarves for my cousins. I don't want *things*. Frankly, if you want to give me something, do it by giving *yourself* a gift…the gift of joy, some peace. What would truly make me happy is for you to be happy."

She brushes her cheeks with her hand, and I cannot be sure whether she is brushing away tears or merely brushing away the icy drizzle.

"You are a true friend, K. Burke," I say.

"I try to be," she says, her voice choking just a bit. "But it's hard to be a friend to a lucky man who has had some very bad luck."

"You are doing just fine," I say.

We continue our walk.

We are about to turn onto the Place Vendôme when she says, "By the way, Moncrief, you can stroll if you want to."

"I am walking slow because I am contemplating a problem," I say.

Burke looks nervous, serious.

"What's the matter?" she says.

"I have a problem that only you can solve."

"And that is?"

"That is this: we are going to a place where I had planned on purchasing you a combination Christmas–New Years–Friendship–Thank You gift. And now you say…" (I do a comic imitation of an angry woman) *"I don't want you to buy me anything!"*

"That's the problem?" she says.

"For me, that is a problem. Can you solve it?"

"Okay, *mon ami.* You may buy me one more thing. Just one. And then that's it."

CHAPTER 36

THE FLAG THAT is pinned over the doorway is not too big, not too small. It is surely not an elegant sign, although the small building itself is a beautifully designed nineteenth-century town house. The sign is wet from the rain, so it is wrinkled in many spots. Dark-purple letters—only three letters—are printed against a white background.

JAR

Quite logically K. Burke says, "Is it a store that sells jars? Or do the letters stand for something?"

"The letters stand for something," I say. "It is a man's name. Joel Arthur Rosenthal. He is the finest jeweler in the world, and, not surprisingly, he is here in Paris."

"Moncrief, when I said one more gift, I did not say jewelry. This is out of the question. I'm not going to allow…"

I put an index finger gently on her lips.

"I am going to ring the bell. I have an appointment. Let's try to keep our voices down."

Within seconds we are greeted by a very handsome young man in gray slacks and a blue blazer. We exchange greetings in French, and then I introduce him to Detective Burke.

"*Mademoiselle Katherine Burke, je voudrais vous presenter Richard Ranftle,* the assistant to Monsieur Rosenthal."

"*Je suis enchanté, Mademoiselle.* I am also very much admiring of your coat. The North Face ski jacket has become everyone's favorite."

"*Merci,* Richard," Burke says. Then she smiles at me.

"Monsieur Rosenthal regrets that he is not here to assist the both of you, but your phone call came only this morning, Monsieur Moncrief, and Monsieur Rosenthal had already left for his home in Morocco. He likes to escape Paris during the Christmas season."

A maid enters. She is dressed in full maid regalia—starched white cap, black dress, starched white apron with ruffle.

She asks if we would like tea or coffee or wine.

We decline.

"Perhaps some champagne," says Richard.

We decline again.

We follow Richard a few steps into what looks like the parlor of a small elegant apartment on the rue du Faubourg Saint-Honoré. A two-seat sofa in gray. A few mid-century wooden chairs with darker gray seats. A very bright crystal chandelier in the center of the ceiling. The only thing that distinguishes the room from a private residence are the four glass jewelry showcases.

Katherine Burke runs her hands along the glass enclosures. I watch her closely. We both seem to be nearly overwhelmed by the beauty of the jewels. Not merely the size of the diamonds but the unusual designs of the bracelets and earrings and necklaces and rings.

"I know very little about jewelry, and it has been a few years since I have visited here, but these stones all seem to be enormous," I say.

"Joel...er, Monsieur Rosenthal, likes to work on a large canvas. You see, even when he uses small stones, as in a pavé setting, he sets them so close to one another that they look like a wall of diamonds."

He points, as an example, to a ring with something called an "apricot" diamond at its center. The tiny diamonds around it look like a starry night.

Richard Ranftle shows us something called a "thread ring." If there were a piece of sewing thread composed of tiny diamonds, then flung into the air, then eventually landing in a messy heap, it would be this enormous ring. For good luck, Rosenthal seems to have decided that a very large amethyst should sit on top of this pile of extraordinary thread.

"Mademoiselle seems most interested in the rings, eh?" says Richard.

I note with amusement that Richard has perfected an amazing style. He is helpful without being condescending. He is courteous without being obnoxious. We are three people having fun. Million-dollar fun, but fun nonetheless.

Burke is slightly stoned, I think, on the jewelry on display.

"Look at that," she says, and she points to an enormous round green stone.

Richard immediately goes to work.

"It is a twelve-carat emerald. Monsieur Rosenthal was inspired to set the stone upside down. Then he surrounded it with a platinum and garnet rope. It is beyond nontraditional. He says it looks like 'a turtle from paradise.'"

Richard removes the ring from the glass case. He places it on a dark-purple velvet tray.

"Let me slip it onto your middle finger," says Richard. Then he pauses and says, "Unless you would care to do so, Monsieur Moncrief."

"No, no. Go right ahead," I say.

"My God," says Burke. "This is about the same size as my Toyota Camry."

"If you like, then, you can drive it out of the showroom," says Richard. We all smile.

She looks at the ring. She holds up her hand.

"I wish you'd told me we were coming here, Moncrief. I would have given myself a manicure."

The ring looks spectacular, huge and spectacular, beautiful and spectacular. I tell Burke to take it. She says, "Oh, no." I insist. She insists no. I say that it's a Christmas gift. She says this is ridiculous. I tell her that she promised I would be allowed to give her "just one gift." Then as an extra argument I say something that is probably not even true: "Look, Detective, how expensive can it be? It's only an emerald, not even a diamond."

For about three minutes the room remains completely silent. I do not know what is going through her head, of course. But when she finally speaks, she says, "Okay."

I smile. She smiles. Richard smiles. Richard hands me a small blue paper on which is written: "540,000 EU." I slip the paper into the wet pocket of my coat, and I continue to smile.

And that is how Detective Katherine Burke came to own the ring that came to be called "The Emerald Turtle."

CHAPTER 37

CHRISTMAS DAY IN PARIS is for family. Grand-père carving the goose. Grand-mère snoring from too much Rémy Martin. It is a day for children and chocolate.

I will not violate the spirit of the feast. Indeed, Reynaud, my late father's exceptional chef, will roast the tenderloin of venison. I have invited Babette and Julien and Julien's girlfriend, Anne. (Who knew Julien had a girlfriend? Who knew Julien had a life apart from Valex?)

So that will be Christmas Day. For Christmas Eve, however, I have made a special plan. Burke and I will have a night of fine dining.

"It will be a night perfect for wearing 'The Emerald Turtle,'" I say.

"I'm so nervous wearing it," says Burke. "If I lose it…if…"

"If you lose it, there are plenty more emeralds in the world," I say. "And if I sound like a spoiled rich kid, so be it. I am. At least for Christmas."

"I'm still nervous."

But, of course, she wears it.

The evening begins with—what else?—chilled Dom Pérignon in the warm and cozy backseat of the limo.

"Our first stop will be Les Ambassadeurs inside the Hôtel de Crillon," I tell K. Burke.

"Our *first* stop?" says Burke.

"*Oui*. The first course of seven courses," I say. "A different course at a different restaurant. I can imagine no finer way to welcome Christmas. This took much planning on my part."

We arrive at the Place de la Concorde. Five minutes later we are tasting artichoke soup with black truffle shavings. Exceptional.

Fifteen minutes later we are back in the car and headed for *le poisson,* the fish course. At L'Arpège my friend, Alain Passard, has prepared his three-hour turbot with green apples.

Just when we think nothing can surpass the turbot we move on to Lasserre. Here the magical dish is a delicate pigeon with a warm fig and hazelnut compote.

The maître d' at George V's Le Cinq describes a dish that both Burke and I think is ridiculous—a seaweed consommé with bits of turnip, parsnip, and golden beets floating on top. It is, of course, magnificent.

When we return to the car Burke announces, "I don't know how to say this properly. But I am full without really being full."

"You are *satisfied,*" I say. "Small portions of exquisite food. The French never fill themselves. They eat. They think. They enjoy."

"Sure. That's it exactly," says K. Burke. Then, with a giggle in her voice, she says, "A bit more champagne, please."

The first four restaurants we have visited are classic Parisian restaurants. They have been filling famous bellies for many years—royalty and food writers and a few pretentious snobs. But always the food has remained magnificent.

"Now we are going to have something completely modern," I tell my dining companion. "We are going to one of the famous new places that I call 'mish-mash-mosh' restaurants. You don't know whether you are eating Indian or French or Hungarian or Cambodian food. The classical chefs turn in their graves, but it is the future, and we must try one of them."

So Burke and I, a little tipsy from champagne and wine, sit at Le Chateaubriand, a fancy French name for a restaurant that looks like a 1950s American diner. The duck breast we are served is covered with fennel seeds and bits of... "What is this?" I ask the captain. He replies, "Tiny pieces of orange candy." This fabulous concoction sits next to a purée of strawberries that tastes a little bit of maple syrup, a little bit of tangerine.

K. Burke describes it perfectly: "It tastes like something wonderful, like something you'd get at a carnival in heaven."

"You have the vocabulary of a restaurant critic, K. Burke," I say.

We leave the heavenly carnival, and a short time later we are at Le Jules Verne, the foolishly named restaurant on top of the beloved *tour Eiffel*.

The alcohol is making me too happy, too giddy, and surely too talkative. "This is a restaurant that has maintained its integrity, even though it is in the very tourist heart of Paris," I say.

"I'm not ashamed to be a tourist," says Burke.

"Nor am I," I say. Then we sit down and look out at the marvel of Paris at night while we eat an impeccable piece of filet mignon—big beefy flavor in every meltingly tender bite.

"And now. On to dessert," I say.

"I should say 'I couldn't.' But the truth is…I could," Burke says.

"We will finish at my favorite place in all of Paris," I say. Soon our car is making its way through the narrow streets of the Marais.

All the chic little shops are closed. A small kosher restaurant is shutting down for the evening. "The best hummus in Europe," I say.

A few students are singing Christmas songs. They swig from open bottles of wine. Lights twinkle from many windows.

The car stops at a tiny corner shop on rue Vieille du Temple, very near the rue de Rivoli.

Burke reads the sign on the shop aloud, "Amorino." Then she says, "Whatever it is, it looks closed."

"Un moment," I say, and I hit a few numbers on my phone. *"Nous sommes ici."* We are here. A young woman appears at the shop door. She is smiling. She gestures to us. We go inside.

"It's an ice cream parlor," Burke says.

"Yes and no. It is a gelato shop. When I lived in Paris—before moving to New York—no evening was complete unless we had a two-scoop chocolate and amaretto cone at Amorino. What flavors do you like? The pistachio is magnificent."

She looks away from me. When she faces me again she is blinking her eyes.

"Would you think I'm rude if I skip the gelato?" she says.

"But you would love it," I say.

"It's been a great evening. I appreciate it. I really do," she says. "But I've had enough."

Then it hits my thoughtless French brain. Suddenly, as if a big rock fell on my stupid little head.

"Oh, K. Burke. I am sorry. I am awful and stupid. I am sorry."

"You have nothing to be sorry about," she says. "It was a wonderful night. It is a beautiful ring. This is the nicest Christmas I've ever had."

Then I find the courage to say what I should say.

"Forgive me, Katherine. I gave you a night of glamour without the romance that should accompany it. Forgive me." She smiles at me.

"There's nothing to forgive, Moncrief. You're terrific. You're the best friend I've ever had."

EPILOGUE

IF I REALLY wanted to stretch the truth, I could say that my partner K. Burke and I are spending New Year's Eve at the Plaza Hotel. But as I say, that would be stretching the truth. A lot.

The fact is, the two of us are spending New Year's Eve in the underground loading alley under the kitchens of the Plaza Hotel.

It seems that our boss, Inspector Nick Elliott, wanted to bring us back to reality after our time in Paris. So Burke and I are on a drug stakeout in the repugnant, disgusting garbage zone beneath the fancy hotel. We are waiting for a potential "chalk drop." That's cop-talk for a major delivery of methamphetamine, a fairly wicked drug for some of the New Year's Eve revelers.

The smell of garbage, the whip of the winter wind, and the knowledge that most of New York is dancing the night away does nothing to relieve our boredom. And as with most stakeouts, the boredom is excruciating.

"So this is how it goes, right, Moncrief?" Burke says. "A week ago we were on top of the Eiffel Tower. Tonight we're in a hole under the Plaza."

I laugh and say, "That's life. Even for a rich kid." I pause for a moment as I watch a rat scurry past us. Then I say, "You know, K. Burke, the truth is, I am enjoying this surveillance routine almost as much as— but not *quite* as much as—our Christmas Eve in Paris. Simply put, I love doing detective work. Can you believe that?"

She does not hesitate. She says, "Yes, Moncrief. I can believe that."

Before I can even smile there is a great eruption of firecrackers and noisemakers and the noise of people shouting with joy.

"Listen closely, Moncrief. You can hear the music," Burke says.

She is right. From somewhere inside the hotel the orchestra is playing "Auld Lang Syne."

I lean in and kiss her on her cheek.

"Happy New Year, K. Burke," I say.

She leans in and kisses me on *my* cheek.

She speaks.

"Happy New Year, my friend."

FRENCH TWIST

JAMES PATTERSON
AND RICHARD DiLALLO

CHAPTER 1

"I HAVE ABSOLUTELY NO appetite! Absolutely none! So don't waste your money, Moncrief!"

This is Katherine Burke speaking. K. Burke is my NYPD detective partner and she is furious with me. This is not an unusual state of affairs between us.

"We're supposed to be on the job, and instead we're sitting in this ridiculously fancy restaurant having a thousand-dollar lunch," she says.

"But you have never tasted anything so magnificent as the oyster and pearls appetizer served here at Per Se," I say.

I raise a small spoonful of the appetizer and move it toward her.

"White sturgeon caviar, icy just-shucked oysters, a dollop of sweet tapioca and…"

"Get that food away from me," she says. "I am way too angry to eat."

"But I am not," I say, and I pop the spoonful into my mouth and put an exaggerated expression of ecstasy on my face.

Don't get the wrong impression. K. Burke and I are great friends *and* a great detective team. Our methods, however, are very different. Burke is a tough native New Yorker. She plays by the book—strict procedure, always sticking to the rules. I, on the other hand, believe in going with my instinct—feelings, intuition. By the way, I am a native Frenchman, Luc Moncrief.

These different approaches lead to occasional disagreements. They also enable solutions to very tough cases.

I eat my appetizer in absolute silence. Then I say, "If you're not going to eat yours…"

She pulls the plate back toward herself and takes a bite. If a woman is able to chew angrily, then K. Burke chews angrily. In a few seconds, however, her mood transforms into peacefulness.

"This time you are pushing things too far. It's almost three o'clock. We should not be sitting here still having lunch."

"K. Burke, please, if you will. Our assignment is completed. And I must remind you that it was an assignment that amounted to absolutely nothing. A complete waste of time. In any event, we did what we were told to do. Now we should enjoy ourselves."

I signal the waiter to pour us each some more Bâtard-Montrachet.

I am, by the way, telling K. Burke the absolute truth about the assignment. And she knows it. Here is how it all went down…

Per the instructions of our boss, Nick Elliott, we arrived at Pier 94 on 54th Street and the Hudson River at 5 a.m. Let me repeat the time. Five a.m.! When I was a young man in Paris, 5 a.m. was when the evening ended.

In any event, Inspector Elliott said that he had unimpeachable, impeccable, irreproachable information that the stolen parts of rare 1950s-era American automobiles—Nash Ramblers, Packards, Studebakers—were being shipped to collectors worldwide, ingeniously smuggled into supply boxes for cruise ships at the 54th Street shipping pier.

We arrived (at 5 a.m.!) with detectives from Arts and Antiquities, four officers from the New York Motor Vehicles Bureau, and three NYPD officers with .38 Special handguns.

Beginning at 6 a.m. the officers, using crowbars and electric chainsaws, began uncrating large wooden boxes that were about to be loaded on board. Or, as K. Burke informed me, "laded on board." Apparently her second cousin was a longshoreman. K. Burke is full of revelations.

To no one's complete surprise, the crates marked "Steinway & Sons" contained pianos. The crates marked "Seagram's" contained whiskey. The crates marked "Frozen Ostrich Meat" contained…you guessed it.

By eleven o'clock we had uncovered properly tax-receipted crates of video games, mattresses, antacids, bolts of silk, *but* no automotive parts.

At noon I texted Nick Elliott and told him that we discovered nothing.

He texted back an infuriating, Are you sure?

I refused to answer the insulting question. So Detective Burke texted back, Yes, Moncrief is sure.

While Burke was texting Elliott, I was texting Per Se, making a lunch reservation. And that is where we now sit.

"You always make me sound like a hard-ass workaholic, Moncrief," Burke says.

"Hard-ass?" I say. "I think not. A little difficult. A little stubborn. But not a hard-ass. You are a woman, and because you are a woman…"

"Don't you dare say anything vulgar or sexist, Moncrief. I swear I'll report you to NYPD Internal Affairs."

"But I never say anything vulgar or sexist," I say.

Burke squints for a moment, puts down her salad fork, then says, "You know something? Come to think of it, you never do. I apologize."

"*Ce n'est rien.* It's nothing."

Burke lets a small smile sneak on to her face. We're aligned again. And that's truly important. Her friendship means the world to me. I've had a very bad year, to say the least. My beloved girlfriend, Dalia, died, and I was left with an impossibly broken heart. Shortly after Dalia's death my *not* very beloved father died. This left me with an obscenely large inheritance, but a great sum of money did nothing to repair my heart. Only my friend and partner K. Burke kept me sane through all of it.

Two waiters now swoop in and lift our empty appetizer plates from the table. Almost immediately two different waiters swoop in with our main course of butter-poached sable with a mission fig jam. The sable is accompanied by toasted hazelnuts and…

K. Burke's cell phone rings.

"I asked you to turn off that foolish machine," I say.

"Yes, you did, and I told you that I would not."

She looks at her phone. Then she looks at me.

"We are wanted at 754 Fifth Avenue," she says.

"Bergdorf Goodman, the store for rich women," I say.

"You got it."

"Well, we cannot leave before we are served our main course."

"Yes, we can. There's a dead woman in a dressing room at Bergdorf Goodman. Inspector Elliott will meet us there in fifteen minutes."

I toss my napkin onto the table.

"I know we cannot decline the job, K. Burke. But I am disappointed," I say.

She stands at her chair and speaks.

"Why not ask the waiter for *le petit sac pour emporter les restes*?"

"This is a French expression that *you* know and that I do not," I say.

She smiles broadly.

"Translation: a doggy bag."

CHAPTER 2

THE VERY EFFICIENT K. Burke calls for a squad car as I sign my Per Se house account receipt. The police car speeds us along Central Park South. In five minutes we are at Bergdorf Goodman.

We exit the squad car, and we both immediately realize that something very weird is going on. Burke and I are *not* greeted with the usual crime scene madness. There's *nothing* to indicate that a homicide has occurred inside this famous store. *No* flashing lights, *no* zigzag of yellow DO NOT CROSS POLICE LINE tape, *no* police officers holding back a curious crowd.

"What the hell is going on here?" Burke asks. "It looks so…so…not like a crime scene."

For a second I think we may have the wrong location. As if she could read my mind, Burke says, "I know this is the right place. But…let's go in and see."

Inside, the same thing. A busy day for the wealthy. Everything is calm and beautiful. Elegant women and an occasional man examine five-thousand-dollar handbags, perfumes in crystal bottles, costume jewelry as expensive as the real thing.

Our boss, Nick Elliott, is waiting right inside the entrance for us.

Elliott looks serious and concerned. His greeting is typical: "You two are finally here." Then he gets right to the point.

"Before I take you upstairs I've got to tell you something. This scene plays out like a typical natural death. A twenty-five-year-old woman, name of Tessa Fulbright, suddenly drops dead in a dressing room. Maybe a heart attack or a drug OD or a brain aneurysm. But it's not. It's a shitload bigger than that."

Elliott says that he'll give us the most important details upstairs in a few minutes.

"They gave me details in the car on the way over, but nobody thought to mention what floor it's on. Lemme check," Elliott says. He begins to punch into his cell phone. Before he gets the correct floor number, I speak.

"It's the sixth floor," I say.

Almost in perfect unison Elliott and Burke say, "How'd you know that?"

"Floor six has the youthful designer clothing."

They know what I am not going to say: I am remembering the days before Dalia died.

Two minutes later, with a store detective and a floor manager accompanying us, Burke, Elliott, and I are standing in a very large, very lovely dressing room. It is furnished with two armchairs and a small sofa, both of them upholstered in pale purple, the signature color of the store.

One other thing: there is a stunning, beautiful, red-haired young woman lying on the floor. She is wearing a Chloé summer gown with the price tag still attached.

Burke and I kneel and examine the body closely. Other than the dead woman's beauty, there is nothing unusual about her.

"I assume you noticed the tattoo behind the right ear," says Burke.

"The tiny star? We got it," says Elliott. Then he looks down at the deceased, shakes his head, and speaks to the small police staff around him.

"You can take Ms. Fulbright downtown. Don't dare release the body. She belongs to us until I say so."

The medical examiner nods. Then Elliott looks at me and Burke.

"Here's the deal," he says. "In the last two weeks there have been two other deaths *exactly like this one.* The first one was in Saks Fifth Avenue, ten blocks away."

Elliott explains that a twenty-three-year-old woman, Mara Monahan, died suddenly—literally dropped dead—while she was paying for shoes. Elliott and his teenage daughter were having lunch around the corner at Burger Heaven when the call came in. So after lunch, when Elliott's daughter took off, he went over to Saks to take a quick look-see.

"So this Mara Monahan turns out to be the wife of Clifton Monahan, the congressman from the Upper East Side. Maybe you've seen her picture online or something. This Mara Monahan is a beautiful, I mean *beautiful,* blonde."

"I heard about this," K. Burke says. "The *Post* and *Daily News* were having a field day with their covers. She was beautiful."

I interject. "I was at her table at the gala dinner for the Holy Apostles Soup Kitchen. She was a knockout."

"Could we refocus on the *pertinent parts* of the case, gentlemen?" Burke says.

"Anyway. I figure I'd better make nice to her husband, the congressman. I'll be under a crushing amount of pressure and scrutiny to close this case. So I go see him. He's broken up. Really broken up, I mean. Two days later there's a funeral. I go. Lots of big shots. Cuomo's there, Cardinal Dolan does the service. Over and out. Sad stuff."

But there's one more chapter in Nick Elliott's story. He tells us that the following Monday, almost a week after the Monahan woman dies, a few days before today's date, a second-string Broadway actress dropped dead in one of the only restaurants in New York as expensive as Per Se. It's called Eleven Madison Park, and yes, the woman was young and beautiful and...

"Brunette this time," I say.

"No," Elliott says. "This one is blond, also."

One quick glance at Burke, and I can tell that she's pleased that my hunch was wrong.

Elliott explains that this woman is the understudy to the female lead in the latest Broadway smash hit. But, perhaps as a measure in case her acting career doesn't work out, the woman, Jenna Lee Austin, recently married a multimillionaire hedge funder. Elliott also points out that the medical examiner's reports in both deaths show *no* sign of trauma, *no* injuries, or, almost as important, no sign of any foreign substance in the victims' systems, nothing that could indicate a cause of death. And looking at victim number three here, she seems like she's going to match the pattern.

So, NYPD has three young, beautiful, rich women, all of them apparently dead from natural causes, all of them dead in the middle of an ordinary day in three of the fanciest places in Manhattan.

"What do you need us to do?" K. Burke asks.

"Frankly, everything. Hit the computers. Pull all the

info on all the women, their husbands, their friends. The first one seemed like a tragedy, the second more suspicious, and now with three—there's obviously some sort of connection. And we don't have one god-damn idea what it is. So I want you two to take over from Banks and Lin, who are working the first two. See them and get caught up."

I nod. Burke gives her typically enthusiastic "Got it, sir."

Elliott says, "I'll see you at the precinct tomorrow."

"A small problem, Inspector," I say. Then Burke jumps in.

"We have one of our rare long weekends. But we can cancel all that and come in to work."

I interrupt her quickly, almost rudely.

"No, we cannot," I say. "Detective Burke seems to have forgotten. We *do* have some plans for the weekend."

K. Burke looks slightly startled, but she is smart enough to know that she'd better trust me on this one.

"Okay," Elliott says. "Bang the hell out of the computers tonight. See what you can find. By Sunday you'll have the ME's report. I'll assume you two will be in on Sunday?"

"But of course," I say.

He nods to the store detective. They both begin to walk toward the elevator. Then Elliott stops for just a moment. His face has the barest trace of a smile. Then he speaks, "Have a good time." God only knows what he is assuming about Burke and me.

Nick Elliott makes his way through the sea of Carolina Herrera dresses and Stella McCartney jackets. Katherine Burke looks at me. Her eyes narrow slightly.

"Okay, Moncrief. What the hell is going on?"

"What's going on is this: I shall pick you up at your apartment tomorrow morning at six. And please, K. Burke, be sure to bring some nice clothes. Yes, this case looks very interesting. But, my friend, so is this little trip that I've planned."

CHAPTER 3

VERY LITTLE TRAFFIC IN Manhattan. Very little traffic on the Hutchinson River Parkway. Very little traffic on Purchase Street. Everything is going our way. So, in thirty-five minutes K. Burke and I are walking through the Westchester County Airport in White Plains, New York.

Burke is, after all, a detective, accustomed to ridiculously early hours. So she is wide-awake and bright-eyed, and also a trifle confused. We walk through a small gate marked PRIVATE AIRCRAFT. I am about to show my driver's license to the security guard as ID, but the young man waves his hand casually and says, "No need, Mr. Moncrief. Welcome aboard."

Five minutes later we are in the sky.

"First question," she says. "What's with this fancy jet? Don't tell me you rented a private plane."

"No. I did not rent it," I say. "I bought it. It is called a Gulfstream G650, and it contains enough fuel to fly for about seven thousand miles. That's my complete knowledge of the vehicle."

She shakes her head slowly and says, "They should give one of these planes to every NYPD detective. It would make days off so much more fun."

Then she says, "Question number two. Tell me where we're going, Moncrief, or I'm walking off this plane."

"No need to prepare your parachute, K. Burke. We are going to a city named Louisville, in the state of Kentucky."

As I say the word "Kentucky," the attractive young woman who greeted us as we boarded crouches beside us, rests her hand on mine, and asks if we would like some champagne or coffee. (I hear K. Burke mutter, "Oh, brother.") Both Burke and I decline the offer of champagne and settle for a perfectly pulled cappuccino. As if the coffee was a magical elixir that filled her with special knowledge, K. Burke suddenly shouts.

"The Derby!" she says loudly. "Tomorrow is the Kentucky Derby!"

"Congratulations. You are a detective *parfaite,*" I say.

"Since when did you become a horse-racing fan? And please don't tell me you bought a horse and managed to get him into the Kentucky Derby."

"No, although I did think about it. But the dearest friends of my late parents have a horse running tomorrow at Churchill Downs. They have been racing horses ever since I can remember. Madame and Monsieur Savatier, Marguerite and Nicolas. The name of their extraordinary horse is *Garçon,* although his full name is *Vilain Garçon,* which means 'naughty boy.'"

"So, they named the horse after you," she laughs.

"An easy joke, K. Burke. Too easy."

"Irresistible," she says.

"In any event, the Savatiers have been in Louisville for two months while Garçon was training. For Nicolas and Marguerite the Kentucky Derby has been their dream. They have rented a house, and we will be staying with them. They will meet us when we land."

Burke and I each have another cappuccino, and less than an hour later we arrive at Louisville International Airport.

We exit the plane. At the bottom of the steps waits an elegant old woman wearing an elegant gray suit and a large white hat. Next to her stands an equally elegant-looking man of a similar age. He, too, wears a suit of gray. He also wears an old-fashioned straw boater. They both carry gold-handled canes.

"Bienvenue, Luc. Bonjour, mon ami bien-aimé." Welcome, my beloved friend.

We embrace.

"Madame et Monsieur Savatier, I wish to present my best friend, Mademoiselle Katherine Burke," I say. "Miss Burke, Marguerite and Nicolas Savatier."

The three of them exchange gentle handshakes. K. Burke says that she has heard wonderful things about them as well as "your great horse, Vilain Garçon."

"Merci," says Madame Savatier. "And I must say this. Since Luc just called you *his* best friend, that makes you also *our* best friend."

Monsieur Savatier speaks. I immediately recall what a stern and funny old Frenchman he can be.

"Please, everyone," he says. "This is all very touching. But we must hurry. In less than a half hour they will be having the final workout of the horses. And no friendship is worth being late for that."

CHAPTER 4

THE FIRST SATURDAY IN May. That's the date of the Kentucky Derby. May promises sunny weather. But today, May does not make good on that promise. The sky is overcast. The temperatures are in the mid-forties. The only sunshine is the excitement in the noisy, boozy, very colorful crowd. Katherine Burke, the Savatiers, and I are standing outside the super-elite Infield Club. This is where the horse owners and their friends gather. Here most women are dressed as if they are attending a British royal wedding: huge floral print dresses, most of them in bright primary colors; necklaces and brooches and earrings with sparkling diamonds, emeralds, and rubies. The women's hats are each a crazy story unto themselves—huge affairs that must be pinned and clipped to remain afloat, in colors that perfectly match or clash with the colors of their dresses.

The men are in morning suits or are dressed in classic-cut blazers—each a different rainbow color. Bright club ties, striped ties, bow ties. The whole area has the feeling of happy anxiety and big money. And of course no one is without a smartphone, constantly raised to capture the moment. This has to be the most thoroughly photographed Kentucky Derby in history.

I give K. Burke two hundred dollars.

"Bet one hundred on Garçon for me, one hundred on Garçon for yourself," I tell her.

"I'm not going to take your money," she says.

"But this time you must. To watch the race with a bet riding on it makes it a million times more exciting. But I must prepare you for the worst."

She looks surprised.

"Garçon has little chance of winning. The odds-makers have his chances at forty to one."

"I don't care," she says, in the true spirit of the Derby. "He's our horse." And she is off to the betting window. She's become a real racing fan.

K. Burke clutches our tickets tightly. She is dressed more casually than most of the women in the infield, but she looks enchanting. Marguerite Savatier has given Burke a piece of Garçon's silks—a red, white, and yellow swatch of cloth. Burke has tied it around her waist as a belt. She looks terrific in a simple white billowing cotton dress. And if anyone present thinks Burke is out of her social element, all they need do is glance at the huge emerald necklace, the gift that I gave her this past Christmas in Paris.

Then it is time for the race.

Grooms snap lead shanks onto their horses and escort them out of their stalls. Then comes the traditional parade. The horses are conducted past the clubhouse turn, then under the twin spires of Churchill Downs. Finally, the horses are brought into the paddock to be saddled.

Nicolas and Marguerite Savatier speak to Garçon's

jockey and trainers. They save their most important words for...who else? Garçon. Both Savatiers stroke the horse's nose. Marguerite touches his cheek. Then they move away.

Now comes the moment that most people, myself among them, find the most touching. It begins with a simple, sad piece of music. A college band begins playing a very old Stephen Foster song. Everyone at the Derby sings along, right down to the heartbreaking final verse:

> *Weep no more my lady.*
> *Oh! Weep no more today.*
> *We will sing one song*
> *For my old Kentucky home.*
> *For the old Kentucky home, far away.*

And the race begins.

For me there is no sporting event that does not excite me when I am watching in person. Boxing. Basketball. Tennis. Hockey. But nothing compares to horse-racing. And nothing in horse-racing compares to the Kentucky Derby.

It is even more incredible to be watching the race with owners of one of the racehorses. It is almost as exciting watching K. Burke transform from a no-nonsense NYPD detective into a crazed racing fan. She clenches her fingers into fists. She screams the word "Garçon" over and over, literally without stopping for breath.

And the race itself?

If I could have "fixed" the race, I am ashamed to say, I would have taken all of my father's inheritance and done so. Nothing would please me more than to see my frail elderly friends, Marguerite and Nicolas, break down in tears as Vilain Garçon crossed first at the finish line. Nothing would please me more than to see my best friend in her white cotton dress jump for joy, her emerald necklace flapping up and down. Yes, it would have been worth my fortune to see that happen.

As it turns out, I did not have to spend a penny.

The voice on the loudspeaker, above the cheering, came out shouting, with a perfect Southern accent, "And the winner, by half a length, is VILL-EN GAR-ÇON!"

CHAPTER 5

THE BEST THING ABOUT being the governor of Kentucky must be hosting the Winner's Party for the Kentucky Derby.

We watch the giant wreath of roses being placed upon Garçon. Then we head to the Kentucky Derby Museum for the Winner's Party. K. Burke and I are sort of maid of honor and best man at a royal wedding. We get to enter with the bride and groom, Marguerite and Nicolas. Shouts. Cheers. Music.

"I bet that most of the people here think that we're the son and daughter of the Savatiers," K. Burke says.

"Or the son and daughter-*in-law*," I say. Burke acts as if she did not hear what I just said.

Armand Joscoe, the tough little French jockey who is hugely responsible for Garçon's victory, is carried around the room on a chair, like a bride at a Jewish wedding.

"He's adorable," says K. Burke.

"When I was a lad everyone called him *Petit Nez*, Little Nose. He has been with the Savatiers forever. This win is a wonderful day for him."

"No more *Petit Nez* for him," says Burke. I now look at the commotion around the Savatiers.

The charming old couple is, as always, composed and courteous as they field the questions from society magazines, racing magazines, newspaper and TV reporters from all over the world, and gossip blogs. Marguerite's gentle voice is barely audible among the thousands of clicks from the cameras and cell phones. It is their show. Burke and I stand many feet away from the stars.

"Have you tasted the mint julep?" I ask K. Burke.

"I'm an Irish girl. I prefer my whiskey straight up," she says. "I just don't understand the combination of mint and bourbon."

As if on cue a waiter passes by with a tray of chilled mint juleps. I take two from the waiter and hand one to K. Burke.

"As a good guest and adventurer you must try the local drink," I say.

Reluctantly she says, "Okay." We both hold our drinks in the air.

"To Garçon and his owners," I say.

"To you, Moncrief, with a big thank you for this trip," Burke says.

"My pleasure, partner," I say. We clink. We sip. She speaks.

"Hmmm. I think I may have been wrong about bourbon and mint leaves. I could easily get used to this concoction," she says.

I frown and say, "Not me. A white Bordeaux will always be my drink."

"Over there," Burke says, pointing to a nearby waiter with a tray of good-looking hors d'oeuvres. Then she adds, "What do you think those things are?"

"Hush puppies with country ham," I say.

"I didn't know you were such an expert on Kentucky food," Burke says. "You're just full of surprises, Moncrief."

We are poised to grab a few bites from the hors d'oeuvres tray when the orchestra suddenly lets go with a musical fanfare. A commotion seems to be taking place in the area where the Savatiers are being interviewed and photographed. Always on the job, Burke shoots me a look and heads toward our friends.

As we push our way through the crowd, a spotlight hits the older couple. A gigantic arrangement of red roses is being carried in. It's even larger than the garland of roses that was draped on Garçon. The floral arrangement is so large that it takes four men to carry it. They place it in front of the Savatiers. Marguerite and Nicolas's heads disappear behind the huge red rose arrangement.

One of the unidentified four men holds a mic. It clicks on with a screeching noise.

"Five hundred American Beauty roses for one wonderful French woman," he says. His accent is tough, New York–ish.

Both Savatiers seem confused. The two Derby officials with the Savatiers also seem confused. The four men walk away quickly.

"Was that some official part of the winner's ceremony?" Burke asks.

I shrug my shoulders. "So much of what you Americans do is a little bit crazy. Let's go find the waiter with the hors d'oeuvres."

In the next hour Burke and I set some kind of record for "Most Hors d'Oeuvres and Canapés Consumed at Churchill Downs." We set a similar record for "Most Mint Juleps Consumed at Churchill Downs."

We are drunk enough to have trouble forming words

when we kiss the Savatiers farewell. Our thanks are heartfelt and garbled. Fortunately, the Savatiers' chauffeur drives us to the airport. Moments later we are aloft. On our way back to New York. On our way back to the murders of the three beautiful young women.

I try to do some mental theorizing about the case. But I am tired, and my brain is muddled, and K. Burke's head is resting on my shoulder.

CHAPTER 6

KATHERINE MARY BURKE UNLOCKS
the three dead bolts that will allow her to enter her
apartment. After the door is finally opened, she surveys
the one-room apartment on East 90th Street where she
has lived for the past five years.

All those keys and locks to keep this little place safe.
Is this cramped little studio even worth protecting? she
thinks. The dark-green sofa, dotted with stains. It's the
sofa that her cousin Maddy was going to throw out.
The two needlepoint pillows that a friend made. The
first one says, THERE'S NO PLACE LIKE HOME. The second
one says, YOU CALL THIS PLACE HOME?

When she first rented the apartment it seemed
spacious and bright. That was before she set up the
fake-pine IKEA coffee table with the wobbly fourth leg.
That's before she made the decision to keep the Murphy
bed permanently opened and unmade. That's before
the club chair from the Salvation Army became the *de
facto* storage unit for her pile of shirts, jeans, slacks, and
tights, plus an occasional shoe, boot, or sneaker.

310 JAMES PATTERSON

Yet Burke came to love the place. It was simple. It was sweet. Most of all, it was hers. Okay, her best friend Moncrief may live in a loft big enough to host a basketball game, but life has a way of evening out sorrow and joy. She would never trade her simple life for Luc's wealthy world, a world scarred by death and tragedy. Sometimes she wonders how he gets through the day without crying.

And what the hell, right now Burke is feeling rich, too. The $4,000 she won on Garçon is the biggest single amount she has had since…since…well, since ever. She could pay her Time Warner Cable bill, she could buy a really cool first communion gift for her niece Emma Rose, she could bank some of it so that when Christmas came she could buy Moncrief something a bit fancier than a fake Cross pen and pencil set (which he does, however, keep on his desk and actually use).

Burke drops her luggage on the floor. Then she plugs in her laptop and her smartphone for recharging.

She unpins her hair and removes her bright silk belt. The juleps are catching up with her.

One last look at her email. It has been a few hours since she checked it. There might be important info on the three murder cases that she and Moncrief are jumping on top of tomorrow.

Nothing urgent. Some new files about the victims' cell phones, no important DNA material from any of the crime scenes, a few useless pieces from the gossip sites TMZ and Dlisted about the alleged affair between Tessa Fulbright's husband and a twenty-year-old Yankees farm-team player. Hmm. He's in the closet? Interesting but probably irrelevant.

Finally, there is an email from Mike Delaney. Mike is part-owner and weekend bartender at a place called, what else? Delaney's. Mike isn't the sharpest guy Burke has ever met, but…Mike is sort of like her apartment. Mike is simple. He's sweet. And she knows she could have him for the asking.

She falls backward on the bed. Her head hurts. Her feet hurt. But she is full of happy memories of the Derby, the roses, the party, the juleps…and a friend like Moncrief.

Friend. The word "friend" seems to stick uneasily in her mind. What do you call a male friend who's rich and handsome and funny, and when you accidentally-on-purpose fall asleep on his shoulder you feel warm and comfortable?

I guess you just call it…a Moncrief, she thinks.

Then she falls asleep.

CHAPTER 7

"**ALL RIGHT, I HAVE** it entirely figured out," I say as K. Burke, wearing I've-got-a-hangover sunglasses, walks into the precinct.

"Can it wait five minutes until I put a little coffee in my engine?"

"K. Burke, it is ten o'clock Sunday morning. We agreed to meet at nine a.m.? I assume you were not at church," I say.

"Moncrief, already you're making me crazy, so I'm going to give you my mother's two favorite words of warning," Burke says. "Two simple words."

"Please, nothing obscene," I say.

"Obscene? My mother? No way. Here are the two words." Then she shouts: *"Don't start!"*

I am stunned for a moment, but just for a moment.

"But why would I not *start*?" I ask. Then I launch into my analysis.

"There was no cause of death determined in the postmortem on the first two victims, but you have no doubt read the autopsy report from the medical examiner concerning Ms. Tessa Fulbright, the dead woman in Bergdorf?"

"No, I have not, but I'm sure you'll tell me what I need to know," says Burke.

"With pleasure. As we noted, there was no physical abuse, no bruising, no fractures. Beyond that there were no unusual substances in her blood…"

"Unusual? You mean like poison?" Burke says.

"Correct. Unless, like me, you consider a small amount of instant oatmeal and trace amounts of pomegranate juice to be poison."

"That's it?" Burke asks. I can tell by the wrinkled forehead and the speed with which she gulps her coffee that she's listening hard.

"Yes, that's it for the examination, but that's not the end of the information I have found. I called Tessa Fulbright's pharmacy this morning and received some interesting information."

"How'd you know what drugstore to call? From her husband?"

"No. But I figured it out easily. We knew she bought her wardrobe at Bergdorf's. So I correctly assumed that she bought her medicines at C.O. Bigelow, the most glamorous pharmacy in Manhattan. Tessa Fulbright did not seem like the kind of woman who would wait on line at Duane Reade."

"So what did you find out?"

"Not much. Not really much at all. She was due for a refill on Nembutal, which as you know is…"

It's K. Burke's turn to show off a bit.

"It's a pretty popular antidepressant, a pentobarbital pill-pop. You'd have to swallow an awful lot to kill yourself. Marilyn Monroe left town on it. Anyway, if it wasn't showing up in Fulbright's autopsy, I'd rule it out."

"*Moi aussi.* Me too, but, I am sad to report that the only other thing the postmortem examination showed in her blood was a high amount of sugar and a certain amount of a medication named…"

Here I pause and refer to my iPad for the name. "Dulcolax. It is a stool softener."

"I know what Dulcolax is," she says.

"Ah, so the hardened stool is a problem that you suffer from, K. Burke?"

"I'm not going to say it again, Moncrief. *Don't start!*"

CHAPTER 8

I AM, OF COURSE, laughing at my little joke. And I believe that she, too, is suppressing a smile.

"Okay," I say, almost ready to rub my hands together with enthusiasm, "Now for the big insight. Turn on your computer. I have something more to show you. Something important."

Burke quickly boots up the desktop and enters a code. She turns away from the beeping computer sounds as if they are making her head hurt.

"Okay, the computer's ready. I'm ready. What's up?" she says.

"Here's what's up!" I say, and in my enthusiasm begin very quickly calling up some pages on the screen.

"Alors!" I shout. "Look at this."

She studies the screen for a few moments and then eyes me suspiciously.

"It's photographs of the three dead women," Burke says. She gives a short shrug. "So what? We have photos of…lemme see if I remember right…this is the redhead from Bergdorf, Tessa Fulbright. This one is the blonde who died in the restaurant. The 21 Club."

I interrupt. "No, *not* 21 Club, *but* there is a number in the restaurant name—Eleven Madison Park."

"Her name is Jenna Lee Austin. She's the actress. The understudy. Married to the hedge funder."

"*C'est magnifique*. Now. The final *Jeopardy!* answer is…?"

Katherine Burke does not hesitate. She taps the screen photo of the third victim.

"Mara Monahan. Shoe department, Saks Fifth Avenue."

"You go home with a million dollars!" I yell.

"Great," she says. "I'll just add it to the four thousand bucks from yesterday."

"And now I will show you something else," I say.

I quickly tap a few keys on Burke's computer. "See?"

Under the photo of each dead woman appears a photo of a different man. Beneath Tessa's photo is a strapping young blond lifeguard type. Under Mara's is one of those nerdy-handsome guys, the black eyeglass frames, the slightly startled smile. Under Jenna's photo is the "older gentleman," who looks amazingly like the former French Minister of Agriculture (but is not).

"Who are these guys? Their husbands?" K. Burke asks.

"A good guess," I say. "*Mais non.*"

"Do I get a second chance?" she asks.

And then she knows.

"They're the boyfriends, aren't they?"

"Precisely," I say.

"How'd you figure it out, Moncrief? Instinct?"

"No, no, K. Burke. Not at all."

"Then how'd you find them?"

"On Facebook, of course."

CHAPTER 9

WHEN KATHERINE BURKE AND I go to work we really go to work.

On the sixth floor of Saks Fifth Avenue, where a simple pair of Louboutin heels can cost more than the monthly rent on a Sutton Place one-bedroom, we ignore the exquisite merchandise (and I ignore the smooth, sexy curves of the customers' legs).

"If you could just take us through the movements that Mrs. Monahan made as you remember them," Burke says to Cory Lawrence, the department manager. Young Cory looks as if he'd be right at home on a prep school tennis team or a Southampton polo club.

"Well, as I understand it from the store representative helping her…"

Burke interrupts, "That store representative is the same thing as a *salesman?*"

"That's right," Cory Lawrence says. He is not unpleasant, but his voice does have a touch of *you're obviously unfamiliar with the ways of fancy stores.*

"Okay, if you could walk us through it," I say.

Cory Lawrence speaks softly. He says that he would like to do this as quietly and unobtrusively as possible, so as not to annoy the "clients." "Clients" is apparently the new word for "customers."

"Okay, Mrs. Monahan tried on some shoes, made her choices, and then she slipped back into her Tory Burch sandals. I escorted her to the sales counter. Because she's a frequent, valued customer she has access to our exclusive app, available only to customers who spend a hundred thousand a year with us, where she can just pay with a tap of her phone. And that was it."

"Did she say anything? Did you have any sense that she wasn't feeling well?" Burke asks.

"No, not at all. She said something when the phones tapped, like 'Oh, this is like a little kiss.' Then I noticed that she stopped smiling. I was about to ask whether she wanted the shoes sent to her home, and...*bam*...she just sort of collapsed to the ground."

"What did you do then?" Burke asks.

"What did I do? I thought she had fainted. I touched her face gently. Her eyes were adrift. And then a young man—in a black Ferragamo suit, I couldn't help but notice—rushed over and began calling her name. Then there was store security, and we called 911. But then the EMT said...that she was...she was dead."

"Anything else?" I ask.

"Well, the police came with the ambulance, and then some important police boss arrived. His name was Elliott something, I think. And then they took Mrs. Monahan away."

"What about the young man in the black suit?" Burke asks.

"I guess that he left with them. I assumed he was Mrs. Monahan's assistant or her driver," says Cory Lawrence.

"Did you really *assume* that?" I ask with a tiny smirk.

"I always assume that," says Cory Lawrence.

"You are a wise young man, Mr. Lawrence. In a decade or so you will be running this store."

"Thank you, sir."

"But for the time being...Don't look now, but I would discreetly direct your eyes to the woman seated approximately ten yards to your left. She is wearing white slacks and a black silk shirt. You will notice that she has slipped on a brand new pair of Isabel Marant ankle boots, replacing them in the box with her scuffed and worn-out Blahnik pumps. *Merci et au revoir, Monsieur Lawrence*."

CHAPTER 10

AN HOUR LATER DETECTIVE Burke and I walk into the art deco splendor of Eleven Madison Park.

"My God," says Burke. "I feel like I'm in an old black-and-white musical."

Suddenly, Marcella, the tall, thin, copper-haired beauty from the front desk, walks quickly toward me with her arms extended. Her smile is huge.

"Oh, here we go," says Burke.

She and I embrace.

"Luc, you're back. It's been at least a month," she says, shaking her hair. "Let me check on your table," she adds. "Have a flute of champagne while you're waiting. It's on the house, of course."

"*Merci,*" I say.

As the lovely Marcella walks away, Burke says, "*Merci,* my foot! What's going on, Moncrief? She's checking a table? We're on the job."

"But if the job takes place in one of New York's

finest restaurants, it would actually be foolish not to partake of lunch."

"No. It would actually be foolish if we *were* to partake of lunch. About as unprofessional as you can get."

"Oh, K. Burke. You know I can always be much more unprofessional than this."

Needless to say, Burke does not laugh. She also refuses to join me in a glass of champagne. So we stand and wait in angry silence.

A few minutes later we are seated at a corner table.

"I'm not going to eat," says Burke.

"Didn't we have this identical conversation just last week?" I ask. As soon as I finish asking that question, a handsome fifty-ish man with close-cropped gray hair approaches the table.

"Mr. Moncrief, a pleasure, as always."

"This is my colleague, Detective Burke," I say. "This is the restaurant's manager, Paul deBarros."

As K. Burke gives a quick cold nod, deBarros pulls out a chair from the table and sits down.

Burke looks surprised, until I explain that deBarros witnessed the death of Jenna Lee Austin.

"Mrs. Austin was here at least once a week for lunch, and often for dinner," says the manager.

Burke and I follow the training rule: when the witness starts talking, do not interrupt. Let him get going. Sit back and listen.

"Sometimes Mrs. Austin dined with her husband. Sometimes she was with her mother. But the unfortunate day she died, she was dining alone. She told the front desk—Marcella was on that day—that perhaps she would be joined for coffee. She was not sure."

DeBarros takes a deep breath and shrugs his shoulders.

"Honestly, there's not much more to say. I welcomed

her. I asked after her health. I asked after Mr. Austin. She was, as always, very bubbly and happy. I asked if she'd like something to drink before she ordered. She said she'd like a glass of San Pellegrino. A minute later, when I delivered it, she looked up at me. Then her head crashed onto the table."

"Who else saw this happen?" Burke asks.

"I'm not sure anyone else saw Mrs. Austin pass out. But when her head hit the table I shouted for help. So, of course, other diners looked, but it was early in the luncheon service, only a bit before noon. So there were not that many people here."

DeBarros describes how Jenna Austin was unresponsive to anything, although he admits that he did not follow the 911 operator's explicit instructions not to move her.

"I did not want to cause a disturbance for the other diners. So we carried Mrs. Austin to the passageway between the kitchen and the dining room. I'm certain she did not want people to see her in that condition."

"In *that* condition?" I ask. "Did you think she was drunk?"

"Oh, but of course not," he says. "I did not think she would want to be seen unconscious."

"Anything else, Detective?" I ask Burke. "The police? The ambulance?"

"Yes, all that. They gave her oxygen, I think, but the EMT said she was dead. I think they took her to Beth Israel hospital."

"Actually, it was NYU," Burke says.

"Thank you, Paul," I say. Burke thanks him also.

The captain rises from his seat. He gently pushes the chair back into place.

"Now, to travel from something tragic to something peaceful…if indeed you have no further questions…"

I have no further questions. The pattern is emerging, and that pattern is simple: no clue from any eyewitnesses. We will have to make sense of the boyfriend angle.

I ask K. Burke if she wants to ask anything. She shakes her head.

"In that case, Miss Burke, Mr. Moncrief, I have ordered a simple but interesting luncheon. To start with, a refreshing lobster ceviche with watermelon and lime ice. Then, if you agree, a Muscovy duck breast with lavender honey."

"Sounds wonderful," I say.

"Just coffee for me," says Burke.

"Bring Detective Burke the lobster ceviche. She may change her mind."

As soon as deBarros leaves, Burke hisses at me, "No. I told you I'm not doing this. I'm not eating. This is outrageous."

A few minutes later, after I've selected a Hugel Riesling as our wine, the lobster ceviche appears.

It is my pleasure to inform you that K. Burke ate every bit of it.

CHAPTER 11

ABOUT FIVE SECONDS AFTER Dalia died, I was certain of only one thing—that life was truly not worth living.

Yet everything else around me remained the same. People clogged the subways at rush hour. The *Mona Lisa* still smiled at the Louvre. Washington still crossed the Delaware at the Met. I was rich enough and skinny enough to wear the idiotic Milan fashion show suits, but I could bring myself to wear only Levi's and black T-shirts. People made love. People made war. I did neither.

Although I did not eat much, I made dinner reservations. I scheduled sessions with my personal trainer. And when my impeccably restored '65 Mustang needed work, I drove it to the mechanic in Yonkers who loved the car like a man loves his child.

I did go back to work, and that—along with my friendship with K. Burke—kept me from leaping from the rooftops.

I did make one big change, however. I never

returned to the apartment I had shared with Dalia. I could not go back.

I lived briefly at the St. Regis Hotel. It was pleasant, and midtown Manhattan was certainly convenient. Hotel services made life easy—clean, crisp sheets every day, 4 a.m. room service deliveries of Caesar salads and Opus One wine. But after K. Burke persisted in jokingly calling me a "rich vagabond," I did as she suggested. I purchased a new apartment. A temple of simple luxury—cement flooring, spacious uncluttered walls, an occasional piece of iron or copper or steel furniture.

I return here this evening. After a day of investigation at Saks and Eleven Madison Park, I should be invigorated. Case work is my joy in life. Instead, the inevitable gloom of loneliness passes over me. I knew if I returned to our old apartment, I would never stop expecting to hear Dalia's voice from another room, to see her coat and scarf and pocketbook on the hallway chair, to hear her sound system blasting Selena Gomez. I wish. I wish I could hear her playing that obnoxious music again. I wish I could yell, "Turn off that crap!" I wish.

I do what I always do when I first arrive home from work, whether it is early in the evening or five in the morning. I take a shower—piercingly hot, Kiehl's coriander body wash, rinse with icy cold water. I step into sweat shorts and walk into the kitchen.

Lunch at Eleven Madison Park with K. Burke was delicious (and yes, I admit that we shared the orange chocolate bonbon for dessert), but it was a long time ago, so now I crack three eggs into a bowl. I whisk with a fork. Then I move to the eight-burner Wolf oven. (No, I did not forget the salt; Dalia was trying to make me cut down.) I melt a big knob of (unsalted) butter until it bubbles from the heat. I am about to pour the mixture into a pan when an echo-like disembodied voice fills the air. I know it well. The phone message machine is programmed to speak to me twenty minutes after I turn off the entrance door security alarm.

"You have two new messages," announces the small silver box on the kitchen island. Two? I seldom share my landline phone number, so there are usually *no* messages. Tonight there are *two*.

The first message promises to be a long, boring, and complicated piece of information from one of my late father's accountants. Something to do with German bonds and electronic stock certificates. I know that the accountant will call back. I move to the silver box and click Next.

The second message is a potentially important one.

"Mon cher enfant." My dear boy…with those three words I recognize the voice of Nicolas Savatier. He continues in French: "We have just arrived in Baltimore…preparing for the Preakness Stakes.…It would be most helpful if you could get in touch with us soon, very soon. We are heading to the Four Seasons on the harbor, where we are staying, but we always have our cell phones at hand. Please, if you would call soon."

In the background I hear Marguerite Savatier speaking loudly, *"Immédiatement."*

Then, from Nicolas, another *"immédiatement"* followed by a soft and courteous *"Merci."*

I return the call *immédiatement*.

CHAPTER 12

"MON CHER LUC, WE did not want to alarm you," says Nicolas, ever the perfect French gentleman.

"Give me the phone, Nicolas," I hear Marguerite say, in French. Then I hear her voice clearly on the phone.

"Luc. It is you?"

"Mais oui," I say. "What is the problem?"

We both switch to French.

"We are not quite certain that it is an actual problem. And, of course, we do not want to alarm you…"

"Or trouble you," comes the voice of Nicolas, now relegated to the background.

"Please," I almost shout. "You are *not* alarming me. You are *not* troubling me. What is the matter? Speak, please, speak."

Marguerite continues.

"Perhaps it is not worth getting excited about," she says.

I am thinking that if they were with me in person I would wring their aristocratic necks, or at least toss a glass of Veuve Clicquot in their faces. Finally, Marguerite speaks. Her voice is trembling:

"I have received two dozen red roses," Marguerite says. "A deliveryman was waiting with them when we landed in Baltimore."

I, of course, instinctively know that there is more to this phone call, that not everything has been revealed. Even a slightly dotty elderly couple would not become frightened by a box of flowers. However, I proceed as if all will turn out normally.

"How delightful. Who sent the roses?" I ask.

"We do not know," Marguerite says. "It is anonymous. And *c'est ça le problème.*"

Suddenly, Nicolas's voice is on the phone.

"You see, the greater problem is that, yes, it is unsigned, *but* there *is* a note with the roses. Let me read it to you."

Nicolas's frail voice becomes strong: "'Win the Preakness. Or you will suffer the consequences.'"

I keep my own voice calm, but this is surely not the sort of note anyone wishes to receive.

"Did you try contacting the florist?" I ask. (Yes, I know, a foolish and obvious question.)

"*Encore une fois, mon cher Luc.* We may be old but we are not stupid," says Nicolas. "There was no name on the card or on the box. We signed for them without thinking, figuring it was just more congratulatory flowers. It wasn't until we were in the cab that we even thought to look at the card. It is so mysterious."

I am thinking that it is not just mysterious, but it is so creepy, really creepy. Is it a threat? A joke? A mistake?

To put the Savatiers at ease I say something that I don't fully believe. "This is nothing to be alarmed about."

Then I quickly add, "Listen. The Preakness is next Saturday. I've got work to do up here. But if you need me, I'll drop everything and join you. Okay?"

"Okay," says Nicolas.

In the background, just before I hang up, I hear Marguerite's voice in a loud stage whisper: "Tell him to come down now."

Click.

The butter for the eggs is now burnt to a foul brown grease, and the smoke detector is screaming at me. So my dinner becomes a bowl of Special K and two large glasses of Bouchard Montrachet.

I don't sleep. Not a wink. My bedtime companion is the relentless stream of grim BBC detective shows and one more glass of the soft chardonnay. Between the ending of *Wallander* and the start of *Vera* comes dawn.

CHAPTER 13

Mara Monahan
2 East 79th Street

TODAY BURKE AND I visit the Manhattan apartments of the three beautiful murder victims. Burke has made some interesting connections in the three cases: Each one of the murdered women was, of course, beautiful and wealthy. But there's something more. Each of them had an only child below the age of three. All these rich women, of course, also had household help—maids, drivers, housemen, housekeepers, cooks, nannies. It's the nannies who interest Burke and me. In reading the reports, Burke noticed that all three of the nannies were placed by the same employment agency in London. Funny. In detective work you have to be very careful of coincidences, and then again, you can't be *too* careful.

An attractive, excessively energetic young woman with a demure hairstyle opens the door of the Monahan apartment.

The young woman wants to appear properly somber, but she cannot hide the sometimes chronic American characteristic of perkiness.

"I'm Congressman Monahan's District Assistant, Chloe Garrison," she says. "Please come in." We walk into a big foyer with traditional Upper East Side black-and-white tiled marble floors.

"The congressman wanted to be here himself to speak with you," she says, then quickly adds, "But he was on the first flight down to DC today. There's an environmental waste bill in debate…and…well, he thought it would be most helpful if he got back to work." We agree again.

"NYPD has already spoken to Mr. Monahan," Burke says. "He's been very cooperative…especially given the painfulness of the situation."

Chloe nods. "Congressman Monahan is taking Henry, their little boy, out to Montauk this weekend. Like you said, the whole death thing is pretty…tough."

"No doubt about it," Burke says.

The assistant grants our request to speak to Henry's nanny, Mrs. Meade-Grafton. "If it's all right, you'll meet in Congressman Monahan's home office."

The home office has a spectacular view of Central Park, and Mrs. Meade-Grafton does not remotely look like what I thought a British nanny named "Mrs. Meade-Grafton" would. She is wearing stretch jeans that cling quite snuggly to her ample hips and thighs. She sits on a black leather sofa, and her legs are tucked beneath her. Her white T-shirt has these words printed on the front:

I LISTEN TO BANDS THAT DON'T
EXIST YET.

We introduce ourselves. Mrs. Meade-Grafton does not stand to greet us, but she does extend her very fleshy hand. The congressional aide leaves the room.

"Is young Henry around?" Burke asks.

"Oh, the little one is watchin' telly. Cook's keepin' an eye on 'im," the nanny says. English is definitely *my* second language, but you don't have to be 'enry 'iggins to know that it is a fairly lower-class accent.

I ask how she and the late Mrs. Monahan got along.

"Like two peas," she says. "An' why not? We didn't see very much of one 'nother. I was with little 'enry when she wasn't. And when she was seein' to the little lad then myself mostly wasn't there. But Mrs. M was a decent enough sort. Quite a loss, o' course. Not sure the 'usband 'as took it all in yet. An' to be honest, little 'enry might be thinkin' his mum's still just out shoppin'."

She laughs. A lot.

CHAPTER 14

Jenna Lee Austin
156 Perry Street

JULIA HIGHRIDGE PREFERS TO be called *Miss* Highridge, *and* she prefers to be called a governess, not a nanny. Wardrobe? A dark plaid tweed suit, sensible shoes, hair in a bun. Miss Highridge is probably forty years old, but with her grooming and wardrobe she could pass for fifty. She is as formal as Mrs. Meade-Grafton was informal.

We sit in the first floor Victorian parlor of an impeccably decorated Greenwich Village town house. We are only a block from the West Side Highway, the Hudson River just on the other side of that.

"So, you look after Ethan?" Burke asks.

"That would be *Master* Ethan. And yes, Master Ethan is my charge."

Then she gestures to a small table. On the table is a silver tray covered with a silver teapot, teacups, a large plate of cookies, and various pastries.

"I thought you might need some tea. I've also had the cook bring in some puddings and cakes. You may not be familiar with all of them, these especially..."

"I am happy to tell you that I am completely familiar with these. They are *canelés,* and I have not seen them ever before here in New York," I say. *"Je les adore."* I adore them. "They are my favorite."

I am not merely being a polite guest. I am telling the truth about the crunchy little dome-like butter pastries that are in every patisserie in Paris. I've not found any that taste as good as they do there.

"Ah," Miss Highridge says. "An authentic Frenchman. Perhaps you would like to conduct the interview in French. I'm fluent."

"No," I say. "I think English is the more appropriate language for an NYPD investigation. Plus, my colleague might not…"

Burke interrupts. She is not at all amused. "Have a canelé, Detective Moncrief. And let's get on with it."

Miss Highridge goes on to tell us that she was enormously fond of Mrs. Lenz—"That would be *Mrs.* Austin to you."

Burke, losing none of her edge, says, "We know her husband is Bernard Lenz. He's been interviewed twice already."

We ask for her opinion of Jenna Lee Austin.

Her answer: "She was an actress. That should tell you everything." Then she proceeds to pop a third canelé into her mouth.

"That really does *not* tell us very much, Miss Highridge," I say.

"Then let me explain. She knew how to *act* like a mother. Just as she knew how to *act* like a good wife. But…please, have another cake…"

Both Burke and I decline.

"In any event, I suppose she wanted to be a good mother. But her career came first. She cared so very much about her career. The lessons, and the private trainer and the yoga instructor and the homeopathic doctor and the nutritionist and…oh, so many people to help her. But Mr. Lenz didn't seem to mind."

Miss Highridge pauses, pops another pastry, then speaks: "Her husband had *his* life. She had *hers*. And Master Ethan had *me*."

We talk some more. Miss Highridge says that Jenna Lee seemed to have a lot of friends.

"How about her marriage?"

"The marriage was what most marriages are. A series of small compromises."

When we are ready to leave, she agrees to get in touch if she thinks of anything helpful. But, she tells us, "That seems unlikely."

Then she says, "Let me have these extra canelés wrapped for you. You can take them with you."

"*Non merci, mademoiselle.* You enjoy them."

"Oh, dear. It's the last thing I need," she says. She pats her significantly round belly, and we escape without the little cakes.

CHAPTER 15

Tessa Fulbright
River House, 435 East 52nd Street

MAZIE McCRAY LOVED TESSA Fulbright. My instincts tell me that immediately.

"First I raised her mother, Mrs. Pierce. Then I raised Tessa … I mean, of course, Mrs. Fulbright. And now my last job will be raising Andrew. But I never expected not having his mother by my side while doing it."

Mazie dabs at her eyes with a crumbled tissue. Mazie is Black and round and perfectly charming. Mazie, Burke, and I are sitting on low, children-sized benches in Andrew's bright-yellow nursery. Andrew toddles around, chubby arms extended. He falls. He giggles. He laughs. He gets up and walks some more.

Suddenly Mazie stands up and walks quickly to Andrew. Mazie lifts the child. He rests in Mazie's arms, and Mazie uses her free hands to cover the boy's ears.

"Tessa, Andrew's mother, was fine, absolutely fine, a wonderful child, a wonderful woman. Then she married Mr. Fulbright. Then she started in with 'I'm not pretty enough. I'm not young enough.'" Mazie shakes her head thoughtfully, and then fixes her eyes on Burke and me.

"You two saw her," she says. "You must've seen photos. She was beautiful. The most beautiful woman. Even more important, she was a *good* woman. I knew her. I raised her. I knew her better than anyone."

A long pause. Then K. Burke speaks softly.

"What do you think happened?"

Mazie places Andrew back on the floor. The little boy returns to his giddy, happy walking. Mazie takes a deep breath, shakes her head, and speaks.

"I wish I knew. Dear Lord, I just wish I knew."

CHAPTER 16

I SLEEP WELL. BUT don't assume that sleep comes to me easily. No, not at all. My sleep is a chemical and musical trick. It requires 10mg of Ambien, followed a half hour later by 5mg of Xanax, and then I queue up the Luc Moncrief Artist of the Week on the sound system. This can be anything from Chopin to the Rolling Stones. This week, I'm sleeping with the little-known Vienna Teng. Her music is just slow enough to lullaby me a bit, just fast enough to let me know I'm still breathing.

Sleep arrives suddenly. And just as suddenly I am awake. The telephone is ringing. It is morning. The big bedroom is filled with soft morning light.

I grab the receiver.

"Yes, what is it?"

"Luc? It is so early," comes the old woman's voice. I recognize it immediately.

"Marguerite, what's wrong?" I say.

My neck hurts. My lips are dry. An Ambien-induced sleep brings sleep, but it rarely brings peace.

"Many things. I'll put Nicolas on."

"The news is bad," he says.

I can only imagine. And I want to know everything right this moment. I do not want the Savatiers to begin dithering.

"Stop! Do not tell me anything except what the goddamn problem is," I say. I have purposely chosen the curse word to demonstrate my seriousness.

"It is a murder!" the old man shouts back at me.

"A murder. A murder of whom? Tell me. Keep talking."

I don't understand what he's saying at first…then I deduce a horse has been killed.

"Which horse?" I ask. Nicolas says something I don't understand in half-French, half-English.

"Say it again, sir. Say the horse's name again." I hear something like "Charlene Bay."

"Charlene Bay?" I ask, just one impatient step away from a shout.

"No. Not Charlene," he says.

"A bay? The horse is a bay?"

"Luc. You are not listening properly," Nicolas says.

I restrain myself from becoming angry at the anxious old man.

"Speak slower…slower and louder," I say.

He says the name again. Slower and louder.

This time I get it. "Charlie-Boy? The horse's name is Charlie-Boy?" I ask.

"Ah, oui. Son nom est Shar-lee-Boy. Charlie-Boy."

He continues.

"The security people say they heard a noise. They go into the stable, and there he lay. His throat was sliced, they think, with the electrical saw, the machine a man uses to cut down a tree. It made me sick. Marguerite wept."

My response is "Holy shit!"

Nicolas has yet more information.

"Charlie-Boy was the Pimlico exercise horse. The warm-ups. As you know, the warm-ups are so important."

I remember. Only a few days ago Nicolas described the important job of the warm-up horse to K. Burke and me. But the lesson here, in the most graphic terms possible, was: Do as I say, or Garçon is next.

As I am recalling that excellent lesson, Nicolas passes the phone to his wife.

"What should we do?" says Marguerite.

I am, of course, thinking of the note the Savatiers received. *Win the Preakness. Or you will suffer the consequences.*

There is just one thing to do. I tell them what they want to hear.

"I have to come down there immediately," I say.

She conveys this news to Nicolas. I can hear him talking loudly in the background.

"No, Luc. We do not want to be a bother. We only…"

"*Au revoir, mes amis.* I'll see you both soon."

"But Luc…" I hear Marguerite, and I am forced to be an American.

"Gotta go, guys." Click.

CHAPTER 17

WE WALK TOWARD STABLE A-2 at Pimlico Race Course.

It is almost noon on Wednesday. The sky is clear. The temperature is seventy-six degrees.

"I wish we could bottle this weather and save it for next Saturday's race," says Detective Kwame Clarke of the Baltimore Police Department.

I am walking with Detective Clarke, Marguerite and Nicolas Savatier, two Pimlico officials, and Nina Helstein. Miss Helstein is an investigating officer from TOBA, the Thoroughbred Owners and Breeders Association. They have kept the scene intact for us.

We walk, almost like people in a funeral procession, into the stable.

We stare down at the lifeless body of Charlie-Boy.

My father raised horses at his home in Avignon, but they never particularly interested me (especially since Avignon was only a two-hour drive to the beaches of Nice, with their beautiful waters and topless women).

Perhaps because I have spent so little time with horses,

whenever I see these animals I am always surprised that
they are so big.

This dead horse, Charlie-Boy, looks…well…
gigantic. A huge dead pile of tremendous muscles, a
heap of giant thighs and legs and torso. Yards of white
linen bandages are tied tightly around Charlie-Boy's
massive neck. The bandages are splotched with red
blood. Bloody hay is scattered around the horse's neck
and head. The straw is also caked with blood.

Marguerite looks down at the floor. Nicolas looks
up toward the wooden rafters. After what feels like an
appropriate amount of time, Detective Clarke speaks
quietly to me.

"There's a trainers' lounge in Stable A-4. I'll wait
for you there. Say, in about ten minutes."

I nod yes, and then I walk with the Savatiers to
another stable, the stable where Garçon is being kept.
Both Marguerite and Nicolas break into sobs when
they see their horse. Armand Joscoe, Garçon's jockey,
smiles gently. Joscoe and a tall young man are method-
ically stroking Garçon's neck and back.

"Ah, Monsieur Moncrief," says Armand. *"Une véri-
table tragédie."*

The young man with Joscoe addresses me: *"Bonjour,
Monsieur Moncrief."*

I have no idea who this teenager is. Then Armand
Joscoe tells me in French that "Perhaps you remember
Léon, my little boy. He is all grown up."

"He certainly is," I say. I am amazed Léon has
become a veritable six-footer. He is quite handsome,
freshly showered, and I can't help but notice that he
is impeccably dressed. I also can't help but notice how
expensive his clothing is. He looks more like one of the
well-heeled spectators than his hardworking father.

The Joscoe men and I· all smile at the different

heights of father and son, but our smiles do not come from the heart. It is impossible. The stable is too filled with sadness and fear.

Here, the second step on the way to the Triple Crown, a wonderful horse with wonderful owners, an occasion that should be so festive. Now it is all so terribly grim.

A few minutes later I walk into a room attached to Stable A-4. The room is small, with two worn leather sofas, a stack of dirty, smelly jodhpurs in one corner, a soda machine in another corner.

Detective Clarke smiles when I enter.

"You were probably expecting something a bit fancier for Pimlico," he says.

"I never expect anything," I say. "That way I'm never disappointed."

"That's a perfect New York philosophy," says Clarke.

"It is also a French philosophy, I think."

Clarke is a small man, Black, and completely bald. He also wears a suit (I can't help myself from comment here) whose cut and quality seem quite elegant for what I know a detective's pay level to be, especially in Kentucky. In any event, he is smart, and he is extremely likable.

"Your friends have filled me in," he says. "And Miss Helstein is talking to yet more of the track officials."

"The Savatiers are terribly frightened," I say.

"With good cause," he says.

He hands me a neatly folded letter-sized piece of paper. I open it and see that it is a copy of the threatening note that was sent to the Savatiers.

Win the Preakness. Or you will suffer the consequences.

"What do you think?" I ask.

"I think that it is very much what it appears to be—a scary, gruesome, inscrutable threat. I really wish you or the Savatiers had contacted me earlier…"

"They only told me about it yesterday."

"Doesn't matter. Anyway, I sent the original note to the lab. Frankly, I don't think they'll come up with anything. Prints and stuff like that only happen on TV. All we can do is keep watching Pimlico, up and down, east to west."

"Any other suggestions?" I say.

"Well, I would strongly suggest they try to persuade their horse to win the race on Saturday."

"I wish I had thought of that," I say.

Kwame Clarke laughs. We both give very weak smiles. Then Clarke says, "My instincts tell me that the horse-murder and the threatening note are *not* connected. I've got absolutely no proof. But I just feel that if there was a connection we'd see it. The whole thing is just a little too baroque, bizarre. You know what I mean?"

Another detective with *instinct*. I knew I liked this guy.

"My instinct's the same as yours," I say. Then I add, "Two cops with the same unsubstantiated idea. We must be wrong, huh?"

We're in no mood to laugh. I speak.

"Look, my friends are scared. And I don't blame them."

"I don't, either. We've put three plainclothes people—two men, one woman—around the stables. We've got three other detectives checking everyone and everything coming in—florists, caterers, workers, setup people, tent people."

"How about you assign some protection for my friends?"

"Detective, I don't know about the NYPD, but here in Baltimore there's always a shortage in manpower. I can't loosen one or two people for a civilian guard."

"Let me ask this. Do you have anyone who's looking for some freelance work on their days off?"

"Plenty of those, but like I just said, there's no budget for it."

"Do me a favor, if you don't mind. Get three people to follow the Savatiers. I'll feel a whole lot better. And I'll come up with the cash. I'm going to be back down here next Friday night for the race on Saturday. I'll give you cash to pay your guys."

Clarke does a goofy over-the-top double-take.

"Way to go, New York!" he shouts.

Kwame Clarke throws his right hand up into the air. *Shit.* I must try to execute a high-five, always a disaster for me. We complete the gesture clumsily (on my end, at least), and almost immediately my cell phone rings.

Of course, I know who it is, and I know what the greeting will be. I click on the phone.

"Where the hell are you, Moncrief?"

I answer the question.

"And good day to you also. I'm afraid, K. Burke, that our work has followed us to the races."

CHAPTER 18

AFTER MY PLANE TAKES off from Baltimore's Thurgood Marshall Airport we receive information that travel from our reserved airport, White Plains, into Manhattan is a mess. I don't know how my pilot does it, but he manages to get last-minute clearance at LaGuardia.

I walk through the private aircraft gate and immediately hear a shout.

"Moncrief! Over here!"

It can only be K. Burke.

"I've got a patrol car and driver outside. We've got to get our butts over to Central Park West. We can catch up on the way," she says. I follow her quick step toward the exit.

Instead of asking why "our butts" are so urgently required on Central Park West, I ask, "How did you know I'd be here, at *this* airport?"

"I have top-secret access to a special communication device. It's called a telephone. I used it to track you down."

I stop myself from saying that I thought perhaps she had the powers of a gypsy woman. Instead I simply say, "Ingenious, K. Burke. You should become a detective."

"And right now you should become familiar with what's going on at 145 Central Park West. It seems…"

The police siren blares as our car enters the expressway.

"One-forty-five?" I say. "That's the San Remo. 74th Street. *Très élégant;* I have a good friend who lives there…"

"Why am I not surprised?" Burke says. "Who?"

"Juan Carlos Vilca, the Peruvian polo player, and his wife, Gabriela," I say. "She's a professional model. She is exquisite."

"Do you know anyone who isn't exquisite?" A quick pause, then she says, "Wait. Don't answer that. I just thought of someone who isn't. And you're sitting next to her."

"That is *your* opinion, K. Burke," I say. That conversation goes no further. She moves on.

"Meanwhile, there are a few facts you should know about a dead neighbor of your Peruvian friends."

Burke tells me that at two o'clock this afternoon a personal assistant to a rich young woman by the name of Elspeth Tweddle found her dead in her bedroom.

"Tweddle?" I ask. "That is a real name? It sounds like the name of a talking duck in a child's storybook."

"Elspeth Tweddle is a very real name, and Elspeth Tweddle is a very dead woman. And, there's a bit of background information. She's twenty-five years old. And take a look. As you would say, truly exquisite."

K. Burke clicks a photo of Elspeth Tweddle on her iPad. The woman may be twenty-five, but she could pass for eighteen.

This woman *is* exquisite, truly beautiful. A big pouty look on her face, with light-green eyes, and chestnut hair with the fashionable blond streaks.

Burke tells me that they are called champagne streaks.

"When the streaks have more gold in them than blond," she explains, "the color is called champagne."

"I love to learn, K. Burke. And that is good, because you love to teach."

Burke ignores me. Then she tells me more about the woman with the champagne streaks.

The woman's personal assistant came in at two. He usually arrived at ten, but the woman had a dentist appointment and he had arranged to not arrive until after lunch.

"The assistant found her sprawled on the floor, and since Tweddle was rich and beautiful, 911 actually remembered to call us. She was dead when the ME got there."

At this moment our squad car pulls up to the first of the two San Remo apartment towers. The doorman opens the car door.

"Good morning, Mr. Moncrief. Is Mr. Vilca expecting you?" he asks.

"No, Ernie. I am here today on official business."

K. Burke takes charge. "I'm Detective Burke, and apparently you already know Detective Moncrief. We will be joining a few other members of the NYPD on the…"

Ernie finishes her sentence. "The twelfth floor. There are quite a few people up there already. Take a left at the end of this hall, and that'll be your elevator."

As we wait for the elevator I ask Burke, "So, what are you thinking? Do we know if this case fits the same pattern as the other three?"

"The only thing that fits is that the victim or the 'dead woman,' if you prefer, is very pretty, very young, and very rich. There the similarities end. Miss Tweddle is *not* married. Miss Tweddle does *not* have children. And so Miss Tweddle does *not* have an overweight nanny."

"Hmmm. Yet it *feels…it feels…*" I begin to say. Burke holds her hand up like a traffic cop. She speaks.

"I'm with you. It sure as hell smells like the other three deaths."

"Mademoiselle Tweddle lives alone?"

Burke looks down at her notes.

"Well, there's a live-in cook, a live-in maid, and another maid who doesn't live there. Miss Tweddle's personal assistant comes in five days a week. But there are a few other things I've got to tell you…"

Then the elevator arrives. The elevator man pulls wide the bronze gates, and two young boys wearing blue blazers and gray flannel slacks get off the elevator.

Burke and I ride up to the twelfth floor in silence. She's not about to tell me anything in front of the elevator man.

We finally arrive on twelve. Two police officers nod and gesture toward the open apartment door. But Burke pauses before we enter.

"Let me finish the background," she says. "Elspeth Tweddle lives here, but this is her mother's apartment. The victim grew up in this apartment. Elspeth never moved out."

"The mother is deceased?"

"No, she's very much alive. Elspeth's mother, Rose Jensen Tweddle, is currently the American ambassador to Italy."

CHAPTER 19

THE POLICE SCENE HAS not been touched. Pristine. Just the way we like it when we show up.

The victim is lying on her back on the bedroom floor. She wears only a sports bra and cut-off gray sweatpants.

Jonny Liang, the assistant medical examiner, approaches us immediately. Jonny handled Tessa Fulbright's case.

"A quick on-site blood test is telling us no drug abuse, but we won't know for sure until we get the full autopsy going," Jonny says.

Jonny's a smart guy. Before Burke or I can say a word, he anticipates our next question.

"I know. From a circumstantial point of view, it looks just like your other three 'rich gal' cases. Yet so far the forensics don't support that conclusion. Wait until tonight or tomorrow morning. I'll get you the information fast."

"Assuming there *is* information," Burke says. I share

her skepticism, but something is bugging me. Before I can even think about what that nagging feeling might be, a handsome young blond man—no more than thirty years old—approaches us.

"Good morning, detectives. I'm Ian Hart. I'm Miss Tweddle's personal assistant."

"I'm happy to tell you what I told the police officers," Hart says. My instinct is that this guy is a sleazebag—too handsome for his own good. I notice his four-hundred-dollar jeans, and consider that he spends each day with the ambassador's beautiful daughter.

I immediately glance at the bed and consider if more than one person has been in it. No. Just one side of the king-size bed looks slept in.

But I rethink that instinct as he speaks. This guy comes across as smart and strong. He's also somber, like a guy who is authentically sad that he's lost a friend.

For the most part I learn nothing that I haven't already heard from K. Burke. He does, however, point to a small desk near the window. On that desk is a coffee mug with the initials "ET" on it.

"She had a lot of ET stuff," Hart says. "Her initials, you know."

Burke nods. She obviously figured that out. Elspeth Tweddle.

I also nod. I would never tell this to Burke, but I did not figure that out.

Burke tells one of the officers to "bag" the coffee mug contents and get it to the lab.

"What exactly were your responsibilities with Miss Tweddle?" I ask.

"The usual PA stuff—lunch reservations, dinner reservations, dealing with what little correspondence she had. But a lot of the things she did…well, we did together. We played squash. We went to parties together. We'd run in the park. We went riding in the park a lot. And she was working on this documentary. She had all these home videos of her and her family's summers on Fishers Island."

Clearly Ian Hart interprets our silence and our occasional nods as indication that we thought his boss's life—not to mention his own job—was pretty frivolous.

He says, "Listen. I know it kind of sounds like I was being paid to be Elspeth's friend. And in a way I was. But I really liked the days I spent with her. She was smart and she was pretty and she was fun."

He looks away from us. He blinks his eyes quickly. He looks back at us, composed. He smiles.

"She was my friend," he says.

Later, as we wait for the elevator, Burke says, "You know one of the toughest things in detective work?"

She does not wait for my answer. Instead she gives her own answer.

"It's whether grieving people are telling the truth. In those moments, I never quite know for sure when someone is bullshitting me—or even being honest with themselves."

"I am not so good at it myself," I say. We are silent for a few seconds.

Then Burke says, "So, they went riding a lot. You've got quite a few horses in your life these days, Moncrief."

As we walk from the elevator to the door I say to Burke, "*Alors.* You have reminded me. You know that white dress in which you looked so magnificent at the Kentucky Derby?"

"What about that dress?" She asks the question suspiciously.

"Have it washed and ironed. Next Friday night we are leaving for Baltimore. The next day is…"

She knows. She yells, "The Preakness!"

CHAPTER 20

THE SAVATIERS' HORSE, GARÇON, came to Louisville as an anonymous foreigner. He comes to Baltimore as a worldwide celebrity, the favorite.

Garçon now has a really good shot at capturing the Triple Crown, the honor that goes to the rare horse who wins the Kentucky Derby, the Preakness Stakes, and the Belmont Stakes. This possibility is beyond thrilling—only twelve times, in more than one hundred years of thoroughbred racing, has a horse won the Triple Crown.

Only a few days ago I was here to view the remains of a horse, a mysterious and disgusting slaughter. But we carry on. We have tried our best to tuck the event in the back of our brains. Even the ominous threats and flowers sent to the Savatiers cannot eradicate our nervous hopes. The Savatiers are worried, but they are certainly not defeated. The hired bodyguards and Detective Kwame Clarke have been staying very close to them.

Now, if only the weather would cooperate.

It is a miserable day. Cold rain everywhere. Umbrellas are everywhere. Serious raincoat weather. Pimlico Race Course is becoming Pimlico River.

K. Burke and I wait in the stable with the Savatiers. Wet hay sticks to our water-soaked shoes. Rain pelts the stable roof.

But Garçon's jockey, Armand Joscoe, keeps smiling and tells Burke and me not to worry. Then he gives us some information to keep us calm.

"Le cheval aime la boue," the little guy says.

"Très bien, Armand. Très bien." Then I turn to Burke and translate.

"The horse likes mud!" I say.

"Merci," Burke says. "And may I remind you for the hundredth time that I speak French." She speaks sweetly, but there is a touch of irritation in her voice.

"Where is your son, Armand?" I ask. He tells me that Léon is occupied elsewhere. But of course, he will be watching.

Burke speaks.

"Have you noticed, Moncrief, that you, me, Marguerite, and Nicolas are all wearing the same clothes we wore at the Derby?"

I look.

"Mon Dieu," I say. "Unbelievable." But it is not really unbelievable.

The four of us seem to be honoring a superstition: Everything must be as it was in Louisville. Marguerite is in her bright floral suit. Nicolas in his perfectly cut gray slacks and blue blazer. Katherine Burke in her white linen dress with the Savatiers' racing silk colors belted around her waist.

I move in close to K. Burke and whisper, "Do you think Madame Savatier is wearing the same undergarments as she did in Louisville?"

K. Burke looks away from me, as if I am a naughty-minded schoolboy and she is the little girl I chose to shock.

Then a tremendous blare of trumpets. The moment is upon us.

CHAPTER 21

THIRTY SECONDS LATER AN announcement comes from the loudspeakers: "Horses and jockeys will now proceed to the track!"

We walk a few yards with Armand Joscoe and Garçon. After a few minutes the horse and rider turn. They walk toward the water-drenched track, and the rest of us find our places in the owners' circle.

The parade is magnificent, a combination of beauty and strength. Marguerite is seated to my right. She holds my hand. Katherine Burke sits to my left. She holds a pair of high-powered binoculars. Me? I occasionally glance at the equine parade, but mostly I keep a keen eye on the many people seated near us. Who might be watching us? Who might want to harm the Savatiers?

I would like to report that the sun broke out before the race began. It did not. The rain keeps on raining, but it seems a little more cooperative. It seems to fall in a softer, more peaceful rhythm. We wait for the race to start.

I say, "You will recall, K. Burke, that during the plane ride down here you insisted that I was *not* to place a bet for you on Garçon?"

"Of course I do. It was just a sudden superstition on my part. I didn't think he'd win this time if we placed a bet."

"Well, I disobeyed and did so anyway," I say. "But I bet only a hundred dollars."

She's pissed. She turns away from me and mutters, "Damn it. Do you ever listen?"

I say nothing. So she speaks again.

"When I specifically asked you not to? It's bad karma, Moncrief. You're pushing your luck…my luck…our luck."

"But, K. Burke, we are trying to do everything in the same way as we did in Kentucky, *n'est-ce pas?*" I say.

"*N'est-ce pas,* my foot. I think it feels selfish to bet, to feel so smug about winning. If Garçon loses, I'm blaming it on you."

"We shall see. And please, not to worry. This time cannot be exactly like last time. At the Derby Garçon was a long shot. Today he is the favorite. Today his odds are a measly two-to-one. Even if he wins you will only…"

But my attention is suddenly elsewhere. A few yards away from K. Burke I see Detective Kwame Clarke taking a seat. Clarke watches us. Our eyes meet. He tips his umbrella handle in my direction. We both nod to each other.

Marguerite speaks to me.

"I am scared, Luc. Very scared," she says.

"There is no reason…"

"Yes. Yes. I know that you have the private guards watching us. And I know Detective Clarke is nearby. But I am nonetheless frightened."

"You have no need to be," I say. "All is secure."

But I am wise enough to know that, like me, Marguerite is thinking about that dark and threatening note.

Win the Preakness. Or you will suffer the consequences.

"What if Garçon does not win?" she says.

I don't have time to answer. We hear the sound of a bell. Marguerite grabs my hand.

The race begins.

CHAPTER 22

ARMAND JOSCOE, THE JOCKEY *extraordinaire,* turns out to be a psychic *extraordinaire*.

Joscoe's assurance that Garçon "likes mud" turns out to be absolutely true! It becomes clear in the first few moments of the race that Garçon doesn't merely *like* mud. Garçon *loves* mud! Physically, spiritually, indisputably. With mud painting his hooves and legs, Garçon does not merely gallop, he flies.

Yes, we remain nervous. We are still anxious. But it is so much better to be nervous and anxious with a winning horse.

But not only does he win, he wins *decisively*. We all go nuts, and for the second time in two weeks, we are celebrating like crazy people.

The Savatiers are ecstatic, but it is also clear to me that both of them are anxious. Marguerite's hands tremble. Her head keeps turning back and forth. Officials (including Kwame Clarke) arrive quickly to lead the couple to the presentation circle.

"My friends must come with us," Marguerite says to Detective Clarke.

"No, no," I say. "You will be well cared for, and Detective Burke and I will be standing nearby."

Burke leans into me.

"Moncrief, she's shaking. She's a nervous mess. What difference does it make? Let's go with them."

Burke's logic is impeccable, of course.

"Very well," I say. Marguerite Savatier turns to Burke: "*You, Mademoiselle Burke,* are a very fine influence on our Luc." Hmmm. I could swear there was a flash of romantic mischief in Marguerite's eyes.

So we join the owners. Then, a few moments later, the four of us join the triumphant horse and the smiling jockey. Garçon is covered in a huge blanket of yellow flowers.

"Those are Viking poms. They're meant to look like Black-Eyed Susans, the official state flower of Maryland," Burke says to me.

"Is there anything you do not know, K. Burke?" I ask.

"Well, I don't know how much money we won on that race," she says with a twinkle in her eye. Then we both turn our attention to the trophy presentation, as well as the presentation of a large bouquet of Black-Eyed Susans to Madame Savatier. The old woman smiles for the cameras. Applause. Smiles. The thousands of *click-click-click* from cameras.

I feel a buzz from my cell phone. I try looking at the screen as discreetly as possible. A message from Inspector Elliott.

Where the hell r u 2?

I text back. See u soon.

He texts back. WTF?

I slip the phone back into my pocket.

The speeches from corporate sponsors and the governor of Maryland are mercifully short. Then we stand at attention—for the third time—and listen to yet another rendition of "Maryland, My Maryland."

CHAPTER 23

THE MOMENT BURKE AND I break from our group and head to the after-party she says, "That message you got was from Elliott, wasn't it?"

"Indeed it was. He asked about our whereabouts. I told him that we would be in touch soon. Not to worry," I say.

"We should get back up to New York now," she says.

"In due time, K. Burke. For the moment, a celebration."

The party in the Pimlico Club room is lavish, even more so than the post-race party in Louisville. Instead of mint juleps, Pimlico serves a cocktail called the Black-Eyed Susan.

"I think they put every fruit juice in the world in this drink," says K. Burke.

I ask a nearby waiter what goes into this concoction. He practically quotes Burke: "Any fruit juice you can name—orange, pineapple, lime. Then a lot of vodka and a little bourbon."

Burke and I each put down a few drinks. Indeed,

will Burke and I ever find a race-party cocktail that we do *not* like?

It should be a festive day. Garçon has won. The party is noisy and happy and fun. Instead of Louisville's tiny hush puppy hors d'oeuvres, we are served miniature crab cakes. The crowd is elegant. The music is loud. The DJ plays Randy Newman and Bruce Springsteen and Lyle Lovett and even Counting Crows. And every song is—amazingly—a song about Baltimore.

I pull out my phone and pull up my favorite horse-racing blog. I have to yell to be heard over the music and celebration, but I read this part to K. Burke:

"As a Frenchman loves champagne, so does Preakness favorite Vilain Garçon love mud. Yes, Vilain Garçon easily grabbed hold of step two in his bid for the Triple Crown. This extraordinary steed, owned by a charming elderly French couple, Marguerite and Nicolas (no "h," *s'il vous plait*), and ridden by the until-now unknown jockey Armand Joscoe, won the Preakness decisively this afternoon. Not by a nose, but by a full length. The rain-drenched crowd is reacting with wild shouts. As for this reporter, I will suggest to the Savatiers that, when the Belmont Stakes comes along, that they pray for rain. If their prayers are answered, then the Triple Crown is certain."

Burke pretends to listen, but she's chewing on the orange peel from her cocktail. As always, however, she is on the job.

"Shall we check in with your buddy Kwame and the Baltimore PD?" she asks.

"Certainly. If you ever finish your orange peel," I say. She makes a face and puts the peel back in the glass. Then we both walk to the entrance archway where Kwame Clarke and two men in gray suits are standing, bodyguards for the Savatiers. The cut of their boxy suits immediately tells me that these are two officers.

Introductions all around.

"Aha, now I finally meet the extraordinary K. Burke," says Kwame Clarke.

Burke nods her head in my direction and says to Clarke, "You didn't hear that word 'extraordinary' about me from Moncrief, I'm sure."

Smiles all around.

K. Burke and Kwame Clarke shake hands. Perhaps an unusually long handshake, I think.

It occurs to me that Burke and Clarke have noticed…how to put this?…how good-looking the other is.

Why does this annoy me?

Clarke introduces me to the officers—Vinnie Masucci and Olan Washington. They explain that they are eyeballing everybody who comes in.

"If the name's not on the invite list, they're not at the party," says Masucci.

We discuss the rain, of course. The weather and the triumphant Garçon are the subjects of the day. Then Clarke says that he and his "guys" are going to check out the kitchen once more.

"We can hang here," K. Burke volunteers.

And we do. We even have a serious discussion concerning the merits of crab cakes versus hush puppies. Then K. Burke, who must have been reading *Horse Racing for Dummies,* lectures me on the wonders of American Pharoah, the most recent horse to win the Triple Crown.

K. Burke ends her lecture abruptly and says, "I'm worried, Moncrief."

I shrug and say, "We have done all we can. They have put ten plainclothesmen at the stables after the training horse was killed. They put thirty officers in the crowd today, two of them directly behind the Savatiers and us. They randomly tested all the food. They did backgrounds on the caterers, waiters, band…"

"Moncrief!" K. Burke says. "Over there."

She points to two young men walking toward us, wearing jeans and yellow rain slickers, carrying either side of a huge arrangement of roses. Holy shit! The floral display is identical to the arrangement Marguerite Savatier received at the Kentucky Derby.

"Where'd these roses come from?" asks K. Burke.

"I don't know. Some kid, a teenager, dropped 'em off. Matt and I were just working out there, parking cars, trying to stay dry. Then this kid shows up in this shitty old van. He gives us each twenty bucks and tells us to bring it inside to the party. He says they're for some old lady."

He then pulls a small gift card from his pocket and hands the envelope to Burke, who then passes it to me.

The roses are, of course, for Marguerite.

"You know where the old lady is?" says the guy who's helped carry in the floral arrangement.

"Yeah, we do," I say. "We'll make sure she gets them."

CHAPTER 24

BACK IN NEW YORK, at the Midtown East precinct, K. Burke and I receive an exceptionally warm welcome from our boss, Inspector Nick Elliott.

"Where the hell on Christ's green earth have you two lovebirds been?"

K. Burke now makes a huge mistake. She talks.

"Excuse me, Inspector Elliott. I just want to make it clear that Luc Moncrief and I are not—in any way, shape, or form—involved in a romantic or…"

Elliott interrupts.

"Thank you, Detective Burke. Your private life is your business."

K. Burke won't let go of it. Bad idea. She tries once more.

"This is the truth. Moncrief and I have never…"

Now Elliott interrupts loudly. No one is going to interrupt him again. He's moved back to the work discussion.

"As I was saying. Take a look at this. It's a surveillance video of a drug dealer in Central Park."

This time I speak.

"Inspector, forgive my rudeness, but finding a drug dealer in Central Park is as common as finding a blade of grass in Central Park."

"I don't disagree, Moncrief, but just take a look." Then he adds, "And do it quietly." By now both K. Burke and I have annoyed him.

Elliott motions to us with his finger from his desk chair. Burke and I move behind him and lean into the computer screen.

The black-and-white picture portrays—in muddy shades of light and dark gray—what looks like clouds. Eventually, as the scene comes into focus, everything is more easily identifiable as an unkempt area of trees and weeds and stone boulders.

"It looks like Sherwood Forest," Burke says. "Is it the Ramble?"

The Ramble is a wooded area of Central Park totally un-manicured and un-landscaped.

"Yup. During the day you see bird-watchers with their binoculars and notepads," says Elliott. Then, "At night it turns into a kind of playground for gay guys."

"I have been to this area. To the Ramble," I say.

Elliott looks up at me, slightly startled. Burke turns her head and looks at me. Also slightly startled.

"No. I am not a bird-watcher. But when I began working for you, Inspector, you may recall, my first assignment was searching for criminals who stole bicycles. For three weeks myself and Maria Martinez spent two days at the Bethesda Fountain, two days in the Sheep Meadow, and two days in the Ramble, all in pursuit of bicycle thieves."

"And as I remember, you and your partner didn't catch one goddamn bike thief," says Elliott.

"Ah, but I learned a great deal about the geography. Right now, in this video I can tell you the scene is located precisely between Harkness House on the East Side and the Museum of Natural History on the West Side."

"Great. Keep watching," says Elliott.

The camera suddenly makes a sharp downward turn. We zoom in for a medium close-up to record who is standing on the stone pathway that rambles through the Ramble.

Burke and I study the screen. It now shows a fairly sharp image—for a police surveillance video: a teenage boy. Tall, thin, with a great deal of blond hair. Perhaps he is seventeen.

"New York City rich kid," K. Burke says. "A common species."

She is correct. He wears a blue blazer with an indecipherable gold insignia on the front pocket. A white button-down shirt of the Brooks Brothers variety. Striped blue-and-yellow silk tie in a thin sloppy knot. Gray pants.

"In fact," she continues thoughtfully, "didn't we see one of those recently?"

I am distracted. "His rucksack is bursting," I say.

"Speak English, Moncrief," says Elliott. "What the hell is a *rucksack*?"

Burke cuts in again. "At Miss Tweddle's. Didn't we see…"

She trails off as two similarly dressed teenage boys approach. The blond boy reaches into his… backpack…and hands each of them a plastic bag.

"No exchange of money," says Burke. "Maybe the next customer."

"I think his clientele pay in advance or put it on the tab," says Elliott.

"The latter—the tab—that is the way the rich do it," I say.

No sooner has Burke predicted a 'next customer' than a pretty—and very curvy—brunette woman, maybe thirty years old, in athletic clothes approaches. Again, the blond boy reaches into his satchel and hands over a small plastic bag. And again no money is seen.

"This is why I called you to look at this," says Elliott. "Do you recognize that woman?"

"Oh, my God," says Burke. "The Monahans' nanny."

"Mrs. Meade-Grafton!" I remember her unsettling laughter.

"One of the officers who was at the Monahan apartment happened to be on this as well. Lucky stroke for us. Especially while you two are gallivanting around," Elliott says, with insinuation.

Burke's face is very red, but she lets it pass. "What I was going to say is that we saw two boys wearing blazers and gray pants exiting the elevator when we entered Miss Tweddle's building."

"Very good, Burke!" I exclaim. "I had forgotten. Your sartorial eye is getting better every day."

I do not think I deserve her glare.

We watch more transactions. Most of the buyers are young. Most of them are white. The entire video will continue for twelve minutes before the blond boy leaves the frame.

"We had no trouble identifying the teen pusher. He's been booked before, petty thievery once. Ready for this? He and his girlfriend bolted a bill at Daniel. The most expensive restaurant in the city. Plainclothes caught them two blocks away on Fifth Avenue."

"Beware the couple who attend the restroom at the same time," I say.

Elliott smiles slightly and recites the rest of the rap

sheet: Weed outside a dance club on 28th Street. Assault of another student at a school basketball game.

"And no arrests that stuck?" Burke says.

"No. The kid's name is Reed Minton Reynolds. His father, Bill Reynolds, is that big deal weight-loss specialist, and, if you want, he'll give you a side order of plastic surgery. I've met him twice—actually a nice guy. Full disclosure, he's also responsible for 50 percent of the funding for the Police Athletic League."

"And 50 percent of the facelifts and breast augmentations in Manhattan," K. Burke says.

I can't resist. I turn and say, "You sound like you know something about these procedures, K. Burke."

Elliott shoots me an angry look.

"Don't start." A pause. Enough time for K. Burke to give a *somebody got in trouble* kind of smile. Elliott continues.

"Anyway, this Reed Reynolds kid is about to graduate Dalton, and he's signed, sealed, and soon-to-be-delivered to Yale. I'd like you two to track him for a day or two or three. Stay close to him. I want you to see where he goes, if he works anywhere else in the park. Do a 'smother job' on him. I'm not that interested in him, but…I think if we get a good fix on him, we can find out who's supplying him with his stash."

K. Burke gives one of her energetic responses: "Gotcha, Inspector."

As we reach Elliott's office door to leave I cannot resist saying: "Oh, and by the way, Inspector. While we're in Central Park, I'll keep my eyes open for any stolen bicycles."

"Get the hell out of here, Moncrief."

"Gotcha, Inspector."

The last word I hear from Elliott's mouth is simple. "Asshole!"

CHAPTER 25

WE SPENT ALL YESTERDAY afternoon trying to track down this kid, but only saw him as he arrived at home at the end of the day, and never came back out. But we never saw him leave this morning, either, unless he left before dawn, so now K. Burke and I are waiting on the north side of East 89th Street. We watch students straggling out of the Dalton School. Some light cigarettes. Others hold hands. Reed Reynolds doesn't show.

"Let's get over to Central Park. Maybe he cut out of school early," I say.

"Or maybe he never went to school today," says Burke. "I remember my own last few days of high school. Once we got accepted to college or had a job lined up, we didn't care anymore."

We enter the park just south of the Metropolitan Museum. We walk over a wide grassy area where shirtless men and near-shirtless women are sunning themselves. We then make our way down a small dirt pathway that leads us into a large dark wooded area. The Ramble.

The skunky-sweet smell of weed is in the air. Burke and I quickly locate the general area where Reed Reynolds was recorded distributing drugs. A few people are around—tourists, dog-walkers—but there are others in more secluded corners, kissing and smoking. But it's the same as the wait at his house this morning and at his school this afternoon—no Reed Reynolds.

I suggest we walk farther into the woods. It pays off. Thank you, instinct. A slightly swampy overgrown area, a few people, a few pairs of people. And there he is, holding court on a bench, like a little kid running a lemonade stand. We watch, taking care to remain hidden in the trees.

There he is, smoking cigarettes, an occasional finger snap to the beat of the music coming through his phone. He pauses only when a buyer comes along. Reynolds hands out his little zip-lock bags, his plastic orange bottles of bennies or red balls or good old reliable speedballs. He's got a steady flow of customers. He seems to know exactly what they came for. No money changes hands. In about twenty minutes he's supplied about a dozen people.

Who are these folks? Your basic mixed bag of New Yorkers: the old, the young, the Black, the white. Some are dressed for sleeping on the street. Some are dressed for sleeping at the Carlyle. They're as varied as the crowd at a Knicks game. People like Mara Monahan and Tessa Fulbright, two of those young women who died, would fit seamlessly into this group.

"You're starting to get agitated, Moncrief," says K. Burke.

"It is true, K. Burke. I have a great agitation to put handcuffs on this little preppy shithead," I say.

"Our job right now is to watch him and follow him. Nothing more. Nothing less."

"Oui, maman," I say.

Suddenly, K. Burke elbows me.

"Take a look at that guy with Reynolds now," she says.

I look to see a middle-aged man in annoyingly good shape. Sinewy muscles and forearms. He is wearing a ridiculous costume: tight black lycra shorts, a colorful yellow bicycling shirt, and a yellow helmet.

"I think that man has escaped from the circus," I say.

"No. He's that guy who gives massages. Remember that gift certificate you gave me for massages? That's him."

"Ah, *oui*. The Armenian masseur. Louis."

"Non. The Hungarian masseur. Laszlo."

"Whatever his name," I say, "he's spending my money on skag."

We study the other customers. Two of them are teenagers—very distressing. Two of the female purchasers are what are known as "yummy mummies," in a way that is also distressing.

We watch the ebb and flow of buyers.

"Aha, K. Burke," I suddenly say. "Now it is my turn to push my elbow into your side. You will please look at that woman who is approaching young Master Reynolds."

I point to an attractive Manhattan-type: Her perfectly cut chestnut-colored hair falls over a snug white T-shirt. She wears a pair of baggy black linen shorts. The woman is not beautiful, but she is impeccably put together. This woman is evidence of an observation my late beloved Dalia sometimes made: "She's done the best she can with what God gave her."

"Okay, Moncrief. Who is she?" asks K. Burke.

"You do not know her? You met her just a few days ago. She…"

"Holy shit!" says Burke, perhaps a little too loudly. "It's that frumpy English nanny…what's-her-name… the one who worked for what's-her-name."

"Well put, K. Burke. What's-her-name is correctly named Julia Highridge, who appears to have been transformed from a dowdy Miss Marple into a chic Manhattan mademoiselle."

"It's amazing how much better she looks," says Burke.

"A touch of makeup. And a six-hundred-dollar Frederic Fekkai haircut," I say.

Reed Reynolds hands Julia Highridge a plastic bag, and she walks in the direction of Central Park West. She seems to be the day's final customer.

Reed Reynolds stands alone. He makes a few quick notes on a small pad. Then he takes a silver flask from his bag and takes a long swig. He recaps the flask and slips it into his backpack. Reed Reynolds heads east to Fifth Avenue. He half walks. He half runs. He has youth on his side. We take off after him. Skipping, hopping, jogging, racing, or leaping over a stone wall, K. Burke and I keep up with him.

Now we're out of the park. He crosses Fifth Avenue. We stay on the Park side and watch him. Reynolds stops at 930 Fifth Avenue, a large gray-stone building. He nods to the doorman. The doorman touches the rim of his cap. Then Reed Reynolds enters the building.

He's home.

"Damn."

Now it is *my* turn to calm *her* down.

"K. Burke. Please. You will settle your nerves. We will follow him. Tomorrow. And the next day. We will learn from him. Then once we know how he does it and where he gets his inventory...*Voilà!*

"This young man believes he's going to Yale. But first...well, he may have to do an internship on Rikers Island."

CHAPTER 26

Tuesday
3:00 p.m.

EARLY THE NEXT MORNING, K. Burke and I visit the office of Megan Scott, the dean of students at the Dalton School. We have shown her our ID and begin our questions, politely of course.

"We need to know if Reed Reynolds was in class today," we say.

"Why do you *need* to know?" asks Megan Scott.

"That's an expression, Miss Scott," says K. Burke. "And this is an NYPD investigation."

Burke and I know that many of the students at this school are the children of the rich and powerful. That means little to me, and it means absolutely nothing to my partner.

"We give information out on our students only when it's necessary," says Megan Scott.

"Mademoiselle," I say. "We have asked you for one piece of information. Was the boy in school today? That is not an inflammatory or provocative question."

Burke gives me a look that seems to say, "We're not going to let this bureaucrat obstruct our investigation."

"Very well," says Scott. "Reed was *in* class today, but he was not in this building. He's finishing up a special project at the Metropolitan Museum of Art. Okay. There's your answer. Now if I may ask a question, what's the problem?"

"Not a problem, really. We just want to talk to him," Burke says.

"This Reed Reynolds, he is a good student, a good young man?" I ask, trying hard to use as much French charm as I can muster.

"Yes, 'this Reed Reynolds' is a very good student. He's on his way to Yale. He's a wonderful young man. If you could see this project he's doing with the curator of Dutch Renaissance portraiture at the Met…"

K. Burke has heard all she cares to hear. She puts an end to it.

"Thanks, Miss Scott. Thanks for letting us take up your precious time," she says.

Later that day, we're back in the Ramble, witnessing a similar-looking stream of buyers.

Reed Reynolds is still, of course, totally prepped out—white button-down, striped tie, loafers. He looks like he should be on the front of a prep school recruitment brochure.

We watch the distribution of the plastic bags of… heroin? Weed? Speed? Buttons? The possibilities are endless.

Then I turn to Burke and say, "Okay. I'm going to try something."

"What?" she asks.

"I think I'll make a purchase," I say.

"It won't work, Moncrief. These are regulars. Don't be stupid."

I know that she's right, but there's nothing to lose.

And if I make a buy we can hook him into cuffs without chasing all over the city. As I walk toward him, I can practically *hear* K. Burke rolling her eyes.

"I was wondering if you could help me out?" I say.

"Probably not," he says. His voice is flat, dead, weak.

"Maybe just some loose weed," I say.

"No."

"I have two hundred dollars."

"No, man. Go away."

"Five hundred for two ounces?"

This time he doesn't even bother to say "no." He simply walks away.

I return to K. Burke.

"Please notice, Moncrief. I am not saying a word."

But Reed Reynolds doesn't go far, once he sees I'm gone. We watch from our hiding place as, like yesterday, he makes some brief notes and then takes a swig from his silver flask. This time, he does not head toward the Upper East Side but heads south through the park. We tail him past the lake, past Bethesda Fountain, on through the Sheep Meadow, then we are out of the park.

At 59th Street, just opposite the Plaza Hotel, Reed Reynolds hails a cab. We do the same. We follow them down Seventh Avenue, to the downtown corner where it changes to Varick Street. We're in SoHo now.

Reed Reynolds gets out of his cab at 300 Spring Street, a cement and steel monstrosity, a modernistic pile of crap in the midst of the great old SoHo ironclad buildings.

Burke is on her iPad.

Seconds later she says, "It's his father's office and clinic. William Reynolds, MD. Let's go up. We can take a service elevator, maybe, or..."

"No," I say. "I know something better to do. And *you* will do it tomorrow."

"Me?" she asks. Burke looks confused. And suspicious.

"You will visit the eminent plastic surgeon, Dr. William Reynolds, *and* you will see if he will sell you some drugs."

"I'm not so…"

"Come, come, K. Burke. I can tell… You also think it is a good idea."

"Well… maybe… yes," she says. (Oh, how she hates to agree with me.)

"And for now I have another good idea."

"And that is?" she asks, also suspiciously.

"We are a mere three blocks from Dominique Ansel Bakery. Let's go and have some good coffee *and* one of Ansel's famous cronuts. *Allons-y!* Let's go!"

"I know how to speak French!" she explodes.

"Please, no angry attitude, K. Burke. Let's hurry! The bakery may soon be out of cronuts."

CHAPTER 27

I HAVE JUST SHARED with K. Burke my precise plan for tomorrow morning. The blueprint is not without some danger. And Burke will be the major player, practically the only player.

"Have you cleared any of this with Inspector Elliott?" K. Burke asks. I think she is nervous. And I don't blame her.

"Share it with Elliott? Of course not," I say. "I have cleared it with you, and I have already cleared it with myself. I think that will be sufficient approval."

"Sweet Jesus, Moncrief," she says.

We walk a few steps to the children's playground next door to Dominique Ansel Bakery. We begin eating our extraordinary cronuts.

As I watch the children in the wading pool and beneath the gentle sprinkler, I am transported—but just for a few moments—to that small unknown children's area in the Jardin du Luxembourg, a mostly hidden area of slides and swings and climbing ropes, an area where a grumpy old man performs absolutely terrible puppet shows, a childhood memory that...

"Moncrief, the plan. You were about to give me the details," Burke says.

My memory of the Jardin du Luxembourg explodes into the New York air, and I tell Burke the plan.

She will make an appointment to visit Dr. William Reynolds, father of drug dealer Reed Reynolds. Only an hour earlier we followed the son to his father's medical office. Only yesterday we watched an employee of one of the beautiful dead women purchase drugs from Reed Reynolds. Beyond that, we know that Dr. Reynolds is the go-to weight-loss specialist for the wealthy women of Manhattan.

"Listen, K. Burke. You are perfect for this job. You are attractive. You are slender. You are articulate. You are the perfect 'insecure rich woman.' We will buy you some decent clothing..."

Burke sneers a very tiny sneer. "Watch it, Moncrief."

"What did I say?"

"Just go on."

"No. It is simple. You go in. You say you are interested in...oh, I don't know...a little Botox here...a little lifting of the butt...maybe you discuss the nose, although I must say that your nose is a sweet little button, a gift from your Irish ancestors."

"Okay, Moncrief, let's stop right there," she says. "I'm actually with you on this idea. I hate to admit it, but it's good. As an idea. But I'm going to change something. Instead of surgery, I'll try asking Dr. Reynolds for drugs—weight-loss, relaxants, stimulants, that sort of thing."

"It is your setup and your scene. It is all up to you," I say.

I have been googling around on diet and weight-loss

sites. I have learned about, I tell Burke, a desire on some women's parts to supplement their amphetamines and appetite suppressants with laxatives. I hand Burke my iPad. She reads a highlighted piece from Dr. William Reynolds's website, BeautifulYouInstantly.com.

> Some patients believe that the additional use of diuretics and laxatives aids in reaching their weight-loss goal. This is a matter in which I try to dissuade them. Strong emetic medication, while fostering the sense of weight-loss, is a worthless medical methodology.

"But you're contradicting yourself. Reynolds is saying here that he does *not* approve of laxatives…" says Burke.

"*C'est vrai.* That is true, but my instinct tells me this: I am beginning to suspect that our four victims were using very strong purgatives. Such medications either contributed to their death or actually caused their death. Reynolds is invoking the 'reverse psychology' approach. Tell someone they don't need something, and, of course…"

Burke finishes my sentence: "And, of course, they will want it even more."

"Here's what I think. You remember the ME's reports, yes? No drugs, they said…except for an antidepressant or two, and a seemingly innocent laxative. So what do I think? That our victims died of laxative overdosing."

"Oh, my God," says Burke.

I continue. "I also believe, consciously or not, that he was supplying his son's business with items that have street value. But to our victims, he supplied massive doses of laxatives—over-the-counter, prescription, even holistic herbs and teas. In any event when you go to see Reynolds, ask him to sell you one or two of the high-powered laxatives. Okay?"

I can see that Burke's enthusiasm is growing stronger.

"I'll do it, Moncrief, but I'm nervous."

"Not to have the worry. I will be there. I'll have a SWAT team on standby. Emergency medical will be standing by," I say.

"Medical?"

"Precautions, K. Burke. Laxatives can be… unpredictable." She doesn't laugh at my joke. "Don't worry. It is a harmless setup."

"Well if it's so easy, why don't you do it, Moncrief?"

I cannot resist. I say, "I would not be credible. What possible imperfection could Dr. Reynolds find in me?"

"Maybe he could change you from a smug asshole into a normal person," she says. Neither of us speaks for a moment.

"I will call." I dial the number from the website. A receptionist with a warm, calm voice answers. I exaggerate my French accent.

"Yes, I'd like to make an appointment for my client. She has not seen Dr. Reynolds before, but he is highly recommended. I am afraid my client needs to be seen right away—as in tomorrow. Her name is Marion Cotillard. Can you fit her in?"

I watch Burke's eyes widen. "Oh, you can? Thank you. She will see you tomorrow at five."

I hang up and she sputters, "Marion Cotillard?! She's a famous actress! I don't look anything like her."

"Does not matter," I say. "Now you're in. We never said you were *that* Marion Cotillard."

"What about when they ask for my identification?"

"You will have this."

I hand her a rolled-up wad of cash.

"Take this. Buy everything with cash."

"Why? The NYPD never allows personal money to…" she begins.

I ignore her. "It is thirty one-hundred-dollar bills. Three thousand dollars. Take it, and use it."

K. Burke nods. She takes the cash. We finish our cronuts and coffee.

Now the only thing left to do is to persuade K. Burke to walk with me to Alexander Wang and buy an outfit that's just a little bit more chic than her khaki pants and yellow Old Navy polo shirt.

"The weather is cooler," I say. "Let's walk around SoHo for a little bit."

"Sure," she says. "And while we're walking, let's stop at Alexander Wang and buy me some very cool clothes."

I laugh. Then I say, "You are something else, Katherine. I know that this plan will go very well."

"Holy shit," she says. "You must think this is important."

"And you say that because?"

"Because you actually called me Katherine."

CHAPTER 28

BURKE BLUSHED BUT WAS secretly proud when Nick Elliott first introduced her to Moncrief: "She learned it, she earned it. She's one of the best detectives around. *And* she's got guts to go with her brains." She knew it was true. She didn't often have the chance to do undercover operations, and was looking forward to this. Even so, Burke couldn't help feeling nervous about this operation.

She walks into Dr. William Reynolds's office the next day at 4 p.m., and her mind's eye virtually clicks a photograph of the waiting room—furnished with objects she only recognizes due to Moncrief's shopping addiction.

Creamy white walls. Two authentic—Le Corbusier, she thinks?—black leather couches facing each other. A glass-topped coffee table sitting between the couches. An authentic and huge photograph hanging on the wall that Burke recognizes thanks to an art crime case. It's Jeff Koons's *Made in Heaven*—a near-naked man and woman in a passionate embrace.

The couches, the Koons. Click. Brain picture.

Burke is the only patient in the waiting room. A receptionist sits behind a glass Parsons table. The only item on her table is a very small MacBook Air. Next to the table is a small gray cabinet.

The receptionist is gorgeous. Long blond hair. Perfect features on a perfectly shaped face. Burke remembers what her mother used to say about a beautiful woman or a handsome man: "God took extra care when He put that one together." The receptionist wears a simple sleeveless gray shift, matching the gray cabinet. Nice touch.

Burke approaches, and as she gets closer she notices a slightly theatrical shininess to the woman's face. Could she really be using pancake makeup? Greasepaint? The woman's figure is not merely thin, it is thinner than thin. Her clavicles are sharp and prominent.

The receptionist is possibly twenty-five years old, or thirty-five, or forty-five...Burke really cannot tell. The receptionist exists in plastic surgery time.

"Ms. Cotillard, welcome," she says. A warm voice, a quiet voice. Burke senses disappointment, but there is no comment. A moment later she is filling out forms on a tablet—the information is fictional, but she trusts she would be done before this was discovered. After a short wait, the receptionist leads Burke into a changing room. Burke slips into an unusually elegant examination gown—pale yellow, soft thick cotton, matching slippers.

A knock on the changing room door.

A man's voice. "Miss Cotillard. It's Bill Reynolds. May I come in?"

Burke opens the door. William Reynolds is a bigger-sized cosmetically enhanced version of his son the drug dealer. No classic white doctor coat and stethoscope here. His blond hair is perfectly cut, his black suit fits perfectly, and his shirt is bespoke, like Moncrief's, allowing his slim frame to show some muscle.

He shakes Burke's hand. Reynolds does not indulge in ordinary clichés of greeting, no "Nice to meet you," no "Good to see you."

Instead he tenderly moves both his hands to Burke's shoulders and speaks gently: "Let me help you, Marion. Will you please let me help you?"

It should sound creepy, she thinks, but instead it sounds soothing. Burke wants to hear something dangerous or, at the very least, phony. Instead his voice makes her feel restful, trusting, and…oh, shit, she thinks…ever so slightly aroused.

CHAPTER 29

"MY OFFICE IS THIS way. Please, come with me, so we can talk before the exam."

Why am I wearing a gown? Through another door. Reynolds's office is sparse: another glass desk, a small gray cabinet. Some solemn-looking medical books on the shelves. An examining table with three measuring tapes and a small camera. Nothing else. It barely reads like a doctor's office. Reynolds gestures to the chair opposite his desk.

"What is your trouble? What is your dream? How can I help?" he asks.

She knows she must slip into the role she has come here to play. Reynolds's voice soothes her. But, damn it, she will, of course, be tougher. She's smarter. Clear the decks. Light the lights.

"I am just starting to hate the way I look. I mean, I know I'm sort of pretty. I also know the world's falling apart, and I'm worrying about the millimeter droop in my neck and my ears. But, well, I guess I should start by doing something about my weight…"

Burke knows that she is perfectly proportioned. She knows that if she ever truly complained to her cousins Maddy and Marilyn they'd laugh and criticize her for such self-involvement. God forbid she ever said something to Moncrief. He would force-feed her a hot fudge sundae.

"There's always room for improvement," Reynolds says. "That's the wonder of life."

That's the wonder of life? Burke thinks. *Jesus.*

Reynolds reaches into his filing cabinet and takes out two pamphlets. He hands one to her.

"Read along with me, Marion. Let's start on page three."

The page is titled "Help on Your Journey."

He begins reading:

"The judicious use of diet pills may lend you exactly the support you and your willpower need in order to learn and maintain sensible eating habits. Small doses of Dexedrine in limited quantities will give you the resilience you never knew you had."

Burke nods. Dexedrine, huh? On the street, in the clubs, in the best and worst neighborhoods, they're called Black Beauties.

"By the way," he says. "I know, of course, that my assistant, Nora, asked for the name of your pharmacy. That will be used strictly for emergencies. I will, for the sake of precision, put together a weekly packet of medication for you. It's a much wiser system, a safer system."

"But how do you know what…" Burke begins.

"I know, Marion. The Reynolds system is always the same, always foolproof. When you see a truly beautiful woman on Fifth Avenue, chances are great that she once sat where you're sitting now." He continues reading, in what is becoming the most bizarre doctor's visit she's ever had:

"Random and unpredictable sleeplessness is sometimes the result of even the most well-planned and supervised weight-loss plans, like the one you'll be embarking on. To compensate for the possible problem of insomnia, you will also be prescribed limited doses of Flunitrazepam, the medication that has been proven helpful to many European women."

Again Burke nods. She is sure that she remembers Moncrief saying that Flunitrazepam is called *le petit ami parfait,* "the perfect boyfriend," by wealthy Parisian women.

The reading from the gospel according to Reynolds continues. He tells Burke that her pill packet will also contain two forms of mescaline, as well as what Reynolds calls "a late afternoon relaxant."

Burke knows that on the streets of New York, these tablets are called roofies.

Reynolds stands at his desk.

"So that's it," he says. "I'll see you a week from today, anytime that's convenient and available."

"That's it?" she says, and she realizes that she may have sounded too surprised. Quickly she adds, "What I mean is: aren't you going to weigh me or take blood or urine or look in my eyes?"

"No need to right now. If we need those things at a later date, then we'll do them. But for now, it's better to just relax."

He hands her a small bag. It is made of a gray velvet-like material. The bag has a gold thread closure; it looks like it would contain a piece of silver given as a wedding gift, or a piece of jewelry given to a loved one.

Then Reynolds hands her a five-by-seven manila envelope. The envelope has nothing but the letter *A* written on it.

"These are helpful also. They're a mild laxative. Sometimes my clients find the act of bowel emission to be a helpful signal of how they're doing."

Burke has studied Moncrief's notes. She knows exactly what this medication is: Amatiza, a prescription laxative.

Reynolds keeps talking. "They're fairly large pills. So be sure to take plenty of water with them. Of course, you'll be staying away from all fruit juice. Too much sugar. Sugar and carbs. The dual enemy."

As he speaks she cannot resist squeezing the metal tab on the manila envelope. She pulls out one of the light-blue pills. By any estimation it is huge.

"Can I cut these in half?" Burke asks.

"You may get them down any way you choose," he says. "Put them on the tip of your husband's…" he begins to say. Then he laughs. Burke tries hard not to show that she's both surprised and repulsed by his joke.

"In any event, the medication chart for when you should take these pills is in the little bag," he says. "If you have any questions, Nora or I are always available."

Reynolds removes his suit jacket. He hangs it carefully on the back of his desk chair. He walks around the desk to where Burke is seated.

She thinks: *Why am I wearing an examination gown if he's not going to examine me?*

Now Dr. Reynolds stands in front of her, close to her.

"Do you have any questions?" he asks.

"No, I guess not," Burke asks.

But she realizes that this is now or never. She's got to get him to *sell* her some drugs. She pretends as if some new thought has just crossed her mind.

"Oh, yes. There is something. I'm glad you brought up the laxative thing," she says.

"Yes?"

"A friend of mine told me she occasionally uses something called…oh, I'm not sure…it's like…clementine…clemerol…some sort of laxative that really relaxes you inside…she says."

Burke is setting herself up to request an illegal drug, one banned by the FDA. It should be powerful. It's formulated for horses.

"You're probably thinking of Clenbuterol," Reynolds says. "And it *is* highly effective. But I'm not sure it 'relaxes you inside.'"

"I could swear that's what she said."

"It could help. Some women like it."

"I'd give it a try. I'm pretty serious about losing weight."

"I'll add it to the prescription package. But I must warn you…"

Oh, Burke thinks, this is when he warns me of serious side effects.

No. Reynolds says, "…that there will be an extra charge. I'll give you seven pills, until next week's visit. Like I say, they're pricey. One hundred dollars each."

"That's fine," says Burke.

"Very well. Now go get dressed, and on your way out stop and see Nora. I'll tell her to add Clenbuterol to your 'goody bag.' It's been a pleasure meeting you."

"Same here," Burke says.

With a big smile on his face, Dr. William Reynolds speaks again. "Next week we can discuss what we might do about those droopy breasts of yours."

CHAPTER 30

KATHERINE BURKE DRESSES quickly. The baggy black linen Alexander Wang pants tie easily at the waist. The simple white cotton T-shirt slips quickly over her shoulders. She grabs her pocketbook and she does a fast check of its contents: iPad, personal iPhone, work cell phone, roll of thirty hundred-dollar bills, and finally, the "Austrian Baby," which is what Moncrief calls the Glock 19 handgun that Burke and Moncrief carry.

Burke walks down the short hallway to the waiting room. She is certain that the lighting is dimmer than when she first entered. Yes, her quick police detective mind registers that the two Sonneman table lamps have been turned off. The track lighting has been turned down. The spotlight on the Koons photo is no longer on.

It's not scary, she thinks. *It's just gloomy.*

The very skinny, very pretty receptionist/assistant—Reynolds called her Nora—is not at the glass desk.

Then suddenly a noise, a human sound, not quite

a cough, not quite a sniffle. Burke turns in the
direction of one of the black couches. The back of
the couch is facing her. Then Burke watches the receptionist beginning to sit up. Nora yawns the tiniest
of yawns.

"Oh, Miss Cotillard, I'm sorry. I was just catching a
nap while I was waiting for you. You're Dr. Reynolds's
last patient. Forgive me," she says as she stands.

"What's to forgive? I wish I could grab a nap right
now myself," says Burke.

Nora goes to her desk and begins tapping away at
her iPad. "Let's just see what the total payment is. The
consultation is one thousand…"

One thousand!

Burke tries not to show her astonishment when she
hears the amount.

"The weight-loss medical package is another thousand," says Nora. "And I see here that Dr. Reynolds has
dispensed additional medication, Clenbuterol. That's
seven…"

Now Burke hears a noise coming from behind her.
Nora must be hearing that noise also. Both women
look toward the black couch where Nora had been
napping. The cough comes again, louder. It is an
intense cough, a man's cough, a sick man's cough,
Burke thinks.

Suddenly a young man stands up. Burke can only
assume that he also has been lying on that couch. The
young man squints in the direction of both women. He
seems confused, disoriented. He is blond, young, thin.
The young man is Reed Reynolds.

"That's Dr. Reynolds's son. I think they're meeting
for dinner," says Nora, who delivers the information
calmly, matter-of-factly. Burke nods, as if this actually
explained something.

"Your dad will be out momentarily, Reed," says Nora. Now she looks back to her iPad and says, "That will be a total of twenty-seven hundred dollars, Miss Cotillard."

Katherine Burke begins counting out hundred-dollar bills.

"Excellent," says Nora. "Cash."

Burke speaks. "Oh, and I'll need a receipt."

"I'll just email it to you," says Nora.

"Oh, I'd prefer a hard copy."

"If I email it you can just print it at home."

"Yes, but I really would prefer to leave with a piece of paper. I'm a dinosaur when it comes to receipts."

Suddenly a loud harsh voice comes from Reed Reynolds.

"Are you deaf *and* stupid, lady? She said she's going to email it to you."

"Reed, please…" says the receptionist.

The young man comes from around the black couch and approaches the glass desk.

"I know this bitch," says Reed Reynolds. "She doesn't *know* that I know her, but I do."

"I don't remember ever meeting you," says Burke, who is now really on edge. This kid is stoned or at least buzzed.

"You were with that asshole who tried to buy shit from me in the park. Like I didn't know you were feds or cops or some other kind of asshole."

Burke is not quite certain what she should say. But facing Reynolds, her arms and hands are shaking. Her stomach is churning. This operation is about to go up in flames. She turns away from Reed Reynolds to face Nora.

"Just ignore him," Nora says.

But Burke cannot. Reed Reynolds is walking toward

her. His long legs bend dramatically at the knees. His walk is almost cartoonish.

The combination of sneer-and-smile on Reynolds's mouth, the dramatic deep red outline of his dead eyes... there's nothing cartoonish about that.

She snaps open her pocketbook. She reaches in, but immediately realizes that her cell phone is in the compartment where her Glock should be.

Reynolds's voice comes at her, loud but slurred: "Move to the goddamn door, lady."

Burke freezes.

Reynolds's voice again: "Get her! Are you fucking deaf? Get her."

It takes Burke a millisecond to realize that Reynolds is shouting at Nora.

If the cell phone is sitting where the Glock should be, then the Glock should be where the...

Burke reaches into her pocketbook. Yes. *I am a lucky sonofabitch,* she thinks. Burke spins to face Nora.

Nora is holding a gun.

Burke's arm is still in her bag. Her hand is on the gun. But Nora is a second ahead of her. Nora aims her pistol in Burke's general direction.

Nora fires—and misses. The bullet hits the couch.

This is astonishing... to everyone except a cop. *"The 'general direction' IS NEVER GOOD ENOUGH!"* She can hear her firearms instructor's voice.

"Even if you're only three feet from your target it's still READY, AIM, and SHOOT. If you forget the AIM part, then chances are you're dead."

Katherine Burke does what Nora didn't do.

First she *aims.* And then she shoots.

Blood sprays from Nora's neck. She falls on top of the desk. Nora's blood is smearing like children's finger paint on the glass desk.

Then suddenly a hideous, retching, gagging sound comes from Reed. Sick and savage and loud, like a cannibal war cry.

Now Burke is alive in a kind of crazy way. She spins around and sees the boy fold at the waist. His head is almost at the floor, but he is still standing. He begins spewing a fountain of vomit, which splashes to the floor. Some of it hits his black pants as she uses her phone to call for Moncrief.

CHAPTER 31

I DIAL 911 AS I enter the reception room, along with Dr. William Reynolds. I see a dead woman facedown and bleeding out over a glass desk. I barely recognize Reed Reynolds, who is so unconscious that he appears to be dead, his head resting in his own pool of vomit. I ignore William Reynolds, staring at his dead receptionist and son. They will be dealt with when more officers arrive, which should be any minute.

When I look to the other corner, I see K. Burke standing, looking out the window. Her shoulders are shaking. She is sobbing, really sobbing, big bursts of tears mixed with squeaks and grunts and coughs.

I walk to her and from behind I put my arms on her shoulders and gently turn her around. She puts her head on my chest.

"It is all right, K. Burke. You behaved admirably. You have much to be proud of," I say softly.

I hold her, rubbing her back with my hands. Silence. Seconds. Minutes. Then Burke speaks.

"Moncrief, I just killed someone."

I imagine page after page after page of police forms and reports. Thousands of finger taps on so many cell phones and laptops. Photographers and photographs and the whooshing sounds of expensive cameras. More detectives. Medical examiners. More police officers. Inspector Elliott. A deputy mayor. The newscasters. The newswriters. The news photographers. The people in the neighborhood. The conversations.

"They say they killed Dr. Reynolds."

"No. Not Reynolds. They killed his girlfriend."

"No. They killed the nurse."

"The nurse *is* the girlfriend."

I can see in my head what is coming, a spectacle for a summer's night in New York City.

I tell Burke that I will take her home to her apartment, and, to my mild surprise, she does not object. She does, however, remain completely silent as the patrol car takes us from SoHo to her apartment in the East 90s.

At her apartment door we step over the messy pile of shoes, boots, and magazines.

"What sort of alcoholic beverages do you have here?" I ask.

"There's a bottle of Dewar's in the cabinet over the fridge, and there's some Gallo Hearty Burgundy next to it," she says. She cannot see the disgust on my face when she mentions the wine. But this, of course, is hardly a time for humor, even between such great friends. Also, these are the first words she has spoken since we left the mad carnival in Dr. William Reynolds's office. Reynolds has been taken to the precinct. Burke has been brought to her home. All has ended the way it should. Yet the air is heavy with misery.

Burke pauses only a few feet into the apartment. She stands perfectly still. Her hands hang at her side.

"K. Burke, what can I do to help you?" I ask. "We

have had no nourishment since luncheon. I will order something. A little soup, some bread, some pastry."

"Nothing," she says. Her voice is soft.

"Do you need to refresh yourself? Do you want me to draw you a bath?"

Burke turns her head toward me. She speaks, "'Draw me a bath.' You said 'Draw me a bath.' That's so old-fashioned. So foreign. So…Moncrief-like."

"Well, what is your answer? A bath? A shower? A Dewar's on the rocks?"

It looks as if a small smile is creeping onto her face. I am delighted. The breaking of the ice, as they say. But I'm very wrong. The smile continues without a stop. It curves up and over her cheeks. Her eyes squint hard. Her entire face becomes contorted into sadness. Tears. Loud. Shaking shoulders. Hands to face. Then through her tears comes her ragged voice.

"I think she would have shot me, Moncrief. Do you think so? Moncrief, tell me that you think if I had waited she would have killed me."

I grab her by the arms. And I speak sternly.

"You do *not* have to ask me or torture yourself. You did what your job called for you to do."

She leans onto my shoulder. She sobs, but the sobs do not last long.

"I want to take a shower," she says.

"That is wise," I say. "Perhaps it will help to wash the day away."

"Perhaps," she says. Then, "Thank you for helping. You don't have to stay. I'll be fine."

"No," I say. "I will wait until you are ready for sleeping. I will have a Dewar's waiting for you when you come out of your shower."

Before she enters her tiny bathroom K. Burke turns to me. Her smile is small, but it is real. She speaks.

"Draw me a bath? I don't think anyone has ever said that to me." She closes the bathroom door.

The room I'm left in is cluttered with small piles of clothing, an opened but unmade Murphy bed, stacks of magazines, a desk computer whose screen frame is littered with decals and Post-it notes.

I am suddenly thinking: *Who is this woman and what has she become to me? A friend? Of course. A sister? Somewhat. A daughter? Absurd. A woman who might be my lover? No answer to that one. More "no" than "yes." But maybe not.*

I walk to the bathroom door. I hear the shower. Somehow the mere sound of the shower water raining down helps soothe me also.

I do not believe that time heals everything, but in this case, this time...I so very much hope and pray that it will. This is not just anybody in my life. This is Katherine.

CHAPTER 32

I STAY THE NIGHT.

K. Burke and I drink our glasses of Scotch. She lies down on the "always-down" Murphy bed. I retreat to the green Barcalounger, which, I discover, is both incredibly ugly *and* incredibly comfortable.

When Detective Burke finishes her drink she holds out her glass. I move to the tiny kitchen area to pour more Scotch. I'm gone maybe thirty seconds, but K. Burke is sound asleep when I get back.

I remove my shoes, my socks, my shirt.

I do not remember falling asleep. But I certainly do remember being awakened by the buzzing of my cell phone. I am not exactly surprised by the caller.

"Luc, as always we call at the most inconvenient time. It is me, Nicolas." I glance quickly at the Felix the Cat clock on Burke's wall and see that it is ten minutes after three in the morning.

"Wait just one moment," I whisper. I take the phone into the bathroom and close the door so not to wake K. Burke. I still keep my voice low.

"Yes, yes. What is the problem?" I ask.

"It is the same. Only different. We are here in New York City, as you know, of course, for the upcoming Belmont. We are at the St. Regis, and...all of this is *très mal*...this..." he begins. I want to scream "Get to the point!" Then mercifully, the inevitable occurs: I hear Marguerite say, *"Donne-moi le téléphone, Nicolas."* And Nicolas gives Marguerite the telephone. She begins talking.

"Luc, do you know what the time of day is?" she says.

Oh, shit. Is she going to be polite and long-winded also?

But I stay cool. Instead of saying, "Of course I know what the goddamn time is," I say, "Yes. Tell me the problem."

"There was a phone call from the lobby desk. Just a few minutes ago. The man at the desk said that there was a delivery for us. He said that the deliveryman insisted it be brought up to the room immediately. We are, you know, traveling without a maid or a secretary. So Nicolas answered the door buzzer and...*Voilà!*" She pauses.

This time I do not edit or censor my reaction.

"What was it, goddamnit?"

"An extraordinary wreath of roses. Hundreds of them. Hundreds and hundreds. Just like the roses we previously received."

"A card? A message?"

"Yes. I shall read it to you," she says. "'Lose at Belmont. Or suffer the consequences.'"

I am silent. I am thinking. Then I say: "But of course. In the past they have delivered the roses at the victory party. This time they are certain that there will be no victory party."

Silence. Then Marguerite's voice again on the phone.

"Luc, are you still there?"

"Yes," I say. But I'm not completely *there*. My brain is traveling—filtering and sorting and clicking away. But it clicks slowly. I am weary from lack of sleep. My skin is wet with sweat. My eyes burn. My instincts fail to bring cohesion to my brain.

Marguerite's voice is just short of frantic. "What should we do, Luc?"

"Go back to bed. Try to sleep. I shall stop by your suite at nine a.m."

"Is there nothing else for us to do until then?" she asks.

"Yes. There is one thing."

"Of course," says Marguerite.

"Order coffee and croissants for a nine o'clock room service, and tell them to make certain that the coffee is very strong and the croissants are very flaky."

CHAPTER 33

I DO NOT FALL back to sleep. K. Burke, however, sleeps soundly. Indeed, she is still sleeping when I leave her apartment at 7 a.m.

Back at my own place, a shower, a shave, fifteen minutes in the sauna, another shower, and then a phone call to Jimmy Kocot, the man who is known as "Bookie to the Stars." He is so named because he does not accept bets below a thousand dollars. Further, he does not necessarily accept your bet if he does not personally care for the person placing the bet. How do I know all this? Via the recommendation of Inspector Elliott.

Yes, I know. Amazing. My police boss recommended my bookie. Here's how: Approximately one year ago I told Nick Elliott that I had a good friend who was competing in a—don't think me too foppish— cribbage tournament in Lyon. Because there was a one-day electronics strike in France I could not get through online or by phone to place a "win" on my friend.

Inspector Elliott said that he sometimes used a bookie

("Betting isn't really betting unless you can bet odds," he said, by way of explanation of his own breaking of the law). And so I spoke with Jimmy Kocot. I bet five thousand euros on my friend Pierre Settel. And so I lost five thousand euros.

"So, you got another frog buddy in a cribbage match, Mr. Moncrief?" Jimmy asks this morning when I call.

"No. I'm interested in the Belmont Stakes," I say.

"So's everyone else," he says.

"A great deal of wagering?" I ask.

"A very great deal," he says.

"What sort of odds are you giving on Garçon?"

"I'm not. The smart money is on Millie's Baby Boy and Rufus. They're both three-to-one to win. My clients are not keen on Garçon. I couldn't tell you why."

"No idea?" I ask.

"No. I've got no clue. But the other two nags are coming in, like I say, three-to-one for winning."

"And nothing new to cause this change?" I ask.

There is a pause. When Jimmy speaks again his voice is quieter, intimate, almost a whisper.

"Two guys told me the horse has a sesamoid fracture. That's the bones down around…"

I finish his sentence, "…the ankles."

"Ridiculous," I say. "I'm going with Garçon. I know the owners, and they've told me nothing," I say.

"Whatever you want. I make my money either way. If you'd rather listen to those two old French people instead of me, it's your loss." He says it as a joke, but there is a note of malice in the joke.

"In any event, what are the odds on Garçon?"

"I've got him at seven-to-one."

"I'll take it," I say.

"You say you don't know any inside stuff, but I'm sure you know stuff that I don't know," says Jimmy

Kocot, Bookie to the Stars. "Anyway, how much you betting?"

"Fifty thousand."

"You want to tell me that one more time?"

"I think you heard me."

"You doing a group bet, huh?"

"No. It's all mine."

"Fifty is a mighty big bet, even for me. How are you covering it? You know I can only do cash."

"You'll have it in less than a minute. I'll wire it to you right now."

Jimmy and I say our good-byes. I punch in the codes and numbers that deliver fifty thousand to a site called starsbook472ko.com.

CHAPTER 34

AN HOUR LATER, PERFECT luxury is on perfect display in the Savatiers' suite at the St. Regis on East 55th Street.

The elderly couple is, of course, dressed elegantly, Marguerite in a simple white suit with navy-blue piping, as if she had stepped out of a Chanel showroom in 1955. Nicolas in a dark-gray suit with a vest, a wide red silk tie with a diamond pin.

A waiter and waitress are pouring coffee into the exquisite St. Regis china cups—cups and plates that ironically are designed with a delicate border of roses.

Nicolas quickly reminds me that there are real and dangerous roses to deal with. "The floral arrangement is in the bedroom," says Nicolas.

I step into the adjoining bedroom—the beds are already made, the carpet already vacuumed. I check this arrangement of roses against the photographs from the Derby and the Preakness on my phone. Indeed, all three arrangements are identical.

When I return to the living room Marguerite thrusts

the accompanying note toward me. A quick glance verifies that the request is to "Lose the Belmont." All I can do is read it and nod.

"Your croissants are getting cold, Luc," says Nicolas. There is a teasing smile on his face.

"My husband is not nearly so nervous as I am," says Marguerite, as we all sit down at the breakfast table.

"I am nervous, of course," explains Nicolas. "But what can happen to us? What are these 'consequences' we will suffer should we actually win—not lose—the Belmont tomorrow? Will they shoot us? So what? We will have won the Triple Crown. We have lived long and happy lives. People have died in far worse circumstances."

Marguerite sighs.

"No one loves her horses as much as I do, but I am not sure that I am willing to die for a horse race."

"Let me ask," I say. "Have you been in touch with the trainers and Belmont management about Garçon's health?"

"Of course, we speak to the head trainer every few hours. And our jockey Armand calls constantly…" begins Nicolas.

"He calls almost too often," Marguerite adds with a tiny laugh.

Nicolas: "And he is nervous but very optimistic about Saturday's race."

I am not surprised by this information. These trainers and Armand Joscoe have been with the Savatiers and their horses for many years. I nod, and then I take a big gulp of my coffee. I break off a crisp end piece from my croissant.

"Please, Luc. Tell us. What should we do?"

"First, we should finish our *petit déjeuner*. Then we should proceed as if all circumstances are normal. We will drive out to Long Island and watch Garçon go through his paces. Then we can decide what to do."

"Just one more question," says Nicolas.

"And that is?"

"Where is the delightful Mademoiselle Burke?"

"Merci," I say. "How could I forget about her?" I click the contact list on my cell phone and call K. Burke.

"Where are you, Moncrief?" comes the very grumpy, very sleepy voice of K. Burke.

"I am at breakfast with the Savatiers, downtown. You must brush your teeth and comb your hair. Put on your clothing and put on a smiling, happy face. The Savatiers and I will come fetch you in less than fifteen minutes."

"No way that I can…"

"We are on our way out to Belmont," I say.

"I don't know, Moncrief. I don't think I can."

"Please, K. Burke. Life goes on. Today is a day for working."

CHAPTER 35

Belmont.
The day before the race.

THE MERCEDES SUV THAT carries Marguerite and Nicolas Savatier, K. Burke, and myself is allowed through three different gates. At the last gate hangs an enormous red-lettered sign:

> WARNING: TRACK OFFICIALS,
> OWNERS, AND EMPLOYEES ONLY
> BEYOND THIS POINT.

As we pass through, Marguerite says, "Now *that* is a sign to warm the heart of a frightened old lady."

I nod, but I am more taken with the exceptional beauty of Belmont racetrack—the hundreds of yards of lush ivy blanketing the walls, the freshly painted blue and white grandstand. Men and women in police uniform, men and women in official Belmont Park uniforms nod at us as we pass. The skies are cloudless and clear.

As we walk toward the stables I say, "The weather is a perfect seventy-seven degrees."

K. Burke catches sight of Nicolas's puzzled look and

translates. "Seventy-seven degrees Fahrenheit is equal to about twenty-five degrees Celsius."

"Merci," says Nicolas. "I am afraid our beloved young friend Luc has become transformed very much into the red-blooded American."

At the stable the Savatiers move as quickly as they are able toward Garçon. They stroke the horse's back. Nicolas looks into the horse's eyes.

There is a great deal of embracing and cheek-kissing between the Savatiers and the jockey, Armand Joscoe; between the Savatiers and *le docteur* Follderani, the vet that they've imported from France. Then begins the hugging and kissing between the owners and the trainers and the groomers. Finally, I receive a warm embrace from the jockey's tall son, Léon Joscoe. He looks very satisfied.

"Good to see you again, Léon," I say.

"And I'm tremendously happy to see you again, Monsieur Moncrief. It's been quite a ride for my father and me."

Now we have a great crowd of Frenchmen, all babbling excitedly at once. Actually a lovely occasion. Voices overlapping. Nervous laughter. Marguerite raises her voice; very unusual. Nicolas's eyes tear up; even more unusual.

K. Burke looks at me and says, "Okay. You win, Moncrief. I *do* speak French. But these folks are going way too fast for me. I don't understand very much."

"I assure you, it doesn't even make much sense to me."

Burke and I walk a few yards away from the small crowd of Frenchmen.

"So, we are alone for a moment. I am anxious to know: how are you feeling, K. Burke?" I ask.

"Not terrible," she says.

"*Not* terrible. Ah, compared to last night that is wonderful."

"And by the way," she says softly, "thank you for helping me."

My voice now turns serious, a shift from banter between good friends.

"You shall feel even better in a very short while. I have deduced who it is that is threatening the Savatiers with the grotesque notes."

"You know who is…?" she begins. But I keep talking.

"*Ah, oui.* This must be the same person who murdered the training horse. The same person who has stolen all the joy and luster from winning the races. But that person is now done for."

"Who is it, Moncrief? How did you…"

"In a moment," I say. We move back near the French group.

I interrupt, but my voice has a genuine smile in it.

"Please, I must ask a favor of all of you: if you speak only French, please speak slowly. Better yet, if you can speak reasonable English, please try to do so. It would be helpful to all the Americans."

With a laugh Nicolas says, "Because English is the official language not only of our new American friend, Katherine Burke…but now it has also become the official language of our *old* American friend, Luc Moncrief."

Most of the crowd laughs.

Armand Joscoe, usually a quiet, shy man, says, "It is for me not much English. So I speak not much. But Léon speaks so good English. He will have to translate for me."

Almost everyone looks in the direction of Léon, who is fiercely tapping keys on his cell phone.

A sparse round of applause. Spirits are high. Nicolas shouts out, "Léon! *Ah! Quel bon garçon!* Such a good boy!"

Léon looks surprised at the sound of his name echoing through the stable. He looks up at the gathering. A moment of confusion on his face. I walk toward him slowly, without threat.

Léon speaks. His voice is thick with the nasal sounds of French pronunciation.

"*Mon papa,* he is very not correct. Very bad I am with the English," says Léon with the forced trace of a smile.

"I'm surprised to hear you say that. You spoke such fine English when I first came in. To quote, 'I'm tremendously happy' and 'It's been quite a ride.' Now that's impressive, excellent…impeccable English, each word used properly, spoken properly."

At first it seems as if he's going to remain silent. But he's a smart lad. Smart enough to trust his own brain. He speaks.

"You know how, *monsieur,* in the classes of English they teach first the American conversational English. The idiom expressions. *Oui.* It is a challenge they teach me good."

I interrupt.

"Did they teach you to say 'I'd like to bet ten grand on Rufus' or 'I'd like to place twenty thousand on Millie's Baby Boy'? How did you learn that?"

He is now a frightened little boy.

I snatch the phone from his hand. I find the last message sent and I read out loud the recipient: "starsbook472ko.com."

Then, holding the phone above my head, I say to the crowd, "It appears that Léon and I use the same bookie. Only this time Léon is betting *against* the horse his father rides."

I hand the cell phone to K. Burke. She looks at the screen and shakes her head.

"Jesus Christ!" she says. "Who would have thought?"

I move in, close to Léon. Then I speak. Directly to Léon.

"First, you thought you'd spread a rumor to get longer odds on Garçon. But you realized you stood to earn more from sabotaging and betting against the expected winners. How could you do this? To your father? To the Savatiers? How could you hurt and betray the best people in your life?"

K. Burke gets it, too. Her mind works fast.

"You needed the money, Léon, didn't you?" I say.

Burke begins explaining—in French—to Armand Joscoe and Madame and Monsieur Savatier what has happened.

Léon is the person who sent the threats and the arrangements of roses to Marguerite. Who murdered the training horse. That Léon threatened the Savatiers and told them to order his father to lose.

"Léon would make a fortune if Garçon lost this race," I add. "Though he wanted Garçon to win the Preakness—and knew he could, due to his father, since Garçon runs very well in mud—so that the bets would be sky-high for this final race in the Triple Crown."

The Savatiers' faces are saturated with shock, horror, and confusion. How could such a thing be? How could someone so close to them execute a scheme so hideous? They simply don't understand such an evil world.

Armand's face also looks sad, then horrified, and then…his face quickly turns to a red and wild rage.

"Comment as-tu pu?" he screams it over and over. How could you? How could you?

"J'ai le diable pour fils!" he screams. I have the devil for a son!

K. Burke and I move to either side of Léon.

Armand also moves closer to his son. He faces Léon. Tears are rolling down Armand's cheeks. I am expecting the symbolic slap across the face.

But there is no slap. Instead Armand moves swiftly. He throws his fist up high. That fist travels to his son's jaw with enormous force and a great cracking sound. Léon falls to the floor of the stable. He moans.

Armand looks down at his son and spits, then he screams and runs from the stable.

CHAPTER 36

Belmont.
Race day.

AT TEN IN THE morning, Marguerite and Nicolas
Savatier, K. Burke, and I watch a young Cuban jockey
taking Garçon on a gallop around a training track. Also
watching the "audition" of the replacement jockey are
assorted trainers, sports writers, Belmont officials, and
even four competing jockeys. Garçon appears relaxed
and ready.

"*Que pensez-vous, mes amis?*" I say to the owners.
What do you think of it, my friends?

"He will have to do," says Nicolas.

Marguerite says what we are all thinking. "It is a
tragedy. To come this far. To be this close. The Triple
Crown within sight…"

The most senior of the Belmont officials says, "You
can still withdraw the horse, Mrs. Savatier. It's happened before."

"No. I could not do that to Garçon. My wonderful
horse has waited all his life for this," says Marguerite.

Everyone present has a point of view. One of the
trainers thinks the Cuban jockey is "almost as good as

Armand." Another thinks the Cuban jockey is *"trop rapide avec la cravache."*

"Okay, Moncrief. I can't translate that one," K. Burke says.

"The jockey is 'too quick with the riding crop,'" I answer.

The talk grows faster, more passionate. I hear Marguerite say, "Garçon will race even if I have to ride him myself."

Then I watch Nicolas look toward the vibrant blue sky and say, *"Aidez-moi, s'il vous plaît, mon cher Dieu."* Please help me, dear God.

Then a man's voice comes from behind us. Startling all of us.

It is sudden and strong.

"Who is riding my horse?" he shouts.

The voice belongs to Armand Joscoe.

"Armand..." says Marguerite. "We have not seen you since yesterday. We had no idea where you were."

Armand tells us that since yesterday morning he has been dealing with the Belmont New York police, as well as an assistant New York State attorney general, two representatives of the New York State Racing Commission, two attorneys who represent Belmont Park, and a son who has committed a serious and unforgivable crime.

Quickly Marguerite interrupts.

"No," she says. "Nothing is so serious that it cannot be forgiven."

"So true. So true," says Nicolas. "You are here with us now. We shall all be friends once again. You will see."

The Cuban jockey has alighted from Garçon. Armand Joscoe rushes toward "his" horse. Then he shouts for the trainers.

"Get the drying cloths immediately. He's wet. Walk him slowly. Cool him down. Feed him half of his usual food. Get him inside. Hurry!"

The only way to describe the faces of Marguerite and Nicolas is "joyful."

I turn to my partner.

"So, what do you think, K. Burke?"

"Well, with all the Savatiers' talk about forgiveness and everyone being friends again, I can only think one thing: those two would never make it in New York City."

I laugh and say, "K. Burke, *vous êtes un biscuit dur.*"

She smiles, but not with her eyes. "Not as tough a cookie as I seem."

CHAPTER 37

Belmont.
The race.

K. BURKE, NICOLAS AND Marguerite Savatier, Luc Moncrief. Together again at a horse race, for the third time.

In the owners' circle. The weather is perfect, even cool for summer. We are all tense, tired, a little shaky from raw nerves and too many glasses of pre-race champagne.

"You know, K. Burke, two years ago, when American Pharoah won this race, it had been almost forty years since any horse had captured the Triple Crown. The wise guys, the smart money, 'the horse guys,' they all say it will be another forty years before it happens again. They have weighed the odds. They know the facts. I worry for Garçon's chances."

Burke makes a skeptical face.

"That's what 'the horse guys' say. I guess I'm getting more and more like you, Moncrief. I say, 'Don't always go with the facts. Sometimes you have to go with your heart.'"

Nicolas has been listening to our conversation.

"My heart says that I am enormously grateful that Armand has returned to the job of jockey. You know, I don't really care if Garçon wins the race."

"Don't be insane, Nicolas. I certainly care," says Marguerite. "Indeed, feel however you like. I care enough for the both of us."

The four of us could easily banter and bicker until night falls, but the trumpet blows. The horses assemble within the starting gate. Of course, our attention is focused on Garçon. He seems under control, calm. I glance at Millie's Baby Boy. He's equally calm. Rufus, the only other real contender, is skittish.

The gun.

The race.

The cheers.

I am no expert at calling races, but from the start we all can see that it's going to be close. Garçon and Millie's Baby Boy take the lead together. They are, as the inevitable saying goes, neck-and-neck. So close that the two riders could carry on a conversation.

As always, Burke is amazingly excited. She shouts. "Hey, Millie, get off Garçon's ass!"

The two horses seem almost to run as a team. But then...as they close in on the finish, I am ecstatic to see that Millie's Baby Boy is falling behind. Not behind a great deal at first. Just a bit. Then a length. Then perhaps three lengths.

But now...as they approach the finish...what should be a glorious win for Garçon turns into a problem.

From fifth in the pack, Rufus has become Garçon's new partner.

And now...and now...

My eyes cannot see even a slight difference as they cross the finish line.

Different people erupt with different shouts. Rufus!

Garçon! Rufus! Garçon! An announcement. The crowd quiets.

The photo sign will be posted and the results will be announced.

The waiting, of course, feels like a few hundred lifetimes.

The crowd turns even quieter.

Video screens play the finish over and over.

Finally, a voice echoes out of the loudspeakers:

"The winner, by a head, is Garçon."

EPILOGUE

K. BURKE AND I are together in Paris.

Why Paris? Because the Savatiers have decided to forgo the final important race in America, the Breeders' Cup. Instead, Garçon has been brought home to Paris to compete in the most important of French races, Le Prix de l'Arc de Triomphe.

Why together?

Frankly, because I find it impossible now to be in Paris without her. After our previous visits, visits that were touched with both tragedy and tenderness, Katherine Burke has given me new eyes to see Paris, from the glamorous shops on the Champs-Élysées to that perfect little bistro in Montmartre.

Burke and I are walking slowly through the Bois de Boulogne, the great forest-like park on the outskirts of Paris. It is also in the Bois where Parisians keep their own famous racetrack, Longchamp.

"Leave it to the French to build a racetrack smack dab in the middle of a beautiful park," says K. Burke.

"The park is for *fun*. The track is for *games*. Fun and games," I say.

"Whatever you say. Anyway, I'm always happy to be here," she says.

"And you will be even happier if tomorrow Garçon wins."

"Yes, I will. Especially that it's my own one hundred euros that I bet on him."

We walk without speaking for a few minutes.

It is October in Paris. Usually a rainy time of the year. But today the air is cool and the sky is bright. The trees are dripping with color—autumn reds and yellows.

"I hope the weather will be this great tomorrow," I say.

We are now walking so close to each other that our shoulders occasionally touch, our hands occasionally brush against each other's.

"And if the weather isn't so great, at least we're in Paris," she says.

"You have grown to like this city, eh, K. Burke?"

"I've grown to *love* this city," she says.

"Maybe we should both move here, live here," I say.

"If you'd said that a year ago I would simply say that you're crazy," she says. "But now I almost feel the same way."

I stop. I talk.

"That means we have become crazy together."

She says, "So now we're *both* crazy. I guess that's good."

I take her hand. We continue our walk.

ABOUT THE AUTHORS

James Patterson is the world's bestselling author. His enduring fictional characters and series include Alex Cross, the Women's Murder Club, Michael Bennett, Maximum Ride, Middle School, and Ali Cross, along with such acclaimed works of narrative nonfiction as *Walk in My Combat Boots, E.R. Nurses,* and his autobiography, *James Patterson by James Patterson.* Bill Clinton (*The President Is Missing*) and Dolly Parton (*Run, Rose, Run*) are among his notable literary collaborators. For his prodigious imagination and championship of literacy in America, Patterson was awarded the 2019 National Humanities Medal. The National Book Foundation presented him with the Literarian Award for Outstanding Service to the American Literary Community, and he is also the recipient of an Edgar Award and nine Emmy Awards. He lives in Florida with his family.

Richard DiLallo is a former advertising executive. He lives in Manhattan with his wife.

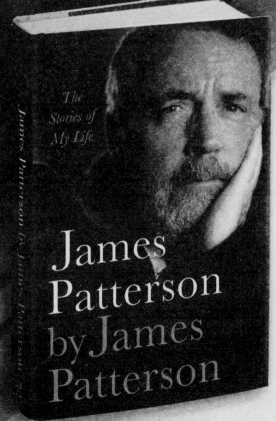

JAMES
PATTERSON
RECOMMENDS

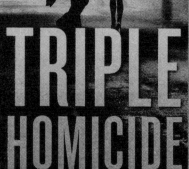

JAMES PATTERSON

TRIPLE HOMICIDE

TRIPLE HOMICIDE

I couldn't resist the opportunity to bring my greatest detectives together in three shocking thrillers. Alex Cross receives an anonymous call threatening to set off deadly bombs in Washington, DC, and has to discover whether it's a cruel hoax, or the real deal. But will he find the truth too late? And then, in possibly my most twisted Women's Murder Club mystery yet, Detective Lindsay Boxer investigates a dead lover and a wounded millionaire who was left for dead. Finally, I make things personal for Michael Bennett as someone attacks the Thanksgiving Day Parade directly in front of him and his family. Can he solve the mystery of the "holiday terror"?

JAMES PATTERSON

"No one gets this big without amazing natural storytelling talent— which is what James Patterson has, in spades." —Lee Child

THE FAMILY LAWYER

THE FAMILY LAWYER

The Family Lawyer combines three of my most pulse-pounding novels all in one book. There's Matthew Hovanes, who's living a parent's worst nightmare when his daughter is accused of bullying another girl into suicide. I test all of his attorney experience as he tries to clear his daughter's name and reveal the truth. Then there's Cheryl Mabern, who is one of my most brilliant detectives working for the NYPD. But does that brilliance help her when there's a calculating killer committing random murders? And finally, Dani Lawrence struggles with deciding whether to aid in an investigation that could put away her sister for the murder of her cheating husband. Or she can obstruct it by any means necessary.

JAMES PATTERSON

THE WORLD'S #1 BEST-SELLING WRITER

THE HOUSE NEXT DOOR

BIG THRILLS. SUSPENSE THAT KILLS.

THE HOUSE NEXT DOOR

There's something absolutely bone-chilling about a danger that's right in front of you, and that concept fascinates me. Everyone always thinks there's safety in numbers, but it isn't always true, and those closest to you can sometimes be the most terrifying. In *The House Next Door*, Laura Sherman's neighbor seems like he's too good to be true; maybe he is. And then in *The Killer's Wife*, Detective McGrath is searching for six girls who have gone missing but finds himself dangerously close to his suspect's wife. Way too close. And finally, I venture out there in *We Are Not Alone*. Robert Barnett has found a message that will change the world: that there are others out there. And they're watching us.

For a complete list of books by

JAMES PATTERSON

VISIT
JamesPatterson.com

 Follow James Patterson on Facebook
@JamesPatterson

 Follow James Patterson on Twitter
@JP_Books

 Follow James Patterson on Instagram
@jamespattersonbooks